GIVE US THIS DAY

Give Us This Day is the final triumphant book in the bestselling trilogy of the Swann family.

God Is An Englishman began the saga, introducing Adam Swann in the middle of the Victorian era. Then came *Theirs Was The Kingdom* which took the narrative down towards the final years of the Old Queen's reign. And here is the last part, *Give Us This Day*, in which Adam Swann is an old man in Edwardian England.

The whole adds up to a panoramic vision of the British Isles. For Ronnie Delderfield was a storyteller of genius, a practitioner of an art that will always be popular and always be influential.

Give Us This Day was originally published in paperback in two volumes entitled *Three Score Years And Ten* and *Reconnaissance*.

Give Us This Day

R. F. Delderfield

CORONET BOOKS
Hodder and Stoughton

Copyright © 1973 by Mrs. May Delderfield

First published in Great Britain 1973 by
Hodder and Stoughton Limited

First published by Coronet in 1974 in two
volumes: Book 1—Three Score Years And Ten;
Book 2—Reconnaissance

*This Coronet edition published in one volume 1981
Third impression 1983*

British Library C.I.P.

Delderfield, R. F.
 Give us this day.
 I. Title
 823' .912[F]   PR6007.E36

ISBN 0 340 25354 1

Printed and bound in Great Britain for
Hodder and Stoughton Paperbacks, a
division of Hodder and Stoughton Ltd.,
Mill Road, Dunton Green, Sevenoaks,
Kent (Editorial Office: 47 Bedford
Square, London, WC1 3DP) by
Richard Clay (The Chaucer Press) Ltd,
Bungay, Suffolk

For May

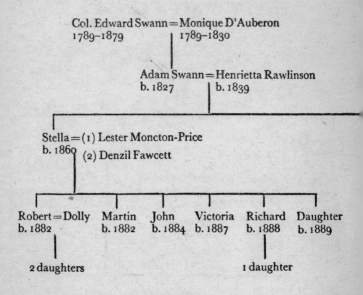

Col. Edward Swann = Monique D'Auberon
1789–1879   1789–1830

Adam Swann = Henrietta Rawlinson
b. 1827   b. 1839

Stella = (1) Lester Moncton-Price
b. 1860   (2) Denzil Fawcett

Robert = Dolly | Martin | John | Victoria | Richard | Daughter
b. 1882   b. 1882 b. 1884 b. 1887   b. 1888   b. 1889

2 daughters   1 daughter

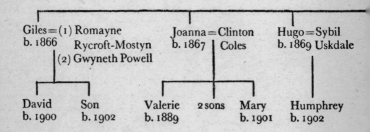

Giles = (1) Romayne | Joanna = Clinton | Hugo = Sybil
b. 1866   Rycroft-Mostyn | b. 1867   Coles | b. 1869   Uskdale
          (2) Gwyneth Powell

David | Son   Valerie | 2 sons | Mary   Humphrey
b. 1900 b. 1902   b. 1889   b. 1901   b. 1902

THE SWANNS OF 'TRYST'

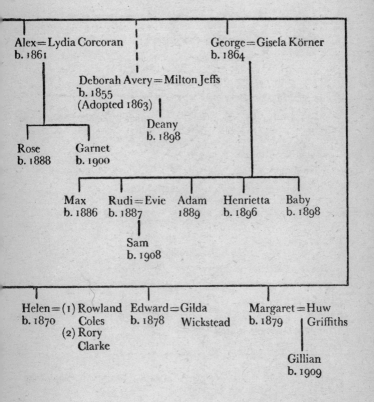

Alex═Lydia Corcoran
b. 1861

George═Gisela Körner
b. 1864

Deborah Avery═Milton Jeffs
b. 1855
(Adopted 1863)

Deany
b. 1898

Rose
b. 1888

Garnet
b. 1900

Max
b. 1886

Rudi═Evie
b. 1887

Adam
1889

Henrietta
b. 1896

Baby
b. 1898

Sam
b. 1908

Helen═(1) Rowland
b. 1870   Coles
        (2) Rory
        Clarke

Edward═Gilda
b. 1878   Wickstead

Margaret═Huw
b. 1879   Griffiths

Gillian
b. 1909

SWANN·ON·WHEELS
REDEFINED REGIONS

SCOTLAND

Glasgow Edinburgh

NORTH
EAST
REGION

Whitby

Belfast

THE
POLYGON

IRELAND

Manchester

Dublin

THE FUNNEL

Macclesfield

Newark

Beddgelert

WEST
MIDLANDS

Derby

Norwich

Birmingham

THE
MOUNTAIN
SQUARE

Worcester

THE LINK

Pontnewydd

Cardiff

THE
SOUTHERN
SQUARE

London

Tonbridge

THE KENTISH
TRIANGLE

Salisbury

Barnstaple

THE
WESTERN
WEDGE

Taunton

Exeter

TOM
TIDDLER'S
LAND

Truro

Contents

PART ONE

Three Score Years and Ten

I

Clash of Symbols

ON THE MORNING OF HIS SEVENTIETH BIRTHDAY,
in the Jubilee month of June, 1897, Adam Swann, one-
time cavalryman, subsequently haulier extraordinary,
now landscaper and connoisseur, picked up his *Times*,
turned his back on an erupting household and stumped
down the curving drive to his favourite summer vantage
point, a knoll sixty feet above the level of the lake overlooking the rustic building entered on the 'Tryst' estate
map as 'The Hermitage'.

His wife, Henrietta, glimpsing his disapproving back
as he emerged on the far side of the lilac clump, applauded
his abrupt departure. Never much of a family man,
preoccupied year by year with his own extravagant and
mildly eccentric occupations, he had a habit of getting
under her feet whenever she was organising a social event
and preparation for a family occasion on this scale demanded concentration.

By her reckoning there would be a score sitting down
to dinner, without counting some of the younger grandchildren, who might be allowed to stay up in honour of
the occasion. She knew very well that he would regard
a Swann muster, scheduled for dinner that night, as little
more than an obligatory family ritual but she was also
aware that he would humour her and the girls by going
through the motions. Admittedly it was his birthday and
an important milestone in what she never ceased to

regard as anything but a long and incredibly adventurous journey, but she knew him well enough, after thirty-nine years of marriage, to face the fact that celebrations of this kind had no real significance for him. Whenever he gave his mind to anything it needed far more substance and permanence than an evening of feasting, a few toasts, a general exchange of family gossip. That kind of thing, to his way of thinking, was a woman's business and such males who enjoyed it were, to use another phrase of his, 'Men who had run out of steam', an odd metaphor in the mouth of a man who had made his pile out of draught horses.

As for him, Henrietta decided, watching his deliberate, slightly halting progress down the drive and then hard right over the turf to the knoll, he would almost surely die with a full head of steam. Increasing age, and retirement from the city life eight years before, had done little to slow him down and encourage the repose most successful men of affairs regarded as their right on the far side of the hill. He had never changed much and now he never would. Indeed, to her and to everyone who knew him well, he was still the same thrustful Adam of her youth, of a time when he had come riding over a fold of Seddon Moor in the drought summer of 1858 and surprised her, an eighteen-year-old runaway from home, washing herself in a puddle. He was still a dreamer and an actor out of dreams. Still a man who, unless his creative faculties were fully stretched, became moody and at odds with himself and everyone about him. In the years that had passed since he had surrendered his network to his second son, George, she had adjusted to the fact that old age, and the loss of a leg, had diminished neither his physical nor mental energies. He continued to make many of his local journeys on horseback. He still followed, through acres of newsprint, the odysseys of his hardfisted countrymen and the egregious antics of their commercial imitators overseas. All that had really happened, when he moved over to make room for George, was the exchange of one obsession for another. Once it had been his network. Now it was the embellishment and reshaping of his estate that had filled the vacuum created by his retirement. He still made occasional demands on her as a bedmate, but she was long since reconciled to the fact that there was a part of him, the creative part, that was cordoned off, as sacrosanct as Bluebeard's necropolis, even from George, his business heir, and from Giles, who did duty for his father's social and political conscience; even from network cronies out of his adventurous past, who occasionally visited him and were conducted on an inspection of the changes he had wrought in this sector of the Weald since taking it into his head to make 'Tryst' one of the showplaces of the county. There were some wives, she supposed, who would have been incapable of acquiescing to this area of privacy in a man for whom they had borne five sons and four daughters. Luckily for both of them Henrietta Swann was not one of them. She had always been aware both of her limitations and her true functions and had never quarrelled with them, or not seriously. To reign as consort of a man whose name was a household word was more than she had ever expected of life and fulfilment had been hers for a very long time now. Her place in his heart was assured and their relationship, since she had passed the age of childbearing and become a grandmother, was as ordered as the stars in their courses. Any woman who wanted more than that was out looking for trouble.

*   *   *

He paused on the threshold of The Hermitage, doing battle with his sentimentality. The thatched, timbered building was a Swann museum, housing practical personal mementoes he had carted away from his Thamesside tower when he retired, in the spring of 1889. He was not a man who revered the past but the exhibits in here symbolised his achievements and it struck him that a man had a right to sentimentalise a little on his seventieth birthday. He went inside the shady, circular barn and glanced about him, his eyes adjusting to the dimness after the June sunlight.

Originally, when he first conceived the notion of a Swann depository, there had been no more than half-a-dozen items. Since then many more had been added, the most impressive being the first coachbuilt frigate the firm of Blunderstone had delivered to him when he started his freight line, in '58. It looked old-fashioned now, a low-slung, broad-axled structure, with a central harness pole for the two Clydesdales that had pulled it all over the Home Counties. He had kept its brasswork polished and the hubcaps winked at him conspiratorially. He glanced up at the framed maps of the original regions, drawn in his own hand after that first exhaustive canvass of his head clerk, Tybalt, probing what they might expect from haulage clients in competition with the ever-expanding railways of that race-away era.

The maps seemed to him very crude now, but he saw them for what they were, the spring from which everything about him welled. Today, with the network almost forty years old, they certainly qualified as museum pieces, for George, his son, had abolished the regions as such, promoting a variety of other drastic changes that had rocketed some of the older area managers into premature retirement. The original regions had had queer, quirkish names, yet another fancy of their creator – the Western Wedge, the Crescents on the east coast, the Northern Triangle, where it lapped over the Tweed into Scotland, Tom Tiddler's Land, that was the Isle of Wight, and the like. Now these had been condensed into huge areas, embracing the entire British Isles – South, North, Far North and Ireland. Prosaic names and very typical of George, who was still known, among the older waggoners, as the New Broom.

He thought about George, isolating his good points and his bad. The good far outweighed the bad, for the boy had shown tremendous application and a high degree of imagination in the expansion period, although he had not as yet succeeded in banishing the horse and replacing it with one or other of those lumbering, ungainly machines that people in transport said would soon be commonplace on the roads. Rumour reached him that the New Broom had bitten off more than he could chew in this respect. Here and there, egged on by the younger managers, he had experimented with machines spawned by that snorting, fume-spewing monster he had lugged all the way from Vienna ten years before. The older men had jeered at them and their scepticism had seemed justified. Four times in one month waggon teams had to be harnessed to them to tow them home and Head Office had been taxed to explain a pile-up of delivery delays. But George's other changes had been happier. Frigates, the medium-weight vehicles of the kind that stood here, had been all but withdrawn and their teams used to increase the firm's quota of light transport, resulting, so they said, in a wider range of deliveries and a faster service for customers trading in more portable types of goods. George had also made his peace with the railways, contracting with them in every region to offload goods at junctions and then sub-contracting for most of their local deliveries. He had also broken the despotic power of the regional men at a stroke, sub-dividing the depot functions and installing sub-managers answerable, individually, for house-removals, railway traffic and the holiday brake-service. Well, Adam mused, you would look for this kind of thing in a new broom, especially one like George, whose amiability masked a ruthlessness and single-mindedness not unlike Adam's own in his younger days.

He went out of The Hermitage and ascended the tree-clad knoll that gave a view of the frontal vista of house and grounds. It was a prospect that always gave him the greatest satisfaction. Other men had contributed to his founding of Swann-on-Wheels but this, the transformation of a rundown manor house and its surrounding fifty-odd acres, had been his alone, expressing his developing aesthetic taste over all the years he had lived there. It proclaimed the three phases of his life. Young trees, from all over the world, bore witness to his years in the East up to the age of thirty, when he had dreamed of a positive participation in the era and made up his mind to renounce a game of hit-and-miss with the Queen's enemies and the near-certainty of getting his head blown off. The neatness and precision of the layout, with its lawns, spaced clumps of flowering shrubs, belts of soft timber, lake and decorative stonework, signified his middle years and his unflagging passion for creativity within precise terms of reference. The colour, form and enduring mellowness of the scene, with the old, stone house crouching under the spur of rock were indicative of his tendency to opt for the attainable in life, an unconscious compromise between the turbulence of youth and the sobriety of a man who had made his pile and put his feet up. Surveying it, he thought, 'That's my doing, by God! It owes nothing to any man save me,' but he had second thoughts about this. No man, perhaps, but at least one woman, his wife, Henrietta, child of a coarse, comic old rascal now in his dotage among a wilderness of stinking chimney-pots up north. Sam Rawlinson, who had made two fortunes to Adam's one, and thoughts of Sam led directly to his daughter, the tough, resolute, high-spirited girl he had found on a moor and carried off like a freebooter's prize on the rump of his mare.

Regard for her, generous acknowledgment of her fitness for a freebooter's bride, had grown on him year by year. A girl he had married almost absentmindedly, in the very earliest days of the network, who had been able, surprisingly, to stir his senses every time he watched her take her clothes off; even now, at a time of life when a man with a truncated leg was lucky to be mobile, much less intrigued by the spectacle of her wriggling free of all those pleats and flounces.

The thought made him smile again as he remembered a

coffee-house quip of thirty years ago, something about 'that chap Swann reinvesting half his annual profits in his wife's wardrobe'. Well, for anyone who cared to know, he had never been over-impressed by Henrietta Rawlinson dressed for a soirée or a garden-party. He had always seen her as ripe for a bedroom romp, and a ready means of escape from the cares of empire. More of a mistress, one might say, despite five sons and four daughters, each born in that crouching old house under the spur, and a very rewarding mistress at that considering the profound ignorance of her contemporaries concerning the basic needs of a full-blooded man of affairs. All but two of their children had been by-products of these moments of release, but George, and his younger brother Giles, were exceptions.

And even this was odd when you thought about it. George, his commercial heir, had been sired almost deliberately the night of their truce at the one important crisis in the relationship of man and wife. George he had always seen as a tacit pledge between them, acknowledgment that he should look to his concerns as provider and she to hers as gaffer of that rambling house up yonder. And so it had transpired, for Henrietta's maturity had flowered from that moment on, reaching its apogee three years later, with the loss of his leg in that railway accident over at Staplehurst, and the birth, forty weeks later, of Giles, keeper of the Swann conscience.

He turned half-left, glancing across at the belt of fir trees marking the limit of the estate to the north-west, the spot where, in a matter of hours before the accident, the pair of them had found something elusive in their relationship in the way of a hayfield frolic, belonging to a time before the British put on their long, trade faces, their tall hats and that mock-modesty ensemble that everyone expected of a prosperous middle-class merchant and his consort. And out of it, miraculously, had emerged Giles, the family sobersides, whose cast of thought was alien to the extrovert Swanns of 'Tryst', and whose absorption into the firm had proved a counterpoise to George's enterprise. For Giles, to Adam's mind at least, supplied the balance so necessary to any large organisation employing men and materials to make money. Giles was there to safeguard the Swann dictum that every unit counted for something in terms of human dignity and had proved his worth in every area where the waggons rolled. Giles was the adjuster, if that was the right word, between profit and people.

*　　*　　*

His random thoughts, gathering momentum, descended from the pinnacle of the particular to the plain of the general, so that he saw both himself and his concerns as a microcosm of the Empire, currently preparing for an orgy of tribal breast-beating, the like of which had never been witnessed since the era of Roman triumphs. A Diamond Jubilee. An Imperial milestone. A strident reminder to all the world that the victors of Waterloo and the battle for world markets were there to stay, for another century or more, perhaps for ever.

The papers were full of it. The streets of every city, town and village in the country were garlanded for it. From every corner of the world, coloured red on the maps by conquest and chicanery, a tide of popinjays flowed Londonwards, to share in what promised to be the most emphatic event of the century. Homage to a symbol, the pedants would call it, but a symbol of what? Of racial supremacy? Or trade and till-ringing? Of military triumph on a hundred sterile plains, deserts and in as many steamy river bottoms? He had never really known, despite his diligent observation of the antics of four tribes over five decades. Once, a long time ago, he had seen it all as a matter of trade following the drum in search of new markets and fresh sources of raw material essential possibly for a nation that lived on its workshops. But forty years of trading had taught him that this was no more than an expedient fiction. For now, when inflated jacks-in-office and glory-seekers gobbled up remote islands, he knew that the helmsman was away off course, and that most of these acquisitions would cost, in the long run, far more than they could ever yield.

Gladstone, that self-righteous old thunderer, had told them that years ago and every city clerk who could balance a ledger must be aware of it today. Yet all the time, across the Channel, the laggards, no less greedy and certainly no less vainglorious, were jostling for what they called 'a place in the sun' and he isolated them one by one. There was Germany, led by that loud-mouthed ass Wilhelm; there was France, obsessed by her sense of inferiority since the 1870 debacle; and across the Atlantic there was America with a commercial potential that could, given time, reduce the status of all his rivals to those of nonentities. And thinking this he did what he had always done when his mind ranged far beyond his concerns. He withdrew, thankfully, into the realm of the predictable, represented by his own brood and his own business.

George, no doubt, would forge steadily ahead, pushing the network to its limits. And beside him, as a safety-valve operator, was Giles, placator of ruffled clients, temperature-taker of the Swann work force, adjudicator of every grouse and dispute that came humming down the threads of the network to the heart and brain of the enterprise beside the Thames. It was enough, he supposed, for a man of seventy that morning, with a tumultuous family dinner party in the offing and little hope of repose until his own and the nation's affairs had steadied. He tucked his unread *Times* under his arm and descended to level ground, sniffing the fragrance all about him and cocking a countryman's ear to the murmurous summer noon.

*　　　*　　　*

The wire came within an hour of the family exodus, when the last touches were being added to her Jubilee ensemble and the gardener had delivered the carnations and roses for the ladies' corsage sprays and the button-holes the men would wear in the lapels of their newly pressed frock coats.

Henrietta, her mouth full of pins, could have wept with vexation as she glanced at the buff slip from Hilda, her step-mother: '*Father worse. Advise coming immediately*', a mere five words capable, providing convention took precedence over inclination, of spoiling an occasion she had been anticipating for months.

For a moment, without removing the pins from her mouth, Henrietta Swann weighed the substance of the message, calculating, on the minimum of evidence, Sam Rawlinson's chances of hanging on to life for an extra twenty-four hours or so, long enough for her to sandwich the Imperial spectacle between the present moment and a long, hot journey to Manchester in order to put in a dutiful deathbed appearance.

Almost forty years had elapsed since Sam had forfeited any affection she had for the old ruffian, for how could anyone love a father prepared to bargain a daughter for a scrap of wasteland adjoining his loading bays in the mill town where she had waited for Adam, or Adam's equivalent, to rescue her from obscurity. A wily old rascal, ruthless and disreputable, who had kicked his way up from bale-breaker to mill owner, who had reckoned every-thing, including his own daughter, in terms of brass and done his level best, God forgive him, to mate her with a simpering nobody. Adam, of course, had forgiven him long ago, and had even tried, over the years, to soften her approach, but he had made little or no headway. For her, Sam Rawlinson continued to stand for vulgarity, male arrogance and the seediness that attached itself to his entire way of life, and remembering this like a line out of her catechism, she removed the row of pins from her mouth, hitched her petticoat and called, "*Adam!* It's from Hilda! A wire, saying we should go at once . . . What *are* we to do, for heaven's sake? Today, of all days!"

He came out of his dressing-room, took the wire, read it and laid it on her dressing-table among her vast array of bottles and lotions.

"That's for you to say, isn't it, m'dear?"

She said, bitterly, "No, it isn't! Or not altogether. Everything's so nicely arranged. We were very lucky indeed to get that balcony and a thing like this . . . well . . . it's once in a lifetime, isn't it?"

"I fear so," he said, making no effort to keep the chuckle from his voice. "The Old Vic isn't likely to last another ten years even if we do."

He picked up the wire again and took it over to the window, musing. Her frown disappeared then for she knew very well what he was about. Calculating times and distances, as though the dying Sam was an impatient shipper and he had been asked to deliver a haul of goods within a specified time. He said, "I don't know . . . family obligations . . . how would it look, Hetty? An only child, exchanging final farewells in favour of the Lord Mayor's Show?" and hoisted himself round, sitting on her plush dressing-table stool, sound leg bent and tin leg, as he always called it, thrust out.

She knew then he was teasing her as he so often had over the years in this room where few serious words ever passed between them. She said, protestingly, "Really, Adam, it's not a thing to joke . . . !" but he reached out, grabbed her by the hips and pulled her close to him.

There had been a time when his big hands comfortably encircled her waist. They didn't now and recalling this he thought, 'Even so, she's trim for a woman who has produced a tribe of nine,' and his hands passed over the rampart of her corset to her plump behind straining below the rim of a garment that he sometimes referred to as her cuirass. It was an aspect of her that had always captivated him and he pinched so hard that she exclaimed, "Adam! Be serious! We've simply *got* to make up our minds, haven't we?"

"You've already made up your mind," he said, genially.

"All you want now is to shift the guilt on to me. Well, here's how I see it. Sam's eighty-eight and Hilda's a born worrier. But the fact is anybody would find it damned difficult to travel north until the exodus begins, tomorrow night. Nine trains in ten will be heading south-east and most of the upcountry traffic will be shunted to make room for them. We'd best make arrangements to travel on overnight, from London. I'll wire Hilda. Finish dressing. The carriages will be round at noon. If we get up to town by four we'll take a stroll and have a preview of the decorations."

She kissed him then, impulsively and affectionately, and he stumped across to the door to tell one of the girls to bicycle into the village with a reply. But then, on the threshold, he paused. "He's had a damned good innings, Hetty. And any last words he wants to say will be to me, not you. He was proud of you, mind, in his own queer way, but he saw me as the son he never had. Don't let it spoil your day."

2

In the old days the Swanns, in the way of the middle-class, celebrated national occasions *en famille*. As recently as the Golden Jubilee, ten years ago, a small balcony near St. Clement's Dane had accommodated man, wife and such of their family who were still home-based. But in a single decade the tribe had proliferated to an extent that astounded Adam whenever he thought about it. Unlike Henrietta he had never had it in mind to found a dynasty.

Today the royal balcony at Buckingham Palace would have been taxed to accommodate the entire Swann tribe even though two offshoots were out of the country, one in faraway China and another across the Irish Sea. But proliferation was not the only reason for dispersal. In spreading their wings each Swann had swung into an individual orbit, so that their occupations, their associates, indeed, their whole way of life and cast of thought presented a kind of spectrum of Imperial enterprise.

Thus it was that an occasion like this found them, as it were, picketing the royal route, dotted here and there at intervals along its four-mile route. Each of them prepared to cheer certainly, and wave hat, handkerchief or miniature Union Jack, but for different reasons, dictated by private conceptions of what excused this display of self-aggrandisement. Their individual and often contradictory standpoint was highlighted by their acceptance of what the newspapers were already calling 'Queen's Weather', as though, in dominating one-fifth of the world's surface, the British had tamed not merely tribes but elements.

Stationed at Hyde Park Gardens with his eldest daughter Stella, her farmer husband Denzil, four of Stella's children, his own youngest son, Edward, and youngest daughter, Margaret, Adam was content to view it as 'appropriate' weather. There had been times, during his long climb to affluence, when he had quarrelled with the cult of national arrogance but success had mellowed him. At seventy, he saw nothing remarkable about a cloudless day for a tribal rite of these dimensions. It was to be looked for and, in the nature of things, it had arrived. God, he had often jested, was an Englishman. Nothing else could account for the astounding luck of the English since Waterloo. Today the jest was muted. It had to be in the face of the evidence spread below as the procession unrolled, before his eyes, like a vast, vari-coloured carpet. There would come a time, his commonsense predicted, when the balloon would burst, possibly with a Godalmighty bang, but that time was not yet; and it occurred to him, as the throb of martial music was heard from the direction of Constitution Hill, that he might have been over-hasty in his claim that national pride was hurrying towards its inevitable fall. Every race and every creed under the sun was parading down there and at the very head of the procession, mounted on the huge grey he was said to have ridden to Khandahar, was a small, compact figure, reminding him vividly of an occasion forty years ago when he and Roberts of Khandahar had shared barrack and bivouac in an India torn by strife and had later parted company with a touch of mutual acrimony, Roberts in pursuit of the new Rome, himself to join in the free-for-all at home.

Forty years had not blurred the clarity of his recollection of that parting. He had been convinced then that the little man on the grey was a romantic visionary, who would soon get himself killed in a village that was not even marked on a map. Well, he never minded admitting a misjudgment, and here was the most glaring of his life. Roberts had not only survived and seen his boyish dreams translated into fact. He had gone forward to become a legend in his own lifetime and here were the cheers of a million Cockneys to prove it. He said, as the grey curvetted below, "He had it right after all then . . . !" and when Henrietta asked him what he had said he smiled and shook his head, saying, "Nothing . . . nothing of any consequence, m'dear. Simply reminding myself that Roberts and I once rode knee to knee in battles neither of us expected to survive." But although he dismissed his association with Roberts in such lighthearted terms Henrietta took pride in it and showed as much by squeezing his hand. It wasn't something you could let drop at a garden-party or a soirée – that one's husband was on Christian-name terms with the most famous soldier in the world – but one could bask in the knowledge just the same.

*   *   *

Half-a-mile to the east, at a tall window looking over Green Park, Major Alexander Swann, eldest of the Swann boys, and the only one among them to follow the traditional Swann profession of arms, might have seen it as good campaigning weather. Under a sun as brassy as this the ground would lie baked and the rivers would run low,

permitting the rapid movement of troops across almost
any kind of terrain, yet there was scepticism in his survey
of the colourful assembly that passed, with its companies
of colonials, its emphasis on variety, sounding brass, good
dressing and spit-and-polish turnout. Alex, who regarded
himself as a forward-looking professional, saw it as a circus
rather than a demonstration of military might. It was a
parade rooted, not in the future and not even in the present,
but in an era when his grandfather had ridden down from
the Pyrenees to bring Marshal Soult to battle. A single
Maxim gun, well-sited and well-served, could cut it to
ribbons in sixty seconds flat, and the thought occurred
to him, as he watched the company of Hong Kong police
step by in their comical coolie hats, that this was mere
window-dressing and had nothing to do with the art of
war. And it was no snap judgment either. Not only had
he fought tribesmen and savages in half-a-dozen Imperial
battle areas, his had been the hand that guided the hand
of the Prince of Wales to the trigger of the first Maxim
gun ever fired in England. He said, voicing his scepticism,
"All very pretty, so long as it never comes up against anything more lethal than an assegai or muzzle-loader . . ."
And his wife, Lydia (she who had transformed him
from regimental popinjay to professional) concurred, but,
being herself a daughter of the regiment, added a rider:
"They'd learn," she said, "just so long as some of us bear
it in mind."

*   *   *

A muzzle-loader's range from the vantage-point of Alex
and Lydia was the third Swann picket, denied the privilege of a first-storey view but not needing one, for he
measured six feet three inches in his new boots, and could
see over all the heads between himself and the kerb.

Hugo Swann, Olympic athlete and winner of as many
cups and medals as Victoria had colonies, would think
of it as good track weather, the ground being hard

underfoot and it even put the thought into mind. "Hope it holds," he told Barney O'Neill, the celebrated pole-vaulter. "If it does we'll get a record gate at Stamford Bridge tomorrow and they need the cash, I'm told."

It would be difficult to define Hugo's conclusions on the spectacle, other than a spectacle. His father and brothers had long since come to the conclusion that Hugo, bless his thick skull, had never had a serious thought in his life and his presence in the network, where he put in token appearances from time to time, was that of a thirteen-stone sleeping partner. None of them resented this, however, for Hugo, as a Swann advertisement, was worth five thousand a year on George's reckoning. His name appeared on the sporting pages of every journal on Fleet Street nowadays, so that when it cropped up, as it frequently did in coffee house and country house, no one could ever be sure whether the speaker was going to pronounce upon sport or commerce. All one could guarantee was that the name stood for rapid movement of one kind or another, and time schedules had always rated high on the list of Swann priorities.

*   *   *

Four hundred yards nearer St. Paul's, where the procession was channelled into the Strand and marched blaring, thrumming and jingling between phalanxes of hysterical Imperialists (few among them could have said in which continent British Honduras or Tobago were located) was George Swann, managing director and New Broom Extraordinary. He was perched, together with his wife, his family and his host, Sir James Lockerbie, in a window that would have fetched a hundred guineas had Sir James been in need of ready money. And George would have defined the brassy sunshine as ideal hauling weather.

On a day like this, given a fit team, a waggon carrying a full load could make fifteen miles from depot to offloading point providing the teamster knew his business and gave the horses a regular breather. For years now George had taken weather into his calculations but his mind was not on business today. With the yard closed down, and every employee enjoying a bonus holiday, he was wondering what new and plausible excuse he could offer Gisela for not making holiday himself. The problem not only took his mind off his work. It drew a curtain on the procession below so that he saw, not an ageing dumpy woman in a gilded carriage drawn by eight greys, not the clattering tide of blue, gold, crimson and silver of her cavalry escort and not even the Hong Kong police in their incongruous coolie hats, but a diversion that had interposed between him and his concerns since his chance meeting with Barbara Lockerbie a few weeks ago. For the New Broom had lost some of its inflexibility of late and those within close range of it noticed, or thought they noticed, a wholly uncharacteristic irresolution in the way the broom was wielded. A strange, unwonted peace had settled on the network. Dust had been allowed to settle in out-of-the-way corners at Headquarters, and in the regions beyond, so that regional managers who had been at the receiving end of George Swann's barrage of watch-it-and-wait-for-it telegrams ever since Old Gaffer put his feet up, told one another the gale was easing off a point or two and that the Young Gaffer, praise God, was 'running out of steam' as the Old Gaffer would have put it. They were men of the world, mostly, who had been around Swann yards long enough to remember George as a pink-cheeked lad with an unpleasant tendency to pop up in unexpected places when least expected. They fancied, therefore, that by now they knew him as well as they had known his father, but they would have been wrong. For George Swann had not run out of steam. On the contrary, he could have been said to have built up such a head of steam over the years that it became imperative that somebody came forward to open a safety-valve on his explosive energy. And this, in fact, was what had happened the moment Barbara Lockerbie crossed his path. Any steam that remained in George's boilers was now at her disposal, not Swann's.

It was nine weeks since they had met, seven since he had become her lover and a long, fretful week since he had held her in his arms, shedding his packload of responsibilities much as Christian shed his sins and watched them roll away downhill on his journey to the Celestial City. Unlike Christian, however, George had reached the Celestial City at a bound, for Barbara Lockerbie, saddled with an ageing husband and currently between lovers, had an eye for men like George Swann, recognising him instantly as someone in such desperate need of dalliance that he was, in fact, likely to prove virile, generous and unencumbered with jealousy concerning competitors past and present.

She was right. He took what she offered gratefully, without seeking to lay down conditions and without a thought as to how deep a dent she was likely to make in his bank balance. He did not enquire why her elegant boudoir was slightly tainted with cigar-smoke, or who had paid for that cameo set in emeralds that had not been on the dressing table the night before last. He was as eager as a boy, as trusting as a spoiled mastiff, and as uncompromising in his approach as a shipwrecked mariner beached by sirens after years of toil and celibacy. That was why, when she declared these Imperial rites vulgar, and took herself off to her country house in Hertfordshire before they were due to begin, she knew with complete certainty he would find a way of accepting her invitation to join her while Sir James Lockerbie, rival gallants and his little Austrian wife, Gisela, were city-bound by the national junketings. She was not often wrong about men and she was never wrong about George Swann. Before the tail-end of the procession had passed under the Lockerbie window George had composed and rehearsed an urgent summons from his Midlands viceroy. With luck he could make Harpenden by suppertime and a Lockerbie carriage would convey his wife and family home to Beckenham. He rejoiced then that he had granted the network an extra day's holiday in honour of the Jubilee. It meant that no one would look for him until the following Thursday.

3

For Adam Swann, seventy, it was appropriate weather and for Alex, thirty-six, campaigning weather. For Hugo, twenty-eight, it was athletes' weather and for George, thirty-three, hauling and whoring weather. There remained the Swann Conscience, not quite silenced by the jangle of bells and the boom of royal salutes and for Giles, its keeper, it was something else again. Protest weather, possibly, for Giles, almost alone among that vast crowd was not present as a sightseer but as an actor. Evidence, as far as the Swanns were concerned, that all that glittered down there was fool's gold.

His observation post was a first-floor window above the display windows of Beckwith and Lowenstein's, the once-fashionable Strand branch, now set on its slow decline since the carriage trade had drifted east to Regent's Street and Oxford Street. It was almost the last shop in the north façade of the Strand and he was there as lookout on behalf of the forlorn band of leaflet-throwers stationed two storeys above. Among them, at her urgent insistence, was his wife, Romayne, disinherited daughter of one of the wealthiest merchants in the land.

It was not the first foray in which they had been involved but because of the occasion it promised to be the most sensational, certain of earning press coverage, which was more than could be said of earlier protests, even the abortive one they staged at the Lord Mayor's Show last November.

Soper, the fanatical Secretary of the newly formed Shop Assistants' Action Group, had conceived it, a pallid, tireless and, in Giles' view, a very reckless campaigner who had won a majority vote in committee on the grounds that a gesture of this kind, a challenge thrown at the feet of the most powerful and influential people in Britain, was irresistible and perhaps he was right. Few among those who were offered the Group's standard leaflets in the street, or at Hyde Park Corner, accepted them, and even those who did discarded them ten steps beyond. "We have to move on," Soper had argued passionately, "we have to force the campaign on the national press and what more certain way of doing that than putting our case to the Queen on her way to St. Paul's?"

Put like that it was unanswerable and Romayne, her imagination fired, shouted "Hear, hear! Bravo!" as if the proposal of such a bold gesture represented its accomplishment. But Giles, to her private dismay, had argued against it, first publicly in committee, where he had been outvoted, then privately on their way home. She did not often run counter to him but she did now, saying, "But don't you *see*, Giles? It's dramatic, something they can't laugh off in the way they did when we paraded with placards!"

"It's certainly that," he said, trying to locate the springs of his instinctive misgivings, "but there's something about it I don't like. It's not just the risk of arrest on some trumped-up charge – obstruction, creating a public nuisance – they'd find something if they laid hands on any of us. And it's not the pleasure of reminding all those popinjays that there are more important issues than waving flags. Maybe it's the timing."

"The timing? I don't follow, Giles, dear."

He said, grumpily, "Well, there's no point in us falling out about it. It was a majority decision and we'll go ahead. I only lay down one condition. They leave the wording of the leaflet and the tactics to me."

"Oh, but they'll do that," she said, and he thought she was probably right. The Shop Assistants' Action Group did not lack ideas and enthusiasm but it was woefully short on funds and prestige, both of which Giles Swann, a director of a nationwide haulage network, could provide.

The Jubilee ambush continued to bother him. They lived in a pretty little Georgian house at Shirley, within easy reach of East Croydon Station, and the back looked over woods and pastures to the Kent–Surrey border. That same night, unable to sleep, he got out of bed and went on to the terrace looking across the fields to the blur of Addington Woods and here, in uncompromising moon-light, his misgivings crystallised. He saw the leaflet raid as a single jarring note in a national overture. It was easy to imagine the wrapt expressions of the Jubilee holiday-makers, each of them revelling in a day's release from monotonous toil to witness an unprecedented display of pomp and martial display in which they would feel them-selves personally involved, and a majority, regarding the Queen's personage as sacrosanct, would surely regard the descent of a shower of leaflets on her entourage an act of impiety. It would be irrelevant too, on a day when London was out to enjoy itself, and when every man, woman and child assembled there personally subscribed to the mystique of Empire and took pride in the spread of red on maps hung on the blackboards of the redbrick Board Schools.

Of all the Swanns, Giles saw himself as the only one involved in the present. Alex, George and Hugo were forsworn to the future, to an increasingly modernised army, to the spread of commerce and the triumphs of the sports arena as the might of the tribes increased year by year. His father, who had once had a social conscience, had slipped back into the past, to the battles for franchise and human rights of the 'sixties and 'seventies. But it some-times seemed to him that he alone was equipped to lift the lid on this treasure chest they called the Empire and examine, piecemeal, the terrible injustices concealed under the plumes and moneybags stowed there. As a child he had witnessed an aged couple evicted and despatched to separate workhouses, and as a youth he had penetrated the galleries of a Rhondda coal-mine and seen, closehand, the filth and degradation of the industrial cities in the

north. Everywhere, it appeared to him, was gross im-
balance; wealth and power on the one hand, grinding
poverty and naked cruelty on the other, but so few
acknowledged this boil on the body politic. They chanted
patriotic music-hall ditties, put their money on the Grand
Fleet and thought of themselves as actually taking part
in an eruption of power and plenty, unique in the history
of mankind. Then they went blithely about their concerns, the privileged making money, gallivanting on
river and race-course, snug under a mantle of rectitude
woven for them by Providence. For the others, who made
all this possible, it was very different. The conditions
worked by shop assistants in the big emporiums were only
one of the blatant contradictions in an age of tremendous
technological progress and the flagrant contrasts within
the system tormented him for it seemed to him that, once
they were publicly recognised and acknowledged, they
could be so easily adjusted. Romayne's revelation was
a case in point.

He remembered her as she had been in their courtship
days, a pampered, highly-strung child of an industrialist,
who had seemed never to comprehend his smouldering
quarrel with the status quo, who had taken all her privileges for granted and had indulged in a fit of temper
whenever anything was withheld from her. But all that
had changed and under pressure of what he looked back
on as absurdly melodramatic circumstances. Unable
to adjust to her selfishness he had jilted her, abruptly and
finally after a scene in an Oxford Street milliner's a minute
to closing time one Saturday night, and had glumly
assumed that the incident marked the end of their bitter-
sweet relationship. Yet it was not so. Something had
rubbed off on her, enough to project her out of her
cushioned surroundings and into the workaday world,
there to test his theories in the light of personal experience.
Eighteen months later, against all probability, he had
found and reclaimed her, earning her living in the cash
desk of a northcountry haberdasher's, and sharing the

submerged life of living-in shop assistants working a sixty-hour week under what was really no advance on the lot of slaves. The experience had transformed her utterly, and if that could happen to her it could happen to others, providing the point could be brought home to them with equal emphasis. Yet how to achieve it, without revolution and blood on the streets? Not by protest meetings at Hyde Park Corner. Not by leaflets, placards and parades and letters to the press. Surely by legislation, and the slow reshaping of public opinion it would be possible. There was a lesson here somewhere, for him and for everybody else. Possibly, just possibly, Soper was right. The public needed a shock, a whole series of shocks, and perhaps his underlying misgivings concerning Soper's tactics stemmed from an excessive respect for law and order and an instinctive distaste for involving himself and his family in scandal. Romayne, out of regard for him, had not succumbed to those pressures and remembering this he discerned the real source of her enthusiasm for Soper's paper bombardment. Standing there in the moonlight he thought, forlornly, 'She *did* that. She endured that purgatory for eighteen months, and for no other reason than to prove that we belonged to each other, paying in wretchedness for her tantrums, her ridiculous involvements with grooms and music-teachers, her gross extravagance and the capacity, hardening like a crust, to see the dispossessed as serfs. Well, then, to hell with what I think about the proposal. I'll do it. Not for Soper and not even for the poor devils he claims to represent, but for her.'

He went in to find her sleeping soundly and studied her in the shaft of moonlight that fell across the pillow. A beautiful child, robbed by sleep of the strange contradictions imposed upon her by the past, that included her failure to present him with a child, something she would probably see as a fresh source of inadequacy, although he did not. There were already too many children in the world. Many of them would never have enough to eat.

Many of them would grow into spindle-legged, weak-chested adults with no alternative but to work out their lives at the dictates of some stonefaced overlord like her father or his grandfather. Like his own father, even, despite Adam Swann's national reputation as an enlightened gaffer. He slipped in beside her, still troubled certainly, but comforted, to some degree, by the completeness of her transformation.

2

Paper Ambush

IT WAS DIFFICULT TO RID HIMSELF OF A SENSE OF melodrama as he went about his preparations, beginning with the drafting of the leaflet and ending, an hour or so before the procession was due to pass the corner-site, on the day itself. It was as though all the time he was planning, counselling, conniving, he was standing off watching himself masquerade as a nihilist, a Balkan assassin or a bearded anarchist resolved upon some stupendous masterstroke instead of what it was, an insignificant discord in the national overture.

More than once, as the day drew near, he came near to admitting he was a pompous ass to involve either himself or Romayne in the charade, yet he persisted, partly because he had his full share of Swann obstinacy, but more because, below the level of self-mockery, he acknowledged his cause was just. And then, when every last detail had been perfected, and he was alone in the airless little annexe, partitioned off from the empty showrooms, excitement liberated him from the sense of the ridiculous and he told himself that he would not have been anywhere else. But it still nagged him that Romayne had insisted, as the price of his involvement, on becoming one of the four selected for the perpetration of the actual deed.

They had all wanted a part, even if it was limited to throwing a handful of leaflets apiece and then running for it, as Giles and his chosen three planned they should.

37

But four, he said, was the maximum number within a safety limit. Their escape route lay down four flights of stairs, into the corridor between shop and staff entrance, past the janitor's cubicle and out into Catherine Street, there to lose themselves in the crowd. The plan was as perfect as he could make it. There was a more than even chance that they would all be clear away before the distributing point was located and searched, for Soper, himself an employee of Beckwith's, laid long odds that Meadowes, the janitor, would quit his cubicle at the side entrance the moment cheering heralded the vanguard of the procession.

This part of the premises, the western end, was deserted. The entire staff of the emporium, some fifty of them, were now lining the row of windows nearer the Law Courts, and it seemed very improbable that anyone would leave them at the climactic moment, so that the stairs leading to the upper stockroom, where the ambush was centred, were likely to remain free. Soper and his fiancée, a fragile girl with huge, trusting eyes, who served at Beckwith's glove counter, were positioned there, with five hundred leaflets apiece, laboriously blocked out on a child's printing set, for printers could be traced. The wording was direct and, in Giles' view, necessarily inflammable. It ran:

AFTER THE SPECTACLE THE RECKONING! MILLIONS OF HOURS OF UNPAID OVERTIME WERE WORKED BY COUNTER-JUMPERS TO MOUNT THE SPECTACLE YOU ARE WATCHING! THE AVERAGE SHOP ASSISTANT WORKS AN ELEVEN-HOUR DAY ON A SMALLER WAGE THAN AN AGRICULTURAL LABOURER. TAKE ACTION NOW TO ORGANISE THE TRADE AND OPPOSE:
Low Wages
Fines for 'refusing'
Unjust dismissals without a character or right of appeal
Prison diet, fed to living-in staff
Abbreviated half-days.

THESE ARE BUT FIVE CURRENT GRIEVANCES OF THE MOST EXPLOITED WORK-FORCE IN BRITAIN.

Soper and his committee had been ecstatic about this broadside, embracing, as far as it could on a leaflet measuring about six inches by eight, most of the major ailments of this industrial lame duck. Privately Giles thought it could have been condensed to a point where it could be read at a glance but there was no time to redraft so he let it pass, concentrating on the strategy of the ambush with particular emphasis on the escape route. And now, in the stifling heat of a room piled with the paraphernalia of a haberdasher's window-dressing team, he watched the eddying crowds below, ten deep he would say both sides of the Strand, with a dribble of latecomers drifting down sidestreets in the vain hope of finding a chink in a kerbside phalanx.

Time passed slowly. About nine, as Soper had predicted, the distant throb of drums and the cheers of spectators lured Meadowes, the janitor, from his cubicle and he went out, leaving the staff door open. Soper's key had ensured their entry before he was on duty, and Soper and his fiancée, Miriam, had climbed to the second storey with their bundles of leaflets. Romayne had been stationed as signaller on the third landing. His own job was to watch for the head of the procession, give the signal, and keep a close watch on the escape route and the movements of the janitor.

Timing, he had insisted, was vitally important. It would do far more harm than good to throw the leaflets over the sills before the royal entourage was safely past and on its way down Fleet Street. He hoped to select a section of the cavalcade that was marching rather than riding, for it was always possible that a shower of leaflets would frighten a horse and cause casualties. If there had been the faintest hint of a breeze most of the sheets would have drifted the width of the Strand but the bunting and flags on the lamp-standards hung motionless and it seemed likely that nearly all would find pavement level on the north side. It didn't matter, so long as Soper and the girl followed his orders and waited for the signal passed on by Romayne. Soper was an impatient chap and waiting there, with the sounds of the drums and brass drawing nearer as they battled with the almost continuous roar of the crowd, Giles wished he had had someone steadier to take his own place as scout in order that he could oversee the leaflet bombers in person. He stepped out and tiptoed halfway down the last flight of stone steps to a point where he could see the empty cubicle, then back again, calling softly to Romayne to tell Soper and Miriam that the janitor was safely out of the way. Then he resumed his place at the window and concentrated on the area immediately below. And it was at that moment, his eye ranging the north pavements, that he noted the movement of the thickset man wearing unseasonably heavy brown tweeds and a brown derby hat.

He was clearly more than a spectator and seemed to have some official purpose down there, for he walked purposefully along the carriageway, head tilted, eyes scanning the façades instead of the carriageway, as though he was some kind of policeman or marshal, assuring himself that all was well among the tiers of patriots massed at the windows of the northside premises. There was no menace about him, only an unwavering watchfulness, and when the blaring bands and the cheering engulfed them all like a tumbling wall of masonry he still sauntered there, turned away from the oncoming procession. By then, however, Giles had all but forgotten him, his attention caught and held by the spectacle in spite of himself, as the royal entourage rolled by, eight rosetted greys pulling the open carriage containing a little old woman under her white parasol, the splendidly mounted and richly caparisoned bevy of royalty in its immediate wake, then the glittering, jingling squadron of Horse Guards, and behind it rank upon rank of blue, scarlet and gold, a thousand or more men with brown faces and martial step, their presence representing the flag at the ends of the earth.

The moment was at hand and he was on the point of turning to call up to Romayne when, once again, the man in the brown derby caught his eye, insistently now for he had stopped sauntering and was standing squarely on the kerb, staring up at a window immediately above. It was the window where Soper and his girl were stationed. With a grunt of alarm, Giles saw the first of the leaflets flutter down, drifting idly and aimlessly, like birds dropping out of the sky, and in the same moment he saw the man below stiffen, gesticulate and run swiftly round the angle of the building and out of Giles' line of vision.

There was really little but instinct to tell him the watcher had spotted something amiss up there and for a second or so he dithered, his eye roving the fringe of latecomers in search of Meadowes, the janitor, but as he hesitated more and more leaflets floated down, separating in flight so that they seemed to multiply out of all proportion to the number printed. Then, whipping round, he heard the scrape of a boot on the stairs and leaped for the landing, almost colliding with a thickset figure in the act of tackling the third flight.

The man must have moved with extraordinary speed. Ten seconds or less had brought him this far but his step, notwithstanding his bulk, was as light as a boy's. In a few strides he would be level with Romayne, staring over the stairwell. A moment later he would have Soper and his girl trapped with his back to the door.

Giles shouted, "Run, Romayne, *run!*" and flung himself at the steps, grabbing the heavy material of the man's trousers, then enlarging his hold on one brown boot, so that the man lurched and stumbled, falling heavily against the iron stair-rail and half-turning, so that Giles caught a glimpse of a red face with heavy jowls, a large moustache of the kind made fashionable by Lord Kitchener, and eyes that glared at him with a baffled expression. He was so occupied with holding the man that he did not hear Romayne's warning cry, or the rush of feet on the stairs heralding the frantic descent of Soper and Miriam, the girl still clutching a double handful of leaflets. He was aware, however, of Romayne darting past or over them and into the store room he had just left and almost at once, it seemed, her reappearance with a dust-sheet that billowed like a sail and all but enveloped him.

Then, amid a rush of movement and a confused outcry, the man he was holding let go of the stair-rail and whirled his fists, aiming a blow capable, he would have said, of felling a prize-fighter had it not been deadened by the enveloping folds of the dust-sheet, but was still powerful enough to knock him clear of the stairs to a point where he cannoned into the scampering Miriam, sending her crashing against the door of the store room. After that all was the wildest confusion, the intruder heaving under the sheet and the four of them arriving in a body at the foot of the stairs and bolting headlong down the corridor to the staff entrance where Meadowes stood, mouth agape and hands upraised to ward off what must have seemed to him a concerted charge. He was swept aside, steel-rimmed spectacles flying one way, peaked cap another, and then they were clear and running through the crowd in the direction of Drury Lane.

There was no immediate pursuit, or not so far as a glance over his shoulder could tell him as they doubled two more corners before arriving at the eastern arcade of Covent Garden, deserted now but shin deep in litter and baskets and barricaded with costers' barrows half seen under their tarpaulins. He stopped then, catching Soper by the arm and saying, breathlessly, "Into the market – a dozen places to hide!" and they both scrambled over the barrows, pulling the girls after them and found cover in the semi-darkness of the grilled caves beyond.

Nobody said anything for a moment. The girl Miriam was grimacing with pain, and holding her right hand to her shoulder where it had come into violent contact with the store room door. Soper was spent but otherwise intact. The white of Romayne's petticoat showed through a rent in her skirt and she was already fumbling in her reticule for safety-pins. Then Soper said, soberly, "My God! That was a close shave! Who was he, Mr. Swann?"

"How would I know? A plain-clothes detective maybe, keeping a lookout for something like this. He seemed to pinpoint the place at a glance."

Soper's eyes widened as he said, "You mean somebody peached? Someone on the committee? He was stationed there waiting for us?"

The narrowness of their escape put an edge on Giles' tongue. "I don't think anything of the kind. He was checking the route and saw something unusual. You and your leaflets probably. Why the devil didn't you wait for my signal like we arranged?"

"We had trouble getting the window open. The frame stuck at less than an inch." This from the girl, still massaging her bruised shoulder.

"But you actually threw leaflets. I saw some go down."

"We broke the glass," Soper said. "We had to, there was no other way," and Giles growled, "Well, at least we know how he spotted us. Not that it matters."

"I'm sorry, Mr. Swann. We muffed it. Most of the leaflets are still up there."

Giles replied, sourly, "You don't fancy going back to finish the job?"

Romayne said, sharply, "That's not fair, Giles! What else could they do in the circumstances? At least some leaflets went out."

The girl Miriam began to cry, quietly and half-heartedly – a child warned that she will be given something to cry about if she doesn't watch out. Giles was suddenly aware of the overpowering might of the forces ranged against them, ranged against everybody in their situation, including the cheering crowds who would soon go home, sun-tired and satisfied with their brief vision of world domination, but expected to make it last until the next free show vouchsafed by the élite. A coronation, a royal wedding or a Lord Mayor's Show.

He said, more to himself than the others, "It's no use ... these demonstrations ... leaflets, placards, with every-one involved risking their jobs. There must be another way, a way that doesn't put everyone at risk." He looked directly at Soper. "You and Miriam would have been recognised by the janitor. You daren't go back to Beck-with and Lowenstein's now."

"I don't have to. I've given notice. I told the floor manager I was moving to another billet up north. I was paid up last Saturday."

"You've got another billet?"

"No. That was a cover, in case something like this happened."

"You've got a character?"

Soper shrugged. "I'll use the ones I used to land that job, ones I wrote myself. I was in trouble at my last place. It soon gets around if you're a militant."

"And Miriam?"

"She can go back. Meadowes didn't see her."

"How can you be sure?"

"I'm sure," Romayne said. "She was last out and I knocked his glasses off while she was still in the corridor."

Pride in her took possession of him, going a short way to soothe the frustration and humiliation of the day. He said, "You all came out of it better than me. I was supposed to be lookout but I let him get that far. If Romayne hadn't been sharp with that dust-sheet none of us would have got clear. I'm sorry I sneered, Soper. I had no right to. Your stake is a much bigger one than mine and I don't have to remind you what can result from using forged references."

"That's all right, Mr. Swann." He put his arm round his girl and she winced. "It hurts horribly," she said. "Do you suppose we could find a chemist open and get some arnica?"

"You stay here," Giles said. "I'll find a chemist's

and a pie-shop too. You'll be safe enough here until the crowds start dispersing. Then we can all go home. Will you wait with them, Soper?"

"Anything you say, Mr. Swann."

He went out into the blinding sunshine, working his way west towards Trafalgar Square and King William IV Street where, on his way to the rendezvous, he had seen shops open. 'Anything you say, Mr. Swan . . .' They all looked to him for a lead, not because he was more qualified to give one than the least of them, but because he was a renegade from the far side of the barricades, a man who owned his own house, wore tailored clothes and had a famous father. It wasn't good enough, not by a very long chalk, and somehow he would have to improve on it or leave them to get on with it alone. He found a chemist's and bought a bottle of arnica, then a market coffee-stand where he bought four meat pies and four bottles of ginger beer, carrying his purchases back to their refuge in the labyrinthine corridors of the market. Romayne took charge of the girl, coaxing her to unbutton her blouse and expose a great purple bruise above the prominent collarbone. He noticed that she flushed when her neck and shoulders were bared and he turned aside, taking Soper over to the grille. He said, quietly, "You'll never get a billet after this and you know it. Have you any experience of clerical work?"

"I was a ledger clerk at Patterson's, the wholesalers, soon after I left school."

"Why didn't you stick to book-keeping?"

"I got sacked after asking for a rise. No shindig at Patterson's, just a straight case of Oliver Twist on that occasion. Don't bother about me, Mr. Swann. I'll look out for myself."

He liked Soper's spirit and wry sense of humour. Headstrong he might be but if there were three Sopers in every city emporium the rough-and-ready tactics they had used today would be unnecessary. Real solidarity among the helots was what was needed and it wasn't impossible. It had already been successful in the heavy industries up north. Bargains could be struck between the vast numbers of have-nots and the Gradgrinds in their plush suburban houses. But there were not three Sopers anywhere, much less in a drapery store. More often than not there wasn't one prepared to risk his livelihood for a cause of this kind. He said, "I'll get you a billet with my father's firm. I can tell the truth about you to him. It'll be a fresh start."

"And the Action Group, Mr. Swann?"

"We shall have to work for parliamentary backing. It's not impossible. Other trades have achieved it. What we need is some kind of charter to cover all the retail trades."

"That's looking 'way ahead, isn't it?"

"It's better than this hit-and-miss campaign and I'm going to put my mind to it. Have you got enough money to stay on in your digs for a week or so?"

Soper grinned. "For a month. On credit if need be. The landlady's daughter fancies me and she doesn't know about Miriam."

"Where does Miriam live? She isn't living-in, is she?"

"No. She lives with an aunt in Maida Vale."

"Get her home and let her rest. She'd better show up tomorrow and if she should be questioned tell her to give my wife's name as a reference. We'll say she spent the entire day with us and the janitor is mistaken."

He looked relieved at that, Giles thought, and his estimation of Soper soared another point. "You could get married on the wage my brother George pays his warehouse clerks," he said. "It's above average."

* * *

They said little to one another on the way home. The heat in the suburban train was insufferable and everybody in the world seemed to be making his way out of the city. It was only later, when they were standing at the window watching the Jubilee bonfires wink across the Shirley

46

meadows that he said, suddenly, "How much does all this mean to you, Romayne? This house, servants, security, comfort?"

"Why do you ask?"

"It's important I should know. Apart from that brief spell, when you ran away and worked in that sweat-shop, you've always been cushioned against poverty. Like me. Like almost everyone we know. We're really no more than salon revolutionaries and I'm tired of facing two ways. But it wouldn't be fair for me to make the decision alone."

"What decision?"

"To throw up the firm and get myself adopted as a Liberal candidate, if anyone will have me. Then work full-time at what I believe in, what I've always believed in from the beginning."

She turned and looked at him speculatively. "You'd do that? You'd walk out on your father's firm for good?"

"I would. Would you?"

"You know I would."

"It's that important to you?"

"Seeing you spend your life working at something you believe in is important. It doesn't matter what. It never has really."

He bent his head and kissed her. "I haven't the least idea how to go about it, but . . ."

"I have."

"*You* have?"

"I've thought about it a long time now but I didn't say anything. It had to come from you. I think I know how I could get you taken up, with a real chance of getting to Westminster."

"If you're relying on your father he wouldn't lift a finger . . ."

"It's nothing to do with my father. It's an idea I had a long time ago, when we were on holiday in Wales, but don't ask me about it now."

"Why not?"

"Because I have to think about it, about the best way of going about it. Just let me work it out and put it to you when I'm ready."

He thought, distractedly, 'I'll never know her. Not really, not like old George and Alex know their wives and certainly not like my father knows Mother. I know no more about her now than that day I fished her out of that river below Beddgelert, when we were kids. But the devil of it is she knows me. Every last thing about me!'

The long day was almost done. From across the meadows came the faint, meaningless sounds of revelry, persistent celebrants sporting round their bonfires, reluctant to write 'finis' to a day they would talk about all their lives. He said, as they settled under the flimsy bed-coverings, "Our joint resources won't run to more than three hundred a year, if that. We should have to sell up and move to wherever I was chosen. A terrace house or a cottage maybe."

"Three hundred a year is six pounds a week," she said. "People bring up big families on that and there's only two of us. Go to sleep, Giles."

It was a clue, he thought, linking her sponsorship with her apparent inability to bring him a child. In a curious way their relationship had shifted of late, ever since her fourth and last miscarriage. Perhaps she saw him as the only child she was likely to have and was determined, in that queer private way of hers, to make the best of it. His arm went round her but she did not respond, although he could tell she was wide awake. He had a sense then of complete dependence on her and with it a sudden and inexplicable onrush of confidence in the future. Perhaps the day had not been such a failure after all.

3

Bedside Whisper

MOST MEN, ADAM REFLECTED, WERE DIMINISHED by deathbeds, but Sam Rawlinson, his eighty-eight-year-old father-in-law, was clearly an exception. Sam, half-recumbent in a bed that had never been adequate for him, looked so excessively bloated that he made the ugly, over-furnished bedroom seem very cramped for visitors, who were obliged to squeeze themselves between bed and wardrobe and then sit very still for fear of overturning the bedside table littered with Sam's pills and potions.

Adam was surprised to find him not only rational but loquacious, as though, in the final days of his long, bustling life, he was in a rare ferment to get things tidied up and sorted out, and he received Adam almost genially, croaking, "Now, lad!" in that broad Lancashire accent of his he had never attempted to convert into the city squeak that many men of his stamp affected once they had made their pile. Henrietta had already been in with Hilda, Sam's statuesque second wife, who seemed, improbably, to be giving way to the strain of the old man's final battle against odds, the only one, thought Adam, he was certain to lose. She warned Adam, "You'll find him low but he's tetchy with it. He's had me on the jump for more than a month now. Try and keep him off his dratted affairs, will you?"

He climbed the gloomy, paint-scarred staircase, reflecting as he went that no one had ever succeeded in keeping Sam off his affairs, for they had been meat and drink to the old reprobate ever since, as a slum-bred lad in Ancoats in the first years of the cotton boom, he had kicked and throttled his way from coal-sorter, to bale-breaker, to the looms and, at thirty-odd to part-ownership of his first mill where he worked his hands like galley-slaves. He was already a man of substance when Adam met him, forty years ago, and the fact that Sam still addressed him, at seventy, as 'lad', made him smile. Long, long ago they had come to terms with one another, rarely referring to their first confrontation, when Sam had stormed into the Swann homestead threatening to prefer charges against him of abducting his eighteen-year-old daughter. In view of this understanding they were spared soothing bedside prattle, customary in the circumstances. Adam said, bluntly, "Is there anything special you want doing, Sam?" a clear enough indication to a man as forthright as Rawlinson that time was running out.

"Nay," Sam said, "nowt special, lad, tho' I'm reet glad you've come an' no mistake. Couldn't have said what I'd a mind to say to t'lass. Women don't set a proper value on these things."

"What things, Sam?"

"Brass," Sam said, uncompromisingly, "and what to make of it. Eee, they can spend it fast enough, the least of 'em, but I never met one who could put it to work. Now that lass o' mine, she'll have made sizeable holes in your pockets over the years."

"I'm not complaining," Adam said, "and neither should you with an army of grandchildren, and great-grandchildren to spare. There'll be plenty to share whatever you're inclined to leave."

"That's the rub," Sam said, heaving himself up in an effort to make himself more comfortable in the rumpled bed. "Ah've had second thowts about that. One time I had it in mind to see after our Hilda and split t'rest so many ways. Then Ah got to thinkin'. Most o' the bene-ficiaries wouldn't have a notion what to do with a windfall that came their way, so I went to old Fossdyke and drew up t'new will. Hilda'll pass you a copy of it if you ask her."

He was breathing noisily and his broad, battered face had a deep purple flush, so that Adam said, "We don't have to go over it, Sam. You can trust me to follow your wishes."

"Aye," said Sam, emphatically, "I can that. Come to think of it you're one of the few Ah've always trusted, and there's none so many o' them." He paused, as though reflecting deeply. "I were luckier'n I deserved about you but I've owned to that times enough, haven't I?"

"I've been lucky myself, Sam. What do you want to tell me about your money? That Henrietta is getting the whole of the residue?"

"*Nay*," Sam said, clamping his strong jaws, "she's getting nowt, or not directly. Nor young George either, tho' I still reckon him the flower o' the flock."

It astonished him to hear Sam say this, and with such emphasis. He could understand a man of Sam's temperament fighting shy of splitting his money into so many insignificant packages, thereby making it seem a less impressive total, but he had always believed Henrietta, as Sam's only child, would inherit the bulk of his fortune, and that George, who had been championed by his grandfather when the boy threw everything aside to redesign that petrol waggon he had brought home from Vienna, would come off best among the children.

"What are you going to do with it, Sam? Leave it to charity?"

To judge by his father-in-law's expression the question came close to killing him on the spot. He said, gesturing wildly with his fat, freckled hands, "*Charity?* Sweat bloody guts out for close on eighty years to cosset layabouts who never took jacket off for nobody, 'emselves included? Nay, lad, you can't be that daft! You know me a dam' sight better than that! *Charity!* There's too much bloody charity nowadays! No wonder country's not what it were in my young days, when it were sink or swim. Ah'm leavin' the lot to you, to do as you please with. And it'll amount to something when all's settled up, Ah'm tellin' you!"

"Good God, *I* don't want it, Sam. I'm already the wrong side of seventy, and I've got all the money I'm likely to spend!"

"Aye, I daresay, though a man can always do with a bit more. Besides, it's not as cut an' dried as that, as you'll see if you'll hold your tongue, lad. I've had Skin-a-rabbit Fossdyke make a trust fund in your name. That way you can spread it around whichever way you've a mind, so long as it stays in t'family."

"How do you mean, exactly?"

Sam was silent for a moment or two, seemingly occupied in getting his breath and marshalling his thoughts. Finally, he said, "Put it this way. You and me, we had nowt to begin with, but we each of us finished up with a pile big enow to make men tip their hats to us, didn't we?"

"You could put it that way."

"It's the on'y way to put it. Use that brass o' mine to feed any one o' them lads or lasses who shows my kind o' gumption. And *your* kind of gumption. Any one of 'em, mind, man or maid, who'll stand on their own feet an' look all bloody creation in t'face, same as we have. Do you follow me now?"

It made sense, Sam's kind of sense. Bloated and dying, in an ugly house in a Manchester suburb, Sam Rawlinson obviously looked back over his life with immense satisfaction, hugging his commercial success (the only success worth having in his view) as a just reward for his prodigious and profitable endeavours over the years, thereby earning the respect of all men dedicated to the same object and a man with any other objective was a fool, counting for nothing. He would want to see that money well spent and in a way he would spend it if, by some miracle, his youth and vigour were restored to him at this moment. There was a kind of merciless logic in the gesture, for Sam would restrict the deserving to those who, like himself and his son-in-law, backed themselves against all comers. He said, with a shrug, "Well, you might do worse, Sam. I get the drift of it, and you can rely on me to do it your way. Is that all?"

"Nay," said Sam, "it's not all. Ah've been wanting a word in your ear for long enough. Mebbe I won't get another chance."

Adam waited, but for some moments Sam's gaze remained blank. Then, unexpectedly, he rallied and said, very carefully, "It were about young George. Him and that kiss-your-arse manager he sets such store on. What's the name? Same name as that old maid of a clerk you had down there, before you took it into your head to back out and leave t'lads to run your business."

"You mean Tybalt? Wesley Tybalt, the son of my head clerk?"

"Aye, that's him. I got word he wants watching."

It crossed Adam's mind then, and for the first time since entering the room, that Sam was wandering. Wesley Tybalt, the only child of his old friend in the rough and tumble days, had lately established himself as the most dynamic administrator they had ever had. George himself said so, others echoed his judgment and even his excessively modest father, now retired and devoting himself full-time to his East End mission work, agreed with them. Sam had always been keenly interested in the expansion of Swann-on-Wheels but he had never had anything to do with its day-to-day administration. It seemed extremely improbable that now, at nearly ninety, and a housebound invalid into the bargain, he could have discovered anything of importance about the firm's affairs. Wesley Tybalt had served his time up here, but so had everybody else who held a position of responsibility at Headquarters. It was a Swann rule that promising executives should spend six months in every region before joining the London staff so that Sam might well have met and evaluated Tybalt when he was based in the north. That could hardly account, however, for so direct a warning. He said, sharply, "You'll have to be a damned sight more explicit than that, Sam. I'm out of things now, as you well know. George is gaffer, and Giles is next in line. My other two younger sons, Hugo and Edward, are in the network, but I've never once had reason to suppose George wasn't making a thorough go of it. If there was a flaw in young Tybalt I would have heard about it. One or other of the boys would have told me, and asked my advice, no doubt."

"Not George," Sam said, once again clamping his aggressive jaws like a rat-trap. "George is a loner, as you've good cause to know. Your memory's not that short, lad."

That much at least was true. Ever since taking over George had gone his own way without seeking anyone's advice but the business had prospered under him, despite an occasional misjudgment, like the premature introduction of those mechanical vans some years back. As for young Tybalt, Adam had been prejudiced in his favour a long time now, partly, no doubt, because he had received such unswerving loyalty from his father over a period of thirty years. He had met him often during his visits to the yard, a tall, loose-limbed, toothy young man, with thin sandy hair and an ingratiating manner. Not a boy you could like, perhaps, but one who knew precisely what he was about when he came to having charge of the network's clerical concerns. Every single question Adam had ever put to him concerning stock and trends and routes had prompted a concise and realistic answer. He said, doubtfully, "What put this into your head, Sam? Where did it come from? Has George been up here lately?"

"He came once. A few weeks since, when I was still up and about, but he weren't the same lad as back along. There were no flies on him then but there are now. One in particular, I'd say."

"Who would that be?"

"Nay, I can't swear to that. I could've one time, when I was around to put the ferrets in if I wanted to know anything partic'lar. But I'll lay long odds it's a woman. He were dressed to the nines and had his hair smarmed down and smelling like a garding."

"Did he talk to you about business?"

"Nay, he didn't. And that was what made me sit up an' take notice, for he alwus had before, whenever he looked in on me. Like I say, he weren't t'same lad at all, so I got to talking with one or two of the old uns who dropped in to pass the time o' day wi' me and I got a hint or two."

"What kind of hint?"

"That Swann's New Broom was cutting a dash wi' the quality an' leavin' too much to his clerks. I seen many a good man go bust that way. So have you, I daresay."

"And young Tybalt. Have you ever met him?"

"Can't say as I have but old Levison has. Come to think on it Levison was the one who tipped me the wink."

"Who the devil is Levison?"

"Levison and Skilly, big warehousemen, Liverpool way. Done a deal o' business with 'em in my time but they don't haul by your line. Their stuff goes south on the cheap with Linklater's outfit. These things get around. They always have an' they always will among folk who count."

"What got around, exactly?"

"Nowt to speak of . . ." He was tiring rapidly and his breathing became laboured so that Adam thought, 'I can't press him now, although I'd give something to know what put that bee in his bonnet.' He rose, massaging the straps of his artificial leg. "I'll think on it."

Sam said, watching him narrowly. "Bloody memory's not what it were, dam' it!" He fumbled for his hunter watch, hanging by its heavy gold chain from the bedrail. "Time for me green pills," he said, vaguely. "Better fetch our Hilda up, lad. You'll be staying over a day or so?"

"We're staying at the Midland. Hilda has enough on her hands, Sam."

"Aye," Sam said, listlessly, "she's a good lass, but she never did the one thing I expected of her." He rallied momentarily, glaring the full length of the bed at an atrocious seascape hanging on the far wall. "Ah'd have liked a son to follow on. Hetty's litter is well enough but a lass isn't the same, somehow."

His chin dropped and his thick red lips parted. Adam went out, closing the door softly and calling to Hilda that it was time for Sam's green pills. Hetty asked, handing him a cup, "How did you find him, Adam?"

"Very talkative," Adam said, thoughtfully. "He'll soldier on a bit yet if I'm any judge." And then, as if she had expressed a contrary view, "He's a man of parts, is your father. There aren't many of his sort about nowadays."

"There never were," Henrietta said, "even when I first remember him. That was twelve years before you saw him ride a boy into the ground the night they were burning his mill." Then, in a more conciliatory tone, "Do you suppose he remembers things like that now, Adam? Now that he's dying, I mean?"

"If he does he doesn't regret 'em."

"But . . . shouldn't he? I mean, now that he's going? I'm sure I would. You too."

"That's the difference between us and between the times, too. In Sam's day, in my early days come to that, it was kill or be killed. You can't expect a man reared in a jungle to fall to his prayers in his dotage. Not without his tongue in his cheek that is. He asked me to ask Hilda to show us a copy of his will."

"I don't want his money."

"You're not getting any, m'dear," he said, enjoying her swift change in expression that told him that, in so many ways, and notwithstanding her lifelong disapproval of Sam's ethics, she was still Sam Rawlinson's daughter.

2

He was wrong. Sam died in his sleep three days later and they were obliged to stay on for the funeral. In the interval he had chatted with the old chap several times but neither made further reference to that curious warning about the dash George was cutting with the quality or the dubious reliability of his yard manager, Tybalt. Instead they talked about old times, and mutual acquaintances in the cotton world, and Adam was not surprised to see several of his cronies at the graveside, heavy, unsmiling men, watching the committal of Sam as though his coffin contained money as well as a corpse. It was not until the journey home that Adam re-addressed his mind to the hints Sam had dropped, turning them over and over as the train rushed southwards at nearly twice the maximum speed it had attained when he escorted Henrietta, an eighteen-year-old bride, on her first journey out of the north. George was cutting a dash among the quality. George was taking time off to squire a woman, obviously not Gisela, his pretty little Austrian wife. George was leaving too much to his manager and the manager needed watching. It didn't add up to much and finally he asked, of Henrietta, who was deep in the *Strand Magazine* he had bought her at the bookstall, "Is everything all right between George and Gisela, Hetty?"

She looked up a little irritably. "All right? So far as I know. Whatever made you ask a question like that?"

"Just something Sam said, but he might well have been rambling. George was there a few weeks back and looked in on them. 'Dressed to the nines an' smellin' like a garding' according to Sam."

"Is that all he said?"

"More or less. He hinted that George was gadding about and maybe neglecting the business, but I couldn't make head nor tail of it at the time. Do you see much of Gisela these days?"

"Not as much as I did but that doesn't signify anything. She's four children now, and a big house to run." She prepared to re-address herself to her magazine and he said, with a grin, "Don't you care that much, Hetty?"

"No," she admitted, frankly. "I can't say as I do. They're all old enough and ugly enough to watch out for themselves, as my nanny Mrs. Worrell would have said. George in particular, for George has always gone his own way. How old is he now?"

"Thirty-three last February." He had a wonderful memory for trivia but he had a special reason for remembering George's exact age. The boy had been born on St. Valentine's Day, 1864, a day when the fortunes of Swann-on-Wheels, near to foundering at that time, had taken a dramatic turn for the better, paving the way for what Adam always thought of as their *sortie torrentielle* into big business. Because of this, and the boy's temperament, he had always seen George as a good-luck talisman. They had never looked back from that moment, not even when he was away from the yard for a whole year learning to walk on one sound leg and an ugly contraption made up of cork and aluminium.

"Well," she said, "there's your answer. He was always a wild one but Gisela knows how to manage him. You've said so yourself many a time."

"So I have. Go back to that story you're reading. It must be a good one."

"It is," she told him, "it's a Sherlock Holmes," and the conversation lapsed, but he continued to think about it, trying to make a pattern out of the few stray pieces but not succeeding, no matter how many times he fitted one into the other, so he fell to marshalling his recollections on the boy's past.

For years now George had been a slave to that yard, devoting even more time to it than had Adam himself in his early, strenuous days. That much was known about George, not only inside the family and firm but all over the City, where men talked shop over their sherry and coffee. It was hard to imagine George as a masher, a gadabout or even a dandy. He had an eye for the girls, certainly had always had, ever since, as an eighteen-year-old, he was all but seduced by one of the manager's wives up in the Polygon. What was her name again – Lorna? Laura? – Laura Broadbent, that was it, who had

a brute of a husband, a man George had ultimately un-
masked as a thief. It was on account of that he had sent
the boy abroad and he seemed to remember that George
had had a high old time in Paris, Munich and ultimately
Vienna, where he lodged in the house of a carriage-
builder, with four pretty granddaughters. One of them,
Gisela, George had married and not before time, if Adam's
arithmetic was correct.

Since then, so far as he knew, George had never had
time to sow wild oats. For two years or more he had been
besotted by that engine he brought home and after that,
when he had proved his point by actually making the
thing run, he had taken over as gaffer at the yard. The
relationship of father and son, once strong, had weakened
over the years. Since his retirement, eight years ago,
Adam had leaned on Giles harder than any of them, but
he seldom talked shop with Giles. Mostly they discussed
politics and social issues, subjects that interested them
both. As for young Tybalt, he would take a lot of persuading that a young fellow in his position would play
fast and loose with his future. Wesley Tybalt came from
exceptionally sober stock, and his father was always on
hand to hold a watching brief. It therefore seemed very
unlikely that a man like Levison, head of a shipping
business in Liverpool, could have heard anything but a
rumour to the contrary, and yet . . . old Sam was certainly no fool when it came to a man's commercial worth.

He recalled then that Levison's firm used a rival haulage
line. Linklater's it was, a tinpot outfit, not regarded by
any big haulier as a serious rival and maybe it was there
he should look for clues. A dispute between Swann-on-
Wheels and Linklater's maybe, in which the latter had
been worsted by young Tybalt or George, or both, and
had gone away with a grudge of some sort? A long shot,
so long that it was hardly worth looking into, especially
as he was supposed to be out of it these days. But he knew
he was not out of it, and would never be out of it. Swann-
on-Wheels had been his life for thirty-odd years. All his

possessions and personal triumphs derived from it and a man could never slough off a burden as big as that, certainly not when his own kin were carrying it forward into the new century.

He was glad then that he had arranged for Hetty to travel home while he stayed a night in town to view a furniture sale at Sotheby's. Some choice pieces were coming up, part of the collection of Sir Joseph Souter, and he rarely missed an important furniture, picture or porcelain sale these days. They filled the vacuum caused by his exchange of the roles of haulier and connoisseur. He would drop in at the yard after the viewing, and have a word with both George and Tybalt, scratching around for confirmation of Sam's hints if any was to be found. And having decided this he made his mind a blank, as he had trained himself to do over so many tedious train journeys in the past. In seconds he was asleep.

3

He stood with his back to the familiar curve of the Thames looking the width of Tooley Street at the sprawling rectangle that had been the heart and pulse of his empire since he came here in the steamy summer of '58. A jumble of sheds, lofts and stables, crouched around the slender belfry tower, all that remained of the medieval convent that had once occupied the site. When the Plantagenets had used that bridge, the tower had doubtless summoned a few dozen nuns to prayer. During his long tenure up there it had overseen hauls the length and breadth of the island, a lookout post from which, in a sense, he could see the Cheviots and the Cornish moors, the Welsh mountains running down to the Irish Sea and the fenlands that drained into the German Ocean.

A slum, his wife and customers called it, and technically it was, pallisaded by a tannery, a glue factory, a biscuit factory, a huddle of tiny yellow-brick dwellings and the grey-brown tideway where a thousand years of South

Bank sewage had hardened into a belt of sludge, making its unique contribution to an overall smell of industry that he never noticed, not even now, after he had been inhaling the furze and heather scents of the Weald throughout years of lazy-daisy idleness. He knew every cranny of the enclosure and loved what he knew, seeing it as the powerhouse of the four clamorous tribes that had used this tideway as a base to conquer half the world. Not with sabres and muzzle-loaders like traditional conquerors (although the British had resorted to these times enough) but latterly with merchandise, spewed from their clattering machines and the gold that poured into these few square miles of avarice, expertise and grimed splendour.

He was proud of his contribution, although he would never admit it, not even to his intimates. It was a pride he kept locked away in his big body and restless brain, to be taken out and contemplated at moments like this when he thought, vaingloriously: 'All the others had a part in it. Josh Avery, who traded it all for a Spanish whore; Keate, the waggonmaster and Tybalt the clerk, whose hearts were in piling up credit in heaven; that foul-mouthed old rascal Blubb, who pulled us out of that shambles at Staplehurst and died doing it; Lovell, the erudite Welshman; Ratcliffe, the Westcountry clown and all the other viceroys. *But it was me who created it and set it in motion.* And "the fruit of my loins", as old Keate would put it, are keeping it rolling to this day.'

He crossed the road and entered the open gate that led to the weighbridge and the weighbridge clerk jumped off his perch, giving him the quasi-military salute all the veterans reserved for him after it got about that he had seen the Light Brigade go down at Balaclava, and later helped Lord Roberts, the nation's darling, to empty that stinking well at Cawnpore. The clerk said, "Afternoon, Mr. Swann. We don't often see you nowadays," and he replied, jovially, "No, Rigby. I was seventy this month and I make damned sure you don't! Is Mr. George in his office?"

"No, sir, I think not. Can't be sure, sir, but I think he's off in the regions somewhere. Mr. Tybalt'll know."

"Thank you, Rigby."

He had a continuing liking for the older men, still seen about the yard but falling away year by year now that younger ones were pushing from behind. Lockhart, the master smith was one, directing his four journeymen and three apprentices at the glowing forge. Bixley, the night watchman was another, but he wouldn't show up for an hour or so. Everyone, old and young, greeted him respectfully and it occurred to him that they still thought of him as the real gaffer, despite the New Broom's many innovations, of which there was evidence everywhere in enlarged warehouses, a new exit in Tower Street, the new clerical block where the old wooden stables had stood, now replaced by the red-brick building running the full length of the north side.

His own quarters in the tower were used as a lumber room now and he climbed the narrow, curving staircase, to find the queer octagonal room strewn with crates, sacks and discarded harness, its narrow window, where he had watched many sunsets and not a few dawns opaque with dust and grime. He took a piece of sacking and rubbed a pane, catching a glimpse of the Conqueror's Tower on the far bank and the swirl of river traffic east of the bridge. It was still as heavy and continuous, a never-ending stream of barges and wherries skimming down to the docks where funnels outnumbered masts by about two to one. It made him feel old and lonely up here among debris that was not his any more and he stumped down into the open again, pausing to examine a heavy double padlock on one of the last original warehouses, with its own exit into Tooley Street.

In his day they never locked warehouses in the daytime and he wondered whether this was the result of one of George's edicts, or whether the place contained a particularly valuable consignment. He hoisted himself up on a baulk of timber and glanced through the grilled window but all he could see in the gloom beyond was a tall stack of packaged cotton goods, awaiting shipment to Madras or Calcutta, no doubt. A polite voice at his elbow startled him a little.

"Can I be of service, Mr. Swann?"

He turned, stepped down and faced Wesley Tybalt, sleek and tidy as a solicitor's clerk in his dark, waisted frock coat and high cravat stuck with a gold pin. 'George must pay the fellow well to enable him to dress like that,' he thought, remembering that Tybalt's father had always worked coatless with slip-on sleeves to spare his shirt-cuffs, but he said, casually, "No, no, Tybalt, I was only poking about, taking in all the changes you've made. What's in there, for instance?"

Wesley said, very civilly, "Long-term storage, sir. We've taken to locking the warehouses that aren't in daily use. We had an epidemic of pilfering last year. Mr. George thought it a good idea, sir."

"It is," Adam said. And then, "Do you get much yard pilfering these days? In my time it was limited to waggons making overnight stops."

"We've put a stop to it, sir. No reported case since just before Christmas and then we nailed our man. He's doing two years' hard, I'm glad to say. Can I offer you tea in my office, Mr. Swann?"

"No, thank you," Adam said, wondering what it was about the fellow he didn't like, and asking himself why he found himself making an unfavourable comparison between the spruce Wesley and his fussy little father. "I'm catching the five-ten from London Bridge and merely looked in to have a word with Mr. George. The weighbridge clerk said he was away in the regions."

"Yes, sir, that's so. Since the weekend, sir."

"Do you know where, exactly?"

"Er . . . no, sir, or not since he moved on into Central. He'll let me know, however. He always wires or telephones in when he's away. Any message, sir?"

"No, no message. You'll give my regards to your father when you see him?"

"Certainly, sir. But I don't see a great deal of him now. I moved out to Annerley when I married."

"How often do you see him?"

"Oh, whenever he looks in, sir. Are you sure you won't take tea, sir?"

"Quite sure, thank you. Haven't all that much time," and he drifted off, wondering whether the crumb or two he had picked up during the brief exchange had any significance outside his imagination. There had been that split second hesitation concerning George's whereabouts, and a defensive narrowing of sandy eyebrows when he asked about the pilfering. Nothing much, certainly nothing to justify Sam's comment that Wesley Tybalt wanted watching. All it might mean was that he was covering up for George's philandering and that spelt loyalty of a sort. There was the swanky way the chap dressed, an impression that he considered he had hoisted himself a niche or two above his Bible-punching father, and one other thing that might or might not have significance, the fact that Wesley watched his progress the whole way across the yard to the gate and only slipped out of sight when he stopped to speak to the weighbridge clerk on the way out.

"Are we busy, Rigby?"

"On the jump, sir. Things slacked off during the celebrations but they've picked up since."

He put a spot question, striving to make it sound offhand. "Do we sub-contract to that northcountry haulier, Linklater? I came across him in the old Polygon this week."

"Linklater? No, sir. We used to but they've got their own yard in Rotherhithe now."

"Ah. Well, good day to you, Rigby."

"Good day, Mr. Swann," and he left, stumping slowly down Tooley Street in the direction of the river but stopping opposite what had once been his favourite coffee stall, run by an ex-cavalryman with a long, facial scar, acquired, so he said, serving with the 9th Lancers, known as the Delhi Spearmen after their fine performance in the Mutiny.

He crossed over and ordered a cup of coffee for old times' sake and Travis, the proprietor, greeted him with enthusiasm. "My stars, it's time enough since you looked in, Mr. Swann, sir! Alwus reckoned you was my most reg'lar earlybird in the old days."

"I've taken to lying in at my time o' life, Travis," he said, recalling how often he used to stand there sniffing the early morning tideway reek after an all-night session in his tower. And then, seeing the barred entrance to the yard a few strides up the street, a freak line of enquiry occurred to him and he added, "Did that new exit improve your trade, Travis? I would have thought carters coming and going there would have been your regulars seeing there are two coffee stalls nearer the main gate."

"I thought it would but it didn't," Travis said. "They don't use it during the day, tho' vans call in for stuff night-times now and again."

"Light traffic?"

"All kinds but not your waggons. Stuff you've hauled into town for local carriers. I see one o' Gibson's beer drays waiting there one evening last week. And on'y last night a Linklater two-horse took a load aboard. Short run hauls, they'd be and short-haulers were never much good to me, sir. My best reg'lars were the chaps who had been hauling long-distance and were dam' sharpset by the time they got here. I do see Mr. Hugo from time to time. You must be right proud of him, sir."

He forced his mind away from the disturbing knowledge that one of Linklater's vehicles had been here within the last few hours, despite the weighbridge clerk's assurance that their sub-contract work had fallen off since they opened their own yard at Rotherhithe nearer the docks, and contemplated the new Englishman's obsessive interest in sport. A man like Travis, he supposed, would see

Hugo as the superior product of a commercial family. In his own youth railway kings and engineers had been the popular idols. Now reverence was reserved for muscular oafs who could break track records, kick footballs from one end of the field to the other and hit cricket balls for six. He said, "Ah, Hugo, he's the best free advertisement Swann-on-Wheels ever had, or so my other sons tell me," and finishing his coffee moved off towards the station, his mind still occupied assembling the fragments of information his visit had accumulated.

They were beginning to multiply. George's unexplained absence; Wesley Tybalt's defensive manner; a new gate that wasn't used during the day, although it opened directly on that padlocked warehouse; the weighbridge clerk's ignorance that Swann was still subcontracting for the firm of Linklater, the original source of Sam's information that 'young Tybalt wanted watching'.

It made no sense any of it and he supposed, in the end, he would have to come right out with his suspicions, if his vague uneasiness justified the word, and ask George whether, in his view, there was anything worth investigating. But then another thought occurred to him and he wondered whether, in the circumstances, George was the right one to approach. George might be reticent about his own frequent excursions into the provinces, and almost surely resentful if neglect of duty was implied. What was needed was more detailed information concerning George's alleged 'gadding about', and how much reliance he placed, in his absence, in Wesley Tybalt. The obvious source concerning the first was Gisela, George's wife. As regards Wesley, Tybalt senior would be worth a visit, especially as, according to his son, he called in at the yard from time to time.

He caught his train and settled grumpily into a corner, watching the evening light play tricks with the smoky labyrinth down there under the ugly complex of bridges and viaducts and telling himself that he was an ass, at his time of life, to bother himself with what was amiss, if anything, with the network. He had pledged himself long ago to leave all the worrying to his successors and so far he had honoured that pledge, occupying himself with landscaping and collecting down there in the fresh air. It had kept him out of mischief for years now, and doubtless prolonged his active life, but he began to understand, for the first time since his retirement, that it was really no more than a substitute, and a poor one at that. His real ego, all that he was as a man and creator, had gone into the network, and the merest hint that it was threatened roused him like a man menaced in his sleep. George had made one bloomer over the introduction of those petrol-driven waggons and a dog was allowed one bite, so they said. But not two and not at the vitals of Adam Swann's lifework. Not if he could help it, by God!

4

He had always been a man of action, compelled to put theories to the test at once and after no more than cursory contemplation, so that anyone who knew him would not have been surprised at his decision to leave the train when it stopped at Petts Wood, on the way to Bromley. George had set Gisela up in a fine house here, where the south-eastern spread of the metropolis had petered out and the countryside was still unspoiled. It was a more convenient base than his own, deep in the Weald, and miles from the nearest station. The train service was excellent and George could be in the yard within thirty minutes of quitting his doorstep.

He took a four-wheeler to the cul-de-sac where George's windows looked out over a spread of arable fields and birch coppices, enjoying the prospect of surprising Gisela, for, although a foreigner, she had always ranked as his favourite in-law. She represented nearly all that Adam expected of a wife, concerning herself exclusively with home and children, and making no attempt to fashion her husband into the Galahad brides-in-waiting dreamed about before they had their corners rubbed off. He had never had the least doubt but that she loved his boy dearly, and both he and Henrietta had taken to her the moment she stepped ashore from the Dover packet all those years ago, soon after George confounded them with the news that he was married.

They had four children now, the eldest, Max, aged eleven, the youngest a rosy little bundle born last year and christened Henrietta, just as the third child, Adam, had been named for him. The stamp of the Continent lay heavily on this branch of the family. All the boys favoured their mother, with hardly a trace of their Anglo-Saxon father. Their manners were impeccable and their approach to him reverential. Like their mother, they used the word 'Grandfather' as though it were a title. He had no doubt but that one or more of them would prove a useful addition to the firm in the new century, for they already showed signs of that Teutonic application that had made the Germans Britain's nearest rivals in trade and industry.

The house, taken over from a failed speculator (George had a nose for failures and the bargains that went along with them) stood in its own grounds and was comfortably furnished, although its decor was too Germanic for his taste. Gisela was delighted to see him and pouted when he told her he was only stopping off on his way home, that Henrietta expected him at dusk, and that he was keeping the cab. "I only looked in to find out where I could locate George," he said. "I tried the yard but he's away off somewhere. When do you expect him back, my dear?"

She said, dutifully, that she could never predict George's comings and goings. Sometimes days passed before he turned up, his arms full of gifts for the children. "He spoils them," she added. "It is not good, and I tell him so often. He is very busy just now, yes?"

"It seems so," he said, "but no matter how busy a gaffer he is he shouldn't cut himself off from his base.

Tybalt senior always knew where to find me, even if Henrietta didn't. I was told he had been in the Midlands."

She turned away suddenly, so abruptly indeed that she gave herself away, for his sharp eye caught the droop of the lip. She said, with a shrug, "Then perhaps it is not business this time. Perhaps it is that woman!" He was so taken aback at her frankness that he gasped.

"George keeps a woman?"

"I do not think that he keeps her. I believe she has a rich husband."

"God bless my soul! He's told you about her?"

She turned and studied him with an expression that could have been mistaken for one of patronage. She was flushed, certainly, but he would have said that was due to irritation rather than embarrassment. Irritation not with him but with the entire British race, whose approach to this kind of thing continued to baffle her after years this side of the Channel. "George has told me nothing. How could he, being English, and brought up as an English gentleman?"

"Then how . . . I mean . . . are you telling me he doesn't love you any more? You and the children?'

The pink flush deepened. "I cannot say as to that, Grandfather. He is very fond of the children and spoils them as I said. But there are two kinds of mistresses, are there not? One is a . . . how would you put it? – a toy, he will soon discard. The other is a substitute for a wife put aside, yet without losing her rights." She paused, concentrating hard. "Perhaps 'rights' is not the word. Would 'status' be more exact?"

"Who gives a damn about that?" he burst out. "I heard he had taken to gadding about. The rumour had reached as far as his grandfather, up in Manchester, so it follows I'm probably the last to hear he's off the rails! How does that come about? Why the devil didn't you come to me or the boy's mother? We could have straightened him out. We always have before."

She said, considerately, "Please sit down, Grandfather.

It is not good that you should become so excited over something that is perhaps of small importance."

He sat down, hypnotised by her placidity. 'It's too long since I crossed the Channel,' he thought. 'Here I am, looking at everything through English eyes,' but said, with a lift of his hand, "I don't understand how any woman in your position can take that view, Gisela. George has no right to treat you in this way. His mother would be outraged."

"Then do not tell her, Grandfather."

"I'm not sure I will. I should have to think about it. But I'll tell you this. Whoever she is that woman is making nonsense of his responsibilities at the yard and that's important. To me at all events. It's what brought me here in the first place!" He was rewarded by a frown on the girl's pleasant features, as though he had found a chink in her complacency.

"Ach, that is not good," she said. "You are sure of it?"

"I'm sure of it. Who is this woman? Do you know her? Have you met her?"

"Wait," and she got up, crossing to a huge bureau bookcase that occupied most of the south wall, an item of furniture that he would have thrown out as a baroque monstrosity, better left in Central Europe where it originated. She opened a drawer, rummaged there and returned carrying a copy of *The Illustrated London News*, open at a page of social gossip. There was an illustration of a meet of the Quorn, featuring half-a-dozen celebrities and hangers-on, guzzling their stirrup cup. There was only one woman in the group, a handsome wench with what he recognised as a first-class seat. The caption below told him she was Lady Barbara Lockerbie, wife of the well-known Scottish industrialist, Sir James Lockerbie, 'An exceptionally able horsewoman, whom readers will recall excels not only in the hunting field but in the pursuit of winter sports.'

"If he hasn't told you about her how can you be so sure?" he demanded, returning the magazine and this time she smiled. "George is not a good liar, Grandfather. And I am not a fool."

He decided not to press the point and take her word for it, racking his brains for anything specific he might remember about James Lockerbie, who had bought his Scottish title, they said, with a sizeable contribution to Scottish Liberal Party funds when they were in low water after the last election. He knew nothing at all of his wife, save that she was obviously half his age, for Lockerbie had been prosperous in the days before Swann-on-Wheels surged over the border to capture the Lowlands trade. He made, if he remembered rightly, sanitary units, designed by that slightly risible genius, Thomas Crapper, supreme in the field of water-closets. It all added up to a very bad joke and the taste in his mouth was so sour that he rose abruptly, saying, "You leave this to me, Gisela. When he shows up don't tell him I've been here, do you hear?" But then, recollecting her pronunciation on the two types of women who lead husbands astray, he said, "What do *you* think about her? I mean, is it a passing fancy, or is it something more serious?"

"Ah, I am not qualified to tell you that yet, Grandfather. It began only last March, when he met this woman at the launching of his first trading vessel in Scotland. It is still only July, is it not?"

"But you must have some idea."

She said, pacing slowly across to the window, "All I can tell you is this. When George came to us, as a young man at Essling, he was very gay and nothing mattered to him. Nothing but laughter and picnics and kissing the girls. My sisters, Sophie, Valerie and Gilda, they were his companions at that time, without a serious thought in their silly heads. But then George became interested in Grandfather Maximilien's invention. It changed him. After that, when Grandfather was stricken, he stopped being a boy and we married and he brought me here, as you remember?"

"I remember. You and that damned engine."

"You put him to work, and he pleased you very much, I think. But later you quarrelled over the engine and we went to Manchester to live."

"I remember it all very well. What's all that got to do with George gadding off with the wife of one of his best customers?"

"It has everything to do with it. George has been hard at work for thirteen years. You have a saying for it, 'Nose to the milestone'."

" 'Grindstone'."

"Ah, so. Perhaps he thought it was time to laugh again before he grew old. The way he laughed when he first came to Vienna."

"But he's thirty-three now, and has a wife, four children and a damned great business to watch over. Why can't he do his laughing at home?"

She was still holding the magazine and glanced at it. "Husbands are not horses," she said, so gravely that he suddenly felt like laughing himself. "That horse she is sitting so well was a colt once but somebody took it and trained it and broke it to the bridle. You cannot do that with men like George. One day, for a little time, they will want to frisk again and it is better to let them. At least until they are tired."

He thought, grimly, 'I never did underestimate her. She's got her head screwed on and no mistake . . . !' He said, kissing her, "You're very wise, my dear. I was always fond of you but never more so than now. Would you like me to handle this my way, so long as I keep in mind what you just said?"

"You do what you think is right, Grandfather. George has no right to neglect the business you gave him so generously. As for me, you must understand it is a matter of waiting."

"I understand that," he said, "and I'll promise you something into the bargain. This is between you, me and George, and I'll make damned sure I tread warily, and that he never discovers we confided in one another. Will you bring the children over on Saturday and stay until Monday?"

"Thank you but no," she said, "I would not like George to return to a house empty of everyone but the servants."

She showed him the door and the cabby hastened to settle him comfortably, but he brushed him aside impatiently. "Catch that nine-ten to Bromley and I'll tip you a florin. Miss it and it'll be sixpence."

Suddenly he felt his years.

4

Reconnaissance

As a tactician Adam Swann was decisive, seeing what required to be done and doing it without preamble. As a strategist, working on a long-term plan, he could be both cautious and diabolically tenacious.

In his army days he had a reputation among senior officers as a good man to send out on reconnaissance. His eye seldom missed much of importance. His sketch-maps were models of neatness and accuracy, and it was much the same in the world of commerce. Before he cashed in a looted necklace of rubies, representing his entire working capital, he rode the full length of England, making meticulous notes on local industries, road and railway communications, terrain and a hundred and one other things likely to be invaluable to a haulier. His eye for detail was excellent and his memory phenomenal. He had a few sound precepts from which he never departed and one of these precepts was 'Know your enemy'.

Thus, on returning to 'Tryst' in the first days of July, 1897, he took no immediate action but continued to probe, using his personal contacts, his treasury of social and industrial trivia, and his library of reference books, to follow up his two definite leads, one heading for Barbara Lockerbie, the other concerned with the haulier, Linklater, currently using the Tooley Street exit of the yard to load goods stacked in one of his warehouses. Ten·

days elapsed before he was satisfied that he had learned all he was likely to learn concerning both.

Barbara Lockerbie was a high-class whore, who had emerged from obscurity with no capital beyond undeniable physical attractions and ruthless self-interest, deploying both to capture a rich and presumably excessively tolerant husband, then lead the kind of life that a selective harlot of her kind found agreeable. That is to say, to spend around three thousand a year on clothes, to stay looking young, to go everywhere, see everything and, more important, to be seen by everyone. She had reached Sir James and his fortune via one husband and many lovers. Even the Prince of Wales was rumoured to be numbered among her admirers but that Adam discounted, reasoning that if half the charmers reputed to have shared a bed with Edward had enjoyed his patronage, Edward would have declined years ago, as enfeebled as a Sultan of Turkey reared in a harem.

Her first husband was an architect and her abandonment of him had led to a soon-forgotten scandal, the poor devil having thrown himself under a train at Liverpool Station soon after her desertion. The woman, he decided, was lethal, and his appraisal of her steeled him to take swift intervention to head off possible disaster, even though he doubted whether the hardheaded George was the type of man who would ruin himself over a woman, no matter how much he was besotted by her. You could never tell, however, in situations of this kind. Avery, his former partner, had been cynical and world-weary at forty, and an experienced roué into the bargain, yet he had sacrificed everything he possessed, and ultimately laid himself open to a charge of double murder, in order to spend himself between the legs of a Spanish music-hall artiste. Adam even recalled his self-justification when they met for the last time, a few hours before he smuggled the idiot out of the country. He had asked, "Have you ever been sexually enslaved?" and when Adam said he had not, "It happens. It happens to the cockiest of us. Take care it doesn't happen to you, Adam . . . A man can turn a blind corner as I did when I first took Esmerelda to bed . . ."

Avery was surely an object lesson for, like him, George's weakness had always been women. He wished he knew more of George's early life in those days when the boy had been opening oysters in the network and on the Continent. The character of Gisela was no real guide to his taste. A man seldom married the kind of woman who could bring him ecstasy, plus a brief escape from care and responsibility. Usually he looked about for something more maternal and mature.

His investigations into Linklater's, the carriers, were more positive. They were a relatively small firm, dealing mostly in sub-contract work, but currently expanding. They had a fleet of about three hundred waggons and bases in a few of the big manufacturing cities in the North and Midlands. Starr, Linklater's partner and son-in-law, had a dubious reputation in the trade. There had been a lawsuit some years back, concerned with the loss of a valuable consignment of agricultural machinery, and Starr emerged from it technically innocent but with his reputation tarnished. The discrepancy between the comments of the weighbridge clerk and those of the coffee-stall proprietor continued to puzzle him, and he decided that it was here he must resume his investigations and that it must be done with delicacy.

George was back at work now, no doubt, albeit temporarily, and a direct approach in the circumstances seemed inadvisable, precluding another visit to the yard. He could have questioned one or other of George's brothers, notably Giles, who was close to him, but he rejected this as putting too much strain on family loyalty. After turning the matter over in his mind he decided his best course was to approach Tybalt senior, who could make innocent enquiries on his behalf, not only about Linklater's, but also concerning the relationship of his son and George, how often George was absent and for how long at a stretch, and maybe the precise function of that padlocked warehouse on the east side of the yard. He told Henrietta that he was going up to town for a day or so to attend sales and she accepted the excuse without question. His only excursions these days were concerned with landscaping and collecting.

He packed a bag and set off for old Tybalt's terrace house in Rotherhithe, where he busied himself with mission work, in company with his lifelong friend, the former waggonmaster, Saul Keate. Tybalt received him rapturously. He had always seen Adam as the temporal equivalent of his nightshirted Jehovah, for whom he was at pains to rescue fallen women, alcoholics and destitute children. His dedicated service to Swann, over a period of some thirty-five years, he regarded as tribute to Caesar, sanctioned in the Good Book, and Adam, while mindful of his idiosyncrasies, held him in high esteem, for he had brought tremendous devotion to his job as chief clerk, sometimes sitting up half the night to trace a missing sovereign or run down a mislaid invoice. He was a small, undistinguished-looking man with a round bald head and huge trusting eyes that blinked nervously behind spectacles. He almost dragged Adam into his house, demonstrating such enthusiasm that it made initial enquiries somewhat embarrassing, until Adam confessed that he was worried about the immediate future of the firm.

That stopped his fussing. He said, looking almost agonised, "Worried, Mr. Swann? But surely there's no need . . . I mean, all the information I have is that we're booming along, positively booming along!"

"Oh, I daresay we are from an outsider's standpoint, and you and I are numbered among the outsiders these days. Financially the firm is sound enough, I can assure you of that. No, it's more specific. You might say a family matter, to do with my son George, as a matter of fact."

Tybalt still looked grave but his concern moderated. "You're telling me Mr. George is trying to re-introduce those mechanical waggons?"

77

"I wish he was. That at least would indicate he was still absorbed. The fact is, Tybalt, he's fancying himself as the man about town and, to my mind at least, neglecting his responsibilities as gaffer down there."

"I'm very surprised indeed to hear that," said Tybalt, and looked it. "I always thought him . . . well . . . forgive me, Mr. Swann, a bit too go-ahead . . . and, how shall I put it? Experimental? But he's always struck me as a young man with a very astute head on his shoulders, and an absorbing interest in the work."

"Me too," Adam said, "but he's falling off, or so I'm told, from a very reliable quarter."

Tybalt looked evasive and twiddled his neat penman's hands. "I . . . er . . . I earnestly hope that source isn't my boy Wesley, sir. Oh, I know Wesley is very dedicated to the firm, but I wouldn't like to think he's been talebearing. At least, not without seeking my advice first."

"How often does he seek your advice, Tybalt?"

Tybalt looked down at the plush tablecloth, stacked with buff envelopes he had been addressing to mission subscribers. "I'll be as frank as you've been, Mr. Swann. Not nearly as often as I should like. Hardly ever, in fact, since he came in from the regions, and Mr. George appointed him in my place." He paused and Adam looked away. It went against the grain not to take Tybalt into his full confidence but what proof had he got, or was likely to get, that Wesley, in Sam's quaint phrase, 'needed watching'? Time enough if proof turned up. It would likely break the old chap's heart.

But Tybalt went on, with difficulty, "Mind, I don't complain, not really. Wesley's twenty-eight now, and holding an important position in the firm. He's married too, and feeling his feet, I daresay. The truth is, Mr. Swann, all these young people tend to regard our kind as silly old buffers, with old-fashioned notions as to how a business should be conducted. Have you been into the clerical department lately?"

"No."

"You'd be astounded, I think. It isn't at all like it was, not even when I retired, a mere three years since. They've got two of those telephones now, an automatic letter-copying machine, and three young women clacking away at typewriters. I've even seen a little horse-play there when I've looked in, and Wesley has been out and about. I never did approve of young women going out to business. It must present a great moral temptation, even to girls properly brought up."

"Tybalt," Adam said, hiding his smile, "I'm not talking about new business equipment. Or even about a kiss and a cuddle between a clerk and a typewriter operator. I've been given a hint that there's some well-organised hanky-panky going on down there, and the only clue I can give you is that it's centred on that warehouse on the east side, the one they keep locked, even during the day. That, and the exit behind it into Tooley Street, another innovation since our day."

"Er . . . could you be a little more precise, sir?" asked Tybalt, wringing his hands, and Adam said no, he couldn't, because he didn't know anything more, save that the firm of Linklater might be implicated, and he repeated Sam's remark as to his source and the discrepancy between the testimony of the weighbridge clerk and the observations of Travis, the coffee-stall tender. As he expected Tybalt made very little of it. "I'd trust the clerk," he said, "he's one of the old hands. I think that other man must have been mistaken. I knew about the exit, of course, and the padlocking of the doors, but I think you'll find we haven't done business with Linklater for some considerable time."

"Can you swear to that?"

"Well, sir, how could I? It's three years since I handled ledgers and invoices. But Wesley could tell me on the spot."

Adam said, carefully, "I'm not sure that's the right way to go about it, Tybalt."

"Why not?"

"Because it implies loss of confidence on my part. Wesley would know I've asked you to make enquiries and I had my own chance to do that when I was there, less than a fortnight ago. I didn't take it because . . . well, because I've got a suspicion that both your son and mine are being systematically hoodwinked by trained thieves, men actually serving in the yard. Wesley told me they had had an outbreak of pilfering but my guess is they only nailed the small fry." He took a deep breath. "Will you do something else for me, Tybalt? Something you might find a little distasteful?"

"I'd do anything for Swann-on-Wheels. You surely know that, sir."

"Yes, I do, but it isn't all that difficult. I'd like you to drift into the yard on some pretext and keep your eyes open. Make it around six, when the clerks are in a rush to be off, and you can get a look at the day-book without anyone knowing. They won't mind leaving you in there. Would you do that, without consulting Wesley? I've a reason for it."

Tybalt said, diffidently, "I think I should know the reason, Mr. Swann. The boy means everything to me now his mother's been taken. We only had the one chick."

"Well, it's very simple. My impression is that Wesley and George are very close, as close as you and Keate and I were in the old days. He'd regard it as his duty to warn George that I was about to pull him up for playing the fool and George is sharp enough to set matters right before I can get at him. What I'm really saying is, I don't want to be left with half a case. If I challenge him I've got to be able to quote an actual instance of neglect on his part and I think I can do it. Does that satisfy you?"

"Perfectly," said Tybalt, and came as close to winking as Adam recalled in their long association. "It isn't easy to show them a pint of experience is worth a quart of enthusiasm, is it, sir?"

"No, but neither is it impossible, Tybalt."

They talked on awhile about old times but when he left

Tybalt he did so gladly. In a way, he supposed, he was cheating the man but there was no alternative so far as he could see. Sooner or later Tybalt might have to face up to the fact that Wesley was either an idiot, being gulled by his own underlings, or was himself a skilful thief.

*   *   *

It was four-thirty when he left Rotherhithe, finding a cab in Jamaica Road and clip-clopping along the familiar South Bank that had so many lively memories for him. It was here he had walked with the giant waggonmaster, Keate, in search of Thameside waifs, whom Keate later recruited as vanboys and a happy notion that had been too. At least a dozen of the gamins, dredged from the mud, had gone on to hold responsible positions in the firm. One had become a regional manager and was still entrenched in what had been, in his time, the Southern Square, and recalling that Rookwood was now a man of substance, with a grown family of his own, nostalgia assailed him. He thought, 'I told myself I could slough it off when I marched out, and left George and the others to get on with it, but it's not so easy as all that. There's something to be said for taking one's ease but I miss the rough and tumble of life down here in the thick of it.' And in a curious way he felt grateful to George and Wesley Tybalt for drawing him back into the swirl of the enterprise.

The cab dropped him off at his hotel in Norfolk Street, the Strand, and he went up to his room with the evening papers, wondering how he would pass the time while Tybalt did his probing.

The city editors, after a surfeit of national junketing, seemed to be turning their attention to the outside world again. One had almost forgotten its existence this last month and it was now seen to be in its customary turmoil. There was trouble in the Balkans again. Germany was yelping over the murder of two of her missionaries in

China. France and Russia were getting together, with a view to giving Kaiser Wilhelm something to worry about. The Americans were slamming high tariffs on imports, in order to stimulate their own industries. They were a restless, quarrelsome lot, with no clearly defined purpose, of the kind that had brought Britain to the forefront, that unwavering conspiracy among homebased men of affairs to make money and let politics take care of themselves. Germany had the commercial potential and if she concentrated on trade, instead of trying to get herself elected bully of Europe, she could soon learn the tricks of underselling her competitors. That was the source of real power, not a rabble of clockwork soldiers marching here, there and everywhere, like overgrown children. But they would never learn, or not while that grandson of Old Vic was in charge, insisting that everybody referred to him as The All-Highest.

He turned, impatiently, to the inside pages, where a domestic item caught his eye. Trunk telephone wires were being transferred to the General Post Office, a sure sign that the contrivance Tybalt had spoken of slightingly was now generally accepted and would soon, he supposed, link every business concern in the country and perhaps, given time, every home as well. He hadn't installed a telephone at 'Tryst'. With half-a-dozen servants to run his errands, and the telegraph system in the village, it hadn't seemed necessary, but perhaps Henrietta might like to think about it, if only to gossip to her friends about her interminable round of fêtes and croquet parties.

On the following page was a news item of more relevance to him, a debate on the Employers' Liability Bill, aimed at making hirers of labour responsible for injuries and compensation to men injured on their premises during working hours. He wondered if George had given any thought to it. Swann-on-Wheels had its own provident scheme covering this contingency, a measure he had introduced years ago, so that once again he saw himself as a pioneer and preened himself a little as he shaved and changed for dinner. They would all come round to it in time – that precept of his that a man's profits were directly related to the way he treated his work force – but for years most city men had regarded him as an eccentric and a radical in this respect. You never got much out of men you regarded as animated tools of the trade. You had to isolate them as individuals, and invest them with some kind of dignity, and Giles had seen to it that his well-defined policy in this respect had survived his father's retirement.

He thought about Giles for a moment, asking himself if the boy found fulfilment in his job at the yard and deciding, not for the first time, that he hadn't, and probably regarded his post there as a stop-gap. Not that it was, of course. He was a necessary counterpoise to George, his ideas equating more with Adam's own than with any of his brothers. 'I should have made a parson out of him,' he thought, 'for money doesn't interest him and never will. He's always seen himself as some kind of standard-bearer and standard-bearers need a sound organisation at their backs if they are to survive.'

Thus ruminating, and in a relaxed frame of mind considering his purpose here in town, he took a constitutional along the new embankment, winked up at Boadicea's statue, wondered again at the incongruity of Cleopatra's Needle, returned to the hotel for a nightcap and finally toddled off to bed. Tybalt might well draw a blank at the yard tonight and, in any case, he was very unlikely to report in until tomorrow. It would be interesting, to say the least, to learn if the old chap had uncovered anything about Linklater's.

He already had his nightshirt on, and was in the act of opening the window to get a breath of riverside air, when somebody rapped at his door and he called, gruffly, "Who is it?"

"Me, Mr. Swann! Tybalt! Could I have a word with you, sir?"

He opened the door and the clerk was on the threshold,

looking, Adam thought, as though he had met a headless spectre in the corridor.

"I was just going to bed. I didn't expect you tonight, man!"

"I'm sorry, sir, but I didn't feel I could leave it. Might I . . . might I step in, sir?"

"Of course. You look about done. Would you like me to ring for a drink?"

"No, Mr. Swann . . . no drink, thank you . . . but I had to see you and came as quickly as I could. I did what you asked, I went down to the yard tonight. It was a few minutes to six and everyone was leaving. I said I'd lock up and give the keys to the watchman as usual, so I had the place to myself."

"Well?"

"You were right. There is something queer going on. There's no mention in the current ledgers or day-books of a sub-contract with Linklater's, but I wanted to be quite sure, so I had a word with that coffee-stall proprietor and he confirmed what he'd told you. He said one of Linklater's vans had been there again last night, about nine-thirty. It stayed about ten minutes, no more, and was backed in so tightly that he didn't see what was offloaded or taken aboard."

"What then?"

"Well, seeing that the man seemed so positive I looked in at Linklater's yard on my way home. I pass near the gate, it's in a cul-de-sac off Jamaica Road. There were several vans in the yard so I . . . well, Mr. Swann, I slipped in and I looked inside a half-dozen of them. Most of them were empty but the last one was fully loaded. There were several of our crates, Mr. Swann, with our brand on them."

"What was inside? Did you get a chance to look?"

"No, sir. I was going to, even if it meant prising one open, but then two men came out of the shed across the yard." Tybalt paused, drawing a deep breath, and blinking twice a second. "One of them was Robsart, our

84

yard foreman. I didn't know the other. It was getting dusk then so I thought it best to slip away behind the vans and make my way out. I signed Robsart on myself, sir. He'd been with us four years on suburban runs. I remember I was surprised when he told me Wesley had promoted him yard foreman. There were several men there with more experience but later Wesley said Robsart was the brightest of the bunch and thoroughly up to the job."

"He's certainly up to something," Adam said. "Did you come straight here after that?"

"Yes. Though I had it in mind to do something else."

"What was that?"

"Take a train out to Annerley to talk it over with my boy."

"I'm glad you didn't, Tybalt."

He turned away, moving over to the window. The night was clear and there was very little river mist about. The light of a thousand lamps reflected on the sliding Thames and the muted roar of the city came to him like the long roll of muffled drums. He had little doubt now but that Wesley Tybalt was implicated, and that some really massive 'shouldering' was going on down there. He remembered coachman Blubb introducing him to that word, a phrase the old coachees applied to the practice of picking up passengers at intermediate stops on a regular run, dropping them off one stage short of the terminus, and pocketing the fare. Only in this case it was not passengers but goods that were being shouldered, and suddenly two-thirds of the pattern became distinct to him, incorporating Sam's hint, the leak from Linklater's Northern headquarters, that warehouse with an unobtrusive exit that they kept locked, back and front, during the day and Travis's reports of vans calling after the yard had closed and only one or two men would be on duty.

The goods, he imagined, would start out from Northern

and Midland bases in Linklater's vans, to be offloaded close to the starting point and hauled South in Swann's waggons, stored in that warehouse, uninvoiced of course, until one of Linklater's vans could collect them, with nobody a penny the wiser save a sprinkling of rascals in both firms operating the swindle. He said, quietly, "You realise there must be at least half-a-dozen of our chaps involved in this, Tybalt. Waggoners from the original depots would have to be squared, as well as the yard men like Robsart. They've been making a very good thing of it, I wouldn't wonder, and it must have been going some time to develop to this stage."

"You're saying we've hauled hundreds of pounds' worth of goods into London for Linklater, Mr. Swann?"

"That's putting it very mildly."

"But it's the most outrageous confidence trick I've ever heard of! To do that, openly, night after night . . . A regular smuggling run, practised on that scale? I simply can't imagine what Wesley could have been about to let something like that happen under his nose! I mean, the boy must be a complete fool not to have checked the contents of that warehouse from time to time."

"What about my George?" but Tybalt went on tut-tutting, so that he thought, miserably, 'He'll have to know but I'm damned if I can tell him. How the devil does a man convince an old friend that his own child is a cutpurse heading for gaol? No wonder Wesley covered up for George that time. That young fool's whoring must have been a Godsend to him. I daresay he stages a pick-up every time he knows George is off somewhere with that woman . . .' He said, "I'm very indebted to you, Tybalt. For the time being let's face the fact that both your son and mine are hard at work proving neither one of 'em is fit to put in charge of a waggon, much less a fleet of 'em. I'll locate George tomorrow somehow, and lay it all on the table for him. There's nothing more you can do except go home and go to bed. It was sharp of you to check on Linklater's yard. I'll see that place has its shutters up before another twenty-four hours are past."

"There's no possibility of some other explanation?"

"None that doesn't nail your boy and mine as victims of a three-card trick, Tybalt. Are you sure you won't take a drink?"

The little man shuffled, then threw up his round head. "I've faced a good many upsets in my time, Mr. Swann, and I've done it on tea."

"Then let me order you a pot of tea," and without waiting for Tybalt's assent he rang the bell and summoned a waiter. When the tea appeared Tybalt poured, his movements as precise as an old maid's, and Adam thought, dolefully, 'I wish to God I hadn't involved him now. This is going to hit him damned hard,' and he urged the clerk to drink up, get a cab and go home to bed.

When Tybalt had left he sat in his nightshirt at the window looking over the river, musing on his tactics from this point on. He had a penchant for French metaphors and one occurred to him now, *offensive à outrance*. There was no point in nibbling around the edge of this unsavoury mess. George would have to be located and brought back, by the ear if necessary, and both he and Wesley would have to be confronted with the situation as far as he knew it. That foreman Robsart would have to be threatened until he told all he knew. The thieves would have to be run down, here and out in the network, and sent packing. There would be prosecutions, no doubt. Charges would have to be formulated against Linklater and Linklater's operators. It was likely to be a long, sordid business, with half the yard men under suspicion during the investigation. He lit one of his favourite Burmese cheroots, a solace granted him over the years, ever since, as a youngster, he and Roberts, and other men long since in their graves, had ridden across the Bengal plains. Beyond his window the roar of the city subsided to a soft, insistent murmur.

2

He had his first piece of luck next morning. He was dawdling over his second cup of coffee in the breakfast-room when a waiter brought him a message that a Mr. Giles Swann had called, but could only stop a short while. Adam said, eagerly, "Tell him to come in and fetch some fresh coffee, will you?" Giles, dressed for travelling, entered from the foyer, taking the seat indicated but saying he only had twenty minutes as he was anxious to catch the ten-ten Westcountry train from Waterloo. "I'm going down to clear up that Gimblett claim," he said. "That old Scrooge is still bucking at paying up, although the adjudicators declared for us a month ago. That collision at Taunton was his liability."

"How the devil did you know I was here?" Adam asked, and Giles said, smiling, that he was always here when he was in town, and Hugo had word from Henrietta yesterday that he was off on one of his junk-buying jaunts. "My words, not his," he added. "I think you've got a collector's eye."

They talked as equals, something he was unable to do with his other children, but Giles, unlike him in so many ways, had a maturity that the more extrovert of his family lacked. "As a matter of fact, I'm here to ask a favour, Father. A small one."

"It wouldn't have to do with George, would it?"

"No. Why should it?"

"I don't know. Just a hunch. Is George at the yard?"

"No, he isn't. He hasn't been for a day or so."

"Where is he? I can never find him these days. He's here, there and everywhere and I particularly want a word with him while I'm up here."

"He's in the regions," Giles said. "They expect him back sometime tomorrow."

"Do you know where in the regions?"

"No, but Wesley Tybalt would tell you."

"I don't think he would." He looked at Giles narrowly. "How do you hit it off with that chap, Giles?"

88

"Not all that well," Giles said, looking a little puzzled. "He's a first-class yard manager, according to George, but I don't find him as likeable as his father. He's a bit of a know-all, and talks down to the men and up to us."

"My sentiments exactly," Adam said, "and he resents my poking my nose in when I feel like it. He probably takes his cue from George in that respect."

He toyed with the notion of taking Giles into his confidence but quickly decided against it. All his life he had been jumping on people for coming to him with untidy briefs and his own was far from complete. "What was the favour, boy?"

"It's about a chap called Soper. I promised him we'd take him on. He's out of a billet and I'm obligated to him. He's a member of the Shop Assistants' Action Group and has had about as much as he can take from the drapery trade."

"There's more to it than that, isn't there?"

Giles hesitated. "Yes, there is. If I want your help I owe you the truth. Did you read about that leaflet raid on the Jubilee procession in the papers? Fleet Street end of the Strand?"

"Yes, I did. A very juvenile business, to my mind. That sort of gesture is spitting into the wind. Did Soper get the sack over it?"

"He can't go back. And he's nothing put by to keep him while he looks for another billet."

"He won't get one without a character."

"That's why I'd like to help him." He looked Adam in the eye. "How do you feel about the shop assistants' cause, Father?"

"Sympathetic. If I was in drapery it would have been a bomb not a leaflet. Time they organised themselves like other trades. But that's their business. It certainly isn't mine at my time of life."

Giles said, slowly, "I'll not keep anything back. I organised that 'spit in the wind'. I was there at the time. Me and Romayne."

Adam wasn't much surprised. He knew Giles was mixed up in various campaigns, all of which were probably as abortive as this one. He said, "It's the wrong way to go about things, boy. Old Catesby, up in the Polygon, could have told you that. He was your kind, always chasing the millenium, and even went to gaol for it in his time. But he learned and started from the bottom up. Got a proper trades union organised, and then went right after parliamentary representation. You don't get far over here, marching around with banners and distributing leaflets at public assemblies. People are too lazy and too indifferent. Legislation is the only lever the British will accept. Germany excepted, we're ahead of others in capital and labour relations. This chap you're telling me about, is he the wild man type?"

"He wouldn't be if he worked for a firm like yours."

Giles always gave him the impression he was only helping out at Swann-on-Wheels, that he had never been fully integrated, like George, Hugo or even young Edward, and that his post as Claims and Provident Scheme Manager was a stop-gap while he went on looking for a purpose in life. Yet his work had never been in question. Adam had heard George say that Giles' tact and patience was worth five thousand a year to the network, if only on account of cases settled out of court, thus saving a sheaf of lawyers' bills. Adam said, "This Soper, has he had any clerical experience?"

"Yes. Before he became a floor-walker at Beckwith's."

"George would have signed him on on the strength of your recommendation."

"In a case of this kind I'd sooner approach you, Father."

That was another thing about Giles. He still addressed him as 'Father', instead of the more familiar 'Gov'nor', used by his brothers. It stemmed, he supposed, from the boy's attitude towards him since the time they had first begun discussing history and politics when Giles was a child of thirteen. Adam always had the impression that

Giles still regarded him as his mentor in these fields and would see that as far outweighing his vast commercial experience.

"If I'm to catch that train I must hurry," he said. "Here's Soper's address." He wrote rapidly in his note-book. "Maybe you could find time to call and look him over."

"I don't need to do that," Adam said. "I'll tell George he's been highly recommended to me by an old customer and I want him given a chance. Good luck in the West, boy. Wish I was coming with you. I always liked that part of the country."

"Why don't you? I'll be returning first thing to-morrow."

"Things to do," Adam muttered and escorted him into the street, where Giles had a hansom waiting. He watched him get in and responded to his hand wave, thinking, 'Queer chap, old Giles, but so likeable . . . lovable even. More brains than any of 'em if he'd put 'em to better use but you can't have everything . . .' Then he climbed up the stairs to his room, still undecided on his next move in the confrontation he knew must occur within twenty-four hours.

He sat thumbing through his notes on Barbara Locker-bie, dismissing as improbable the possibility that George was engaged in genuine network business, gambling on the likelihood that they were off together somewhere and telling himself that his first priority was to intercept George before he turned up at the yard. He had Sir James Lockerbie's town address, in Sussex Place, but it was unlikely George was holed up there. He had a country place somewhere but Adam did not know where it was, so he went down to reception and buttonholed the manager, whom he knew well, demanding to know if Sir James Lockerbie was a telephone subscriber. "I can soon find out, Mr. Swann," the man said, "for I keep a list here," and he popped into his inner office, re-emerging a moment later with the information that Sir James was listed as subscriber two-seven-five in the London area.

"Could you connect me?" Adam asked, "I've important business with him and don't want to waste time calling on him if he is out of town."

"Certainly, if you'll step into my office, Mr. Swann. The hotel telephone is in there. Very few of my guests ever seem to have need of it."

"That doesn't surprise me," Adam said, "we managed well enough with pen and ink in the old days," but he followed the manager into the office and watched him twirl the handle before asking the London exchange for number two-seven-five. After a few moments he offered Adam the earpiece. "Speak slowly and distinctly, sir," he advised, "and don't hold the mouthpiece too close. No one will disturb you in here," and tactfully he left, closing the door.

A disembodied voice at the end of the line said, "Sir James Lockerbie's residence. Who is calling?"

"Swann," Adam said. "Director of Swann-on-Wheels. Is your master in town?"

"No, sir," the voice said, "he's abroad. Could I send a message, sir? Is it social or business?"

"Social," Adam said, heading off a switch to Lockerbie's London headquarters. "Is her ladyship at home?"

"I'm afraid not, sir. This is Medley, the butler speaking. Her ladyship is in the country."

"Well, see here, Medley," Adam said confidentially, "I'm very anxious to send her an invitation she's expecting. Could you oblige me by giving me her country address?"

"It's not usual, sir. Mr. Swann, you said?"

"Yes. Your master has been doing business with me for thirty years and my wife is extremely anxious that this invitation reaches Lady Lockerbie by today at the very latest."

"I see. Well, Mr. Swann, I think I would be exceeding my duties by withholding the country telephone number.

I think you'll catch her there later, sir. After six, I would say, for I understand she's attending the local regatta today."

"I'd be uncommonly obliged," Adam said, trying to keep the jubilation out of his voice. "What is it?"

"Swanley Rise, number six, sir. It's in Hertfordshire and you get it through the Barnet exchange."

"Thank you very much indeed," Adam said. "I'll get in touch with her before dinner," and he hooked the earpiece on to its gilded standard, reflecting that he might have been unjustly prejudiced against telephones. They certainly saved time and trouble on occasion.

He went out into the sunshine, wondering how to pass the hours until early evening. He intended staying clear of the yard, where his presence, twice in ten days, would certainly alert Wesley and there were no auction sales advertised that he cared to attend. He had no wish to run over to Gisela's either. The wretched girl had enough worries, without him adding to them, and momentarily he was at a loss as to how to put in the time. Then his eye caught the destination board on the front of a 'bus – 'The Tower & Minories', and fancy jogged him like the elbow of a playful uncle. The Tower of London. The grey pile he had stared across the river at for thirty years when isolated in his Thames-side eyrie, but had not visited since he was a lad. He said, aloud, "Damned if I won't look in there, like any gawping provincial. Why not? I need something to take my mind off my worries for an hour or so," and he moved out into the crowded roadway and swung himself aboard.

The 'bus set him down on Tower Hill, where some of his favourite characters from the past had taken their final glimpse of the world in the upturned faces of ten thousand Cockneys, assembled to witness a spectacle that was even more popular than a bear-baiting or a cock-fight. Strafford, who put too much trust in Princes, old Lord Lovat, for his share in the Jacobite rebellion, and that nincompoop Monmouth, who died gamely they said, but only after crawling on his knees before that bigot James. Well, they managed these things more discreetly nowadays, and he wasn't at all sure that the condemned thanked them for it. He had a notion that a man needed an audience on occasions like that and might even look for a chance to show his paces at the last minute. He went down to the public entrance and past the Traitors' Gate, once again making a character assessment on the men and women who had climbed those slimed steps from the river. Tom Moore, too holier-than-thou for his taste, Tom Cromwell, the prototype of many a crafty merchant he had bested in his salad days, and young Elizabeth, who learned her lesson well during the period she lived here in the shadow of the headsman. Then up to Tower Green, where a raven gave him a speculative eye, as though the old ruffian queried his purpose there.

He stood for a minute beside the slab marking the spot where the scaffold had stood, remembering the luckless Ann Boleyn and rekindling his lifelong resentment for the least likeable of England's monarchs, who had her pretty head lopped by the Calais executioner. They said the damned scoundrel (Adam had never regarded Henry as anything else) waited outside the city wall for a cannon shot, announcing the fact that he was a widower, before riding off to Jane Seymour, and he wouldn't put it past him.

He looked in at the tower that had held so many state prisoners, thinking: 'If you played for high stakes in those days you earned anything you took away from the table.' Then he tackled the winding stair to the horse armoury, peering at the exhibits with the eye of a man who had seen more carnage than most and afterwards stumped down again and crossed to the battlemented walk overlooking the river, where Raleigh was said to have spent most of the daylight hours during his long imprisonment here. He must have been in a particularly fanciful mood today for he found himself thinking of Raleigh as a kind of Giles, a man full of promise who somehow never achieved much, perhaps because he attempted too much, and never learned the trick of concentrating his energy. Yet anyone who could write that valediction of Raleigh's was a man of parts, surely . . . What was it again . . . ? A few lines that had appealed to him so strongly when he learned it at school that it had remained with him all these years:

> *E'en such is time that takes in trust*
> *Our youth, our joys, our all we have*
> *And in the dark and silent grave*
> *When we have wandered all our ways,*
> *Shuts up the story of our days.*
>
> *But from this grave, this earth, this dust,*
> *The Lord shall raise me up, I trust.*

It occurred to him to wonder how much store his own family set upon hope of a personal resurrection. Not much, he would say, for all their regular church-going when they were youngsters. Henrietta, he knew for a fact, never let herself contemplate death, her own or anyone else's. Alex, professional soldier, would have come to terms with it long ago. George wasn't the spiritual type, or Hugo either. The one might see Paradise from a Turkish janissary's standpoint, a perfumed garden, full of houris, and the other as a super sports stadium, where he won every event on the card. Giles was more difficult to predict. He was too intelligent not to have renounced conventional doctrine long since, but, like Adam, he had a powerful belief in man's potential and in the never-ending struggle between good instincts and bad. As for the girls, they had almost certainly given a great deal more thought to their clothes, looks and figures than they gave to their souls, and not for the first time he envied men like Raleigh their deeply-rooted faith in an all-seeing, all-caring Creator, universal at the time, he supposed, before tiresome fellows like Darwin and Huxley set about confusing everybody.

The sun was moving down towards the higher reaches of the river now and he glanced at his watch, taxing his long memory regarding the likelihood of one or other of his many business cronies about here who would be likely to possess a telephone and let him borrow it for an out-of-town call. He decided on Crosby, a timber importer, with offices in Cannon Street, and went out on to Tower Hill again where, after some tea and a cake in a bunshop, he whistled a hansom and gave the cabbie Crosby's address. A few moments later they were threading their way through westbound traffic, very thick about here, and not getting any better, despite so many road-widenings since he had become a regular user of these streets forty years ago.

The man set him down outside Crosby's place at the very moment a three-horse fire-engine dashed past, moving in the direction of the bridge, the epitome of urgency with its clanging bell and rattle of equipment, gleaming brass and straining greys, moving over the ground as though they were quite aware of the fact that they took precedence over drays, four-wheelers, hansoms, bicycles and even the odd motor in the press. The driver's handling of the team was a pleasure to watch and every-body did his damnedest to give the vehicle clearance. Then, in its wake, came another, and finally a third, so that the cabbie said, "Someone's in trouble, sir. Looks as if it's on the South Bank. They usually manage with their own brigades," and he pointed with his whip at a blur of smoke hanging in the clear air above the south-eastern angle of the buildings.

"That'll make traffic worse," Adam said, recalling the clubbed approaches to the bridge on that side whenever anything of this kind was afoot over there, but then his quick ear caught a single word shouted by a newsboy at a customer buying his paper a few yards along the kerb and he almost ran over to the lamp-standard where the boy had his pitch.

"*Where* did you say? *Where* is it?"

"Swann's, sir, the carriers . . . Going well, they say . . . !"

Adam threw himself round and caught his cab in the act of turning, shouting, "Get over the bridge! Half a sovereign if you make it in ten minutes . . . !", and dragging open the door he flung himself on to the leather cushions he had quitted a moment since.

5

River Scene

THE MAN EARNED HIS HALF-SOVEREIGN. TAKING
advantage of every chink in the traffic, and three times
mounting the pavement with his nearside wheel, he
brought Adam to the junction of the Borough High Street
and Tooley Street in eight minutes. As the cab drew up
yet another fire-engine clattered up from the direction of
Southwark so that to Adam, scrambling from the hansom
and hurrying breathlessly as far as Grubb's glue factory,
the yard was seen to be ringed with fire-engines and arched
over with hissing jets from their hoses.

The confusion about him was that of a city captured
by storm. Great banks of yellow smoke gusted towards
the river on the light breeze, more and more sightseers
arrived every minute, some of them scuffling with the
harassed police, and trapped vehicles from the Old Kent
Road side tried to fight their way out of the press, striking
one another glancing blows so that their drivers' oaths and
shouts of warning added to the general tumult. And
beyond it all, like the continuous crackle of musketry,
came the menacing sputter of the flames at the heart of
the fire some hundred yards lower down the street.

He stood there a moment dazed by the uproar, telling
himself that it was all a mistake on the part of that newsboy, that it was someone else's empire that was burning
and that his presence here was part of a nightmare. But
beyond this the core of his brain kept reminding him

that the fire was no coincidence, that the crooked trail
he had been following ever since Sam Rawlinson had
croaked out his warning, led directly to this scene of
destruction and the suspicion, close to a certainty, made
him swear aloud as he chopped his way through the press
of spectators, shouting, "I'm Swann! I own the damned
place . . . ! Let me pass!"

The police nearer the bridge gave way to him but
halfway down Tooley Street, at a point where he could
see the pulse of yellow and crimson flame beyond the
weighbridge gate, a sergeant caught him by the arm and
said, "Don't go in, sir . . . They're driving the horses
through! The stables have caught," and he watched,
appalled, as four Cleveland Bays dashed through the
gate heading directly for the section of the crowd held at
the junction of Tower Bridge Road. At the same time he
saw a terrified Clydesdale caught by a triumphant urchin
outside the scent factory and led away, to await receipt of
its captor's tip.

He said, to the sergeant at his elbow, "How bad is it?
How much of the yard is involved?"

The policeman replied, "Bad enough! It's only been
going forty minutes and look at it. All this side is well
alight but they say the Southwark brigades are getting a
grip on the other side."

"How did it start? Does anyone know?" and the man
glanced at him. "How do they ever start? Carelessness
nine times out of ten, and Mr. Nobody's the culprit!
Stand *back* there! *Jarman! Hoskins!* Stop those fools
crossing the road!" and he bustled away, fully absorbed
in his job of controlling the ever-increasing swarm of
spectators, now surging in from the bridge and all the side
streets connecting Tooley Street with the Old Kent Road.

A moment later Adam saw his youngest son, Edward,
wild-eyed and stripped to his shirt and shouted, "Edward!
Over here, boy!", and the youth spun round, knuckling
his eyes and exclaiming, "Gov'nor! How did you get
here? I thought . . ."

"I was in Cannon Street and heard of it. Were you here when it started?"

"Yes, in the clerical section . . . Somebody rushed in and said a warehouse was well alight . . ."

"Which warehouse?"

"Number Eight, that new one behind the tower. There was a frightful panic. Everyone rushed out and did what they could but it was little enough until the brigades got here. We only had the hand-pump and buckets. Then the roof of the counting-house went up . . . must have been sparks."

"Are either of your brothers around?"

"Hugo is. Over on the far side, turning the horses loose. The waggon-shed and forge are alight and two other warehouses, I believe. Everything was as dry as tinder, sir!"

Adam said, "Keep by me, I'm going in," and taking advantage of the sergeant's back he slipped across the road and through the dense smoke shrouding the weigh-bridge.

It was a little clearer beyond, where the river breeze was driving the smoke to the west and he was able to make some assessment of the overall scene. The heart of the fire was in the immediate area of Number Eight warehouse, the one they kept padlocked, but there seemed no hope of saving the counting-house, or the stable block and forge that ran at right angles to it. Three pinnaces, one-horse vans that served the suburbs on short-run hauls, had been dragged out of the waggon-shed and were burning in isolation in the centre of the yard. Maddened horses clattered past on either side, making by instinct for the main exit. A group of helmeted firemen were playing four jets on the counting-house but even as they watched a superintendent detached them to concentrate on the stable block, leaving the one-storey building to burn itself out. Smoke from the gutted warehouse set them both coughing and wheezing and all around the steady crackle of the flames proclaimed the certainty that Swann's headquarters, as he had known it over half a lifetime, was doomed.

He said, grimly, "Where's the yard manager? Where's Wesley Tybalt, Edward?"

"I don't know, sir. George is away, and Giles too . . . Shall I try and find Tybalt?"

"Yes . . . you do that. I'll stay as close here as I can. They seem to be containing it about here."

"Hadn't you better get back to the street, sir?"

"Do as I say. Find Tybalt, and if you can't bring Hugo."

The boy dashed off, moving in a way that reminded Adam of Henrietta's claim that, of all the Swanns, only Edward favoured her father Sam. It was true. He had Sam's big head and squat, squarish frame, Sam's bustle and air of guarded alertness. In a matter of seconds he was lost in the swirl of smoke from the stable block but he re-emerged a few minutes later with Hugo in tow. It was the first time Adam had ever seen Hugo blown, despite his string of triumphs on the running track. He gasped, "It's a regular shambles, Gov'nor. All happened so quickly. Never seen a fire get a hold like that. But we got the horses out. All seventy of 'em."

"Anybody hurt?"

"No, sir, I think not. But the superintendent says he can't save Four and Five warehouses. He's concentrating on the others, giving them a rare soaking. The waggons are our property but there are customers' goods in all the sheds."

"Water will spoil what the flames don't get," Adam grunted. "How about Tybalt? Is he over there?"

"I haven't seen him," Hugo said. "Come to think of it I haven't seen him all day."

"I have," Edward volunteered. "He came into the counting-house and went through to his office some time in the afternoon."

"When was it? Think, boy, think hard!"

"It must have been about an hour or so before the alarm was given."

"You didn't see him go to the key rack?"

"No, sir, but he doesn't have to. He has duplicates in his office over there."

"Where, exactly?"

"In a rack on the wall behind his desk in the annexe," and Edward pointed to the butt end of the clerical building, the one portion of the block that was still more or less intact. Even its window, facing the yard, was unbroken.

He said, "Come with me, Edward. Hugo, go back and tell the superintendent to make his major effort on the warehouses. You're quite right. The waggons are fully insured but we've only minimum cover for goods in transit, once they're stored in the yard!" As Hugo hurried off he led the way to the abutting end of the clerical section, Edward following with a bewildered expression on his pink, squarish face. There was a pinnace axle-tree resting against the brickwork and Adam lifted it, smashing the frame and the four panes of glass with a few swift blows. The heat here was intense but under the wall they were protected from the dense clouds of smoke issuing from the burning half of the building. He turned to the boy. "Scramble in and look at that desk and key rack. Jump to it. Desk first . . ." and Edward dived through the aperture and was at once shrouded in smoke.

He called back, "All the drawers are open or thrown down. He must have saved his papers."

"Are his keys there?"

"Yes, sir, I think so."

"Bring 'em out, boy. Sharp about it," and Edward came tumbling out, his hands full of keys, each with its oval label.

"Shall I give them to the firemen?"

"No, I'll take them. They'll hack their way in if they have to but it mightn't be necessary. You say the desk was cleared?"

"More or less. There were papers on the floor."

"Right, now listen here. I'm staying in town, at The

Norfolk, and there's nothing I can do here. Tell Hugo where I am, and tell him to notify the brigade chief and the senior police officer. I need a drink and a good wash while I'm at it. You and Hugo watch out for yourselves, and don't take chances saving property. We can always replace property," and he walked away, leaving the yard by the main entrance and pushing roughly through the ranks of sightseers now contained behind a rope barrier. He was more than halfway across the bridge before he saw an empty cab going his way. He said, clambering inside, "Norfolk Hotel," and settled back in the interior, his mind juggling with so many factors that it finally abandoned any attempt to relate them. The stench of woodsmoke clung to his clothes and he had inhaled so much of the stuff that he felt sick and muddleheaded. But then, as he stretched his legs, he heard the keys jangle and thought, sourly, 'That was a bonus, anyway. I don't know as it will prove anything but it's a lead having regard Tybalt's jumping the gun in order to empty that desk.'

2

His over-riding desire, before he so much as ordered a drink, was to have a bath. The stench that hung about him was not merely unpleasant. It darkened his thoughts to a degree that the fire could not have achieved. The depression was at a different level, the deepest level of his consciousness. He probed its source, asking himself why a fire, even one so fierce and destructive, should make him feel lonely and desolate. Then it came to him in the whiff of his jacket as he peeled it off, a stink of frustrated wretchedness and personal degradation that took him back to a time years before Swann's waggons roamed the highways, to places on the far side of the world. It was the once familiar reek of burning towns, the stench of Delhi, Cawnpore, Lucknow and Jhansi, ravaged, looted and fired. It struck him that the nose was the best barometer of the spirit, that certain smells one associated with hope and happiness, and others, like this one, with bitterness and defeat.

He muttered, "Here now this won't do! You're responsible for it in a way, so keep your nerve and see what can be salvaged from the mess!" and he spread the keys Edward had given him on the bed, examining each label carefully.

There were seventeen in all, eight giving access to warehouses, two to the main entrances of the yard, one to the head clerk's office, one to the clerical building itself, one marked 'postern' (he assumed this opened the new Tooley Street exit) and four belonging to other sectors of the yard, the tack room, the waggon-stores and the forge. He set aside all but the warehouse keys and studied these again, marking off in his mind the buildings they represented, the row of one-storey warehouses facing his old tower that were used, in his day and since, for goods awaiting shipment and onward transmission into the Kentish Triangle and Southern Square.

At first the set seemed complete but then it came to him that one was missing. The key to that smaller, newer warehouse across from the counting-house, with its exit at the rear, and the significance of this occurred to him at once. It told him that Wesley Tybalt, slipping into the office to empty his desk, had hooked this key from the rack and used it to further some purpose of his own.

Cautiously he pondered that purpose, forgetting his need for a wash and a drink but sitting there in his shirt-sleeves, his mind reviewing every factor in the case.

Wesley had not been seen about the place all day, save for that fleeting visit to his office. Wesley had been nowhere around when the fire started and gained its hold. The fire had begun in that quarter of the yard. Wesley had not returned the key, a golden rule at the yard all the time it had been Swann's headquarters. It pointed, he would say, to two certainties. One, Wesley was the last to visit the small warehouse, and two, Wesley had been warned by someone that the hunt was up and he would be required, within the next twenty-four hours, to answer a number of awkward questions. Concerning himself and Robsart, seen in Linklater's yard last night, and concerning, above all, the contents of that warehouse and the invoices representing the goods inside. Dramatically a pattern emerged revealing so much that it had the power to make him leap up, putting so much reliance on his tin leg that he stumbled.

'Great God, the fellow's not only a thief but an arsonist, covering his tracks!' he thought, and almost choked with rage, calling himself an absolute fool not to have spotted the grand design days ago, or at least last night, after Tybalt senior told him about the Swann packages in the Linklater waggon.

His first impulse was to contact the police and put them in touch with their colleagues at the seat of the fire. His second, on the heels of the first, was more complicated. It involved not only Wesley Tybalt, but Tybalt senior and maybe a dozen subverted men at headquarters and out along the network. Detection on this scale called for skilful timing and absolute secrecy if the entire gang was to be rounded up and the network purged from top to bottom. And he was unequal to the demands of that task right now, when he was tired, hungry and filthy.

He looked at his watch, surprised to find it was coming up to eight o'clock, four hours since he had stampeded over London Bridge to the burning yard. He shrugged off the rest of his clothes, put on his dressing gown and slippers, took his towel, soap and razor and went along the corridor to the bathroom, an innovation up here, for until recently guests had made do with tin bowls and cans of hot water carried up three flights of stairs. For half an hour or more he soaked and scraped, turning the finer points of his assumptions over and over in his mind and then, feeling ready for battle, he sprinkled himself with lavender water and went back along the corridor to his room.

He had not locked it and on crossing the threshold it

seemed that the place was full of people. He drew back, rubbing eyes that were still smarting from smoke and yellow soap. Then he saw that there was only one person in there but the man by the window was so huge, and possessed such a commanding presence, that he seemed to fill the room. It was Saul Keate, his former waggon-master, who had been his friend and confidant since that first summer evening in '58, when Avery had introduced him as the likely recruiting sergeant of a South Bank work force. A gentle giant, standing six feet six in his socks, with a great, slabsided face and mild blue eyes, a man who had searched the docks night after night for lost souls with potential that could be channelled into the network. Another Bible-puncher, certainly, and a prude who winced every time he heard a carter swear, but a person of immense positiveness for whom he had always entertained the greatest respect.

He said, "Have you just come from the yard?" and Keate, surprisingly, said no, although he had heard about the fire from one of the men who lived in his street. "According to him there was little I could do," he said, "so I thought it best to come here and give you this, sir. It had this address on it or I would have travelled down to 'Tryst', late as it is." He handed Adam a sealed envelope addressed to him in Tybalt's hand and marked 'Urgent and Personal'.

"Where did you get it?"

"At Tybalt's home. It was on his sitting-room mantel-shelf when I called round for some mission funds appeals he asked me to collect this afternoon. His front door was ajar but he wasn't there. I called up the stairs and then made enquiries. He lives alone, as you know, except for a woman who comes in and does for him since his wife died. I found her eventually. She told me he was there at midday, when she left, but she hadn't seen him since." He waited in his grave, self-effacing way that recalled so many orders-for-the-day sessions down the years.

Adam said, "Very obliging of you, Keate," and carried

the envelope over to the window, opening it, taking out two closely-written sheets and reading them with his back to the light.

The first lines made him catch his breath for Tybalt began:

My dear Mr. Swann,

When you read this I shall have moved on, and I pray God Almighty finds it possible to forgive me for what I am about to do. But I thought it only honourable to admit that I did not follow your advice last night. I was far too agitated to let it rest until morning. I took a train to Annerley to discuss this grave matter with my son, and try and discover whether he had remained in ignorance of the fact that Robsart and others were robbing the firm. I learned a great deal more than I bargained for.

He looked up, glancing across at the impassive Keate. "You say you couldn't locate Tybalt? You're sure he wasn't somewhere about the house?"

"As I said, I called, sir . . ."

"Then listen to this, Keate. I'll read it first and explain on the way over there. You and I are going back as soon as I've got some clothes on . . .

". . . You will understand, Mr. Swann, how excessively painful it is for me to write this, so I do not propose to go into details. You will do that as soon as you confront my boy, Robsart and that scoundrel Linklater. The truth is, in a word, Wesley was implicated so deeply that he heard me out and then offered me a substantial bribe to forget what I had seen and deduced, saying he could concoct some plausible explanation to satisfy you and dispose of Robsart and his associates overnight. I do not think I need tell you I spurned his offer and counselled him there and then that there was only one course open to him now, to lay everything before you and Mr. George, and throw himself on your mercy.

"At first he brushed this aside, saying you would make certain he went to prison, but I went on and he finally promised he would consider taking this course, provided I would allow him a few hours to make up his mind. It seemed to me I owed him that, or rather I owed it to his wife and child, so I left and went home. No words of mine can express the shame I feel on his behalf. I can only assume he was a far weaker vessel than I thought and was led away by Linklater or Robsart, but one thing he did add and I pass it on for what it is worth. The pickings were trivial at first but when Mr. George took to travelling more, and gave Wesley a free run of the yard, he plunged deeper and deeper into wickedness and began organising big-scale runs from the North and Midlands, roughly along the lines you suggested – that is to say, our vehicles making the long hauls and Linklater's onloading from that warehouse whenever the occasions were propitious.

"I can only add that never, under any circumstances, could I look you in the face again. Our long association has been, to me at least, a very happy one and I will carry with me to the grave a deep appreciation of all your trust and kindness since I came to work for you in the earliest days of Swann-on-Wheels.

"I remain, sir, your very humble servant, Hubert Tybalt."

He had never seen Keate so blanched and tense. The big man seemed dazed with shock and when his lips moved no sound issued from them for a moment or so. Then he said, hoarsely, "He can't . . . he wouldn't do anything so . . . so foolish, so dreadful, Mr. Swann?"

Adam said, sharply, "He certainly will if we aren't lucky enough to run him down and persuade him a man can't take upon himself the guilt of others, no matter how close they are. Go down and get a cab. Pick the youngest horse in the rank and tell the cabby we want him to risk his neck in a dash to Rotherhithe. Don't say anything more now, we haven't time. I'll be with you in less than five minutes." And without waiting for Keate to leave he tore open the wardrobe and threw his spare suit on the bed, struggling out of his dressing gown and flinging himself into his clothes. He went out in such a hurry that he left the door open and the bed strewn with keys.

3

Traffic had eased off at this hour but the journey seemed a tedious one, for it did not take him long to acquaint Keate with the basic facts of the situation and afterwards, following a futile speculation or two, the pair of them jolted on in gloomy silence. It wanted a few minutes to ten when the cab drew up beside Tybalt's little house and he bundled out of it, calling to the cabbie to wait. Keate was close behind him and they paused in the narrow hall to light the gas, then went on into the front-room, where Tybalt's mission appeals lay in neat stacks on the red plush tablecloth. He said, gruffly, "You stay here. I've got to make sure before we alert the police. I'm pretty certain it'll be the river, and I only hope it takes him a long time to screw up his nerve!", and he clumped upstairs, finding a candlestick on the tiny landing and lighting the wick.

Tybalt's bedroom, tidily done over by the woman who looked after him, was empty, and the bed had not been disturbed, but that meant nothing, for she had been here until midday. He went back across the landing and examined the other two rooms, scarcely more than boxes. One, that was furnished, had been Wesley's all the time he was growing up here, and a text hung over the bed, one of those framed Biblical quotations that hung in the homes of all men like Tybalt. It read 'I am the Way, the Truth and the Light'. He went out and was beginning to descend the stairs again when he noticed a door midway between the bedrooms that he had mistaken for a cupboard. He now saw that it was not a cupboard but a recess, converted into a water-closet. On impulse he turned back and flung open the door, holding the candle high above his head.

Tybalt looked back at him, a baffled, outraged expression in eyes that were wide open, as was his mouth. His feet reached to within about six inches of the floor. The knotted cravat about his neck was hooked over the trigger of the cistern and entangled, somehow, in the short length of chain and even as he stared the final irony of the situation jumped at him in the form of the raised lettering on the cistern. It announced that the water-closet was the product of James Lockerbie & Company, Ltd., Sanitary Engineers, Glasgow, the man George was cuckolding. George had given Wesley Tybalt so much rope that he had succeeded in hanging not Wesley but Wesley's father.

He would have thought himself proof against the shock of witnessing a violent death but this death was more than violent. It was obscene, a bizarre and shuddering mockery of all the man hanging there had believed in and practised throughout his blameless life. It was as ritualistic as the death of a terrified savage, willed to destroy himself by a witch-doctor and it was acknowledgment of this, rather than the spectacle itself, that made him recoil retching, steadying himself by throwing up a hand to grasp the lintel of the makeshift door frame.

In that moment Keate was beside him, the pair of them crowding the narrow door frame as Keate said, quietly, "Leave him, sir. I'll see to him. Go down, sir, I'll not be a moment," and Adam turned and groped his way down the stairs to the front door, standing there with his back to the hall gulping the river breeze and telling himself that he was past this kind of thing, long done with meddling in other men's affairs, and yearned only to be safely back at 'Tryst', with Henrietta, his trees and his flowers.

He was still standing there when Keate came down,

saying, in the same steady voice, "Take the cab and get along home, sir. Leave everything to me. I'll inform the police and do what has to be done," and when Adam made a gesture of protest, "He was *my* friend, sir! The best a man ever had," and practically propelled Adam to the cab, calling to the driver, "Back to the hotel but take it steady this time. The gentleman is in no hurry now."

But later, an hour or so later, Adam decided that Keate was wrong. He was in a hurry, a tearing desperate hurry to call George to account, and he only waited long enough to down a couple of stiff brandies before searching through his notebook for the number that butler had given him earlier in the day, a day that seemed to have stretched itself into a month and a month in which disaster piled on disaster in a way that was somehow new to him, and that after a lifetime of adventure. He went down to reception and saw the night manager, asking if he might use the inner office for a private telephone call, and when the young man had ushered him inside and offered, as was usual he supposed, to get the callee for him, he waved his hand, saying impatiently, "No . . . I'll get it. I know how to work the damned thing. Mr. Irons showed me this morning."

It took longer than he thought, a matter of ten minutes or so, and he was close to giving up when a woman's voice said over the wire, "Who is it? Who is calling?"

"Is that Lady Lockerbie, ma'am?"

"Yes it is." The voice was snappish and decisive, the voice of a woman who did not suffer fools gladly. "Who is it calling?"

He said, very meekly, "You won't know me, Your Ladyship, but I'm calling on very urgent business. This is Mr. Wesley Tybalt, yard manager of Swann-on-Wheels. I was given this number by Mr. George Swann and told to use it in emergencies. There has been an emergency, Your Ladyship. I'd be very obliged indeed if you could put me in touch with Mr. Swann."

He waited, counting the seconds and perhaps ten elapsed

before she said, carefully, "What *kind* of emergency, Mr. Tybalt?", and he said, eagerly, "A fire, Your Ladyship. I'm afraid I have some bad news for Mr. Swann. Half the yard has been burned down. The brigades are still there."

That rattled her a little. He heard the swift intake of breath but the voice was casual when she said, "I think I might be able to locate Mr. Swann for you. He is one of my house guests."

"You could reach him soon, Your Ladyship?"

"Possibly. I'll pass your message to him."

"I'm sorry, ma'am . . . at the risk of sounding impertinent it is essential I locate him as quickly as possible. I could wait while you enquired for him."

There was a longish pause. Finally she said, "Very well, Mr. Who-is-it?"

"Tybalt, ma'am."

"Tybalt."

She went away and he settled himself as comfortably as possible in a cane chair that was too deep and too small for his bulk and customary sitting posture. Minutes passed and he yawned, trying to keep awake by equating the faraway voice with that lovely imperious face of the horsewoman Gisela had shown him. Presently a polite male voice enquired, "Did you get your subscriber, sir?" and he said, "Yes, I'm waiting." Slowly, as minutes passed, the exhilaration the success of his ruse had injected into him waned, the mild glee insufficient to hold at bay the memory of Tybalt's baffled eyes and short legs dangling six inches from the closet floor. His head nodded and the confines of the uncomfortable chair enfolded him in a way that made him yearn for release. And presently, against all probability, he dozed.

6

Return of Atlas

THE GARDEN-HOUSE, A PRETTY, TIMBER-CON-
structed building, set in a secluded part of the grounds
of Sir James Lockerbie's country home, was his wife's
favourite resort when she was temporarily disenchanted
with cities. It was comfortably furnished and out of
sight and sound of the big house, an ideal place to re-
enact a kind of Marie Antoinette Arcadian fantasy, and
Barbara Lockerbie was given to fantasies. Indeed, she
would have argued that fantasy (judicially translated into
fact whenever the opportunity offered) had been responsible for her spectacular climb from the daughter of an
Irish emigrant, to the late Victorian equivalent of a
Regency courtesan. George himself would have acknowledged this. In fact, every young spark and kept doxy in
London's second-grade society acknowledged it, and it
was generally assumed that even Sir James Lockerbie
must have adjusted to it, for there were certain commercial
advantages accruing to the husband of one of the most
talked-of women in London. It kept the name of Lockerbie in the eye of men with money to burn, especially in
a society where, despite so many impressive technical
achievements, the earth-closet and the close stool were
still much in use, where few country houses boasted a
bathroom and the habit of daily bathing was still regarded
as a mark of eccentricity.

Thus Sir James, who spent a great deal of his time

travelling, and whose ambition it was to die the wealthiest man in Scotland, gave his wife a notoriously long leash and appeared to pay little heed to gossip concerning her virtue. She was gay, undeniably pretty, an excellent hostess when he had need of her services as such, and wore a romantic halo that went some way to encourage tolerance regarding her alleged shortcomings in other respects.

Her father, it was rumoured, was a Kerry landowner, whose gambling debts had obliged him to live abroad where he subsequently married a Portuguese heiress. Her mother, some claimed, was a Polish ballet dancer, and had been a mistress of Czar Nicholas II who had married her off to a British embassy official. She had, according to other random tongues, been born in Trieste, in an Indian garrison town, in the American West during the '49 gold rush, in Bergen, in Egypt and any number of places with exotic connotations, like Samarkand, Baghdad and a village high in the Caucasus.

Not one word of these colourful stories was true but this was no loss to romance. Real romance resided in her survival, and promotion to a position where she could pick and choose wealthy lovers and receive them, more or less openly, at the Garden House, on a Hertfordshire estate of four hundred acres, or in her apartment in the Avenue Wagram, in Paris. Promiscuous she undeniably was but she was not a fool and London had never been the setting for a single indiscretion. She had more than enough commonsense to realise that nobody moving in her circle credited the fact that anything important, including an act of infidelity, could occur outside London. Incidents rumoured to have taken place across the Channel, or in the British provinces, could therefore be dismissed as fiction.

As to the truth concerning her origin, perhaps she herself had never known it and had been obliged to invent a pedigree. In fact, she was the illegitimate daughter of a scullery-maid, employed on an absentee landlord's estate in County Mayo at the time of the Irish potato famine, and Bab Casey, as she began life, was the deferred price paid by a starving girl for one square meal a day. Her mother must have had a certain shrewdness, however, for she at least prevailed upon her lover to give her enough money to emigrate to Canada on one of the Cork coffin ships, and the scullery-maid must have been hardy, too, for she and her child survived when three-fifths of her fellow passengers died on voyage, or during the quarantine period in the St. Lawrence River, where they were buried in mass graves on an island before the survivors were set ashore at Montreal.

It was here, in the shanty town, that Barbara spent her brief childhood until she followed her mother's example and ensured her own survival by sailing away as the fifteen-year-old mistress of a German sea captain, later drowned off the Newfoundland Banks. She next turned up in Liverpool, as part of the travelling equipment of an animal trainer, who exhibited at one-night circus stands in the cotton towns of the North-west. It was here, while assisting her employer in his alligator act, that she attracted the attention of a professional gambler, who took her to Glasgow, graveyard of many a gambler, and his too after Barbara moved from half-world into broad daylight by leaving him and marrying a Paisley architect of respectable family.

From then on her career was at least on record. She divorced her husband when she was twenty-three and married Sir James Lockerbie a few months after his wife had died of jaundice. Few women could have come this far without learning the basic rules of survival in a world shaped by men for men and Barbara learned more than most. Her philosophy was simple, and based on the assumption that a busy man, obsessed with the business of coaxing a good living from a gullible public, may prattle a lot about domestic felicity but invariably ventures beyond the range of his own hearth in search of it during his brief intervals between stints of hard grind. Another thing she learned about men was that few of them ever matured, as a woman matures. From adolescence until senility the simple gratification of their senses was more important to them than all their wealth and status and almost any man, however thrustful and ambitious, is a slave to his carnal appetites. It was therefore in this direction, and no other, that a personable woman should look for advancement. Had she been asked to summarise her conclusions in this field she would have said that a help-mate, however dutiful and accomplished, invariably lost the battle to a bedmate, providing, of course, that the bedmate knew her business as well as Barbara Lockerbie, alias Mrs. Creighton, alias Barbara Tracy, Barbara Villeneuve, Barbara Schmitt and so on, all the way back to little Babs Casey, fighting to stay alive in a Canadian shantytown.

*   *   *

She had tested this theory on a string of lovers, some chosen for gain and lustre, others, as she passed the thirty mark, for diversion, and her involvement with George Swann, head of a national transport network, was proof that her theory was sound. George attracted her for a variety of reasons, chief among them being his indifference to competition. It was as though his headstart over every other haulier in the country equipped him with an ability to discount her other admirers, past and present, and this added up to a kind of amiable arrogance that she found very agreeable. George took what she had to offer boisterously and gratefully, but he left it at that, using her, she suspected, much as she had used a succession of men in her rise from the gutter. He never probed her past, or speculated on their future as lovers, seeing her, no doubt, as a prolonged holiday treat and, God knows, the poor man badly needed a holiday when she ran across him at his ship launching last April. As far as she could decide he hadn't had one for years and was not even aware that he had earned one, and it might have been the memory of this that prompted her to lie about the telephone bell that broke in upon their idyll towards midnight the day of the regatta.

He was shaving now in the tiny dressing-room adjoining the bedroom and from the bed she could hear the rasp of razor on stiff bristles that required him, so he said, to shave night and morning. She felt very much at peace with the world after a tiring and somewhat boring day on the river, for the regatta and the sunshine had brought everybody out, and she had had her fill of chitter-chatter with local sportsmen and their frumpish wives. George, thank God, was not a sportsman, and had no interest in fashionable games and pastimes. He evidently enjoyed his work and manifold responsibilities. He must have done, in order to keep his nose to the grindstone ever since he took his father's place as head of the network, but he had no social ambition and this in itself was refreshing. He was, she would have said, a man who preferred to save his vitality for his network and her, and she was not disposed to let him go until she had exhausted all his possibilities.

She now lay spreadeagled on the silk coverlet of the bed, speculating whether the long day by the river had exhausted him as much as it had her, and how this was likely to affect his performance as a lover. She was clinically interested in such performances, and his, a little storming and clumsy at first, was improving rapidly under her tuition. She even thought he was aware of this and gave her the credit for it, and this was very exceptional in the male animal. She called, lazily, "Do you know why I'm always pleased to see you, George?"

He called back, "Because you don't have to flatter me."

"No," she said, "although that's a point. It's because you're the only man I know who doesn't decorate his face with a lot of bristly undergrowth."

He said, laughing, "Got it from the Gov'nor. Never seen him with a beard or whiskers."

He often mentioned his father, usually in terms that

implied they got along much better than most reigning monarchs and their heirs apparent. "You're very fond of him, aren't you, George?"

"I've got a hell of a lot of respect for him."

"Does he keep a mistress somewhere?"

"He's turned seventy, woman."

"Did he ever keep one?"

"Not to my knowledge. Personally I doubt it. All his energy went into the network. He started from scratch."

He drifted in, dabbing his tanned, good-natured face with a towel, and contemplated her a moment before lowering himself on the edge of the bed. He was in no hurry. He never was nowadays and this was something else she found rewarding about him.

"What's your mother like, George?"

"You're not interested in my mother."

"I'm interested in any woman whose husband reaches seventy without him getting goatish."

He said, thoughtfully, "Come to think of it, I daresay you're right. She probably had a good deal to do with it."

"How, George?"

"I always got the impression she wilts every time he comes into the room. She still does."

"That wouldn't account for it, would it?"

"It would in her case. She never troubled to conceal the fact and that has a steadying effect on a man."

"Tell me."

"It enlarges his domestic conscience. Makes him feel shabby when he does cut loose."

"Your wife thinks a deal of you. Do I bother your conscience?"

He said, quite seriously, "Yes, from time to time. But then I tell myself that a man must have fun sometimes. I had a good deal up to the age of twenty-one but not much since."

"Where did you find your fun, George?"

"In Munich."

"Tell me about Munich."

He told her something of his time in Munich, where a statuesque German widow, almost old enough to be his mother, had seduced him before he was twenty. He still remembered Rosa Ledermann with great affection. It was she who had shaped his tastes in women. He had a preference for well-covered women, with generous hips and busts, and now that he looked at Barbara Lockerbie he realised that it was her figure that had attracted him, even though she had delicate features and a beautiful skin. He said, voicing his thoughts, "If I had met you a few years ago I wouldn't be here dancing to your tune. You were skinnier then, or so I've heard. Is that so?"

"Yes, it is so," and she subjected him to a long, careful scrutiny, noting his jauntiness and the half-smile about his clean-shaven lips. She thought: 'He could keep me quiet for a year or more, I daresay. Maybe even longer, providing he didn't begin taking me for granted.' Aloud she said, "Kiss me, George."

"I'll do more than that. Move over."

Her arms arched over his strong neck, pulling him down and pressing his mouth to hers with a kind of playful determination, as though willing him to take the initiative. And when her mouth opened he did, losing his jauntiness and letting his hand run as far as her thighs but it was never her habit to yield to the first overtures. As his head came up she turned hers sideways and he saw that she was laughing.

"What's the joke, Babs? Is it us? Saying good night all round and slipping away here?"

"No, not that."

"Something that came to mind unexpectedly?"

"That's very sharp of you, George. Sometimes you're a little too sharp. I was thinking of that poor little man on the other end of the telephone."

"What little man? You said it was your town butler, ringing about tomorrow's enquiries."

"Well, it wasn't. That was a wicked lie."

"Why?"

"To keep you here. It was someone who works in your yard. A man called Tybalt."

He sat up, instantly attentive. "*Wesley* Tybalt? My yard manager?"

"Yes, and it was very naughty of you to give him this number to use in emergencies."

His face clouded now as he said, "Tybalt's had that number ever since our first time up here but he's never used it. What was the emergency?"

"I'll not tell you."

"You damned well will tell me!"

It was a long time since Barbara Lockerbie had felt menaced and the experience was rare enough to excite her. She said, "Now listen here, Mr. Waggonmaster, you might be God Almighty in your network but here . . ." but he cut in, taking her by the shoulders in a grip that would leave bruises.

"I'm not fooling any longer. It might be very important, so you'll tell me why Wes Tybalt rang."

"It wasn't important."

"You let me be judge of that."

She had learned, over the years, precisely how much teasing a man could stand. There was no sense in antagonising him beyond a certain point or he might turn sulky and sulks in a lover meant a dull evening.

"All right, let me go. It was a fire at the yard."

"What kind of fire?"

"How should I know? He said a fire, and asked if I could get hold of you."

"And you left him on the end of the telephone?"

"The line is still open."

"But good God, I heard that bell tinkle when I started shaving fifteen minutes ago. You had no right . . ." and he would have made for the landing where the telephone was but she felt challenged and grabbed him by the hand, throwing her full weight against his arm so that he staggered and fell on her.

"Let go, Babs! I've got to talk to Tybalt if he's still there."

"He's waited fifteen minutes. He'll wait another ten. At least long enough to prove I'm more important than a transport yard," and she tried to enfold him in a way that would have delayed some men even if the bed had been on fire.

She got a real shock then, of a kind that was unique in her experiences over the last few years, although it was by no means the first time she had been manhandled. He got his right hand under her chin and pushed with sufficient force to break her embrace and throw her against the bedhead where the impact made her teeth rattle. And then, before she could regain sufficient breath to swear, as only Barbara Lockerbie could swear given provocation, he was gone and she heard him snap, "*Tybalt?* Are you still there, Tybalt?", and after that, while she was deciding whether she enjoyed or resented being rough-handled by a man again, a sharp exclamation on his part followed by a long, mystifying silence.

2

The voice reached Adam like a hail from the top of a mountain. George's voice certainly, but distorted by distance and his own drowsiness so that it was small as a child's yet charged with a child's urgency.

"Is that you, Tybalt? Tybalt, can you *hear* me?" and he dragged himself fully awake, stared down at the earpiece still held in his numbed hand, and said, "It's not Tybalt, George. Tybalt's skipped." And the gasp at the far end of the wire reached him as the ultimate in surprise and apprehension.

He was alert now and wondering how he could have slept so soundly without relinquishing his grasp on the heavy earpiece. There was a sour taste in his mouth, the straps of his tin leg had cut into the flesh of his thigh and he could still smell that damned smoke.

"*You*, Gov'nor?"

"It's me, George. Come on home you young fool, and get about your business."

"What . . . what's happened? I heard there'd been a fire. How bad a fire?"

"As bad as a fire can be; short of loss of life. Two-thirds of H.Q. is in ruins but that's the least of your troubles, lad."

It was rubbing in salt but he didn't care. If anyone had sat up and begged for punishment George had over the last few weeks.

"Two-thirds? What *could* be worse?"

"Your credit. And the life of someone who gave everything he had to the network."

"But you said no one was hurt . . ."

"Not in the fire. I'll give it you short and sweet, George. Young Tybalt's made a monstrous fool of you. He robbed the firm right and left and his father caught him at it."

"*Old* man Tybalt?"

"Yes, *old* man Tybalt. He was one year junior to me. What the devil has his age to do with it? He was so damned ashamed that he hanged himself before I could get to him and I hold you responsible for that. Can you still hear me?"

"I can hear you."

"Then I'll add something to that. Do you know what Tybalt used to anchor the cravat that strangled him? One of Lockerbie's flush cisterns. Go in and tell that woman as much. I daresay it will make her laugh. Then come home and don't waste time doing it, d'you hear?"

He replaced the earpiece on its hook and put his hand to his aching thigh, massaging it with the slow circular motion he had employed ever since he wore an artificial limb. The night manager looked in.

"Were you able to get your subscriber, sir?"

"I got him and I'm obliged to you. Put the cost of the call on my bill and make it up for the morning. I shall be leaving after breakfast."

"Certainly, sir. Good night, sir."

"Good night."

He climbed the stairs feeling older than Pharaoh and as oppressed as Atlas. There was no satisfaction in bludgeoning George in that ruthless way but it had to be done. Only a shock of that nature would bring the boy to his senses and even that might fail when he surveyed the ruin of the yard. He might see it as something hardly worth redeeming.

*　　　*　　　*

She was still sitting on the bed. Naked now, her back to the bedrest and slowly combing her blue-black hair as though, by unmasking all her batteries, she could be certain of capitulation on the spot. He was stubborn but not as stubborn as all that, or not unless the sum total of all she had learned about men was less than she had assumed all these years. She said, gaily, "Well, George? Did the little man tell you to report back for duty?"

"The little man wasn't the yard manager. The little man was a very big one."

"Oh? Who would that be, George?"

"My father."

She was not so much alerted by that as by his changed expression. It was drained yet glowering, as though news of the fire had reduced him to total insignificance.

"But he's retired, isn't he? How does he come to be mixed up in it?"

"No time to explain," he said, thrusting his legs into his trousers and hitching his belt so tightly that it emphasised his small waist and the impressive breadth of his shoulders.

"Listen, George," she said, earnestly, "I'm sorry I kept it from you but I really couldn't imagine you would be concerned to that extent. After all, what do you pay men for if it isn't to run the place when you're away?"

"Wesley Tybalt did that all right," he growled. "He's been practising large-scale fraud and coinciding every fresh haul with my absences. If I ever run across him he won't live to betray anyone else who trusted him!"

"How much has he stolen from you?"

He glared down at her. Her promise seemed to arouse in him no more interest than if he had been looking at a bale of merchandise.

"What the hell does it matter? I get a message that my place is in ruins, that my manager has skipped with everything he could get his claws on, that Tybalt's father, one of my Gov'nor's oldest colleagues has hanged himself for shame of it. What the devil do you expect me to do? Call it a day and snuggle into bed?"

"*Hanged himself?* You mean the manager's father was involved?"

He paused, at least long enough to give her a pitying glance. "How could you understand? Some people have scruples. You might be amazed to learn it but they do. Wes Tybalt's father worked for Swann-on-Wheels from the day it sent its first waggon out on the roads. It was his life, and he lived to see it in ruins at the hands of his son and successor. It's no use asking how you might feel in those circumstances. You probably wouldn't feel a damned thing, not being put together that way. But *I* feel something. I feel it wouldn't take much to put me in the frame of mind of old man Tybalt!"

He was scrambling into his clothes all the time he was talking. She said, with a shrug, "Well, you still have to be practical. There's no transport out of here until morning. All the servants are in bed, the stables are locked, and there isn't a train to town until six in the morning."

He paid no further attention to her so she climbed off the bed and put her arms around him. "George, dear, think! I can arrange for you to be driven to the station in time to catch the first train. I daresay it's a shock, and naturally you'll feel yourself needed. But for heaven's sake . . ."

He freed himself from her with an air of resignation.

"I'll walk to the main road and hope to hop a night

haul into Covent Garden. Market gardeners pass through the village from time to time." He gave her a final, searching look. "This is goodbye, Babs. I'm wide awake now and you aren't likely to catch me napping again. Good hunting."

The flatness and finality of the parting stunned her, striking a shattering blow at her vanity, so that, for the moment at least, she felt as vulnerable as the fifteen-year-old waif who had staked her future on Captain Schmitt, in the St. Lawrence River, all those years ago. She said, wonderingly, "Don't I count for anything any more?"

"Not a thing, my dear, but it's not your fault. Like I say, it's the way people are put together and you're patchwork mostly."

She had no answer to this, and stood there, hands on hips, watching him go. The front door slammed and she listened to the scrape of his feet on the wooden steps leading to the lawn. He was a man entirely outside her experience and her sense of humiliation, although overwhelming, was tinged with curiosity. She went over to the window and pulled aside the curtain. In the light of the waning moon she saw his shadow cross a gravel path and melt into the coppice that shut off the view of the big house. She realised then that she would never see him again and the certainty of this generated in her a yearning that was more urgent than anything in her past. She would have given all she possessed to have been able to will him to turn about, re-enter the room, throw her on the bed and share his strength with her for a few riotous moments, absorbing a little of the ethos of the first real man she had ever held in her arms. Frustration welled in her to a point where she could have screamed and hurled things about the room but she lacked even the spirit to do this. Instead she sat astride her dressing-stool, staring into the gilded mirror and seeing there a parody of the woman who had purred back at her reflection an hour ago.

3

Adam stood in the narrow casement of the tower looking across an acre of desolation at the familiar curve of the river, finding a crumb of satisfaction in the knowledge that the stone-built belfry had survived while all about it were heaps of ashes and charred timber, broken here and there by the rotten tooth of a chimney-stack where the stoves of the various buildings had been centred. Here, on this side of the yard, his tower was all that remained. The Tooley Street warehouse, the counting-house, the waggon-shed, the forge and even the high clapboard fence had been consumed, together, he assumed, with a hundredweight of documents, ledgers, invoices and records of goods in transit to the docks and goods awaiting transit in the network. How did one set about sorting out a mess on this scale? Old Tybalt could have attempted it but Tybalt was lying under a sheet in the Rotherhithe mortuary.

At right angles to the main gate the stable block was all but destroyed and two of the original warehouses, timber-built, were roofless and windowless. Of the rest, on the far side, where the Southwark brigades had been first on the scene, warehouses had been saved but it was likely half the goods inside had been spoiled by jets played on the roofs and through the windows. Tiny eddies of smoke still rose from a jumble of waggons at the centre assembly point and word had come that a total of forty-seven vehicles had been destroyed or damaged. All the horses had been saved, thank God, but to use them someone would have to borrow transport from Southern Square, The Bonus and the Kent Triangle, dislocating all the schedules in those regions for as long as Blunderstone the coachbuilder took to replace what was lost.

He heard footsteps on the stairway and turned back into the room as George came in. His face, clothes and hands were smudged and blackened. He looked like a man who had himself narrowly escaped death in a blazing building.

He said, "They told me you were here at first light, George. Is that so?"

"I was lucky. I got a lift as far as Barnet in a market gardener's van, then caught a train around four."

"Have you had any breakfast?"

"I've no appetite for breakfast, Gov'nor."

"You'd best have some, none the less. Send one of the men over to the coffee stall. You've had a good look round?"

"I've seen all there is to see." He glanced round the octagonal room, littered with debris that might just as well have been burned. "I'm glad this place is intact. It means a lot to you, doesn't it?"

"Aye, it does." He lowered himself on a crate, spread his legs and rested his hands on his knees. Pity for the boy was beginning to invade him. He had never seen George look or move in this listless way. "It's not the end of the world, lad. You'll make it all good, I daresay, providing you pull yourself together and go back to that nice gel of yours. There's not much you can do here until the assessors have had a look. Why don't you go home to her. She'll be right glad to see you."

George said, "I can't get two things out of my head. How I could have been so wrong about Wes Tybalt, and why his father had to take it so hard."

"As to the first," Adam said, "young Tybalt fooled us all, me included. I never liked the chap. He was too smarmy for my book. But it always seemed to me he knew his business."

"He knew his business all right," George said, savagely. "It's hard to estimate but my guess is he's taken us for thousands, apart from the fire. I screwed that much out of Robsart before the police took him away. I got a list of his confederates too. These fellows have no more loyalty to each other than they have for us."

"How many are involved?"

"Eight. Three in Northern Region, three in the Midlands and two in the South. Robsart told all he knows and I think he's telling the truth. Probably too scared to do less. I've sent wires to lay the others by the heels, but they're small fry. Tybalt was the brains behind it. Robsart says he even organised Linklater's side of it and where the devil are we to start looking for him?"

"Overseas, I'd say. Providing you want to."

"Don't you?"

"No," said Adam, "I don't think I do. He'd be hard to find, anyway. He probably had it planned and is heading for some country without an extradition treaty. He might be snug on any one of a thousand vessels by now. My guess is he crossed to France last night and will keep moving from there. Take my advice. Don't spend yourself chasing Wesley. You've got more than enough to keep you occupied."

"That isn't the reason, is it? I mean, not the reason you don't want Wesley brought back and charged."

"No. The real reason is the loyalty I owe his father. Used to bully him unmercifully in the old days, when he came up here fussing about one thing and another. But Swann-on-Wheels owes him more than it owes any single man and if I could have reached him in time I'm sure I could have talked him round. However, there it is. Any fool can chart a course when he's home and dry. It never occurred to me he'd go to his son and give him a headstart in that way."

"Do you really think he started the fire, Gov'nor?"

"He started the warehouse fire. Probably didn't intend to do more than destroy what was in there, so that we should have trouble proving anything. Unsupported evidence of men like Robsart wouldn't have convicted him."

"Then why didn't he stay and brazen it out?"

"He slipped up admitting as much as he did to his father. Or maybe the size of the blaze scared him, or someone saw him entering or coming out of the place. Who can tell? Forget Wesley and take a look at your own affairs, George. Care to tell me how it started? I'm not poking about in a midden heap. It might help to talk to someone other than your wife."

"Gisela won't even refer to it. Most English women would but a Continental goes to the heart of the matter."

"Isn't that woman Lockerbie the heart of the matter?"

"No, Gov'nor, not really. There was nothing permanent about that relationship. What happened here in the meantime is what counts."

"You're saying you were never in love with that woman?"

"I've never really understood that phrase . . . 'in love'. Have you?"

"Not in the way poets peddle it. Love? I suppose I've always seen it as a crop raised by an association between a man and a woman after they've been trapped by their senses. Your mother and I were like that. I didn't 'love' her in that sense when we married. And she was far too green and too flighty to know what she was about, apart from choosing a wedding gown, and having some kind of status conferred upon her. But she fancied me and I fancied her, and we grew important to one another, the way people do when they find 'emselves saddled with shared responsibilities." He beetled his brows and stared at the floor. "If you had to cut loose for a spell why didn't you go to the places men frequent when things get on top of them?"

"It wasn't that kind of need."

"What kind was it?"

George said, slowly, "I was twenty when I met Gisela. I'll tell you something I never told anyone else. You've met her tribe of sisters. They were all as pretty as pictures, and very saucy with it in those days. I might have settled on either one of them, or all three of them maybe, if it hadn't been for old Grandfather Maximilien and his engine. He steered Gisela my way. Quite deliberately. You probably never did believe our eldest boy was a seven-month child."

"You married her on that account?"

"I didn't even know she was pregnant."

"Then what's all this got to do with you staking every-thing you worked for on a frolic with a high-class whore, like that Lockerbie woman?"

"As I say, it goes all the way back to Max and his engine. Until I found myself hooked to that, life was all cherry pie. Afterwards? Well, it was never quite the same again. I put everything I had and hoped for into that brute Maximus and I still think I was on the right track. About transport, I mean, about petrol-driven vehicles being much more than fussy little toys, replacing the carriage and pair. Then, when I thought I'd made a breakthrough, you handed the business to me on a plate and the fact is I wasn't ready for it. I had no idea how much it involved, and how many demands it made on a man."

"You seemed content enough. You appeared to be making a rare go of it."

"I was content, and I was making a go of it. But then, one day last spring, I suddenly realised it was taking over. To the exclusion of everything else, including Gisela and the children. It was my bad luck that this should hit me in Barbara Lockerbie's company. Do you want to hear the rest?"

"Only if you want to tell me."

"We met at that launching of mine. The Lockerbies invited me to spend a weekend with them at their lodge in Skye. Have you ever been to Skye?"

"No, though I've looked across at it."

"It's a magic place. Or it seemed so to me at that time and in her company. Sir James didn't turn up and I see now she planned it that way. We were out on the lower slopes of a mountain and the weather was fine and warm for the time of year. I suddenly realised what I'd been missing all these years and that soon I'd be forty. It all stemmed from that realisation, a matter of letting off steam, I imagine. The trouble was I didn't realise, until I heard your voice over the telephone last night, how much steam was there. That, and the fact that women have always been more important to me than they seem to be to you and Alex and Giles and the others. I don't mean all women. I mean lively, high-spirited women like Barbara Lockerbie, and that landlady of mine I once told you about in Munich."

He understood. Far better, perhaps, than George knew, for in her own way Henrietta was such a woman. Had it been otherwise it seemed probable that he too might have needed a change when he was George's age. The trouble lay, he supposed, in the fact that Gisela was a serious-minded little body and wouldn't know how to coax him out of such a mood, whereas Henrietta would, and had done so time and again without him being fully aware of it until now. He said, "Well, some of us drive ourselves hard and when we do there's generally a price to pay. You've paid yours, lad, and been overcharged to my way of thinking. I'm glad you told me as much as you did, but where do you go from here?"

"I know the answer to that," George said, "but I haven't the gall to tell you. Maybe I'll tell you when this place is ticking over again."

"No, tell me now. You've laid all your other cards on the table. Play out the hand."

George said, with a ghost of a grin, "You'll kick me downstairs I daresay, but I'll chance it. I need a longish spell clear away from this place. Not to blow off more steam, at least not that kind of steam, but to follow a dream. Your kind of dream."

"Something new?"

"Not entirely. We went over the same ground when we parted company that last time. As I say, I've never ceased to believe the real future of road transport is in the mechanically propelled vehicle but everything I've attempted so far has gone off at half-cock and I know why. You can't approach a job as demanding as that with half your mind on a business this size. You need isolation, and time to concentrate on every last detail, every modification, every scrap of information that comes in from the States and the Continent. Steam waggons aren't the answer, not for our kind of work. But there *is* an answer and I'd find it if I had the time and money."

"You've got the money, haven't you?"

"Not really. All I've put by is earmarked to pay shareholders what Wesley Tybalt filched but I could scrape by on next-to-nothing until I had a blueprint that satisfied me. Do you remember Jock Quirt, that Scots mechanic I had by me, when I was working on Maximus up at Sam's place in Manchester? He was an ugly little chap, with very little to say for himself, but he was a bit of a genius to my way of thinking. He's still working on that prototype up in the north."

"You're suggesting you set him to work right here?"

"No, I'm suggesting I go to him and we work on it together, but it would mean someone who really knew the ropes taking over here until next spring. I think I could guarantee results by then and we'd have motor transport that would give us a two-year start over every haulier in the country. I've absolutely no right to ask this . . ."

"But you are asking it?"

"Yes."

His head came up and the quick gesture reminded Adam again that, of all his children, George came closest to the Adam Swann who had made his grab on the strength of three guarantees. The yield of a looted necklace, sold to shady rascals in the city; a dream, not unlike George's; and an invincible belief in his own star. He said, doubtfully, "I'm turned seventy, George, and past it. Go ahead with your dream if you have to and you'll be no use to me or anybody else if you don't. But find someone else to sort this lot out and get things moving again."

"There isn't anybody else. And you aren't past it. It's my belief you don't really think you are either."

"I wonder."

He turned and crossed to the narrow window and this

time he did not see the desolation below but the broad curve of the river and the many-turreted tower he had explored only yesterday. He stood there a long time, thinking back and assessing himself in terms of profit and loss, failure and achievement, hopes fulfilled and un-fulfilled. He thought of 'Tryst' too, and the showplace he had made of it in the years that had passed since he turned his back on this slum. He would miss that and he hadn't much time to squander. How would Henrietta think of it? What would his doctor have to say about him shouldering a packload like this at his age? But did it matter what Henrietta, or the doctor, or anybody else thought? He did a kind of equation with the various factors of the case. A headquarters burned to a cinder. A criminal prosecution in the offing that would expose him and his as fools, milked by their own employees. George himself, at a crisis in his life, wanting desperately to atone but in his own way and on his own terms. He thought, distractedly: 'I wonder if he's right and whether I'm right to sympathise with him? I was wrong about mechanical transport. It's plain enough it's almost here now. I might even live to see the day they put the last of the horses out to grass and clutter the roads with clumsy galleons, like his precious Maximus. Everyone said I was mad to carve up the area the new railways had neglected but I saw further than most of 'em. Maybe George does now, for he's my flesh and blood, and there's a lot of old Sam Rawlinson in him. But none of these things count in the long run. The heart of the matter is, would I care to come back here and spend a St. Martin's summer in this room, gathering all the loose ends together and adapting, if I could accept them, to all the changes he's made already?' And suddenly his heart gave him the answer and he understood that, in an odd, clownish way, he would enjoy the exercise enormously, would relish being fully extended again and needed, not only by George, but by all those Johnny-Come-Latelys George had planted out along the network, cocky youngsters

mostly who had long since written him off as an old codger, well past his prime. He said, "I'll do it, George.
For one year from today. And God help the whole boiling
of you if I prove unequal to it, for then you'll all be in a
worse mess than ever. As to money, well, you don't have
to worry on that score. Your grandfather didn't trust
any one of you come to the end. He left his pile to me,
with orders to dole it out as I saw fit, and you'll get your
slice of it. If you want to pour it down the drain in some
murky workshop that's your business. I only want two
pledges from you and here they are. You'll be back here to
take over twelve months from now, hit or miss. And you
take that wife of yours north with you."

"Gisela won't leave the family."

"You can dump the family with Henrietta. It'll keep
her out of mischief while I'm slumming it right here."

George said, eagerly, "You won't regret it, Gov'nor.
Not when the final score is totted up."

"I'm not so sure about that but I've followed my nose
in situations like this all my life and I'm too long in the
tooth to change. I see too much of myself in you, George,
and that's a fact. Though I do flatter myself I had better
brakes at your age."

"Giles will back you."

"Oh no, he won't. In case you haven't looked hard
enough, Giles has a dream of his own and it doesn't run
on four wheels. As for Hugo, well, I've never seen him
as anything more than Swann's barker in the market-
place. Young Edward is more promising. He showed his
mettle yesterday. I'll take him under my wing for he's
merchant through and through, I wouldn't wonder."

He got up stiffly. "Go down and get a wash under the
pump and we'll drink to it before I catch my train. I've
still got to break this news to your mother. She won't
have heard of it, tucked away down there."

George went out without another word and a moment
later, watching from the window, Adam saw him splashing
head and shoulders in the pump trough. He thought,

'I don't know . . . I could have wrung his neck twelve hours since, and here I am, giving him his head again just as if he was all I had to show for my years here.' And suddenly, as clear as a picture on the wall, he had a memory of coming home to 'Tryst' one frosty February night, in 1864, and being greeted by the news that Hetty had been delivered of her third child and second boy, and going upstairs to look down on a merry little bundle in the cot, wide awake, knuckling his mouth, and staring back at him with an expression he could only describe as conspiratorial. And then, he recalled, a droll thing had happened, reminding him of the pact he and Hetty had made nine months before, after he learned from his father she had gone off the rails in his absence and come near getting herself seduced by a gunner who had fancied her. As if the baby in the cot was aware of the circumstances accounting for his presence, he had winked in a way that made Adam laugh aloud. He understood then why George was so easy to forgive.

7

A Titan, Fishing

THE NARROW COASTAL ROAD, REACHING THE
tiny village of Llanystumdwy, crossed the boulder-strewn
river Dwyfor by a humped-back bridge, just beyond a
cottage on the right. Where the bridge wall was broken,
giving foot access to the river below, she stopped the dogcart, saying, "Down there, Giles. That cottage is his old
home but I learned from that man back there he'd gone
fishing. He spends a lot of time fishing when Parliament's
not sitting and he can slip away up here."

He looked at her with amused incredulity. "I can't
just buttonhole him in that way, Romayne. Not him,
not a man with his reputation. He'd snub me and I'd
deserve it."

"L.G. has never snubbed anyone in his life. Sat on
them, talked them down and carried them along in his
wake, but not snubbed. It's not his nature and I should
know, for I'm one of his constituents seeing that Beddgelert house is still in my name. You do as I say. March
right up to him and tell him what you have in mind and
he'll admire you for it. Nobody in the world is cheekier
than Lloyd George."

"Let me see that letter again."

Romayne opened her reticule and took out a single
folded sheet, straightening it and passing it to him. The
secretary's reply was couched in a single paragraph on
House of Commons paper. It said:

Dear Madam,

Further to your enquiry concerning your husband,
Mr. Giles Swann, Mr. Lloyd George has asked me to
say that he will be in your area for one week when the
House rises and would be happy to see Mr. Swann if he
could come to Llanystumdwy before midday between
Monday, 15th, and Thursday, 18th.

Nothing else but the signature was written on the paper.

He said doubtfully, "It's a bit chilly, isn't it? A chap
like that must get hundreds of similar requests and if he's
on holiday . . ."

"Trust me, Giles. I know exactly what I'm about!"
and he thought, 'Well, I can stand a snub from a stranger,
and afterwards, maybe, she'll let me go about things in
my own way.' And he got down and went through the
gap to the steep, fern-clad bank where there was a tiny
path, hardly more than a rabbit run, leading inland
through close-set trees growing above the stream. He had
only gone about fifty yards when he saw him, sitting on a
rounded boulder holding what looked like a boy's fishing
rod made from a bamboo cane and a ball of twine.

He recognised him instantly, not only as the rumbustious politician who was always getting into the news
and its backspread of photographs, but at a much longer
remove – a jaunty, rather cocky young man he had encountered all those years ago at the door of the empty
Chamber of Commons, on his very first visit to Westminster, the incident that had inspired Romayne's impulsive letter to the member for Caernarvon Boroughs.

He recalled the circumstances vividly. Himself a shy,
thirteen-year-old, awed by the place where he stood;
the young Welshman, brash and confident, despite his
sing-song accent and country clothes. Slightly patronising
yet friendly and informative, with his talk of the miserly
wages Llanberis quarry-workers were paid and his intention, implied rather than uttered, of doing something
about it if the opportunity offered. And since then he

had, proving that his talk on that occasion was no adolescent boast but the pledge of a man already aware of his potential.

All that, however, had happened eighteen years ago and since then 'Mr. George' (who had dismissed the hallowed Chamber as 'crabbed and poky') had moved on to capture headlines as the noisiest, wittiest, most trenchant member of the Liberal Party whereas Giles, by his own reckoning, had stood still looking on.

He went down the narrow path until the fisherman, hearing the crackle of dry twigs, looked up and smiled, calling, in a slightly moderated brogue, "Lovely morning, Johnny Peep! Come and join me in the sun. The fish aren't rising. I did much better here as a boy poacher!"

He still wasn't sure of his welcome, despite Lloyd George's jocular greeting. 'Johnny Peep' implied an intrusion and he could pinpoint the source of the gibe:

> *Here I am, Johnny Peep,*
> *And I saw three sheep,*
> *And those three sheep saw me.*
> *Half-a-crown apiece pays for their fleece,*
> *And so Johnny Peep goes free . . .*

It was a verse quip of Robbie Burns, who had used it to win an evening's entertainment from three northcountry drovers.

He said, "I'm Giles Swann, Mr. George. My wife wrote for an appointment and later persuaded me to follow you here. I realise that's a liberty but she seems to think you don't mind seeing constituents."

"I never mind meeting an old acquaintance, Mr. Swann."

"You remember me?"

"Perfectly. A small, over-awed boy with knobbly knees and a reverence for politicians they don't deserve."

It was astounding, he thought, that he should recall their first meeting but the politician had another surprise for him. "Why do you suppose I addressed you as Johnny Peep?"

"That was understandable, me dropping in on you in this way. You must value the few hours you get to yourself."

"Not all that much. I never did care for my own company. The truth is I like an audience. Anyone about here will tell you that. As to recalling you, it came back to me the moment I saw the name 'Swann' on your wife's letter, and why not? It's a very famous name and you mentioned your father's profession on that occasion." He laid his improvised rod aside. "So you know the identity of Johnny Peep?"

"It was Burns, wasn't it?"

"One of my best stories. Robbie was a rare spirit. Do you read him still?"

"Not in dialect," Giles said. "He's too broad for me." Then, "I . . . er . . . didn't see my wife's letter. To be frank, she wrote it without my knowledge and sprang it on me when she got a reply."

"Sounds an enterprising lass, Mr. Swann."

"She's Welsh."

"That accounts for it. Join me," and he made room on the boulder. "I take it you know what she wrote *about*?"

"She knew that I was anxious to be considered by the Liberal Party as a prospective candidate and thought a direct approach to you was the best hope. I must be frank again, however. I live and work in London. We have a holiday house up here, and come as often as we can. We met about here when we were eighteen."

"Where exactly?"

"I fished her out of the river at Aberglaslyn. I thought she was drowning but she wasn't, just fooling. She's the daughter of Sir Clive Rycroft-Mostyn, the industrialist."

The politician whistled softly. "Dynastic alliance?"

"Far from it. My father-in-law and I are not on speaking terms, and haven't been since before Romayne and I married, eight years ago."

"Political differences?"

"Not really, although I never did care for his way with people. He's a big Tory subscriber."

"Yes, he is," Lloyd George said, thoughtfully, "and a bad man to work for they say. But your father is a radical, I'm told. Did he bring you up the way you should go?"

It was difficult to withstand the man's charm, even though, behind his amiability, there was irony, and that hint of patronage, as though Giles had been a small public meeting of the faithful. He had the most winning smile Giles had ever seen on the face of man or woman and he could understand why he had a reputation with the ladies. His personality played over you like a warm draught, but a searching one at that, Giles thought, telling himself that it would be dangerous to be less than frank with a man whose shrewdness showed in his eyes – merry, teasing eyes, but feeding every impression back to the calculating brain in that big, proud head. He said, "You've probably heard about my father's methods. His above-average pay-scale and his provident scheme. He was a pioneer in that field and many City men dislike him on that account."

"But he never tried to enter politics?"

"No. He's a merchant first and foremost."

"Probably more useful to us in that capacity," Lloyd George said, chuckling. "At least he's demonstrated that it isn't necessary to chain his workers to the oar in order to balance his books." He broke off, looking down at the tumbling water with a relaxed but watchful expression. "And how about you, Johnny Peep? Are you a convert, or have you always had a conscience? No, that's not what I'd like to know. Put it this way. Suppose we found you a constituency to nurse, and after times out of mind addressing lukewarm audiences in draughty church institutes, the walls of Jericho fell and you clawed us another seat from the privileged? What qualifications would you claim to enter that pint-sized chamber where we met and make your maiden speech to gentlemen who weren't listening?"

It was not at all the kind of interrogation he had been

expecting. The man's complete lack of formality and touch of irony ran contrary to one another, so that it was difficult to decide whether he was posturing or deliberately seeking to discourage. Giles said, finally, "I've had far more administrative experience than most applicants. I'm in charge of a provident and pension scheme for two thousand hands and I've read most of the social prophets in my time, deeply enough to quarrel with most of them."

"That's a point in your favour. Nearly all were theorists. Anything more?"

It was a time, Giles thought, to gamble and he had the advantage of having Celtic ancestry on his mother's side. Irony was a weapon in this man's armoury but it wasn't the one he employed very much in his attacks on every aspect in the system where he saw, and bitterly resented, injustice and inherited privilege. Colourful detail and dramatic licence spiced every public address he had ever made, either as courtroom solicitor or a member of Parliament and it followed that he would be likely to respond to his own stock-in-trade. Giles said, "When I was a boy of ten I watched an elderly farm labourer and his wife expelled from a tied cottage and sent off to separate workhouses. I never forgot that. It had a direct bearing on what I read and what I thought about when I was still at school. The month I left, thirteen years ago now, I walked from North Devon to Edinburgh to see things for myself. One incident made a deeper impression on me than anything else. It was on the deepest level of a Rhondda coal-mine. A young miner had his foot crushed by a runaway tub and I visited his parents that same night."

"Well?"

"They saw the accident to their son as a piece of rare good fortune. It meant he could still earn money but in safety, on top, a cripple with a sporting chance of survival. If we can't do better than that, as the richest and most powerful nation on earth, something's wrong with our thinking as Christians."

He saw at once that the gamble had paid off. The politician was looking at him with interest and the gleam of mockery behind the eyes had gone. "That's what we're looking for, Johnny Peep. But I wouldn't have expected it from a man with your background. Where is your holiday home in Beddgelert?"

"On the Caernarvon Road, about two hundred yards this side of the village. It's called 'Craig Wen'."

"The white rock. I know it. Might I invite myself to call and have tea with you and your wife tomorrow?"

"My wife would be delighted, Mr. George. But you could meet Romayne now if you wish. She's waiting for me in the dog-cart up on the bridge."

"Ah no," he said, "that would be taking advantage of the lady. Anyone sharp enough to write that letter and steer you here would want to do the honours. Tomorrow. Around four."

It was a polite dismissal and he got up, extending his hand. "You've already been more patient than I had any right to expect."

"And you've been more entertaining, Mr. Swann. Constituents who buttonhole me as you did usually want to talk about the disestablishment of the Welsh church, or get a shilling off their rent. Good day to you."

He shook hands, casually, and picked up his amateurish rod and line. When Giles looked over his shoulder halfway back to the bridge he was still hunched there. He looked very boyish for someone they said would end his career in the Cabinet or in prison.

2

Neither of them ever forgot one detail of that first visit of the Welsh Cyclone, as some of his admirers were calling him, to the pleasant house under the chain of mountains that enclosed the Nant Gwynant Pass all the way to Capel Curig, and on through the softer Vale of Conway to the sea. It was a house that had happy memories for him, for it was here, when he was no more than a schoolboy, he had lost his heart to the lovely restless girl Romayne Rycroft-Mostyn had been in those days.

The memory of the visit remained a red-letter day for him because it was here, rather than beside the tumbling Dwyfor, that he fell under the hypnotic spell of this strange, magnetic being, a force rather than a man, embodying, as Giles saw it, the romantic fervour of the Celt and a shrewdness that was Norman rather than Celtic and served the purpose of brake, spur and generator of a man whose life, up to this point, had been a calculated advance towards the limelight and the source of power. For Romayne it had deeper, more personal significance. She saw Lloyd George's patronage as the first practical attempt she had ever made to channel the potential of Giles Swann into a course where others, as well as herself, would accept him as a teacher and interpreter of his own uniquely compassionate philosophy. That, and the first real opportunity he had ever had of justifying himself in his own eyes.

For two hours by the grandfather clock, the Welshman talked about himself. Not vaingloriously, and certainly not tediously, for it was like listening to a saga out of the remote past where a king without a kingdom set about searching for his destiny. He told them of his obscure but happy childhood in these hills, fathered by a shoemaker uncle who emerged from the tale as a kind of Chiron preparing Jason for the Argosy. He told how, having decided to make his protégé a solicitor as a first step, his Uncle Lloyd had coached him in Latin by first learning Latin himself from a sixpenny grammar, bought on a bookstall. He laughed over his adolescent exercises in oratory, in the pulpit of a Welsh chapel, his early forays into journalism and the dramatic incident that made him famous throughout Wales when he successfully defended quarrymen flouting the law by forcing churchyard gates and burying a Nonconformist father beside his child in ground forbidden to Dissenters.

The rest was familiar, at least to Giles. His challenge, at the age of twenty-six, of the local squire at the hustings, his early days at Westminster and his rise to prominence as a politician who paid scant tribute to parliamentary procedure in his onslaught on the social sicknesses of his age.

But then, as the sun passed beyond the mountain summits in its swing down towards the Irish sea, he returned briskly to the purpose of his visit, the possibility of settling Giles in a constituency where hard work and, as he put it, the gathering might of the people, would elect him to Parliament and enable him to help convert Britain into a real democracy instead of a sham one.

"For mark you, it's almost here," he prophesied, with one of his extravagant gestures, "this landslide that will sweep us into power and enable us to implement reforms centuries overdue. Five years, ten at the most, but not more I promise you, and maybe you'll be there, Johnny Peep, to hammer out a constitution based on principles of justice, merit and equality of opportunity."

But it was not all rhetoric. He had a shrewd eye, for instance, for advantages to be wrung from the fact that Giles Swann bore a nationally-known name in commerce and it was while questioning Giles on his father's secure foothold on the southern perimeter of the region that he pounced on one specific area as an ideal jumping-off place.

"Pontnewydd?" he exclaimed, after Giles had told him the name of the valley where he had descended a coal-mine in the company of Bryn Lovell, for so long his father's viceroy based on Abergavenny, "I know it well and I've heard tell of Lovell, too. Isn't he the man who hauled a Shannon pump to the flooded shaft, and saved the lives of nearly sixty entombed miners? Why, man, it's a legend down there and legends are stock-in-trade. Pontnewydd is in Usk Vale country, that will likely fall to us after a couple of campaigns. Evan Thomas, the candidate down there, is over sixty and I doubt if he'll weather it."

He was silent and contemplative for a moment. Then

he said, "It would mean full-time campaigning, lad. Over a period of years unless you were exceptionally lucky. How dependent are you on your father?"

"I've money saved and my holding in the Swann Company would bring me a small income. But wouldn't it be possible to campaign up to the next election on a part-time basis?"

"No," Lloyd George said, uncompromisingly, "it would not. Winning a seat in Parliament was once a rich man's hobby but it isn't any longer, praise God. People stopped playing at politics when Gladstone broadened the suffrage. In a place like Pontnewydd it would be a fight with the gloves off, much like my first fight against Squire Nanney up here."

"Couldn't he be chosen as a North Wales candidate, Mr. George?" Romayne asked and he said, smiling, "No again, my dear! He's an Englishman, who doesn't speak a word of Welsh. In the south that isn't important. They've had the English on their backs for so long they're half Anglicised themselves I'm told, although they wouldn't admit it. We might try for an industrial seat in England, but I wouldn't have much influence there. Many English Liberals regard me as a potentially destructive element. The more respectable among them have already joined the club."

"What club is that?"

His eyes danced. "One that I hope you'll avoid if you ever get to Westminster. The Pro-Consul's Club as I think of it, where the lions lay down with the lambs. Or the wolves. Dramatic personality changes occur in revolutionaries, once they've put on the Westminster strait-jacket. You might even have difficulty distinguishing them from their opponents after a year or so in that hot house. It's a rare place for raising hybrids." He looked at his watch. "I'm due in Caernarvon for a constituency meeting at eight and must leave you now. May I take it you're prepared to put yourself in my hands? Well, you might do worse in your situation, for I've taken a rare fancy to you, Johnny Peep. A little more fire in your belly and you'll emerge as a very promising recruit to my way of thinking. A Tory-orientated young man, with every-thing to gain by accepting the advantages conferred on you by a rich background and good education, who accepts the radical as the arbiter of the twentieth century." He turned to Romayne. "You can play your part, my dear. The role of a politician's wife isn't easy. You'll soon learn that, I daresay. In any other profession a man can use what cover is available. Out there in the arena he's a sitting target and it isn't only his hide that takes a walloping from time to time."

They were both well aware of what was explicit in the warning. As recently as last July Lloyd George had been cited in a divorce suit that threatened to topple him but he did not act like a man under a cloud. His denigrators, Giles decided, would have to get up long before sunrise to catch David Lloyd George napping.

*   *   *

Adam was in his tower working by lamplight when Giles came to him with the letter. An invitation to present him-self at an Usk Vale constituency meeting, where pre-liminary steps would be taken to replace the retiring Liberal candidate at a rally of the Executive in the new year. Evan Thomas, a local councillor who had fought three unsuccessful elections had stepped down earlier than anyone expected on grounds of failing health. Almost certainly, Giles decided, he had been nudged by younger elements of the party in the area, men working in close liaison with Lloyd George, who was already accepted by the thrusters as the real leader of the Welsh Liberals.

Giles had kept Adam informed to date but there hadn't been much to pass on and, in any case, his father's energies were fully absorbed in the gigantic task of reorganising and rebuilding headquarters while still exercising control of the provincial network. Giles had not been able to help him much. His own experience was confined almost wholly to welfare on the one hand, and the investigation of claims on the other, and he rarely spent more than two days a week in the capital. But Adam had not complained. Indeed it had seemed to Giles, through those busy autumn months after the New Broom had vanished from the scene, that his father relished the task thrust upon him by George's leave of absence, and the havoc wrought by the fire.

"You'll be going down to look them over, I take it?" he said, and Giles reminded him that it was more a case of being looked over.

"Swanns do the looking," the old man said, half in jest.

But Giles replied, "Oh, I don't give myself much of a chance. They'll be sure to choose a local man in favour of a candidate who can only pay flying visits to the valleys," and failed to notice his father's abstracted look as he took the letter and held it closer to the circle of lamplight. "I thought I should let you know I'll be out of touch Monday and Tuesday of next week. I'll get those Swansea claim forms from the clerks and deal with them over the weekend."

Adam said, sharply, "Wait on, son. Don't be in such a confounded hurry. I need time to mull this over. Pour me a noggin and help yourself to one while you're about it."

"But you're swamped with work. Look at that desk."

"I'm getting on top of it."

Giles went to the wall cupboard his father had reconverted into a cellarette. Ever since he could remember his father seemed far more relaxed in this queer octagonal chamber than in his more comfortable surroundings at 'Tryst'. The place still had the air of a bivouac, tenanted by a campaigning general with spartan tastes and a passion for work.

"How do you feel about going the whole hog, boy?"

Giles looked at him, encouraged by the smile plucking the corners of his mouth.

"You mean shifting down there permanently? Leaving you to cope with this mess alone?"

"I'm not alone. Keate has come back four days a week. And that young brother of yours is a damned quick learner."

Giles noticed he said nothing of old Hugo. He had always been disposed to dismiss old Hugo as an amiable oaf. Anywhere outside a sports stadium, that is.

"One of us ought to stand with you, apart from a kid Edward's age."

"Not you, boy. For one thing your heart's never been in it and for another this letter tells me you've got bigger fish to fry. Well?"

"I don't know. I as good as told Lloyd George I couldn't accept a full-time candidacy."

"Question of money?"

"No. We could get by on a modest income down there."

"That won't get you far, son."

"How do you mean?"

"The Liberals are not only short of young talent at the moment. I happen to know they're desperately short of ready money."

"I didn't promise them any money."

"You didn't have to. I'm not saying that chap Lloyd George doesn't recognise good political potential when it comes knocking at his door, but it wasn't that that got your foot in the door. If you could bring the local party a sizeable annual subscription they wouldn't give a local man a second look. I know that much about party politics. You've got your share of Sam's residue. It's more than enough to win that seat, backed by hard graft."

"Isn't it a bit like buying your way in?"

"You have to buy your way into everything, son. You always did, even in my day. Only now it's twice as expensive. Only those Keir Hardie crusaders see politics in any other light and they'll come around to it as soon as the Labour Party settles down."

"Lloyd George got himself elected without financial backing."

"So he did. But who keeps him there, pitching away at the coconut shies? His family practice mostly. I've had that on good authority."

"It still doesn't entitle me to leave you in the lurch."

Adam sipped his brandy. "Tell you something I've not told anyone else, Giles. Something I wouldn't admit to your mother, if only for fear of hurting her feelings. I'm happier here, back in this slum, than I've ever been ever since the day I walked out on it, and turned my hand to making something of 'Tryst'. That was a challenge while I was doing it, but now all that's left for me to do is to watch the trees and shrubs grow and I'll be gone before they mature. Oh, I daresay George regards what I'm doing here as a sacrifice, and I mean to let him go on thinking it. It might help to keep him in line, after that silly business with that Lockerbie woman. The truth is I put myself out to grass before I was used up and it does a man a power of good to realise that when he's seventy and get a chance to prove it. Lift your glass, boy, and drink to the first Swann to make laws. They've been busy bending 'em ever since Agincourt. It makes a change."

Giles finished his brandy, reflecting that nobody ever stopped learning about the Gov'nor. His queer passion for this squalid place. His unquenchable faith in himself and his potential. His gruffness, forthrightness and swift, unexpected touches of kindness, gentle as a woman's. He said; "If I won a seat, would that make you glad? Proud, perhaps?"

The old man crossed to the cupboard and poured himself another measure. "It's important I should know, sir."

The 'sir' arrested him. Like his brothers, even young Edward had stopped calling him 'sir'. It was Gov'nor or Father, according to their estimate of his mood.

"Glad? Yes, I'd be glad for your sake. Proud? I'm not so sure. You've got respect for that place and I once had. But most of it has leaked out my boots over the years."

"It's still the best governing instrument in the world, isn't it?"

"Yes, you could claim that I suppose. But looking round the world nowadays I sometimes wonder if we couldn't have set a better example."

"Because other democracies are younger and greener?"

"Not necessarily. Put it another way. Ours should be better than it is by this time. We had a long start over everybody else and I'm not sure I like the use we're making of it nowadays. 'Strutting' doesn't become us."

He knew what was in his father's mind and it was not merely the recent exercise in what he had dismissed as 'tribal breastbeating'. It was an attitude taken for granted by almost every living soul in the islands, from tiara-wearers, walking the red carpet between ranks of cooing shopgirls outside Devonshire House, down to the hardest-driven slavey in the basements of their town houses. It was in their ditties and their folk lore, and taught alike in their redbrick elementary schools and ancient seats of learning. It could be heard in the clamour of their half-penny press and seen in the swagger of their sailors on shore leave. You could see it reflected in stock-market quotations and hear its voice in the rattle of money pouring into a million tills. It decked itself in feathers and pearl on Hampstead Heath on Bank Holidays and in scarlet and gold in garrison towns all over the world, and perhaps Adam was speaking for his son as well as himself when he added, "It's not all bad, mind you. The devil of it is most radicals would throw out the baby with the bath-water. There's a lot here worth saving but it needs pruning and we'd best set about it ourselves before some-body does it for us. If you get into that place, give 'em a prod from me, will you?"

"If I ever did get there," Giles said, "I'd look to you for a briefing before I threw my hat in the ring."

Adam watched him cross the yard as he had watched

his brother George go, thinking, 'Well, that's another of 'em. It's lucky Hetty wouldn't call "whoa" when I wanted to, for we're going to need reserves before we're through,' but this didn't depress him unduly. Swann-on-Wheels had been his life's work and the patrimony was there for the taking, providing any one among his five sons was equal to it. But he wasn't a man enslaved by the notion of seeing his own flesh and blood dedicate themselves to it, in the way he had done when he had turned his back on soldiering and took the plunge in the 'fifties. He would see that as vanity and although reckoned as proud as Lucifer by friends and enemies alike nobody had ever called him vain. He drained his tot, stumped round the end of the desk and settled himself in his wide-bottomed chair. Outside the evening sounds of the yard reached him, muffled in river fog. A Goliath, or fully-loaded man-o'-war creaking in from the Midland sector; a vanboy's quip as he leaped down from a tailboard; the dolorous hoot of a tug heading down river towards the docks. Sounds that were the symphony of his life and enterprise about here, able to comfort him as he settled back to his work.

8

Swanns at Large

SHE THOUGHT ABOUT THEM ALL A GREAT DEAL.
The big old house was quiet as a convent these days and
seemed half-empty too, despite its four indoor and four
outdoor staff. Adam and Edward were away at work all
day and the only one on hand was Margaret who, notwithstanding the fact that she had put her hair up four
years ago, and was now an unusually pretty child of
eighteen (it was natural that Henrietta should think of
the youngest of nine as a child); she was inclined to be
solitary and spent so much of her time painting.

Sometimes, indeed, whenever Henrietta pondered it
deeply, she resented his decision to return to the yard,
having come to believe he was done with all that. It was
only after that long gossip with Deborah, when her
adopted daughter returned here for a holiday in August,
that she adjusted to his abrupt return to the city.

There had been the unlooked-for bonus in the permanent presence of George's four children, Max, Rudi,
Adam and her namesake, Hetty, the first of her grandchildren she had a chance to spoil, but they were all so
like their mother that they did not seem children to her,
more like a quartet of little adults, with their impeccable
manners and ingrained habits of obedience instilled into
them by their Austrian mother. Familiarity with Gisela's
children led her to reflect upon the curious choice of
mate made by the most extrovert of her sons. She would

have thought George would have sought out a very
different girl, pretty possibly but fashionable and as self-
willed as himself, whereas Gisela was by far the most
complaisant of her daughters-in-law.

Henrietta knew all about that shocking lapse of his by
now, although the menfolk had done their best to fob
her off with half-truths. Secretly it hadn't surprised her
much. In so many ways he was more like Adam than any
of them, and she imagined Gisela's placidity would have
exasperated him in time and set him thinking of more
exhilarating romps between sheets. A man of his type,
and Adam's, needed more from a woman than
acquiescence, and she even went so far as to discuss this
with Deborah when they held a stimulating inquest on the
scandal in August.

She had always been able to confide in Deborah, ever
since that awful time after the Staplehurst rail crash, when
she would have gone out of her mind had it not been for
the child's unwavering faith and ability to communicate
it to others. Deborah Avery, a love-child of Adam's
former partner, Josh Avery, had never seemed less than
a daughter to her, and marriage to that nice young journalist, Milton Jeffs, had done nothing to weaken their
relationship. She had taken it for granted that Deborah,
with her quick brain and ready access to Adam, would
know more about George's wobble than she did and she
was right. Somehow, although Deborah lived in far-off
Devonshire, where her husband ran a local newspaper,
she was in possession of all the facts – George's shameful
neglect of work, wife and family, his scandalous affair
with the wife of Sir James Lockerbie, his misplaced confidence in that scoundrel Wesley Tybalt (who had since
disappeared from the face of the earth) and finally that
awful fire that had drawn Adam back into the network.
What Henrietta wasn't sure about was Adam's motive in
letting the boy have his head about that obsession of his
and this Deborah had been able to pass on, saying, with a
chuckle: "But it's so characteristic of him, Aunt Hetty!

He isn't really a stick-in-the-mud, you know, he just likes to pretend he is. He knows George is absolutely right about the advantages of getting a flying start with mechanical transport, and I think he did it for Swann-on-Wheels rather than George."

She had been surprised by that, thinking that Deborah would have had more sense than to assume the time was fast approaching when Swann's merchandise would be rattled about the country in horseless vehicles, of the kind George had played with for so long in the old stable across the yard.

"You can't mean to say you agree with him, Debbie? You can't think we'll soon be selling off all those Clydesdales and Cleveland Bays?" and Debbie had replied, laughingly, that of course she agreed with him, and that George's sense of dedication, when one thought about it, was another Swann characteristic.

"Adam looked far ahead when he threw up soldiering to start the network in 1858, didn't he? Everyone thought he was daft then. Even you, I suspect, when you married him. Come now, be honest, Auntie, you would have much preferred to marry a boneheaded soldier in scarlet and gold, wouldn't you? Uncle Adam always declares that you would and tried to persuade him to stay in the army."

"Adam Swann has too long a memory for my liking," Henrietta grumbled, remembering this was true at the time Adam rescued her from a shepherd's hut on a rain-soaked moor. "But surely, a haulier's business with teams and waggons is one thing and that snorting monster George brought home from Vienna is quite another. I mean, it's really no more than a toy, is it? Oh, I know we have motors on the roads nowadays, and there are even one or two about here, although whenever I see one it's always being towed home by cart-horses."

"That's what I mean. Until now motors have been regarded as expensive toys, even by their inventors, but that won't last. They're getting better and faster and more powerful every day and it's quite obvious they'll have to be used for much more than road racing and one-day excursions to the seaside. But I didn't come in here to talk about motors or George either, Auntie. I've got a piece of family gossip that you'll be the first to learn, but you must promise me you'll keep it a secret until I give you the word. Even from Uncle Adam."

Henrietta fidgeted. All her life she had relished secrets, and had been flattered when one was entrusted to her. So rarely, however, had she kept faith with her confidante that fewer and fewer secrets came her way now that she was a grandmother many times over.

"Tell! You know I won't breathe a word to anyone."

"I doubt it but I'll take the risk. I'm going to have a baby."

The shock was so great that it precipitated Henrietta out of her chair. "A *child! You*, Debbie? But goodness gracious me, you're . . . you're *forty-one* by my reckoning."

"You don't have to shout about it. Yes, I'll be forty-two in November, and Milton and I had long since given up hope, but it's true, thank goodness. It will be born in late January, and there's no more doubt about it. In fact, that's one reason why I came up without Milt, to see a specialist. I've never spent a night away from Milt until now."

"Eight years!" Henrietta exclaimed. "Eight years and now . . . now *this*?", and an expression of anxiety crossed her face, so acute that it touched Debbie. "Aren't you scared half out of your wits?"

"Of course I'm not. It's unusual, I'm told, but it's not unique. All the medical men I've seen – and Milton has fussed no end in that direction – tell me I'm exceptionally healthy and, given luck and good care, I'll be all right. It might have to be a Caesarean section but they can't be sure until nearer the time."

Henrietta gazed at her with awe. Debbie had always seemed so wise, even when she was the child Adam brought in here out of the snow thirty-odd years ago. She had heard vague and rather frightening talk about Caesarean sections at her croquet-party gossips but she had never met any woman who had one or even anticipated having one.

"Well, it would scare the living daylights out of me! I'm pleased for you, of course, for I've known all the time you longed for one. But after eight years trying . . ."

"Trying is about right," Debbie said, merrily. "I'm sure nobody could have tried harder," and saying that brought Debbie even closer, for Henrietta would have been too inhibited to talk this way with any of her daughters, even Joanna who had been pregnant, stupid girl, when she ran off with that young scamp, Clinton Coles.

"Have I *got* to keep this a secret?" she wailed, and Deborah said she had, for at least a month, for if anything happened between now and January she would prefer to nurse her disappointment in secret.

"Oh, I'm sure nothing will," Henrietta declared, slowly adjusting to the stupendous news and finding herself able to share Debbie's pleasure. "To think you'll be ahead of Giles and Romayne after all and Romayne only thirty!" and she kissed Debbie on the cheek and begged her to write soon and give her permission to confide in Adam and the girls.

"And now you tell me all your family gossip, aside from George," Debbie said. "Gisela's tribe will be in to lunch any minute and we shan't get another chance. Has Margaret got a beau yet?"

She recounted all the Swann trivia, the kind of detail Adam would never bother to pass on, for she suspected he and Debbie discussed nothing but politics whenever they met. No, Margaret hadn't got an admirer, and didn't seem to want one. Instead she spent hours and hours painting about the estate, and never had much to say for herself at a soirée or fête. Alex, the eldest son, was in India now and so was his wife Lydia, of course, for she accompanied him everywhere. Their daughter Rose, and son Garnet (named for Sir Garnet Wolseley, Alex's commander in Egypt) were expected home soon to get their education here but Alex was on a five-year tour and would be forty before she saw him again. It was very depressing, she admitted, to have to acknowledge a son of nearly forty, but there it was, she didn't feel fifty-eight, and she didn't think she looked it when she was well corseted. Giles and Romayne led a strange, bizarre life, bereft of all social occasions and as obsessed with politics as George was with his engines, surely the two dullest preoccupations on earth if one discounted cricket. Stella, eldest of the brood, was apparently content with her peasant's life over at Dewponds and her tribe of mop-headed peasant children and that lumping husband of hers, Denzil Fawcett.

"The girl really let herself go after she married a second time," Henrietta said, "and I can never understand why. She turns the scale to twelve stone now and never wears anything but straw bonnets and gingham. It's odd, for you remember how fashionable she was when she was growing up here, and how she could have taken her pick from the hunting set in this part of the county. But there it is, it's her life, I suppose, and when I remember that frightful first marriage of hers, I really ought not to grumble. Denzil still treats her as though she was one of those Gainsborough ladies, stepping out of a picture frame." Then there was Hugo, still a bachelor, and likely to be, poor boy, for he never stood still long enough to fall in love, although his sisters told her girls swooned at the sight of him. As for young Edward, Adam seemed to think he had a rare head for business and a passion for work, and *that* was a comfort, now that George had disappointed everybody.

"And how about Joanna and Helen, Auntie?" Debbie prompted, remarking privately that Henrietta had always been disposed to dismiss girls as afterthoughts.

"Oh, they might just as well be dead for all I see or hear of them. Joanna is stuck in Dublin with Clinton and their family, and Adam seems well satisfied with all he hears of the Irish branch. And poor Helen and that stuffy missionary she married are in China. They moved on there from Africa last Christmas and she's written saying Rowland is worked off his feet, for they have all the diseases in the medical dictionary out there. I *do* wish she'd make him throw it all up and buy a nice practice here in Kent. He could well afford it. His father is rich as Croesus and it can't be doing the girl any good in all those terrible climates. She lost her first baby, you remember, and never had another. I've only seen them twice since they married."

"She's probably happier with a man absorbed in what he's doing," Debbie said, "and from what I remember of Rowland Coles he isn't a husband to be 'talked' into anything." She glanced at Henrietta shrewdly, adding, "Anyway, who are you to advise a wife to take the initiative? You never did, save that one time when Uncle Adam lost his leg and wasn't around to keep you in order."

"Ah," said Henrietta, unabashed, "but nobody in their senses could compare Clinton or Rowland Coles with Adam, could they? I mean, he's a very remarkable man, isn't he, and I'm not alone in thinking so, am I?"

"No, Auntie, you're certainly not," Debbie said, laughing, "but even if you were nobody could persuade you to the contrary."

Out across the paddock Phoebe Fraser's lunch-bell jangled and as Henrietta bustled off Margaret came in, wearing a sun-bonnet and a linen dress plentifully be-daubed with paint. She held a sketch under her arm and Deborah said, "Let me see it, Miggs. And don't tell me it isn't finished."

"Finished or not it's no masterpiece," Margaret said, and held it up, to reveal what Deborah at once thought a very colourful and exceptionally strong watercolour of a corner of the paddock wood, where the path ran under a stand of beeches towards Adam's Hermitage. The picture centred on the beech clump but the foreground was a riot of colour, composed of one tall foxglove, some yellow toadflax and a sprinkling of trefoil. The composition was uncontrived and the painting of the leaves, petals and seed-pods impressionistic, yet definite enough for individual flowers to be identified.

"It's very good indeed, Miggs. And I believe you think it is."

"Oh, I'm coming along," Miggs admitted, "but this is far too free to impress a professional. An Academician would dismiss it as woolly."

"I think half the pictures they exhibit are woolly," Debbie said, "and all paintings should be 'free' as you say. At least, they should give that impression. Do you ever paint in oils, Miggs?"

"Not landscapes and never outdoors. Foliage and flowers require softer treatment, I think. At least, mine do. I should concentrate on oils if I was a real painter."

"But you *are* a real painter, Miggs. You've got a very individual style. Why, I've seen hundreds of amateur flower paintings and landscapes and I'd sooner have this one on my wall than the best of them."

She noticed the girl's cheeks flushed, and thought, 'Poor Miggs! Growing up here among all these Philistines. It must be very discouraging for her sometimes,' and said, "Have you ever sold a painting, Miggs?"

"Good heavens, no! Who would buy one?"

"I would. I'd buy this if you'd sell it. It would remind me of growing up here every time I looked at it."

"Then I'll give it to you."

"Oh, no, you won't. People only value what they pay for. I'll give you a sovereign for it," and she took a purse from her dress pocket and extracted the coin.

Miggs said, "But I'd sooner give it to you, Debbie . . ." But Deborah pressed the coin into her hand and closed her fingers on it.

"At least let me frame it for you. There are plenty of frames in the old Colonel's cupboard." Deborah recalled then that the old Colonel, Adam's father, had spent his old age down here painting and then she remembered something else that struck her as singular, Henrietta telling her, in an expansive moment, that Margaret had been conceived the night they buried the Colonel in Twyforde Churchyard. Well, maybe it proved something, for who else among the Swanns ever put brush to canvas, and now that she thought about it Margaret was the spit of that French wife of the Colonel's whose portrait hung in his old room in the east wing.

She had a few minutes before lunch so she went upstairs, moving along the wainscotted gallery to the eastern side of the house, pausing here and there to wonder at all the laughter, loving and heartache that had gone on between these old walls since that old pirate Conyer built his house on this spot. She remembered a great deal of it herself, since that winter's day Adam winkled her out of the convent and brought her here to live among his own sons and daughters. What would have happened to her if he hadn't? Not long after the place was closed down and the nuns went back to France, and she had never set eyes on her own mother. Adam was, as Henrietta claimed, a very remarkable man.

She moved on into the old Colonel's room, glancing up at the portrait of Monique d'Auberon, Adam's Gascon mother and the old Colonel's Peninsula and Waterloo trophies. The cavalryman's busby, with its numerals, '16th Lt. Dragoons'. The field-glasses through which Cornet Swann had looked across the Bidassoa at Marshal Soult. The sabre that killed the cuirassier who lopped two fingers from his hand at Waterloo. Henrietta would never have any of his things moved nor allow the room to be used by any of the children, and Deborah, knowing her so well, could understand why. The old chap had championed her when his son brought her home on the rump of his mare all those years ago and Henrietta would see him as the sponsor of her marriage and all that emerged from it. It was a pleasant thought and did her credit.

She went out and moved back towards the broad staircase, thinking of all the children she had seen scampering and quarrelling along these waxed oak floors. Stella, Alex, George and Giles, and the post-accident spread, Joanna, Hugo, Helen, Edward and Miggs. All but the two youngest were scattered and although the house was very old, and full of ghosts, her recollections of the Swann tribe belonged in that category now for what did she know of them today apart from scraps of information contained in their occasional letters or comments on the small change of the day? They wrote or said little of their secret hopes, fears and frustrations and nothing that singled them out as nine men and women, born in that master bedroom across the gallery. All the same, she experienced the strongest urge to give birth to her own child in this house for it was a house of high adventure and anyone born in it would be inoculated against dullness and mediocrity. She smiled at the notion and went down to lunch, wondering if Milton would understand why the place exerted such a pull over her at a time like this and whether he would dismiss it as a pregnant woman's fancy.

2

Deborah's guesses concerning latterday Swanns had substance. Each of them, in their own way, was an adventurer, with a strong dash of their father's enterprise and their mother's tenacity of purpose.

George, at that moment in time, was working against the clock alongside his acolyte, Jock Quirt, a fierce, wholly dedicated man, whose approach to the apparatus of his trade was that of a pilgrim handling fragments of the true cross. They were making rapid progress up here, in the oppressive heat of a Manchester summer. Yet the ten months left to them, before Adam's ultimatum expired, did not seem long enough to surmount so many hurdles. Once embarked on a project like this there was no knowing how many blind alleys one had to explore for a means to increase power while stripping down overall weight, and grappling with repetitive problems like overheating, friction, warped metals and technical anticipation of the fearful shaking and jolting inseparable from the passage of a vehicle over roads that had served the coaching era. There was a new mountain to be climbed each day and a desert of speculation crossed after dark, so that he was now very glad indeed that Adam had persuaded him to take Gisela but leave the children behind. Released from them she could play a woman's part in the undertaking, appearing at regular intervals with hot food and drink and in between running his errands to every forge and workshop in the city.

It was thus a new Gisela he came to terms with up here, a person as resolved as himself to assemble something practical from this jumble of rods, bolts, brackets, wheels and cannisters, and when, after a twelve-hour stint he was ready to peel off his filthy overalls and take a bath, she was always there, even-tempered and giving, so that one night, holding her in his arms, he was moved to say, "I must have been mad to take you for granted all these years . . ." And she replied, in her modest way, "Hush, George. A man has his work, and his own way of going about it, and I'm a part of it now. It's something I've always hoped to be since the time Grandfather Max found you a purpose . . . sleep now." So he had slept, dreaming of a time when they were skylarking beside the Danube, and he had isolated her from her fun-loving sisters, put his arms about her and decided that here was a woman who could reveal to him his inner self and nurse such creativity as he had inherited from that ageing Titan beside the Thames.

*　　　*　　　*

Thousands of miles east of George Swann's north-country workshop, Alexander Swann, who after the Jubilee had been posted to India, wrestled with frustrations that were akin to those of his brother, inasmuch as they were concerned, in the main, with marketing a piece of hardware to his generation. But perhaps Alex's task was the more formidable, for his circle of activity was that much narrower, one in which prejudice and ridicule was the norm.

For years now, urged on by his wife Lydia, daughter of a military buffoon, Alex had been hard at work convincing his masters that increased fire-power was the only guarantee to success in confrontation with the enemy – with any enemy, be he savage, armed with sword and spear, or with a Western rival, who was also busy perfecting his own means of aggression.

Specialising in small-arms, particularly the new Maxim gun adopted by the British army after Alex himself had fired the first prototype on the Wimbledon ranges, he had never ceased to advocate the multiplication of the quota of two guns per battalion, arguing that outmoded weapons like the lance and sword, and the use of cavalry as anything other than reconnaissance troops, were as archaic as Hannibal's elephants once the Prussians had annihilated the Painted Emperor's legions at Sedan, in 1870.

That was already twenty-seven years ago but so few professionals above the rank of major appeared to have learned the lesson inherent in the arrival of the breech-loading rifle. They continued, confound their sluggish wits, to think in terms of headlong charges against infantry equipped to mow them down like so many partridges, and most of them did not even think as far as that, seeing an army career as an eternal round of polo matches, pig-sticking forays and the maintenance of a military etiquette that belonged to the time of the Black Prince. Sometimes it was like battering one's head against a wall or journeying on through a morass of Lyle's Golden Syrup, and he was already aware that his unquenchable enthusiasm was regarded as a bore in the messes.

Yet he persisted, not only because he was his father's

son but because, at his elbow throughout all those years
of sapping and mining, was the counsel of his wife, Lydia,
she who had rescued him from permanent involvement in
among those self-same regimental pigstickers. Year after
year he persisted, hawking his hardware and his theories
from Africa to India, to Egypt and back again, until
regimental wags found a derisive soubriquet for him –
'The Barker', the chap who, due to a touch of the sun
maybe, had evolved into a travelling salesman trudging
from fair to fair with a packload of nostrums and cure-
alls on his back. Yet all the time Lydia continued to
sustain him, sometimes locating an eccentric colonel, or a
major-general, who would at least listen to him, but more
often counselling patience with her prophecy that one
day he would be seen to be right and could make history
as the unsung saviour of the Empire.

*   *   *

Stella Fawcett, once Stella Swann, was untroubled by
opposition. In her own tiny world, bounded by the frontiers of a three-hundred-acre Kentish farm, the word
'Mother' (as everybody thought of Stella now) was holy
writ. Denzil, titular master of Dewponds, had deferred to
her ever since he had installed her as mistress of the farm
she had helped him to rebuild and everybody else, the
straggle of children, the farmhands and even the wholesalers who bought Fawcett crops, took their cue from him,
so that it became a matter of; 'We'll see what Mother has
to say about it', or 'Go to Mother and get your orders from
her unless you want to do it all over again.'

She was thirty-seven now, as broad in the beam as
one of her own butter churns, and with massive freckled
arms that could, so they declared, have boxed the ears
of a fairground prize-fighter, yet she was not all brawn
and maternal majesty. Under her direction Dewponds,
almost alone among local farms, had ridden out the
agricultural depression of the early 'nineties, and the

Fawcetts, it was rumoured, had money in the bank as well as the best strain of beef cattle in the Weald. For Stella too was her father's daughter, although she had been late to discover as much and came near to foundering at the time of her marriage to a dissolute wastrel over the Sussex border. Denzil it had been who rescued her from that impasse and when her marriage was annulled, and Dewponds had been rebuilt brick by brick by the pair of them, he had married her, or, as village gossips preferred, Stella Swann had married him, carrying him off like a prize turnip and using him to sire a spread of blue-eyed children, between their stints of labour on the farm.

Did she ever think, as she waddled between farm-kitchen and henyard, of her brief, inglorious spell as the Honourable Lady Moncton-Price, in a ratty old country seat some twenty miles from here? Did she ever remember being spied upon through a knot-hole by a homosexual husband and his lover? Had she completely erased from her memory that climactic night when old Moncton-Price, her father-in-law, had prodded and pinched her as though she was a horse at a fair, and gone on to propose that she lived on as his doxy, while maintaining the farce of a marriage with his son? If she did she gave no sign of it, but perhaps the subconscious memory of these terrible humiliations prompted her outward respect for Denzil and the fact that, at intervals of less than two years, she presented him with a lusty son or a rosy-cheeked daughter. Possibly she still saw him as the bearer of that storm-lantern under the lambing copse, that had been her beacon light the night she fled from the Moncton-Prices in a tearing south-westerly. It may have been so but it is open to question. Strong in Swann obstinacy and will power, she was woefully deficient in Swann imagination.

*　　*　　*

Far to the north-west, across the breadth of the shires, the mountains and eighty miles of Irish Sea, Joanna Coles,

née Joanna Swann, was living in much more ease and
comfort than her older sister. Joanna was an essentially
lazy woman, who needed a definite stimulus to deflect
her thoughts from clothes, race-meetings, fox-hunting,
and her husband's prospects of promotion in the Swann
hierarchy. For it was generally assumed the Irish branch
was a managerial proving ground.

Clinton, who shared her enthusiasm for race-meetings,
had taken her along to the Curragh that afternoon and
she was not much surprised when he excused himself on
the grounds of placing a bet on the three-thirty but went
instead to pay his respects to the handsome Deirdre
Donnelly, this season's toast of Dublin. Joanna did not
resent his devotion. She had long ago taken the measure
of Clint Coles (still referred to as 'Jack-o'-Lantern' by her
father, on account of the elopement nine years before),
confident that he was unlikely to compromise himself with
a woman like Mrs. Donnelly. For one thing she was much
sought after, and Clint was too sure of himself to compete
for favours. For another she was the wife of one of his
best customers and Clint had his eye on the main chance
over here where the branch had thrived under his
management.

It was true that Clinton, left to himself, could be
dangerously impulsive and she should know this better
than anyone, but Joanna reasoned that impulsive men
kept on a tight rein were those most likely to bolt, even
if they waited years to do it, and over here it was generally
accepted that husbands were free to flirt at all sporting
assemblies. Wives, too, if opportunity came their way.

There was no harm, however, in reminding him that
she was not stupid and had not been taken in by that
excuse for leaving the enclosure. So, after making sure
there was no man of her acquaintance in the stand whom
she could use as a light foil against Deirdre Donnelly, she
scrawled a note on a page of her pocket-book, and tipped
a steward to give it to Mr. Clinton Coles on his return.
The note told him she could be reclaimed in the mixed

refreshment buffet. It would bring him there at a run, she calculated, for although Dublin etiquette was more relaxed than across the water, it was unusual for ladies to enter either of the buffets unescorted.

On the way through she passed a cheval-glass and caught a glimpse of her reflection, finding it moderately pleasing for a woman of thirty, eight years married and the mother of three children. Her mother had always declared her the flower of the flock as regards looks and elegance, and Joanna noted with satisfaction that her figure had not suffered as a result of her last pregnancy. She did not look more than twenty-five and her best feature, a wealth of soft tawny hair, carefully arranged under a wide picture hat, was as arresting as it had always been. Her complexion was good too, for the Irish climate suited it and she gave herself a little nod of encouragement before passing into the pavilion and looking round for a waiter to bring her tea.

Several men glanced at her approvingly, among them Tim Clarke, owner of 'Spanish Flyer', placed third in the last race. Like everybody in the Pale she knew Tim, a rare character in a city teeming with characters, and wealthy to boot, having made his fortune as an importer of Continental wines and spirits, of which he had what amounted to a monopoly hereabouts. He had two famous sons, she recalled, Rory and Desmond; the first an M.P. for a Meath constituency, and a prominent fillibuster in the Home Rule campaign at Westminster, the second holding a commission in the 2nd Dragoon Guards, a brilliant steeplechaser who had twice come close to winning the Grand National at Aintree. Thus old Tim, fat as a wine vat and oozing a geniality that ran counter to his reputation for striking hard bargains, had a foot in both camps. Rory's fiery speeches at Westminster established him as a true patriot, and Desmond's profession, plus his sporting reputation in England, ensured the goodwill of Dublin Castle. Tim was also said to have a gallant reputation with the ladies and at once proved it by being the first

to catch her eye, doff his hat and take advantage of the
fact that she was the only unaccompanied woman in the
buffet. He said, with a bow, "Mrs. Clinton Coles, I
believe! Allow me to get you something. Glass of champagne, eh?" And without waiting for assent he snapped
his fingers and two waiters came at the double.

"Tea, if you please, Mr. Clarke. I'm parched for a
cup, and I've lost my husband."

"You mean he's lost you and it's mighty careless of
him," he said, ushering her to a seat. "Why, if you were
my wife, Mrs. Coles, I wouldn't let you out of my sight
at the Curragh. A rare lot of garrison mashers on the
prowl today, ma'am."

"He went to place a bet," Joanna said, enjoying the
small stir she seemed to be causing in here.

"He didn't back my horse, I hope," Clarke said.

"No, indeed," Joanna said, matching his sauciness,
"Clinton said Spanish Flyer isn't due to win until next
time out, Mr. Clarke," and he laughed heartily, his sharp
blue eyes lost in ripples of rosy flesh.

"Very spry of him. Tell him I'm saving the colt for
something better but I'm not such a fool as to be more
explicit in here, my dear."

He somehow managed to imply that a few moments
privacy with her might prove a worthwhile investment
and it suddenly struck her that she could exploit this
encounter to her own and Clinton's advantage. She
recalled Clint grumbling, only last week, that he had
underquoted for Tim Clarke's all-Ireland distribution but
still lost out to an Irish haulier, Brayley. She also remembered what Clint had said on that occasion, telling
her that old Clarke would not risk his son's displeasure by
putting money in English pockets. She thought: 'If I
can put in a word for the firm with someone of his standing,
Clint is going to look very foolish when he shows up here
as soon as he's done flattering the Donnelly filly,' and she
said, carefully, "I'm not sure I should be civil to you,
Mr. Clarke. My husband tells me he pared an estimate

to the bone on your behalf last week, and you accepted Brayley's tender in spite of the fact that his quotation was higher and his service far less reliable."

The thrust seemed to delight the old fellow. He wheezed for a full half-minute before saying, "Bless my soul, Mrs. Coles, you're a chip off the old block and no mistake! I knew your father when he opened up over here. Shrewd man. He brought haulage costs down with a bump and not before time. The Dubliners were holding the lot of us up to ransom. Now when would that be? Five years ago?"

"Eight. My husband replaced Mr. O'Dowd as Irish manager, soon after we were married. Now be so good as to tell me, Mr. Clarke, why did we lose the contract? I have to know, for when Clinton finds I've been talking to you he'll quiz me all the way home. Was it simply because Mr. Brayley is an Irishman?"

The attack, pressed home in this way, momentarily disconcerted the wine merchant, so that he welcomed the respite granted him by the arrival of the tea-tray. But then, before he could counter, Clinton arrived out of breath, and not seeing Clarke at once, scowled his displeasure and said, "Really, my dear, wasn't it rather silly to disappear like that? I wasn't gone but ten minutes . . ." but broke off when he became aware of Clarke's grin across the table.

Tim said gently, "Come now, don't scold her, man. She's only here to argue your case and how many wives would do that in public? Especially young and fetching ones like yours. Here, let me buy you a drink to take the sour taste of that contract out of your mouth," and again he summoned a waiter, this time ordering two whiskies and sodas. "I know that's your tipple, Coles. It's my business to know these things. Don't let your tea go cold, my dear."

Then followed, for Clinton Coles, one of the most bewildering intervals of his sojourn in Ireland, for it soon became clear that a man whose patronage could mean as

much as two thousand a year to the firm and who had
resisted all his efforts (including costly backhanders to
warehouse clerks) to point custom Swann's way, had
taken a great fancy to his wife and was vulnerable on
that account, if half they said about Tim Clarke's gallivanting was true. For ten minutes they talked horses
but they soon got around to business, and the upshot of
the occasion was a promise from Clarke that he would
review the contract when it came up for confirmation at
his quarterly Board Meeting next month.

By then the last race was run and they had downed a
couple of whiskies apiece while Joanna sipped her tea
and concentrated on looking excessively demure. It was
when they rose to leave, however, that Clinton Coles
became fully aware of his wife's potential as a business
asset. Clarke said, "If you're thinking of attending the
garrison supper-ball on Thursday week, could I prevail
on you and your charming wife to join my party as my
guests? The fact is, I'm short of young people this year,
and we ought to take advantage of a gel as decorative as
Mrs. Coles."

Clinton murmured that he would be delighted to
accept and Joanna, glowing with triumph, added that
they would anticipate the occasion with the greatest
pleasure. She reasoned that old man Clarke would have
no means of knowing that year after year had passed
without the Coles having received a coveted invitation to
the liveliest event of the Dublin season.

They were bowling homewards before Clinton, slowly
recovering from the shock of acknowledging his wife as
an emissary extraordinary, squeezed her hand and said,
feelingly, "My dear, you were sensational! We've as good
as hooked that old rascal and it's all your doing. How did
it come about? You went into that buffet in a pet, didn't
you?"

"Oh, not really," Joanna said, generously, "I was
aware you were one of the wasps buzzing round Deirdre
Donnelly's jampot, but why should that bother me? I

really did need some tea, and as soon as the old goat started sidling up to me I thought I'd take advantage of it. After all, where's the harm? He's over sixty and only playing games with himself, isn't he?"

"Well, I wouldn't go as far as that," Clinton said, chuckling. "They tell me he can still give a very good account of himself with the barmaids, and seeing how dashing you look today no one can blame him trying his luck. I would have thought, however, he'd turn glum as soon as I appeared on the scene. Maybe he reasoned I'd turn a blind eye for two thousand a year."

"Ah, and would you?"

He looked outraged. "Good Lord, woman, you surely don't mean . . ." but she laughed and pinched his knee, underlining the tolerant and cheerfully sensual relationship that had developed between them since she and her sister Helen had switched beaux at a Penshurst picnic in their youth. She knew very well that he was not in love with her in the way she had been with him since she had surrendered to him on a Kentish hillside, but she flattered herself that she could still make him forget the Deirdre Donnellies of this world when she had him in her arms.

"I'm only teasing," she said, "and you surely know it. Well, we didn't back a winner, but, taken all round, I'd call it the most profitable day we've had at the races, wouldn't you?"

"I would indeed," he said, "and it isn't over yet, my dear."

Neither was it, in the sense he implied. That night, in their pleasant bedroom overlooking the Kingstown busy harbour, he was a boy again and she reflected that he was never likely to be anything else, despite his cares of office and a propensity to spend rather more than they earned each year. And yet, in the event, she was wrong in assuming today had been a profitable day for the Dublin branch of Swann-on-Wheels. She had no means of knowing that her chance encounter with Tim Clarke, at a Curragh race-meeeting, was the very first detonation in a chain of explosions down the years that would, by the spring of 1916, divide her loyalties and Clinton's, and that the wounds inflicted by the breach would not be healed until Dublin itself was a battlefield.

*   *   *

Two months' voyaging and a week's uncomfortable land trek from the Dublin Pale, where the London Mission had its pitch under the walls of Peitang Cathedral in the Imperial City of Peking, Helen Coles, once boon companion of Joanna, and sister-in-law to Clinton was also recalling the famous picnic on the wooded hillside above Penshurst Place, in April, 1888, an event that had led to her marriage with Rowland Coles and her presence here in the enervating summer heat of the Chinese land mass. The heat, the smells and unceasing clamour of the great city were factors that disinclined her to continue the battle to persuade herself that she had the best of the bargain on that occasion.

In the years of trapesing that had followed her acceptance of Rowley's proposal, she had made sustained efforts to convince herself that she was very privileged to be the wife of a man whose sole ambition in life was to relieve suffering, teach aliens the rudiments of Western hygiene and bestow upon them the benefits of a Christian way of life. Having her full share of Swann tenacity, however, she stuck gamely to her endeavours, but here in Peking, a mild improvement on their billet in East Africa, she was conscious of losing ground rapidly. Her temper was not improving and neither was her health but, what was more depressing, she was coming to terms with the certainty that she was thoroughly unsuited to the life of a medical missionary dedicated to his calling, and was wishing heartily that something would stifle her yearning for a humdrum life in the company of Europeans, living out selfish lives in a comfortable background. And this made her feel shamefully disloyal to poor Rowley, whom she still cherished, but in the way one might cherish the chief of a tribe, or the austere and remote father of a large and indigent family.

She had come to look upon Rowley in this way by slow and arduous stages, signposted over nine years of marriage by his expectations of her as a helpmate and deputy, rather than someone licensed to release him, from time to time, of his fearsome responsibilities, but she had proved miserably unequal to the task and awareness of this made her a failure in her own eyes.

She knew, at the deepest level of consciousness, that it was not her fault, that no mere woman could wean him, even momentarily, from his resolve to work miracles among the heathens, first upon their bodies, and then (providing he had the time) upon their souls. She learned this very early in their marriage, possibly by the manner in which he made love to her on the rare occasions he could be coaxed from this quest in savage, fly-pestered backwaters for his personal Holy Grail. On all occasions, even when on leave, and at a remove from his flock, it was she who had to initiate each encounter and remind him shyly that she was his wife as well as his dispenser, and when he acquiesced, in his quiet, grave way, he performed his marital functions absentmindedly, as though he was carrying out some repetitive task, with a particle of his mind. Then he would lie flat on his back, pondering some problem concerned with the spread of typhus, or the contamination of drinking water, or an antidote for the bite of some lethal reptile, and was quite lost to her in the physical sense until the next occasion.

It had a very depressing effect on her, this withdrawal, as though, each time it occurred, he was saying that she was incapable of stimulating his senses, and fleetingly, with a kind of terrible nostalgia, she remembered the frolics of other, less exalted men, who had embraced her in dark corners of 'Tryst', sometimes letting their hands stray over her breasts and buttocks, proclaiming what she had always assumed a male compulsion to fondle and be fondled. Sometimes she found herself envying his convert nurses when he lost his temper on account of their clumsiness or dilatoriness and snapped at them in a way that sent them scuttling. It would be gratifying, she thought, to goad him to a point of fury where he would unhitch his belt and thrash her and make her smart and cry out, for this would at least establish that she stood for more than a mute, unpaid assistant in the wards where his patients queued for a few moments of his time.

All the other missionaries' wives, and there were more than a dozen here in Peking, seemed to adapt to this passive role, but mostly they were middle-aged, with complexions dried and skins wrinkled by equatorial suns, whereas she was still only twenty-seven and could never banish from her mind the greenness of Kentish hopfields and the freshness of meadows and coppices in the Weald. The death of their child, after a few sickly weeks of life, had been a double tragedy for her. Its survival might have prevailed upon him to send her home to await his next leave. As it was, he seemed to take it for granted that she would remain as isolated from civilisation as a female Crusoe, and she had begun to doubt whether she had the hardihood to endure a three-year stint at the Peking Mission.

The possibility of their being shifted, she gathered, was remote. Nothing dramatic ever happened out here, as China pursued its timeless journey down the centuries. The Chinese had developed a way of life that nothing could hope to alter, and the great powers, Britain, America, Germany and Austria, enjoyed their limited concessions in this incredibly old city. She discounted rumours of a growing opposition to the foreigner building to northern and eastern provinces. The wily old Empress would never be so stupid as to challenge the might and technology of the West and any move against isolated missions and trading outposts would be savagely repressed by Imperial troops.

She re-addressed herself to the monthly task of writing

to Joanna in Dublin, the only member of the family with whom she maintained a regular correspondence. 'My Dear Jo ... Nothing much to report ... kept busy from dawn to dusk ... thank you very much for the dress patterns but I don't know whether I shall ever find time to make anything ... Rowley very well, although I must confess I feel drained of energy in the summer ... my love to Clint and the family ... I do envy you two boys and a girl but perhaps I shall be lucky soon ...' Random, inconsequential thoughts that were hardly worth committing to paper yet her sole link with a world that sometimes seemed as remote as the stars.

*　　　*　　　*

George tinkering with machines; Alex peddling lethal hardware. Stella dominating a dutiful array of sons, daughters and farmhands; Margaret filling her canvases. Joanna as a Swann emissary in Ireland; Helen eating her heart out in Peking; Hugo touring the country from one sports meeting to another; Edward following in George's footsteps, it seemed. Henrietta saw them all as a queer, rootless, self-centred lot, not in the least like the orderly spread of soldier sons she had envisaged when, as a girl living in a rackety industrial town, she had dreamed the hours away, waiting for a prince to ride over the hill.

She granted them a rather breathless individuality, and a trick of fixing the attention of whoever looked in the direction of any one of them but they lacked, to her mind, a common theme, a resolute and clearly defined purpose that had been hers all the years they had been growing up in this old house on the spur. Their various aspirations confused her, for they were not, she would have thought, the ambitions that should activate conventionally reared sons and daughters. Their fulfilments to date eluded her. The best she could do was to number off their progeny and hope that a coherent pattern would emerge from the following generation. But having settled her mind as to that she went about her chores contentedly enough, cocking an eye at the clock now and again to remind herself that a predictable husband and youngest son would be home soon, wanting their supper.

But Adam, in his stone eyrie above the sliding Thames, did not view them in these slightly censorious terms and did, indeed, perceive a pattern in their collective pursuits, seeing them as children of their tribe and times, widening an ever-larger circle in a way that soldier sons would never have done and on the whole he was not displeased. 'At all events they're *positive*,' he thought, 'every last one of 'em, and that's as much as a man has a right to expect at my time of life.'

The verdict mellowed him, leaving his mind free to pursue his self-imposed task of restructuring the network and going about it in a way that would probably astonish George when he scrubbed his hands and re-addressed himself to paperwork. For this restored to him his pride and pride, to Adam Swann, was a power-house that set all his other generators to work and helped to balance the nation's books. He seldom gave a thought to his grandchildren. The past he had renounced at the age of thirty and the future was not his business. All his nervous energy was engaged with the present on a purely day-to-day basis and on that basis Swann's waggons would continue to roll.

PART TWO

Tailtwist

I

Breakthrough

THE VALLEY WAS NOT AS GILES REMEMBERED IT.
When, as a scholar-gipsy, he had first passed this way
on his marathon walk from Devon to Edinburgh in 1884,
he had seen it as a monument to squalor that yet retained
a few subtle undertones of an older Wales, when unsullied
streams ran between folds in the hills and islands of green
showed on the ragged escarpment behind the town. Dirty
and depressing, especially under lowering skies, but raising
a few of its tattered banners of the time before the English
first came here with their mail-clad men-at-arms, later
with their prospectors and surveyors, finally with their
armies of scavengers to claw the wealth from the ridges
and darken the mountain with spoil.

Today, a mere thirteen years later, the whole area was
given over to the money-grubbers, with no vestige of
green remaining and tips everywhere, dark against the
sky on the northern edge of the town. Housing had proliferated as the mines expanded and more and more
Welshmen yielded hard-won acres to the thistles and came
out of the interior to earn their bread. The winding gear
was silhouetted against the winter sky, a stark symbol of
Anglo-Saxon dominance, like a gallows in the market-
place of a conquered town. The steep terraces of the tiny
dwellings began higher up and stretched all the way down
to the grey-black blob that was Pontnewydd, where there
were a few grubby shops and a rash of chapels, each built

like a fortress of local stone. The overall picture now was one of stupefying drabness, and yet, knowing these people, Giles was fortified by the certainty that this was not the whole picture, only its frame and outer edges. Down there in the heart of the place, and up here on the serried terraces, there was warmth and comradeship that one could seek in vain in more wholesome places. There was human dignity too, a plinth for loyalty, courage and the dreadful patience of men and women who, while admitting defeat, had never signed the articles of unconditional surrender.

Lovell, his father's former viceroy about here, found them the house, one of the few about here with privacy, for it stood at the end of an unsurfaced road running at right-angles to Alma Terrace and ending in a cul-de-sac under the lowest ridge of the mountain, the house, Lovell said, of an official of the Blaentan Company, that could be bought for a couple of hundred pounds. Stone-built and four-square to the winds that cut their way through the northern passes all winter and the south-westerlies that blew in from the Atlantic in spring and autumn. A three-bedroomed house, reckoned grand by Pontnewydd standards, for it had a small, walled garden front and back, and a rear view of the mountains of mid-Wales.

Lovell said, giving him a steady look: "Sure you want to buy it? Will your wife care to bide here, within washing-line view of cottages and tips? Pontnewydd is the central point, I'll grant you, and will shorten your journeys about the constituency, but we could find something more salubrious if we looked nearer the coast, and you'll have the horse and trap to get you around."

"I'll hang out my sign here," Giles told him. "If I'm to represent these people I've got to know them both in and out of the mine. Where else could I hope to do that?"

"It's not you I'm thinking of," Lovell said. "You were always something of a Romany, even when you looked in here as a schoolboy, and talked me into taking you down a pit. But Mrs. Swann deserves some consideration.

With a man like Rycroft-Mostyn for a father, and eight years soft living in London, she'll not take kindly to slumming, will she?"

"She might," Giles said, smiling. "You can decide that when you meet her," and on impulse told Lovell the story of her flight on the eve of their wedding, and how he found and reclaimed her, working for a few shillings a week in a northcountry drapery store.

"I never heard that," Lovell said, wonderingly. "What made her do a daft thing like that?"

"All manner of motives, adding up to a need to break free of her background. In fact, I might as well admit that, but for her insistence, I wouldn't be here now, throwing my hat in the ring. She seems persuaded I'm tailor-made for the role."

"Ah," Lovell said, nodding, "that tells me more about her. I've had the same notion ever since you looked in on me on that tramp of yours." He mused a moment, toying with the heavy key of the front door. "Tell you something else. You'll win this seat, in spite of Carey's grip on the farming and docking interests further west. In a year or so the Tories will have shot their bolt about here. Maybe you're right to camp on the battlefield. It might help overcome the prejudice against the English. That'll be my line of attack, anyway."

"You'll come out of retirement to be my full-time agent?"

"I will and gladly," Lovell said, "and I'll tell you something I never dared tell your father. I did my best about here, and made a success of the branch, but trade was always second best with me. I always did have a hankering to get at their throats. Any true Welshman has and I'm free to please myself now that I'm a widower and the boys are grown and off my hands. I'll see Hughes Brothers about the house. They'll need a deposit, for a place like this wouldn't stay on their books long."

He led the way into the open and paused at the rusted iron gate between the two stone pillars of the front patch. "Christ Almighty!" he said, "but they've made a rare midden of it, haven't they? I used to fish down there as a boy. All you could catch now would be an old boot and a tin can. I wonder if they'll ever go away again?"

"They'll go, when the seams run out. Meantime we'll give as good as we get, I promise you."

*　　　*　　　*

The weather had broken when he drove her up here for the first time. The valley was screened in a curtain of slanting rain and the mountains were unseen under great grey banks of low cloud. It was a pity, he thought, that she couldn't see the one redeeming feature of the landscape, but she made no complaint, following him round the squarish house that was littered with crates, a few of which he had already unpacked, for they had planned to move in at once and be on hand for the adoption meeting on Saturday. He had chosen the back room as their bedroom on account of the view it offered but now that he entered it the drabness of the vista depressed him a little. He said, "You're sure about this, Romayne? After all, as Lovell pointed out, we could look about for a more cheerful aspect beyond the main line. There's a belt of agricultural land there and one or two stone-built villages."

"With populations of a hundred or so?"

"No more. Almost everyone about here works in the pits. The electoral roll shows a population of around twenty thousand in Pontnewydd alone."

"Then here is the place we start. Anything less would be a compromise, wouldn't it?"

"Well, yes, I suppose it would, but you'll spend a good deal of your time up here and you ought to have the final say in it."

"It was all my idea, remember? So now that it's shaping up don't apologise for it, not ever. To do that is cheating, Giles."

"Cheating who?"

"Me. This is the first worthwhile thing I've ever done for you, to bring you up to the point of making a clean break and I want to remember that, always. It's a fresh start for me too. Those years in London were no more than an interlude."

She walked slowly round the little room, with its peeling wallpaper and brass bedstead set against the inner wall between sash window and door. Most of his unpacking had been done up here. The folded bedclothes were piled on the mattress. A bedside table had been set up with its oil-lamp and there was a new dressing-table in the opposite corner, looking like a piece of furniture that had come in here out of the rain and been unable to find its way out again. "I'll tell you something, Giles, that might convince you that this isn't a fad of mine . . . settling here, I mean. This place, this house, is going to mean a great deal to me. A new beginning for me as well as you, for we've never been man and wife in the full sense of the word or not until this moment. No, don't quarrel with that for you know very well what I mean. We've loved each other, yes, but neither one of us has ever been . . . well . . . fulfilled, in the way those miners and their wives are fulfilled in those brick boxes down the hill."

"You're talking about children?"

"Partly. I'll give you children here. I feel it, inside here," and she touched her breast. "But I'll give you more besides and the feeling that I can makes me happier than I've ever been. Safer, too."

He kissed her mouth, surprised by the eagerness of her response. She said, "Let's not unpack anything more up here. Uncrate some of the kitchen stuff and light the fire. I'll make the bed up and cook supper. It will only be bacon and eggs and cheese but I'll improve on that without a cook. It won't do for you to have people waiting on us up here. Just a woman to pop in and help clean up in the mornings, that's all I want from now on," and she addressed herself to the blankets and pillows, going about it so briskly that he had to remind himself he had never seen her make a bed before. He went down the narrow stairs and soon had a crackling fire going with sticks and a bucket of coal he had brought up in the trap. By the time supper was cooked and eaten, and the crocks scoured in a sink half-full of water boiled on the hob, darkness had closed in, pressing against the uncurtained windows. She said, "Do you want to tackle those voters' registers now, or shall we make an early night of it?"

"I'm doing no paperwork tonight. I was travelling from first light this morning, putting in the time getting to know the beat until your train arrived."

"Give me fifteen minutes," she said. "There's something I've a mind to do," and she slipped away upstairs, leaving him with the impression that they were alone for the first time in their lives. When she called down he damped the fire with dust, extinguished the lamp and went upstairs, pausing on the threshold of the bedroom and blinking into the lamplit room. It was a room magically transformed. Rose-pink curtains screened the window. Rugs covered the shredded linoleum. The bed had been made up and turned back and she was sitting at the dressing-table mirror brushing her hair.

"Well, bach?"

"It's marvellous! I've never seen those curtains before."

"I made them and the rugs were set aside before the inventory was made out at Shirley. It's cosy, isn't it? Much cosier than I expected. The heat comes from that chimneybreast and it'll stay warm all night, so long as the fire stops in. Feel here."

He put his hand on the chimneybreast and found the bricks warm. "I think you got a bargain," she added. "This place is far better built than Craig Wen but that's because it was built by Welshmen for a Welshman. In Beddgelert they were just fleecing the English."

It amazed him how quickly she was adapting, but then he remembered that she was pure Welsh on her mother's side. "I daresay you'll end up speaking Welsh fluently," he said. "You've got the hang of it from old

Maggie, up in Beddgelert." And as he said this there came to him, fresh as a rose, the memory of that first morning she had led him into her father's house in his dripping clothes, and Maggie had scolded her in Welsh and dried him off while Romayne, full of mischief, had changed into a gown of crimson velvet, with gold facings and rows of gold buttons on the bodice and sleeves. She said, "What are you remembering now?"

"Your 'Camelot' gown," he said, "and how you looked when your hair was cut short and combed close to the head, so that it matched the gold buttons on the sleeves."

"You've forgotten something not so far back."

"What's that?"

"Today's our wedding anniversary."

"My God, so it is! And I *had* forgotten, although how . . ."

"I didn't," she said, triumphantly, and reached beyond the bed and pulled out first a stone hot-water bottle, wrapped in her nightgown, then a bottle of champagne and two glasses. "There," she said, "but it's not fair to crow over you because I made up my mind our first night here would have to be a special occasion. That's why I persuaded you to leave me behind to finish the packing. Open it, but don't let it shoot over the bed-clothes. They're all we have until the van gets here."

It was years, he thought, since he had seen her in this mood, as sparkling as the child she had been the day they met. She was wearing a blue silk dressing gown he had bought her on their first visit to the Continent, a dashing affair, trimmed with Lille lace and sashed with blue velvet. He drew the cork and filled the glasses, saying, "What do we drink to?"

"To winning Pontnewydd from the enemy!"

"No," he said, "to us, and to you especially, for I've never seen you like this since . . ."

"Since before I ran off?"

"Since before that really, for we seemed to squabble our way through that interminable engagement. Since that day on the mountain just before you went back to London to be presented. You flew into a temper because I argued against us getting married right away."

"I remember and I was right. You should have taken me at my word. My father would have agreed, he was so relieved to find anyone who would take me off his hands. At least we should have been spared all those silly squabbles."

"But you wouldn't have seen how the other half lived and then we shouldn't have been here at all."

"That's so. I'd forgotten how it began."

She drained her glass and set it down on the dressing-table, crossing to him where he sat on the edge of the bed. "It's permanent," she said. "You believe that, don't you?"

He unhitched the bow of her dressing gown, slipped his hands behind her and ran them lovingly down her back and over her thighs. "I not only believe it. I feel as if we were beginning our honeymoon, with all the benefit of experience. There's Welsh magic left in this valley after all. Those tips haven't been able to banish it."

She slipped out of her gown and threw it across the only chair in the room. "Stop making speeches," she said. "They'll be needed later. If we're on our honeymoon let's get on with it, bach," and she kissed him, lifted the hot water bottle from the bed and slipped between the sheets.

The pleasant languor of her body encouraged a state of mind enabling her to isolate the uniqueness of the occasion in a way that had never been possible in the past. For then, like a heavy shadow, the shame of her encounters with other men prompted by curiosity on her part and uncomplicated lust on theirs, had stood between her and physical fulfilment in the arms of a different kind of man, one whose chivalry and essential tolerance had been recognised by her from the first day she met him.

He knew of those earlier follies, of her seduction, before she was seventeen, by a groom and later a Belgian musician. She had allowed them to fumble her with clumsy fingers, then possess her for a few sweaty moments in isolated corners of the house. Her father had made sure that he did know when, washing his hands of her, he was still resolved to use Giles Swann as a go-between in his relations with his work force. He had laid the unsavoury facts before him like items in a police report but it had not freed him from the need of her, nor scared him off, as it would have scared most men. Rather it had enlarged his area of compassion so that their subsequent relationship had never been soiled by the knowledge. As for herself, her lovers, if you could call them that, had never come close to teaching her anything of the least significance about the way to search out a relationship that promised to assuage the loneliness of spirit that had clouded her childhood and adolescence. Indeed, it was not until this moment, the culmination of the long haul that had led them to this unremarkable little house overlooking a ruined valley, that she recognised the act of physical fusion, even with a man she could respect, as little more than a starting point in the journey of the soul towards personal fulfilment. It was imperative that she should acknowledge this and acknowledgment was made with a gesture. She reached out and found his hand in the darkness, lifting it gently and mooring it under her breasts. Its presence somehow confirmed her full acceptance of the active role in their partnership.

2

George versus the Clock

FOR GEORGE THE WORK WAS REMINISCENT OF
housebound hours spent over jigsaw puzzles in the nursery at 'Tryst', a methodical sorting and shifting of segments of a battle scene, or a farmyard, until the four
cornerpieces were in place, and the straight edges in
approximate alignment, so that a start could be made
towards completing the picture but the analogy went far
beyond that. Just as, bent over the tray holding the puzzle,
the selection of a fragment was suddenly seen to be the
correct one and a segment slotted into place, so it was with
the third prototype of Maximus, whose assembly presented
so many experiments, frustrations and disappointments.
There was a penalty of error too. On the workshop floor
a misconjecture could represent a wasted day, perhaps a
wasted week and he was working against the clock.

He had been through it all before. Once beside the
Danube, sorcerer's apprentice to old Maximilien Körner
assembling his giant carriage that had ultimately crawled
through the morning river mists like Jupiter's war-chariot,
and later during his earlier severance from the firm, when
he had improved on Max's model to a degree that had
half-persuaded his father that the days of the dray horse
were numbered.

But now the challenge was more immediate. All over
Europe and the Americas men were bending brain and
will to the solution of these selfsame problems, although

a majority of them still regarded the mechanically propelled vehicle as a substitute for the brougham rather than the waggon and dray. He made the fullest possible use of their discoveries, however, adapting and often blending gleanings from word-of-mouth information, sketches and sometimes spare parts, run down by the indefatigable Scottie Quirt, who had spent ten years drifting about the north and midlands, hiring his skills to whoever would pay for them.

Like a jigsaw, yet he sometimes saw his task in a more majestic light. A range of mountains, with a few major peaks and innumerable smaller ones, each presenting a peculiar challenge of its own. Nothing was predictable in this wilderness. Sometimes the loftier peaks were easier to scale.

One such peak represented the ratio between thrust and laden weight, another the variation of gears to adapt to gradients, including a reverse gear, for without the ability to reverse a vehicle was as cumbersome as a barge fighting a strong current. He estimated that he should be able to generate sufficient power to haul a five-ton load, more than any load Swann's four-horse or two-horse waggons could haul over indifferent roads and this had been achieved by constant modification of the carriage until the overall weight of the vehicle was reduced to a point where its chassis did not fracture under the strain. The main structure of a Swann man-o'-war, the heaviest category in use with the exception of purpose-built Goliaths, was of oak, four inches thick in places. A petrol-driven Maximus of corresponding strength would be impossibly heavy, so he switched to nickel-steel that was found equal to anything Swann was likely to haul, excluding heavy machinery. The gear changes operated through a gate, with a retaining bar to prevent reverse gear being engaged in error.

The third and fourth mountains to be scaled, however, presented greater challenges. They represented over-heating, and a tendency for vital parts to be shaken loose by vibration and passage over uneven sections of carriage-way and he was assaulting these most of the winter. Over-heating was eventually cured by the introduction of a perforated jacket made of copper and the summit of the fourth major peak was reached on the unforgettable day that he and Scottie fitted their double semi-elliptic front and rear springs, affording the first real flexibility Maximus had ever achieved.

There remained the minor peaks, each with a range of problems of their own, so that it was sometimes like inching his way up a shingled incline sown with brambles and quickset thorn. They represented braking, solved at last by internal expanding shoes operating in drums, uneven transmission, overcome by a new type of carburetter intake copied from a French model, lubrication and a hundred and one other problems, each of which proved desperately time-consuming. Even so, by late April, ten months from the day he had stripped son of Maximus down to its last rivet in the Salford yard, he had done what he had set out to do. He had, he told himself, a vehicle capable of hauling a sizeable load south to H.Q. in two days, averaging seventy-five miles a day from the final testing ground, a mile east of Macclesfield, to London Bridge.

"Will you take me with you, George?" Gisela asked, when he was ready for the gamble, and he said, regretfully, that he could not. A passenger meant extra weight and, aside from that, the driver would have to face a formid-able buffeting. It was a silly risk to take in view of the fact that she was now five months pregnant.

"Then I shall go by train," she said, "and it's a great pity. I should enjoy your father's expression when he comes down from that tower and finds a Maximus in his yard."

"Oh, you could still do that," he said, anxious to acknowledge her loyalty and invaluable help over the past ten months. "Set out by train the day after I leave and when you get there wait for me in the yard of the old

'George', somewhere between five and six. If I break down I'll telephone Bendall's factory in the Borough and he'll send someone over with a message. In that case catch the train on to 'Tryst', but say nothing about the trial run. I'll catch them bending or not at all."

She said, gravely, "You will make the journey, George. If you had doubts you would not set out."

"But this is a pure gamble."

"No, George. Your father, he is a gambler but you are not the same. Your father would gamble on his luck, but you? You would not put one pennypiece on a horse unless you owned it, trained it and rode it in the race. That is the difference between you."

It increased his confidence to hear her talk that way and he went blithely about his final preparations after Scottie Quirt had left them to take a holiday with his family in Glasgow and she had packed her things to follow him to London. She saw to it that he should lack nothing for the journey that was in her power to supply and it was while she was baking pasties for him, the night before he was due to set off, that he said, "I'll make it up to you, Gisela, I swear it."

"Ach, but you already have, George. I have been very happy up here. It has been like the old days, when grandfather Max was alive. Will you travel loaded?" she replied.

"Part loaded. I'm taking two tons of rice down to the Madras Trading Company, in Cheapside."

"Why rice?"

He grinned. "Proof, of a kind. A four-ton load is due to go south by road tomorrow. I've shipped half of it aboard and given Carstairs, the yard goods manager, instructions to despatch the other half at seven o'clock, the same hour as I leave."

"And you plan to get there well ahead of him?"

"We'll see. I've worked out a route and my worst gradient is one in twelve, but I'm still scared of over-heating."

She said, "Suppose the motor is as good as you think it is and suppose you prove it to all of them, what are your plans when you take over from father again?"

"A fleet of 'em," he said, briefly, "with all the four-horse waggons withdrawn and their teams allocated to frigates and some extra Goliaths, for it'll be years before we can develop a non-rigid vehicle to haul the really heavy one-piece loads – boilers, generators and the like. There's only one thing I should enjoy more than making it in two days."

"And what is that?"

"Grandfather Max to wish me luck."

"He's here," she said, "I dreamed of him last night. Both of you, locked away in that stable at Essling." Then, remembering how Max had died, "There's no danger, is there?"

"None for me. Plenty to oncoming traffic. I'm resigned to being cursed by every carter from here to London Bridge."

*   *   *

The rice had been loaded the day before and every foreseeable contingency guarded against. Twenty gallons of fuel was stowed in ten-gallon drums forward and he had even shipped a water-cask in case she boiled at a point on the route where no water was readily available. He had a spare tyre too, although, if one left the rims, he was doubtful of replacing it without Scottie's help. After he had run the vehicle out and warmed her up he went over all his preparations again, while it stood there trembling like an over-trained racehorse at the tape. He thought of the Swann-Maxie as female, although he had seen its two predecessors as male. Maybe it was because she was so much trimmer, or perhaps because all the months he had sweated over her she had reminded him so often of the maddening unpredictability of a woman. He thought, 'Maximus doesn't suit her now and Maxima doesn't sound right. If we do build a fleet on this model it will have to have a trade name and Max ought not to be forgotten.' He finally settled on a hyphen-ated name, 'Swann-Maxie', and looked up at the clear April sky, praying for propitious weather, at least as far as Market Harborough or Kettering, where he planned to let her cool off for the night, depending on his progress.

The first leg of the journey, as far as Cheadle, was encouragingly uneventful. Gradients rather than mileage had dictated his choice of route and the roads thus far were level and fairly free of traffic at that early hour. He averaged seventeen miles an hour over the first thirty-five miles, and she seemed to be behaving impeccably. In all the villages crowds of boys ran alongside shouting up at him, some of the bolder ones in ribald terms but the older folk just stood by and gaped, and only one old chap, mounted on a spirited bay, shook his crop threaten-ingly when the horse reared at a farm gate. He thought, 'There'll be plenty of that before people get used to motors. I daresay a majority would like to see that damned Red Flag Act back on the Statute Book but that won't happen. It's already cost us the lead we might have gained over Continental mechanics.'

It was after Cheadle, as he was following the valley of the Trent in a south-east direction, that he had his first scare. He had tackled a long incline at a slow walking pace and breasted the summit with a great sense of relief. Below him, curving eastward in a wide, scimitar sweep, lay the white road running between low hedgerows, with a straggle of farm buildings at the bottom where the river was crossed by what appeared, at this distance, a shallow ford. He thought, gratefully, 'Well, here's a mile or two of coasting,' and changed gear, forgetting for a moment the down thrust of the load behind him but sensing its compelling weight when he realised the slope was much steeper than it looked.

There was nothing to give him an accurate indication of his speed but by the time he was two-thirds of the way

down it seemed to be far in excess of the limit he and Scottie
had agreed upon when they were planning the route
mile by mile. His teeth rattled every time the wheels
struck a dried-out puddle crater, where underground
springs had been at work all the winter, and then, as the
road flattened out, he saw a herd of cows crossing from left
to right, and it seemed to him that nothing could prevent
him ploughing into them.

He had rigged up a handbell on a short length of rope,
the bell itself fitting into a bracket on the canopy support,
and he took his left hand from the spokes of the steering
wheel to ring it furiously so that an aged cowman, emerging
from the nearside gate with a pair of yapping collies at
his heels, glanced up and saw his approach at a distance
of about eighty yards.

George had never seen a man look more astounded and
for what seemed like seconds he stood there, hand on
gate, mouth wide open. But then, with remarkable
agility for a man of his years, he turned and ran up the
hedge, diving head first through a clump of ash saplings
that grew there and disappearing in a flash while his cows,
unimpressed, pursued their leisurely progress across the
road to the opposite gateway.

A violent collision seemed inevitable, even though only
two or three cows still remained on the road, and a
collision would certainly have occurred had it not been
for the dogs. Almost equally terrified, but more conscientious than the cowman, they bounded forward
nipping the heels of the laggards, while George threw his
entire weight on the brake lever without, it would seem,
doing much to check the thundering onrush of the Swann-
Maxie, for now it was as though the weight at his back was
propelling man and vehicle down the last stretch of road
straight into the river.

And then he saw something else, the narrow entrance
to an old packhorse bridge marking the ford, and he knew
that to stay on the road was to gamble the entire enterprise on his ability to steer a straight course between

the stone parapets. He did not possess that much faith in his own skill. There was no more than an inch or so to spare on either side and in response to a split-second decision, he chose instead the nearest of the two ford approaches as looking the shallower of the two. He shot off the carriageway at an angle of about sixty degrees and the sheet of water that rose on impact enveloped him, rising in a solid column like a waterspout. And then, without so much as a lurch, Swann-Maxie stopped dead in about a foot of water, and people came running from all directions, converging on both banks and dancing and gesticulating as the hiss of steam from the radiator sounded the knell of his odyssey.

There was no one to blame but himself. No rustic cowman could have anticipated the onrush of a monster weighing some five tons laden weight on a country byroad miles from the nearest city, and no medieval builder could be blamed for building a bridge only inches wider than the largest haywain then in use. The fault lay with himself, for changing gear at the summit and putting too much reliance on his powerful handbrake, and he climbed down into the current cursing himself in German, still his favourite language for abuse.

The water rose to the level of the hubcaps so that he saw at once it was not a matter of the engine being flooded but rather doused in that first surge of water. As he realised this his spirits lifted for he reasoned that the automatic inlet, the valves, the surface carburetter and the ignition tubes could be stripped down and dried, although the process would occupy him at least two hours, even if no vital piece of mechanism had been dislodged by the jolt.

An enormously fat man in a moleskin waistcoat and a hard hat seemed to be in authority among the wildly excited group of onlookers on the far bank and George called, "Can you tow me clear on to level ground? I'll pay a sovereign an hour for the labour and the hire of horses."

The fat man swallowed twice, licked his heavy underlip, pushed his hat brim an inch higher on his forehead and said, ignoring the offer, "Christ A'mighty! Whatever iz un?"

"It's a petrol-driven waggon," George said, impatiently. "Can you do what I ask? I've got to make Leicester by dusk."

At that the man removed his hat altogether and passed his hand over the full extent of his balding skull, saying, "I thowt at first it were a locomotive running loose from up the line. A horseless carriage, you zay? But that'n iz ten times the size o' the doctor's," and at that George's heart leaped and he said, eagerly, "The doctor here owns a motor? Will you send for him? He'll have the tool-kit, no doubt. Will you do that? For an extra half-sovereign?"

"Christ A'mighty," the man said again, "youm pretty free with your coin, maister." And then, after ruminating a moment, "Arr, I'll vetch 'im, for he'd give me the length of his tongue if I didden and he missed this carnival. *Ben!*", and he whirled about and roared aggressively at a gap-toothed boy beside him, who was still surveying the vehicle as if it were a stranded dragon, "Stop gawping and rin an' vetch Doctor Bowles. Look sharp about it! Seed 'im go in Fanny Dawkins', minnits back. Tell 'em us've something in the river he'd like to zee!" His speculative gaze returned to George. "A sovereign an ower, you're offering?"

"That's what I'm offering but every minute counts. If I'm out of here in less than two I'd add to it, sixpence on every minute saved."

The bribe now seemed to animate the man who shook himself in a way that caused his gross body to quiver. In less than five minutes two enormous Percherons were trotted out, yards of plough harness were produced, and with a single, squelching heave Swann-Maxie was dragged out on to dry ground and into the lee of a barn where the horses were unyoked and led away, and George crawled

under the vehicle for a close inspection of the complex
of tubes and rods assembled there.

No damage was visible but every part dripped water
and he was already removing the feed pipe to the carburetter when a cheerful voice greeted him from the
offside, calling, "Hey, there! Come on out, man, and
tell me what happened. Maybe I could help, although
this is a new one on me. Is it a Daimler?"

George crawled out, leaving one end of the feed pipe
uncoupled, to see a man about forty in a neat broadcloth
suit that at once distinguished him from the rest of the
crowd still gathered about the machine. "Desmond
Bowles," he said, extending his hand. "Anything shaken
loose? Or is it a case of stripping down and drying
out?"

George shook his hand and although time pressed on
him like a goad he found the doctor's smile so engaging
and his interest so obvious, that he decided the least he
could do was to introduce himself and his product.

"My name is Swann," he said, "and I'm in transport.
You'll know my firm, no doubt, the hauliers, Swann-on-
Wheels. I'm making a trial run to our London head-
quarters and planned to get as far as Leicester tonight.
Do you own a motor, doctor?"

"Yes, I do. A Panhard-Levassor," Bowles said. "I
brought her over from the Continent last year but she's in
dry dock at the moment so I'm back to the buggy, confound it. Do you mind if I crawl under and have a look?
I've done a lot of tinkering with petrol-engines. It's a
hobby o' mine. These people think I should be put away,
of course, and the same probably applies to you. I've
never seen anything like that before, however."

"Nobody has. I only finished work on her this week.
She's purpose-built for commercial work and not designed
for joy-riding as you can see. Have you got a tool-set
with that Panhard? A smaller screwdriver is what I need
to detach the intake pipe from the carburetter. That's
where the damage is, if any. One drop of water through a

joint and I'm stuck unless I can clear it," but he was addressing no one in particular for the doctor had slipped out of his jacket and scrambled underneath the rear wheels where his findings reached George in a series of short, authoritative pronouncements, as though he was diagnosing a patient.

"No need to remove the intake pipe. Not yet anyway. We'll try blowing bubbles first. Been stuck here myself but in far worse trouble. Your chassis is much higher and your casing took the brunt of it. Damned good idea that casing. Bellows might help." His head emerged, and he bellowed at Ben, the boy who had summoned him, "Slip across to the forge, Ben. My compliments to Vosper and tell him I need his hand-bellows again!" The boy darted off as Bowles said, "Dry the externals with the bellows. Done it myself and it works sometimes. You're right about the intake, though. She's blocked. Grit washed in, I wouldn't wonder. That or an airlock. It can happen crossing a puddle sometimes. Come on under, Mr. Swann."

George joined him and found him supporting the loosened end of the intake, holding it between finger and thumb of his gloved hand. "A steady blow," he said, "can't use the bellows on here. Careful, she's piping hot. Use your handkerchief," and George fascinated by his air of knowing precisely what he was about, found his handkerchief, wrapped it round the detached end of the intake and blew gently and unavailingly for a moment until, with a faint plopping sound, the blockage cleared. He said, excitedly, "I can dismantle the carburetter with the tools I've got already, Doctor Bowles. Then dry 'em out piece-meal. Will you give her an overall dusting?"

"The moment Ben gets back with the hand bellows. My stars, but she's a powerful brute! How far have you come today?"

"From Macclesfield. I've planned a two-day haul to our London H.Q. If I can make it, I'll be building a fleet to replace our four-horse vans," and the Doctor sat up so

abruptly that he dinged his hat on the crank casing.
"*Build!* You built this yourself? It's not patented?"

"Parts of it are. It's my third prototype, based on an
Austrian model built by a man called Körner. He was
quite unknown, but I happen to be related to him. She's
been running sweet as a nut up to here. You can blame
this on my damn foolishness, taking that hill too fast."

"Here, I'm teaching my grandmother to suck eggs,"
Bowles said. "I took you for an engineer. 'Swann' you
said. You're *the* Swann's son?"

"I'm more than that. I'm his managing director,"
George said, smiling, "and I'm extremely grateful for your
help in spotting the trouble at a glance. I should have
wasted an hour eliminating various factors. Here's your
bellows, Doctor," as a breathless Ben joined them,
carrying a brass-nozzled bellows of the kind found in
every forge in the country.

"Pity you can't stop over," Bowles said, methodically
setting to work with his bellows on every exposed section
of the engine. "Between us I daresay we'd have my Panhard on the road again in a jiffy. You're sure you can
reconnect that intake with tools you've got?"

"I'm already doing it," George said, gaily, congratulating himself on his luck, and they worked on in silence
for ten minutes or so, drying out and dusting off every
section of the engine with the bellows and clean pieces of
sacking supplied by the obliging Ben.

"That'll do, I'd say," Bowles said, squirming out into
the open. "Crank her up and see if she turns over," and
George followed him out, reaching into the driver's cabin
for the heavy crank lever and noting, as he slotted it in
and prepared to swing, that the crowd, now grown to about
a hundred, edged away leaving himself and Doctor Bowles
alone in the clearing.

He brought all his concentration to the first swing,
remembering to cock his thumb inside on account of the
powerful back-kick the engine produced on several occasions, once putting Scottie in hospital for close on a week

The initial cough was one of the sweetest sounds he had ever heard, and then, using the full strength of his arm, he swung furiously and the engine burst into a stuttering roar, gloriously sustained and magnificently full-throated, proclaiming that Swann-Maxie was no worse for her ducking.

"Are you going to risk stopping her?" roared the doctor, above the beat of the engine.

And George shouted back, "No, by God! I'm off, while I've got the chance! Where's that fat chap in the moleskin jacket? I owe him a sovereign."

"I'll give it to him," Bowles shouted through cupped hands, "up with you and the best of luck," but the fat man, seeing George on the point of climbing aboard, overcame his caution and waddled forward, pointing to his watch that showed the delay had cost George fifty minutes from the moment he plunged into the stream. He threw the doctor a coin and engaged low gear, heaving at the steering column and regaining the flint road at about four miles an hour. Bowles waved his dinged hat, the crowd edged forward and a ragged cheer sped him on his way over the level stretch to a fork in the road where a signpost indicated the ways to Derby and Lichfield. He bore off to the right and slowly built up his speed to around twenty miles an hour, presently seeing the triple spires of Lichfield Cathedral away to the south-west and calculating (he had his father's trick of memorising routes, mileages and local products) that he was now within a hundred and twenty miles of London Stone and reflecting that Swann's waggons had been hauling beer and market produce from this area for forty years.

Tamworth, Atherstone and Hinckley – he skirted them all, adding a dozen or more miles to his journey to avoid the risk of getting caught up in a traffic jam in busy streets and around five o'clock, after one brief halt for a cool-off at Polesworth, he was heading almost directly eastward towards Market Harborough, sixteen miles south of Leicester, and eighty-one from London.

There was still an hour or more of good daylight but it seemed like pressing his luck to push on, taking pot-luck when he stopped for the night and, in any case, his head was aching and his eyes were sore with dust, so he pulled on to the broad grass verge short of the little village of Sibbertoft, ate two of Gisela's pasties and spent an hour carefully rechecking tomorrow's route sheets. He had a yearning for a pint of country-brewed ale but he dared not leave the vehicle unattended and nobody came by whom he could tip to go to the nearest tavern, so that he was about to make do with water when he remembered Gisela had put tea, sugar and condensed milk into his knapsack. "Just in case," she had said, when he told her he wouldn't have time for a picnic. "You may find yourself stranded miles from anywhere and be glad of some tea while waiting about for spare parts to arrive."

In a few minutes he had a roadside camp fire going downwind of Swann-Maxie and brewed his tea in a billycan he kept among the tools. He was grateful for Gisela's forethought then, for never had tea tasted so good, easing the ache from his brow and washing the dust from his throat.

It was dusk by then and to stretch his legs he walked along the country road as far as a stone monument, pausing to read its inscription and learning that he was camping on the field of the battle of Naseby. He thought, grinning, 'Old Giles will laugh at that and see something symbolic in it – *The old order changeth, giving place to new.* He'd remember the Johnny who wrote that too, but I'm hanged if I do.' He lit his pipe and leaned against the memorial, inhaling the freshness of the evening breeze and the scent of the hedgerows for it seemed he could never free his palate of dust motes and fumes of Swann-Maxie's exhaust.

His progress, despite the mishap, had been remarkable. By the route he had come he estimated he had travelled over a hundred miles in ten hours. With ordinary luck he should now fetch up at The George Inn, Southwark, about tea-time tomorrow. No other experience could have taught him so much in such a brief span of time and he reviewed the lessons learned one by one. Somehow the steering would have to be lightened and some means would have to be found of extending the range of gears, for gradients far in excess of one in twelve would have to be faced when the vehicle went into mass production. The vibration, although greatly reduced by the new springing system, was still a source of anxiety and that plunge into the river had set him thinking hard about the hazards of descending hills as well as climbing them. Shoe-brakes were adequate to check the progress of the vehicle itself but when one added on the thrust of a load it was asking for trouble to tackle gradients commonplace in many areas of the country. There were aspects, however, that encouraged him. Transmission problems seemed to have been overcome, and over-heating, although a factor that had to be watched, was not the ever-present menace it had been on the two earlier models. He knocked out his pipe and went back to the machine, draping it for the night in a tarpaulin, then crawling inside and making a nest for himself on a palliasse wedged between fuel drums and rice sacks. In a few minutes he was asleep.

*　　　*　　　*

He made a dawn start in the morning. Before the chill was off the air he had brewed himself tea, breakfasted on chocolate and apples and refuelled with the help of a watering-can fitted with a funnel. To do this, in the stiffish breeze that was blowing, he had to make a windshield out of the tarpaulin, for a gust was sufficient to spray the spirit in all directions and he could not discount the high risk of a fire caused by a spark from a roadside fire. This set him thinking about the positioning of the fuel tank, so that he mused, 'The devil of it is you can only go so far in a workshop . . . The real solution to every problem is out here on the open road, where theory and practice merge. I could improve on this model in a dozen ways right now and I suppose that will be the way of it from here on . . . a slow climb towards perfection, if it's ever possible to perfect a wayward brute like this. Well, now for the physical jerks!' He took the starting handle and swung and swung until he was scarlet in the face and sweating freely, despite the nip in the air. On the twenty-eighth swing, when his arm felt as if it had been stretched on the rack, she started with the now familiar stuttering roar and he tuned the engine and moved off, taking the road to Dunstable.

For two hours his progress was smooth and uneventful, apart from the sensation his appearance caused in villages and one or two small country towns. It was just short of Letchworth, after passing over a particularly rough stretch of road, that disaster struck again. Part of his cargo had shaken loose, promoting a snaking motion on a mild descent that ended in a hump-backed bridge, where he pitched so heavily that he had to slew the vehicle hard right on to the verge. In that swerve the nearside tyre left its rim.

He managed to stop almost at once but the damage dismayed him. The tyre was twisted into a loop and half-severed by the iron rim and he saw at a glance that it would have to be cut away and replaced with his spare.

He was still wondering how this could be done without lifting gear when the knife-grinder appeared, riding a trap with a high, hooped canopy and a sad-looking cocker spaniel crouched on either side of him where he sat on the box. The man was a singular-looking wayfarer, tall, spare and narrow-faced, with sad, brown eyes to match those of his dogs, a Romany no doubt, who preferred his own company and obviously lived in his ancient two-wheeler.

His professional apparatus was stacked in a tailboard box or suspended from the canopy struts on short lengths of string, so that it jangled and rattled as the trap approached. Unlike most of the wayfarers George had encountered, however, he seemed to find nothing menacing about Swann-Maxie and looked her over with mild interest before pulling in, tying his horse to an overhanging bough, and saying judiciously: "You'll have to cut that loose, brother. And you'll need something more business-like than that clasp knife." He foraged among his tools and produced a murderous-looking butcher's knife. With a few swift slashes he rid the wheel of the ruined tyre which he then examined, with what seemed to George a professional interest. "The best Malayan rubber," he said, sniffing it, "and you've given it a rare pounding, brother. Do you carry a replacement?"

"Yes," George told him, "but to fit it I'll have to raise the front wheels at least four inches and muscle won't do it. I'd gambled on this happening near a farm or a forge where I could hire labour and borrow levers. By my reckoning I'm still five miles short of Letchworth."

"Four and a quarter," the man said, "but I have something better than a lever," and he went back to his tail-board and dug deeply into it, dragging out what appeared at first to be a large bench vice but on closer inspection was a multi-purpose tool with both curved and flat expanding surfaces, operated by large butterfly nuts, a marriage between a bootmaker's last and an anvil. "A legacy of my father's," the grinder said. "He was a Jack-of-all-trades and made his own tools. He was a file-cutter at one time and I find this useful for straightening agricultural implements. Scythes mostly and plough-shares. Do you carry a heavy wrench, brother?"

The man's serious, methodical air made an immediate impression on George, so that it crossed his mind that the country must be teeming with inventors and would-be mechanics, grandchildren of the Industrial Revolution with inherited skills of every variety. He fetched his largest wrench and the grinder selected a section of the front axle as an anchor for his expanding vice, spinning the heavy butterfly nuts with long, supple fingers until the tool was about one-third extended. Then, together, they applied the wrench and George was greatly relieved to see the rim inch from the ground until it was spinning free, after which they took a breather before tackling the job of fitting the spare tyre George had trundled out.

The man said, incuriously, "What would you be hauling south, brother?" When George told him it was Madras rice he said, "Now there's a queer thing to be taking into London, and London is your destination, no doubt. Wouldn't rice come in by sea and be offloaded on the spot?"

"Not this consignment. It's an assortment of high-grade samples and came ashore at Liverpool. I only happened to stow it because it was there. I could have made up the weight with anything handy." Although time was pressing he felt obliged to give the man an explanation of his presence here on a country byroad, with a stranded vehicle and two tons of Madras rice. The traveller was a difficult man to surprise. All he said was, "To replace the draghorse, brother, you will need to do one of two things in the new century. Either you will have to prevail upon a niggardly Government to surface every main road in the country, or you will have to find a means of cushioning those wheels in a way that will enable them to absorb the shock of every dip on your route. Springing alone won't do it, although you have some powerful springs there. Are they making any progress with heavy, air-inflated tyres, on the lines of those fitted to the latest bicycles?"

"If they are I didn't get to hear of it," George said, "and I made enquiries everywhere, here and abroad. The weight of a vehicle like this would be enough to puncture air-inflated tyres every mile or so, except on a first-class Macadamised road. This kind of mishap could happen twenty times a day."

"Ah," said the grinder, thoughtfully, "God is a great husbander of secrets, brother. He will reveal that one, no doubt, when the time is ripe. Will you join me in a short prayer, brother?"

"For the patenting of air-inflated tyres for heavy vehicles?" asked George, too surprised to smile.

"Why, no," said the grinder, gently, "for God's blessing on the remainder of your journey."

"I should be obliged if you pray on my behalf, brother," George said, not in the least disposed to laugh now, whereupon the man closed his eyes and said:

"Lord God, please to look kindly upon this traveller, and grant him a safe arrival. He is about Thy work, I think, and is not prompted by usury. Amen." And, while George was still debating whether or not the grinder was correct in his charitable assumption, the man picked up the spare tyre and began to fit it to the rim of the wheel, motioning George to hold on to the spokes while he inched the taut rubber in place with the help of a broad-bladed file he had fetched when he brought his winch.

It was the work of a few minutes to lower the chassis and when it was done George said, "I'm uncommonly obliged to you for your help. I hope you will allow me to pay you for your time and trouble."

But at that, for no particular reason, the more sedate of the two spaniels gave a short, scornful bark and the knife-grinder said, "The dog rejects your offer of payment, brother," and said it without the merest hint of a smile, so that George had no alternative but to suppose the grinder found nothing whatever surprising in his dog's ability to form moral judgments or, for that matter, to understand every word that had passed between them.

He shook the man's hand warmly, thanked him again, and went on his way in a mood of quiet exaltation, boosted not so much by the man's skill and kindness but by his evident belief that the horseless carriage came within the orbit of the Almighty's plans for mankind's progress. 'My stars,' he thought, as he moved off towards Dunstable, 'you learn a thing or two on the open road. I daresay that's where the Gov'nor learned most of his lessons. He'd relish that chap, to be sure.'

By noon he was skirting St. Albans and an hour later, on Barnet Heath, he was drinking a pint of ale and munching beef sandwiches, sparing a thought, as he refreshed himself, for the woman whose home lay a few miles to the north-east and who had, in a sense, shown him the way home again. His entanglement with Barbara Lockerbie seemed to have happened a long time ago and yet, in terms of the calendar, it was only ten months since he had walked out of her summer-house and begged a lift on a market cart to the scene of what could have been, but for his father's tolerance, the wreck of his fortunes. And the thought of surprising Adam, with eight weeks in hand, added zest to the final stage down the old Roman road where carters, waggoners, bicyclists and a few horseback-riders gave him a wide berth and sometimes shouted a jest into the wall of sound isolating him from other traffic.

At three-fifty-five by Cricklewood Church clock he was moving through traffic that reduced his speed to a crawl. By four-thirty, he was traversing Oxford Street to approach London Bridge from Cheapside, crossing the river and edging into the yard of The George at precisely four-forty-five. And there, on the flower-decked gallery, sat Gisela with tears in her eyes, so that he forgot Swann-Maxie for a few moments, abandoning her to a crowd of stablemen and urchins who approached her less reverently than his rustic audience north of Lichfield, for hardly a day passed now when a motor or a mechanically-propelled waggon of one sort or another did not turn on the cobbles where coaches had discharged their passengers in the days before Stephenson laced the country with his grid-iron and made the 'Shrewsbury Flyer' as obsolete as a chariot.

She said, "It doesn't even look out of breath . . . and you're ahead of time. I hadn't expected you until dusk and ordered dinner for seven-thirty. Shall I cancel it, along with the room, George?"

"Not on your life, my love, for if she's none the worse for it, I am. I could eat a five-course meal and sleep the clock round but I'm not foregoing the spectacle of the Gov'nor's eyebrows lifting half the length of his head.

Have you got a wrap and a veil?" When she nodded he told her to fetch them. Fifteen minutes later he had swung Swann-Maxie in a wide arc, repassed the arch of the inn and was heading for the yard.

2

Adam was in his eyrie when Edward rushed in, almost incoherent with excitement; and this was enough to bring Adam to his feet, for Edward, a dour boy, went about his work with the air of wary concentration characteristic of old Sam Rawlinson when he was satisfying himself that a customer got what he had paid for but nothing in the way of a bonus.

For a moment he could make little sense of the lad's jabberings but finally he gathered it was something to do with George and said, "Hold it, boy! Start from the beginning. What's George been up to now?"

Edward, pointing to the window, said, "He's here. With that petrol waggon and a load of rice for Dickenson's!"

"George here? With Dickenson's rice . . . ?" and following the direction of Edward's finger he hastened round the end of the desk to the window. What he saw made him grunt with surprise for there below, in a tight circle, was every waggoner, clerk and farrier on the staff, all gazing up at his son and daughter-in-law, enthroned on a streamlined version of the juggernaut he had seen thunder past his holly bush ambush on its test run up in Cheshire nine years before. The boy was right about the rice too. The tailboard was down and already a couple of jubilant warehousemen were offloading Dickenson's sacks.

He called, scarcely less excited than Edward, *"George! Gisela!* Wait, I'm coming down!" as if he expected them to vanish in a cloud of blue exhaust gas, and in reply to Edward's "Hold a bit, Gov'nor, I'll fetch 'em up here!" snapped, "Nay, you won't lad! This is one time I bend

the knee to George! He's two months in hand, by God!"
He followed the boy down the winding staircase, sniffing
the unfamiliar stink of engine oil that introduced an
entirely foreign element into the blend of smells about the
yard. He called, as George handed Gisela down, "Hi!
How far have you come in that thing? When did you set
out?" and Gisela answered, saying, with just a hint of
triumph, "Yesterday morning! He left Macclesfield at
seven a.m."

"You're telling me he took *you* along?"

"No," she said, descending and kissing him, "of course
he didn't, Father. I came on today by train, and met
him by appointment at The George. But he's not to stay.
He hasn't had a hot meal since he set out, and he slept
by the road last night."

"He's time for a drink, none the less," Adam said, and
bawled, more to express his elation than to disperse the
crowd, "Get on with whatever you were doing, the whole
lot of you! Damned thing won't run away. Jenkins, tow
it in the man-o'-war shed. And if there isn't room make
room, d'ye hear?" Then he led the way up the stairs
again, with George, Gisela and Edward at his heels, and
Edward, bright lad, didn't have to be told their various
tipples, bringing out brandy, sherry and ginger-beer
for himself. Alone among the latterday Swanns, Edward
had no head for liquor.

Adam said, raising his glass, "Well, here's to the two
of you, and I'm more pleased to see you than you can
imagine. Your mother hasn't stopped nagging me since
I took up this packload again and I'm re-abdicating
tomorrow, like it or not!"

But then curiosity overcame everything else as he
remembered those rice sacks and he said, "Just how much
freight did you haul? Edward said something about two
tons."

"Edward had it right. It's sample rice, from Monday's
Liverpool shipment. The other half set off by waggon the
same nour as me but I'll lay you long odds it doesn't get

invoiced until sundown tomorrow. And even then they'll have to hustle."

The calculated subtlety of it tickled Adam. It was the kind of trick he would have played on doubting Thomases a generation ago and he did not begrudge George his moment of triumph. "She came out of it well, then. Damned well, I'd say. A hundred and seventy-five miles in – what was it? – two legs of ten hours apiece? Well, you've proved your point, and I'll make sure everybody about here knows it. How long will it take you to build more of those snub-nosed monsters and get 'em into commission?"

"All of two years," George said, "but that will be Scottie Quirt's job as soon as I've approved the blue-prints for modifications. There'll be Swann heavies on the roads for a long time yet."

"Ah, that's what you say. A sop to my pride, no doubt."

"No, it's true. We've got our lead and there's no point in going off at half-cock again. I nearly came a cropper twice and on both occasions I had more luck than I deserved. A man needs training to handle one of those on the open road and apart from production we'll have to school a team of likely lads as drivers," and he sketched his adventures, as much for Edward's benefit as his father's.

Adam could see the boy was exhausted and took Gisela aside, telling her to take a cab back to The George. "If only to wash all that grime from his face," he said, and to George, "You'll be coming on to 'Tryst' with me and the lad after we close up?"

"No, Gov'nor. Gisela's booked overnight at the inn. Tell Mother we'll be over tomorrow. How are the children? They haven't tired her too much, have they?"

"She'll not like parting with them," Adam said. "The old place is quiet these days." And then he noted with approval that Gisela was pregnant again, and this added to his satisfaction for it surely meant that that foolishness had been worked out of the boy's system and he told himself he could take most of the credit for that.

She must have realised what he was thinking, for when she raised herself on tiptoe to kiss him she whispered, "In October, Father. Tell Mamma for me," and they went out, with the enslaved Edward in their wake, leaving him alone with his thoughts that were among the most cheerful he had had up here since he was as young as the man who had just toted two tons of Madras rice nearly two hundred miles without a horse to haul for him. Provided, of course, one discounted the Percherons who pulled him out of the river.

He gathered up his papers and took what he thought to be his final valedictory look at the broad curve of the Thames and its procession of barges, tugs and lighters shooting the arches of a bridge that had spanned this point of the stream for centuries. 'And that's another thing,' he thought. 'They'll have to think about replacing that for the passage of brutes like that one below.' But it wasn't his business, thank God. He'd had his fill of problems and there were plenty over for the Georges and the Edwards to solve.

*   *   *

The sun was setting in its familiar orange glow upriver as he crossed to the new, brick-built stable block to look the vehicle over. It was neater, and far more compact than either of its predecessors but it had none of the grandeur of a four-horse man-o'-war, a two-horse frigate or even a well-turned-out pinnace. It stood there looking sullen and impersonal, a tool rather than a partner in the never-ending struggle of man to save himself time and trouble and ensure that he claimed his portion of luxuries from the scrimmage. It was very difficult to visualise a day when the stink that still hung about it banished the prevailing odours of horseflesh, leather and trampled manure. But he had no doubts at all on the prospect now.

Transport would make another leap forward, almost identical to that of the 'thirties and 'forties, when coachman Blubb and his ilk grumpily dismissed Stephenson's locomotive as 'that bliddy ole tea-kettle'. And was it so surprising when you pondered it? The history of a tribe was and always had been the history of its transportation.

He went out and crossed to the main gate, looking about him at the rows of new buildings that surrounded his belfry like an army of youngsters bringing an old warrior to bay. Old George would have a fresh start at all events, for a great deal had happened here in his brief and busy St. Martin's summer as The Gaffer; his Swann-song as the local jesters called it. The insurance had paid for most of the rebuilding and old Sam Rawlinson's pile the rest, but although the layout was his it wasn't his yard any more. It was the domain of that engine in there and he had no authority over it now that George was back.

The weighbridge clerk had a cab waiting and he got in, riding the short distance to London Bridge Station alone, for young Edward wasn't to be found and he welcomed the solitude. Edward too was in the other camp now, and in a year or so he would be little more than a left-over of the century that had begun with cheers for Trafalgar and would go out with salutes from fourteen-inch guns and the cough and stutter of those snub-nosed replacements for Cleveland Bays, Suffolk Punches, Clydesdales and Percherons. He didn't mind, or not all that much. He had done what he set out to do and a little to spare.

3

Drumbeat

MUCH AS HE HAD ENJOYED BEING IN COMMAND again of the affairs of Swann-on-Wheels, Adam was glad to return to the peace of life at 'Tryst' with Henrietta, and found plenty to occupy himself, planting a bed of new roses in the garden, and studying the art dealers' catalogues. He was still a keen observer of the firm's activities, however, and it gave him great satisfaction in the year following George's historic journey from Macclesfield to London to see his son tackling the problems still facing him with such determination. Now George was reunited with Gisela, Adam had no doubts in George's ability as his successor. In spite of Adam's own doubts earlier about a future for petrol-driven vehicles, he was now convinced that it would be George's Swann-Maxie which would ensure that Swann-on-Wheels remained the largest and most progressive hauliers in the country. Though it would take at least two to three years before a complete change-over to petrol 'lorries' could be made. There was certainly plenty to occupy George, improving the technical performance of the new vehicle, and also in planning out what reorganisation and re-routeing was going to be necessary once the majority of long-distance journeys were being made by Swann-Maxies.

They still sought him out in the last years of the old century, coming singly for encouragement, for consolation, or for a nugget of counsel from his bran tub of experience, and he was sometimes amused by their deviousness for they often disguised their visits as duty-calls on Henrietta and needed a little prodding to come to the point.

Giles was a regular caller and the most outspoken, a man picking his path among Celtic caltrops sown for unwary Englishmen. George looked in oftener, with or without Gisela, giving a brash account of himself and his affairs but often seeking to draw him out on a choice of routes, the breaking-strain of an executive, or the credit-worthiness of a customer.

Hugo was not such a frequent visitor at 'Tryst'. For him it had been a frustrating and puzzling year, but it wasn't until several months after Lady Sybil Uskdale's nursing benefit sports meeting, in the Putney arena on August Bank Holiday, 1898, that he found it necessary to come to see his father for some advice.

*   *   *

It was a very fashionable event and Hugo, ordinarily disdaining what he would have styled 'a bunfight meeting', would not have been there had it not been for the fact that Lady Sybil, president of the Volunteer Nurses' movement, was a forceful and persistent woman, able to appreciate the drawing power of a track champion who held European records in amateur athletics for the mile and the marathon. At twenty-nine Hugo should have been past his prime as an athlete but he showed no sign of a decline during that first circuit, loping along with the measured stride that sports editors claimed did not vary by a centimetre and apparently in no hurry at all to prove he could lap the best of his opponents when the time came. But then Springer, the London harrier, crossed to the inside, inadvertently implanting a track shoe on the arch of Hugo's right foot and causing him to swerve in a way that disconcerted a knot of competitors on their heels.

The result was a mix-up that steered the lamed cham-

pion into a marker post and the impact was violent
enough to stun him.

When he opened his eyes, wincing with the smart of
a lacerated foot, he was lying on a stretcher in the shade
of some elms and Lady Sybil herself was ministering to
him with that compound of authority, despatch and professional tenderness that made her so popular with
photographers selling plates to the fashionable periodicals.
On this occasion, however, she was not wearing her
standard regalia of gleaming linen but a Paris creation
of striped silk that emphasised, as her rustling uniform
could not, the graceful contours of her figure with its
high bust and impossibly girlish waist. This, together
with a tiny straw hat, gently angled and worn high, made
the very best of her plentiful blonde hair that was wreathed,
German fashion, over her temples.

It was a very reassuring spectacle to a champion
wincing with pain and aware that he had lost his chance
of fresh triumphs in the tail-end of the season, and Hugo,
forgetting his troubles for a moment, gazed at the vision
with rapt attention, almost as though the track tumble
had translated him to an Anglo-Saxon Garden of Allah
where the queen of the houris awaited his pleasure.

The illusion faded, however, the moment the vision in
striped silk spoke, saying, in a tone of voice that had never
been challenged since nursery days, "Lie *quite* still, Mr.
Swann, do you hear? You've had a nasty tumble and I
feel entirely responsible for it. You must stay here until
the doctor has examined that foot."

He blinked once or twice but then the pain of his wound
increased, as someone out of his line of vision applied a
salve, and had it not been for the soothing touch of Lady
Sybil's white hand on his brow, he would have sat up and
cursed the fool who had blundered across his path in that
uncouth manner. Attendance at foreign sports stadiums
had enlarged Hugo's vocabulary, and bystanders, held at
a respectful distance by Lady Sybil's acolytes, might have
learned an interesting variation of the British equivalent

of, say, 'clumsy fellow, born out of wedlock'. As it was, there was no alternative but to lie still until a doctor arrived, going over him as though he had been the heir-apparent savaged by would-be assassins.

He heard Lady Sybil say, in a more peremptory voice than she had employed to him, "Into the committee tent! Move the chairs! Take the trestle table away! Bring the chaise-longue from the terrace! Cushions too, lots of them!" People scurried in all directions, two stewards lifting the stretcher and bearing him away, like a dying warrior king, across the trampled grass to the welcome coolness of the pavilion where, under Lady Sybil's expert direction, he was made very comfortable and given a glass of iced lemonade, held to his lips by the mistress of ceremonies.

Then, quite suddenly, it seemed, everybody except Lady Sybil disappeared and the sound of distant cheering came to him from the arena, rising to a climax as the winner, whoever he was, breasted the tape. He asked, a little petulantly, "Who won?" and she said, gently, "Never *mind* who won, Mr. Swann! You won't be concerned with who wins or who loses for quite some time. I'm having you taken to my town house as soon as the brougham comes round. I'm afraid you must regard yourself my patient until that foot has healed."

It crossed his mind to remind her that stunning good looks and extreme elegance did not entitle her to prescribe his comings and goings for as much as an hour but meeting the level gaze of her cornflower blue eyes all he could mumble was, "It's nothing, Lady Uskdale . . . a mere scratch . . ." She smiled down at him in such a bewitching way that he was deprived of the will to get up and limp outside to discover who had carried off the trophy he had expected to win at a canter. Instead he lay back among his cushions, wondering why a woman as celebrated and socially exalted as Lady Sybil Uskdale should make so much of a few foot punctures and mild concussion Being Hugo, a stranger to the world of high fashion, he decided it must be because she regretted having enticed him to appear at a bunfight meeting and inadvertently eliminating him from more serious events in the near future.

His surmise, of course, was a long way from the truth. Nothing so trivial as a twinge of conscience had ever prevented Lady Sybil Uskdale from acquiring anything she coveted, and at this moment, having made up her mind in a single intuitive flash, she coveted Hugo Swann so jealously that he would have blushed had he discerned her motive.

He was not necessarily stupid to so misread the situation. More sophisticated men than Hugo Swann had pondered the secret motives of Sybil Uskdale for years without arriving at any significant conclusions. The eldest and by far the most decorative of the famous Uskdale girls, she was now within two weeks of her thirtieth birthday and the only one among them unmarried. And likely to be, so most London hostesses predicted, for her hauteur was a legend, and all the eligible bachelors she seemed to find repellent and she scared away less exalted candidates with a mental superiority that was the very worst card an eligible spinster could display in the presence of a suitor. Even her detractors (among them the frustrated mothers of a dozen or more spurned eligibles) had to admit that Sybil had had her chances, some of them splendid chances all the way back to her coming out ball, twelve years before. Yet here she was, within days of the spinster's Rubicon, still pottering about first-aid posts, obsessed with some horrid plan of luring nice girls from the real business of life in order to learn how to alleviate the sufferings of the victims of road or railway accidents, as if these things couldn't be left to the professionals and lower-middle-class girls who went in for voluntary nursing in the hope of finding a husband. It never seemed to occur to the most discerning of them that Sybil Uskdale saw her vocation in precisely these terms.

In the course of her long, semi-regal passage through the

ballrooms and drawing-rooms of fashionable London Sybil Uskdale must have encountered a regiment of gallants who would have needed no more than a soft glance, a blush or a mere hint, to bring them to the pitch of proposal. Yet so far not one of them had been given the signal and the simple reason for this lay in the impossibly high physical standards Sybil Uskdale set herself when her thoughts turned to marriage.

It was not that she did not desire to be married. She did, and with all her heart. Indeed, had the more staid of her hostesses been granted access to her secret fantasies in this field it is doubtful if she would have received invitations into their homes. For the truth was Sybil Uskdale panted for a man, providing he was one who was neither a middle-aged widower or a member of the younger set that she thought of, in her eccentric way, as a 'pebble'.

The origin of this line of thought is interesting, illustrating her singularity in that closed society. As a child she had paid occasional visits to Folkestone, where it was fashionable at that time to rent a villa by the sea, and there she had witnessed a group of local boys diligently throwing pebbles at a shelving ledge twenty feet up a cliff overlooking the promenade. Every now and again a pebble lodged itself among a small pile but nearly all of them rebounded and fell among the gorse growing below. When, some time afterwards, she was introduced to the young men who were paraded round Belgravia's drawing-rooms like so many colts each season, she at once equated them with the pebbles flung by little Folkestonians in the hope of making a lodgment. She never had and she never could think of herself as anything so commonplace as a ledge, and throughout a succession of seasons no single pebble lodged with her but this was the fault of the pebbles not the pitchers. In a later era, when Victoria had at last made way for her more relaxed heirs, newspaper editors found certain labels for young men making regular appearances at these exclusive mating functions. They called them 'chinless wonders' and 'debs' delights', and

Sybil Uskdale would have regarded the soubriquets as very apt. Their chinlessness offended her estimate of what a husband should look like. Not one of them had ever looked remotely like Hugo Swann, as he lay concussed on the stretcher under the elms at Putney on that hot August afternoon. It was then that Sybil suddenly realised, and with a sense of liberation so compelling that it required strict self-control not to proclaim it aloud, that here was the man she had been looking for all these years and that her quest was now at an end.

She had always been attracted to athletes and was herself an ardent bicyclist and tennis player, so that she knew all about Hugo Swann when she invited him to participate in her nursing fête. It did not matter to her that he was a prosperous tradesman's son, and the fourth in line at that. The notion that like should mate with like was passing out of fashion anyway, and it was now considered almost chic to marry into trade, so long as the word was elevated to 'commerce' and so long as the commerce had resulted in wealth. All the Uskdale wealth reposed in land, and, as everybody knew, land was at a discount now, what with successive agricultural depressions, and millions of pounds of refrigerated food were pouring into the ports from the dominions and colonies. Far better a tradesman's son with a beautiful body than a pebble with an uncomfortable country house, his father's mortgages and a thousand unproductive acres in the shires. Particularly a tradesman's son of Hugo Swann's splendid proportions, who looked, she thought, like Achilles lying on his shield as she ran her approving glance the length of his bronzed body, happily open to close inspection in his singlet and running drawers. A shaft of sunlight, striking through the branches, teased his thighs, sown with short golden hairs that grew all the way down to calves knotted with solid muscle. A long ecstatic sigh escaped her as she contemplated those hairs, and the thicker growth just visible above the hem of his singlet, and she had a vivid impression of what it would feel like to lie beside him and

feel the weight of that huge sword arm across her breasts.
Then her fancy went further and she contemplated the
extreme satisfaction it would give her to stroke those short,
curling hairs and the limbs they grew upon and she made
up her mind in a matter of seconds. Hugo Swann's
days of bachelorhood were numbered.

*   *   *

Hugo came to see Adam a few months later when it
had finally dawned on him that Sybil Uskdale was resolved to land him, weigh him and, for all he knew, mount
him in a glass case and hang him on her boudoir wall,
but because he was Hugo, childlike in a situation of this
kind, Adam handled him gently, managing to persuade
him that he had reached a stage in life where he would
be well advised to settle for a rich, influential wife, who
regarded him as a person of enormous consequence and
would coddle him in a way that would compensate him
for the sacrifice of bachelorhood.

"The trouble with your line of country is that it gets
tougher in direct ratio to your weight and wind," he
said. "You're what age now? Thirty, is it?" and Hugo
conceded ruefully that he would not see twenty-nine
again. "Well, then, you're past your prime, old lad, and
may as well admit it. She's wealthy and well-born so they
say, but not as grand as she pretends. Her grandfather
was in Chilean nitrates to my recollection and *his* father
was a Pennine weaver with a few bright ideas. However,
that's neither here nor there. The important thing is,
do you want middle-aged freedom at the price of lonely
old age? Some men reckon it's the better bargain and for
all I know you might be one of 'em."

It was the first time in his life Hugo had aspired to such
an intimate level of conversation with his father and
confrontation of this kind embarrassed him horribly. He
said, grimacing, "I dunno, Gov'nor, I always reckoned
I'd marry and settle down sometime. It didn't seem to

matter when or how but Sybil, well, she's a rare sport for a woman."

"What do you mean by that?" asked Adam, relentlessly. " 'Sport' is an ambiguous word in that context, isn't it? Are you implying she was free with her favours among her kind before she met you?"

"Lord, no, Gov'nor, not that! She doesn't give a fig for polite society and never did, according to her sisters. They told me she could have married time and again but she wouldn't have anyone picked out for her, the way all those girls do." He shuffled a moment. "What I mean is – she, well . . . she doesn't *crowd* a man, and tag him along to all those soirées and at-homes. She's a top-class tennis-player, she's bicycled across France and can handle a racing skiff better than some of the undergrads you see at Henley."

"She sounds tailor-made for you, Hugo. Grab her while the going's good, boy. Your mother will be delighted, I'm sure, for it'll be a dressy wedding, no doubt."

"I haven't said a word about a wedding," protested Hugo but when he saw his father's twinkle he grinned and mumbled, "Well, everyone seems to *think* I'm spoken for tho' I haven't actually proposed so far."

"You leave that to her. She'll do it more gracefully than you and it's my belief she won't be long about it," and it seems that he had sized up Sybil Uskdale as accurately as he had been wont to take the measure of his customers, for the announcement of the engagement appeared in *The Times* the following week, and within twenty-four hours (another accurate prediction) Henrietta came to him wailing she had nothing to wear for the great occasion.

All of which, he supposed, was run-of-the-mill stuff, no more than his due as the father of nine.

*　　*　　*

It was otherwise with Alexander, when he looked in to ask his father to use his friendship with Lord Roberts in order to enlist him as an ally in the campaign to increase the number of Maxim guns per infantry battalion.

The prospect of button-holing anyone as celebrated as 'Bobs' (as everybody seemed to call him these days) and then preaching him a secondhand sermon on field tactics, was not one that Adam relished. There had been a time when this would have presented no difficulties to a man holding equal rank with the old campaigner, but that was so long ago that it belonged to another age. They had kept in touch over the last forty years but their correspondence had been intermittent and more or less formal, a matter of mutual congratulations mostly, although he remembered he had turned to Roberts for help once before, when Henrietta badgered him into using his influence to get the boy into a good regiment. Roberts had been kind and helpful about that, he recalled, and there might be no harm in an invitation to luncheon, at Pall Mall Club, to which they both belonged although, now that he thought about it, he had rarely seen Roberts about the place. He considered very carefully before he assented, however, saying, "You're absolutely sure you want me to do this, son? I don't mind getting snubbed, or not so long as I'm persuaded it's in a good cause. But if it got around that you had been using backstairs methods with a lion like Roberts it could spell trouble for you, I daresay."

Alex said, emphatically, "I don't mind a snub either, Gov'nor. I've already had more than my share in that direction, nor do I mind the backdoor, for they all use it whenever they can. That's why chaps like me, who take their work seriously, get more kicks than ha'pence. Ninety per cent of the men who outrank me got where they did by a word in the right ear at the right time, and the cavalry have the edge on all of us when it comes to patronage. Suppose you invited him to lunch, I was around and you called me in and introduced me when you'd got as far as coffee and cigars? That's all I'm asking. I'd play it from that point on."

And thus it was arranged, so blatantly yet so neatly

that Roberts went to his grave without knowing the 'chance' encounter had been stage-managed, and because Roberts was another man who took his profession seriously, he listened attentively, Adam noticed, when Alex paraded his hobby-horse round the most famous soldier in the Empire, showing it off like a nagsman at a fair.

Roberts said, when Alex excused himself, "Does you credit, Swann. More than you deserve, a straight-talking young chap like him. Sound on theory, and far more battle experience than most of the well-heeled youngsters you meet in the mess nowadays. How old is he?"

"Thirty-eight. Eight years older than I was when you and I parted company in India."

Roberts smiled and Adam remarked that, although his face was furrowed, and burned the colour of elm bark after half-a-century in the sub-tropics, his eyes were still young. 'And nothing remarkable about that,' he thought, 'for if they weren't so he wouldn't have given me the time of day after all these years,' and would have reverted to talk of scenes and companions of their youth had not Roberts said, suddenly: "Matter of fact, I've had my eye on him, Swann. Ever since you wrote and told me how he survived that shambles in Zululand. Did you know the subs dubbed him 'Lucky' Swann on account of that?"

"Yes, I did," Adam said, quick to seize his advantage, "but they have less flattering names for him now. One of them is 'The Barker' he tells me. I don't have to tell you that one pays a price for setting up as an expert before one's within a step of retirement, or that most professionals play at soldiers all their lives. Those who don't usually acquire reputations as mess-bores."

"And that's happening to him because he's refused transfers that meant promotion to stay on as a small-arms specialist? Well, that's you emerging in him, I daresay. You always were an obstinate cuss, Swann."

"No more than you, although your convictions were the more fashionable, even then."

"Not everywhere," Roberts said, thoughtfully. "My concept of Empire was rejected by you, if I remember correctly, but it's true that a majority of career men aren't interested in anything but polo, pigsticking and cutting a dash with the ladies. I wouldn't have got this far if I hadn't had more than my share of luck. Kitchener, too, I can tell you, and some of the others. We chaps need luck more than most and we're all going to need a lot more before we're much older."

"Where, particularly?"

"South Africa. Nobody will frighten Kruger into toeing the Imperial line and anyone who argues otherwise is a fool. You've read it all in the newspapers, I daresay."

"I've read a lot of bluff on both sides. The question is, if it did come to a showdown, who is likely to back Kruger? The German Kaiser wouldn't, and the French wouldn't. As for the Austrians and Russians, I daresay they'd have to be told who Kruger was. So who is bluffing who?"

"Kruger is bluffing himself," Roberts said. "That's his grief and ours, so long as those get-rich-quick Johnnies in the gold mines keep clamouring for the franchise and want us to take over the Transvaal." And then, as though his mind was off at a tangent. " 'The Barker', eh? Well, if I read that youngster correctly it's not promotion he needs so much as a backer or two on the staff, and that shouldn't be difficult to arrange. After all, he's talking sense. How many casualties did Kitchener's outfit suffer at Omdurman? Twenty-eight, and they killed ten thousand of the Mahdi. That was only achieved by automatic fire-power. I'll turn up the boy's file the minute I get a chance."

He sipped his brandy and they smoked in silence for a minute. Then Roberts said, "I've got a son about his age. Fine young chap who might go far, but not as far as your boy. Too amiable for one thing. I'm glad you put one of them in the army."

"It wasn't my choice, it was his own and his mother's. Tell me – that dream of yours about the destiny of the British. Does it look as rosy as it did to you then?"

"Can't answer that," Roberts said. "It's only half-fulfilled as yet. Need a century at least to bring something as big as that to full growth."

"But you must have a good idea how it's shaping."

"It needs pruning, I can tell you that."

"Ah, then you're coming round to my way of thinking. When I watched you ride by in that procession it crossed my mind that I was watching a lot of greedy children who had eaten enough confectionery to make 'em tolerably sick."

"They can do with a purgative," Roberts said, "but there's one coming and they'll be the better for it, so set your mind at rest as to that."

He got up, moving briskly as a boy. "Pleasure to see you again, Swann. We should do this more often. There aren't so many of us left nowadays."

They went out into the sunshine, a slim, short man loaded with honours and a very tall one, loaded with cash, and as they shook hands and took separate cabs, it occurred to Adam that they represented two sides of the national coin. Glory, a more mystical, less strident equivalent of the French 'gloire', and trade. The bray of the trumpet and the chink of the till, combining to produce a jingle that could be heard all the way round the world. 'Well,' he thought, 'I don't know what will come of all that in the end but something might. Can't but help the boy to have someone like Roberts behind him. Queer that . . . what he said about South Africa. Hadn't thought it was that serious myself, but he should know . . .', and he used the train-journey to Bromley to study the political correspondent's column in the *Pall Mall Gazette*, – 'that chap Stead's rag' as he still thought of it.

There wasn't much about South Africa there, only a paragraph announcing Paul Kruger's steadfast refusal to extend the franchise to the riff-raff that had invaded his

Old Testament domain once gold and diamonds had been discovered in the Witwatersrand, and he wondered what he would do in Kruger's place; bow the knee, to what most men would accept as the inevitable march of progress, or fight to the last ditch for the way of life adopted by the Cape Dutch after they had trekked north to their Promised Land?

The train ran into the station and he left his *Pall Mall Gazette* on the seat to beguile someone else's journey. The older he grew the more insular he became; the slow growth of his own cypresses and Himalayan pines interested him more than international rivalries these days. That was one of the troubles about growing old – one ceased to have any convictions about anything save those affairs, necessarily trivial, that lay under one's own hand.

2

Henrietta remembered other wars but never one like this one, with everyone, from scullerymaid to Duchess caught up in it, knitting, nursing, arguing, advising, one could almost say advancing against Kruger alongside the Yeomanry and any number of fancy volunteer units, all falling over themselves to singe Kruger's beard.

The earlier wars had been occasions for ceremonial for all who were not actually fighting, and so few had been in those days; hardly anybody one knew, more's the pity, for she had always wanted to be personally involved in an Imperial adventure.

There had been those colourful cutouts of Imperial warriors to paste on to nursery screens, awarded as Sunday School prizes; and reports in the weekly journals of last stands, broken squares and Highland pipers sitting on rocks puffing away at their bagpipes while shot and shell exploded all around them. But everything had always been at a remove, an intriguing succession of slides projected on to a magic-lantern screen.

Today, as the mother and grandmother of Imperial

soldiers, she knew that it wasn't quite like that, that sometimes men were speared and mutilated, as Alexander had
so nearly been at that Zulu battle with the long unpronounceable name, but she had no earlier experience
to guide her when Stella appeared at 'Tryst' demanding
to know how she could go about erasing young Robert
Fawcett's name from the muster roll of the Kentish
Yeomanry, after the boy had been silly enough to sign
on for the duration. Robert was still a month or two short
of his eighteenth birthday and had no business at all to
do a thing like that without consulting his father.

Stella was right to be angry, of course, and Robert,
senior among Henrietta's tribe of grandchildren, deserved
a severe scolding but she could not stifle a thrill of pride
at the lad's spirit, prompting him to go all that way from
home in order to confound the Queen's enemies. She said,
distractedly, "I really don't know how to advise you,
Stella. In my day wars were fought by soldiers, not
farmers' lads. Even Alex, only a year older than Robert
when he went off to fight the Zulus, was preparing to be
a soldier and Robert isn't, is he?"

"I really couldn't say," Stella grumbled, "but he'll feel
the weight of my hand alongside his ear the minute he
comes home. His father has learned to rely on him for he
does two men's work around the place, or so Denzil says."
Henrietta thought it odd that Stella should put Denzil's
crops and cattle before the honour of the flag. She was
therefore mildly shocked when Adam took an identical
view, dismissing Robert's gallant gesture as a piece of
schoolboy nonsense.

"He's absolutely no call to risk his skin in that quarrel,"
he growled. "The Boers are outnumbered by ten to one
to begin with, poor benighted devils." Although she had
always entertained great respect for Adam's knowledge of
public affairs she did not feel she could let this pass without
protest.

"But surely the boy feels he *ought* to do something,"
she said. "I mean, I think Stella is being very parochial

about it. She's got two younger boys and three lumping great farmhands . . ." But she stopped, seeing his brow cloud and feeling, in any case, out of her depth on a topic of this kind.

By then, of course, Alex had sailed, but this was in the natural order of things. Fighting the Queen's enemies was what he was paid to do and she had come to believe nothing much could happen to Alex for he obviously had a charmed life, like a sailor born in a caul. The situation grew even more perplexing when Croxley, 'Tryst's' second gardener, left at a day's notice, explaining that he was a reservist and had no choice. And after Croxley young Ricketts, the stable-lad, took himself off, also volunteering for the Yeomanry, so that Henrietta decided privately that Adam must be in error for once, for surely all these people would not be needed to deal with an enemy outnumbered ten to one.

The news, that autumn of 1899, seemed to prove her right. Nobody, it seemed, could get within singeing range of Kruger's beard and anyone who tried was shot down like a partridge. Defeat followed defeat and the sense of shame they brought spread outwards from London, like a wave of bitter-tasting medicine that everyone was obliged to swallow in droplets. Larger doses were on their way. When everybody was busy dressing their Christmas trees, news came of three shattering reverses in a single week, a week the newspapers called, justifiably in Henrietta's view, 'Black Week', for she could not recall a single occasion (apart from that temporary one at the hands of Zulus) when anyone challenging the British on the field of battle had come away the victors.

Adam, for all his lofty talk of the Boers being outnumbered ten to one, was clearly depressed, especially when he heard that his old friend Roberts had lost his only son, killed trying to save guns at Colenso. He said, gloomily, "Only mentioned him to me last occasion we met, that time I put in a word for Alex at the club. I gathered he was the gallant-idiot type. They invariably get themselves killed in the first skirmish. But how the devil do they expect a father, facing grief of that kind, to pull Buller's chestnuts out of the fire, now we're fully committed? Damned politicians should never have let it come to this. The country's gone mad and the whole world is laughing at us. Giles is the only chap I've met who takes a sane view of the silly business."

Henrietta was intrigued to learn that Giles, by nature such a quiet, studious boy, had taken the war fever, and said, innocently, "What does Giles think we ought to do, dear?" and Adam administered one of the biggest shocks of their married life by growling, "*Do?* Why, what any Government in their senses would do in the circumstances. Find a face-saver, pull out and let the Boers go their own way."

She did not think she could have heard him correctly. It was so uncharacteristic of all she knew of him to advocate such a craven course and concede victory to the enemy, just as if positions had been reversed and the British were a small republic facing an opponent with vastly superior resources.

"Pull out!" she gasped "You mean . . . let them *win?*"

"Dammit, woman, they are winning!"

"But only temporarily. I mean, they're bound to be beaten in the end, aren't they?"

"Yes, they are," he said, "but we won't emerge with any credit. They've already given us the hiding of our lives and demonstrated that the only possible way to beat them is to wear 'em down, burn their farms and slaughter or capture every able-bodied male between fourteen and seventy. By God, if I met a Boer now I wouldn't have the gall to look the chap in the face. We're behaving more like Prussians than Englishmen."

She gave it up after that. Clearly he had got some bee in his bonnet about the Boers and was deaf to the opinions of everyone around him. She only hoped he would keep his mouth shut in the presence of any of her friends she invited in over the Christmas holiday.

There was to be the usual family party, with a coming and going of the whole tribe of children and grandchildren, and she wanted to make a special impression this year. Hugo would be bringing his aristocratic wife on Boxing Day, the first time she had been offered an opportunity of getting to know the exalted creature, for the brief introductory visit before the wedding didn't count and at the ceremony itself she caught no more than a glimpse of the bride among all those fashionably dressed guests.

*　　　*　　　*

As it happened, however, Hugo and his wife appeared long before Boxing Day, bowling up to the forecourt in a very elegant equipage just as she was emerging from the kitchen in a grubby apron, after helping one of the girls to unstop the clogged runaway of the well-trough. She found it hard to believe that even Hugo could be so dense as to spring the girl upon her without a warning and would have blushed scarlet if she had not had her mind switched by the vision of Hugo in a well-tailored uniform of dark blue, with a broad yellow stripe running down his trouser-leg. Daughter-in-law Sybil escorted him up the steps and presented him like an impresario introducing his star-turn.

"There now!" she cooed, "doesn't he look perfectly *splendid*? Aren't you proud of him, Mrs. Swann? My word, but that tailor did a wonderful job once I put a flea in his ear! 'Swamped with orders, ma'am,' he said, if you ever heard such nonsense. As if Hugo didn't take precedence over a queue of stockbrokers and pen-pushers! Kiss your mother, Hugo, I'm sure she expects it."

Henrietta wasn't at all sure what she expected, apart from the floor to open and engulf her after being confronted by the daughter of the Earl of Uskdale in a flowered apron and a sewing dress, two years old. She was seized in Hugo's bearlike embrace and lifted clear of the floor but Sybil did not seem to pay the least attention to her embarrassment. She had no eyes for anyone but Hugo. Henrietta had time to note the soft shine in her ice-blue eyes as she patted and prodded her exhibit, straightening non-existent tunic creases and flicking imaginary specks of dust from the frogging. And then, to make bad worse, Adam had to come downstairs, pause on reaching hall level and exclaim, "Lord God Almighty! What's he joined, a German band?" and she could have cracked him over the head with the sewing-room door-stop. Luckily his daughter-in-law was not only blind to everyone but Hugo but deaf to opinions that he looked anything but every inch a soldier. Then Adam moved all the way round him in a cautious circle and said, "That's a City of London badge, isn't it?" and Lady Sybil said that it was and that Hugo was now a member of the Inns of Court Volunteer Company.

"But how does that come about?" he protested, giving Henrietta a chance to doff her apron and stuff it behind a row of leather fire buckets that stood alongside the stair cupboard, "He's not reading law, is he?"

"Oh, I managed that easily enough," Lady Sybil said, implying that she could, if she wished, secure Hugo a seat in Kruger's war cabinet. "All it needed was a word here and a push there, and here he is, come to say his goodbyes before joining General Gatacre's staff as a supernumerary. We're both sailing on the *Empress of India* the day after tomorrow."

"You're going too?" Henrietta gasped.

"The entire nursing unit is going," confirmed Sybil. "Eighty-six of us, not counting the surgeons. Daddy telephoned me before it was released to the newspapers."

"But Hugo has had no training for staff work, has he?" asked Adam, whose face still expressed incredulity, "he's only fooled about in the Yeomanry."

"Does one *need* training for a post of that kind?"

"Well, military men are in two minds as to that, my dear," said Adam, his features relaxing somewhat.

Lady Sybil said, "I daresay they'll see you get trained

in the field, Hugo. And now . . ." she turned her best hospital-fête smile on the cringing Henrietta, "I really *would* like a cup of that nice China tea you gave us when Hugo first brought me here, and we've at least an hour for a gossip, because we aren't due at the Overseas Comforts concert until ten o'clock, and that will give us plenty of time to change. It's a nuisance really but I did promise to appear."

It was not Henrietta's idea of a gossip. She hardly contributed a word and Hugo said very little but sat there beaming at his wife as she described in detail how she had set the stage for Hugo's début as a national hero. When they were leaving, and Hugo embraced her again, Henrietta shed a tear or two, for the bovine Hugo had always seemed the most helpless of her sons. But then she reflected that he was in extremely capable hands and Lady Sybil's manipulations would almost certainly ensure that he climbed the military ladder at twice the speed of his brother Alex.

Adam, it seemed, had more sombre thoughts as they watched the brougham sweep round the curve that ran between the leafless limes to the gate. "I don't know, I never did credit Hugo with much grey matter, but I would have thought he had sense enough to stay clear of that shambles. That woman's a menace. And to think I urged the boy to marry her!"

"She's obviously very much in love with him," Henrietta said.

But he replied, glumly, "Is she? Is that love? I don't think it is. Not our kind of love at all events. She's using him as a kind of reflector, something to catch the public's eye and bend it in her direction," and he withdrew to his study without another word.

3

He could talk to Giles, had always been able to talk to him ever since he was a boy, with his nose stuck in all those heavy tomes in the library and his flow of questions about the meaning of existence.

Giles and Romayne were among the Christmas visitors and Romayne was far gone with child, and seemingly happily settled in that Welsh valley where Giles had at last found anchorage. He used this as an opening gambit when they took a walk together on the last afternoon of the old century, climbing the spur behind the house and crossing the bracken-clad slope towards the river that fed Adam's lily ponds. He said, "That wife of yours, boy, she seems to have found contentment that eluded her all this time. I must say I never realised she was genuinely interested in social reform. To be honest I always saw it as a bit of a fad."

"I don't think she's more than marginally involved in politics," his son told him, "or not in the way Debbie is. You're right about her adjusting, however. Our relationship has changed in Wales. I'm not saying we were unhappy before but . . . well . . . she always seemed to me to be looking for something."

"Want to tell me?"

"If I can."

They walked on down the gentle slope to the river where it split into two streams to form the islet that Henrietta always thought of as Shallott, a grey-haired man, born in George IV's reign, and his serious-faced son of thirty-four, who always seemed detached from everybody around him.

"She's identified with me now," Giles said, "in a way that's almost miraculous. Or so it appears from my standpoint. It was she who brought it about, you see, something she did without prompting from anyone, and it's made a place for her that didn't exist before. Given her a clearly defined purpose, I suppose, that was missing all the years she was growing up surrounded by lackeys and neglected by that old devil of a father. I've got to win that seat, if only for her."

"How do you rate your chances?"

"Fair to middling. Better now that I've taken L.G.'s line on the war."

"How can that be? It's a very unpopular line, isn't it?"

"Not among my people. They've been an oppressed minority for generations and some of them see Kruger as a South African Llewellyn, fighting for freedom. L.G., and all the other pro-Boer Liberals, have had a very rough ride these last few months but I haven't. I've had some rousing meetings and our party machinery improves all the time. If I don't win the next election I'll win the one after that, once reaction sets in and people begin to see that L.G.'s line was the right one. This jingo mood isn't a natural one for the British. By and large they're a fair-minded lot when they're sober. Right now, of course, most of them are blind drunk."

It was a good enough analogy, Adam thought, approving his son's clearheadedness. He said, pausing for breath, and looking between the willows at the winter flood swirling round the butt end of the islet on its way to the sea, "By God, I've seen a thing or two in my time, since I was a boy growing up in the fells. Railways lacing the country. Trade figures multiplying fifty times over. The nation swelling itself up like the frog in the fable and edging everyone else out of the sun. It took Rome five centuries to do what the British have done since Waterloo, yet how long is it in terms of the calendar? Eighty-five years. Just over a single life-span. Would you believe I once saw a poor devil hanged in Carlisle for setting fire to a barn? When I fought my first skirmish in India, Germany, as we know it today, didn't exist and most of America was a desert. It's the pace that makes one dizzy. The entire cast of society has been broken and remade since those days. Everyone's expectations are upgraded, even those of your miners, although you probably wouldn't get them to admit there had been much change in their standard of living. There has, tho', and I don't know where it began, exactly. Was it with steam-power and greater mobility? Or with the emergence of trade unions?

Or with Gladstone's compulsory education acts? Or a social conscience among an élite minority, with leisure and time to digest the philosophy of Tom Paine and company? Damned if I could pinpoint it, or predict its future course. It's like that river there, made up of a hundred streams welling out of the hills until it's strong enough to carry everything along. Can you make a guess where we're heading, lad?"

"I try every time I make a speech or finish a canvass," Giles said, smiling, "but I come up with different answers once a week. I suppose it depends on the calibre of the men on top, and what kind of course they've set themselves."

"What course are you setting after midnight? The end of a century is a good time for stocktaking, isn't it? Not at my time of life, mind, but certainly at yours."

"To adapt the new technologies to the needs of the average man, woman and child, I'd say. That's the heart of the problem. All those innovations you've been spouting at me aren't worth a damn if all they do is to help make rich men richer, and are used to browbeat sixty thousand Boer farmers into changing their way of life to please diamond diggers and gold prospectors. You can only work, argue and fight within the law. The law's very far from perfect and still bears down on the majority but less than it did. And, anyway, it's a lot better than a street full of people throwing bricks at one another."

They took the short way home across the bridge and through the five-acre ornamental landscape Adam had conjured out of the two paddocks, a few coppices and some rough pasture. He was silent as they climbed the rise but as they emerged in the forecourt he said, thoughtfully, "We'll be lifting our glasses tonight, when the village bells ring the old year out and the twentieth-century in. I don't know what the others will be drinking to but I'll raise my glass to you, boy. At least two of us speak the same language and that's a comfort for a man with a family as big as mine."

He went in, reminding himself that it was less than just for a father to acknowledge a family favourite but how could one avoid a preference, with five sons and four daughters of such diversity? He had a flash of insight then, concerning this particular son, his wife and that child in her belly, and all three acquired special signifi-cance in relation to this mellow corner of England that he had shaped and made his own, in a way that the network was not and never would be a durable monu-ment to him. Alex had his career and George the business. Hugo had that extraordinary wife dancing attendance on him and the girls had their husbands and families. Something told him it was Giles and his successors who would live here some day when he was dust and maybe some of them would come to think of it as he was beginning to think of it, the only worthwhile legacy one generation could pass to another. Land, and what grew on it; contours, cunningly adapted to the eternal round of seasonal colours that nothing could change or distort, no matter how many cleverdicks came forward with their inventions. It comforted him somehow, a conviction that continuity was attainable, providing a man had patience to keep striving for it.

4

Sacrifice to Dagon

IT WAS DEEMED A SIGNAL HONOUR TO RIDE ON
reconnaissance with Montmorency. The Empire, woefully short of heroes of late, had plugged holes in the
Pantheon Wall with a hotchpotch of newcomers. Small
fry, by yesterday's standards. Captains, sergeants, pipers
and even bugler boys, but welcome none the less under the
present humiliating circumstances.

Captain the Hon. R. H. L. J. de Montmorency was at
the apex of this improvised pyramid, having, so to speak,
secured a year's start over his competitors by winning
the V.C. serving with the 21st Lancers, in Kitchener's
Sudan campaign, in '98, and since added other dashing
exploits to his credit, so that his name was familiar to the
readers of every penny journal in London. It followed that
anyone who rode with him was shortlisted for reflected
glory.

Glory, after such a laggardly start, was rallying out
here along the farflung battlefront. Times were already
on the mend when Hugo landed at East London, and
trekked north-west through Queenstown to the sector
where General Gatacre was doing his best to wipe out the
shame of earlier defeats on the central front. He was
having some success too, or so it was rumoured along the
route. The Boer generals, De la Rey and Schoeman, were
already giving ground and falling back to the north, the
price paid for their inexplicable failure to exploit the rout

237

of the British in this area when the tide of invasion lapped
into Cape Colony.

The enemy moved slowly, however, far too slowly for
Gatacre, who was now deploying his cavalry to chivvy
them as the main offensive developed on the right flank.
When Hugo received orders to ride ahead with Montmorency's column he was delighted, not so much because
Montmorency was a popular leader but because he had a
suspicion that the long and purposeful arm of Lady Sybil
would soon reach out from her field hospital at Queenstown and keep him out of Mauser range of the Boers
while he was, as she herself had put it 'easing himself in',
a phrase that suggested a cushy billet well behind the
lines.

He was not to know that his selection for a forward
post was the direct result of a message Gatacre's chief
of staff had received from the daughter of the Earl of
Uskdale, informing him that the famous athlete she had
married, and shipped out here along with her nursing
unit, had no aptitude for paper work and would need
careful coaching. It was an unfortunate admission so
far as Lady Sybil was concerned. A staff officer, mounting
a massive advance against an alert enemy, was not likely
to fancy the job of coach to civilians in uniform and merely
did what seemed to him the next best thing for a serving
officer sponsored by the daughter of an earl. He attached
Hugo to a proven hero, reasoning that this was the shortest
route to newspaper acclaim and likely to please the lady
concerned. Only that day he had received news that the
Boers were pulling out at Bloemfontein. A token rearguard resistance was the worst Montmorency's column
were likely to meet while feeling their way across the
Kissieberg hills to Stormberg Junction.

Like so many others in the great arc of Imperialists
between the Orange River and the Tugela that winter,
Gatacre's reckoning was seriously at fault. The Boers
were moving back certainly, and faster than his Intelligence had deduced, but they were determined to make

the British pay for any gains they made. Montmorency's column rode headlong into a well-laid ambush that emptied fifty saddles at the first volley and the survivors, milling about in the wildest confusion, could not see so much as a hat to aim at after they had galloped for cover.

Hugo had been enjoying the ride up to that moment. Half-dozing in the saddle he jogged along, dreaming of conquests past and yet to come, seeing his presence here as little more than an exciting interlude in a lifetime of pot-hunting. He did not share the general view that an athlete approaching his thirtieth year was past his prime and should be casting about for the means of acquiring other laurels. After all, he was neither a sprinter nor a leaper, and long-distance runners often continued to compete well into middle age. An Italian, over forty, had just won the marathon at an international meeting.

Then, in a sustained crackle of rifle fire that reached him like the flare up of dry sticks on a fire, he was jerked back into the present, with wounded and riderless horses cavorting past him in all directions, dismounted troopers looming out of the flurry of dust and Mauser bullets going over him like a swarm of bees.

He did what seemed the only thing to do, wheeling and dashing for the nearest cover, a scatter of low rocks at the foot of a broken hill on his immediate right, and when he got there, flinging himself to the ground and making a grab at his horse's bridle, he was astonished at the scene of chaos that presented itself, not only along the track ahead but right here, in the shelter of the rocks.

Dead and dying troopers were everywhere among terrified horses, some of them hit and screaming with pain. Dust rose in a red cloud, obliterating the field of fire. Equipment, including a scatter of long, useless lances, lay everywhere. A sergeant sat with his back to a rock, trying to staunch a spouting wound in his thigh and his blood spattered Hugo as he stepped over his legs, making for a knot of unwounded men cowering behind a larger rock and emptying their magazines at nothing. He recognised none of them and this was not surprising, for he had only joined the column the day before. The only man he could have identified was Montmorency, now lying dead, someone told him, a hundred yards higher up the pass. His informant, another sergeant, had something else to say about Montmorency. "Led us right into a rat-trap," he shouted, above the uproar. "Didn't even scout the bloody hills with a flank guard, and we'll not hold out here for long the way those fools are loosing off!" Then, ignoring Hugo, he darted among the marksmen bellowing, "Hold your bloody fire! Wait until the dust settles! Save your ammo! For Chrissake, save your ammo!"

The dust was a long time settling and in the interval Hugo's horse rolled over, shot between the eyes and falling on its right flank where Hugo's carbine bucket was strapped. He only looked long enough to satisfy himself that the horse was dead before drawing his revolver and accosting the frantic sergeant again.

"Aren't there any officers left?" he demanded.

"Yessir," the man said, breathlessly. "Mr. Cookham over there. But he's plugged, I believe!" He pointed to another outcrop twenty yards higher up the slope where a group of about a dozen survivors were gathered round a young subaltern with a wispy moustache, who was supervising the erection of a barricade of loose rocks.

The rate of Boer fire had slackened somewhat by then, but it was still inviting certain death to venture on to open ground. Hugo decided to risk it and tore across the exposed patch, a bullet striking his spur and making a sound like a finger snapped on a wine-glass. He got there unscathed, however, and Mr. Cookham seemed relieved to see him. "You a regular?" he demanded and Hugo said no, just a supernumerary who had joined the staff earlier in the week. The sergeant was right. Cookham had been hit in the upper arm and his left sleeve dripped blood.

"Well, here's a how-de-do," he said gaily. "It looks as if I've got my first command." He glanced around the circle where the dead and wounded outnumbered the living by two to one. "Don't think I'll have it long, however. What's your name, Supernumerary?"

Although he had been in Africa less than a month, Hugo was well aware that any regular, even a nineteen-year-old subaltern, would hold the Yeomanry and Local Volunteer units in contempt. He said, diffidently, "Swann, Mr. Cookham. Hugo Swann . . ."

The officer let out a whoop and said, "Swann, the runner?" and at once transferred his revolver to his left hand, grabbed Hugo's right and shook it. "Heard you were around. A rare pleasure to have you here!" he said. "You'll set up a new record today if we get out of here alive," and the joke seemed to remind him of his duty, for he turned away and issued a stream of orders concerning the barricade, rate of fire, transfer of badly wounded to the patch of shadow under the tallest rock and several other instructions that Hugo did not catch, for a wounded horse, dragging itself round by its forelegs, struck him and sent him staggering off at a tangent as another bullet shattered his wrist-watch and grazed the skin along the joint of his thumb. It was no more than a scratch but enough to project him the far side of the dying horse at a bound. He landed on a dead lancer, spreadeagled behind the barricade.

Gradually the dust began to settle and the blue of the sky showed through the haze. A long outcrop of rocks some two hundred yards distant in the left foreground became visible, clearly the point of ambush, for intermittent flashes revealed where invisible marksmen were peppering them from two angles.

Cookham said, breathlessly, "Have to hump ourselves higher up. They'll pick us off one by one so long as we stay here!" And under his direction the ragged group of survivors began to claw their way up the slope in short, individual rushes, aiming for a bulkier outcrop thirty yards above their first position.

Most of them made it, although a trooper scrambling

up beside Hugo spun round and went tumbling head over heels down the incline again, his carbine making a tremendous clatter among the loose stones. Up here it was possible, by risking a bullet between the eyes, to get a grasp of the battlefield as a whole, a shallow valley with larger outcrops clothed with scrub on the Boer side and a long, steep ascent, bare of cover, at the rear of their own position. Cookham shouted, "How many of us, Supernumerary? Count 'em for me, will you?" Hugo, counting, said there were two dozen on the ledge and some lightly wounded still firing from below.

Cookham had his binoculars unslung now and used them to sweep the valley left to right at the price of losing his helmet that whipped from his head and sailed away like a clay pigeon. He said, "Well, it's better than I thought. They've only wiped out the head of the column. There's no firing for'ard. Murchison's lot have pulled back out of range, lucky devils! They'll have sent someone back for reinforcements and guns by now but that won't help us, frying up here." He paused, frowning with concentration, and Hugo was struck by the contrast between his outward immaturity and his calm acceptance of responsibility involving the lives of every man between the ridge they occupied and the floor of the valley. Images of two of his brothers presented themselves, Alex, a veteran soldier by the time he was Cookham's age (and very like Cookham now that he came to think about it) and Edward, at home beside the Thames, who was young enough to have been at school with Cookham. He thought, 'Either one of them could pull their weight in a show like this but I'm not much use, damn it. I feel like a passenger in a ditched 'bus, waiting for someone to tell me what to do,' and the thought of those rows of silver cups, urns and medals in the showcase at 'Tryst' returned to him, as though heliographing their puerility and trashiness across thousands of miles of land and water. He said, ruefully, "I can't even hit 'em with this, Mr. Cookham. And my carbine's back there, under my horse."

"None of us can hit 'em," Cookham said, cheerfully. "I doubt if we could even if we could see 'em. The sun is at their backs and their worst marksman could shoot the feathers out of our bonnets. Still, so long as they know we're here they'll hold off, and that'll stop them moving south and laying another ambush for relieving troops. Something else too – they can't even guess at our numbers." He bobbed up again and took another quick squint through the binoculars. This time a flight of bullets passed over, the Boers firing high and overestimating the height of the ridge for the bullets ricocheted from the rock face above.

"Checkmate," Cookham said. "We can't stir but they dare not hold that position for long. By that time the batteries will be up and they'll have to look lively getting away over that broken ground behind them." He sucked his teeth. "We're snug enough by that reckoning. There's no time for them to work around behind and fire down on us, but suppose . . . Pity you're a miler, Swann."

"Why?"

"If you were a champion sprinter we might have a sporting chance to nab them . . . Remember that track, branching left two miles back?"

"I remember it."

"I'll lay a pound to a penny it passes behind that range of hills. If the relieving force sent cavalry and horse artillery down it, and they looked lively, they could cut the line of retreat before the Boer pulls out. Look . . ." and he whipped a pencil from his notebook and propping the sheet against the rock face sketched the manoeuvre, a narrow sweep behind the Boer position, masked by high ground at the junction of the tracks.

"Won't they have posted lookouts above that track?"

"If they're as smart as I think they are, but no more than two or three men. Murchison could pin them down if you got word to him."

"How far back is Murchison's column?"

"Under a mile. But to get down from here you'd have

243

to move over the ground faster than you've ever covered it. Those chaps over there are the best shots in the world. I wouldn't order anyone to take a chance like that."

"You don't have to order me."

"You'd try it?"

"I'm no use up here, with a six-shooter, Mr. Cookham."

Cookham considered him gravely. "You're game, Mr. Supernumerary. We'll give you covering fire, but for God's sake raise the dust the minute you reach level ground."

"They won't stop me."

He knew, somehow, that it was his moment. All the pounding over the Exmoor plateau as a boy, all those circuits of tracks over the years, all those cheers and trophies that had come his way in the last decade had led to this, a dash down a valley whipped by bullets from the rifles of the deadliest marksmen in the world, carrying a message from a wispy-moustached boy to a rearguard picquet. He knelt half upright, stripping off his spurs, tunic and helmet.

"When you're ready, Mr. Cookham."

The boy said, slowly, "I saw you win the Stamford Bridge two thousand metres when I was on leave last year. You've got one hell of a stride, Swann. And more puff than a blacksmith's bellows. Good luck – sir."

He saw the 'sir' as an accolade, a singularly graceful compliment from a professional to an amateur. It brought him more satisfaction than any victory in the sports arena. They shook hands and Cookham passed the word along to give covering fire at rapid rate the moment Hugo left cover. Then, with a single prodigious leap, he was off, bounding down the slope and swerving at every obstacle in his path, dead men, dead horses, jettisoned equipment, loose rocks, everything between him and the brown surface of the beaten path over which they had ridden not half-an-hour since.

He had no awareness of being a target on the way down. His concentration was centred wholly on his swerves and leaps and the placing of feet encumbered by heavy cavalry boots. Then he was running south, faster it seemed than over any straight stretch to the tape. Once on the level he heard the impact of individual Mauser bullets striking the rocks in his path but none struck him and gradually the fusillade reverted to the odd whining plop as a spent bullet ricocheted into the slab-sided hillside to his left.

He came upon Murchison's rearward picquet behind an outcrop on the Boer side of the path, a little short of the distance estimated by Cookham, for he had run, at a guess, a little over half-a-mile from the point where he reached level ground. A man stood up and called, making a trumpet of his hands, and he changed direction, breasting a slight slope and leaping the low parapet into a shallow depression where a few dismounted lancers were huddled, commanded, it seemed, by a middle-aged trooper. He said, between laboured breaths, "Thirty survivors still holding out a mile back. Orders from Lieutenant Cookham in command. Boers occupying high ground on this side of the valley. Mr. Cookham says to find Major Murchison and tell him to send cavalry and guns behind the range to cut 'em off."

"There's a Boer outpost overlooking that track, sir. That's why we daren't move back."

Hugo thought, glumly, 'He's waiting for orders, for a direct order, and there's no one else to give it.' He said, "Take all three troopers. One of you will make it if you move fast. Give me your carbine and a bandolier. I'll climb higher and try to pin them down for a spell. I'll wait until they're firing on you before I move."

The man was an old sweat, conditioned by years of service to rely on an officer, even a volunteer. He called his three men by name, telling them briefly they were to make a run for it, one at a time. Anyone who got through was to pass the order on to Major Murchison. Then, his confidence restored, he turned back to Hugo. "Just how far for'ard *is* Captain Montmorency, sir?"

"Captain Montmorency is dead. Lieutenant Cookham's

commanding all that's left of the column. Tell them that too if you make it."

"Can they hold out long, sir?"

"Indefinitely. But the Boers will pull out by the time reinforcements move up. Get going, man."

The man handed over his carbine and unslung his bandolier. "There's around twenty cartridges, sir. Good luck, sir."

"You too," Hugo said and watched as, one by one, the four of them leaped from cover and ran a zig-zag course down the track. The old campaigner went last, in less of a hurry than the others and taking full advantage of the overhang of scrub this side of the path. One man fell but picked himself up again and Hugo had no chance to watch their further progress for he had to turn his back on them to scale the tumble of rocks screening him from the snipers' outpost on the crest.

The hill here was a series of small fissures and easily scaleable, partly on account of its milder gradient but also because every cleft was sown with a prickly, tough-stemmed growth sprouting leaves not unlike the umbrella plants that grew down by the ox-bow below 'Tryst'. He went up very carefully, hugging the slope, for the crackle of shots from above and a short distance to the left, told him the Boers posted immediately above the fork were still trying to pot the troopers as they made their way to the rear.

He had expected to find the summit of the spur open ground, with no cover worth mentioning, but as soon as he reached it he saw that he was wrong. For some reason there was more scrub on this side of the valley and the umbrella-like plants had straggled all the way up a donga that might, at one time, have been a tiny watercourse. There was no advantage in him making his way along the ridge as far as the outpost snipers. Sooner or later, probably the moment they saw a sizeable body take the left hand branch at the fork behind the Boer position, they would withdraw, moving at the double all the way along

the crest to warn the main body. He realised the logic of
Cookham's assumptions. 'Damn it,' he thought, 'that kid
has more brains than Montmorency. If he'd been commanding the column we should never have run our necks
into the noose like this,' and he opened the lowest pouch
of his bandolier and found there five bullets, enough to
fill the half-empty magazine of the carbine.

The sun was blisteringly hot and he lacked the protection of his helmet. By raising himself to his knees he
could just see the track down which he had run, two dead
horses marking the southern limit of the battle and the seam
where Cookham's survivors were still holding out judging
by the occasional burst of fire from one side or the other.
He could have seen a good deal more had he stood upright but the tallest umbrella only grew to a height of
about two feet and if his presence here was so much as
suspected, all his trouble would have gone for nothing.
The outpost party would fan out and fire at him from
several angles, rushing him if they failed to hit him because
they would see a warning to the main body as worth the
sacrifice of some of them. So he lay very still, carbine
thrown forward and ear to the ground listening for the
scrape of a boot and trying to calculate how many Boers
he would have to deal with. Presently, however, the
outpost's rifles fell silent. Either they had accounted for
the troopers or had reverted to their task of watching the
ox-path a hundred feet below where Murchison or base
reinforcements would soon be beginning the outflanking
movement.

About twenty minutes passed in almost complete silence
to the north and south, the cessation of fire implying that
the main body to the north had already begun their
withdrawal towards Stormberg. Then, quite close at
hand, he heard guttural voices and the chink of metal on
loose stones, but although the voices seemed to be
approaching he could see no movement in the scrub when
he raised his head above the cluster of parchment-like
leaves at the top of the donga. He had just lowered it

again when he heard someone shout an order in an urgent tone, and in the same second he saw his first man, a grey-bearded, thickset Boer, with a slouch hat and his rifle held at the trail, moving at a crouching run immediately to his front and already less than thirty yards from where he lay. He raised himself on one knee and took a snap shot, with no pretence of aiming and the man stopped in his tracks, his legs set widely apart and his free hand stretched out, as though to ward off the bullet.

He remained in that curiously rigid position long enough for Hugo to get an unforgettable glimpse of his expression. Not so much startled as abstracted, the expression of a man who, quitting his front gate for work, suddenly remembers something he should have done before slamming the door. Then, quite slowly, the Boer toppled sideways, his rifle dropping soundlessly into the scrub, his body falling away down the incline out of sight and sound as it rolled down the western slope of the hill and at that precise moment his following companion showed, hatless, beardless and with Mauser in firing position. The face behind the levelled rifle was that of a boy, fourteen or younger.

He was obviously firing blind for his shot went wide by yards and he had no time to work his bolt and press the trigger a second time. Hugo's second slug hit him squarely in the chest so that he staggered backwards, dropping his rifle and pressing his hands to the point of impact. Then he fell flat on his back in a small open patch so that Hugo, peering through the stalks, could see the upturned soles of his hobnailed boots.

A long silence followed, unbroken by the staccato crackle of fire higher up the valley, or by a rustle or boot-scrape further along the spur. The sun, now directly overhead, scourged his neck and sweat dripped in his eyes, blurring the sight of the upturned boots in a grey-green haze that undulated like a curtain in a draught.

The shot from the right and below almost did for him, ripping through the rucked up folds of his shirt and cutting the shoulder strap of his bandolier so that it fell free and would have bounced into the donga had he not made a grab at it. He swung half-right and fired twice but whether he hit anything or not he had no means of knowing, for at that moment a fourth Boer fired from the left, the bullet coming close enough to slice the scrub six inches from his nose.

He had to take a gamble then on whether there was a fifth or sixth Boer somewhere behind the dead boy, for there was better cover there in the form of a spur of rock. Once behind it the marksmen on the lower terraces would be in his sights. He half-rose to his feet and dashed forward and was within a yard of it, his left foot braced on the outflung arm of the boy's corpse when his head exploded like a rocket, painlessly yet with a kind of deliberate wrenching movement that stretched every nerve and muscle in his body.

*　　*　　*

He was still breathing when they found him, sprawled half across a spur of rock at the very summit of the ridge, with the dead boy touching his foot and the other man he had shot some ten yards lower down the western slope of the hill. Kneeling over him the stretcher-bearers debated among themselves whether or not it was worth their pains to carry him down to the ambulance behind the company of Devons now advancing in open order towards Cookham's survivors half-a-mile down the valley. On one side of his temples was the familiar small puncture. On the other, exactly opposite, a jagged gash, welling blood. The middle-aged trooper, identifying and reclaiming his carbine and bandolier decided the matter for them, saying, laconically, "Stop yer gab an' take the pore bleeder where he can snuff it in shade. But for 'im that bloody look-out detail woulder made it all the way back an' give their mates the tip. Looks like he got two of 'em before they got 'im." He moved on, walking upright to the spot about two hundred yards on, where the two other members of the outpost lay, one dead, shot from below at long range, the other holed in the leg and biting on a plug of tobacco while a medical orderly applied splint and bandages to the shattered shinbone. So Hugo's gamble had been justified in a sense. There could have been no fifth Boer crouched behind that spur of rock and one more bound would have won him the contest. The stretcher-bearers, grumbling at his weight, worked their way slowly to level ground and the wound was plugged pending closer examination, providing he survived the ride back to the nearest field ambulance tent. Two wounded troopers of the 21st Lancers, salvaged from among the casualties higher up the valley, tried to divert attention from the smart of their own wounds, by having a bet on the issue.

2

Sybil, eldest daughter of the Earl of Uskdale, currently directing her dynamic energy into the administration of the military base hospital at Queenstown, had two public faces. To her intimates, in the enclosed circle in which she had been reared, she was cool, sophisticated, uniquely purposeful and self-contained. To the public at large, particularly those who devoured bulletins from the war fronts, she was rapidly qualifying for a niche in the pantheon of English heroines alongside Grace Darling, Boadicea and Florence Nightingale. Both images were too facile to equate with the truth. To a great extent Sybil Uskdale's life up to this point had been a masquerade for, contrary to all public and private estimates of her character, she was a complex personality and her positivity concealed a canker of self-doubt.

There was logic in this. Rejecting, instinctively, the social strictures of her times and, more especially, of her class, she had not yet succeeded in filling the vacuum that renunciation implied and was still, in a sense, preoccupied with her quest for a credible alternative. Her obsession with nursing was one aspect of this search and her acquisition of Hugo Swann as husband was another, her most daring decision up to that time. Both spiritually and physically she yearned for fulfilment in a changing world where the tide was beginning to run against wealth, privilege and social protocol, and had long since set her face against the purely decorative, submissive role that most well-endowed women accepted with equanimity. But one does not slough off the habits and training of childhood and background at a bound, and there were times, particularly of late, when she questioned not only her ability to fly in the face of convention but her right to pursue the course she had set herself.

Physically, as a vigorous and exceptionally robust woman of thirty, she had coveted Hugo Swann ever since she saw him stretched out in that committee tent at the Putney fête. But so far the marriage had been oddly frustrating, for she soon decided he was really no more than an overgrown boy, disinclined, unable perhaps, to use her as she longed to be used. Awed by what he obstinately regarded as her social superiority his demands, so far, had been faltering and inexperienced, so that she had been forced back on her original resolve, that is to use him as a crutch and fanfare in her drive to develop into what she dimly realised might be a fulfilled woman. He was young and lusty and there was time enough ahead. But then, before she had time to come to grips with this new situation, the war had engulfed them both and she found herself running a hospital overflowing with maimed and desperately sick men, all of them young and full of promise, each calling to her to be nursed through a personal crisis involving stomach wounds, shattered limbs, devastating facial and head wounds and, more pitiful still, the ravages of enteric fever, now accounting for three out of every four patients brought in on the hospital trains. In the strain of facing up to her responsibilities she had almost forgotten Hugo.

The death rate was appalling by any standards. At

some hospitals, they said, men were dying at the rate of fifty a day from this scourge alone and the nursing staff and doctors were hopelessly inadequate to deal with such a situation. They did their best, God knows, and Sybil among them, working stints of up to twenty hours but with the advance to the north the rate of casualty increased and the strain thrown on the administration became intolerable. She was tough but she did not know how long she could survive the demands made upon her and then, a challenge that made every other shrink to insignificance, they wheeled in what was left of Hugo, shot through the head in a skirmish up in the hills and certain, so the surgeons said, to die.

*　　　*　　　*

Her immediate reaction was one of terrible guilt for she reasoned that, but for her, Hugo would be safe at home, jogging round the running track and turning up every now and again with another of those silver trophies. She saw herself, at that moment, as a murderess who had deliberately plotted his death and in her misery she wanted nothing else than to die herself and ahead of him.

But then, when he refused to die, when Udale, the chief surgeon, told her that he had a chance, she rallied, by no means shedding her crushing packload of guilt but finding sufficient resolution to set it aside, a parcel that would have to wait its turn to be opened, and gradually she not only reintegrated herself into the daily rhythm of the hospital but delegated herself Hugo Swann's guide back to the land of the living.

She had him isolated in her own quarters and although this isolation would be seen as an exercise of privilege on her part, she did not care. Hugo was her personal responsibility, the victim of her vanity and if, by sheer force of will, she could restore him to even partial health, nothing was going to be allowed to stand in her way.

These were her attitudes during the initial period, when

Hugo, head swathed in bandages, lay silent in his cot, a hulk with a fingertip grasp on life. Her first reaction was the deliberate postponement of the acknowledgment of guilt. Her second a resolve to atone for the terrible wrong she had done him and when Udale came to her to report the successful conclusion of his third operation she allowed herself to hope, after the surgeon, in response to her persistent badgering, gave it as his opinion that the patient's reason did not seem to have been affected by the clean passage of the bullet.

"How can you be sure of that?" she asked, breathlessly.

"He talked, more or less rationally, under the anaesthetic. For what it's worth that in itself is unusual with a wound of that nature."

"What did he say?"

"Mentioned a Lancer subaltern by name. 'Cookham' it sounded like. That, and a young Boer who pointed a rifle at him."

"Does that alone signify anything?"

"A little. For your sake I took some trouble to find out the names of officers involved in that scrap. A Lieutenant Cookham was the fellow who sent him on that run with the message."

"What about the Boer?"

"That might mean anything or nothing. Some fleeting impression of the battle that stayed with him possibly."

She derived some comfort from this and spruced herself up for her next spell of watching at the bedside, where she combined the office of nurse with that of general administrator. The mirror in her tented quarters showed her a gaunt, hollow-eyed stranger, quite unlike the bustling woman who had presided here before the Stormberg ambush. She even went to the lengths of using papier-poudres on the dark areas under her eyes, and a touch of rouge to her cheeks against the time when they removed his bandages for the first time.

But then Udale insisted on a fourth operation and the night it was performed, again successfully, he piloted her to a secluded corner of the convalescent sector and admitted the true source of his evasiveness during earlier discussions on the case.

"Someone has to tell you, Lady Sybil, and everyone else shirks it. He'll recover all right. Not much need to worry on that score. But he won't see again, not a glimmer."

It was as though a mailed fist had crashed into her abdomen and then the same assailant had grabbed her by the throat and squeezed until tears streamed from her eyes and she had the utmost difficulty in breathing.

"Won't *see*? He's *blind*? Hugo Swann, *blind*?"

He nodded, reaching out to steady her but she shook him off.

"But that's . . . that's monstrous! It can't be so! It can't!"

"You must have considered it."

"Never! Never once! I thought of everything but not that . . . *not that*!"

He said, his eyes on the scorched turf, "The bullet severed the optic nerve. Only vital damage it did. A pure freak. Chance in a million it didn't kill him outright, or leave him a cabbage." He took a silver flask from his pocket and unscrewed the stopper. "Take a swallow of that. Please, I insist!" and she took the flask and gulped down the raw spirit but it did little to steady her. She whispered, presently, "Go back to the wards, Mr. Udale. Tell everybody I'm not to be approached, not for any reason," and surprisingly he went, leaving her on the threshold of a little pergola they had built for sitting-out patients.

She stood there without moving for a long time, only half aware of the medley of background noises of the vast, tented purgatory, the dolorous squeaks of unoiled ambulance axles, the continuous murmur that rose from the huge convalescent marquee, housing men who were short of a limb, and permanently disfigured perhaps but not one, so far as she could recall, deprived for ever of his eyesight and reduced to the helplessness of Samson in the camp of the Philistines. There was a bitter analogy here. Samson Swann, noted not for his strength but his fleetness that seemed to her, indeed to all who knew him, the very essence of his being. Samson made a sacrifice to Dagon, the Philistine God. Not by his enemies, not by the Boer who had fired that freakish shot but by her, Sybil Uskdale, who had coveted him, won him and led him out to make sport for the multitude. Surely no woman since the world began had gratuitously laid upon herself such a mountain of guilt and shame.

And then, without warning, there burst from her a terrible sob that was like a soft explosion between her breasts, yet so violent that she sagged and almost fell, clutching the upright of the pergola porch and groping her way to the seat beyond. She would have given all she possessed, life itself, to be released into tears, but her eyes were dry and her throat, fearfully constricted, once more in the grip of that merciless fist. The thought of self-destruction came to her, warm and welcome as a fur-lined cape in winter, and she conjured with various possibilities – the row of bottles marked 'poison' in the dispensary, a razor at her wrists, a rope about her neck to anticipate the slow strangulation of the mailed fist. She considered them all, clinically and objectively, but neither one nor the other seemed adequate as a means of escape or retribution, and as she rejected them the idea slipped away like a rebuffed beggar and she was left with nothing but a tiny spark of defiance that had never ceased to glow in her from the day she put aside the frivolities and proscriptions of her caste.

She said, acknowledging as much aloud, "It was my doing and I'll finish it for no one else can," and she got up and walked jerkily to her quarters, lifting the tent flap and averting her eyes from the still, mummy-like head on the pillow. She sat down and looked in the mirror again, flinching but forcing herself to study the reflection, a small-boned woman in a starched coif with a blue, scarlet-lined cloak about her shoulders. A woman with good features and light blue eyes ringed by sallow areas below the lids. A wide mouth firmly compressed and drawn down at the corners. The famous Uskdale chin, small and resolutely pointed, jutting slightly out but softened somewhat by the central cleft. Behind her the man on the bed shifted and muttered, then relaxed as his breathing became heavy and regular. She said, again aloud, "I'll tell him and I won't put it off. No sense in holding out hope, in breaking it gently over a period. That's his due and my obligation."

3

She was there when they removed the bandages four days later and watched an orderly scrape away at his bristles, seeing the familiar face emerge from a cloud of lather and marvelling that the scars were so small and insignificant. A pinkish circle on the right temple, puckered and no more than a centimetre across. A zigzag line like a small hedge tear in the left temple, where the bullet had emerged and the stitching remained to be cut. And about this second wound an area of heavy bruising, fading from dark blue to coral where new hair was growing in a ragged sideburn. They left the eyes covered with gauze and cotton wool, and then, as arranged, the doctor shooed everybody out and she waited for Hugo to speak.

He was talking freely then. Two days earlier he had asked them what had happened upon that ridge, whether young Cookham and his survivors were saved, whether the Boers had made good their escape and, at length, how long it would be before they removed all these damned wrappings from his head.

Mr. Udale told him what he knew of the battle. Cookham and his survivors had been rescued. He and Cookham had been recommended for decorations. The main body of the ambush party had slipped away but they had captured the rearguard, thirty-odd marksmen who came down off the ridge under a white flag.

As to his wound, his wife, Lady Sybil, would tell him about that, for right now, Udale said, he had too much on his hands and so, for that matter, had she. "All I can say is you're lucky, Swann. Couple of months and you'll be out of here and sailing for home."

Sybil fed him then, spooning broth into his mouth, crumbling bread between her long, slim fingers and jokingly pushing it between his bearded lips. He said, when she told him they were alone, "Odd, me turning up here so quickly. Seems only a day or so since I said goodbye and went off with the new draft. How long have I been in hospital, Sybil?"

"More than a month," she said, "but we'll talk about that later. Right now you must sleep. You were in very bad shape when you came in, dearest, but Mr. Udale thinks you've done splendidly."

"Where was I hit?"

"In the head. Just once but it was as the surgeon said, you were lucky not to be killed."

He lifted his hand to the bandages and canvassed them from ear to ear, from the crown of his head down to the chin. "My God, it must have come close," he said. "That chap lower down the hill. One of two of 'em, firing from either side, crafty devils. Simply never occurred to me they'd move off the crest." And then glumly, "Sorry about that kid, though."

"What kid, Hugo?"

"The one I had to shoot. Couldn't have been more than fifteen. Stood there bold as brass after I'd got the older one. Who the devil would want to kill a kid that age?"

"Don't think about it. The fault lies with the men who sent him there. Try and sleep."

She could have told him then, she supposed, but it seemed wiser to wait and build up his strength a little, and once they had the bandages off he made tremendous strides, so that she wasn't surprised when he sat up as soon as Udale cleared the tent and said, "When can I see you, Sybil?"

She choked at that and had to summon every scrap of courage to prevent herself breaking down there and then but at least he had given her an opening. She took his hand, lifted it and pressed it to her lips.

"Hugo, dear."

"Yes?"

"I've got something bad to say. Can you take a grip on yourself? Can you hear me out without . . . without shouting me down, trying to get up, making a . . . a fuss?"

His brow contracted. Clearly the statement puzzled him very much. She took a tighter grip on his hand, still covered with the tape they had put over the long bullet crease on the palm. He said, finally, "There's something else? I was hit somewhere else? But you said . . ."

"No. You've just the one wound but that . . . it was as bad as could be. The bullet went in one side and came out the other . . ."

"My face is smashed up?"

"No, dearest. You're as handsome as ever. The most handsome man in the world," and she kissed the freshly shaven face twice, still without releasing the hand.

"What then?"

She braced herself, as for a leap across an impossibly wide chasm.

"Your eyes, Hugo."

She felt him stiffen and at once extended her hold to his shoulders, drawing her chair so close to the bed that she was dragged sideways by his weight. "It was the optic nerve. It's damaged . . . enough to affect your sight."

He tore his hand free and lifted it, passing his fingers over the gauze.

"How badly affected?"

"It's very difficult to say. It might be a long time before we know."

It seemed best to tell a white lie, to leave him a ray of hope. He would need time, years perhaps, to adjust to the truth. Yet even now he did not cry out or give any kind of vocal reaction.

"That doctor. He said I'd be going home."

"You will. We both will."

"But if there's more treatment . . ."

"You'll get treatment in London. The very best there is. Far better than anything they can do for you out here."

"Then I might . . . might see again?"

"It's possible."

"*Possible?* Dear Christ . . . !"

The reaction came at last, a convulsive heave that lifted her clear of the chair.

"*Please*, Hugo! . . . You never know about these things . . . Surgeons nowadays can do amazing things . . . impossible things!"

"Like making a blind man see again?"

"Don't *say* that word . . ."

"Why not? Why not, if it's true? Oh, Christ! Christ help me! . . . Sybil, tell me there's hope . . . real hope. You must know . . . you're in charge here."

Little by little she was getting a grip on herself and it derived from a defiance of the kind she had cultivated and practised all her life. She said, "I'm matron because of whom I am, not because of what I know. I'm not a surgeon and I'm not a doctor. I was only playing at the job until I came out here, and saw what awful things can happen to people. But I know this. We'll go everywhere and we'll see everyone. In London and on the Continent. Maybe there's someone who could give you partial sight . . . I don't know about that yet, and can't even make proper enquiries from here, in this awful country. All I can say is your sight is badly affected and all I can be glad about is that you're alive and I'm here to help and will always be here, right beside you. Will you try and remember that, and never forget it, and think about it all the time, Hugo? Will you do that for your sake and mine? It's terribly important for both of us that you should. For me especially because . . . because I brought you here, I put you in the path of that bullet." Mercifully, at that point she began to cry, the tears flowing silently as she rocked to and fro, a woman racked with unbearable pain. A little of her stress communicated itself to him. Not much, perhaps, but enough to cause him to lift his free hand to her face and touch her eyes with the tips of his fingers. He said, "Don't cry, Sybil. Not now. Not yet. Just . . . just *be* there and talk . . . Say something . . . anything . . ."

"I'll always be there. Anything you need, Hugo, and all the time. Every day and every night, my love."

"Kiss me again."

She turned her head and drew her lips slowly across his cheek and mouth, enlarging the caress into a kiss and lifting his hand to the swell of her breasts under her taut bodice. In the year of their marriage she had never kissed him in that way or known how to, and her body quivered when she sensed the impact it was making on his senses, as if close contact with her flesh raised a barrier against the onrush of the murderous despair bearing down on him like a runaway express. She slipped her hand inside the loose linen gown that covered him and ran it lovingly over his massive shoulders and down the length of his ribs, consciously doing battle with the malign, destructive forces that were intent on destroying him.

"Oh, God, I love you . . . love you . . . I'll care for you . . . make it up to you somehow. *Trust me*, Hugo! Never stop trusting me . . . !"

An orderly appeared at the flap of the tent, glanced inside, hastily drew back and stole away, stepping quietly over the seamed earth of the parched compound.

5

The Fists of Righteous Harmony

TAPSCOTT, THE METHODIST MISSIONARY, BROUGHT them the first hard news, hammering on their bungalow door about an hour after dawn and almost falling over the threshold the moment Rowley drew the bolts. Tapscott, the little man who always reminded her of Peter the Hermit, shorn of his zeal but pinned here, it seemed, by dwindling hope that the Lord would finally take cognisance of his settlement along the Hun Ho River, in the apex of the Lu Hun and Peking-Tientsin railways, where he ministered to a flock of two dozen converts.

It was not, of course, the first news they had had of the campaign against the Foreign Devils, and their contemptible converts, the Secondary Devils. All that spring rumours had been creeping north from the Honan province and west from Shensi and Kamsu, where the Fists of Righteous Harmony, jocularly referred to by the representatives of various sects in the Chihli province as 'The Boxers', had been promoting their hate campaign for more than a year and were now openly threatening to erase every trace of the foreigner from Peking to Hong Kong and the vast hinterland of Mongolia. Their aim, it seemed, was to restore the ancient culture of China and the Manchu dynasty to the omnipotence it had enjoyed before the scattered trading posts were established, and the missionaries arrived with their gospel of a risen Christ and their meddlesome opposition to the rituals of a civilisation that was flourishing hereabouts when the Foreign Devils were living in caves on the other side of the world.

Rowley had showed her one of their propaganda posters, a drawing of a crucified pig transfixed with arrows and a Mandarin presiding over the execution of goatheaded strangers. She had dismissed it, as he had done at the time, as a crude expression of the almost total ignorance that predominated in this land of absurd contrasts. A land where female children were of so little account that many were left to die at birth, and an exconcubine enjoyed absolute power over countless millions of idolators. But the breathless arrival of Tapscott changed all this, converting what had been a crop of rumours into indisputable fact. For Tapscott told of a descent on his settlement by men with red headgear and red ribbons at their wrists, who had butchered two of his converts and forced the rest to act as their labour force, pending an advance, they said, on the capital itself, where every foreigner who refused to leave would be instantly decapitated.

She was not really surprised by Rowley's reaction and realised the futility of reasoning with him. He said, "They mightn't take much account of our spiritual advice, Tapscott, but my experience is they've still got respect for our drugs and surgery. There'll be sickness down river, no doubt. And wounds to be dressed. Turning one's back on the situation will only make it worse for all the outposts strung out along the railway and river line."

"What alternative is there?"

"There's one. I'm going down there to find someone in authority and give him a piece of my mind, before they get too uppish. The legations in Peking are already threatening the Court, I'm told. Sooner or later the Government will have to act against these ridiculous bandits. You'll be safe enough here and you obviously need rest. Wait until I've something to add to your report before we go on to Peking and get an audience with

the British Ambassador there." After which he issued
orders for the saddling up of his riding and pack ponies,
summoned his interpreter and set off while the badly
shaken Tapscott was still soaking in his bath.

They were not in their usual location. When the temperatures began to soar they had moved south-west to
within half-a-day's ride of Machiapu where they rented
a summer bungalow and supervised an outlying post
catering for the coolies working on the new railway
branch to Paotingfu. Some Belgian engineers were camping five miles nearer the present terminus and there was
no danger in his absence for a day or so. He kissed her
gravely and rode away and she did what she could to
counter the chattering rumours among the converts, set
in train by the initial outburst of that fool Tapscott on his
arrival. The heat was building up all the time, even here
away from that stinking slum of a city, and she thought,
'I doubt if he'll want to return north when he comes back
but if he does I'll put my foot down in favour of staying out
here for another month or so. Right here we can at least
keep to surgery hours and that's more than we can do
in the city, where queues are still waiting at sunset . . .
As for Tapscott, well, it's high time he was recalled and a
younger man sent out. He's finished, that's plain to see.
Another six months here will kill him . . .'

She did not mind the comparative isolation, having no
taste for the society of the legations and the company of
missionaries' wives in Peking, with their malicious gossip
and outward piety, their eternal round of race meetings,
amateur theatricals and sewing bees. In a way she half-
sympathised with the unconverted Chinese, who regarded
their presence here as an unwarranted invasion of privacy.
The very rawness and brashness of Western civilisation
was apparent to any thinking person who had spent a
couple of years in China and the striking contrast between
Chinamen and the East African and Papuan savages of
previous stations was so demonstrative that she sometimes
wondered why an intelligent man like Rowland Coles did

not throw in his hand and demand a transfer back to settlements where the natives were children and could at least be relied upon to defer to the white man's right to call the tune. She could only suppose he had more or less withdrawn from all but the medical sphere and found his work here more absorbing and varied than it had been in less settled communities. She read a little from the latest batch of periodicals her mother sent out, took a long siesta, conducted an impromptu surgery at sundown, coping with a dozen or so simple cases, mostly dressings, and wrote a long letter to Joanna ready for collection by the first Belgian railway surveyor who called in at the post. Then, relishing her first lazy day for weeks, she ate supper with the worried Tapscott and retired to bed.

*　　　*　　　*

She was awakened by what sounded like a crash of glass and glancing at her watch in the thin morning light that filtered through slatted blinds and mosquito net, saw that it was coming up to five. The initial crash, half-heard beneath a blanket of sleep, did not worry her much and she dismissed it as a kitchen accident on the part of the cook, but then she heard the wailing voice of Tapscott right outside her door and she jumped out of bed, struggled into bedgown and slippers, and called, sharply, "What *is* it now, Mr. Tapscott? What's broken?" but the only response was a kind of squeak and she threw open the door and saw him standing there in his nightshirt.

He looked more like Peter the Hermit than ever in that get-up and was shaking from head to foot and jabbing his finger in the direction of the compound. She was aware then of a sustained buzz beyond the shuttered door, and, realising that it was early for the staff and converts to be abroad and making so much noise, she went back into her bedroom, held the blind aside and glanced out across the verandah. About twenty Chinese were gathered there in two groups, standing near the compound entrance, but there were strangers among them and she told herself again that Tapscott's nerve must have gone to let himself be scared to that extent by what looked like a quarrel among the staff, for she recognised Li-Yung, their major-domo, among the smaller group and he seemed to be making strenuous efforts to drive the others away from the gate. She said, impatiently, "Li-Yung has caught some-body stealing. Or it's a casualty brought in and he's trying to explain the Doctor is away," and she went out of the front entrance and down the steps to the compound fence.

They made way for her with great haste, scattering in both directions, all save the major-domo who stood rigidly against one of the gate uprights, with a curiously blank expression on his face. She said, "What is it, Li? What did they want?" but he made no reply only pointing across the track to a tethering-pole nailed to two stakes, each about five feet in height. Balanced on top of the further one was an object that she took to be a large round stone to which trailers of grey and russet-coloured moss were attached. She said, "What *is* it, for heaven's sake?", but still he made no reply so she hitched her robe and went out to see for herself. It wasn't a stone. It was a severed head, draped in bloodied hair and whiskers and she stopped short about five yards from the pole, gazing at it with a revulsion that paralysed her senses. Li-Yung shuffled closer to stand immediately behind her. "A horseman brought it, a Kansu warrior. Hai saw him and said he carried a Kansu banner."

She hardly heard him, much less understood what he was saying. She was slowly coming to terms with the frightful certainty that this was Rowland Coles' head and in the few seconds that elapsed between seeing it and identifying it she noted aspects of it that stamped them-selves on her memory like a brand on the flesh. The eyes were half-closed and the mouth open so that the expression was a parody of a man caught in the act of yawning. She marked this and several other aspects; the length of the iron-grey hair with its premature white streak; the thick growth of the beard below the high cheekbones; the fact that one ear was half-severed, as by a sword stroke that had all but missed. And then the wide landscape beyond the tethering pole heaved and spun and the pale sky merged with the brown folds of the plain as she teetered backwards and all but brought Li-Yung to his knees in his effort to prevent her falling flat on her back.

* * *

When she opened her eyes the room seemed to be full of Europeans, some of them in travel-stained white ducks, others in operatic-looking military uniforms and armed to the teeth with an array of swords, daggers, holstered revolvers and bandoliers. Someone, a young civilian, was holding a metal cup to her lips and she sensed the taste of brandy on her tongue. The civilian said, in near perfect English, "We haven't much time, ma'am. We're taking you along to Peking. Can you sit a pony?"

She pushed the cup away and nodded, holding at bay the memory of that grotesquely decorated post, for the sense of extreme urgency that dominated the room conveyed itself to her, sufficiently strongly to enable her to hoist herself out of the chair and stare about her, recognising the civilians as Belgian railway surveyors from the camp nearer Fentai and the armed quartette as foreign soldiers in battle array. The young man who had given her the brandy said, "The legations sent an escort. These men are Cossacks from the Russian Embassy guard. They were enough to get us out as far as here but we daren't waste a moment, ma'am. If you can ride we can move that much faster. If you hadn't regained consciousness I was going to harness up a cart."

She said, tonelessly, "The staff . . . the converts . . ." and he replied, indifferently, "They've gone. We had to threaten them with our revolvers to leave the horses behind," and they hustled her out into the open where Li-Yung and one other Chinaman were holding the bridles of about eight ponies. The head, she noticed, had gone from the haltering post. She became aware, on mounting, that she was still in her nightgown, bedgown and slippers but Li-Yung fastened her mantle about her shoulders and they moved off at a trot, heading north-east into the sun. The civilians rode in a compact body, the Cossacks, carrying lances, rode in formation, one out on either flank, the others fifty paces behind the cavalcade. She had no other awareness of the journey than the painful friction of her calves on the smooth leather of the stirrups.

2

The trauma isolated her for a long, long time, protecting her to some extent from the stupendous happenings around her; from the noise, heat, stench and deadly ennui of the legations' siege so that, although present, and even, marginally, participating now and again, she could not have given a coherent account of what was occurring in that city within a city. And this, to a great extent, was responsible for the rescue of her reason, for she continued to think of Rowley, and that object crowning the post outside the compound, as totally unrelated to one another.

It was not that her memory was blurred in any respect. Indeed, it was sharp and clear, more so than it had been at any time throughout the monotonous months they had shared out here. She accepted the fact that Rowley was dead, that never again would she see his grave, bearded face across the table, or lie beside him under the mosquito net in some benighted corner of the earth, but he might have died in a faraway land among strangers a long time ago, and this meant that the identity of the head had no significance. It was just a head, anybody's head. Something someone had left there because they were tired of lugging it about.

She came to know the precise moment when she returned to full awareness, cognisant of their perilous situation here between the wall of the Forbidden Imperial

City and the Tartar Wall to the south, where the American and German detachments manned the barricades. It was about halfway through the siege then, the day the Imperial troops and their allies, the Boxers, mined the French Legation and blew it sky high, together with some of the garrison. The roar echoed clear across the city, from the Tartar quarter in the north to the Temple of Heaven on the southern rim of the Chinese quarters and probably across the plain beyond. And at once the tocsin in the bell tower began to toll and on its notes she found her identity restored to her, that other Helen Coles, *née* Swann, who had ridden her new safety bicycle down Kentish lanes and laughed and danced and flirted and played endless games of tennis at the old house in the Weald. She watched everybody else run to the assembly point but she did not join them. The sense of release and self-discovery was too urgent for that. It was like watching oneself born. She just stood by the canal that intersected the defences and listened to the crackle of rifle fire coming from the direction of the shattered French Legation and thought: 'I'll live through this. I'll go home. I'll see 'Tryst' again. I'll survive to see Joanna and tell her what having adventures and escaping to the outside world is really like . . .' For she recalled a discussion they had had on this very subject the night she and Joanna conspired to switch beaux.

But at a deeper level than relief was another, altogether alien emotion and it had to do with this land and these people. With their flies and their smiling perfidy, with their teeming, gimcrack cities, boundless plains and brown, sluggish rivers, and she could only identify this as hate, an intensity of hate she had never felt for anyone or for anything in the past. She wanted to punish every last one of them for the misery and bitterness and frustration they had engendered in her and the terrible anger she felt for them, and for the place they lived in, and her hate was so compelling that it could only find release in action of the kind the British Marines, and Cossack Legation guards and the volunteers known as 'The Carving Knife Brigade' were taking at this very moment. She could not leave here without some act that would stamp the seal of her hatred on the country and its people and this would be more than a mere reprisal for Rowley's death. It would be the ultimate expression of all she felt about her time here and after that, purged and purified as it were, she would take passage home and put this part of her life behind her.

Slowly, a little more each day, she became interested in the plight of the beleaguered garrison, learning the geography of the various bastions of eleven nationalities fighting for their lives inside the shrinking perimeter. She knew the perilous handholds the Germans and Americans had upon the Tartar Wall, the battered Fu, where the forlorn Japanese garrison contested every inch of the area east of Customs Street, the half-ruined French Legation and its comic opera Ambassador, Monsieur Pichon, who was forever declaring that survival was a matter of hours and, above all, the central bastion formed by the crowded British Legation, with its bell tower and its hordes of sick, wounded and clamorous refugees. She identified with the rumours too. How soon the relief column from Tientsin would arrive. How long the rations of stewed pony and champagne would hold out. How many more casualties the garrison could afford before the attackers swarmed in to exterminate every man, woman and child assembled. She was aware of every desperate sortie there into the labyrinth of ruined buildings about here, the creeping advance of the Chinese barricades that were slowly enclosing them in a wall of rubble, the high courage of heroes like Captain Halliday, R.M., the poltroonery of absurd figures like Pichon, the French Ambassador.

But to know these things, to stand off and witness them was not enough, and neither was the offer of officious women in sweat-soiled dresses to stitch sandbags made of silk, satin and sackcloth, or tend the crowded hospital ward where men, women and children died every day. This was women's work, of course, but it wasn't *her* work. She had to do something far less passive, far more definitive and there was no prospect of a woman taking her place at the barricades, where she would be most likely to find her chance to assuage the terrible thirst for revenge and atonement. Whenever she went to one or other of the thinly manned posts she was quickly sent out of range by the officer or N.C.O. in charge, warned off like a venturesome child approaching a tree-felling party of woodsmen in the grounds of 'Tryst' and told, roughly but kindly, "Please to stand away, ma'am!" or "Please to go back, ma'am!" but it was through these persistent attempts to get within killing range of the Boxers that she at length acquired sufficient guile to circumvent their prohibitions. But that was towards the end of the siege, when the temperatures were well over the hundreds every day and the last of the ponies was marked for death and the stewpot.

*   *   *

By then, of course, she knew that the Boxers were not, in fact, within anyone's range, for someone told her they had proved utterly useless wielding their clumsy weapons against anyone but unarmed missionaries and terrified converts. The daily attacks were now mounted by Imperial troops, armed with artillery and modern Mausers, and sometimes she caught a brief glimpse of one of them, darting about behind their maze of barricades on the outer perimeter of the Fu, or slipping by under the Tartar Wall. Colourful figures, in blues and scarlets, greens and golds, with their inscrutable banners and whenever this happened the yearning to down at least one of them became so masterful that she could have dashed over the intervening barricades and flown at them single-handed. But then, towards the end of July, her moment arrived, so unexpectedly and in such mundane circumstances, that it had almost gone before she was aware of it.

She had found herself an approved job by then, carrying rations to men enduring long spells of duty at the loopholes, ordeals that lengthened in relation to the daily reduction of effectives manning the defences. It was in the Fu area, where the Japanese were sometimes helped out by some of the more spirited among the horde of Catholic converts, brought into the legations' quarter the day the siege began and within hours of the murder of the German Ambassador. By then the Fu was a scene of almost complete desolation, with buildings levelled and the open spaces where they had stood strewn with rubble concealing, and sometimes half concealing, Chinese soldiers who had died prising the Japanese from one position after another. The defenders had now retreated to a triangular position terminating in an apex pointing towards the north bridge over the canal, some fifty yards beyond the garrison's barricade and here they had built a six-foot wall pierced with loopholes, some of which were shuttered by hand-carved wooden blocks used to preserve the ancient works among the thousands of books housed in the Hanlin Yuan Library, the oldest library in the world someone told her, but now a gutted ruin, like everything else about here. The blocks were set beside the wall, ready for insertion every time a loophole was vacated. There were strict orders to this effect, dating from an occasion early in the siege when besiegers had used one to fire directly into the defences.

Some sort of attack seemed to be in progress at this moment. From the apex of the triangle came the almost continuous stutter of small-arms fire, punctuated every now and again by the boom of Imperialist cannon engaged in a one-sided duel with Betsy, the home-made gun used by the British marines. She had just crossed an open space carrying her pail of stew and was approaching the wall to make a delivery to the sentry standing there when the man, a Catholic convert, quitted his post in response to a shouted command for stretcher-bearers from the embattled sector. He left in such a hurry that he not only forgot to shutter the loophole but left his rifle leaning against the wall. The battle, at this juncture, was about eighty yards to the north but crouching there, close against the barricade, Helen heard no signs of activity beyond the cloud of smoke and brickdust that masked the sector, so she set down the pail of stew and took a quick peep through the loophole as far as the burned-out ruins of Customs Street.

It was then, without the slightest warning, that she saw her opportunity. A thickset Imperialist was inching along the outside of the wall in the direction of the dust-cloud and she judged him to be an officer of some kind for his uniform was exceptionally colourful and instead of a rifle he carried a revolver and a scimitar-type sword with a broad curving blade and two points, one set above the other. She did not hesitate a second. He was no more than five yards away when she first glimpsed him, but, seeing the unshuttered loophole, he half-turned and took two strides towards it. In that moment she grabbed the sentry's rifle and fired at point-blank range.

She had never fired a gun of any kind before but she had often watched her brothers potting pheasants and partridges in the coverts at 'Tryst', so that the act of levelling and aiming was instinctive. The gun went off with what seemed to her a disproportionate roar and the recoil was so fierce that it struck her shoulder like the blow of a club, causing her to stagger back clear of the wall. Even so she had a clear view of the officer who doubled like the blade of a jack-knife, spun round and then, with a kind of grace, toppled backwards over a block of masonry and lay still, his boots angled to the sky.

At first it did not seem possible that she could have killed him so effortlessly and she remained where the recoil had driven her, one hand holding the heavy rifle across her breast, the other slowly massaging her bruised shoulder. She could see nothing of him but his angled boots but his posture convinced her that he was dead. As dead as those other men half-buried under the rubble. As dead as the

English officer she had seen buried by the bell tower the previous evening. As dead as Rowland Coles, whose headless corpse was lying out there on the treeless plain.

The feeling of wonderment passed, replaced by an altogether different emotion that she could only describe as a kind of omnipotence. It was as though, by that single shot, she had emerged from the flesh, bones and spirit of the jaded woman who had stooped to glance through the loophole and reassumed the personality of the eager girl she had been when she married Rowley and went off with him to seek adventure on the far side of the world. All the bitterness, the frustrations, the disappointments of the last few years dropped away, discharged into the body of a middle-aged Chinaman now lying across a block of masonry with his boots pointing to the sky. She had a sense of repossessing herself, much as a proud woman might cross the threshold of a house where everyone waited to do her bidding.

Mechanically, and with no real awareness of what she was doing, she laid aside the rifle, shuttered the loophole, picked up her stew pail and moved along the wall towards the enveloping dust cloud where the defenders were grouped in the apex of the works and very confident, it seemed, of beating off the unco-ordinated attack mounted from the ruins of the Hanlin.

They saw her coming and a sprucely-dressed Oriental, whom she recognised as Colonel Shiba, came towards her and bowed. The gesture, in that time and in that place, made her smile. It was her first smile in months. Her manner, and perhaps her presence there, seemed to please him for he too smiled, revealing about twice as many teeth as a man should have, but he said, taking her pail, "You should not be here, madam. Not when there is firing. Please to withdraw out of range."

She turned back and made her unhurried way along the wall, then over the open ground to the Legation, bathed in a serenity that was balm to the spirit, and was at once reabsorbed in the fretful routine of the kitchens.

Everything that happened during the remainder of the siege was an anticlimax. Hope of succour came and went, fanned by stories of searchlights in the night sky to the south, by reports of distant gunfire, by the coming and going of couriers who seemed to make their way to and from the beleaguered legations with very little trouble. The truce came and then, in mid-August, the storming relief column, headed by the jovial Colonel Gasalee and his polyglot army of British, American, Russians, Japanese, French, Austrians and Italians. Nothing during those climactic days could ruffle her newfound serenity, not even the unconfirmed story from a fugitive that Rowley's body had been found and given Christian burial some ten miles down the river line from the spot where she had been rescued by the Belgian engineers and the Cossacks. Rowley was dead but then, to balance accounts, so was that thickset officer, shot through the loophole. It only remained to begin all over again. Not here, of course, not anywhere where temperatures soared to 110 degrees in the shade and huge, lazy flies swarmed about one's head and plate. Somewhere cool and green. A place where everybody spoke a familiar tongue and servants wore starched caps and aprons. She had no belongings to pack, nothing but a few souvenirs of the siege and the clothes bought with the grant paid out to survivors to enable them to travel down to the coast and await transport home.

They went out in convoy, the women chattering gaily and continuously of the horrors of the siege but although she listened it was in the mood of an indulgent parent settling to the prattle of children. No one among them had killed a man in a split second of time and because she had said nothing of her exploit they thought of her, she supposed, as a brokenhearted widow, one of so many overwhelmed by deep, personal tragedy. Or perhaps not even that. Simply as a drifter who had helped out now and again in the kitchens of the embattled legations.

6

Study in Black

WHENEVER HER MIND TURNED UPON SUCH THINGS
(it was not often, for Henrietta was a very sanguine person)
it struck her that, over the years, the clan had enjoyed more
luck than most. Not so much because they had prospered,
socially and commercially, but because every one of them
enjoyed splendid health and most troubles, she decided
after she reached the sixty mark, stemmed from sickness
and the disabilities that got between one and one's in-
dulgences.

Apart from that one frightful period in '65, when Adam
had lost his leg, 'Tryst' had never been a home of mourning. Unlike most women of her generation she had
succeeded in rearing the nine children she had borne
between 1860 and 1879 without a single procession to the
churchyard. Their illnesses, if you could call them that,
were trivial and transient and their luck held out in other
ways. Six of them were comfortably settled now and each,
in his or her own way, had found a partner that could, at a
pinch, be reckoned 'suitable'. Not, of course, a unique
being like Adam but someone who adapted to their several
idiosyncrasies and that, she supposed, was rare when you
thought in terms of half-dozens.

Stella had made that unfortunate first marriage, but
luck (plus her mother's despatch and sagacity) had put
that right in no time. Alex had survived any number of
bloody fields without so much as a grazed knee, whereas

275

the younger ones, although getting into innumerable scrapes, all seemed to possess a degree of resilience that equipped them to evade the full consequences of wrong-headed decisions and the occasional folly. Even Joanna, who had played fast and loose with young Jack-o'-Lantern Coles, and got herself with child, had succeeded in disguising a crass piece of idiocy as a romantic adventure. Alone among them Henrietta was privy to the fact that Joanna's eldest child, now eleven, had 'come across the fields' as they used to say. Helen's future worried her a little. It couldn't be good for health or child-bearing to go trapesing round the world in the wake of a medical missionary but it was her life and she had chosen it and if, by now, she wished to change it, then she could use her native wit to persuade that solemn stick Rowland to abandon such unrewarding work, come home and buy a lucrative practice in Kent, for the Coles were known to have made a fortune peddling pills and Rowland, eldest of the family, was likely to be rich when his father died.

As for Giles, he seemed contented enough these days, despite his eccentric approach to a war that had engulfed two of his brothers, and that flighty wife of his had at last succeeded in presenting him with a son, something Henrietta had thought unlikely after thirteen years of childless marriage. George and Edward were both as obsessed with the business as Adam had been until recently, and Margaret, the family postscript, seemed happy enough mooning about the fields and coppices with her clutter of paints and canvases.

There remained Hugo, the family clown, but he too had had an astonishing run of luck so far, first being granted licence to pursue athletics as a career (only a father as tolerant as Adam would have countenanced that!), then falling into the lap of that extraordinary woman who made a positive fetish of a boy whom Adam had often dismissed as 'fifteen stone of musclebound bacon'.

All in all an unbroken run of luck, stretching over a period of more than thirty years and she saw no reason to suppose it would not continue, at least for as long as she retained her faculties and could keep a sharp lookout for squalls. For in a way Henrietta took upon herself most of the credit for this galaxy of achievement. After all, it was she who had borne the brunt of their upbringing, for Adam had always been immersed in that other family of his — the Swann network of depots and establishments that sometimes seemed to her to haul half the merchandise of the Empire from one point to another. If the children had turned out well then they had her rather than him to thank for it. And after her, she supposed, that dear, dogged Phoebe Fraser, who had served them so selflessly since Stella and Alex were toddlers.

As the seasons passed Henrietta came to assume that the Swanns were immune from the disasters and tragedies of less fortunate families and more and more, as she grew older and more prescient, she half-identified with that other matriarch at Windsor, whose even larger brood enjoyed the same ascendancy. It was therefore with a sense of appalling shock that she read the express letter from Alex, postmarked Durban, telling that Hugo, God help the boy, had been shot through the head in a Boer ambush, and although well on the road to recovery, was temporarily blinded. Alex stressed the word 'temporarily', pointing out that Hugo was scheduled for a long and complicated course of treatment on his return home but he added, as a kind of buffer against despair, that he was likely to lose the sight of one eye and have limited vision in the other.

For days after she had received this frightful news, Henrietta was stunned. Nothing Adam could say helped her adjust to it for Hugo, admittedly the slowest witted of the family, had been its prime physical product. Just as she took pride in Alex's invulnerability, George's cleverness, Giles' erudition and the girls' undeniable charms, so she basked in Hugo's rare beauty, seeing him as a reincarnation of a Greek demigod, described in

Mr. Kingsley's book, *The Heroes*. She simply could not picture Hugo as a big, helpless baby, led about by others and sitting mute while somebody cut up his meat or found his trousers. He had always possessed such an abundance of effortless grace and of all the boys he seemed the one less equipped to adapt to a terrible handicap of that kind. But as the shock wave receded somewhat her anger mounted against that bustling, rather overpowering woman who had landed him into such a mess. Adam had to take a stern line with her, pointing out that Hugo was a grown man and could have made his own decision about volunteering for active service. He was also harsh enough to rap her knuckles about her own contribution, saying sharply for him, "Listen here, Hetty. I won't have that! It's not the slightest use taking that line and throwing your dignity to the winds. I seem to recall you were among a majority here who clamoured for war with Kruger and his burghers. I daresay a good many of them have been shot through the head and lost their farms into the bargain. It's a terrible thing for a boy to face a handicap of that kind, and I'm in a better position to appreciate that than most, having stumped through half a lifetime with a tin leg on account of a fool who couldn't read a railway time-table. But upbraiding Sybil Uskdale and the Boers won't help any of us, least of all you. If people go to war some of them come out of it in worse shape than they went in and at least the boy's alive. Do you know how many men have died from enteric fever out there on that veldt?"

"I'm not the least bit concerned with them," she snapped, "for they aren't my sons."

"They're somebody's sons and they lost their lives in what I think a damned poor cause. Sooner or later everyone will come round to that view. Even Hugo."

"Is that going to help him?"

"No, but neither is adding to that wretched woman's tragedy by letting her know you lay the blame at her door. She's all he's got now for he'll never run again and if I'm not mistaken he'll realise that."

"I never thought to hear you talk so cold-bloodedly about your own flesh and blood!" she wailed.

"I'm not cold-blooded!" he growled. "I'm simply trying to make the best of what can't be altered. She'll make sure he gets the best treatment in the world and she's in a better position to do it than we are!"

It provoked one of their rare, smouldering quarrels that persisted right into early July, when a wire came informing them that a shipload of wounded was arriving at Southampton and they could go along the coast and meet Hugo and Sybil on disembarkation. There was no question of bringing him home. He was scheduled to go straight into a private clinic, supervised by Sir Oscar Firbright, the famous eye specialist, there to undergo further surgery for several months.

*　　　*　　　*

It was on the quay, as the wounded were being carried ashore into the waiting hospital trains, that she first questioned her attitude and began to reflect upon Adam's forthright advice. The change was not effected by the sight of so much suffering but by her first glimpse of Sybil during the brief interval before the hospital train pulled out.

The change in her was shattering. She seemed to Henrietta no more than a ghost of the brilliant creature who had bounced up the steps of 'Tryst' seven months ago, dragging Hugo in her wake like a barge towed by a splendidly equipped steamer. Her cold, classical beauty was all but gone. Traces of its sparkle lingered in the hard blue eyes but the cheeks were pitifully hollow, the full, sensual mouth dragged down at the corners, and the famous Uskdale bloom had been drained from her cheeks by the South African sun, the reality of war, or both. Her figure, Henrietta recalled, had been slight but very trim at that spectacular wedding at St. Margaret's. Now it seemed angular and graceless, whereas her voice, hitherto

slightly hectoring, had dwindled to a murmur little
above a whisper as she said, brushing Henrietta's cheek,
"You don't have to berate me, Mama. I've been doing
that for myself all these weeks. But the only thing that
matters now is to get him well and in a frame of mind
when he'll put his trust in his surgeons and doctors.
That's *my* responsibility mainly but you can help if you
will. Remind him he's so much to live for, even if it
takes him a year to adjust to not seeing."

"Won't he . . . isn't he likely to see at all?" Henrietta
had stammered. "I mean . . . isn't recovery a possibility?"

"No, it isn't," Sybil said, staring down at her elegant
boots. "There's no point in lying to you or to myself any
longer. The best we can hope for is a glimmer of sight
in his right eye and I'll thank God to the end of my life
if we can achieve even that. I have to go now. I'm
travelling on with the unit. It was kind of you both to
come all this way for a few minutes."

She boarded the train then, without a backward
glance and Henrietta, eyes blurred with tears, accompanied Adam across the platform to where the civilian
boat-train to London awaited them in a siding. He said,
with something between a sigh and a groan, "Well, there's
the war everybody wanted," but then, in a milder tone,
"He's in good hands, Hetty. Something about that
woman I like, despite everything. Spunk, maybe."

They had arranged to stay at the Norfolk overnight
before returning home and as the cab dropped them off
at the portals her eye caught a newspaper placard reading
'*Peking: Massacre Feared*', and her heavy heart gave a great
leap and then seemed to subside well below the navel for
she remembered Joanna writing to her only last week
saying that Helen had written to her in May, telling her
that she was based on Peking but sometimes accompanied Rowley to help out at out-lying surgeries. She
caught Adam's arm as he was paying off the cabbie and
said, "Look at that! It can't be that Helen and Rowland

are involved . . ." and he said, gruffly, "Come inside and take tea. I can tell you more than you're likely to learn from the *Daily Mail*," and she went into the tea-room where he ordered tea and buttered scones with an air of gravity that warned her he must have been aware of Helen's danger for some time but had postponed telling her, probably on account of Hugo. She said, "Tell me, Adam. I've a right to know."

"Nobody knows anything for a fact. It's all guess-work so far. That, and the kind of sensation papers thrive on. You knew there had been unrest in North China, didn't you?"

"No, I haven't even glanced at a paper since we heard about Hugo. Every page was full of war news and it only made me more miserable than ever."

"Well, there's been an uprising of some kind. A secret society they call the Boxers has been working up a hate campaign against the foreigners, especially the missionaries. They've even killed one or two, but not in her province, somewhere a long way to the north and west."

"But it actually mentioned Peking on that poster."

"There's an unconfirmed report from Hong Kong about the foreign community there. A German diplomat has been killed and our Government has asked their Government to protect British nationals."

"Can't we find out anything specific about her? I don't think I could stand another shock of that kind."

He took her hand and pressed it. "Leave it to me. I'll find out somehow. I've got a good agent in Hong Kong and I'd believe anything he wired me but I can't do it tonight. I'll get the wheels moving first thing in the morning. I know roughly where that chap Coles operates and will put some feelers out." He paused, still holding her hand and regarding her with the vaguest suspicion of a twinkle. "Poor old Hetty, you are having a time of it! Haven't seen you this way for long enough. As a matter of fact, I can't remember how long."

"I can," she said, sombrely, "since the time of that rail crash all of thirty-five years ago."

"Well," he said, "we all get our turn if we hang around long enough." And then, "See here, we're not doing Hugo or Helen any good by moping. How would you like to go to a music hall and don't pretend it isn't 'decent'. It's the best way I know of holding trouble at bay for a couple of hours."

She said, unexpectedly, "I'll do anything to take my mind off Hugo. What time do they start? Is it after or before dinner?"

"Both," he said, grinning, "but I'd best take you to the first house. The second gets a bit rowdy."

She thought: 'That's the really comforting thing about him. He *knows* things. About what's going on in Peking and what time the curtains at music-halls go up. He knows me too, enough to give me that facesaver about the propriety of visiting a music-hall on a night like this . . .', and she finished her tea and went up to their room for a rest and a wash.

He knew the entertainment world too, it proved, for he chose the 'Star' where the bill included the great illusionist Devant and a galaxy of eccentric comedians and daring acrobats, the latter all foreigners, she noted, working in family groups. For two hours she all but forgot her misery watching pyramids of men, women and children in skin-tight costumes pile themselves almost as high as the proscenium arch, girls presumably sawn in half skip nimbly from gaudily painted closets shouting 'Hoi!' as they flashed wide, toothy smiles at the audience, short fat men in baggy trousers screaming abuse at tall thin men in evening dress, soubrettes who specialised in songs that would never have been tolerated twenty years ago but seemed now to delight the patrons and jugglers who whirled clubs so rapidly that it made one dizzy to watch. He said, as they settled into a hansom and made their way back to supper, "Well, Hetty?" and she kissed him impulsively on the cheek and then, quite irrationally, began to cry. Just a little; just enough to require a furtive dab or two between lamp-standards as they bowled down Fleet Street, past the Law Courts and into the Strand. He didn't notice. Or pretended he didn't.

2

As she had half-expected there was worse to come.

She never recalled a period as sustained and depressing as this, for the crisis in 1865, when they came to her for permission to amputate his left leg, had lasted no more than a few weeks. After that, with him absent and on the road to recovery, she was able to adjust, losing herself in his concerns at the yard and watching the calendar against his return.

This crisis needed more stamina and patience than she possessed. Wretchedness and uncertainty stretched into months, right through the remainder of the summer, the autumn and into the new year, when a mantle of sadness settled over the whole nation with the death of the Queen at Osborne.

It was September before they were called upon to face the fact that Hugo would never see again, that further surgery and visits to Continental doctors were pointless but, mercifully perhaps, the sharp edges of Hugo's tragedy were blurred by the long spell of agonised waiting for news of Helen and Rowley, and finally the shattering announcement that Rowley had been murdered by those Chinese fiends and that Helen had survived the horrors of a seven-week siege.

There was relief, to be sure, in the news that she was alive and was on her way home but Henrietta, entirely without experience of this kind of situation, was not in the least sure what she would do with the girl when she arrived. She was sad then that Helen had no children to take her mind off the tragedy and very relieved when Joanna wrote from Dublin saying that, as soon as her sister had rested, she would be glad to welcome her for an indefinite stay. The two had always been very close and Joanna's jolly household would surely have a more beneficial effect on a young widow than a sojourn at 'Tryst' just now, with everyone so cast down about Hugo. Adam approved the plan at once, saying, "Best thing in the world for her. There's only young Margaret here and the age gap is too wide. We're in no fettle to cheer her up, are we?" And then, advertising his lifelong detachment from the brood once again, "How old is she now? I never can remember the order they came in."

"She's thirty. Just a year younger than Hugo."

"Ah," he said, vaguely, "then I daresay she'll marry again soon enough."

"I really don't know how you can say such things," Henrietta protested. "For heaven's sake don't mention such a thing in her presence."

"I've a damned sight more sense than that," he said, smiling, "but it's the best thing she could do for all that. No sense in making a fetish of a dead husband like Queen Vic. Oh, people are sympathetic for a year or so but after that they go out of their way to avoid you. Just remember that when I pop off, Hetty."

He meant it jocularly enough, she supposed, but she did wish he would save his gallows humour for George and his male cronies. The prospect of widowhood, even at an advanced age, terrified her, notwithstanding a tribe of children and grand-children, and she could never forget he was her senior by twelve years. She said, "I daresay you'll outlive me and I hope to goodness you do," and went about her business, getting Helen's old room ready in the west wing beyond the gallery and remembering, as she entered it, how gay and hoydenish those girls had seemed growing up here in the days when their safety bicycles were novelties.

She managed at last to put Rowland Coles and his horrid death out of mind. She could always do that with people who were not her flesh and blood and when Helen did arrive, in the last golden days of October, she was agreeably surprised to discover that the girl, outwardly at least, did not appear to be devastated by her frightful experiences. She looked sallow and peaky to be sure but who wouldn't, after having one's husband murdered and afterwards enduring a seven-week bombardment in a fortress with temperatures into the hundreds, horsemeat for rations and the prospect of butchery held at bay by a few barricades and one's own fortitude?

Adam helped more than he realised, questioning her closely about the siege as soon as he realised she didn't mind discussing it, and as more and more horrific details emerged Henrietta began to feel a glow of pride in her daughter's hardihood. She was sure she could never have behaved so gallantly and upheld the honour of the flag in that way, not even if Adam had been by her side. She was shocked, however, to learn that Helen had not only killed a man but gloried in the fact.

"You mean you . . . you *know* you killed him? You weren't just . . . well, there, with a gun in your hand?"

"I killed him, sure enough," Helen said blandly, "and if you can bring yourself to believe it, killing him did me a great deal of good. I would have killed a few more if they had given me half a chance."

"Well, I can understand you feeling bitter and . . . well, full of feelings of revenge," Henrietta said, turning away from her daughter's hard, rather brittle smile, "but I mean . . . well . . . it couldn't have been a *pleasant* experience. Not even in the circumstances. And I really don't understand how it could make you feel any better about poor Rowland."

"Well, it did," Helen reaffirmed, "but as to expecting you to understand how, I don't think I could do that, Mamma. You would have to have lived in China and been there and listened to those savages howling for blood. Maybe Papa would understand, having served in the Mutiny and buried those women and children slaughtered at Cawnpore."

Adam understood and the curious change in the girl

interested him, bringing her a little closer somehow. He said, when Henrietta had excused herself on some domestic pretext, "Do you mind if I add something to that? Keep up the attack, girl. Don't ever let self-pity creep up on you. That's no road out of the woods, believe me. Came close to letting go myself when I had to learn to walk again at dam' near forty but I held on somehow. Matter of professional interest. What make was that rifle you used to swat the Chinaman?"

"A Martini-Henry," she said. "I found that out later."

"It had a devilish kick, didn't it?"

"It left a bruise on my shoulder as big as an orange."

"And popping that fellow didn't get into the official reports?"

"No. I never told a soul about it until now."

"That was wise," he said, thoughtfully, "for you're full young and can begin again. Go over to Ireland. Take it easy and look around. Ease yourself back into the mainstream as I did. It can happen. I'm proof of it. How are you off for cash?"

"I've still got your two hundred a year and I'll get a pension they tell me. Plus compensation for all we lost at the bungalow but it will take time to come through I suppose."

"I'll double the allowance and see that it's paid through our Dublin branch."

"That's very generous, Papa."

"Is it? I wouldn't say it was. Not for a girl who can tote a Martini-Henry and live seven weeks on horsemeat and champagne."

He kissed her absentmindedly and went out into the autumn sunshine and down the drive to his observation mound behind The Hermitage, pondering with the slow, massive strength of an ancestral tug. Swanns had been in the killing business for centuries and here it was, cropping out in a girl who was the daughter of a tradesman and reared in what most people would regard as genteel circumstances.

* * *

Lady Sybil brought Hugo on his first visit shortly after Helen had left and Adam read them all a brief lecture the day they were due to arrive.

"Don't treat that boy as a helpless invalid," he warned. "Nothing more irritating when you're crocked than people fuming and fussing about you, handing you this and that and telling you to watch out. God knows, you don't need hourly reminders of a handicap of that kind. Leave all the gentling to his wife. She's a professional and knows her business if I'm any judge."

She did, too, as he was very quick to note. She didn't let the boy out of her sight but her ministrations were wonderfully unobtrusive so that he gained the impression she was working round the clock to accustom him to routines that would build up his confidence. As to whether she was making real progress it was difficult to say. Hugo was very subdued and sat about mostly, like a big, ageing collie, too old and tired to frolic. Who could tell what the boy was thinking when he felt the sun on his face or the wind in his hair?

Adam had a private word with Sybil about his future and, as he had expected, she had specific plans for him. "He's going to take a course as a masseur at one of the big military hospitals," she said. "It'll keep him in trim and give him something to think about, as well as contacts with other handicapped men of his kind and age. I'm going to make sure he rides, too, on a leading rein, and I've engaged a retired sergeant-major as his personal batman. Truscott, he's called, formerly of the Duke of Cornwall's Light Infantry. I chose him because he was once a well-known amateur walker. He has as many trophies as Hugo I wouldn't wonder. He'll be reporting here tomorrow if that's agreeable to you, Mr. Swann."

"Splendid idea," he said, his approval of her increasing with each new encounter. "The more mobile he is the easier he'll adjust and after all these months in hospital he needs all the exercise he can get."

Truscott was an instant success, a sunburned man about

fifty with legs like saplings and a jerky way of carrying himself, as though he was forever on the point of breaking into a trot. He had the traditional parade-ground bark, even when he was trying to please and his yell of 'Sah!' every time Hugo summoned him so intrigued the grandchildren that they at once incorporated him into their games. Indeed, within days of Truscott's arrival the game of 'Sah!' took over from hide and seek and prisoner's base and soon Hugo's batman was a firm family favourite.

Adam watched them set off one morning on their first tramp over the plateau that enclosed 'Tryst' from the east and noted with relief that sightlessness had done nothing to shorten the effortless stride that had carried Hugo to victory over so many miles of track and steeplechase course. He thought, seeing the pair move into the screen of elms that topped the spur, 'He'll do, so long as that woman sticks to him . . .' and went into his study to report on both Helen and Hugo in a long and explicit letter to Giles. Of all his children Giles alone shared his complete confidence.

3

On January 22nd the news was broadcast from Osborne to the remotest corners of the world, tapped out on countless telegraph keys, spoken over thickening clusters of wires that were beginning to enclose every sizeable city of the land, passed from mouth to mouth across the island that had once been marked as 'Tom Tiddler's Ground' on the Swann waggon maps, then over the Solent to the mainland, then out across the shires to the coasts of Donegal, Sutherland and the Empire beyond the seas. The impossible had happened. Victoria had slipped away on a grey winter's day and a curtain of black fell on an era.

It was as though nobody had ever died before. As though, to yield up the spirit, and be trundled away in a coffin, was a privilege extended to the very few, a singular dispensation by Providence as a reward for spectacular services on earth.

The face of the nation changed overnight. Every public building was hung with circular wreaths that looked like so many black lifebelts and many were shrouded in yards of whispering crêpe. Black crêpe was at a premium. Top-hatted city gents tied it about their arms, cabbies tipped their whips with crêpe bows and every woman who valued her neighbour's regard (and quite a few who did not) went into full mourning, including the ultra-loyal among the London prostitutes who continued, however, to ply a brisk trade among the thousands of provincials who travelled up to town for the occasion.

Adam, secretly amused, was among them, reminding himself that he had no business witnessing the event for he had been born two reigns ago and could recall wearing crêpe round his straw hat for Silly Billy, the Queen's uncle.

The ceremonial of the four tribes had always interested him, however, and he sauntered about glancing at solemn faces and hoping to catch one of them off-guard. He was unsuccessful. On a 'bus ride from London Bridge to Kensington he did not record so much as a single smile and even the Thameside costers looked as if they were losing money on every hot potato they sold in response to their dolorous cry of "Warm yer 'ands an' warm yer belly for 'apen'y!"

When he read that the royal corpse was being conveyed by state procession to Paddington for its final journey to Windsor he took a fancy to travel up again and avail himself of an old customer's offer to watch its departure from a hotel window overlooking the station approach. Henrietta declined to accompany him and not, as she claimed, on account of the cold, foggy weather. Her dismay was genuine, more genuine than even he realised, for more and more of late she had begun to identify with Victoria and there seemed no point in reminding oneself of one's mortality at this chilly season of the year. So he went alone, staying overnight at the Norfolk and booking an early cab to his vantage point where his host had a comfortable sitting-room with balcony and a supply of hot toddy to keep out the cold.

It moved him more than he would have believed, all those cloaked potentates marching behind the gun-carriage with its pall topped by the Imperial crown; the silent ranks of infantry standing with bowed heads and reversed arms between the cortège and dense phalanxes of Cockneys, Londoners without a speck of colour about them save the odd splash of undertaker's mauve. He had never liked the woman much (though he had always entertained respect for her dead husband), but he did not begrudge her her eight, cream-coloured horses. One had to admit she had stayed the course better than most monarchs and had even succeeded in pulling herself together somewhat after the first twenty-five years of widowhood.

He had plenty of time, as the cavalcade crawled past, to let his mind range freely back and forth across the decades, as it often did on occasions of this kind. Odd, irrelevant thoughts occurred to him, tiny tributaries of the national stream of history personally explored by him over many years. He remembered when the army had discarded traditional headgear in favour of the German pickelhaube, a curious concession to the widely accepted belief among military men that the Prussian army's performance against the French in 1870 entitled them to set military fashions, as though the design of a man's helmet determined his prowess in the field. He found it difficult to see the heavy, tired-looking man riding behind the bier as the future King, remembering, with an inward chuckle, all the fuss there had been about Bertie's frolics with the girls and at the gaming tables, that had earned him his mother's disapproval since he was eighteen or thereabouts and breaking out from the frigid mould she and Albert had cast for him. And on the King's immediate right he had more serious doubts about Vicky's unpredictable grandson, the German Emperor, wondering if he was qualified to run a village skittles team, much less a thrustful nation of eighty millions. He seemed on his very best behaviour, however, reining back as they approached the station entrance in order to allow Uncle Edward to exercise his priority rights. He could see nothing of the new Queen and princesses, in their closed carriage pulled by a mere four horses, so that his mind was free to conjure with the secret thoughts of the spectators, wondering how genuine was their involvement in this splendid panoply of death. Reasonably so, he would imagine, but not for the obvious reasons. Very few of them down there could recall any royal symbol other than the little old woman on that gun-carriage, now on her way to lie beside her beloved Albert so that they would see this, he supposed, as a break in the continuity of their lives. That would disturb many of them. The English did not like their continuity broken, fearing changes in the national pattern as much as the French and Italians welcomed them. All their lives she had been there, as unchangeable as a feature of English topography, the cliffs of Dover or the curves of the Thames. Ever since childhood her double-chinned silhouette had crystallised their awareness of national prejudices and preferences, and whereas her withdrawal, in the 'sixties and 'seventies, had made her unpopular, the two Jubilees had restored her to her place at the pinnacle of the royal pyramid. So that it followed they were watching not *her* exactly but their own past, a past transforming itself into a future, and that meant un-certainty for most. Especially those no longer fortified by the arrogance of youth.

*　　　*　　　*

The kings, princes and flunkeys moved on and he sipped a whisky, awaiting dispersal and a chance to make his way back to Charing Cross and home. His old friend Lord Roberts repassed below, his horse (black like every-thing else today) led by a groom, along with the horse

the King had been riding, and there came to him again a
brief vision of the crossroads he and Roberts had occupied
immediately after the Sepoy Mutiny, when Roberts had
opted for glory while he had seen a military career for
what it was – years of boredom and heartache for all but
the mystics like Roberts. Instead he had devoted himself
to what? To money-making or something more exalted?
What was it exactly? Surrender to a compulsion that had
nagged him since boyhood? To make a mark, to fulfil
his own extravagant fancies in competition with other
egotists? He didn't know. He never had known with
certainty. Yet he was sure of one thing. He didn't regret
his choice and given his youth he would do it again but
sooner, much sooner. The real point was, where did one
go from here, if anywhere? He was seventy-three and
unlikely to see another royal funeral, unless Edward VII,
fourteen years his junior, gorged and whored himself to
death. The long years of striving were behind him and in
the time left he could never be more than a spectator.
A keenly interested one, however, not only of his own
concerns but of the ultimate destiny of his race and he
could make no more than a guess or two at that. They
had passed their apogee, he supposed, a year or two back,
when they involved themselves in this ridiculous war with
a bunch of farmers but the country was still sound enough,
politically and financially, so long as it stopped short of
tearing itself in two unequal halves, the Little Englanders
on one side, the Imperialists on the other. And that
mightn't matter in the end. It was hard to believe that
anything cataclysmic would result from this temporary
schism for the people. Even those like Giles and his radicals howling for social reforms, were conservative at
heart, trafficking mostly in compromise. It seemed more
likely that the real challenge would come from outside.
Not from the Germans as he had once thought – they
wouldn't get far with that ass of a Kaiser raising dust
everywhere he went. More probably from France that
George said was leading the field in the new technologies,

or from that vigorous offshoot of the British across the Atlantic that had its own way to make in the world. If he lived as long as Vicky he might begin to discern some of the answers. Whatever they were they would be interesting . . . interesting . . .

The penetrating cold tormented the stump of his leg and he thought longingly of his own fireside and Henrietta's eager questions about the funeral procession. He said his goodbyes, despatched an urchin for a cab with the promise of a florin if he got one and went downstairs on to the porch. The crowds were rapidly dispersing, already forgetting the bier and its contents in search of something to keep out the cold. The boy arrived with a growler and he climbed in, sitting back in the musty interior saturated with spectacle and turning his thoughts towards home.

PART THREE

Towards the Summit

I

Headstart

THE OLD HANDS ABOUT THE YARD — AND THERE
were still some who remembered Adam Swann's heyday —
exchanged wry jokes when it got about that the New
Broom had retreated to the tower, the only section of the
Thameside premises to emerge more or less intact from
the fire.

It struck them as ironic that a man who preached the
heresy that the horse was obsolete, and was threatening
to supersede them by the spawn of that snorting juddering
contraption he had driven down from Manchester three
years ago, should choose a draughty, fourteenth-century
belfry, approached by a narrow, twisting stair as the hub
of his empire. In deliberate preference, moreover, to the
new red-brick office block they had built fifty yards short
of the Tooley Street exit.

It was out of character somehow. A man who had, as
it were, forced upon them every kind of innovation in the
last decade, was not a likely candidate for withdrawal to
a lumber room lit by oil lamps and not even served by a
telephone but equipped, instead, with the speaking tube
apparatus Adam had employed all the years he had
worked up here. In a way they saw it as a recantation, an
admission that the new ways were, after all, inferior to the
old and when he remained up there fourteen months,
making but fleeting visits to ground level, they told one
another that he had mended his ways and not before time.

They would have been outraged had they realised that what George was doing was to use his father's eyrie as a kind of Guy Fawkes' cellar, to hatch a plot aimed at erasing every familiar aspect of the yard and setting in motion shock waves that would be felt in every corner of the network beyond. Neither did they suspect that the tidal wave that followed would wash every last one of them into premature retirement, making way for newcomers who would talk a language largely unintelligible to them, who would think in terms of horse-*power* rather than horses and whose avowed purpose would be to reduce haulage schedules, routes and laden capacity to a series of formulae that made no kind of sense to them.

For all that, they were not entirely wrong about him. There was about his withdrawal a hint of the Adam of the 'sixties and 'seventies, a man who found it essential to commune with himself in solitude before he could focus his mind on the immensity of his task and solve a thousand closely interrelated hypothetical conundrums. For what George was doing in the fourteen months that succeeded the submission of his engineer's report that a fleet of motor-vehicles was costed down to the last detail, was to redesign the national arena in which the fleet would operate. Such a task, far more formidable than any his father had tackled in his up-and-coming days, needed not merely physical stamina but a very high degree of concentration. To say nothing of access to the hundreds of route maps and trade summaries built up over the forty-two years Swann-on-Wheels had been in operation.

No one else could have done it. No one else could have attempted it and there was a reason for this. George Swann, New Broom Extraordinary, was the firm's only real link between past, present and future. At least, the future as he saw it.

It was, he came to decide, a matter of gradients. Everything in his flirtation with power-driven vehicles over the past twenty years suggested that gradients were the key

to every imponderable. Perhaps others would see it
differently, would give priority to factors like wear and
tear of rolling stock, centres of population, concentrations
of industry, quality of road surfaces and other come-day-
go-day aspects of the hauling trade. But George's experience equipped him to survey each of these factors
separately and make a deliberate choice as to which of
them demanded maximum attention. It did not take him
long, after studying Scottie Quirt's report, to select
gradients as the keystone of the exercise. Everything else
was relative. Everything hinged upon a single, deter-
minable axiom, viz: 'Can a Swann-Maxie waggon haul a
given weight from point A to B if a gradient, in excess of
a given limit, interposes between point of departure and
point of arrival?' If it could, well and good. If it could
not one might as well consign the whole complex of
dreams to the wastepaper basket and indent for fifty
thousand pounds' worth of younger horseflesh and new
waggons, leaving the advancement of power-driven
vehicles to the wealthy amateur with time on his hands
and a bottomless pocket.

It looked at first as if the answer to this equation was
negative. Swann's main routes, according to copies of
Adam's maps (the originals still occupied pride of place
in The Hermitage museum, at 'Tryst') established that a
laden waggon, with flexible traction as regards the number of horses employed per haul, could be dragged over
almost any terrain where business was to be found. All
the initiator was required to do was to increase teams or
change the nature of the waggon in relation to the load
and the natural obstacles in question. Bearing this in
mind the entire country was wide open and Adam Swann
had proved as much forty years ago. Swann's frigates
regularly crossed the Pennine Ridge and used unsurfaced
cart-tracks in the remotest areas of Wales and the Westcountry. Its pinnacles, with one nimble Cleveland Bay
between the shafts, threaded the most congested centres
of the nation's cities, usually without loss of routeing time,

for there was always a maze of side streets available. Even Swann's men-o'-war and Goliaths, eight-, six-, and four-horse vehicles, could, given a leisurely time schedule and diligent routeing, haul enormous loads clear across country, from North Sea coast to Cardigan Bay. But Scottie Quirt's report confirmed that one could not hope for such flexibility if one substituted power-driven vehicles for the drag-horse. Britain was not a level plain, served by modern bridges. There were always, God curse them, gradients, some a mere one in ten but often as steep as one in five, or even four, that could defeat, with a sneer-scream of grit or a flurry of liquid mud, the maximum thrust of a Swann-Maxie engine.

It had not needed his experiences on the trial run south to teach him this, although those experiences highlighted the two-edged sword suspended over the neck of the too-hasty innovator. Two-edged because it involved not only ascents but descents. Whereas it was a matter of routine to apply drag-shoes at the summit of a hill before tackling a sharp descent with a waggon, one now had to rely upon braking power and he foresaw that it might be years before some bright spark evolved a foolproof method of checking a fully-laden waggon on a one-in-four hill. One could not always rely on the presence of an amiable and inventive amateur, awaiting one's thundering descent into a ford, as had occurred early in the trial trip. Neither could one bank on the presence of an evangelist knife-grinder to straighten things out, as had occurred on his second day's run into London. He saw now, looking back, that he had enjoyed the devil's own luck on that trial run south. Who could hope for such fortunate encounters when Swann's new waggons were making daily runs from the Tay to the Channel, from the Wash to Cardigan Bay?

It was then that he began to regret his arbitrary abolition of the localised structure of the network. With the original seventeen territories reduced to a mere five, with the scrapping of the old patriarchal system, and the new (and so far successful) policy of centralisation, the initiative of the regions had been superseded. More and more hauls were planned and routed from Headquarters. Improvisation on the part of provincial viceroys was not encouraged. Indeed, in many respects it was frowned upon. The power of the men out there had been subtly curtailed as they had learned to rely more and more upon the guiding hand of Headquarters, less and less upon their own reactions to local problems and this policy had seemed to pay dividends. For one thing, it put a stop to regional jealousies. For another, it checked indiscriminate exchange of teams, waggons and even contracts between managers who liked one another and overall reluctance to co-operate between men who did not. It knit the entire enterprise together. It encouraged a variety of lucrative by-products, not least among them a far closer co-operation with the railways than any achieved in his father's day. But it had, as he now saw with dismaying clarity, a fatal defect. It introduced a system of long, interlocked hauls over all kinds of terrain, and Maxies could not adapt to such demands. In a month, he suspected, head-quarters would be swamped with reports of ditched vehicles, stranded loads of perishable goods, helpless drivers and infuriated customers. In bad weather half the fleet would be off the roads. And in six months Swann's forty-year-old boast, that he could haul anything any-where in less time than his liveliest competitor, would become a tavern jest. What could result from that but ruin?

It cost him a great deal to face up to this conclusion. His faith in the petrol engine was all but absolute and he never doubted, not even now, that a time would come when nobody but a rural baker's roundsman would invest a penny in a horse as part of his stock-in-trade. But geo-graphy was geography and, although extremely obstinate, he was not so pig-headed as to risk his own future, plus the livelihood of three thousand men, on a fiction that wishing it could reduce Britain to a level plain, like the old

Crescent Centre territory in Lincolnshire. At the same time, as in all human equations, there had to be an answer and he set himself to find it.

      *   *   *

The answer, when it came, was so obvious that it hit him like a piece of falling tackle, projecting him nose foremost into the jumble of maps, sketches and half-finished sums that covered his desk.

It was there in that same summarisation of his father's maps that he had brought up here a day or so after receiving and studying Scottie's report, and it now lay buried under so much clutter that he had to dig for it.

There it was, a curious relic among all those figures and designs and memoranda, a scale condensation of the seven original maps Adam had drawn up in 1858, between them embracing every shire in England and Wales, for neither Scotland nor Ireland featured on Swann maps of the period.

He unrolled it almost reverently, a piece of parchment measuring about three feet by two, with every regional border sketched in and, what was more to the point, every railway line and contour marked in coloured inks. The old discarded nicknames were there – the Bonus, the Kentish Triangle, the Polygon and so on, and as he identified them one by one he was afforded a searching glance into his father's mind when he had split the country into so many irregular and disparate sections. For Adam, at that time, had clearly been beset by the identical problem – gradients, and what they meant in turns of profitable road haulage.

The key was there and he used it to unlock his memories, memories of a hundred conversations he had had with his father about the early days of the network. Some were sharp and clear but others needed to be chased into corners, and it was one of these that convinced him, without a shadow of a doubt, that the answer was almost within his grasp. Something about a railway engineer who had counselled Adam on the subject of investing his capital . . . something to do with natural obstacles standing between Swann and his destiny. And then, with a growl of triumph, he heard his father's voice speak across the years from a time when the two of them had been stuck in a fogbound railway coach on their way home to 'Tryst', when he was little more than a boy. The voice said, ". . . Fellow told me to fill in the empty spaces . . . whole damned outfit emerged from that." And in response to George's query as to the wisdom of staking everything he possessed in a single idea Adam's gruff reply, "Never had second thoughts about it . . . Believed in what was happening around me . . . Most people didn't . . . thought the industrial wave of those days was a flash in the pan. I knew it wasn't. That's why I kept ahead of the best of 'em . . ."

He got up and went over to the wall cellarette, pouring himself a brandy four fingers high and carrying it back to the table. It gave him a lift he did not need. He had his answer. *Re*-regionalisation, and to hell with his pride! A redivision of Swann's four big units into a score of smaller ones, each self-supporting and self-administered. Only this time what would determine the regional frontiers was not the curving lines of the 1858 railway system but the factor that had drawn them in that specific pattern when Stephenson, Brunel and all the other pioneers were assembling their gridiron. *And what was that but contours?* For railroads, even now, half-a-century later, were still the slaves of rock formations and river valleys, shoulders, marshes and plateaux that took shape when the earth cooled and the islands were subdivided by as many haphazard ridges as one could expect to find on a baked apple!

He cleared the desk of everything but the map and an atlas open at a page of England and Wales unscored by his father's inks and crayons. He overlaid the smaller map with a sheet of tracing paper and began to work, drawing a kind of parody of Adam's breakdown with an eye that never strayed from the light and dark brown shading of the highlands, not even when he reached for his glass, put it to his lips and sipped the undiluted spirit. And as his pencil skimmed the tracing a new regional network emerged with startling clarity, a minced and sliced version of an England ripe for conquest by Scottie Quirt's fleet of Swann-Maxies, all but two of them still on the drawing board awaiting Headquarters' go ahead. The borders almost drew themselves, bondsmen of the Cheviots, the Cotswolds, the Chilterns, the Cambrians, the more testing areas of the Pennine Chain and the high plateaux of the Westcountry moors. A few regions were much larger than Adam's but most were smaller, separated from one another by gradients that a petrol-powered waggon could never hope to climb unless it tackled them unladen. And even then, in places like Shap, Dartmoor, the Fells and the North Riding it would do so at risk.

Day after day he sat there, tracing, retracing, noting down, calculating distances in relation to centres of industry where his customers were thick upon the ground, siting motor depots with an allocation of light horse transport, and sub-depots on the lower slopes of the highlands where, at a pinch, he could call on teams of draught horses to help power-driven freight over a hump and ease it down a steep declivity.

It was the evolution of this emergency scheme that established yet another principle in his mind. It was no longer a question of either/or, of retaining or banishing the heaviest of his draught animals and settling for the new at the expense of the old. For here, surely, was an exercise in long-term phasing, of combining horse and mechanical thrust to combat the freakish terrain of the islands. If a haul necessitated the crossing of a frontier, and that frontier ran along a high ridge approached by steep hills on either side, then draught teams could be whistled up in advance to be used in a haulage or braking capacity. But the bulk of the journey, on both sides of such a barrier, could be accomplished at three or four times the speed of an old-style frigate or man-o'-war and Swann-on-Wheels would thus enjoy the best of both worlds.

His fancy, and a sense of deep indebtedness to Adam, led him to conjure with a spate of nicknames for his newly-defined regions. The Mountain Square, generally speaking impossible terrain for a Maxie, was all but abandoned to the horse. So was the long central spine of England, from the Southern Uplands between Solway and the Cheviots, all the way down to the Peak area, west of Sheffield. He called this Pennine strip The Chain, pencilling in sub-depots at Appleby, Keighley, Penistone and Bakewell.

In the old Western Wedge he set about similar fragmentation, establishing sub-depots at Barnstaple and Ashburton commanding Exmoor and Dartmoor respectively. Between the Mendips and the Quantocks, where few really formidable slopes interposed between Taunton and the Bristol Channel, he formed a new unit, naming it The Link, for it served this purpose between the far west and easier territory that stretched away as far as the Thames estuary and the Wash where river roads were plentiful and surfaces among the best in the country.

Away to the east, in the old regions Adam had called The Bonus, and The Crescents, there were no sub-depots. The land was flat and rivers were well-bridged, all the way up from the capital to the Vale of York, then east again to the Humber and the Naze. In the main, this was ideal Swann-Maxie country, where teams could be freed by the dozen to earn their oats on the gradients further west and north. He named this two-hundred-mile section The Funnel because that, on his new maps, was how its shading appeared to him. Then, and then only, he addressed himself to Scotland, where motor-vehicles could operate without much difficulty in the Lowlands whereas the horse would likely hold its own for decades north of the Tay. The same, in a sense, applied to Ireland.

Broadly speaking Ulster, Leinster and Munster were open to the Swann-Maxie but there seemed no profit in sending them into Connaught or down into the far west.

When his maps were completed and neatly redrawn for the brochure he planned, he turned to costing, and after that to compiling a short list of candidates for regional control and the younger cadres who would be given their chance as managers of the sub-depots. He worked from a roll of names sent up on request by Accounts. Some were managers of proven ability, like Rookwood, Higson, Godsall and Markby, men who already controlled regions of their own, but in the longer list were a score of young- sters in their 'twenties, whose latent abilities showed up in last year's bonus slips. Finally he compiled a detailed report for Scottie Quirt, telling him to hold himself in readiness for conference confirmation of a fleet of sixty vehicles, to be put into commission as they emerged from the workshop and sent out to work the day they completed their test-runs.

He did not realise how spent he was until he had de- spatched the brochure to the printers. On the way down the spiral staircase he staggered and had to make a grab for the rail. He thought, 'By God, I need a break and I've earned one! I'll take it before I put it to the directors' conference. They'll need a fortnight to digest it and I daresay I'll have to spend myself all over again convincing the doubters. Some of them are getting set in their ways and I can't really rely on the backing of more than a few . . . chaps like Jake Higson up in Scotland, and Godsall, who has always been the most forward-looking of the originals . . .' So he made his decision on the spot. He would take Gisela and the children down to 'Tryst' for a few days and try it out on the old dog fox before the day set for the conference. It would be interesting to see how the Gov'nor reacted to a scheme that was, in essence, his cartographical grandchild.

2

In the very earliest days of his venture Adam Swann had seen himself as an isolated traveller with his eyes fixed on a far distant objective, separated from him by a wide and varied terrain. But the peak, despite distance and haze, had always been there, stark, clear, beckoning and infinitely desirable.

He did not think of it in fanciful terms, as the Celestial Mountains or El Dorado for he was not a fanciful man, rather a supreme individualist who, although well-endowed with imagination, had learned how to employ fancy to practical purpose, evidenced by the lighthearted nicknames he bestowed upon his vehicles and territories. He thought of it as The Summit and was not deeply concerned regarding the prospect it might offer him when he arrived there.

Very soon after setting out he was joined by Henrietta, then by his motley crew of privateersmen and finally, in late middle age, by his grown sons and daughters, all of whom, it seemed, had their eyes fixed on some adjoining peak, but there never had been a time, not even when he journeyed alone, when he regarded his odyssey as a private endeavour. It was one he shared, willy-nilly, with his tribe as a whole, for he always saw himself as a standard-bearer of the era travelling only one step ahead of his fellow-countrymen, the English, and their proven allies, the Scots and the Welsh. He discounted the Irish as a race of by-roads dawdlers, temperamentally unsuited to a haul of this length and complexity.

As time went on he drew appreciably nearer his goal, adjusting his pace somewhat and taking time to look around him as he progressed, but he was still untroubled by what lay beyond the furthest ridge. A man's life-span did not run to that, he would have argued. Somewhere along the road ahead he would, inevitably, drop out of the line of march, surrendering the vanguard to a seasoned successor and this successor could only be George, the closest reflection, without his experience, of himself in his early thirties.

Thus it was that he welcomed George when the boy at last emerged from his hibernation period, guessing that what he would have to say would concern, among other things, the march-plan into the future. For George, lucky dog, was young enough and strong enough to concern himself with the prospect beyond the summit.

He heard him out in almost complete silence, interjecting no more than an occasional question and that a shrewd one, for the old man, George noted, still retained his fantastic memory for terrain and regional potential. When George had talked himself out he gave him another ten minutes to concentrate on the maps and was relieved when Adam at last looked up and said, "You came up with this alone? Up in that old belfry? No clerks? No brain-picking discussions with Accounts and Routeing?"

"I daren't risk that, Gov'nor. I didn't know the real answers myself until a month ago and I've had my head down ever since. It seemed ... well ... dangerous to start gossip down in the yard. You know what they are. It would have gone out along the grapevine in a matter of hours. Do you approve of that?"

"I certainly do," and he gave one of his hard, tight grins, "for whenever I had anything important on hand I made damned sure I manoeuvred myself into a position to anticipate their tomfool objections. They were a pig-headed bunch in those days. Always had to bully 'em into trying anything new."

"Well?"

"Don't rush me, boy. This is a revolutionary scheme. Far more ambitious than anything I dared to hatch up sitting overlooking that slum. What's your spot estimate of the cost over a twelve-month period of transition?"

George took a deep breath. "A shade under a hundred thousand. Say the round sum to be on the safe side."

"Four-fifths of the Reserve Fund?"

"We could scale it down and borrow from the banks."

"Why do that and pay their interest? The money's there, waiting to be used isn't it?"

"Then you approve?"

"It's a damned good scheme. It's got the smell of success about it." He paused. "Didn't you expect me to say that?"

"No, I didn't. I hoped for your approval in principle. No more than that. Will you show up at conference and give it your blessing in public?"

"Not me," said Adam, fervently. "You're running the show now. It's up to you to win 'em over. If you do it's a bunch of feathers in your hat. If you don't, it's your funeral."

"You think I'll have trouble convincing them?"

"You'll have trouble, boy, but you're completely persuaded it's a practical proposition, aren't you?"

"Absolutely. I've double-checked every figure, every mile of the routes, and even my estimates can't be more than two to three per cent out."

"Well, then, you dig your heels in. Damned hard. Don't budge. And don't whittle against your better judgment. A hundred thousand, eh? That'll rattle their teeth. I shall be able to hear their sighs from here."

"Can I do that? Can I stand by that scheme without compromise if the majority vote against me?"

"Legally yes. The Swann holding is still standing at fifty-one per cent, isn't it? At a pinch we've still got overall control. When I made the network into a private company, and let those rascals invest their own money, I gave them half-a-mile of rein. I didn't throw the curb away."

"But it isn't as simple as that, is it?"

"No, it isn't. You couldn't make it work in the face of a really determined opposition."

"Suppose I do run into opposition on that scale?"

"You hammer away at it, week by week, month by month. And you exploit their rivalries shamelessly. That was my method and I always got my own way in the end."

"That could take a long time, Gov'nor."

"Yes, it could take time. A year, maybe two or even five. But I'll tell you something, boy. You'll win in the end."

"Why necessarily?"

"Because you're my son. Because you're a natural leader and they're natural followers, every last one of 'em. If they hadn't been they wouldn't be there, still in the fold. The best of 'em would have hived off long ago and set up on their own. Even the thrusters like Godsall, and that convert to the kilt, Jake Higson."

There came to him then a heightened appraisal of his father's unique talents. Not as businessman, a gambler and an innovator. These had been apparent to him even as a child. Rather as a superbly accurate judge of potential, especially the potential of men of action, with an ability to distil past experience into a series of considered judgments on any one or any grouping of his associates. It stemmed, he supposed, from the Swann genes, developed over centuries on a thousand battlefields, and in as many embattled siege works. It reached back to the first Swann who had adopted the profession of arms, somewhere around the first years of the fifteenth century or perhaps, unrecorded, long before that, and it had been running strongly in the strain ever since, clear across the patchwork of history and Imperial conquest, from the campaigns of Henry V to the plains of India during the year of the Mutiny. It must have revealed itself in colonel and cornet and in foreign fields and in dynastic clashes in English shires, under or opposed to chieftains like Edward IV, Cromwell, Kingmaker Warwick and Prince Rupert. It had found employment on the Plains of Abraham and in that sorry business when the Anglo-American colonists in buckskins sent Cornwallis' and Burgoyne's redcoats packing. It had helped to tip the balance at Salamanca, Vittoria and Toulouse, and plant the flag on the bloody ramparts of Badajoz and Ciudad Rodrigo. It had made nonsense of Boney's ultimate bid for Europe on a Brussels plain, where his own grandfather had left two of his fingers. He said, as a kind of admission of his unpaid ancestral debt, "I'd sooner have you behind me than the whole bunch of them, Gov'nor. That's what I came seeking. Your blessing."

The old man mused for a moment. Finally he said, with a shrug, "You don't need anyone back of you, George. Not really. Not when the cards are dealt. Edith Wadsworth, the woman they all thought of as my mistress at one time, once likened 'em to a bunch of privateers, planning a descent on someone's coast, and she was about right. But a privateer doesn't cast off without a captain it can trust, and even the share-and-share alike pirates sailed under a quartermaster. You'll do, boy. Always thought you would somehow."

He watched George gather up his papers, throw a knowing wink in his direction and saunter out, seeing himself forty years ago and feeling glad that his battles were behind him.

3

Of the twelve original managers who bought themselves in when Adam (tiring of having his policies challenged by men who claimed the right to hector him without risking their own cash) made a private company of the concern, only five still sat on as directors. The other seven had either died or been replaced by successors in the regions. George thought of these five as the hard core of Swann-on-Wheels, who had seen it grow to maturity and who regarded their stake, rightly or wrongly, as more than financial.

Godsall, once an army officer, had ruled in the old Kentish Triangle. He now controlled the whole south-eastern beat of the network. 'Young' Rookwood (George reckoned his age at fifty-three) was the Dick Whittington of Swann-on-Wheels, having risen from vanboy to the rank of viceroy in what was once known as the Southern

Square. His enlarged beat now extended north to the Midlands and west as far as the rural territory of the late Hamlet Ratcliffe, who had died at his post on the eve of Victoria's Golden Jubilee. Ratcliffe's place on the board had been taken by his nephew, Bickford, a shrewd forty-year-old, known throughout the network as 'Bertieboy' Bickford. Scotland was controlled by another ex-vanboy, Jake Higson. The East Midlands were still under the sway of the Wickstead family, the sons of Edith and Tom Wickstead, whose independence was tempered by their devotion to Adam, the only man in the network aware that Tom Wickstead had once been a professional footpad. Tom, ailing now, had been succeeded in the old Crescent lands by his son Luke, a young man who had always seemed to George excessively shy. Further north, between the Yorkshire coast and the Pennines, Markby, a comparative newcomer, had made great strides of late. Markby was an innovator. It was he who had forced through a policy of purpose-built vehicles and he could usually be relied upon to put forward some constructive propositions at the quarterly conferences. Over in the West, in the old Mountain Square lands embracing all Wales, they had a new viceroy in the person of young Edward Swann, whose coming-of-age present had been a managership and a seat on the board earlier that year. Edward would have to be regarded as a new boy and expected to keep his mouth shut on anything but topics concerning his own beat. Clint Coles, representing Ireland, would also be ham-strung by family ties, although George felt he could rely on his brother-in-law's vote on a major proposition. Clint (the Swann family still thought of him as Jack-o'-Lantern, a soubriquet he had acquired when he eloped with Joanna Swann) was a fine salesman and a very amiable man, and he and George had always seen eye to eye.

There were two imponderables, Morris, once of the prosperous Southern Pickings territory around Worcester, and Dockett, a wayward character who had made a great success in Tom Tiddler's Land, otherwise the Isle of

Wight. Morris was elderly now, and long retired, but he had the keenest financial brain in the network and was very active on the board, where he kept a sharp eye on cash reserves and could bear down heavily on anyone he suspected of relegating the profit motive to any notch below number one on Swann's list of priorities. Dockett was the reverse, a gambler who had no patience with men who played safe. It was Dockett, who, as far back as 1863, had proposed specialisation in his own most profitable line, that of house removals, and had later initiated the saucy slogan painted on all Swann's house removal waggons, '*From Drawer to Drawer*'. He seemed a likely supporter for a scheme as grandiose as George's.

He pondered them all separately, trying to assess their reactions to the fat brochure, illustrated with maps and a diagram of the Swann-Maxie prototype sent to all directors a fortnight in advance of the summer meeting, and his conclusions were guardedly optimistic. Edward and Jack-o'-Lantern were, so to speak, safely in his pocket. He was almost equally sure of Markby, in the North, and of Dockett, who now played a leading role in Swann's coastal and Continental trade. That, with his own vote, meant a nucleus of five but he needed support elsewhere unless he was to face the long-term prospect of ramming the venture down managerial throats. Between them men like Rookwood and Godsall could rally a great deal of support among the relatively inexperienced men around the table, youngsters like Luke Wickstead, known to be cast in a cautious mould, so that it was with some misgivings that he sensed restraint on the part of both Rookwood and Godsall when they greeted him and he took his seat at the head of the table.

In the old days the board meetings had always been held in the original warehouse. Now, the warehouse having gone up in smoke, they gathered in comfort in the board room, south of the tower where the atmosphere, although more comfortable, did not encourage the breezy give-and-take of the old, privateering days. It was a pity,

George thought, that the Gov'nor had declined to chair
the meeting, even in a neutral capacity. The most independent among them still had affection for him, besides
deep respect for his judgments. He was also a terse but
effective speaker, a talent George had not inherited. He
lacked his father's sense of irony that had always helped
to cool tempers and heal feuds. Accustomed to working
alone he lacked the patience to reason with the querulous
and suffer the windbag gladly. In his view a man who had
not studied his subject matter down to the last detail had
best remain silent and he was uneasily aware that no one
around that table knew much about the vagaries or the
potential of mechanical transport. Alone among them
Godsall owned a motor but it was chauffeur-driven and
as a first-class horseman he had a contempt for anything
that went on under the bonnet. Indeed, George suspected that Godsall's car was maintained for reasons of
social prestige rather than personal prestige.

He tried to compensate for this deficiency in his opening speech. After the usual preamble he developed a
theme based on the dramatic headstart a fleet of petrol-
driven waggons would give Swann-on-Wheels over its
competitors. Mechanically propelled transport was not
unique in the trade. Several rival hauliers ran steam waggons, double-crank Fodens mostly of the traction type, used
for short, heavy haulage. A few were experimenting with
the new ten hundredweight Albion 'dogcart' on suburban
routes. But a fleet of sixty heavy vehicles, working from
provincial depots placed at strategically sited points across
the country, was something entirely new in the concept
of road haulage. He was aware, of course, that the staking
of almost the entire reserve fund on a single gigantic project entailed risk, but he argued that it was a carefully
calculated risk. That was why he suggested a slow phasing out of the horse over a period that might extend into
ten or twelve years. The limitation of power-driven
vehicles to comparatively short runs in the initial years
was, he said, designed to accumulate experience without

the risk of slowing down deliveries and increasing insurance rates.

He sat down unconvinced that he had made the best of his case, and telling himself, rather petulantly, that a speech of that kind should not have been necessary. It was all there in the brochure for anyone but a fool to see and if any one of them had failed to understand the tremendous implications of the report that man had no right to be sitting here.

The long, uneasy silence that followed his invitation for comments gave him his second clue to the overall mood of the gathering. It was clearly one of extreme uncertainty and nervousness, based less on the general proposal than on the amount of capital demanded. It was difficult, he supposed, for ex-gamins like Higson and Rookwood to think in terms of a hundred thousand pounds, when they probably recalled the earning of sixpence as the hallmark of a profitable day on the Thames foreshore. He waited, glumly, for what seemed a long minute and then, at a nod from Rookwood, Godsall stood up to address the chair.

George had always enjoyed a good, working relationship with Godsall, seeing him as the most go-ahead of the viceroys, and he looked for a sign of this accord now. Godsall, however, avoided his eye, addressing himself to the wings rather than the head of the conference and his first words were a storm signal.

"For a long time now, gentlemen, it has been an open secret that the Chairman and I have seen eye to eye in most matters . . ." and George took this as an expiatory remark, designed to soften the impact of what followed. He was right, for Godsall went on, "However, at this early stage of the proceedings, I am obliged to confess that I find myself implacably opposed to the project so lucidly set out in the Chairman's brochure. Not, I hasten to add, in principle, but certainly in particular, but if I had to say why, in a few words, it would be difficult. It seems to me – as I gather it does to others present – that we are being asked to swallow at one gulp a meal that might, in the long run be very nutritious but, in the manner of taking, could so damage the digestion as to put Swann-on-Wheels on bicarbonate of soda for years!''

George, looking down at the table, did not see the titter that ran down both sides of the table for what it was, a release of nervous tension. To him, momentarily stunned by Godsall's polite perfidy, it was a barb signifying un-animity, or near unanimity, of their rejection and ridicule of the plan. In a flash he was a boy again, standing in a classroom holding a blotched exercise exposed to the usher's irony, and he thought bitterly: 'God damn him! He could have given me a hint . . . *One* of them could have hinted . . . written . . . questioned the practicality of the project before we assembled here and before I took it for granted any objections would be based on techni-calities . . . !' But then, with a tremendous effort, he got his resentment in hand in order to give his entire attention to Godsall's devastating analysis of the brochure and form some kind of judgment as to the essence and validity of his dissent. He realised then that Godsall's opening ad-mission had been honest. The man was not opposed in principle to the switch. He was merely rejecting its breadth and totality.

He had to concentrate hard to follow the drift of the speech. Odd phrases and deductions evaded him, slip-ping away and drowning in a sea of bile . . . "the Chair-man is aware, as must be everyone sitting round this table, that I have never set my face against the prospect of an eventual phasing out of the horse in favour of power-driven vehicles . . . seen it as inevitable in the long run . . . will admit, unreservedly, that the introduction of, say, a few power-driven vans, as a very useful experiment offer-ing guidelines to the policy of the years ahead . . . but what is proposed here is certainly not that! It is total committal that could put the entire enterprise in jeopardy at a prohibitive cost in order to prove – what? That power-driven transport is on the way in? That it is possible (as our Chairman himself has proved) to make a two-day haul over two hundred miles with a load of over a ton aboard? That a well-designed waggon, powered by petrol or steam, can move over chosen territory faster than a man-o'-war? Or even a frigate, pulled by the best team in our regional stables? But surely, gentlemen, these things don't need proving. Certainly not at the cost of a reserve fund it has taken us years to accumulate against an emergency or series of emergencies . . . !"

Every face was turned away from him now. Rookwood, Markby, Higson and even Bertieboy Bickford and young Edward were straining their ears in order not to miss a syllable of Godsall's merciless rhetoric.

". . . No one here can point a finger at me as a man who sets his face against anything new *because* it is new, but to invest in power to this extent is to walk a tightrope from one end of the country to the other, and for a very simple reason. What is that reason? I believe the Chairman is more keenly alive to it than any of us. His experience with power-driven commercial haulage goes back years, to the time of the earliest prototypes. He is one of the pioneers and we respect him for it. But he will tell you, if you ask him, that the performance of one of these vehicles can be very impressive for two days running. He would not guarantee that performance for ten such vehicles over a month or a year. Or twenty. Or sixty within the foreseeable future. To do that, while running a day-to-day business hauling goods over every kind of terrain, and under every kind of condition, is not so much to put one's head in a noose as to trust one's weight to a single rope, insecurely fastened. I am all for progress, gentlemen, and the widest possible range of experimentation, but I am not prepared to face that terrible risk. Not yet. Not until we have actual proof that the power-propelled vehicle hauling over, say, ten hundredweights, is not only faster but more dependable than a horse bred for haulage."

He sat down rather unexpectedly and there was a buzz

of assent. At least George, glowering at the far end of the table, took it for assent, and when nobody seemed disposed to offer the first comment he said, quietly, "Do I take it you intend to move an amendment to the proposition printed on the last page of the brochure, Godsall?"

"No, sir," Godsall said, promptly, "not at this stage. Not before a full and free discussion."

"Very well, then let me put it this way. If Mr. Godsall's opposition to a fleet of sixty Swann-Maxies *was* couched in an amendment, is there anyone here who would second it?"

Rookwood rose. "I would, Mr. Chairman."

Somehow George had sensed he would endorse Godsall's sentiments. Unlike all the men around the table, with the exception of Jake Higson, his fellow waif, Rookwood had served Swann-on-Wheels in every conceivable capacity over the years, all the way up from urchin vanboy, swinging on a tailboard rope, to staid and highly respected manager of a huge slice of territory in the south. He was a humourless man, slow to make decisions, but when those decisions had been taken he was tireless, inflexible and unshakeably loyal to the interests of the undertaking. He said, looking directly at the chair, "Everything Mr. Godsall said made sense to me. My observation in this field has left me with the impression that petrol-driven vans are superior for light work in congested areas but inferior to reliable teams hauling full loads over long distances. I have even gone so far as to make checks in this respect, on haulage undertaken by Wetherby and Sons, in my area. They hauled a turbine down to Southampton Docks by mechanical waggon last February. The journey, allowing for breakdowns, occupied forty-eight hours. According to my calculations" – he glanced at a sheet of paper he held in readiness – "one of our Goliaths could have accomplished it in thirty hours, allowing two hours lost in city hold-ups."

"Wetherby uses steam-waggons." This from Markby, on Rookwood's immediate right.

"That's so. He operates two on my beat. Traction-engines, that can average nine miles an hour on the flat and the route he took on this occasion was flat in the main. Both breakdowns occurred on gradients. One of one in nine, the other a shade in excess of nine."

You had to hand it to Rookwood. He was a man who very rarely generalised and whose homework could never be faulted. George thought, glumly: 'I wish to God I had him on my side but that's asking too much of Rookwood. He's never taken a real risk in his life, and he'd probably tell you that was the secret of his success.' He looked carefully down both sides of the table. No one else seemed eager to commit themselves. He said, "We'd best give everyone a chance to speak. This thing is far too big for free and easy discussion. I rule we take it in turn. Down one side and up the other. What's your view, Bickford?"

Bertieboy Bickford, operating in the west where, so far, nothing but agricultural traction had been seen, much less used, looked flustered. He was, Adam would have said, a very likely successor to his uncle, the rumbustious Hamlet Ratcliffe, who had always succeeded in surprising them despite mountainous prejudices, a bucolic appearance and a buzzsaw Westcountry accent like Bickford's own. Ratcliffe, no doubt, would have set his face against an innovation on this scale but he would have stated his objections in a way that brought a whiff of humour into the proceedings and Bertieboy was equal to his uncle's memory. He said now, in a brogue that vividly reminded the long-termers of the man who had died hauling a huge statue of Queen Victoria over rough Devon roads when he was in his eightieth year; "They things coulden tackle the roads in my beat Maister, so that lets me out. I dessay the Chairman thowt o' that when he drew up this scheme. Some places you have to hitch four horses to a frigate to haul a load o' turnips over one of our humps and then be bliddy smart wi' the shoes to stop 'er backsliding. I take it these yer trucks would be used on the flat mostly. Did you 'ave that in mind, Mr. Swann?"

"Not entirely," George said, "as you'll see under the sub-heading dealing with branch depots. But you're right about your territory. I wouldn't risk them in the west as yet. That would be asking for trouble."

"Well, then, 'tis none o' my bizness, is it?"

"Yes it is. You're a shareholder, the same as everyone sitting round this table. And in any case, you've always kept your end up down there and I'd appreciate your opinion. Say whatever you've a mind to say."

Bickford frowned, slowly massaging the side of his long, thin nose with his forefinger. "Well an' good, Mr. Chairman. Well, yer's what I have to say. Time was when my Uncle Hamlet was called upon to haul a circus lion all the way down the Exe Valley and put Swann on the map doin' it, as some of you might remember. I was only a tacker at the time but I can tell you this. Uncle Hamlet woulden have coaxed no lion into one of they bliddy contraptions. That old rascal would've been running free on Exmoor yet if Uncle 'Amlet hadn't had a waggon an' team back of him."

It was enlistment with the opposition but George welcomed the comment for all that. It relieved the unbearable tension and went some way towards liberating successive speakers, inhibited by the bluntness of Godsall and Rookwood. Markby was for the gamble, pointing out that the reputation of Swann had been built on innovation and conceding George's claim that a fleet of sixty waggons, designed for heavy traffic, would give them an impressive start over every other haulage firm in the country. "A twopenny-ha'penny carrier on my beat has already captured the Whitby fish trade with one of those light vans," he said. "As time goes on we'll have to face up to stiffer and stiffer competition, not only with other hauliers but with the railways. I've got word they're talking about putting in two-tonners at Darlington, and one or two of the bigger distribution centres up north. I say let's take the plunge and be done with it!"

Young Edward took the same line although, operating

in hilly country west of Offa's Dyke, he had the same claim to neutrality as Bickford. He had read the brochure three times, he said, without benefit of private discussion with his brother, and it seemed to him, a new boy among them, that the entire future of haulage lay with power-propelled vehicles. He sat down, blushing, but then, against probability, Jake Higson came down on the side of caution, and so did young Wickstead. Not because either of them doubted the long-term prospects of motor haulage but solely on grounds of expenditure. A cheaper scheme, with the emphasis on experimentation should be considered, they said, for the virtual wiping out of the central reserve fund would leave every region at the mercy of a bad winter, of the kind some recalled in the past when half the roads in the country turned to slush, river valleys overflowed and an impossible strain was put on teams, waggons and waggoners.

Clinton Coles, speaking for Ireland, took a character-istic line. An inveterate gambler, he was for immediate expansion but his support did not mean as much as it might have done. Careful consideration had been given to the Irish terrain and there was far less competition over there than in the other regions, even in Scotland north of the Tay and in North Wales, where one-man carriers were thick on the ground.

When everyone had had their say, including half-a-dozen comparative newcomers who had nothing new to contribute, George asked Godsall to frame his amendment during a lunch break and put it when they reconvened at one-thirty. He did not join them for the usual convivial session at the old George Inn, judging it best to leave them to argue among themselves over their beer and beef sandwiches. Instead he took himself off to his tower, having no stomach for food but carrying his brandy over to the embrasure where he had a clear view of the Thames, shimmering in summer heat that seemed to slow the pass-age of the tugs and barges shooting London Bridge. He no longer felt like a schoolboy holding a blotched exercise but like a general facing incipient mutiny, and he longed with all his heart for his father's counsel. It was here, he supposed, in every cranny of the ancient chamber, where Adam had spent half his life, but he was too bewildered and too tired to locate it. His mind grappled with the verdict resulting from a show of hands. Markby, Edward and Jack-o'-Lantern were all he could count on. Plus, possibly, two or three of the newcomers, who had little to lose and were still sufficiently awed by his father's ghost to vote for his successor. Seven, more likely six, facing the landslide of hardheaded experience and prestige set in motion by Godsall, Rookwood and Higson, men whose support he desperately needed. It wasn't enough. It wasn't nearly enough. His father said he would win through in the end and so he would, he supposed, when it became obvious to every child in Britain that the horse would follow the longbow and the three-decker warship. But by then he would have lost his headstart and all a switch-over would mean would be a jockeying for position among the nation's leading transporters. He was not interested in that kind of campaign.

* * *

Godsall's amendment, promptly seconded by Rookwood, was lucid. It proposed a scaling down to ten Swann-Maxies, placed at carefully selected depots in favourable terrain, and limited the maximum expenditure to twenty thousand. After a two-year period the whole position could be reviewed. If the figures were encouraging he would withdraw all his objections. George saw the real sting was in the tail of his speech, however, when he said: "Thus restructuring of the entire network will be avoided, for what is this proposal but a return to regionalism? Do any of us want that, with all the wasteful rivalry it entailed in the old days? Let any power-driven vehicles we put into commission prove to us they can run independently of the horse. Don't let us set ourselves up as a target for a *Punch* cartoon, with lame-duck vehicles pulled home by horses, the way half of them are as yet." He sat down and when George did not immediately rise, he said, "I take it you'll exercise your right to reply, Mr. Chairman."

"No," said George, "I won't. Not out of pique but because I've said all I have to say in that brochure. We'll take the amendment. All in favour?"

Three hands went up at once, those of the proposer, seconder and Jake Higson. Two others followed more reluctantly, Bickford's and Luke Wickstead's. Then five of the six new men voted in Godsall's favour, a total of ten. Markby, Young Edward, Clint Coles and Coreless, one of the new men from the Polygon area, stood with George. Dockett, for reasons best known to himself, abstained. The amendment was carried, ten votes to five, with one abstention.

They broke up without the usual jocular exchanges. The tension of the meeting carried over into adjournment but Godsall approached him looking troubled and said, "No hard feeling, George? I only spoke out of my deepest convictions."

"That's your privilege," George said, "but you're wrong, for all that."

"I'm not that much of a gambler," Godsall said. "We've all come a long way since the 'sixties and for most of us it was a hard, uphill pull." Then, hands in breeches pockets, he lounged off, without stopping to confer with his supporters and in ten minutes all but young Edward had gone.

Edward said, falling into step with his brother as he crossed the yard to the tower: "I wouldn't take it that hard, George. Ten Maxies will prove your point in less than two years, won't they?"

"It's not the same, lad. The Gov'nor saw what I was driving at. It's Swann's loss that they couldn't or wouldn't."

"Will you be catching the train at London Bridge now?"

"No. Someone from the Midlands is waiting to see me. He wrote for an appointment four days ago and I told him I couldn't see him until after conference. He's only in town for the day." He took a card from his pocket. '*Jas. L. Channing. Birmingham Castings*'. Have we ever hauled for them?"

"No," Edward said, promptly, "but I've heard of them. Steel people, working exclusively on Government contracts."

George smiled, his first smile of the day. "You've got the Gov'nor's memory," he said. "Tell him how it went, will you? And say Gisela and I will probably be down for the inquest on Sunday."

"I'll do that, George," and he plodded off, with that curious Sam Rawlinson gait of his, deliberate, square-toed, vaguely aggressive, and George thought, 'He'll be a big man in this outfit before long. Bigger than any of us, I wouldn't wonder,' and turned to climb the steps to the turret, having been warned by a clerk that James L. Channing, whatever he sought, had already been appraised of the end of the conference and shown up to the eyrie. It was unusual to receive customers up here nowadays but George had no stomach for the main office, with its clutter of clerks and chatter of typewriters for the story would be all round the yard by now. The New Broom had taken the beating of his life. The wheelwrights and the farriers could breathe again. The turret drew him as a source of respite.

2

Snailpath Odyssey

HE WAS A TALL, ANGULAR MAN, WITH PIERCING GREY eyes that gave George an impression of intense seriousness calculated to reduce the most frivolous to instant sobriety. The kind of man who would stand no nonsense from anyone, who could quell a riot by simply standing there. Very erect, superbly self-contained and resolved to be accepted at his own high valuation. A man of authority and integrity, seldom, if ever, caught off guard. He said, civilly, "Your business is completed, Mr. Swann? You can spare an hour?" George said he was at his disposal and apologised for keeping him waiting. There was only one visitor's chair in the turret so George motioned him to it, taking his own seat behind the desk with his back to the light. It gave him a marginal advantage and Channing was clearly a man in whose presence one looked for such advantages.

"Then I won't waste your time, Mr. Swann. It was courteous of you to receive me at a time when you were obviously fully extended. Birmingham Castings would not mean anything to you as we have never done business, but you will have heard of us, no doubt. We are a firm of armourers, engaged with Government contracts. Naval mostly but we do some commissions for the army. I know your firm rather better, of course. It has an enviable reputation."

His precise manner of speaking was disconcerting,

particularly after a heavy day, so that George thought, 'I was a fool to let the appointment stand ... This joker will want action and immediate decisions and I'm not in the mood to break new ground ...'"

But the man plucked at his curiosity and he said, "Good of you to say so, Mr. Channing. What can I do for you if anything?"

Channing's thin lips twitched. It was probably as close as they ever came to a smile.

"Probably nothing. You were represented to me as my sole remaining hope. By a mutual friend, I might say, Gideon Fulbright. Your father, I believe, hauled for Fulbright over a long period. He seems to hold your father in great esteem, Mr. Swann."

"Most customers did. But my father has retired, Mr. Channing."

"So I understand." Surprisingly he broke off and shifted his searching gaze to the belfry.

"This tower was his office?"

"For forty years. He started here in the 'fifties and never cared to leave it."

"Interesting," Channing said and it was more than a formal comment. But then, with shattering directness, "I probably know a great deal more about Swann-on-Wheels than you know about my undertaking. I understand you are putting motor transport into commission."

"A limited number of vehicles, largely for experimental purposes," George said, more and more baffled by the man, "but none are on the road as yet."

"I see." He paused, placing the tips of his slender fingers together, flexing them rhythmically and breaking contact so that George saw it as a self-energising gesture, almost as though it was a means of lubricating the brain. "My business would hinge on that. Would you be prepared to tell me, in strictest secrecy, how far you are advanced in the field?"

"I don't mind telling you. As a matter of fact it's generally known in the trade. I have two vehicles ready to run up in Manchester. Another eight will be commissioned later in the year. I planned a fleet of sixty but my associates are not prepared to commit the firm to that extent. That's what we've been discussing all day."

He could not have said why he was unburdening himself to a total stranger, and a very unforthcoming one at that, but it slipped out and somehow, in the oddest way, it comforted him, enlarging the area of communication between them. There was something about Channing that suggested he was in the presence of another pioneer, another gambler even. Someone who, like George, was not only able to drive himself but would back himself into the bargain and that down to the last halfpenny in the petty-cash box. He said, "Might I offer you a brandy and a cigar, Mr. Channing?"

"Thank you, Mr. Swann. That's very civil of you," Channing replied.

George busied himself with the drinks and while he was pouring, and reaching into the back of the cellarette for the cigar box, he heard the rustle of stiff paper. When he turned Channing had spread a draughtsman's tracing on his desk. "There's my problem, Mr. Swann. It could be yours too. In passing, are you able to identify it?"

"It looks like part of a gun turret. For a heavy calibre gun, I'd say."

"Thirteen point five. The largest they fit. It's not strictly a turret. It's the cupola, the crown of the mounting and I am bending the rules more than somewhat by showing it. However, I can hardly ask you to haul something of that nature two hundred miles without returning the confidence you have extended to me. That drawing, one could say, represents the biggest single humiliation of my professional life. You see, I'm here in the capacity of a suppliant, Mr. Swann, but my pride and reputation might yet be salvaged. With your help. Your good health, Mr. Swann," and he raised his glass and emptied it without seeming to move his lips.

George picked up the drawing and studied it carefully,

a three-dimensional sketch of a squat, wedge-shaped block measuring, at a rough guess, twelve feet across and six feet in height.

"What's its overall weight, Mr. Channing?"

"Without mountings? Something in excess of six tons. That's confidential, of course."

"You're asking me to haul a six-ton load two hundred miles by a power-driven vehicle? That's impossible, Mr. Channing, even over the flat."

"But you have two such vehicles. Would it be at all practicable to couple them?"

The idea was revolutionary. Even George Swann had never contemplated coupling Maxies in an attempt to double their thrust. But *was* it so unthinkable? With some kind of platform to take the bulk of the strain linked to the sources of power. A flat-car, coupled between two railway box cars?

He said, "Give me a minute, Mr. Channing. Enjoy your cigar," and took a sheet of foolscap drawing paper from the pile he had used for mapping the new network.

For five minutes or more he was sketching, drawing freehand but using the ruler to calculate the overall length of the fanciful cavalcade. The maximum load of Scottie Quirt's prototype was around three tons but, as ever, that hinged on gradients. To drag a load like that up a one-in-eight slope was out of the question, even with a six-horse team of Clydesdales in support. It was a challenge of a kind he had never faced before and it went against the grain to resist it, but only ignominy and danger to man and vehicle could result from a jaunt of that kind. He threw his pencil aside.

"If it was a five-ton load I'd risk it. Six is one over the odds, Mr. Channing."

"Can you tell me why? In layman's language? I've had no personal experience of power-driven transport."

George explained why. It was a simple matter of engine thrusts and gradients. "I could risk hauling around

two tons in excess over the flat, but you couldn't climb
with that weight at your back. You would need vehicles
with caterpillar wheels and even then it would be a
chancy operation. Where does it have to be hauled from
and to?"

"From my foundry, in Bromsgrove, to the naval yard,
Devonport."

"Why can't it go by rail?"

Channing was silent. Finally he said, sourly, "I
wouldn't be here, throwing myself on your mercy, Mr.
Swann, if every other means had not been considered
and rejected. The Admiralty, very properly, won't co-
operate. Why should they? The original section that this
will replace was delivered and fitted, then found to have a
twenty-three-inch fissure. It was my product, personally
guaranteed by me. To get it to the nearest port, Avonmouth, would require a longish rail haul and no railway
will handle it. It's not a question of weight, you understand, but rather of width. There is up-traffic to be considered and lines would have to be cleared over the entire
journey. The Government can arrange that on special
occasions but it requires two months' notice. In fact, that's
our regular route. For the replacement, however, I have
just one week in hand, Mr. Swann."

"Why is it so urgent?"

"The ship is due to begin trials on the twenty-second of
the month. The flawed part has already been stripped
and discarded."

"Couldn't its replacement be fragmented?"

The lipless mouth twitched. "You may be a pioneer in
motor-transport, Mr. Swann, but casting a gun-mounting
of that size and quality is even more specialised. I've been
at it, one way and another, since I was a boy apprentice in
Armstrong-Whitworth's workshops. If it could be done,
and reassembled on board, I assure you I wouldn't be here
begging favours. Any haulier worth his salt could get it
to Devonport piecemeal." He rose and slapped his gloves,
a gesture of resignation. "Thank you for giving me your

time, Mr. Swann. It isn't as if I was a long-standing client of your firm."

"Don't go, Mr. Channing."

A thought occurred to him, emerging from the jumble of the past where mental lumber rooms were crammed with network trivia. Two or more years ago he had watched carpenters at work on a ditched Goliath in the old Polygon headquarters, at Salford. He remembered them using a crane to fit the huge central beam into its sockets and hearing how the Goliath, hauling an ill-secured generator into Rochdale, had fouled an archway and held up traffic for two hours on the main Manchester road. A Goliath, specially braced, could support a six-ton load, providing it was professionally bedded-down. But it would need, he would say, a team of a dozen horses, with post changes every ten miles or so to drag it over that distance. No waggoner, however experienced, could control a string of that size over two hundred odd miles of tortuous English highway from Warwickshire to the Tamar. Everything could happen and everything probably would. The team could become unmanageable in medieval streets, heavy with traffic and presenting any number of right-angled turns and bottlenecks. In the history of the network no vehicle had ever set out from base with more than seven horses in the traces. Yet the memory of that long, lean Goliath persisted. Somewhere, in this jigsaw of factors, there was a place for it, and his imagination conjured up a vision of an improvised cavalcade, a horseless Goliath, sandwiched between two Maxies, one pulling, one pushing from behind. He took up his Atlas and opened it at the two pages portraying the Midlands and the West.

"When you came to me, when you thought the haul might be possible, did you have a road route in mind, Mr. Channing?"

"I did indeed." He took a slip of paper from his wallet and passed it over. It was not a map but a list of place names with notes alongside. Bromsgrove, Worcester, over the Severn at Tewkesbury, Gloucester, down the Severn estuary to Bristol, north of the Mendip slopes to the flat, negotiable country around Bridgwater, due West through the pass between the Quantocks and the Blackdown Hills. Then on to Exeter and the right bank of the Exe, and thence, hugging the coast, a probe for practical gradients across what George thought of as the udder of Devon to Plymouth Sound. It was possible, given minute planning and any amount of luck, with himself and Scottie Quirt at the wheels, and Young Edward following on with the steadiest Clydesdales they had in the stables. It *might* be achieved, with outriders and civic co-operation in every town they traversed but progress would not average more than five miles an hour. Say, sixty miles a day. And again given extraordinary luck. A four-day haul, leaving him three to make his preparations and join Scottie in bringing the Maxies from Manchester to Bromsgrove. Time could be saved by borrowing a Goliath flatbed from the nearest Swann depot, Birmingham, no doubt.

He said, trying to keep the excitement from his voice, "You wield some sort of Government authority. Could you get me an hour's clearance through places like Worcester, Tewkesbury, Bridgwater and Taunton? That's imperative with a haul of this kind. We might – *might*, I say, manage on the open road, and I'll plan a route by-passing every impossible gradient. It would mean extra mileage, of course, but given cooling-off time we could run from dawn to dusk."

"I can get clearances," Channing said. "We've done that before in emergencies by appealing to the local Chief Constables. Plus a certain amount of wire-pulling, I might add. The mountings could go by rail. But I can't get that overall load below six tons."

"That's a risk that has to be taken and I'll take it. My pride is involved too, Mr. Channing. Only today my associates as good as told me I'm living in a dream world on their money and this challenge is tailor-made for a man in my situation. Get those clearances. Send on the mountings, and have tackle ready to load the turret on to a waggon I'll have on your premises by this time tomorrow. I can't guarantee the time schedule as yet. It depends on how long it takes to strip excess weight from my two motor vehicles and get them down from Manchester. Probably Wednesday, to be ready to move out on Thursday." He paused. "I'd be right glad of your company but I can't risk passengers."

"I'll be on hand," Channing said. "Good day to you, Swann." And then, glancing round the octagonal room, "Fulbright was right about your firm. 'Adam Swann,' he told me, 'would haul away the dome of St. Paul's if he was given a free hand and a guaranteed contract.' We've said nothing about mileage rates."

"How can we? Until my father has been consulted as to routeing I couldn't calculate it to the nearest fifty."

"Then your father still has a say in things here?"

"No. He just happens to know every bridlepath between here and the Grampians."

He went down the turret steps behind Channing. The yard was closing down and the skeleton night shift were lounging about the weighbridge hut at the Tooley Street entrance. "There's one other aspect, Mr. Channing. Publicity. Is that out of the question, having regard to the nature of the haul?"

"I don't see why. The cupola will ride under laced tarpaulins, I take it? I might even be able to help in that respect. We have a useful relationship with some sections of the national press." He looked at his watch. "I should be able to catch the six-forty-five from King's Cross."

He clamped his tall hat on his head and moved across the yard to his waiting cab, a tall, angular bird, who moved like a heron searching a river margin for the next meal. George stood a moment, deciding the priority of his consultations. He could be in 'Tryst' in just over the hour, spend two hours with Adam, and still catch the express north by midnight. Gisela would have to wait for a wire telling her he would be absent for upwards of ten days. It wouldn't bother her overmuch. There had been many times of late when his dinner had gone cold and been fed to Laddie, their labrador.

2

The composite vehicle, although outlandish enough to be certain of exciting curiosity wherever it travelled, was yet unlike anything he had envisaged once the cupola was bedded down and shrouded in its tarpaulin.

He had forgotten that the two Maxies, coupled fore and aft, would have to be stripped of their excess chassis fittings, for they would be used exclusively for propulsion and would carry nothing at all. Tailboards and bolted sides were removed within two hours of his arrival in Manchester and it was two very skeletal vehicles that set off on the morning of the sixteenth for Channing's foundry in Bromsgrove.

They arrived without incident and young Edward, bless the boy, was there to meet them, with his Goliath and team of eight Clydesdales, plus a plan to collect fresh teams, if necessary, at two stages en route. Edward had done some weight shedding on his own account, having shortened the central beam of the long vehicle by a good six feet, a mutilation he would be called to explain when he returned the vehicle to Melrose, the waggon-master in this area of the network.

There was no time, unfortunately, for George to get more than a quick rundown on Scottie Quirt's refinements to the Swann-Maxie since that first trial run south, more than three years ago, but he saw at once that they greatly increased his chance of hauling that terrible weight south-west over Adam's devious route, carefully traced on his maps, a job he had been able to do on the night express that rushed him north on the night of the fourteenth. The system of force-feed engine lubrication had been improved, and the rear springing greatly strengthened, but by far the

333

most important improvement was the new water-cooled
braking system. One of his greatest fears had been a brake
fire in the original fabric-lined footbrake. Now Scottie could
assure him that the latest tests had established a safety
margin in descents up to one in six, the maximum gradients
they were likely to encounter on the route planned.

The route itself had all the hallmarks of Adam Swann's
famed familiarity with British highways and byways.
Wherever a detour could avoid a steep hill, up or down,
Adam had devised one, and had also paid particular regard to the width of bridges they were obliged to cross.
There would be no difficulty, he told George, in negotiat-
ing main-road bridges, like the bridge over the Severn at
Tewkesbury. They were all crossed regularly by haywains
as broad in the beam as the Goliath, but it was possible he
would pay a high price for the unavoidable detours over
second-class roads that had never, at any time in their
history, carried a four-in-hand of the pre-railway era.
The odd bottleneck, he warned, might well present itself
here and there (he had ringed one over a tributary of the
river Parret, at a place called Withypool) but his guess
was that the leading edge of the load would clear the
parapet, providing care was taken to load high.

The warning, in fact, presented George with his first
major problem. He had to strike a precise balance between the danger of making his load top-heavy, thus
courting disaster in the form of a spill on uneven ground,
while providing the clearance he judged necessary for
stone walls and parapeted bridges encountered during one
or other of the detours. In consultation with Channing he
compromised, settling for a clearance of four feet four and
a half. The turret was then bedded down sideways, giving
them an overall reduction in width of four inches either
side and while this, in itself, reduced stability, it was a risk
they had to take. A saving of eight inches on some of the
stretches of second-class road included in the itinerary
was essential, despite the headshakings of Channing's
foreman loader.

As to fastenings, apart from four short lengths of chain securing the base of the turret to the staples of the Goliath, he used rope in preference to steel cable. High quality hawser rope offered a certain amount of flexibility. The strain imposed on a chain would prove a source of danger at every pothole and dip in the road.

The cavalcade, when it was lined up, resembled nothing within his experience. Fore and aft were the snub-nosed Maxies, that did not look like first-generation descendants of the vehicle he had driven south with a couple of tons of rice aboard. With their hooded cabins and naked chassis they suggested a couple of half-demolished covered waggons, of the kind American pioneers hauled across the prairie, whereas between them the foreshortened Goliath looked more like a raft than a waggon. In reserve, in charge of two Welsh waggoners Edward had recruited in the Mountain Square, were the eight Clydesdales, four harnessed to a man-o'-war, four more tethered behind and all looking, George thought, ashamed of enlistment in such a caravanserai. The man-o'-war they pulled was laden with stores and tools, including the tool kits of the Maxies, thus saving a little more weight. Edward said, "The team could make the whole journey with that light load at your likely pace, but I've wired for reserve teams to be held in readiness at Gloucester and Taunton. It depends how much you're likely to demand of them."

"I hope to God nothing at all, lad," George said. "They're insurance and nothing more on this kind of haul, but I'm glad you're along nevertheless. Ride in the waggon. Channing has taken upon himself the job as outrider in his Daimler. He'll keep five miles ahead and arrange clearances in the towns."

*   *   *

They moved off in the early afternoon of the sixteenth, with more than five days in hand and at the last minute Channing sent word by one of his clerks that the Admiralty

335

had given them an extra twelve hours, reckoning that the fitting of the cupola, in Channing's presence, could be accomplished in three days. The deadline was thus set forward to one p.m. on Monday afternoon, by which time they were expected to pass the dockyard gates.

It was a perilously tight schedule, even with the twelve-hour bonus, for it allowed for no more than twenty hours for stoppages during travelling time. Quirt, after inspecting the cargo very thoroughly, said, "Could we no' travel nights, Mr. Swann? It would add a good deal to the margin, even if we moved at half speed," but George said he had set his face against night travel. The moon was in its first quarter, and the route was far too involved to risk a wrong turning or too swift a passage over rough ground. "We'll need strict march discipline," he told both Quirt and the waggoners. "At dusk we'll camp and move off again at first light. Thank God it's a June haul. At five miles an hour we could never have made it at any other season of the year."

"Will you be heading us?" Quirt wanted to know and George replied, "No, Scottie, that's your honour. I'll drive number two where I can watch that load. God help us all, it's like travelling two-fifty miles carrying a juggler's end-of-the-act pyramid. At the least sign of trouble I'll give you a long blast on the horn and when you hear that brake, but do it as though you were stroking a crocodile."

"I'll mind that," Scottie said, "and here's my signal to you for synchronised braking," and he reached into the driving cabin of the leading Maxie and showed George a pennanted lance. "When you see that flag, brake. It'll show on the offside, I've tested it."

It was twelve miles to Worcester over the first and largely experimental leg of the journey, and he was thankful there were no detours marked on Adam's route. The surface of the old Worcester–Droitwich coach road was good and apart from Rick Hill, that slowed them to a nervous two miles an hour, they covered it without incident. The load seemed steady enough and the engines behaved well. Positioned immediately behind the turret George could not so much as glimpse Quirt's vehicle but every now and again, on gentle slopes, he could feel its slow, insistent tug that became, over the miles, a kind of Morse code regulating his speed. He thought, thankfully, 'That chap is steady as a rock. I wouldn't have cared to play this cat-and-mouse game with anyone else as a partner. I don't think he's given a damned thought as to what could happen to him, if the load ran away, for I couldn't hold it . . .' But then he made a supreme effort to put such gloomy thoughts out of mind and glanced over his shoulder for a peep at Edward's man-o'-war trailing them by some fifty yards. They passed through Wychbold and Droitwich about tea time and he calculated their progress at a little short of six miles an hour. Men, women and children stopped to gape and shoppers pressed themselves back against the façades of the buildings as they trundled past. Everything on wheels gave them the widest berth possible and one drayman, after a single startled glance, cut a corner over the pavement into the nearest side-street. The traffic here was light but George knew this would not be so in a more populous town like Worcester. He could only hope that the local authorities had responded to Channing's demands for clearance.

It seemed that they had when the outskirts of the city were reached. The road was empty of everything save knots of interested bystanders and with his back to the westering sun a photographer, using a tripod, took a picture of them on the move. The river was crossed at a snail's pace, George noting with satisfaction that there was ample clearance of the low parapet and they took the left-hand fork beyond the Cathedral, clearing the city by six-thirty and heading south for Tewkesbury. Malvern gradients tended to slow their progress now so, at eight o'clock, George gave the signal to halt and a farm cutout enabled them to pull off the road. Scottie's engine was running hot, although his own was still behaving well and while Edward, who had elected himself quartermaster, was seeking the farmer's permission to camp and co-operation as regards stabling, he called Scottie down.

They had checked load and engines by the time Edward returned with news that they were welcome to sleep in the barn and later their host ambled out, a pipkin of a man with a complexion as streaked and rosy as one of his own Worcestershire apples, to stare thoughtfully at the halted cavalcade and wrinkle his nose at the unfamiliar stink of the petrol fumes. His phlegm endured until George, thanking him for his hospitality, told him they had covered the twenty-two miles from Bromsgrove in a little over four hours. The information impressed him. "From Bromsgrove? In under five ower? Wi' that hump aboard? Why, you woulder had to pass the city, then?"

"We got police clearance," George explained.

"Arr, you'd need it, I reckon," and he continued to stare thoughtfully at the nearest Maxie until George, feeling some further courtesy was required, asked him if he would care to look at the engine under one of the bonnets.

"Not I," he said, and retreated into his yard with such precipitation that even the dour Scottie Quirt smiled.

"So far so good," George said, "but we'll have to step up our average tomorrow. I've just worked it out. It's four point six."

"If we can hold it at that I'll no' complain," Scottie said, taking a bottle and two tin cups from his luncheon-box. "Those Taffies are brewing their tea but you'll tak' a drop o' this, will you no'?"

"I'll tak' both," George said, calling to Edward to join them.

*　　　*　　　*

It was too good to last, of course. Around midnight when all five of them were snoring in the barn, thunder rolled down from the Malverns and presently it came on to rain, a heavy downpour on the roof sending Scottie out to check on the tarpaulin bonnet covers draped over the engines. By first light the storm had passed but when George went outside he saw to his dismay that the ground under the Goliath was soggy and an offside rear wheel, where the crushing weight of the cupola bore heaviest, was buried to the rim. They fetched straw, cinders and brushwood and after a warm-up tried to move back on to the road but the wheels of Scottie's Maxie spun dangerously and it was no help to bring George's vehicle round from behind to double the traction. Edward said, dubiously, "Maybe the horses could do it better, pulling on a long trace from firm ground," but all George's experience told him no trace could stand that kind of strain. Time was passing. The sun was up now and they had already wasted over an hour. "We need a solid platform under that wheel," George said. "Planking would do, providing it was heavy enough." He was on the point of seeking help at the farm when Edward said, "The man-o'-war has an iron plate on the waggon bed. It's one of the old type, before we fitted slide rails. Have you got a heavy screwdriver in your kit?"

It was worth a try. After ten minutes' tussle with deeply embedded screws they had the plate off, an oblong of sheet iron worn smooth on its topside by the passage of innumerable crates. They scooped a layer of red mud from the leading edge of the embedded wheel and hammered the metal under the rim with a sledge, too busy to snatch more than a few mouthfuls of the fried bacon the Welsh waggoners, Morgan and Rees, had prepared. Closely synchronising their acceleration they applied maximum power and with a long suck and a rattle the Goliath was heaved back on to the road. George thought, watching Edward plod away to his waggon without comment, 'Damned if he isn't a chip from a couple of old blocks, the Gov'nor and Sam. And that's equal to anything, even a two-hundred-mile haul with this weight aboard.' They moved off under the clear sky, passing Hanley Castle on their right, then heading down the old

coach road to Tewkesbury at a good seven miles an hour.
They were ninety minutes behind schedule.

Channing was waiting across the Severn and jumped
on the step of George's vehicle, shouting above the clank
and rattle of the procession, "Don't stop, Swann! I've
clearance as far as the Abbey. Is she riding well?"

"Better than I hoped," George roared. "The delay
was my fault. Pulling off the road on to soggy ground.
Won't happen again. Learned my lesson!"

"Will you detour this side of Gloucester?"

"Yes, at Longford. I'll look for you where we rejoin
the main road at the Tuffley junction." Channing
stepped nimbly off again and they passed through Tewkesbury before the streets of the old town were more than half
awake.

Channing was as good as his word. Constables held
horse traffic at every junction and the passage was accomplished in under a quarter of an hour. He had time to
glance left at the Norman Abbey, guarding the western
approach to the town, then right towards Bloody Meadow,
scene of the last Yorkist triumph, reflecting, 'A Crown
Prince came unstuck about here more than four hundred
years ago but it won't happen again at this spanking rate
of progress,' and he calculated they had come just under
eight miles in sixty-five minutes. It went some way towards compensating for the unnecessary delay back at the
farm.

Nine miles on, at Longford, they made their first devia-
tion, swinging left on to a flint road towards Barnwood
and aiming to cut a wide semi-circle round Gloucester,
seen in the near distance.

Their route would take them over higher ground on
the northern slope of Robinswood Hill and their speed
was necessarily much reduced here, for the road was
narrow, its surface gritty and the summer foliage thick
enough to swish the tarpaulin of the turret that he now
thought of, in the farmer's terms, as 'The Hump'. Drops of
last night's rain slashed his windshield, blurring his vision,

but they made steady progress through Barnwood and were within three miles of the Tuffley junction when Scottie's lance signalled a halt. He climbed down to discover that the linked vehicles completely blocked the road, with drainage ditches, half-full of storm water, on either side. Scottie said, "Look yon," and gestured ahead.

A huge oak, growing in the nearside hedge, spread its branches overhead, making a green arch and he saw at once that it was far more than a matter of brushing through a screen of twigs and leaves. A low slung bough, thick as a weaver's beam, reached clear across the lane. It would strike The Hump at least two feet below its summit and further progress, pending its removal, was impossible.

He understood then the full hazards of detours and they seemed to him, at that moment, far in excess of narrow city streets, when they could at least rely on police cooperation. Out here was nobody, not even a handy farm to seek assistance and a longish halt could play havoc with their time schedule. He was standing there fuming when Edward nudged his elbow and he turned to see the boy – he still thought of him as such – holding a large bow saw, with powerful, widely-spaced teeth.

"That chap Morgan was a woodsman before he joined us," he said, equably. "He'd make short work of that, George."

"Where did you get that saw?"

"It's standard kit in my beat," the boy said, and looked mildly surprised that his brother, Managing Director of the network, should need to be reminded of such an elementary detail. Morgan, a middle-aged man with a wall eye, came forward diffidently, saying, in his sing-song brogue, "Have it down, I will, in no time at all, Mr. Swann. But she'll have to be hauled clear and it'll take horse-flesh to do it."

He was right, of course. The bough, sawn near the trunk, would fall athwart the road and form a kind of chevaux-de-frise into the bargain. Once again George felt his basic policy vindicated, a partnership of horse and machine, for he would have baulked at using a Maxie for such a purpose in this enclosed country. Even so it was not easy to accomplish. The cavalcade all but blocked the road, the horses would have to be brought forward from the rear and the hedges were high and thickly sown. He said, "Get it down, Morgan. Edward, tell Rees to bring the Clydesdales forward on the nearside. It's just about possible to squeeze past if he uses the ditch. If it isn't we'll backtrack, find a gate and breach the damned hedge higher up."

It was early afternoon now and apart from their hasty breakfast at dawn none of them had eaten. His own contribution was to light a fire, brew tea and lay out home-baked loaves and local cheese he had bought at the farm. Before the kettle was boiling the rasp of Morgan's saw ceased with a long, splintering crash and the road ahead was choked with foliage. But by then three of the Clydesdales had been dragged slithering through the narrow gap, their huge hooves making a ruin of somebody's drainage system. Morgan, in need of a breather, climbed down from his perch in the bole and took charge of the tea while the others went forward to fix drag ropes to the branch, fastening them to the severed butt.

It was even larger than it looked and at first the Clydesdales couldn't budge it, but then Morgan called to Rees to stop fooling and cut away smaller branches, and they went to it with the saw and axes until the main trunk could be prised from its hold on the soggy banks. They had to drag it forward three hundred yards until they came upon a field gate and desperately heavy work it was for man and beast, but within just over an hour from the time of halting they cleared a path through the debris and moved on, munching as they drove, forcing a two-mile-an-hour passage through the lane to more open ground beyond.

The detour still held an unpleasant surprise. Within a mile of the main road the ground rose steeply as it wound under the scree and their rate of progress became even slower as the two engines wrestled with the weight of a load he was beginning to hate like a mortal enemy. It was past five o'clock when they met an anxious Channing striding up and down the road with his hunched, heron's gait, and George made a spot decision to take advantage of an open quarry entrance with a hard-packed surface and call it a day, over-ruling Channing's advice to push on.

"The motors have taken a terrible beating on that incline," he told him. "There's no sense in pushing our luck. We'll give them a good going over while your chauffeur runs my brother and the waggoners to the nearest inn. They've earned a hot meal and a night's rest."

"There's a good inn at Whaddon, a mile or so further on," Channing said, deferring to him. "Will you join us for dinner?"

"Not me," George said, "Quirt and I will stay with the load. We can make do where we are," and Channing, thankfully a man of few words, moved off.

They gave the engines an hour to cool off before going over them part by part, tightening nuts, checking the braking systems, refuelling the twenty-gallon tanks with the aid of a funnel. The long drag had been wasteful of petrol and it was difficult to estimate how much the drum had in reserve. Probably enough to see them through, George thought, for he knew he could not count on the certainty of a fresh supply. Between them they fed and watered the horses, rigging up an improvised corral at the face of the quarry. They were docile giants and would come to no harm in there and when they were dealt with he reckoned up his mileage as a mere twenty-one, the product of eleven hours on the road. It wasn't good enough, and for the first time he felt a prick of doubt. Scottie Quirt, knowing his moods so well, voiced it when he said, "We'll need a clear run tomorrow I'm thinking. Will you risk passing through Bristol?" and the words of his father came to him, saying, after a long squint at his sheaf of maps, "The Avonmouth route is the flattest but that means a snarl up in that city and a stiffish climb out of it to the west. If it was me, with that weight aboard, I'd detour via Keynsham. That's not a bad road, or wasn't in my day."

"We'll take the long way round," he said. "The Gov'nor usually knows what he's about between here and Pentland Firth," and making a pillow of a bag of oats he stretched himself on the waggon-bed and slept.

3

His confidence had returned by the time they moved off, shortly after six the following morning. Channing must have been astir even earlier, for he brought Edward and the waggoners to the quarry by the time the engines were warmed up and George moved out ahead of his rearguard, not imagining he would make such good time over the next leg that they would have difficulty keeping convoy.

It was another fine, clear morning and a chorus of blackbirds and finches whistled them good luck as they swung back on to the main Gloucester–Bristol road and went trundling down the lush green strip between the two cities, sometimes holding the cavalcade at a speed of approaching nine miles an hour and moving over the best surface they had encountered as yet. Just beyond Almondsbury they branched left to begin the wide detour of Bristol, finding the country more built over, and the roads much firmer and broader than during the Gloucester detour. They stopped for a cool-off and a bite to eat in Stoke Gifford and just as they were moving off again Channing drove up with news that Edward and his team were at least three miles behind. "He seems to think you'll want to press on," Channing said. "You aren't likely to need the horses in this area, are you?" George told him no and gave him a careful note of the proposed

route as far as Burrow Gurney, where they were due to
rejoin the main road. By ten o'clock they were under way
again, probing through Kingswood to Keynsham and
encountering no bad gradients, although three slowed
them to under two miles an hour.

The Hump seemed to be behaving with great circum-
spection. Its lashings remained taut and it cleared four
Great Western railway bridges with inches to spare. He
thought, 'That's another astounding aspect of the Gov'nor's
memory. Is there anyone else in the country, even a
veteran railwayman, with his kind of memory for low-
level bridges?' He wondered briefly how Adam had come
by it, for there must have been many changes in the railway network since he reconnoitred the country's highways and byways on horseback, with his little red book on
hand to note down every feature of the landscape likely
to feature in a haulage estimate. It was really no wonder
the Swann veterans still held him in awe, even now, when
he was more concerned with his tulips and cypresses than
the nation's business. He knew all their beats far better
than they themselves knew them and neither was his
knowledge for trivia confined to topography. Near here,
where the Kennet and Avon and Wilts and Berks Canals
converged on the river, he recalled Adam throwing out
one of those stray pieces of information that enlivened any
journey or discussion with him. "It was the scene," he
had told George, "of the first real clash between King and
Parliament, at the very start of the Civil War. The
Cavaliers, so-called, caught their opponents on the hop
and got the impression, poor wights, that the war would
be won at a blow." They pushed on through Whitchurch
and Bishopsworth to the Great West Road, making good
time over narrowing roads. By noon they were back on
the broad highway, having covered upwards of forty miles
in just under six hours.

At Burrow Gurney they took another breather but
Edward did not show. Instead Channing reappeared,
like a daemon in a pantomime, with news that the waggon

team had headed straight through the city to save time and were now leaving it by the western approach. George thought, 'It's damned tempting to push on but I daren't run too far ahead. The long stiff climb at Churchill is less than ten miles ahead and before that I'm going to need the horses as brake-insurance at Lulsgate Bottom.' He was glad then that Edward had showed initiative in taking a short cut and held their speed down to a crawl over the next stretch, halting again at the head of the incline and biting his nails until Channing and Edward showed up almost together and he could use the armourer's Daimler for a preliminary survey.

The hill into Lulsgate was steep, certainly, and would have to be tackled with excessive care, but the road surface was better than average and Channing agreed to drive ahead producing, to everybody's amusement, a large red flag of the type all motorists had been compelled to carry until the 1896 Act of Parliament had been rescinded.

He said, attempting a joke, "Anyone who sees that will assume you've been in purdah for the last five years," but Channing, although taking his point, did not smile. Clearly the trip was playing havoc with his nerves and George thought, 'That's the difference between planners and doers. He's a planner and can design superb weapons in that foundry of his, but I wonder how would he behave if he was called upon to use 'em in action?'

He came back to the stationary cavalcade resolved to use the drag chains, with the man-o'-war shoed on both rear wheels and acting as a holding force. They moved off in bottom gear, inching down the long slope at a slow walking pace and he was very relieved when they arrived at the dip and could unhitch the waggon and take advantage of the flattish stretch towards Bridgwater. Channing, scouting ahead, said there was a cutting sown with flints this side of East Brent and reaching here George decided to curb his exuberance and call it a day. They had come fifty-nine miles in under twelve hours, bypassing one of the largest centres of population in the country and tackling one of the toughest descents on the route map. He helped empty Scottie's bottle of whisky to celebrate.

*   *   *

Their luck seemed set fair now. They moved off to a quick start on Day Four, to tackle the Churchill climb and take early advantage of Channing's traffic clearance in Bridgwater. At the summit of the slope he deployed all eight Clydesdales on chain traces, climbing the hill at a crawl with the draught animals strung out ahead but they kept moving and reached Bridgwater before many carters were abroad.

After that it was flat, easy country to Taunton, eleven miles further on, another town where they were shown every courtesy. The Taunton–Wellington stretch slowed them down, proving hillier than he had expected, but they tackled every ascent with the greatest caution and had no recourse to deployment or the waggon-brake on descents. Edward kept up well and Channing roved ahead with his blood-red flag. By mid-afternoon they were in Cullompton, an hour and a half later in Pinhoe, only a few miles short of Exeter. There was still plenty of travelling time. He pushed on the odd four miles over the lowest crossing of the Exe at Countess Wear and found a halting place in a section where the county authorities had all but completed a road-widening project just beyond the Great Western Railway's coastal stretch on the west bank of the estuary. Their progress, he told them with glee, had been spectacular. They had come, at his reckoning, seventy-one miles in a smooth, uneventful haul. They still had a day and a half in hand to cover the fifty-odd miles to Devonport.

By far the most direct route to Plymouth was inland, heading for Newton Abbot, but the main coach road ran over two very formidable hills, crossing the Haldon escarpment and George, having had personal experience of

347

them during his occasional forays into the Western Wedge, recalled that they were not only steep but tortuous. His father had urged the longer way round, following the coast as far as Teignmouth, then turning sharply inland and moving up the Teign estuary to Newton Abbot.

At many places the road ran beside the railway, said to be the most expensive stretch to maintain in the country, and there were several sharp laps approaching and beyond the little seaside resorts that had grown up under the red bluffs. They reached Newton Abbot without incident, however, and took the road to Totnes, tackling a stiffish slope out of the town, and from there, moving very slowly in this undulating country, heading for South Brent, where the range of tors indicated impossible motoring country to the north.

It came on to rain after they rejoined the main road and he had all he could do to keep moving, with Dartmoor drizzle reducing visibility to fifty yards, but they kept going and were within hailing distance of the Great Western Railway crossing at Wrangton when Channing, scouting ahead, came back signalling a halt. He said, tersely, "What do your maps say about the bridge yonder?" and George, making a check, said there was a twelve-foot nine clearance.

"Somebody is behind the times," he said. "I've just measured it, and it's an inch or so under twelve. Come and see for yourself."

They went down towards the bridge and it was just as Channing had said. New pointing had reduced the clearance below the minimum and even with the tarpaulin stripped off there was no prospect of passing The Hump under the arch. It would foul the bridge two inches or more below the summit.

"Have you got a detour pencilled in?"

"Yes, but the Gov'nor queried it. There's a road bridge on the lower road and the surface is unmade. However, there's no help for it, we'll have to try the Ugborough–Ermington loop."

It was still raining when they nosed their way down a narrow country road south of the main route, then headed west again over an atrocious surface where their speed was reduced to under two miles an hour. He thought, sourly, 'With ordinary luck, yesterday's luck, we could have made Plymouth tonight. We'll never do it now,' and he sent Edward ahead to reconnoitre the bridge.

The boy was back in ten minutes looking glum. "It's even lower than the rail bridge," he said, "and there's only one way of passing it. We'll have to lower the road level by six inches or more."

He went forward to see for himself. The bridge, an old one, had once given haywain clearance but that was long ago. Winter rains had worn away the banks and there was actually a slight incline up to the arch where the road was surfaced with hard-packed rubble.

"It's a pick and shovel job," he told Edward. "Get Morgan, Rees and the tools."

"We'll need more than one pick and shovel to shift that in the time. How about local labour?"

"Is there any to be had at short notice?"

"Farms, I daresay. I'll look around," and he plodded off into the seeping mist while George, momentarily forgetting him, set to work with Scottie and the two waggoners, scrabbling at the surface with such tools as they had.

They had hardly broken the surface when Edward was back in a blue farm-waggon driven by a moorman with straw-coloured hair and a brogue so thick as to be all but unintelligible.

"Us iz zendin' ver Bain," he told George, after a long and hostile scrutiny of the cavalcade. "Youm bliddy well mazed, maister, to bring that gurt contrapsun round yer. Anyone knows you carn taake a wain from Yuish to Ivy-bridge this road." He made no reference to the rail bridge at Wrangton. Presumably local men had adjusted to both underpasses.

"Do you know what he's saying?" George demanded,

irritably, and Edward said, "We don't have to. He understood me the moment I offered him a sovereign an hour for his labour and tools. I had to show him the money, however. No flies on these boys."

'Bain' (subsequently identified as 'Ben', senior hand at the nearest farm) arrived a few minutes later, with two mute assistants and a load of tools. With a labour force of nine they made rapid progress, carting soil and rock chippings away in a wheelbarrow that had an excruciating squeak. Darkness closed in, however, long before the section was cut and levelled, so that George sent for storm-lanterns to hang in the hedges and the work continued in the soft yellow glow, lighting both sides of the arch.

When they were down to a uniform ten inches, and both approaches had been levelled off to some extent, he sent Edward in the moorman's cart for planking, busying himself with Scottie and the waggoners stripping the tarpaulin from The Hump. He took his time now, covering the dip with carefully placed planks two inches thick and it was well past midnight before they were ready to move. Channing appeared out of the murk, a heron with bedraggled plumage, who was already acquainted with the cause of the long delay. Rumour circulated quickly in this kind of country, he said, and Ivybridge was alerted as to their presence a mile south of the main road. "I've sent my man on into Plymouth with a letter to the authorities at Crownhill," he added, breathlessly. "We'll get every co-operation in the city. Will you wait for the light now?"

George told him no. All he wanted was to be out of this bottleneck without further delay and Channing, perched in the dripping hedge on the Plymouth side of the bridge, watched them pass through and tackle the incline towards the main road. The bridge had claimed something in excess of eight hours.

He curbed his impatience then and splashed up a muddy lane to the farm where the farmer's wife, whose

brogue rivalled the carter's, made tea and beef sandwiches, and he paid Bain and his team for their labour
and took his turn to wash under the kitchen pump.
Dawn was lighting the eastern sky now and they made a
fresh start about five, crawling into Ivybridge an hour or
so later and pushing through it without a stop. Despite
the early hour half the town assembled to watch the procession.

The final leg, some twelve miles from Ivybridge to
Devonport, occupied them close on for three hours and it
was nearly eleven-thirty when they trundled through the
dock gates and saw Channing again, miraculously
spruced up, who agreed to superintend the unloading and
find someone to take care of the horses. He said, after a
taciturn naval officer had inspected the naked cupola in
its waggon-bed, "You realise how close we came? Another ninety minutes and they would have refused delivery," and George, stifling a yawn, replied, "They
would have had to haul it back to Bromsgrove under their
own steam for I wouldn't make that trip again for a king's
ransom. We all need a hot meal and twelve hours' sleep.
Did you book any lodging hereabouts?"

"Not me," Channing said, wrinkling his lip in the
second smile George had seen him attempt during their
brief but eventful acquaintance, "but I'm led to believe
your father did."

"*My father?*"

"He's waiting in a local hotel. I forget the name. It's
a half-timbered building, a stone's throw from the dock-
yard gates. Arrived yesterday, I hear." Suddenly, and
with what was clearly an effort for so reserved a man, he
extended his hand. "I won't forget this, Swann. I'm
uncommonly obliged to every one of you. Will you give
this to your men to share?", and he passed over an envelope, later found to contain a cash bonus of a hundred
guineas.

The naval officer summoned him then and George was
watching the mobile crane go into action when Edward

351

plucked his sleeve, pointing to a spare figure in a grey frock coat, standing squarely on the cobbles immediately outside the gates. "You can't keep the Gov'nor away, George. I think he's ruffled you didn't ask him along for the ride."

"I did," George said, "and he laughed in my face. He's nicely placed nowadays. All the fun without any of the grief. I'm beginning to think there's a lot to be said for getting long in the tooth."

They went out together and Adam, deliberately laconic, shook hands with each of them. "You cut it fine, boy," he said, as they crossed to the grill room of the hotel, where Scottie and the waggoners were already wielding knife and fork. "What kept you so long over the final leg?" and George, suddenly recalling his father's stories of old coachman Blubb, the Kentish Triangle manager who had once driven the 'Lord Nelson' coach and four north from the Saracen's Head in Snow Hill before the railways threw him on a scrapheap, said, "You could call it 'that bliddy gridiron', Gov'nor. I daresay old Blubb would have had something quaint to say about it."

"Ah, I daresay," said Adam, "but he would have been equally foul-mouthed as regards your means of traction." He unfolded a *Westminster Gazette* dated four days earlier, indicating a somewhat blurred picture of the cavalcade, moving through Worcester. "I've sent for the negative of that," he said. "We'll use it in the autumn advertisement programme. It should help to win you a handsome majority at the next conference. You'll talk them into going ahead with the fleet of motors, I imagine?"

"Scottie Quirt is travelling north tonight to put the original plan into action as soon as he's caught up on his sleep. They'll be approving a *fait accompli* when they finally get around to it."

"Ah, that was my way," Adam said. "Democracy? It's well enough in theory but it's no substitute for the committee of one, boy."

*   *   *

Adam Swann, whom few would have described as a family man in the literal sense, was none the less an interested observer of family alliances. Down the years he had pondered each of them objectively, feeling that there was something fresh to be learned about people in the shifts and loyalty patterns that went on under his nose. Perhaps it was this curiosity that enabled him to draw what he regarded as the really important lesson from George's two-hundred-and-fifty-mile haul with that bloodless chap's gun-turret.

It was not a reaffirmation of his unwavering faith in George as a pioneer, the only male of his brood in whom he saw himself in the splendour of his youth; neither was it the certainty that George, although moving at a snail's pace, had managed to whip the carpet from under the feet of his colleagues at the board table. Rather, it was a new relationship that had flowered under stress between New Broom and New Boy, his youngest son, Edward. For George, until then, had seemed not to need an ally within the family, whereas Edward (whose reverence for George had been evident since infancy), had been waiting in the wings for a long time now and had at last been summoned, to savour the bliss of what seemed, to Adam, a full and equal partnership. Overnight as it were. Somewhere between Bromsgrove and Devonport Docks. And under what circumstances? The factors contributing to form this interesting new alliance teased Adam all the way home, so much so that he took the very first opportunity that presented itself to satisfy his curiosity, when Edward, leaping out to lay claim on a cab as the express slid into Paddington, left them alone for a moment or two.

"How did the boy shape, George?"

"Edward? To have along on a trip of that kind? First-rate, Gov'nor. Absolutely first-rate." George hesitated a moment, standing with his back to his father and his hand raised to the luggage rack, and in the compartment mirror Adam saw the wide, familiar grin light up his face. Then George turned, heaving at their grips. "Damn it, I'll go further. Why not? Maybe I'm getting woolly. Maybe he's a marriage of your patience and Sam Rawlinson's bullheadedness. I'll come right out with it. He saved our bacon twice over. Without him I'd never have made it. Is that what you wanted to know?"

"I'll own to it, too, George. It's what I suspected and wanted confirmed."

3

Confrontations

IT WAS TIMES SUCH AS THESE WHEN, DROWSY AFTER
an interval of tenderness crowned by a lovemaking he had
dropped away into sleep, that the sense of identity came
to Romayne. A presence, half-shade, half-fancy, yet
almost tangible, standing beside the bed like a fairy god-
mother or like the jovial ghost of Christmas Present in *A
Christmas Carol*. Warm and munificent, a personifica-
tion of the benedictions of a lifetime, so that she was aware
of a fulfilment that had eluded her since childhood.

It had grown a little, this presence, ever since they
settled here, in this scarred monument to greed, with its
tips and its skeletal pithead gear, its undulating seams of
dwellings etched against a ragged skyline, its long tradition of toil and deprivation. Not a presence one would be
likely to associate with ugliness and desecration but at
home for all that, far more so than it would have been in
the pampered circumstances of her earlier life and the
difference lay, she imagined, in her personal contribution
to the serenity of their sojourn and the reality of their new-
found comradeship.

For ever since coming here she had seen him grow,
a little every day, as he moved about among his miners
and their cheerful, extrovert families, healing their small
feuds and weaving their isolated protests against fate into
a force and fervour that would one day carry him to Westminster as their champion. And it was the very certainty

of this that enlarged him so that, looking back to a time when he was dabbling in trade, he seemed small, baffled, blighted and insignificant, with no outlet for his brimming reservoir of compassion.

She acknowledged, proudly and cheerfully, her role in this enlargement. Yet all she had done, when she came to think about it, was to point him in the right direction after so long in the wilderness although her claims in another, more private, area were more substantial. Not only had she brought him a son, and was soon, she felt sure, to bring him another, she was there to offer succour and revitalisation when he came home tired and used up, nurturing him as a lover in this nondescript room when rain came slashing in from the Atlantic and the wind roared down from the mountains, re-inflating his ego in a way that revealed to her not only his innermost secrets but those of every man and every woman who had ever sought and found deep, personal fulfilment in physical fusion. It taught her something vital about the relationship of men like his father and women like his indomitable mother who had, as it were, fed upon one another's being in a long and fruitful association and she was so happy that she feared it was too rich and rewarding to last out their lifespan.

Thus she no longer thought of herself as Romayne Rycroft-Mostyn, the spoiled and wilful child of a money-mad industrialist whose despotism extended over mines, dyeworks and chain foundries. Here, within the easy freemasonry of an enclosed community, where four out of five families wrenched a living from the seams deep under the mountain, she was plain Rosie Swann, the candidate's wife, and she rejoiced in the title. She had come home, out of the long, growling storm.

She withdrew her free hand from the blankets, half-turned and ran her fingertips across his chest and down over his warm belly to the groin, smiling secretively at the limpness and insignificance of her discoveries and wondering briefly if he was capable as yet of re-enacting the climactic surge of an hour ago and dreaming it possible if he was sufficiently encouraged. But then, turning away, she remembered he would need rest for tomorrow's winter foray into the Chamberlain citadel at Birmingham, beside his hero and sponsor, David Lloyd George, for whom their son had been named. She did not fear for him or his mentor on those Midland battlements, despite gloomy warnings of party wiseacres and newspapers, who said the Brummagers would make good their threat to lynch any pro-Boer who ventured among them. Giles Swann and Lloyd George could be relied upon to give a good account of themselves on any battlefield where their deepest convictions were challenged. In the end, despite slanders, violence and mob hysteria, they would win the day.

2

Giles, stepping out into a flurry of sleet on New Street platform a few hours later, did not share her confidence, being under no illusion what kind of opposition they would be likely to face up here and what excesses a Brummagen mob were capable of committing whipped on by the scourge of partisan-patriotism. Patriotism, he thought, was a word that should be expunged from the dictionary. It had become pitifully debased of late and was currently being used to justify every kind of outrage, both here and on the veldt where, so they said, thousands of Boer women and children had already died in Kitchener's concentration camps. A necessary price Tory newspapers claimed, to be paid for denying the enemy access to areas of recruitment and supply. Such facts, if they could be believed (and the latest underground intelligence from the Cape persuaded him they could) dishonoured not only the perpetrators, but the entire nation; especially a people whose boast it was that their homeland was the power house of freedom.

He wondered how his brother Alex would answer such an indictment. Or his mother. Or Hugo, poor devil, whose life had been shattered by impulses set in train by that same word. Surely war against the dependants of a gallant and already defeated minority was indefensible, even when British soldiers were dying at the same rate in tented hospitals behind the blockhouse wire. The entire war was indefensible, had always been indefensible and his loathing for it welled up in him afresh so that he hunched his shoulders against the December sleet and set off, grim-faced, towards the Liberal Club, there to seek the latest briefing on the Town Hall rally where Lloyd George, despite police appeals and a flood of warnings from his own supporters, had pledged himself to speak that night.

He found the sense of foreboding had spilled out of Headquarters into the streets. Police were everywhere, mounted and on foot. Shopkeepers were boarding up their premises, as against a siege or street battle. The very air was charged with strain, the tensions releasing themselves in the thud of hammer on clapboard and the bravado of the party workers, one of whom told him that, although entry to the Town Hall was strictly by ticket, thousands of tickets were known to have been forged and violence was a certainty. Lloyd George himself, he learned, was not yet in the city and his method of entry, and progress to the Town Hall, was a closely-guarded secret, but that he would appear as promised nobody doubted, least of all Giles, for here was a situation the Welshman would relish. All his life he had been moving towards this kind of climax and his personal courage was equal to any of the men who had sworn to silence him, hopefully for ever.

By mid-afternoon, under a sky heavy with snow, he had threaded his way through dense crowds to Victoria Square, where the Town Hall stood on an island, already besieged by patriots, so that Giles wondered how any legitimate ticket-holders could expect to get in without being manhandled. Here again scores of police were on duty but there was little, seemingly, that they could do to control the dense crowds and on a piece of waste land in

Edmund Street he saw a huckster doing a profitable business selling bricks at three a penny 'to chuck at Lloyd George'.

It took him nearly an hour to work his way round to the committee-room entrance, where the presence of over fifty policemen succeeded in keeping open a narrow gangway along which ticket-holders ran the gauntlet of the Chamberlain mobs, screaming abuse and obscenities at everyone whose ticket was accepted as genuine. He thought, on reaching the relative sanctuary of the hall, packed with supporters, 'What the devil has happened to the country? In the old days party rivalry was rumbustious but there was a schoolboy element about its clashes . . . It was never vicious, or never on this scale . . .' and he wondered if it might not have been wiser to cancel the meeting after all, for if the mob broke in something far worse than broken heads and bloody noses would result, and, even if he escaped, Lloyd George's obduracy would be deemed responsible for the carnage.

But then, his confidence returning as he looked at the massed ranks of the faithful and the knots of prowling stewards, he thought: 'Damn them all . . . David is right! Someone has to show the real flag. Someone has to make a stand for free speech and democratic tradition, and who better than him?'

*　　　*　　　*

He slipped in quietly and unobtrusively about seven o'clock, almost unrecognisable under a heavy peaked cap and a rough, workman's overcoat. Utterly composed, and with the familiar twinkle lighting his eye as he said, seeing Giles, "Well, Johnny Peep? How's this for a peaceful exchange of views? A little livelier than a House debate but more productive too, if I'm not mistaken. How is your wife? Did she come along for the fun?"

"She would have if she hadn't been pregnant, L.G. She sent her regards, and said I was to tell you we'll make it next election. We came much closer than I expected last time."

"And she's right, tell her. The mood of the country is changing, despite this welcome party. This is no more than a local fracas, the natural outcome of our Go-For-Jo campaign. Next time we'll give them the shock of the century," and he moved off to chat to Birmingham supporters among whom, Giles noted with some apprehension, were a number of women, already dishevelled by their passage into the hall.

The roars outside beat upon the isolated building like prodigious breakers on a rock, wave after wave of baying that made speech between individuals difficult and would certainly prohibit a public address. Giles shouted, in the ear of a rosetted official, "He'll never make himself heard against that," and the man, his face flushed with excitement, shouted, "He *knows* that! We *all* knew it! It's *being* here that matters!"

It was true enough, he supposed, and Lloyd George, the Welsh Cœur de Lion as they had christened him since the Bangor riot, was already dictating a speech that he knew he would never deliver, seemingly unperturbed by the terrible uproar caused by the use of heavy noticeboards torn down from across the Square now being used as battering rams on the doors. News filtered in, all of it bad. The baying mob had burst through the outer police cordon. The outer doors had yielded to assault. Infiltrators were trickling into the body of the hall. The meeting could only end in bloody chaos, unparalleled in this century.

At seven-thirty Lloyd George led the way out of the committee room on to the platform, fronted and flanked by a phalanx of police. It was soon apparent that the pessimists were right about infiltration. His appearance was greeted by a howl that blotted out the continuous clamour from the Square. Volleys of bricks crashed through the windows as the speaker, leaning forward to address a word to the press bench, was assailed by a boarding party who swept up to the platform in a body, overwhelming the press box in such numbers that it collapsed and precipitated a wedge of pressmen on to the floor. The reporters scattered, notebooks flying. The police and stewards counter-attacked and the storming party was seized and thrust down again. Arrests, in these circumstances, were impossible.

Half an hour passed. Stewards fought, police fought and the mob fought back, drunk and delirious with hate but all the time, slightly in advance of the shrinking party platform, Lloyd George stood there, relaxed, half-amused, fascinated it seemed by the tempest his presence occasioned. Police whistles shrilled, glass continued to shatter along the full length of the hall and the body of the building was jammed with a heavy, scrambling mass out of which rose a cacophony of screams, yells and hysterical appeals for help. The gesture was made and it was time to retreat. Shepherded by police the platform party edged back into the committee rooms, where barricades were instantly erected and all lights were extinguished on the orders of the Chief Constable. Slowly, fighting for every inch of ground gained, police and stewards regained control of the hall but outside the mob now ruled unchallenged. According to police instructions it had been reinforced and the Chief Constable, reappearing, said he could no longer guarantee the safety of the party. There was only one means to extract Lloyd George from the beleaguered building. He would have to pass out under the protection of a policeman's cape and helmet. As for the others, plans were being made for a retreat across the road to the Midland Institute offices, where they might wait until time and falling snow thinned the mob.

Giles watched him don the disguise, protesting that it was ridiculous but submitting, as he explained, for the sake of the Chief Constable's professional reputation. He said, as Giles sidled across, "How do I look, Johnny? Like someone from the chorus of Gilbert and Sullivan?" and Giles said, gravely, "Don't ask me until you're clear

361

of this, L.G. We can joke about it later." They shook
hands and as Lloyd George took his place in the line he
called, "You were here, Johnny! I won't forget that,
lad!"

They passed out in a marching file, heading for Paradise
Street and Easy Row and ultimately, Giles learned
later, the sanctuary of Ladywood police station clear
across the city. But for the platform party the problem
of exit remained and would do so as long as it was believed
L.G. was still inside.

The respite was temporary. Soon a police inspector
arrived from the main battle area, grunting that the line
could only hold for a few minutes. At the committee
room exit, a carriage and pair, assailed from all sides,
and escorted by flailing mounted police, drew the attention of the main body of assailants. Before it was realised
that its interior contained not the arch-traitor but police
reinforcements, the stragglers had made their dash across
the street under another police escort. They were only just
in time. Giles, one of the last to leave, heard the mob
storm back into the hall, climb the platform and range
through every room, smashing and overturning everything
in their path. They were not ejected until the Riot Act was
read and a baton charge could be mounted.

Outside snow was falling in heavy flakes, mantling the
stark outline of the civic buildings and muffling, to some
extent, the roars of the disappointed Brummagers. The
riot petered out. Ambulances collected casualties and
those who could found transport home. Giles walked,
shouldering his way through the stragglers to New Street,
where he caught the night train to Newport, reminding
himself that he lacked L.G.'s ebullience. To him the
evening was bloody, raucous proof of the nation's sickness
and it occurred to him to wonder how long it would take
to cure. L.G., as spokesman for the minority who saw the
war as an exercise in national degradation, had outfaced
the patriots on their own ground and there was, he supposed, some satisfaction to be derived from that. But

divisions, of a kind he had witnessed here tonight, must run clear across the country, driving wedges between man and wife, father and son, and as he thought this he reflected bitterly on his own situation, with one brother away fighting Cronje's commandos and another maimed for life by a stupid, vainglorious quarrel. It was not a happy thought, especially as he and Romayne had promised to keep their Christmas at 'Tryst'.

2

It was not often, nowadays, that Henrietta Swann had an opportunity to bask in her role as matriarch, a privilege she had enjoyed since the eldest of the brood had married and started a family of her own some sixteen years ago. As time passed, and each of them assumed responsibilities in various parts of the Empire, home-comings to 'Tryst' became intermittent and there never had been an occasion, since Christmas, 1888, when she had all of them assembled round her at one time.

This year, however, promised to be a great improvement on recent reunions. All but Alex and Lydia would be returning for Christmas Day and Boxing Day, and even Jack-o'-Lantern and Joanna had promised to appear, bringing Helen home after her recuperative holiday in Dublin.

Adam, permanently home-based at last, took a keener interest than usual in celebrations, personally selecting the Christmas tree and garlanding of the house with holly, ivy and mistletoe, but grumbling, as he worked, that "They owed all this fussy fiddle-faddle to that brace of prize sentimentalists, Prince Albert and Charles Dickens!" He made an impressive job of it. Henrietta never recalled the house looking more festive and welcoming, and when the first of the grandchildren scampered in (George's brood from nearby Beckenham) she was rewarded by their squeals of glee and the grave congratulations of her Austrian daughter-in-law, Gisela, the acknowledged family expert on the Teutonic Yuletide, refashioned for British hearths by that brace of sentimentalists, Albert and Charles, God bless them.

The following day, before luncheon, Hugo and Lady Sybil arrived, with Hugo's soldier-servant in tow, the latter stamping about the waxed and gleaming floors bellowing '*Sah!*', in anticipation of his master's requirements. Hugo, she noted, looked surprisingly fit and Sybil said, in a whispered aside, "The dear boy is adjusting, much as we hoped." Yet it was painful and pitiful to see him so stolid and stationary unless chivvied by that drill-ground sergeant or his wife, and a comfort to reflect that Giles would be along soon, for he and Hugo, she recalled, had been very close as boys during their shared sojourn at the bleak school up on Exmoor. She made a mental note to have a private word with Giles, whom she regarded as the family wiseacre, about a suitable occupation for an athlete who had lost his sight. Lady Sybil had been speculating on a variety of pursuits, among them model ship-making and fashioning things out of potter's clay, but somehow they did not suit Henrietta's notion of Hugo's need. It would have to be something far more positive, especially when Sybil's child arrived, claiming a share of its mother's time and attention. Giles would think of something for Giles always did. And Hugo would likely need him more than anybody.

Romayne, she noted with satisfaction, was holding on to that second child, due in the early spring they announced. A disappointing late starter in the Swann grandchild stakes the girl now seemed to be making amends, for David, their first-born, had only just celebrated his first birthday.

Then the Irish party arrived with a trunkful of presents, all prettily wrapped and ready to hang on the tree, and on Christmas morning Stella, Denzil and their tribe arrived from Dewponds, so that the old house crackled with hilarity and creaked under the impact of so much horse-play, the tenor of good cheer broken every now and again by a short-lived quarrel among the younger cohorts and a constant demand for umpires.

Twenty-six of them sat down to Christmas dinner at eight o'clock that evening, including the senior grandchildren. Upstairs, sleeping it off in readiness for Boxing Day brawls, were half-a-dozen toddlers and three babies, so that even 'Tryst', that had always seemed such a barn of a place with only Edward and Margaret at home, was hard taxed to provide accommodation for the clan. It was a long time since this had happened, Henrietta recalled. The last occasion had been that of Stella's second marriage, when Adam had shocked the county by filling the place with hirelings gathered from all over the network.

Early on Boxing Day Henrietta had another unlooked-for surprise. Deborah, her journalist husband, Milton Jeffs, and their little boy arrived from the Westcountry and she saw Adam's face light up, knowing the soft spot he had always had for the child he brought in like a spaniel out of the snow all those years ago, rescuing her from a convent where she had been lodged, poor mite, by that dreadful father of hers, Josh Avery, whom nobody had set eyes on since he ran away with all Adam's capital.

Two of the children had to be evacuated from an east wing bedroom and accommodated on truckle beds in the sewing room in order to make room for the Jeffs but this was soon accomplished and they all trooped out to watch Stella, Jack-o'-Lantern, young Edward and George's two eldest boys ride off for the Boxing Day meet at Long Covert. With them, at a steady trot, went Hugo and his rough-riding sergeant, who had recently taught him to ride on a leading rein.

"He won't *hunt*, of course," Sybil told her, "but he can poke about the coverts happily enough and I entirely discount the risk weighed against the good it will do him. We tried him out in Rotten Row a month ago and it was a triumph. I couldn't keep the photographers away, unfortunately, for it was regarded as very sensational by all the newspapers and he didn't take kindly to that. I've since warned everybody not to tell him his picture was in *Chambers's Journal*. That's understandable, of course."

But to Henrietta it wasn't, although she thought better of asking her aristocratic daughter-in-law to elaborate on Hugo's excessive modesty. Heaven knows, to her way of thinking, the loss of one's sight in action against the Queen's enemies (hardly anybody had adjusted, as yet, to thinking of them as the 'King's enemies') fully justified the pocketing of any kudos that came his way and she was still puzzled by Hugo's extreme reticence to discuss the war, even impersonally. He had never minded discussing his athletic triumphs and surely they were very small beer matched against what he had achieved, almost single-handed, against those wicked spiteful Boers. She could only suppose it had something to do with Lady Sybil Uskdale's aversion to the vulgar popular press and that she had drilled Hugo into regarding the mention of one's war experiences as putting on side.

All but Young Edward, a rare thruster, were back by mid-afternoon, spattered with mud and well laced with stirrup cup, and they formed an impatient queue at the bathroom Adam had installed adjoining the kitchen wash-house, calling loudly to one another to hurry on out and look sharp about it. Nowadays, she heard, people were actually installing bathrooms upstairs but the plumbing at 'Tryst' would never run to that, Adam said, not without having all its floors up and who knew what might result from that in a house advancing into its fifth century?

Just as dusk closed in over the leafless copper beeches of the drive and all the lamps were lit, there was a vast commotion in the forecourt and George appeared bellowing, "It's old Alex, by God! With Lydia and their girl, Rosie! You never said a word about their arrival, Mother! I thought they were still in South Africa and Rose was at school!" and Henrietta, feeling quite faint, replied, "So did I, and so did your father! But, that's *wonderful* . . .

wonderful for it makes us complete don't you see? And for the first time in I don't know how long!" She hurried into the hall where Alex, in his dress uniform, was helping his plain little wife to shed her mantle and their grave-eyed daughter, Rose, was hurriedly unpacking yet another batch of Christmas gifts.

If she had favourites among them Alex qualified for a place at the top of the list. Aside from Hugo, whose spell of soldiering had been so brief and so tragic, Alex was the only one among them who fulfilled her girlish dream of mothering a race of scarlet-clad warriors but she was fond of Lydia too, whom she realised had given him purpose and direction in his chosen profession. It was more than two years since she had seen them although Rose, their eldest child, had stayed here for the summer holidays, a quiet, well-mannered girl who had inherited, thank God, her father's looks and stature and promised to be quite handsome once she outgrew her coltishness.

Lydia said, kissing her, "Alex was due for another step up and was posted back to Colchester. We didn't write because we weren't sure but it was confirmed while we were at sea. He'll be gazetted lieutenant-colonel in the New Year."

"Why, that's splendid, my boy. Congratulations," Adam murmured, privately wondering if the promotion stemmed from his long-standing friendship with Lord Roberts, also home again after straightening out the mess the army had got itself in out there, and Alex explained that he was to be seconded to an embryo force being assembled at Woolwich for the purpose of consolidating all the experience gained in the field with heavy machine-gun units.

"There's a rumour that we're to be issued with two to a battalion," he said, between greetings, and then, a little uncomfortably, "Is Hugo here?"

"Everybody's here," Adam told him, "George, Giles, Hugo, Young Edward and all the girls, including Helen. You won't have seen her for years, will you? Not since

367

she was last on leave, with that poor chap, Rowland Coles. But I wrote you about that shambles."

"Yes," Alex said, rather absently Adam thought. "It was a shocking affair but I understand Helen came out of it very well. Is she herself again?"

"No, she isn't," Adam told him, "but she's on the mend and looks fit enough. So does Hugo. Surprisingly so. He's been out with the hunt today."

"*Hunting? Hugo?*"

"On the leading rein. That wife of his is a trier and he's got a rough-riding sergeant who bullies him into taking regular exercise. But come along, meet them all yourself . . ."

But instead of following him into the mêlée in the drawing room, where tea was about to be served, Alex hung back saying, "Hold on, sir. I . . . er . . . I don't quite follow. You say Hugo *and* Giles are here? Both? Under the same roof!"

It says something for Adam's ageing reactions that he realised at once what Alex was hinting at and made an immediate response, heading off a squall that could shatter the conviviality of the occasion. He said, quietly, "Come in here a moment, before we get embroiled," and edged his eldest son into Henrietta's sewing-room, now doing duty as a spillover bedroom. He said, shutting the door, "You'll have differences, I daresay. But here and now isn't the place to air them. For mine and your mother's sake. This is the festive season, isn't it?"

"Not as festive as all that," Alex said, tight-lipped. "I confess I don't understand what's happened to Giles, or how he could show his face in Hugo's presence. Damn it, the fellow's unrepentantly pro-Boer, isn't he?"

"Come to that I'm not anti-Boer myself, son," Adam said, mildly. "A lot of people over here think the hammering should stop. We should have made a generous peace with the poor devils by now."

"That's the politicians' business."

"Giles *is* a politician, Alex."

It seemed that this was all but new to Alex. He frowned, as though finding the news distasteful and said, in the same flat voice, "He's also the brother of a man who lost his sight in action. I would have thought that should give him second thoughts about standing on a public platform and supporting that damned traitor, Lloyd George."

He saw the dilemma and a very unpleasant one it promised to be. Not only for Giles and Hugo but for all of them, especially Henrietta, who was riding so high just now. He said, "You'll have to call a temporary truce, son. I can't go into it now and I'm not even sure I'll want to later. You're a professional soldier and Giles is working to become a legislator. You don't have to remind me of the opinion the soldiers have of politicians, 'The Frocks' as you chaps call them. I held those opinions myself in my soldiering days, until I discovered how fiendishly difficult it can be to find a compromise between private convictions and the outlook of men paid to do what they're told to do, no more and no less. Things are getting very complicated as the world moves on, son, but for you chaps there's no question of taking sides. You get your orders and you carry 'em out, best you can. It's not that easy for others. Civilians have to find their own way through the maze and a damned tricky business it is, I can tell you, for anyone with a conscience. And Giles always had more conscience than any of us."

At least Alex paid him the compliment of reflecting a moment but he remained unrepentant. 'War does that to the best of us,' Adam thought. 'Once you've seen men you respect dead and dying you tend to judge everything in black and white and if you didn't you wouldn't be much good at your job.'

Alex said, presently, "That's all very fine, Gov'nor, but surely to God what happened to Hugo would cause a fellow to think twice about getting up on his hind legs and giving aid and comfort to the men who shot his brother's sight away? That's what Giles is doing if I hear correctly. I confess I've publicly disowned him in the mess and I'm damned if I'll shake his hand now, even for your sake and mother's. He and Hugo used to be thick, didn't they?"

"Very," Adam said, "and they still are. And Hugo isn't bitter about what happened to him. If you can get him to talk about it, which I doubt, he'll probably express concern at making several Boer women widows before they got him down. Kitchener wants peace, doesn't he?"

"We all do," Alex said, "and you don't have to preach to me about the cost of war. I've been through half-a-dozen. But a man's loyalty should rest with his tribe, shouldn't it?"

"I'm not so sure about that. There have been reports here that some Boers are coming over to our side, and wishing to God Cronje and his commandos in hell for prolonging the agony."

"Well, as to that, I think no more of them than I do of Giles," Alex said, stiffly. "I'll keep out of his way, that's all," and he went out quickly, his tall boots striking hard on the stone flags as though to emphasise his flat rejection of pro-Boers, Frocks and Boers who were eager to compromise.

Adam thought, gloomily: 'Now here's a how-de-do, to be sure . . . I hope he has enough horse sense to limit his prejudices to a scowl or two. We don't want a family shindig on a day like this . . .' He looked out into the hall, caught one of Stella's boys hurrying past carrying a pyramid of muffins hot from the kitchen and called, "Hi, there, lad! Find your Uncle Giles and tell him I want to see him in the sewing-room. Tell him it's urgent and he's to come whatever he's doing," and the boy said, "Yes, sir!" and scuttled off while Adam, retreating into the little room again, lit one of his favourite Burmese cheroots and puffed at it gratefully until Giles came in, closing the door and saying: "You don't have to break it to me gently. Romayne was bothered about it the moment they showed up and she's slipped away to pack. If Martindale can run us over to Bromley we could get an evening train into town."

He said, sullenly, "I won't have that! You're under my roof and your mother's."

"Wouldn't it be better all round? I've got two choices. To tell Alex and Lydia what I felt about that war or back down and apologise for myself. I couldn't do that, Father."

"I'm not asking you to, son."

"Then what?"

"Let 'em both stew awhile. Bury 'em under a load of paper, in this case Christmas wrappings. I don't ask that for my sake but for your mother's."

"Suppose Alex raises it with Hugo and Sybil?"

"I've ordered him not to and he'll mind what I say. Meantime, steer clear of him, as he means to of you."

"What a mess it all is," Giles said, dismally.

"Nothing new about it, son. It always has been a mess one way and another. That's your problem if you ever get into Parliament. Find a way through it, treading on as few corns as possible."

"Compromise? With people like that mob who tried to lynch Lloyd George a week ago?"

"Not compromise, wait. Give 'em a chance to cool off. They will, if someone throws 'em another bone to gnaw. They'll soon be hurrahing L.G. and throwing their brick-bats at Joe Chamberlain. Some people would call that proof of national instability, I suppose, but it never struck me as that. It's the way a democracy functions. The public take the soundings and you chaps trim your sails to the wind, the way the Frocks do in a free country. It oughtn't to warp your private convictions. Never did mine."

Giles smiled. "You're a wise old bird," he said.

"Not wise, son," Adam replied. "Wily. And I should be. I've had time enough to learn. I've always got my way in the end, and I promise you that you and the fire-eater L.G. won't have so long to wait for a swing around in public opinion. You'll sweep the board at the next election, then everyone will scramble to get on the winning side. You'll have to search for a man who owns up to ever having wanted to wring Kruger's neck."

"You really believe that?"

"I believe it. Seen it happen over and over again in the last fifty years. Go up and tell that gel of yours to leave her packing until tomorrow. You'll leave with the rest of 'em and keep the peace meantime."

And so it might have been but for an unlucky chance the following day when Giles, carrying his grips out to the carriage that was to run Romayne and himself over to the station for the first leg of their journey home to Wales, passed under the horse's head at the entrance of the court-yard archway and came upon Alex at the precise moment he was riding one of the hacks into the forecourt for a canter across the Downs.

There was no way they could avoid one another, short of a deliberate attempt on Alex's part to ride his brother down. He reined back, staring hard over Giles' head to the leafless trees of the avenue and looking so pompous that Giles had to smile. He said, on impulse, "Come, Alex, can't we even shake hands? None of us hold a thing against you chaps. We're opposed to the fools who sent you over there to protect city interests," and when Alex did not respond he shrugged and stood aside, giving Alex room to pass under the arch. He would have passed, no doubt, had not everybody's luck been out.

At that moment Hugo's sergeant emerged, leading Hugo's hack and Hugo himself came out of the tackroom carrying his crop and hard hat. Alex said, glancing at him, "How about Hugo's interests? Don't they count?"

"Good God, of course they do! Do you imagine I get any satisfaction out of what happened to him in a rough and tumble for South African gold and diamonds? He lies as heavy on Chamberlain's conscience as the women and children dying in those damned camps you fellows have set up! Try and see it from the human angle!"

"I'm not concerned with one angle or another," Alex said, slowly. "Only as the difference between one man, doing his duty as he saw it and another, trailing round the country preaching treason," and he gave his mount a sharp cut and cantered off across the forecourt.

Hugo called, urgently, "Hold on, Giles . . . !" and Giles, roused now, tossed the grips in the carriage, stalked round behind the vehicle to where Hugo was standing with an expression of pain on his broad, good-natured face. He said, in a low voice, "I couldn't help hearing that. I'd like you to know I don't see it that way, Chaser."

The use of his forgotten nickname, 'Chaser', acquired after their schoolfellows had learned that he was the son of the Swann whose Western Wedge manager had cornered a circus lion on Exmoor, touched Giles. So sharply that it brought him close to tears, evoking as it did a halcyon period twenty years ago when he and Hugo had loped across the moor together, building calf muscles that were to earn Hugo so many trophies yet lead, ultimately, to the incident that had cost him his sight. He said, "Don't let it worry you. We're well enough used to that kind of abuse, Hugo."

But Hugo muttered, "Take my hack and unsaddle him, Sergeant. I won't be going out on the rein after all."

"Now, sah!" the sergeant protested, "m'lady won't care to hear you've dodged the column! What'll I tell her?"

"Tell her I've gone for a walk instead. With Mr. Giles. Give me a hand, Giles," and Giles took his hand and led him into the forecourt.

"Go up behind, on to the hill. It's a rare place for blowing the cobwebs away."

They went slowly up the winding path, worn into the rocky outcrop behind the house, heading for the wooded plateau where old Colonel Swann had spent so much of his time painting indifferent water colours from the up-ended whaler on the summit. The old, makeshift shelter was still there, its timbers seamed and split by a thousand south-westerlies. They sat together, Giles looking over the winter landscape. Hugo said, at length, "You never heard it, did you? Not the real story?"

"I heard how you got word from an ambushed column and tackled a Boer outpost singlehanded. It was in the papers, the time they pinned the medal on you."

"Ah, the medal."

Hugo moistened his lips and sat very still, hands resting on his enormous thighs. "The Boers didn't traffic with medals, did they? If they did that kid would have earned one, I daresay."

"What kid, Hugo?"

"The kid I shot, just before I was hit. Last shot of the battle barring this," and he raised his hand to the bluish circular depression at his temple. "The last I'll ever fire. Thank God."

"Tell me if you want to, Hugo."

"Don't know how, really." He smiled. "You were the one who always did the telling, Chaser."

That was true, of course. All through their time on Exmoor Hugo had come to him with questions. Questions on every conceivable subject, and had been content to accept any answer Giles gave as the voice of the oracle. To Giles he still seemed pitifully young to carry such a cross but his helplessness and unwonted stillness was beginning to work on him, as though, for the first time in his life, he could sit in one place long enough to think things out and form independent judgments.

"I've come to believe it was tit-for-tat, Giles. My stopping that bullet, I mean, a second or so after I'd shot the kid. I didn't know he was a kid until I looked at him. We'd heard they were using kids that age but I hadn't believed it, not until then. He was about your age when you first went down to West Buckland. I had a quick look at him lying there. Just a second or two. Then it was curtains. Matter of fact, he was the last person I saw. You get to remembering that, you know. At least, I did, sitting about and night times." Then, very levelly, "Do you still believe in God, Giles?"

"Some kind of God, Hugo. I'm never sure what kind."

"Not one that looks out for folks, the way they tell you in the church?"

"No, or not the way they tell you in church. And God is only a word. A useful word but it can fool people, to my way of thinking."

"How about your kind of God?"

"Maybe it's a plan, a providence, with good and evil roughly balanced. Part of the plan is how we tip it, one way or the other and it's our choice. Otherwise there's no sense at all in any of it. But you don't have to go on blaming yourself about that youngster. He was trying to kill you from cover. How were you to know how old he was? The fault lies with the men who gave him a rifle, and sent him out to do a man's job. And even more with our people, who drove those chaps into a corner where they had to fight or hand over to a lot of city sharks. The fault certainly doesn't lie with you, so get that into your head, once and for all."

"Ah, *she* said that. The only other person I ever told."

"Sybil?"

"Yes." Then, "She's a wonderful person, Giles."

"I know. I've watched. You're glad about the baby, aren't you?"

Hugo smiled and seemed, fleetingly, almost himself again. "You bet I am. That's a turn-up for the book, isn't it? Sybil's thirty-three."

"Romayne was almost as old. I daresay you'll have a string now you've started."

"Can't imagine. Me being a father, I mean. Don't think I was cut out for one."

"Neither did I but you'd be surprised when it happens."

They sat in silence for a spell, Giles fighting an impulse to take his big hand and squeeze. It was a long time since he had been so close to tears. Finally Hugo said, "You remember that dream I told you about once?"

"The one you kept having? That dream where you

were lapping everyone else and there was a lot of cheering?"

"You remember it that well?"

"I remember it."

"Funny thing. I never had it once I left school and that kind of thing began to happen all the time. Then I had it again, the first night I was back here, only it was different. I was sprinting across the veldt in those damned great boots, and they were like ton weights, dragging me back. I got there, though, and there was that Boer kid at the tape. Cheering and waving his hat like mad."

Tears began to flow and nothing he could do would stop them. What did one say to that? What was there to say? And anyway Giles could not trust himself to speak. Hugo said, after a half a minute had elapsed, "Does that mean anything, d'you reckon?"

"I . . . I'd say it did, Hugo."

"What, exactly?"

"That the kid understood, sympathised even."

The heavy features relaxed. He said, sniffing the air, "Maybe. Glad I told you." Then, "I always liked it up here. Especially early on, when I was out training before breakfast. I'll get that chap to teach me the way up here on my own."

"You do that, Hugo."

He took his hand now and drew him up. Together they moved off down the twisting track to the forecourt and Adam, standing musing at the long window of the drawing-room, watched their approach. He thought, 'I'm damned sorry Alex isn't here to see that. Might loosen him up somewhat.'

4

Dreams at 'Tryst'

WHO KNEW HOW MANY DREAMS STILL HIBERNATED
under the russet-coloured pantiles of the old house? How
many and how varied, but they were there all right. They
waited in odd corners. Distilled hopes, suppressed hatreds,
thwarted and fulfilled loves and secret fears of ten generations of islanders, all waiting for a chance, maybe, to slip
out of the shadows and find a new post. For the house
itself was the product of a dream, old Conyer's dream of
dredging enough loot from the Lowland banks to build a
home under the crag that had been his trysting place with
the Cecil girl when he was a nobody.

Adam had dreamed there often enough, and so had
Henrietta, but Adam and Henrietta were rarely oppressed
by dreams and when they awoke it was not often they
recalled their substance. No more than an elusive expectation of the good luck or bad they could look for before
the sun set again.

All the children had dreamed here in their growing-up
days and sometimes Phoebe Fraser, nanny to nine, had
been awakened by a cry and hurried in to them, soothing
them in her broad Lowland brogue. Now Phoebe was
past all that, even though she still regarded Edward and
Margaret, the two youngest, as children. She was not
qualified to interpret Hugo's dream, or hoist Helen out
of the slough of the dreams she had had since returning to
'Tryst'.

377

Phoebe Fraser might, conceivably, have gone some way towards interpreting Hugo's dream, but Helen's would have shocked her half out of her spinsterish mind, and this was predictable. Phoebe knew much of boys but nothing of men, and her deep Calvinistic convictions had long since succeeded in repressing any stirrings of the flesh, stirrings she would have accepted as subtle overtures of Satan. In all the years she had worked there nobody had ever seen her so much as flirt with a man, much less lie down in a ditch with one, as some of the maids had when it was high summer and they were out of sight and sound of the house.

Helen Coles' dreams of public ravishment would have struck Phoebe as evidence that she had grossly neglected her duties in the process of Helen's upbringing for a woman, even a married woman, had no business with dreams of that kind. They belonged, if anywhere, in the mind of a harlot. Certainly not in the subconscious of a widowed Christian missionary.

And yet, in a perverse way, Helen welcomed them, for they replaced something more sinister. A recurrent dream she had dreamed often on the long voyage home and during her first weeks in Ireland, surrounded by Joanna's jolly family. In this dream, from which she awoke moaning and shuddering, she saw Rowley's head perched on that gate post, but there was a difference that made her flesh creep. It leered at her, in a way that was altogether uncharacteristic of Rowley, even when his head had been firmly attached to his shoulders, and the dream persisted, with variations, for a long time, so that she grew to fear the prospect of sleep.

But then, settled in the midst of the noisy Dublin family, her night fancies took a sharp new turn. Rowley, and Rowley's severed head, had no place in them. Instead they were dominated by the courteous, businesslike presence of Colonel Shiba, the Japanese military attaché. He who had made such a gallant showing in the Fu area of the legations during the siege. Yet Colonel Shiba's

recurrent behaviour in Helen's dream was not gallant.
Methodically, as though dismantling a barricade prior
to a planned withdrawal, he stripped her naked and
smilingly conducted her to his couch. A makeshift couch
of sandbags sewn in patchwork. And there, with the same
quiet deliberation, and in full view of the entire garrison,
he ravished her, night after night, with a skill and despatch
that Rowley had never once displayed, not even after they
survived the awkward, experimental stage of the earliest
days of the marriage.

The act of ravishment, taken in isolation, was by no
means abhorrent to her. Indeed, once she had recovered
from the shock of finding herself stark naked in the presence
of a passive audience, she offered him no resistance. But
when, at the climactic moment, he vanished in a shell-
burst, she had a sensation of having violated not only her
body but her entire conception of decency and the civilised
code and this was reinforced by the mournful gaze of
some European defenders at an adjoining barricade.
Including, unfortunately, Miss Polly Condit Smith, the
pretty American girl who was the toast of the garrison.

It might have been with the prospect of keeping such
startling dreams at bay that she drank far more than her
quota at the 'Tryst' supper table during her Christmas
stay. Adam kept a good cellar and a particularly fine
claret, so that she sometimes went to bed gay, flushed and
temporarily at peace with the world, feeling herself secure
in these familiar surroundings where everyone behaved
towards her as someone sorely in need of a little cheering
up. But no sooner was she asleep than the businesslike
Colonel Shiba appeared and went to work, methodically,
on the hooks and buttons of her bodice, and now there
was an added embarrassment for, in addition to the
silent garrison, her brother-in-law Clinton Coles was
watching.

One night early in the new year, when all but the Irish
party had packed up and left (Clint had stayed on to attend
the January conference) the dream was particularly vivid

and she awoke from it, less than an hour after lying down, with the virtual certainty that she had indeed been ravished. The claret had left her mouth parched and her head throbbed as she sat up and when she was fumbling with the candle she had a distinct impression that its glow would reveal Colonel Shiba stretched beside her.

But then, coming to terms with the familiarity of the room, and the night sounds from the coppices that were inseparable from 'Tryst', she realised that it was not Colonel Shiba's ministrations that had awakened her but the rumble of voices in the room adjoining hers, a room occupied by Clint and Joanna. She heard Clint's boisterous arrival, guessing that he was the worse for drink, then Joanna's mellow laughter following a stumble on his part, and the sounds, together with evidence of such cosy intimacy on the far side of the wall, renewed in her a desperate awareness of her own loneliness and deprivation, whirling her back to the days when she and Joanna were the conspirators on this corridor, flitting in and out of one another's rooms in order to giggle and gossip about their beaux. So poignant was the memory that tears began to flow and a sense of terrible injustice bore down on her, projecting her from bed to window, there to contemplate the western prospect of the slope bathed in moonlight as far as the blur of woods where Adam's Hermitage sat on the knoll marking the northern boundary of the estate.

It was a prospect that might have soothed her had it not been for the persistent rise and fall of voices in the next room punctuated by Joanna's ripples of laughter. Evidence of such accord and conviviality increased her melancholy, so that she was suddenly aware of an overpowering need to make closer contact with human beings untroubled by her terrible sense of isolation. It was then, with a suppressed cry of excitement, that she remembered the cistern telegraph, a device she and Joanna had sometimes employed when the rest of the household was asleep and they had secrets to exchange. An array of superannuated leaden pipes, that ran the length of the western wing, had long since ceased to serve any practical purpose. They were a relic from an earlier tenant, installed some seventy years ago as a crude means of conveying stored rainwater from the huge cistern in the loft to a few of the more important bedrooms on this side of the house. Adam, reorganising the entire plumbing system soon after he bought the place in the early 'sixties, had done little to disturb the existing network, judging, no doubt, that its dismantlement would do more harm than good to the old structure, and the girls, discovering a practical purpose for this in their early teens, had often used it to communicate with one another after they had been granted the privilege of separate and adjoining rooms.

By removing oaken plugs in the section of pipe that ran under the window, it had been quite practical (and very stimulating!) to communicate with one another, and it now occurred to Helen, standing in her nightgown and listening to the amiable sounds from the next room, that she had only to put her ear to the pipe to be certain of hearing more, if not all, of the exchanges between man and wife.

Ordinarily it might have struck her as a Peeping Tom device but in her present mood she did not give a row of pins about such niceties. She had her ear to the pipe within seconds of remembering its presence and it was just as she thought. Although, presumably, a plug was still in place next door, the voices became distinct and she could hear everything that was said, as well as every movement about the room.

*   *   *

The relationship of Joanna and Clint had been genial and uncomplicated from the earliest days of their association and marriage had simply broadened and deepened it. Joanna, by now, had few illusions about him, seeing him as an amiable, overgrown adolescent, particularly when he was in liquor, but Joanna did not look for rectitude in a husband. Of all the Swanns she was the least exacting. Clint was kind, easygoing, fond of the children, a good provider and a roystering, affectionate lover. What more could a woman expect of a man, seeing that few men matured in any case?

From time to time, in the early days of their marriage, she had been bothered by his extravagance and hurt by his over-fondness for lively company, male and female, but he always returned to her after a brief lapse and she had a serene conviction that he was glad he had married her. Marriage not only provided him with an anchorage, of the kind all men of his stamp needed. It also enabled him to sidestep the gloomy certainty of inheriting his father's pill business, leaving him free to throw in his lot with the free-ranging Adam. When she looked back on their absurd elopement (she thought of it as that although it had been mounted and stage-managed by Henrietta after she had confessed to being two months pregnant) she concluded that Clinton Coles had been a beneficiary rather than a victim of embarrassing circumstances.

On this particular night George had been over again, plotting family tactics for the forthcoming January conference and when Clint and George hobnobbed they could make substantial inroads into Adam's wine stocks, so that she was not in the least surprised when Clint appeared, about one-thirty a.m., drunk as a fiddler and falling flat on his face when he tried to slip his braces and trousers off. He became clumsily amorous the moment she slipped out of bed to assist him, landing a hearty slap on her bottom and grabbing her by the waist as she bent to seize his trouser legs. Together they rolled on the rug, Clint taking advantage of the frolic to hoist her nightgown but he seemed incapable of pressing his advantage. She said, not minding this horseplay in the least, "*Wait*, Clint! For heaven's sake, boy. Stay *still* a minute while I get you to bed!" where she would almost surely have accommodated him, as the quickest method of getting a good night's rest,

had she not, at that moment, heard a sound close at hand
that drove all thoughts of him out of mind.

It was unmistakably a sob. A long, dry sob, indicative
of acute wretchedness, and it came, unaccountably had
she been a stranger to the house, from the direction of the
window-seat. She scrambled up then, leaving Clint in
disarray on the floor and hurried across the room where,
on the instant, she identified not only the source of the
sob but the way in which it had been relayed to her. It
came from Helen's room next door via the old cistern
telegraph they had used as girls.

It sobered her on the instant. She felt neither shame
nor resentment in the realisation that Helen had been
eavesdropping. Only pity and concern that she should
be driven to seek such a means of sharing an intimate
moment of a man and woman whose lives, in contrast to
her own, were so free of strain and misery.

Although excessively outward-looking she was by no
means insensitive, particularly as regards Helen, her
girlhood ally. She had been all too aware of her sister's
taut nerves since her return home and had done everything
she could think of to comfort and relax her, introducing her
into the uninhibited Dublin scene in the hope that, sooner
or later, she would form an attachment with someone that
could lead to remarriage and a chance to forget her frightful experiences in the East. She was a generous soul and
her sincere affection for her partner in so many youthful
adventures had survived their long separation. She had a
certainty now that Helen's marriage had not been a
success, or not as she understood the word. Rowley had
been a worthy, solemn, self-opinionated old stick, so
dedicated to his work that he would have neither time
nor inclination for frolics that made married life so
agreeable, despite the tendency among men, even men
like Clint, to dismiss women as frail, fluttering creatures,
entirely dependent on their mates. Perhaps alone among
the Swann girls she had taken accurate soundings of her
parents' marriage, particularly her mother's approach to

her father. A woman – a wise woman that is – did not quarrel with the fact that it was a man's world. She set about making the best of it and one certain way of doing this was to pander to male appetites, giving them free rein everywhere but in the kitchen. This, at least, kept them even-tempered and any woman with an ounce of sense could manipulate an easygoing man wholly preoccupied with his own concerns that were limited, in the main, to food, bed, counting-house profits and the raising of progeny, approximately in that order.

She turned away from the pipe, jerked Clinton's trousers free, removed his shirt, underpants and shoes and took a firm grip under his armpits, saying, "Now get to bed and sleep it off. I won't be a minute."

His renewed clutch at her was easily evaded and he flopped back on to the bed, grinning foolishly, and saying, in the assumed Irish accent he adopted for these occasions, "You're a *foine* woman, Jo! Said it often and say it again! ... A *foine* woman!" But by then she was gone, not even waiting to slip into her bedgown and had hurried into the gallery and along to Helen's room where, as she half-expected, she found the candle burning and her sister sitting on the edge of a rumpled bed, the very picture of melancholy.

There seemed no profit in beating about the bush, so she said, sitting beside her and throwing an arm about her shoulder, "I heard you at the pipe. Don't worry, love. Clint didn't. He's far too bottled. Now, what *is* it, Helen? How can I help?" She was rewarded by a convulsive embrace on Helen's part and another sob, stifled this time, that released a steady flow of tears.

They sat there for a long time until Helen mastered herself sufficiently to say, "It was unforgivable ... Me eavesdropping like that ... I ... I don't know what's come over me lately ... I remembered the pipe and then ... well, you're so happy, Jo! And for me everything's so sour and wretched. There's no end to it and when I'm alone and have those awful dreams ..."

"What dreams, Helen?"

"The one about Colonel Shiba, the Japanese attaché. And sometimes the frightful one I used to have before about . . . about seeing Rowley's head on the post. Not as it was but alive."

Joanna tightened her grip. She knew all about Rowley's head but the name of the Japanese attaché had no significance for her. She said, "Tell me about the bad dreams then." Helen made no response. "Just saying things, just putting them into words. It makes them less important, Helen. Goodness, it's no wonder you have terrible dreams after what you've been through. Anybody would. Most women would have gone out of their minds."

"Maybe I have."

"Not you. Tell me. Tell me everything."

Outside in the coverts one of the resident 'Tryst' owls hooted. It was a mild night for January and the wind, crossing the Weald from the south-east, went to probing the barley-sugar chimney-pots but without the savagery it showed throughout most of the winter. Joanna draped a blanket over their shoulders without releasing her grip on Helen's shoulders and Helen said, "I don't have the worst one now, or not often. But the new one is almost as bad. It's so real. I can feel it happening to me. And so silly, too, for that man never behaved towards me in any way but correctly. He was a gentleman and brave as a lion. Everybody thought so."

"The Japanese colonel?"

"Yes. He was there when I shot that officer through the loophole."

"What happens to you in the dream, Helen?"

She told her, shamefully and haltingly, but forcing herself to describe both dreams in detail. She told of the macabre leer on the face of a decapitated head. She described the firm, expertly performed ritual of a public ravishment on a couch of sandbags sown from quilts and blankets.

"Do *you* think I'm going mad, Jo? Surely that's a mad dream to have time and again, isn't it?"

385

"No, it isn't mad. And I think the dreams are linked in a way. One's come to blot out the other." And then, without diffidence, "Tell me about Rowley. Tell me about your life together *before* he was killed. How was he? How did he treat you?"

"He was always kind, or tried to be in his funny, absentminded way."

"I didn't mean that. How did he treat you as a woman?"

"He didn't, not really. Whenever he did I . . . well . . . I had to encourage him, to remind him I was his wife even. He wasn't like any other man I've known. You remember how most men didn't need much encouragement that way. Clint still doesn't, does he?"

"No, not Clint!" She came near to chuckling, despite what seemed to her the terrible poignancy of her sister's plight. "But Rowley was never in the least like Clint, thank heavens. Sometimes I used to think Rowley wasn't a man at all, just . . . just a kind of . . . well, a saint, if you like. But saints shouldn't marry, should they? And this one did. It must have been awful for you. I don't know how you put up with it all those years and in all those awful places."

She thought hard, trying with all her might to relate the stray images and conjectures that occurred to her and arrive at some kind of conclusion that would lead her to comprehend Helen's present state of mind. She tried putting herself in her place, not as a woman who had survived unbelievable terrors and hardships, but as a wife lying beside a husband night after night, unable to awaken more than a token emotional response in his body. It was very difficult but because she was her mother's daughter, and because, instinctively, she turned her own sensual nature to very good account, she could get some glimmering of the truth, and in the wake of that truth she saw a possible solution. Or the means of promoting a shock, physical and spiritual, that held promise of a solution. Love and pity rode roughshod over her upbringing, and all the canons of so-called civilised behaviour, for here was her own sister, who had dragged herself home from the threshold of hell, and was now defeated by the clamour of her body and degradation of spirit that Rowland Coles's indifference had invoked. Innocently perhaps, and from the highest motives but mercilessly none the less.

She said, "Listen, Helen. Wait here. I'll only be gone a moment. Wash your face and put a comb through your hair while I'm gone," and she took her sister's hand, jerked her up and pushed her towards the wash-stand, pouring water from the jug and dipping a flannel in it. "Go on! Make the effort, for everybody's sake," and she hovered by the door until Helen began to lave her face. Then she slipped away, moving barefoot along the gallery to the stairhead where Adam left a fixed oil-lamp burning all night in the deep niche beside the sewing-room door.

She went down and stepped gingerly between the two truckle beds inside, then through into the wainscotted dining room, pungent with cigar smoke. In a sliver of moonlight she found and lit a candle, carrying it to the sideboard where, among other decanters, stood one containing Adam's choice port. She poured a beaker and carried it back, lighting her way up the stair to the door of her room and peeping inside to see Clint sprawled naked across the bed. She pulled back the sheets and rolled him in and although he muttered and opened his eyes the lack of focus told her he was still asleep. She went out again and into Helen's room, where her sister was sitting in front of the mirror brushing her long dark hair. She seemed calmer now although her hands trembled violently. Jo said, handing her the port, "Drink it down. Drink all of it. It's what you need. It'll do you good," and Helen, after a single look of bewilderment, began to sip. A little colour returned to her cheeks.

"You're very kind, Jo. You always were the best-hearted among them. I'll manage now."

"Until you sleep you'll manage. Then you'll dream

again, one dream or the other. There's something else you have to do, Helen, and no one can do it for you. No doctor, nobody, you hear? Go into Clint now. I'll stay here until you come back."

"*To Clint?* Me?"

She slammed down the glass so hard that the stem snapped and the bowl rolled across the dressing-table as far as the pincushion, leaving a small pool of dregs on the polished surface. "You can't mean that, Jo. You . . . you *can't*!"

"But I do mean it! You need a man more than any woman I ever saw and I mean to get you one of your own the minute we go home. But you can't wait that long, not to feel . . . feel *wanted* and needed. Not to feel a woman again. You needn't worry about his side of it. He's bottled and won't know providing you use your wits. Just go to him, like I say. Just this once."

"But it's wrong, Jo. It would be terribly wrong with anyone's husband, but yours . . ."

"It's not wrong unless I say it is and I don't! I say it's right. Just this one time. As I say, he's drunk but not so drunk as he won't stir the minute he feels a woman's arms around him. I should know. There's nothing I don't know about Clinton Coles."

The colour in Helen's cheeks flooded back. She sat twisting the ribbon of her nightgown, her eyes fixed on the smears of port on the dressing-table surface.

"How can you be so sure? I mean . . . why would a thing like that help?"

"I don't know why, I only know it will. Maybe it would break that awful sequence of dreams and, anyway, you'd come alive again and that's what's important right now. Besides, what harm would it do? Do you remember how we schemed to switch our beaux that time at Penshurst? Well, it would make you feel young again, ready to start over again. Good grief, Helen, how long is it since a man held you in his arms?"

It was a question she could not answer. Eight months

had passed since Rowley was butchered but long before
that, ever since the first refugees came in ahead of Boxers
rampaging in the west and north, Rowley had been
preoccupied, wholly absorbed in his work as healer and
comforter in the field. Maybe a year or more had elapsed
since he had used her in that way and much longer since
she had felt herself a wife to him. And remembering this
the prospect of lying with Clint did not seem so outrageous,
for she began to discern a kind of logic behind Joanna's
reasoning. The mere thought of lying beside her jolly,
ever boyish brother-in-law and of feeling his arms about
her quickened her blood and breathing. What deterred
her, however, was the cold-bloodedness of such a proposal,
surely unique in the relationship of sisters. She said,
wonderingly, "Don't you love Clint, Jo?"

"I love him in my own way. The way he likes and the
way I'm used to. But I love you too and I won't see you
reduced to this, with no one to help, no one to turn to.
Besides, he's had other women since we married. Not
often, and never seriously, but he's had them. Believe me,
I know what I'm doing, Helen."

"But if he's drunk . . . if he's asleep now . . . ?"

"He'll come half-awake and then he'll drop off again,
thoroughly fuddled. As soon as he does slip out again. I'll
wait for you here."

She got up, both hands still fidgeting with the length
of ribbon. "How do you *mean* exactly? A thing like that
bringing me peace? Helping me to forget?"

"You'll see. Do it, Helen. Just do as I say."

She got up, realising that some act of physical propulsion was needed and taking Helen by the hand she opened
the door. The gallery was in darkness, apart from the faint
glow of the lamplight that touched the head of the stairs.
She could hear Clint's snores, the only sound breaking the
heavy silence of the night. Then she led the way along
to her room, entered it ahead of her sister and blew the
candle out. She said, in a normal voice, "Shift over,
Clint," and surprisingly he obeyed, his snores ceasing as

he stirred. "There, get about it, girl," and she groped her way out, closing the door.

Helen had no certain knowledge now whether he was awake or asleep. She could hear his irregular breathing and it caused her to hesitate a moment longer, telling herself that if he said one word she would turn back and tell Jo that such a thing was not to be thought of. He did not wake and presently she crept carefully in beside him, settling herself so close to her edge of the bed that she barely touched him. She could feel her heart thumping a rival rhythm to his swift, short snores as minutes passed before the warmth of his body communicated itself to hers and she turned, again very stealthily, lifting her right arm and groping for him where he lay just within her reach. She touched his exposed shoulder and fingertip contact with his flesh made her shiver so that instinctively she drew a little closer, touching him lightly with her knees and breasts.

Warmth and comfort seemed to pulse from him, communicating itself to her in a way that soothed rather than excited her but the enlarged contact was enough to increase her rate of breathing so that soon, growing a little bolder, she enlarged her grip and pulled him half round so that he lay flat on his back. He moved sluggishly, almost unwillingly at first but then, or so it seemed, a tiny flicker of initiative passed to him and he flung his arm across her, drawing her closer as his volley of snores ceased abruptly.

Suddenly, outrageously it seemed to her, she wanted to giggle, the sheer absurdity of the situation inflating inside her like a large, coloured balloon, but she mastered the impulse and lay still for a moment, revelling in her own audacity and remembering a time – a thousand years ago it seemed – when she had first shared a bed with Rowley Coles as a girl bride who had entered marriage so confidently but had discovered, all too quickly, that her limited experience as a flirt counted for nothing with a groom cast in his solemn mould.

Time passed. It seemed to her an age had elapsed since

she had joined him between the rumpled sheets and a sense of anticlimax stole upon her as she faced the fact that it was more than likely Jo had been mistaken about the certainty of him making the most of his opportunity. It seemed more than possible that he could lie there snoring until morning and it was the prospect of advancing daylight that prompted her to summon up her courage to resolve the situation one way or another. She could, she reasoned, rely on a few seconds' grace if he was sufficiently roused to open a conversation. She could slip away while he was still bemused and tell Joanna to return at once. She could be clear of the room before he had found matches and candle but in the meantime she felt she owed it to herself to put Joanna's theory to the test. Cautiously, an inch at a time, she lifted his arm and placed it against her breasts, holding it there and was rewarded by the slow glow of satisfaction it brought her, as well as an insignificant signal that his senses were stirred inasmuch as he drew a little closer, stretching out his legs and turning on his side, this time facing her. He did not wake, however, although his snores diminished to heavy, regular breathing and it was this, perhaps, that emboldened her sufficiently to turn her face towards him, and kiss his cheek. Lightly, almost teasingly, as though he had been one of those awkward young men who competed for modest favours in the far off days when she and Jo had been county belles with half-a-dozen swains at their disposal.

The kiss, light as it was, had a disproportionate effect upon her. He was sporting a growth of dark bristles announcing that, with the prospect of male company that evening, he had not bothered to shave for dinner, and the mere touch of his bristles on her lips was a sharp reminder of the contrast between Clinton and Rowland Coles, for Rowley had never needed to shave more than once a day and his whiskers were as soft and downy as a boy's. It emphasised, somehow, Clint's heavy masculinity and awareness of this, together with the weight of his hand on her breast, quickened her desire in a way she would never have thought possible a few minutes since. The initial shame that had restrained her from the moment Jo pushed her into the room fell away like shyness dispelled by a genial greeting and she suddenly felt free and untrammelled by guilt, not caring, in that instant, whether he was awake or asleep. She withdrew her left hand and used it to encircle his head, cradling him closer and kissing him again, more purposefully this time so that his grasp on her breast tightened, then fell away as he made a half-hearted attempt to pluck at the join in her nightgown. He was too impatient or too sleepy perhaps, to loosen the neck ribbons but the effort at least succeeded in banishing the last of her scruples. She plucked the bow loose herself and half shrugged herself out of the shift, her heart pounding like a steam hammer as she bared her breasts and enfolded him, showering his face with kisses now and straining towards him with a fervour she had never once displayed during Rowley's perfunctory embraces for somehow she had always sensed a demonstration of this kind would embarrass him. Asleep, awake or somewhere between the two, Clinton responded, reaching down to grasp the hem of her half-shed nightgown and hoisting it to her thighs. Then, so swiftly that she had no real awareness of the transition, the initiative passed to him and he half-rolled on her, muttering unintelligible words only two of which she caught but she could not have sworn that they were 'fine woman'. Then, with a kind of unconscious expertise he bore down on her and under the stress of his weight and clumsy handling she uttered a low cry, half an expression of protest, half proclaiming an intense physical release akin to the moment of waking after the methodical ravishment by the courteous Japanese colonel. Seconds later he was done with her and sleep reclaimed him again, his fuddled brain suddenly unequal to the struggle against the fumes of all the liquor he had shipped. He slipped away, rolling over on his back again, and his snores recommencing, his inert hand resting on her belly.

She lay very still, aware once again of the night sounds in the coverts and the pale glow of moonlight, almost blue it looked, shafting a gap in the curtains and touching a corner of the bed. Her body continued to tremble but her mind was inexplicably still. She knew then, savouring the knowledge with a deep sense of fulfilment, that Jo had been uncannily right after all. Not only about Clint but about her errant peace of mind.

PART FOUR

Reconnaissance

I

In the Beginning There Was George ...

THE TRANSITION OF SWANN-ON-WHEELS FROM A horse-powered network to a haulage system served by a fleet of mechanical vehicles, supplemented by horse teams where the terrain was more suited to hooves than tyres, was effected so quietly, and so smoothly, that it never qualified as a nine-day wonder in the trade.

Briefly, in city coffee houses frequented by shipping men, and in the loading yards of midland and northern factories, it was seen as a typical foray of that old fox Swann, who had been trying to corner the national hauling trade from the day he recruited his ruffianly army of unemployed coachmen and Thameside waifs back in the 'fifties. Briefly because the 'fifties themselves were now viewed as an era not far removed from that of Stephenson's Rocket.

Swann, they recalled, flaunting his banner-with-the-strange-device, had always been an innovator so there was nothing remarkable about his overnight conversion to horseless carriages. He would likely burn his fingers but he could afford that, having exacted his percentage from almost everything carted over county borders during the last forty years. Even those among his rivals who actually owned a private motor and bumped their wives and families down to the seaside at weekends, considered that he might, for once, have over-reached himself, especially when it got around that he was designing and building

his own transport. But that again was to be expected of
a man who had always been a jump ahead of his competitors and who still qualified as an eccentric in a world where
eccentrics were rare and becoming rarer. After all, no
one could challenge Swann's record as an amateur whose
enterprise, launched with a hundred Clydesdales and half
as many waggons, had gone on to become a household
word in a single generation, and there was no denying the
horseless carriage had come to stay. Only a small minority
of merchants refused to entrust their goods to these clumsy,
vapour-trailing equipages, that people were beginning
to call 'lorries', once their overall performances were seen
to be fairly satisfactory. A majority, remembering Swann's
reliability and punctuality, were content (though not
over-eager) to renew their contracts, reasoning that Swann
and his successors must know their business or how could
they have survived the cut-and-thrust of the last half-a-
century, when something revolutionary appeared on the
world's markets every day of the week.

This then was the impersonal verdict on the transition.
It was otherwise from within, where initial opposition to
the change-over had been so resolute that it had been seen
as a board-room mutiny. Here, indeed throughout the
entire network, there had been a ransacking of conscience
and personal prejudice that was regarded as a rich private
joke by the minority that had voted in favour of George on
what was accepted by Swann veterans as 'The Water-
shed'. That is to say, the period immediately prior to
George Swann's famed cross-country jaunt with a six-ton
gun-turret aboard, a feat that set every transporter in
the country by the ears once they had digested the relevant logistics. The conversion was unanimous and all but
immediate, and perhaps Jack-o'-Lantern Coles summed
it up best in a Biblical parody of the incident that enlivened the otherwise dull speeches at the firm's annual
dinner, in December, 1905. It was an occasion when the
commissioning of the hundredth Swann-Maxie was
announced by Scottie Quirt and Coles said, proposing the

customary toast to the firm: "In the beginning there was Adam. And Adam begat George. But George did much better in that *he* begat the giant Maximus, and Maximus begat the Swann-Maxie that did multiply until it darkened the countryside. But the elders of the tribe murmured against such begetting and took counsel among themselves, saying, 'It is not seemly in the sight of the righteous that so great a strain should be placed upon our pockets.' Yet George set his face against them and persisted. And it came to pass that they were convinced in spite of themselves, and took counsel one with the other again, saying, 'We have sinned and will go forth in sackcloth and ashes manifesting our fault. For this man has found favour in the sight of the Lord and we will henceforth bow down before him and do his bidding . . . !' "

It was recorded that even Young Rookwood smiled (he had never been known to laugh) but the others, Godsall and his fellow doubters, were more generous. Few annual dinner speakers had received such a weight of applause and laughter as Clint Coles, when he sat down and reached for his glass of hock. Converted they were, and to a man, but some went even further, becoming, as George told Adam after the 1906 New Year conference, 'More Catholic than the Pope.' And indeed they were, inasmuch as they were clamouring for vehicles much faster than Scottie could manufacture them. But notwithstanding this, George rejected his father's advice that he should put the patent out to tender among the two hundred-odd registered motor manufacturers now operating in the country.

"No, *sir!*" he said, with emphasis. "Swann-Maxie remains a private company in our name, although it's officially registered under the title of Swann & Quirt, Scottie owning forty-nine per cent of the stock. From here on we sell ourselves all the transport we need, even if we have to dribble it out piecemeal. That way we not only save money, we modify week by week, using our experiences on the open road as blueprint material. Ten

years from now, five maybe, four-fifths of those manufacturers will be broke and out of business. You recall
what happened at the tail-end of the railway boom,
before you set up in business?"

"I remember very well. There were two hundred bank-
ruptcies in as many weeks but there's no real comparison,
is there? The founding of a railway company called for
heavy investment, mostly for rights of way and a motor can
drive anywhere it pleases on established highways."

"I'm saying the majority of those pioneers are amateurs," said George, and when Adam reminded him that
both he and George had been amateurs in their day he
said sharply, "Not in that sense, Gov'nor. We mapped
our markets in advance. That's more than you can say
of this bunch. Most of 'em are financed by loan sharks,
who make damned sure they skim any profit that emerges.
Half of 'em are working in back street stables, buying their
materials retail from blacksmiths and coach builders, and
all of 'em, without a single exception so far as I know, are
concentrating on the joyride market."

It made sense, as George's pronouncements usually did
on reflection and Adam, who had never stood in awe of anyone during twelve years' soldiering and forty years' trading,
confessed to a certain awe of his son when he gave Henrietta
a summary of the discussion that same night.

"I once thought of him as a chip off the old block," he
said, ruefully, "but I'm well on the way to revising that
opinion. Before he's done the trade will think of him as
the block and me as the chip."

It irritated her to hear him talking like that, even in
praise of his own son, for she could never see him as anything less than an oak among saplings.

"He had two advantages you never had. Almost un-
limited capital, and a father egging him on," she said,
sharply, and was rewarded by a self-satisfied grin on his
face as he reached over her to extinguish the bedside lamp.

"Ah, something in that."

* * *

By early summer of that same year he had a much sharper reminder of the debt George owed him when the new Swann maps appeared in the annual brochure. For there, set out for all to see, was the twentieth-century image of Adam Swann's earliest essay in commercial cartography, reproducing so many features of the original company maps, now framed and exhibited in the Swann museum at The Hermitage. For the revised theme of the network now was re-regionalisation and George, he noted, had even restored some of the first names bestowed upon regions by Adam, in 1858.

He carried the brochure away to his perch on the knoll overlooking the southern boundary of the estate, as intrigued as a lad with a complicated mechanical toy. One by one, superimpositions of the new upon the old emerged as though he was looking at George's fleet of mechanically-propelled vehicles through the legs of a hundred Clydesdales, symbol of all the muscle, blood and bone that had hauled his customers' goods from one end of the country to the other.

For to Adam the familiar tracings of old routes and boundaries of the network were clearly visible under the firmly drawn lines of the new frontiers, dictated not by railways, as in his day, but by the factors that had governed the path of the gridiron in Stephenson's day.

First, Zeus among them, was geology, the innumerable stratas of chalk, greenstone, Lias, Trias, Permian, oolite, basalt and granite that had prescribed the movements and habitats of men in these islands since the beginning of time and still, for all man's new technologies, called the tune and regulated the pace.

Then came temperatures and rainfall, and the use man had made of the land in his nonstop wrestle with the elements, and after that, on the heels of climate, came crops, mineral resources and the new concentrations of electrical and industrial power and population.

It was as though he was looking at a potted history of transportation and in the siting of George's new depots he could detect pointers to all the problems and frustrations of man's fight against gravity since stones were dragged across country by weight of muscle for the erection of cromlechs and the building of pagan temples. But, once he had absorbed the general message of the map, he was able to distinguish the domestic patterns that had emerged and found here food for speculation in the way George had set about carving up the realm for the convenience of Swann and Swann's customers. Some basic conclusions leaped from the page but there were others, born of stresses unknown in his day, that he had to search for.

It was quite clear, for instance, that terrain had reprieved the horse in many of the areas of the west and north. In the old Western Wedge, so prolific in humps, bogs and untamed heathlands, the horse still reigned and would, he supposed, continue to reign for a long time yet. Only two depots, Exeter and Truro, fielded a few motor vehicles designed to operate over short distances and the same was true of the Mountain Square, with its main depot shifted from Abergavenny to Cardiff. It would be a long time, he mused, before Taffy took horseless carriages for granted, save in the extreme south of the principality where all its heavy industries were located.

Further north, among the Cumberland and Westmorland fells, few if any Swann-Maxies would run, whereas north of the Tay, horse power, in the old-fashioned sense, would hold its own, probably until he and George too were dust in the churchyard down the road.

Yet here and there, in areas that Adam recognised as a terrible challenge to the newcomer, George had compromised, siting branch depots, furnished with teams transferred from elsewhere to supplement and link Swann hauls on either side of high or soggy ground.

The Pennine depots were a case in point. At six centres, both east and west of the Pennine Chain, George had marked out territory where teams could be summoned at short notice to bridge a difficult stretch, and when they

were not so employed they would doubtless earn their oats
on shorter, local hauls. All down the eastern coast, clear
across the old Southern Square, and over the whole of
Kent, the motor vehicle predominated, but the Cotswolds,
the Northern fells and the Fens were served by emergency
depots. Only Ireland, where the pace was slower, was all
but denied power-driven vans. Belfast had two and Dublin three. The other ninety-five were shared, unequally,
among English and Lowland Scottish shires and the in-
dustrialised regions of South Wales. As Adam refolded the
pull-out map inside the brochure, he wondered how impressive an ascendancy George enjoyed among those
quarrelsome privateers, so jealous of their individual rights
and privileges.

2

He was right to ponder the question. Under the reconstruction, George discovered, the managers were not only
greedy for vehicles but for territory, and the right to
nominate managers of the sub-depots sited within their
frontiers. The preparation of the short lists for these, and
for the new territories, demanded a deal of thought, private
enquiry and tact, and even when they were approved there
were mutterings all round.

There were now thirteen areas, eight of them with all
but unchanged frontiers and in the main he left the suzerainty of these severely alone.

Bertieboy Bickford still ruled in the west, Young Rookwood in an enlarged Southern Square and Godsall in the
old Kentish Triangle, where his influence was undisputed.
Similarly Jake Higson, he who had adopted the kilt, was
left master of Scotland, and the ageing Dockett, who had
at last abandoned his fence-squat, was still in charge of
the Isle of Wight, otherwise known as Tom Tiddler's
Land. Spectacular gambles, however, had to be taken
with new personnel appointed to oversee the new territories and the two biggest of these showed up in The Funnel
– a two-hundred-mile wedge tapering north from Southern

Square to the plain of York and the Polygon territory, where the Lancashire cotton and Liverpool shipping industries were paramount.

Casting round for a promising master of these George remembered his brother Edward's contribution to the now historic snail-crawl from Bromsgrove to the naval dock-yard at Devonport, and on impulse he took a night train to Cardiff, where he found Edward superintending repairs to a ditched Swann-Maxie that had fouled a gateway a few miles from the depot and had to be towed home by horses. Edward said, emerging from beneath the chassis with a broad smear of oil on his forehead, "I've been thinking of you all morning, George When are you going to set up a driving school, and put these damned mechanics through a running repair test? Pritchard can handle a vehicle well enough but he's got no more idea about what makes it tick than a South Sea Islander."

The remark, and its portentous implications decided George in a decision he had been considering ever since reorganisation.

"That's an idea that's been playing hide and seek in my head ever since we made that run, kid. I'll get about it as soon as I can clear a space on the desk. In the mean-time, however, wash your face and join me in a beer for I've a proposition to put to you," and they went across the road to the Prince of Wales' Feathers and ordered two pints from the wood. With Edward one never had to approach a subject deviously. He said, after the first draught, "You've served a long enough apprenticeship in the backwoods, Edward. How do you feel about taking charge of The Funnel?"

The boy pondered, emptying his tankard slowly and all but scowling into it, another trick he had inherited from his Grandfather Sam Rawlinson who invariably frowned on the prospect of a bargain sale, probably because he had a conviction that this might bring the price down.

"That's a big bite, George. It's seventy per cent self-propelled, isn't it?"

"Around that. There are something like twenty teams at auxiliary depots, east of the high ground and Fens."

"Would it mean doing young Wickstead out of the job? It's his beat mostly."

"No, I've got plans for Wickstead. All I'm asking is, do you feel up to it?"

"I could do it."

He was always, George reflected thankfully, a man of a few words but those few were almost invariably to the point. And so it was arranged, and Edward, at twenty-seven, found himself responsible for as much territory as veterans like Markby and Rookwood. It was an impressive step up the ladder and meant promotion for others, too. George took his brother's advice and put Bryn Lovell's two half-caste stepsons, Enoch and Shad, in joint charge of the Mountain Square. Both were native Welsh, with Welsh prejudices and fluent command of the Welsh language. They seemed to be the logical choice, for each had acquitted himself well as a sub-depot manager.

He took a somewhat similar gamble with less confidence on the eldest Wickstead boy, who had all but succeeded his father in Crescent South and Centre, for Tom Wickstead was ailing now and Edith insisted that he conserved his energy. This territory, largely flat, composed of the Eastern Region and the old river lands that Adam called The Bonus had been incorporated in The Funnel. But a large new region had now been created to the west under the title West Midlands. Luke Wickstead, son of 'Edith-Wadsworth-that-was' (some of the old hands still regarded her as the Old Gaffer's ex-mistress) had shown an aptitude for motor transport. Out here, where a score of Swann-Maxies served the engineering plants of Birmingham and the Potteries, George reflected that he would have plenty of scope to prove himself.

He found room, in the reorganised network, to advance his own family. Max and Rudi, his two elder sons were promoted from sub-managerial posts to work under the general supervision of Scottie Quirt in The Polygon, now including the hilly region, The Chain, to the east. Rudi as general manager with the promise of eventual succession and Max, the more mechanically minded of the two as improver in the motor plant at Macclesfield. Gisela was delighted, although her maternal pride in the boys prohibited any overt display of pleasure.

"Your grandfather would have approved wholeheartedly of what's happening clear across the board," George said to her, chuckling and then, recalling, as he tended to do these days, the many hours they had spent tinkering with that cumbersome ancestor of the Swann fleet. "That was the beginning of it all, Gisela – you and me, the Swann-Maxie, the whole box of tricks, and it doesn't seem all that time ago. Do you remember jumping out of that tree during a game of hide-and-seek on Lobau, when I was skylarking with your sisters?"

"Why should I forget? It was the first time you acknowledged me as a woman."

It wasn't strictly true, of course. His real awareness of her came a little later, when that crafty old Austrian grandfather of hers had despatched her to his room early one morning, in the fervent hope that he would seduce her and marry her in preference to one of her pretty sisters. The plot, if it really was a plot, had succeeded and they were married within weeks. He would give something, he reflected, to resurrect old Max and discover how much reluctance he had to overcome on Gisela's part for that little piece of stagecraft but it was not the kind of thing he cared to discuss with her even after this lapse of time.

The mere memory, however, quickened his appreciation of her that same night, when the house was quiet and he lay in bed watching her prepare for bed, noting her singular neatness and precision in her every movement, in the way she folded her petticoats, brushed her long, chestnut hair and gravely contemplated the clean nightgown she took from a drawer. The gentle fragrance of lavender reached him as she slipped it over her head and switched off the light, for George, alone among the Swanns, had installed domestic electricity the moment it became available. He thought, as his arms went round her, 'By God, I had my head screwed on when I married a Continental! How many English women would have buried the past, the way she buried Barbara Lockerbie? That nonsense is eight years behind us now and she's never once hinted at it,' and if Gisela Swann wondered at the display of spirits in the way he handled her, or the genuine affection inherent in his long, contented sigh when, cradled in her arms, he dropped off to sleep, she made no reference to it. She was a very placid woman, with a rare disposition to come to terms with fate but perhaps her mildness stemmed, in the main, from what she recognised as her extreme good fortune. After all, she had exchanged the dullness and obscurity of village life in her homeland, for partnership with a demigod. It was no wonder, therefore, that she enjoyed a happy relationship with her mother-in-law, Henrietta. Adam would have said that in this respect, if in no other, they were as alike as two peas.

*   *   *

There were still one or two stray ends to be tidied up before the Swann facelift was complete, by the spring of 1906. Someone had to be found to oversee The Link, a long, narrow strip of territory connecting the Western Wedge with the Southern Square, The Funnel and the West Midlands, an appointment that would call for tact and flexibility, inasmuch as its next-door neighbours included two new boys, Edward and Young Wickstead, and the proud, touchy Rookwood, who would be inclined, George thought, to bully inexperienced younger men operating on his borders.

He finally settled on Coreless, the energetic middle-aged Northerner, who had voted with him when a majority had opposed him, and when Coreless called in at Headquarters on his way to take up his post at the new Gloucester depot he said, "Word in your ear, Coreless. Keep a fatherly eye on my kid brother, Edward, and Young Wickstead. You're round about my age, aren't you?" When Coreless admitted to forty-four he added, "Just so. I'm forty-two. Old enough to enjoy playing Father Christmas to youngsters like Edward and Wickstead but young enough to remember that at their age I thought I knew all the answers. They might need guidance from time to time. Give it to them if they ask. Otherwise let 'em make their own mistakes and learn from them, for I'd sooner them lean on you than on Rookwood.'

"Rookwood's a top-class man, isn't he, Mr. Swann?"

"Aye, he is, but he knows it, and is inclined to patronise. Even me if I give him half-a-chance. It's often that way with those who came up from the bottom rung, as he did."

Coreless nodded and the nod told George that he understood him completely. Close co-operation was vital to all of them.

'I picked the right chap there,' he mused, as Coreless's hobnailed boots clattered on the tower stairway. 'Maybe I'm developing the Old Man's knack of deputising, and it's time I did . . . for years now I've been disinclined to trust anyone even to lick my stamps,' and he turned to his two remaining problems, recruitment for trainees in the Swann-Maxie depot at Macclesfield, and the more pressing decision concerning the power structure of regional depots, with three disparate sources of income – routine haulage, house-removals and the ever-expanding demand for hired vehicles for holiday excursions known, in the network, as 'The Beano Trade'.

In consultation with Edward he had a half-approved solution for the first problem, so he spent a day concentrating on the latter, weighing the pros and cons of separating the three streams and putting them in charge of individual stewards or leaving one man to co-ordinate all three, as in the old days. He finally chose the latter course and when he explained his reasons to Adam the Old Gaffer approved.

"Never saw a battle won by three generals," Adam said. "Specialists are all very well but a specialist sub-ordinate, aware that the boss is wholly dependent on him, is inclined to get uppity and you can see where that could lead when it comes to priorities. Let one man run the whole circus. He's the only chap qualified to decide whether the acrobats, the lion-tamer or trick cyclists go to the top of the bill. I never did trust that breakdown system you tried after you took over. It looks well enough on paper but it had a fatal defect." And when George enquired what that defect was he said, with a grin, "It puts too much power in the hands of Headquarters who like to play one man off against another. Saw it happening but I wasn't the one to point it out. It's your show now, yours and Edward's and all those downy-whiskered colts you're pushing forward."

He said nothing to his father or to Henrietta regarding a plan he had to offer jobs to two of the Fawcett boys, having a premonition that it might stir up trouble over at Dewponds. He meant to take the risk, however. There was no harm in presenting his nephews with a unique opportunity, and at the same time enlarging the family's hold on the firm for there was no knowing how long he could carry a clear majority with the board. The vice-roys had mutinied once. Under the stress of a crisis, or a series of crises, they might do so again.

He walked the two miles separating 'Tryst' and his sister's farm one blithe May morning, when the Weald looked its best in late spring finery and even George, not one to appreciate pastoral pleasures that would have gladdened the hearts of his brother Giles, or his youngest sister Margaret, could not fail to benefit from the bene-diction of his surroundings.

The belt of woodland to the north-east of 'Tryst' was in full leaf after a long spell of mild weather. Larks sang over the paddocks and every hedgerow sported its galaxy of wildflowers, few of which George could have named. It did occur to him, however, to wonder whether boys

born and raised in these surroundings would take kindly
to working eight hours a day in a northcountry machine-
shed, with its incessant clatter and reek of oil and tortured
metal. He thought, 'My intentions are good enough but
I daresay all I'll get in return is the length of Stella's
tongue,' and he was not so far wrong.

Encountering his sister in the farmyard, where she was
superintending the replacement of a worn-out windlass,
he noticed the entire absence of sisterly warmth in her
greeting. She said, impatiently, "You, George? Wait on a
minute, I must see to this first. We can't do without well-
water. The pond is dry after so long without rain," and
he stood by, watching her with amusement as she berated
two farmhands who were making slow and clumsy work
with the fitting.

The abrupt transition in the character of Stella since
her second marriage, that had taken place when he was
still at school, had always intrigued George. Indeed, he
found it difficult to equate the two Stellas for, unlike the
younger Swanns, he could remember her as a seventeen-
year-old county belle, riding with haughty glance to the
local meets, where every buck in the field was a would-be
suitor. He recalled her mincing ways and her sharp
outbursts of temper when things were not to her liking,
and had not been much surprised by her marriage to
Lester Moncton-Price when she was eighteen. What had
startled him more than somewhat was the dramatic change
that the foundered marriage had wrought in her and how,
within weeks of taking up with young Denzil Fawcett, and
helping him rebuild his farm after the fire in which his
father was killed, she had adapted to the life. Just as his
own viceroys in the regions found no difficulty in switching
their allegiance from horse to motor, so Stella had shed all
the trappings of a fashionable woman overnight and
become a particularly homespun housewife, happy, it
seemed, to work a fourteen-hour stint for a reward that
one of his junior managers would have regarded as inadequate. She had changed physically too, putting on at

least three stones in weight, and getting her once delicate skin gypsy brown in sun and wind. Her voice, pitched low and rather sweet in her childhood, had taken on a sharp, nagging note, and her exchanges with Denzil and the local farming community had introduced into it traces of a Kentish burr.

He was aware that his mother and old Alex (Alex would not have acknowledged her as a sister at this particular moment) had been bothered by the change but Henrietta had adjusted to it over the years and Adam, in his wisdom, let well alone. George knew that his own wife, Gisela, was fond of her sister-in-law but that was predictable. Gisela, too, at heart, still reckoned herself a peasant. What George did not know, and told himself now that he was unlikely to find out, were the underlying factors that had contributed to the change and now, watching her, he pondered them yet again, so deeply indeed that he hardly noticed when his sister was done with her supervision and saying, briefly, "Come into the kitchen then. I can give you a mug of cider if you care for one," and he followed her meekly, entering the big stone room where, summer and winter, a green log smouldered in a fireplace wide enough to roast the traditional ox.

She said, drawing him home-brewed cider from a cask, "Is it a message from mother?" He said no, he had a proposition to put to her and Denzil concerning the boys. "The two middle ones," he added, hastily. "Martin and John." They were no longer boys, he reflected, Martin being twenty-three by his reckoning, and John less than two years his junior, but everyone seemed like a boy in his sister's presence; even Denzil, her husband, who was about forty-six.

"What about my boys?"

"I've been wondering . . . this isn't a very large farm, and a good deal of your acreage is rough pasture. Robert, your eldest, will take over eventually, I imagine. It seemed to me that you might like to place them."

Stella looked very surprised and then equally

disapproving, squaring up to him, both freckled arms on heavy hips. *"Place* them? How do you mean, *place* them? They have a place, haven't they? Right here, working for us."

George said, patiently, "I know that, Stella. I've seen them about in the fields but four sons, on a farm this size, it doesn't seem very practical. I'm no farmer, of course, but everybody knows agriculture is in the doldrums. You can buy farms two a penny in some counties since they began bringing in all these refrigerated Australian and New Zealand products, and buying up millions of bushels of wheat from Canada. Ask Denzil if you don't believe me."

She continued to eye him, with vague hostility. "I didn't say I didn't believe you. But you haven't seen me over at 'Tryst' seeking charity, have you?"

"Damn it," he said, half in mind to tell her and her sons to go to the devil, "I'm not here offering charity! You've got a claim on Grandfather Sam's money, the same as the rest of us, and it's no secret that the Gov'nor makes you an allowance. I'm not talking about money but careers for the younger boys. If you don't care what becomes of them ten years from now then say so."

Denzil Fawcett clumped into the kitchen, nodding briefly in George's direction. George had a swift recollection of Denzil as a youth, walking with long strides and head held high, through a rainstorm to one of his father's pastures east of 'Tryst'. He now looked like a man in his late fifties, with slumped shoulders and grey, balding head. Farming aged a man, George thought and it encouraged him to press on. He said, "I'm here to offer apprenticeships to two of your boys, Denzil. They could learn the motor trade up north and get in on the ground floor. Stella doesn't seem taken with the idea. How about you?"

Denzil glanced at his wife and in that glance, George thought, was the story of their marriage. Lifelong incredulity on Denzil's part, that he had brought home a prize like Stella from the grand house over the hill, complete renunciation of her past on Stella's part, who must, he reasoned, have suffered dismally at the hands of the Moncton-Prices.

"You'm hard agin it, m'dear?"

"Aren't you? The boys' place is here, with their family and acres. Helping you as you get older and slower."

"Arr," he said, thoughtfully, "that's so," but then, to George, "The motor trade? Will that ever amount to anything, George?"

"Good God, of course it will! It'll practically take over ten years from now In your trade as well as in mine. Why else would I have invested a hundred thousand pounds in lorries? It's not a passing fad, man! Why the devil can't everybody see that by now? I had the same job convincing my managers but it hasn't taken them long to decide I was right."

"A 'prenticeship," he said, thoughtfully. "You'd mean, I take it, to learn the trade. But how about after? I mean, who would be likely to employ 'em in that sort of work?"

"I would, if they showed an aptitude. I'm training drivers and mechanics. We'd teach them all we know. After that it would be up to them. My guess is your boy Martin would take to it like a duck to water. I remember how he used to come over to 'Tryst' when I was working on the old Maximus and watch the wheels go round. It was remembering that that made me think of them."

There was a heavy silence in the room. The sap in the green log in the grate hissed an accompaniment to the ticking of the grandfather clock. Stella still had her upper lip clamped over the lower but Denzil, judging by the furrows on his forehead, was thinking hard.

"Would they get paid for larning?"

"Not much. They'd get board and lodging, guaranteed by the firm. And ten shillings a week for pocket money."

"And afterwards? When they knew what they was about?"

"A driver mechanic in the network earns fifty shillings a week, plus overtime. He can soon double that, however, providing he's up to his work. We're expanding all the time. I hope to have two hundred vehicles on the road within two years."

"It's still wrong! Wrong and unnatural!"

This from Stella, red in the face now, and having some difficulty in restraining herself, but Denzil looked at her mildly. "Maybe so, maybe not. You say what you think any road."

"I've told you what I think. Time enough, whether or not things pick up here, as they may and should, we won't be able to keep Ben Gaskell on as a hired hand. And old Trescoe is about finished, what with his rheumatism. What'll we do then, with none but you and Robert and young Richard to farm four hundred acres?"

He said, without looking at her, "That's not the point, m'dear. I don't offen run counter to you, do I? But there's some sense in what George says, for things couldn be worse for farmers. How can we compete with all this foreign muck they're dumping on us every day o' the week? As long as there's Free Trade it'll get worse instead o' better. Maybe we owe it to the boys and I reckon I'd like to sleep on it."

"And talk it over with them if I were you," George said, although something in him responded to the despair in the man's voice and manner. It must be hard, he thought, to see a traditional way of life foundering month by month, with markets shrinking and roots, hard down in the land for a thousand years or more, wrenched up by technologies that, to a man of Fawcett's disposition, must seem as alien as Black Magic. Maybe an answer lay in the adaptation of farms and farmers to the mechanical age, with purpose-built vehicles taking the place of their clumsy ploughs and lumbering, boat-shaped waggons. But this was years ahead, and men who had worked the land with their hands all their lives would be slow to adjust to such a revolution, even slower than would a transport man like Bertieboy Bickford in the far west.

He rose, draining and setting down his cider mug.

"Think it over, both of you. The offer is there. All you have to do is to tell me yes or no," and he went out across the yard, scattering hens who were scavenging there.

Denzil and Stella sat on, silent for above two minutes before Denzil rose and crossed the kitchen, laying his gnarled hand on his wife's shoulder.

"We can't stand in their way," he said. "It woulden be right. Neither of 'em could ever wed on what I pay 'em, and I know how I would ha' felt about that wi' you in mind. They'm both courtin', baint they?"

"Farm girls," Stella said. "Girls reared on good farms over in Lee Valley, but . . ."

"There's no 'buts' about it then. We'll have to let 'em go if they've a mind to go."

He went over to the open window and called Ben Gaskell, still wrestling with the windlass. "Leave that, Ben. Find Martin and John, and zend 'em to me and mother. And tell 'em to look sharp about it, I've something to zay to 'em!"

He went back to where Stella sat by the smouldering fire and stood before her. They had ridden out a number of crises over the years, resolving each as partners in accord, but here, for the first time since they had rebuilt the farm together, was something he had to face alone, shouldering her prejudices to one side, and deep in her heart she understood his motives. They would never fail utterly, and sell up as some of their neighbours had done since the agricultural slump set in like a blight. She had savings of her own and access, as George had reminded her, to capital, but this was irrelevant. In their twenty-five years of marriage he had never once sought help of this kind from her or her family, and she had never offered it, realising that his countryman's pride was as precious to him as the house they occupied and the acres he and his ancestors had farmed for more than four centuries. She took his hand and pressed it to her cheek, holding it there until she heard the scrape of her sons' boots in the yard.

2

Swann Whirligig — 1905/6

ADAM SWANN, IN A WHIMSICAL MOOD, HAD ONCE likened his family's march down the decades as a tribal migration, headed for the uplands. More objective observers, and there were many about the city and the big provincial centres, where money and goods changed hands in volume, saw it rather as a spring gushing from the old fox's enterprise in the 'fifties, and building rapidly to a broad, swift-flowing river in its progress towards a collective destiny. Or perhaps as a tide, beating on a coastline where, ultimately and given luck, it could change the map.

For the Swanns, confound them, seemed destined to advance on a singularly broad front, and before the new century had got its second wind around the fall of the year 1905, they were recognised as a power in the land. Not only in the field of transport (almost from the beginning they had offered a formidable challenge here) but in areas where rival trading clans sought no advancement, that of older, more staid professions, like the armed services and administrative spheres, and even out on the periphery of the national scene, where the vanguards of social reform ranging far ahead of the national conscience, now emerged triumphant at the polls.

As in the flow of all tides and rivers there were stretches down the years when the thrust of the current lost impetus, spending itself in puny forays mounted by individuals, often at odds with one another. Such a period had been

Adam Swann's recession in the early 'sixties, when he and his concerns came close to foundering. Or when, in 1865, he was out of action for a year after the Staplehurst rail disaster. But soon a sportive fate would take a hand in affairs, presenting some challenge that taxed the wits and the stamina of the tribe to the utmost. This had happened, after a long, smooth ride, in 1897, when George Swann wandered off course and the hub of the empire went up in smoke, leaving its spokes in disarray.

But the Swanns, it seemed, were seasoned survivors and these occasional setbacks put them on their mettle so that very soon, in no time at all it appeared to observers, they were in the forefront of the battle again, having used the check to marshal their reserves, mount a series of new attacks in unexpected sectors and push forward as a unit on several fronts.

Then competitors in all their chosen fields acknowledged their merits, numbering among them resilience, original thinking and, above all, the obstinacy of the British squares at Waterloo.

The period immediately following George's display of what mechanically-propelled vehicles could achieve when handled imaginatively, was high noon for the family. Some of George's will to succeed had been siphoned off and distributed among other members of the clan and retainers. Thus 1905 was a time of triumph in a variety of sectors, beginning with the appearance on British roads of over a hundred power-operated vehicles, the very first of their kind, and ending, in December of that same year, with the arrival of Giles Swann at Westminster, as the member for Pontnewydd. But between these two triumphs were a number of smaller victories that could have been grouped under the heading of Domestic Retrenchment.

*   *   *

The first of these modest victories occurred in the early spring of the year and its Boadicea, so to speak, was Helen

Coles, *née* Swann, widow of a decapitated missionary and unsung heroine of the Peking Siege.

It assumed the form, in the eyes of Joanna, her sister and sponsor, of an enchantment for nothing less, in her view, could have accomplished such an unlooked for event. It was as though the malign agency that had reduced Helen to such dependence on her sister when haunted by nightmares of one kind or another, had suddenly relented; or, more probably, been sent packing by a sentimental genie with a sense of humour. For Helen Coles, the pale, brooding widow of a year or so ago succeeded, against well-nigh impossible odds, in capturing Dublin's most eligible bachelor.

Joanna was never quite sure how it came about or why Rory Clarke, most turbulent of the Dublin fillibusters in Westminster, should have been bewitched by a woman five years his senior, when he might have taken his pick of the Dublin belles, most of them pretty, a few of them both pretty and handsomely dowered.

Rory, younger son of Tim Clarke, the vintner Joanna had enlisted as a Swann regular, was a dashing, slightly Byronic man for whom a brilliant political future was forecast, and the two were introduced to one another at one of Clarke père's soirées. Their conversation, on that occasion, was confined to the exploitation in South Africa of Chinese coolies, imported as a source of cheap labour; not, one would have thought, a very promising springboard for a romance. It happened, however, that circumstances favoured the encounter. Rory was in search of a new stick to belabour the British Government, and Helen Coles was the only woman in Dublin with first-hand knowledge of Chinese affairs, so that no other woman present could compete for his attention.

The very next day Rory sent his card round to Joanna's, together with an invitation for a carriage drive the following Sunday. Predictably Joanna was included in the invitation. Equally predictably, somehow scenting a miracle, she persuaded Helen to go unaccompanied.

From that point on progress was spectacular. Something in Helen's new-found stillness (and possibly her aura of tragedy) made a direct appeal to Rory Clarke's Celtic imagination. Bouquets and invitations began to arrive at the house almost daily and soon Dublin was scouting the possibility that Rory Clarke (the new Parnell some were already calling him) had succumbed to the charms of a thirty-four-year-old Englishwoman, who had been romantically involved in a welter of bloodletting on the other side of the world.

At first the neglected matrons and young eligibles of the Irish capital viewed the prospect of a romance with dismay, reflecting that an Irish champion had no business gallivanting with the English, but then certain unseen pressures began to be applied. First by Rory's soldier brother, who had no patience with the quarrel between the Irish and Dublin Castle, then by old Tim himself, who had taken the trouble to inform himself of Helen Coles two likely sources of income, her father and her father-in-law, the famous pill manufacturer. He also discovered, as a kind of bonus, that Helen, on remarriage, would have access to a trust fund from her maternal grandfather's fortune, derived from cotton and the Suez Canal shares.

Yet these were not deciding factors in Dublin's ultimate approval of Helen as the bride-in-waiting of her most promising son. These had their roots in the Irish sporting instinct, for who could fail to respond to the run-up of such an unlikely outsider, who had somehow contrived to lead the field in the Clarke matrimonial stakes?

And then, for Joanna, came a miracle within a miracle. Under the sun of Rory Clarke's tempestuous courtship Helen not only revived but reflowered, recapturing some of the sparkling good looks and high spirits of her youth at 'Tryst', to which was added a maturity and dignity that won approving nods from the senior section of society. Her appearance, in Joanna's view, changed almost overnight. When she had gone to her that night and assessed the damage caused by her marriage and dismal experiences abroad, she had been sallow, hollow-cheeked and listless in movement and manner. She had never been as pretty as Joanna but she had large and expressive grey eyes, a good complexion and, in those days, a trim, athletic figure, moulded by her youthful passion for lawn tennis and cycling. But her best feature had always been her hair, dark brown and thick but very soft in texture.

These starting-out advantages had been sacrificed by her years in the tropics. Hardly a trace of her original sparkle remained when Joanna talked her into a therapeutic frolic with the tipsy Jack-o'-Lantern, and when that sparkle returned in full measure Joanna reasoned that the change could never have been accomplished by a few sweaty moments in Clinton's embrace. Indeed, no appreciable change was apparent in the interval between that occasion and her first meeting with Rory, and yet, little by little, it became apparent that something had been achieved after all, for when they returned to Dublin Joanna noticed that Helen's apathy had changed to a kind of stillness, while privately her sister admitted that her recurrent nightmare had ceased and she was now sleeping and eating normally.

The knowledge made the goodhearted Joanna glad, despite a lingering doubt that Clinton had not been hoodwinked, for she sometimes caught him looking across the table at his sister-in-law with a vaguely puzzled expression, as though there was something about her that eluded him. It would, please God, continue to elude him. Men, Joanna was aware, often joked in their coarse way about all women being identical in the dark but perhaps they deceived themselves in this respect. Perhaps something, smothered under those fumes of alcohol, some awareness of physical unfamiliarity in the woman he had held in his arms so briefly, remained in the morning, when he awakened to find his wife beside him and in an unusually thoughtful mood. If it was so she did not let it bother her overmuch, or not after the forthcoming wedding of

Rory Clarke, M.P. and Mrs. Helen Coles was announced in the Dublin and London papers. One way or another her sister-comrade had been restored to her, whole and healed, and Joanna was never one to quarrel with luck.

2

Adam received the news that his daughter was to take a second husband with reservations. He knew all about the Irish fillibusters at Westminster and was scornful of their tactics. It gave him no confidence that, when, as he predicted, they gained their precious Home Rule, they would govern themselves any better than they had been governed by the British, but he was glad that Henrietta welcomed the match, realising that she had never really ceased worrying about Helen since hearing that story about the girl shooting a man in cold blood and exulting in the deed. She said, "It's positively the best thing that could have happened, Adam, and it doesn't matter a dropped stitch if Clarke is the firebrand you say he is. The fact is she'll be settled again and it's not too late for her to hope for a child to take her mind off her troubles."

That, he reflected with a chuckle, had always been Hetty's way with difficulties of any kind as far as her daughters were concerned. Children represented continuity, and continuity to Henrietta Swann, daughter of a pushing mill-hand and a penniless Irish immigrant, was paramount. Also, he supposed, with another chuckle, the act of begetting them, for no woman in this self-righteous day and age, could have approached that with more enthusiasm. He contented himself with replying: "Well, they're an enterprising bunch, I must say, when it comes to choosing partners. Just tally up our in-laws and try and find the common denominator. We've got a farmhand, a general's daughter, an Austrian peasant, a millionaire's daughter, the son of a pill manufacturer and that social lioness who gobbled up old Hugo. Now, to add variety, Helen is giving us a ringside seat at Donnybrook Fair. And we've still got young Edward and Margaret in reserve. What's brewing in that direction, I wonder?"

He was not to wonder long. News came via Giles that same season that Margaret, postscript of the tribe (conceived, he recalled, the night they buried the old Colonel, in 1879) had found a cogent reason for prolonging her stay in the Welsh valley and would almost surely, or so Giles predicted, marry a Welshman, "Without," as he described it, "two halfpence to rub together."

*　　　*　　　*

Her youngest daughter's shy but prolonged renunciation of the social scene, her seeming inability to make an impact on any one of the eligible young males her brothers had introduced into the house over the years, had been a source of concern to Henrietta for a long time. She reasoned that Margaret, at twenty-five, was in a fair way to becoming an old maid, totally absorbed in what Henrietta thought of as time-wasting pursuits, of the kind once recommended to young girls to keep them out of mischief until a suitor came knocking at the door. And this, in her view, was quite unnecessary, for Margaret had claims to be considered the prettiest (she was certainly the most feminine) of all the Swann girls. She had the kind of face that would retain its youthfulness into middle-age, perhaps even later, a delicate pink and white complexion, despite hours spent outdoors in all weathers, a gentleness of disposition that none of the other Swanns, male or female, possessed, a low, pleasing voice, an equable temper, a quick, shy smile and a trim figure, all of which, in her mother's experience, were qualities young men sought when they came looking for a wife. She had, in addition, two characteristics that were even rarer in girls, especially pretty girls: intelligence and the good sense to conceal it, for it was Henrietta's experience that young men were frightened off by signs of intelligence in a woman, indicating, as it usually did, that they were bad listeners. And yet, as the years passed, nobody came asking and, what was worse, Margaret showed no disposition whatever to worry about her lack of suitors. She was quite content, it seemed, to enjoy her endless love affair with nature, to woo and be wooed by spring landscapes, cloud movements over the Weald, the song of the wind in the larch coppices bordering 'Tryst' to the north, or the older woods that crowned the spur behind the house. She had a predisposition to wear clothes until they all but disintegrated under the tug of briars and hedgerow and her shapely hands (hands that her sisters envied) were usually stained with paint when she answered the lunch bell summons.

Adam, and Deborah, maintained that Margaret had a rare talent for painting pastoral scenes but Henrietta, whose ideals in painting were battle scenes, reproduced in the *Strand Magazine*, was not equipped to evaluate her daughter's artistic potential, for this she would have said had nothing to do with the three essentials in a young woman's life – finding a husband, founding a family and keeping both contented.

It was her doubts concerning Margaret's future, indeed, that encouraged Henrietta to persuade Margaret to accept Romayne's invitation to pay a visit to South Wales and lend a hand with the children. Romayne, who had recently miscarried another child, was in poor health at a time when Giles was fully stretched preparing for the forthcoming General Election.

Henrietta reasoned, no doubt, that Giles, centrepiece of a political arena, would be acquainted with any number of bachelors and perhaps, who knew, a comfortably-off young widower or two. He was, moreover, a kindhearted boy, who would surely do his best to promote any promising friendship, so that she was all agog when Giles wrote in the autumn of 1905 that he was visiting 'Tryst' during a dash to London, 'and would pass on some intriguing news concerning Margaret's debut in the valleys'.

Henrietta could place but one interpretation on this and when he appeared she whisked him into her sewing-room before Adam could bombard the boy with political queries. She said, closing the door and leaning against it, "Tell, then. Tell! That bit about Margaret? Does it mean what I hope it means?"

Giles smiled as he peeled off his overcoat. The relationship between him and his mother was unique in the family. She had always stood in awe of him, even as a child. He was so scholarly, so dangerously knowledgeable about life and people, holding a kind of balance between the clamourings of eight sisters and brothers, a tolerant referee no one cared to dispute. In some ways he seemed even older and wiser than Adam who often, Henrietta had noticed, deferred to him. Giles, for his part, saw his mother in the light of an amiable and impulsive elder sister, but there were aspects of her that he admired, notably her courage and resilience. He said, kissing her, "Oh, it's nothing sensational. Only that she seems to have taken a fancy to one of my party workers. A splendid young chap called Huw Griffiths. They go everywhere together and a day or so ago the poor chap came to me quite lost for words, very unusual for Huw. It seems he thought he should ask my permission to propose."

"Good gracious! And you don't regard *that* as sensational! With Margaret twenty-six next December? What did you say to him?"

"What could I say? I told him it was up to her, to both of them. As you say, she's surely old enough to know her own mind. If she had been younger I should have shuttled him to father. As it was I advised him to throw his hat in the ring."

"But what kind of man *is* he, for heaven's sake? I mean, how old and how eligible? And what does he *do*? Surely even you realise these things are important to us?"

"To you, I daresay. Not to Margaret. She's in love, I think, not only with Huw but with his valleys and the people who live in them. She's even taken to painting pithead scenes and they're very good to my mind, full of truth and humour . . ."

"Oh, *fiddlesticks* to what she's painting!" Henrietta exclaimed, impatiently, "tell me about this man Griffiths. You said 'a splendid young chap'. Splendid in what way?"

"Well, as a party worker for one thing. He's an excellent off-the-cuff speaker and a good organiser . . ."

"Do you mean he's a member of Parliament?"

"Member of P . . . ? Old Huw? Lord, no, nothing like that. He's a miner. About Margaret's age."

"A . . . a . . . miner? A coal-miner?"

"Yes. A big, strapping chap, with hair as black as the coal he digs and a tribe of younger brothers who worship him. They all live in a cottage and look after their mother and one little sister. His father is dead, you see – silicosis, poor devil."

"What would he earn?"

"Oh, about thirty shillings a week, but he isn't likely to stay down the pit. He attends evening classes when he's on day shift and sooner or later he'll get a job on top. I might even persuade him to leave the pits altogether and become my agent. Old Bryn Lovell is getting past it and we're looking for a younger man. If he and Margaret did marry I daresay he'd be tempted. We've got a good organisation and could pay a full-time agent three pounds a week."

The shattering unworldliness of the boy checked her outcry. His values were so alien to her, and no more welcome for being so innocently stated. Looking back over the past she realised that this had always been so with Giles, strangest and most complex of the brood, a boy who, she recalled, always seemed to her to inhabit a different planet from her and the rest of them and even, to an extent, from Adam, the wisest man on earth. And yet, in this kind of situation, there was no place for other-worldliness. She said, gulping down her disappointment, "Margaret can't be serious. You just don't understand these things, Giles. She's probably bored down there and just . . . well, flirting a little. I suppose even that is encouraging in a way, for it's never happened before. But I do think it's time she came back, before she gives that young man silly ideas. You tell her from me I want her home, do you hear? And now here's your father, and you'll be talking politics nineteen to the dozen until luncheon. I'll go and see to it now," and she withdrew into the hall before he could reply, calling to Adam, who was pulling off his gardening boots in the porch, "Giles is here. He hasn't long, he says."

That was the way of Henrietta, faced with unpalatable facts or even trends. She had a trick of reversing them, of picking the meat from the bone of some grisly-looking morsel and persuading herself that it must be good for something, although she wasn't sure what and would have to think about it. If Margaret had taken up with a miner of her own age it must mean that she was becoming aware of herself as a woman and that was hopeful, for it meant that with her daughter safely restored to her own circle, she could begin looking about for a real husband before the girl became restless and out of sorts, as was the way of unwed and uncourted females once they reached their mid-twenties. After lunch she would give her mind to the matter.

* * *

Margaret Swann's renunciation of her former lover, the soft, unchanging Kentish countryside, had occurred within a week of setting foot in the mining valleys. She did not understand what agency brought about such a betrayal, only that some gaunt, looming stranger, brooding but infinitely persuasive, rose out of the mountain under her feet and tugged at her sleeve buttons, bidding her look, ponder and absorb. For here was something unique in her experience and far more soul-stirring than any pastoral scene, with its eternal half-tones of green, brown and gold, its regulated light and the plodding figures seen about its fields and coppices.

Here, her accoster insisted, was vitality, adventure, challenge and an ugliness capable of crippling the spirit if you let it. But you didn't, seeing it for what it was, a stark setting for comradeship, laughter and compassion among all the teeming families inhabiting the terraces that seamed the steep slopes of Pontnewydd bowl. Here was greed, certainly, and probably all the other deadly sins, but they were on the defensive, despite occupation of the landscape reaching up to the rain-heavy sky behind the town. Within this arena, a cheerful, beleaguered garrison manning a battered citadel, were people, a multitude of Joneses, Evanses, Pritchards, Powells, Howells, Morgans, Reeces and Owens. And, of course, Griffiths, like the Griffiths of 107, Bethel Street, where the branch of the tribe lived.

It all began, in fact, within a stone's-throw of the open end of Bethel Street, where it joined the track leading out of the town to the fold in the hill where Giles and Romayne had their stone-built house. Not half-a-mile from the pit that provided some kind of justification for all this clutter, clinging to the side of the hill. Climbing up from the cluster of little shops on the floor of the valley she could just see the winding gear crowning the summit, with its huddle of sheds and sidings and its single rail track that reflected the last rays of the afternoon sun, playing catch-as-catch-can with the clouds.

Huw Griffiths was coming off shift with about a dozen other miners who lived in Bethel Street and she recognised him at once as the impressive young man who had attended last Tuesday's committee meeting in Giles' parlour. He was, she would judge, an inch over six foot and his shoulder span, for a man with such a slender waist, was impressive, but it was not his undoubted masculinity that had imprinted him on her mind but his smile, that was ready and very winning but, at the same time, slightly tremulous, the smile of a child who wasn't sure if he would win some permission he sought, or excuse some fault for which he was about to be blamed. For Huw Griffiths, a man in his mid-twenties she would say, looked no more than thirteen when he smiled and he was smiling now, having seen recognition in her glance across the width of the narrow road. He crossed over to her, his great, clodhopping boots striking harshly on the rocky surface of the track and lifting a filthy hand to an almost equally grimed forehead, said: "It *is* Miss Swann, isn't it, now? I'm Huw Griffiths, the candidate's senior steward. You opened the door to me Tuesday's meeting, Miss."

"I remember you very well, Mr. Griffiths."

Although reckoned shy by Henrietta and others who did not know her well, Margaret Swann was never embarrassed by strangers. Men, young and old, had been coming and going all her life at 'Tryst' and she noted them all, for her eyes were trained to record tiny details and idiosyncrasies about people as well as those of petals, leaf patterns and sun-shadows on gorse and bracken. Besides, there could be nothing to fear from a man with such a childlike smile and she smiled back as he went on, seemingly encouraged, "Might I ask a favour, Miss? I've some draft leaflets, you see – for the candidate, they are. Promised for tonight but there's an evening class, see, and I've scrub-up and tea ahead of me. Our place is only a step and if you'd be so kind . . ."

"I'll take them, certainly, Mr. Griffiths," and she fell into step with him, lengthening her stride over the uneven surface of the road and saying, for something to say, "What exactly *is* senior steward, Mr. Griffiths?" and his smile widened. At the corners of his mouth tiny furrows overlaid with coal-dust seemed to wink large black stars on a white ground. The smile fascinated her so much that she hardly heard his small joke in reply.

"Just a handle. To make a man feel someone, you'd

say, Miss Swann. The candidate's like that, you see . . ." He referred to Giles as though he was a stranger to her, "he likes to haf everybody in there with a part to play. Not just himself, like all the others."

"What others?"

"Oh, the party bigwigs, those who come yer to speak, you know."

"But what do you do, Mr. Griffiths? Write leaflets to put through doors?"

"Ah, no, I only copy them. It's practice, you see, for I'm not much at writing yet. But I can talk when I've a mind to." He expanded then deflated himself with another smile. "All I do is go on ahead to meetings and put out the chairs. Stand by for hecklers too, but the candidate isn't one for clearing the hall, not unless things get too rough, mind. Any old job handy, I reckon, that would cover it. Here's our place, Miss," and he stopped in front of one of the redbrick dolls' houses, identical in almost every detail with all its neighbours, save that its knocker gleamed as though it had just had its daily polish.

"I'll get the leaflets . . ." but then, hesitating, "Won't you step inside, Miss? It wouldn't do to leave the candidate's sister on the doorstep."

She moved in ahead of him, into a narrow strip of passage formed by planks partitioning off the parlour, then, one step beyond, into a kitchen filled with people half-seen through a cloud of steam and drying washing. He squeezed past her, blocking the way. "No, no, Miss, not in there. Mam and the kids are home and my bath is laid out. Into the parlour, please."

She turned and he reached over her shoulder to open the parlour door, revealing a room about eight feet by ten, stuffed with furniture. Inside the tiny house he became a giant but a giant moving over familiar ground, so that every movement was pre-judged. "Take a seat, Miss," and she sat on the one red plush chair, its back protected by a lace antimacassar, while he sidled out again and she heard him subdue a sudden babel from the kitchen, hissing them down as though her presence had converted the kitchen into a chapel. "*Ssh*, Mam! Shssh, Miriam . . . It's the candidate's sister. Mustn't keep her waiting . . ." and after that a long hush, broken only by whisperings and stealthy movements on the other side of the wall.

She looked about her with the keenest interest. The room, vastly overcrowded as it was with table, chairs, a large green plant pot containing a huge aspidistra, knick-knacks of the kind she had seen won as prizes at Ton-bridge Fair, and an assortment of wool mats worked in all colours of the rainbow, was none the less cleaner than any room she remembered. It was, she supposed, the holy place of the house and very seldom used, for it felt cold and damp in contrast to the street and steaming kitchen. Family photographs decorated the walls, dominated by an oak-framed portrait of a thickset man about forty, wearing his Sunday best and gazing down at her as though hypno-tised by her presence. The eyes and the heavy square jaw betrayed him as Huw Griffiths' father, and she wondered where he was, concluding he was probably down the mine on the night shift.

And then, as she sat taking in the contents of the room, and relating it to all she had seen in the few days since arriving here, there came to her a revelation, of the kind she had read about in social and religious tracts, where people renounced one form of life for another, turning themselves inside out and seeing everything about them from a strange new angle. It had to do, in some mys-terious way, with her painting, so far wholly concerned with nature, with rich, colourful, unsullied things that flowered and gave off a wide variety of scents, with soli-tude and stillness. But now, in the presence of these drab, mundane things, most of them lacking colour and form, and with the memory of the scenes outside, dominated by the skeletal winding gear crowning the hill, she had an awareness of stirring from a long, drugged sleep into full and vibrant wakefulness and the desire to capture the experience in pencil lines was so strong that her hands itched for crayons and paper. For here was a new world, with a million subjects awaiting her brushes, subjects of the kind generations of genre painters had found compelling in the past but had never, so far, seemed to her worth reproducing. She could hardly wait to get to her portmanteau containing the materials she had brought from 'Tryst' and stood up, fidgeting with her gloves as he edged himself into the room and handed her a bundle of leaflets tied with string.

"Sorry to keep you waiting, Miss. Nothing's easy to find with so many under your feet. Under Miriam's bed, they were, of all places," and he turned on her that slow, bewitching smile so that she thought, 'I'll capture that too before I'm many days older . . . that smile, against the background of a house like this in a town like this. For that's the essence of it – warmth and cheerfulness dominating squalor and overcrowding, and everything else these people have to put up with . . . Yet not letting these things run away with them, keeping them on a tight rein, just as his mother keeps this place spotless, with all that dirt coming into the house from the black mountain yonder . . .'

She said, facing him as she tucked the leaflets under her arm, "Will you be coming up to Mr. Swann's house in the next few days, Mr. Griffiths?"

"Why, yes, Miss. We've a committee meeting there tomorrow, after tea. The agent, the secretary, the treasurer and the committee men who make out the roster for street-corner meetings."

"When you've done talking will you sit for me?"

"*Sit* for you, Miss?"

"I'm sorry. Let me explain. I paint, you see, and I'd very much like to paint you, Mr. Griffiths. You, holding my brother's little boy David, perhaps, but with the pit-head in the background. It will be light until around eight-thirty and the sketches wouldn't take long. Would you do it for me?"

He seemed so stunned that she was not sure he comprehended her request but apparently he did, for presently he said, "You want to *draw* my picture, Miss? *Me?* You don't mean *take* it, with a camera? Like Dadda up there."

"No, draw it . . . sketch it that is . . . and paint it afterwards. See, I'll show you . . ." and she put down the leaflets and whipped one from the pile, diving into her reticule for a sharpened pencil she kept there. "Now keep quite still, Mr. Griffiths!" and she limned him with a few bold strokes, catching what he obviously regarded as an astounding likeness in a matter of seconds. "There, like that. Only much better, of course."

He took the leaflet and stared down at it. "Why, that's wonderful! Wonderful it iss! Just like that! Like . . . like a flash of lightning!" The awe in his voice made her laugh, banishing the last of her shyness and the strangeness of the encounter in this crowded little parlour. "I spend most of my time sketching," she said, "but I'm not very good at portraits. I think I cou'd be but I should need a lot of practice. Will you do it, after the committee meeting tomorrow?"

"The candidate wouldn't think it a liberty?"

"Giles? Of course he wouldn't. He'd be interested in a change of subject. He's never seen anything of mine but pastoral scenes, in and about the place where we live in Kent."

"May I . . . could I keep this bit o' paper, Miss?"

"Of course, if you want to. But it's only the roughest kind of sketch."

"Mam and the others will be struck dumb when I show them. We never heard. . . the candidate never said . . . I mean, having a sister who could draw pictures like a camera only better . . ." He fell to examining the sketch again, clearly regarding his likeness as the eighth wonder of the world.

She squeezed past him and he followed her out into Bethel Street. The sun had finally won its day-long battle with the clouds and the row of tiny houses was bathed in orange light. Higher up the hill, and down below on more level ground, a veil of smoke had drawn a heliotrope curtain across the sky. The shouts of children at play came to them from lower down the street. She said, as to herself, 'There's so much to paint about here. Why, there's a lifetime of painting ahead of me,' and then, offering him her hand, she walked thoughtfully back towards the track. At the corner of the street she turned and saw him still standing there, silhouetted against the sky, the sketch in his hand.

3

The nine months comprising spring, summer and early winter of the year 1905 was a flood tide for the Swanns. Change, adventure and enterprise, bringing with them individual and collective advances, ran like a string of Chinese cracker explosions along the Swann ramparts.

Tidings of their forays reached Adam at intervals in the form of bulletins and personal reports and, unlike his wife, he was able, from the serene standpoint of a man of seventy-eight, to ponder each objectively. Some excited him but did not surprise him. After all, it was in the nature of things that George should forge into the future with his fleet of mechanically-propelled waggons, and just as predictable that his daughters, Helen and Margaret, should find men to their liking and go their own way up and down the social scale.

Two subsequent developments, however, one concerning his eldest son, Alexander, the other his son Hugo, found a deeper lodgment in mind and heart. The first because he was still able, even after this stretch of time, to see life through the eyes of a professional soldier, the second because, having come to think of Hugo as a permanent casualty, he was uplifted by the boy's re-entry into the lists.

News of Alex's advancement came in late autumn, when he and his wife Lydia spent a period of leave at

'Tryst' and he was told of his son's invitation to join the counsels of the exalted. At the age of forty-five Alexander Swann, with several wars and twenty-seven years' service behind him, was often mistaken for a run-of-the-mill career officer, advancing by seniority, destined, perhaps, for a colonelcy in a line regiment before retirement. Outwardly, he was very set in his ways and his opinions (prejudices, most people called them) were those of a majority of his colleagues. He looked what he was, too, having acquired a slight paunch and the habit of command, and of strict obedience to the whim of superiors, had imposed upon his voice and manner a certain brusqueness. In addition, somewhere along the line, he had forgotten how to laugh at himself, the one quality, in Adam's view, that could prevent an army officer developing into an animated duplicate of the stuffed dummies he had once used for sabre practice on the drill-ground. But Adam, almost alone among those whose path occasionally crossed that of Lieutenant-Colonel Alexander Swann, was not deceived by this veneer. He was aware that, below the skin, his eldest son concealed a brace of Swann traits that could still rescue him from the mental atrophy that overtook almost every serving officer in middle-age. He had sacrificed the saving grace of laughter, certainly, but he had retained and even developed that professional curiosity that lay at the very heart of the Swann empire, as his obsession with the importance of firepower proved. Urged on by his devoted Lydia he had avoided all the popinjay pitfalls in his twenties, and had become an acknowledged expert on the new Maxim gun and its successor, the heavy Vickers machine-gun. Tirelessly, and often with no apparent effect upon his superiors, he had hawked his ideas around the Empire so that now, whenever the question of increased firepower came up in war games and the inquests that succeeded them, Lieutenant-Colonel Swann's advice was sought by men of high rank. Sought and occasionally heeded, Adam remarked, for he kept a sharp eye on the army's technical advances, particularly since the British, descending on South Africa as though it was another Crimea, had taken such a hammering from a few thousand farmers.

The army, he supposed, was changing like everything else about him and modern technologies could not be held at bay indefinitely by an assortment of polo-playing, pig-sticking fops operating at a safe distance from London. Here and there changes were forced upon them, usually by news of French and German innovations, and now that a man of intelligence was in command of the army spring-clean that followed peace in South Africa, it seemed likely that progress would accelerate to the point where it might have some lasting effect upon the cavalrymen crowding the highest rungs of the profession.

And this, in fact, was more or less confirmed by Alex, when he accompanied Adam down to The Hermitage one November afternoon and told him of his recent interview with Haldane.

Adam, who, since his retirement had spent upwards of two hours a day with his newspapers, was familiar with Richard Haldane, one of the brighter stars in the Liberal firmament, judging him a painstaking and unusually imaginative man. Haldane's thoroughness, however, seemingly went far beyond Adam's expectations, for Alex told him that he had been among a group of home-based officers invited to discuss a particular plank in the Liberal platform, grounded on the near certainty that the Liberals would sweep the Balfour Government out of office at the next General Election.

"It's an open secret," Alex told him, "that if the Liberals win, as seems certain, Haldane will be offered the War Office. How much do you know of him, Gov'nor?"

"I've read some of his articles in periodicals," Adam said, surprised to find Alex caught up in politics. "He seems to have some far-reaching ideas about military reorganisation. German educated, isn't he, and spends a lot of his time at Potsdam?"

"He's very impressed with Germany's military

re-organisation. He admitted to me that we could learn a great deal from the Junkers. Well, not the Junkers exactly, for I imagine they correspond to our cavalry caucus, but from the German General Staff. We haven't even got a General Staff. If Haldane gets the opportunity the creation of one is his first priority but that won't concern me, save indirectly."

"You say he sent for you?"

Alex looked a little foxy and Adam guessed, rightly, that he was debating with himself how far he could confide in a civilian.

"I don't know if I should pass all of it on," he said, at length. "I can rely on your complete discretion, of course."

"If you can't, then God help you, boy," Adam said. "I've stopped hobnobbing in city coffee houses, you know." Then, "You had it in mind to confide in me, didn't you?"

"Yes, I did. Well, Haldane aims at instituting some tremendous reforms in the service. Apart from the creation of a staff he wants to amalgamate the Volunteers and Yeomanry into a single unit called Territorials, with a strength of fourteen divisions and as many mounted brigades."

Adam whistled. "That's a big bite. I hope he doesn't give some of his turn-the-other-cheek Liberal colleagues heartburn. They're against army expansion, aren't they?"

"Oh, I know nothing about that," Alex said, casually. "We chaps aren't supposed to meddle in politics but I must say the chap impressed me. For what he's after is the creation of a highly-trained reserve army, plus the founding of a schools' cadre for officers, to be known as the Officers' Training Corps."

"And that, I imagine, is where you come in?"

Alex coloured, never having learned to adjust to his father's badinage. "It would mean an acting colonelcy. And a chance to pass on what I know about small arms to people who . . . well, to put it bluntly, have had their heads in the sand for forty years."

"Why the devil don't you say what you mean," Adam said, irritably, for he had never cared for circular talking when he was young and found it even more frustrating in old age. "Those chaps you've been canvassing for years aren't just ostriches. A majority only took a commission to avail themselves of an idle life, with strong, social advantages. The older ones are fossilised fools, and you've broken your head against them time and again, so don't pretend otherwise. What answer, if any, did you give Haldane?"

Alex said, as though confessing to a felony, "I . . . er . . . I . . . took a chance. I said I was wholly in favour of all the changes he suggested, and if I was given the chance I'd do my damnedest to teach part-time soldiers all I knew on the ranges. Was I right?"

"You were right," Adam said, "and I'll add something to that. I'm proud of you, boy, for if you had wriggled off the hook you wouldn't deserve another step nor a chance to haul the army into the twentieth century." He scowled at the dreaming landscape. "Listen here, as long ago as the eighteen-fifties I saw campaigns bungled and men butchered simply because those in command of them approached every battle with the tactics of Waterloo and Blenheim. The penalty for that was incurred in South Africa and if we didn't learn from that we might as well concede the next war, if one comes, to the Prussians, the French, the Germans, the Russians or the Japs. I wouldn't put a shilling on us beating anyone but the Turks right now, would you?"

He saw that he had gone too far but he did not regret it. Alex, notwithstanding his obstinacy, still needed prodding when it came to making bold decisions, of the kind Adam had made every day when he was his son's age. It was fortunate, he reflected, that Alex had found that funny little wife of his when he was at the crossroads of his career. He said, remembering her now, "Have you told Lydia as much as you've told me?"

"No. I was in two minds whether I should tell you."

"Well, here's one more piece of paternal advice. Confide in her as you go along and you'll never go far wrong. For if anyone can push you to the top of the tree it isn't Haldane, or anyone like Haldane. It's Lydia, who brought you this far without much trouble. Am I right about that?"

He was relieved to see a slow, rather boyish smile crease his son's face so he went on, "Of course I am. You know that better than anyone! Tell her tonight, boy, and see what she makes of it."

Dusk was creeping over the paddocks and Adam went into The Hermitage museum to retrieve his ulster, shed earlier in the afternoon. Alex followed him in, glancing curiously at the Swann paraphernalia cluttering walls and floor of the building. He said, as though voicing a question that had tormented him all his life, "You were trained as a soldier, Gov'nor, and my guess is you were a damned good one. What the devil prompted you to sidestep the chance of a career like General Roberts' for . . . well . . . all this?"

"I can tell you that easier than I could have told you an hour ago. In my day there were twice as many ostriches and no Haldanes about. Come, boy, it's getting chilly and I've a taste for muffins and a dish of tea."

They went out and across the paddock to the break in the sentinel row of trees guarding the drive to the house; father and son, separated not so much by a span of years as by the gulf between wars fought with lance and sabre and an era when weapons could kill at a range of several miles. Between them they represented, perhaps, a dozen generations of professional warriors and the link, to anyone who knew them both, was still strong, despite Adam's early renunciation of the Swann trade. After all, Alex reflected, he had laid aside sword and lance fifty years ago but he was still, in the real sense of the word, a warrior to be reckoned with.

4

Hugo's news came early in the New Year, although Adam and Henrietta got an advance hint of it at the Christmas reunion.

This had gone smoothly enough this year, for Giles and Romayne, caught up in what promised to be the toughest and rowdiest election since the introduction of universal male franchise, were far too busy to leave their constituency and travel down to Kent.

The breach between Alex and Giles, Romayne and Lydia, had not healed during the last few years and Adam sensed that Hugo, innocent cause of it, was still unhappily aware of the family rift, but the paths of the three brothers rarely crossed these days. Furthermore, even Alex had to admit that public opinion had swung in a wide arc since the mood of obsessive patriotism, at the time of the South African war. People, even important people, were beginning to ask themselves if they had not made fools of themselves in public during that spell of euphoria, and a generous peace with the Boers went some way to convincing the electorate that there was a great deal to be said for Lloyd George's opposition to the war, so unpopular at the time.

The fact remained, however, that Hugo was still little more than a hulk, carted round by that tireless wife of his, and that barking parade-ground sergeant he employed as a watchdog. Sometimes, in the long hours of the night (Adam did not need much sleep nowadays) he wondered about the boy, and how he would fare as the years passed, and faced the prospect of travelling down them as a passenger. His faith in Hugo's wife, however, was considerable, and he listened with the closest interest whenever she appeared at 'Tryst', projecting various plans to achieve rehabilitation. Most of them, Adam decided, were harebrained but he admired her audacity, and the way she explored every new prospect of salvaging Hugo's manhood from the wreck of that shambles out on the veldt.

It came, he learned later, during a pilgrimage Sybil and Hugo made to Netley Military Hospital, in the autumn of 1905, with the object of a final consultation with Udale, the surgeon to whom Hugo owed his life.

Udale was permanently stationed at Netley now, caring for several hundred maimed victims of the fighting, and after a prolonged physical check he pronounced Hugo completely fit but privately expressed some concern regarding the patient's state of mind.

"He's too . . . too *passive*," he told her, while Hugo was making a tour of the wards. "Ordinarily this might not matter, might even be a help and a handhold but not with a chap like Swann. More than anyone I know, he concentrated his entire being on physical prowess, and you'll never capture his interest with any of the usual pursuits of the blind. It isn't as if he had ever been engaged in manual labour, or work calculated to tax his brains. We have to hit on something that will focus his mind on some kind of variant of his former occupation, that is give him a renewed interest in his muscles, sinews and staying power."

"He exercises regularly," Sybil told him. "He's walking and riding every day, and he spends a good deal of his time swimming."

"I wasn't thinking of exercise. He needs to use that magnificent body of his to someone else's advantage." Sybil remembered, during the second stage of convalescence, how insistent Hugo had been on regular massage to counteract a flabbiness encouraged by the helplessness of a man without sight. She said, "Do you do much massage here, Mr. Udale?" At once Udale's quick mind sparked and he thumped his desk, exclaiming, "Why, Lady Sybil, that might be the answer! Massage! Professional massage, and I don't mean on the receiving end."

"He once took a course in massage and spent one day a week at a teaching hospital soon after we came home. It didn't seem to interest him at the time."

"But it might here," Udale urged. "You say he learned the theory? Well, why don't I hustle him along to our gymnasium?" And he picked up his desk telephone, the first Lady Sybil had ever seen, and turned the handle with emphasis, asking the operator to put him through to Corporal Corkerdale at the gym. But Hugo confounded them both, so completely that afterwards Sybil speculated seriously on the theory of thought transference, currently fashionable among some of her friends in Belgravia. The N.C.O. in charge of the gymnasium, learning that Mr. Udale intended to bring a blind officer down for a visit replied, instantly, "Would that be Lieutenant Swann, the athlete, sir?"

"That's who I had in mind. How did you guess?"

"But he's already here, sir. Working on Sergeant Toller's legs."

"*Working* on them? How do you mean exactly?"

"Well, sir, manipulating. He and Toller served together in South Africa, and Mr. Swann told me he was qualified as a masseur and would like to give Toller a going over. Did I do wrong to give my consent, sir?"

"No," Udale said briefly, "you hit the bullseye in one, Corkerdale. I'll explain later," and he replaced the earpiece and recounted the conversation to Sybil. "We'll go down and watch," he suggested. "I've time before my next round."

*   *   *

His tour of the wards, in search of two or three men he had met in the early days of his convalescence, had been depressing for Hugo. Failing to find those he sought — Sergeant Toller, hit in both legs by a shrapnel burst at Modder River and confined to a wheelchair ever since, was one of them — he soon discovered that the pity he generated among the crippled servicemen more than outweighed any comfort or cheer he could dispense. As one young officer put it, rather crudely, "I'm short of one leg and one arm, but what's that compared to your problem, Swann? Damned if I feel like complaining when I meet a chap who has lost his sight. Nice of you to look in."

Someone told him Toller was exercising on the bars in the gym so he let his watchdog guide him there. Toller retained both legs but they were little more than props and the two casualties sat side by side on a bench comparing notes. Toller, having seen Hugo canter the open mile at Stamford Bridge just before the war, showed more tact than the officer upstairs. "You're looking pretty fit to me, sir. You must be taking a deal of exercise."

"Oh, I exercise," Hugo said. And then, petulantly, "It's about all I do these days, Toller."

"I can't get enough," the sergeant complained, "but it's not my fault. The quacks tell me I could get the use of my legs back in time but the fact is . . . well, I'm dogtired in five minutes, and have to give up, what with that and the pain. It's no wonder, I suppose. I stopped about two pounds of lead out there and it was a bloody miracle I didn't lose both legs. But I might as well for all the use they are. Feel here, just below the knee joint," and he guided Hugo's hand to scarred and pitted areas of flesh where Toller's calf muscles had once bulged. "I was a bit of a miler myself," Toller went on, "never in your class, of course, but I brought home some pots in my time."

"You could again," Hugo said, unexpectedly.

"How's that, sir?"

"You could again. There's no permanent damage to the bone structure, is there?"

"They say not, not in either leg. There were five fractures at the time but they all healed. It's torn sinew and wasted muscle, I suppose. No damned go in 'em, sir."

There was not much Hugo did not know about leg muscles. Ever since, as the boy wonder on the Exmoor plateau, he had submitted to the routine calf massage of his brother Giles and, later, to that of his trained fag in anticipation of some cross-country event, he had been a student of muscles and how they responded to the strains

442

put upon them. In his championship days he had met, in many a stadium dressing-room, dozens of coaches, most of them professionals, who had taught him how to eradicate the stiffness from overtaxed muscles, how to nurse minor injuries and, above all, how to induce a suppleness that was essential to muscles subjected to the strain of a prolonged training session. Legs, for so long, had been Hugo's stock-in-trade and he knew his own as well as his father knew the main roads of the Swann network. His accumulated knowledge told him that what the doctors said of Toller's legs was probably true. All the man needed to walk again was expert massage over a long period, combined with a graduated course of specially-designed exercises using a few simple items of equipment. He said, "I'd like to have a shot at you, Toller. I'll lay you ten to one in sovereigns I could put some real go into those stumps. Given time and plenty of grit on your part," and after a brief word with the gym instructor, he went to work, hammering away at Toller until he shouted for a respite.

He was so engrossed that he did not notice Udale and Sybil enter and stand beside the gymnast who was watching Hugo with interest. Corkerdale said, in a quiet aside, "He's a dab hand at it an' no mistake, sir. We could do with someone like him to chivvy 'em up. And it's not just the way he goes about it either . . . it's . . ."

"What else is it, Corkerdale?" Udale, unlike most members of his profession, was a good listener, particularly when confronted with a specialist in one field or another. "Well, sir, it's Lieutenant Swann being blind . . . beggin' your pardon, Ma'am . . . I mean, not letting it gripe 'im, the way it would most of us."

"Go on," said Udale, gravely, and when Corkerdale hesitated, "I'm right in assuming there was an idea behind that idea, wasn't there?"

"Maybe, sir, but who am I to talk about it in front of someone like you?"

"Why not? We don't know everything, we only pretend we do. Tell me what you were going to say."

"Well, sir, it's him being blind. Having someone like that, even worse off than most of 'em, that is, makes 'em sit up and take notice and that's very good for 'em, sir, seein' as how so many are down in the dumps. Do you follow me, sir?"

"All the way, Corkerdale, thank you. We'll see what we can do about it," and he watched Hugo shrewdly, so absorbed in the massage that he was still unaware of their entry, so that presently Udale motioned to Sybil to withdraw.

She put it to him that same night, armed with some figures Udale had given her. In Netley Hospital alone there were close on two hundred maimed ex-servicemen, some of whom were permanently crippled, but others for whom there was hope of regaining the use of a limb or limbs under protracted courses of treatment. Toller was a typical case. Encouraged and bullied, he could, in time, make a fifty per cent recovery and might even dispense with crutches. It depended, Udale insisted, more on his own reserves of will-power than upon outside agencies. "Udale swears that you could bridge that gap, Hugo," she urged. "He tells me that one of the biggest handicaps facing them as regards men with a sporting chance is the unconscious resentment patients feel for those who prescribe their courses, and deluge them with advice, from the standpoint of the hale and active. He's very anxious to take you on full-time down there. We can find a house, overlooking Southampton Water, and the sergeant could drive you in every day. Why don't you think about it over Christmas, dearest?"

He thought about it. Indeed, he thought about little else, ranging the coverts and uplands of the Weald on horse and foot, until there grew in him a conviction that here, perhaps, was a field where he might engage his unused stock of energy that could find no outlet in conventional exercise, taken with no other object than keeping his own body at concert pitch. For by now he had adjusted to his blindness in most ways. Moving in a familiar back-

ground such as 'Tryst', or about their home in Eaton
Square, he could walk about almost unaided and he
discovered that an enlargement of his other senses,
particularly those of touch and hearing, had occurred
much the way Udale had prophesied. He was not exactly
unhappy, but he was confused and indecisive regarding a
purpose and self-justification, for until the moment of
his tragedy his athletic prowess had been an end in itself
and he had never ranged as far as the point where he
would be too old and stiff-jointed to compete with younger
men. It was as though, all his life, he had been loping up
an incline, without asking himself why, yet finding a full
measure of satisfaction in the certainty that he could move
faster, and with more precision, than any challenger and
this supreme faith in his physical ascendancy had persisted
right up to the moment he reached the top of that scrub-
sown hill and lay in wait for the Boers manning the
outpost beyond. Then, in a single moment, he had lost
his bearings and paused to ask himself where he was
travelling and why, and what was the nature of the trophy
they would award him, and in the period since his mind
had been mostly a blank, without anything to focus upon
other than moments of guilt concerning that dead boy, or
the transitory repose he found in his wife's body and the
prattle of their child, Humphrey.

He was touched, deeply so, by the kindness of those
about him, sensing that patient efforts to convince him
that he was still at one with them but he knew very well
that he was not and could never be so long as he lived, and
that he must face this formidable truth sooner or later.
And yet he continued, assiduously, to nurse his body,
losing no opportunity of keeping it in the peak of training,
for somewhere ahead there might be a use for it and, in
any case, it was all he had in the way of capital.

A few rare bonuses had come his way since he had
learned how to surmount the worst aspects of his handicap, to think beyond the daily challenges of shaving,
dressing and eating his food without having it cut up by

Sybil or by the sergeant, and perhaps the most rewarding of these was a heightened physical relationship between himself and Sybil, dating from that first embrace in the tented hospital where, or so Sybil declared, young Humphrey had been conceived. At the time he had regarded it as no more than a release of fear and anger, prompting him to use her body as a buffer for his wretchedness, but when, in more tranquil moments, it returned again and again, promoted by her in a way that never failed to stir him, he came to think of it as a source of solace, freely available as an outlet of tensions within him, and would sometimes try and tell her as much, in stumbling, half-articulated phrases, when he was spent and lying still in her arms. And the wonder of it was she seemed to understand, indeed, to revel in her role as comforter, murmuring over and over again, "But I love you, dearest . . . you're everything . . ."

But there was another, more subtle consolation that was harder to understand and evaluate, and it had to do with his frozen memory of the sounds and scents of the countryside where he had spent his boyhood, for these were now intensified to a degree where he could isolate and savour each of them, identifying the smell of autumn and the stir of spring, and images awareness brought to him out of the past; violet mist in the Bray valley on a still October afternoon, rain blurring the escarpment behind 'Tryst', ripening fruit in the cages and orchards south of the house, rows of leather-bound books in his father's library, the steady surge and recoil of winter breakers on the seashore, the rush of hounds breaking covert when the huntsman sounded 'Gone Away', all kinds of things that had once never impinged on him when he had eyes to see them but were now like old friends helping him along the way.

Yet for all this placid acceptance of his limitations there remained the emptiness of his future and it was not until he sensed, through his fingertips, the flacidity of Toller's wasted legs, that he saw, as it were, a glimmer of light in the surrounding darkness, identifying it there and then into hope of a kind so far denied him. Energy surged back into him then, of the kind that had launched him at such speed down the embattled valley among the remnants of Montmorency's shattered column, and something told him that here, at last, was the elusive secret of regeneration, the use of his own bones and flesh to restore the crippled bodies of other poor devils whose youth and vigour had been taken from them out on the veldt.

He went to Sybil on the last day of the old year, saying briefly, "Write to Udale. And look for that house in Hampshire. I'll work at Netley for as long as he needs me, as long as there are men there who can be helped, even slightly."

"There'll always be someone to help, dearest," she said, gladly, and kissed him, but impatiently, for she did not want to waste a moment in setting the seal upon the victory.

* * *

She came to Adam with the news in early February, a week or two after Hugo had joined the Netley staff, with full details of his vocation and their impending move to Hampshire. "As chirrupy as a sparrow," as he afterwards told Henrietta, making no attempt to conceal his own satisfaction. Henrietta heard him out and then had a private session with Sybil, plying her with innumerable questions concerning Hugo and their new base south-west of the Gosport road and overlooking Southampton Water, and when Sybil, with her usual air of setting out on a royal progress, had bustled about her business, Henrietta withdrew to her sewing-room, wondering about her and what strange alchemy had been at work to fuse a woman of that kind with that great son of hers, the splendid young man she recalled so vividly in the days before they shot away his sight. It was a case, she thought, that paralleled Hugo's own pursuit of trophies, for that was how Lady Sybil Uskdale must have thought of him when they met and married. But now, instinct told her, it was different. Something strange and secret had developed between them, that had nothing much to do with Hugo's fame and popularity, but was concerned with a compulsion on the part of that rather overpowering woman to make amends for the wrong she had done him by dragging him off to that terrible war. But there was something else, she sensed, behind Sybil's assessment of him whenever she discussed the boy, or even looked at him, and this was a hint Henrietta could interpret without much fear that she was jumping to a conclusion. Lady Sybil had found in Hugo the kind of fulfilment that she, as wife and mother, had found in Adam all those years ago, and Hugo's blindness, cutting him off from diversions, and making him entirely dependent on her, had proved a kind of boon to both of them, adding something essential to a relationship that had been little more than an arrangement when it began. She thought, 'I never did understand the woman before. I suppose I was always a little scared of her. But I'm not any more, for she's really no different from any of us when it comes down to essentials . . .' And then, whooping like one of those Red Indians in Buffalo Bill's Travelling Circus, Adam hurried into the house, calling for her at the top of his voice, flinging open the sewing-room door and brandishing a telegram that he must have taken from the boy she saw pushing his bicycle up the drive.

"It's from Giles!" he bellowed. "He's in with a thumping majority! Over two thousand, by God!" and she thought, taking the telegram from him and reading it carefully, 'They're such a whirlwind tribe and he's no different from any of them, for he keeps pace with them somehow and that's more than I can do these days.' But she said, trying hard to match his enthusiasm, "How wonderful for him. I *do* hope he likes it when he gets there," and that, for some reason that she did not understand, made him laugh, a fact that underlined somehow the sad but undeniable fact that she was getting left behind with stay-at-homes like Stella and Denzil, in the family's advance into new and frightening worlds.

It was no wonder, really, for things were changing at such a pace, for her and for everyone else who could remember older, more tranquil times, when the social frontiers were fixed and nothing (if you excepted the new railway engines) moved faster than a horse. She remembered that Adam, in one of his jocular moods, had called these changes 'another spin of the whirligig' and they did not appear to distress him at all, even though he was twelve years older than her. Perhaps this was because his newspapers prepared him for them, or perhaps, even without newspapers, he had the temperament to adapt to change. For her part, she found it increasingly difficult, what with daughters finding new and improbable husbands, George rushing about the country on all those horseless carriages, Alex talking about all these frightful new weapons men were using in battles, with Giles becoming a Member of Parliament, Hugo becoming a sort of doctor and every one of them caught up in some cause or invention that hadn't concerned anyone but people like the Royals and Messrs. Disraeli and Gladstone when she was their age. She was sixty-six now, and a grandmother a dozen times over.

She let Adam talk himself out about the election and what it might mean with the Liberals and their allies holding a majority of three hundred and fifty-four over the Conservatives and Unionists, and presently excused herself, going upstairs to try on a green silk dress she had bought for Christmas but had not worn because it was delayed in the Christmas post and hadn't arrived until nearly everybody had dispersed. She held it against her and studied herself in the mirror, a stocky, well-set-up woman who had aged, though she herself said it, very gracefully, for she had never run to fat and her hair still showed no more than a trace of grey. Her complexion was still good, too, and in her eyes was a sparkle that had been there ever since Adam Swann had ridden over the brow of the heath and carried her off, and which would last, she hoped, as long as he was about to share her memories. The reflection in the mirror comforted her somewhat. They might all be much cleverer than she was, and more in tune with the times, but she doubted whether they would look forty-eight when it came to be their turn to be sixty-six and even now none of her daughters-in-law, not even that fashionable Lady Sybil, could hold a candle to her when it came to *style*.

She laid the dress aside and moved over to the tall window, looking down across the new vista Adam had conjured out of the paddocks and seeing, at its northern extremity, the larch coppice bordering the road. It had a bearing on the new family M.P., she thought with a smile. It was there he had emerged from a wayward frolic on her part and Adam's, so long ago as 1865, and today it had the ability, somehow, to laugh back at her across a mile of parkland, as though its treetops were saying, "They know all manner of things you don't, Henrietta, but most of it isn't as important as lessons you learned here, and in the weeks that followed that roll in the hay on a summer day so long ago."

3

The Servile War

HENRIETTA'S AWARENESS OF THE CHANGES AND
stresses of the new century could not be dismissed as the
prejudices of a woman without education, who had spent
most of her life deep in the Kentish countryside. It was
real enough, this terrible quickening of tempo, to anyone
who recalled more spacious times, and it was not necessary
to be an avid newspaper reader like Adam Swann to see
reflected, in the strivings and discontents of the Western
World, the threat to the entire social order. Thrust, turbulence and challenge were everywhere and the rallying
cries of storming parties assaulting strongholds of privilege
and custom were heard in every city from Lisbon to
Moscow, and loudly enough in places like Leeds and
Birmingham to cause countrymen to enquire of one
another what devilry was afoot in those wildernesses of
brick that had tempted so many of their sons and daughters to forsake a traditional way of life in search of advancement and adventure.

It had begun right here in England, Adam could have
told them, and no more than a couple of generations ago,
when Stephenson's railroads quartered the nation, giving
him his own opportunity to make a fortune, but now, far
sooner than even he had judged, the children of the
machines had spread south, west and east, preaching their
brassy gospel as far as the American prairies, calling to the
sod-breakers pursuing centuries-old furrows to make haste

to the fair where the pickings were rich and a man's life was not regulated by the seasons and the yield of the amount of soil he shifted by weight of muscle.

No one under forty, least of all a Swann, could be unaware of what was happening in the big world and for the most part they were more than equal to the challenges offered. Only here and there, in isolated pockets like Dewponds Farm, were fences raised against further encroachments and even here, by the spring of 1906, desertion had begun with the migration of the two Fawcett boys, Martin and John, to George's machine shops in the north.

Elsewhere the challenges were met head-on, sometimes fearfully but more often cheerfully, as in the case of George Swann, already accepted in the city as one of the boldest riders in the field. Yet even George, geared to change, and welcoming every short cut that presented itself, sometimes ran out of breath and would pause to make sure of his path ahead. No longer did he see himself as a pioneer, cutting his way through unmapped territory, as in the days when he had driven singlehanded from Stockport to London Bridge with a load of rice aboard his temperamental waggon. Many others were out there, tinkering, experimenting, disputing this and that with backers and public authorities, and it was no longer necessary to preach his private gospel that the horse-drawn waggon would soon be as outdated as a muzzle-loader on the army's artillery range on Salisbury Plain.

The underground railways, stuck with the slightly derisive name of 'Tube', had been a wonder of the age about the time he negotiated his first contract with a shifty Cypriot tea merchant at Hay's Wharf. Now, as if in answer to his fleet of petrol-driven vans, the City of London Authorities had opened the Bakerloo Line and 'tubes' were accepted as a natural means of cross-city travel. A company, conceited enough to call itself 'Vanguard', was running motor omnibuses in competition with the horse-drawn public transport that had proved such a bane to Swann waggoners in Cheapside and Ludgate Hill, although he noted, with a spark of malice, that their vehicles were fitted with iron-bound wheels, and maintained an average speed over a stage only a little above that of the old horse-buses. A few taxicabs had appeared on the streets, not only here in the capital but in places as far north as Liverpool. Three-horse fire-engines, for so long the darlings of every city urchin, were in retreat and some fire-brigades were going over to petrol, advertising their increased speed by clanging bells with a note that struck Cockneys as more insistent than those of their predecessors. There was even an experimental motor exhibition out at Islington that George attended, hoping to pick up a few tips but leaving with a conviction that he was still ahead of most of them. And, on top of that, in 1906, a few sportsmen who persisted in regarding the internal-combustion engine as a rich man's toy, began holding racing rallies at Brooklands and over winding, hilly courses in the Isle of Man.

It was not only in George's chosen field that progress (Adam, perched on his knoll overlooking his quiet acres, was already beginning to suspect that word) was apparent. Those who looked up from the traditional task of net-mending on a hundred quaysides could see Cunard's floating island, the *Mauretania*, at her trials. With a stupendous displacement of 30,700 tons, and a capability of twenty-six knots, she did for sea travel what a hundred and one George Swanns had been attempting on behalf of road transport. A year or so later she crossed the Atlantic in well under five days. And even overhead, in the hitherto untroubled skies, competitors in balloon races could be spotted over Britain, their occasional appearance causing city urchins to pause in their collection of horse manure (a traditional pursuit enlivened, of late, by the noting down of the names of new motors honking their way among the traffic) and whistle their four-note, rhetorical version of the question, 'Seen the air-ship?'

So much for transport, to which so many other changes

were hitched, but in wider fields, here and abroad, innovators were hard at work, some of them hell-bent on subjecting the social systems of democracies and autocracies to terrible strains.

Making his first hesitant appearance in the Mother of Parliaments, in February, 1906, Giles was soon aware that the pressures that had contributed to his victory in a Welsh valley were even more apparent on the Continent. Russia, still deep in a feudal sleep, was stirring after the lost war with Japan and blood spattered the pavements of Petrograd when the Tsar's Cossacks, shepherds of a once passive flock, tried in vain to stem the tide of revolution that ended, to the delight of radicals all over the world, in the Tsar's summoning of the Duma to approve what optimists were already calling 'The Russian Magna Carta'.

Nearer home old and tried foreign policies were being jettisoned and replaced by new, to the confusion and alarm of men whose grandfathers had fought Napoleon for twenty-three years with one short break, King Edward, he whom men were beginning to call 'Peacemaker', having succeeded, against all odds, in charming the Parisians and cementing the Entente Cordiale, an alliance designed to apply a brake to the upsurge of Germany after Bismarck unified a knapsack of petty kingdoms into a single, aggressive nation.

Adam, reading of this in his morning perusal of *The Times*, did not put much faith in the cordiality of the entente and this was not because his father had left two fingers on the field of Waterloo. It was because, as a lifelong pragmatist, he had no confidence in the ability of the French to wage a sustained war against anyone, with or without allies. They were like some of the tribes he had fought in his youth, bold enough in attack, but lacking the stamina for a protracted campaign. Any war against a resurgent Germany, he reasoned, would call for more than bugle calls, drum rolls, baggy red trousers and the gospel of élan, preached by paunched French generals at every military academy in the land. He would have preferred an alliance (if there *had* to be an alliance) with Germany, whose faith in lance and sabre had been superseded by the breech-loading rifle as long ago as 1866, and he suspected that his view was shared by a majority of his countrymen. But then, as ever, he would demonstrate his impatience with all foreigners by turning to pages of his newspaper devoted to home-based events, noting that at last the new docks serving the Manchester Ship Canal had been opened by the Peacemaker and his handsome consort, who was said to abominate the Prussians for the way they had served her homeland a generation ago. He noted also that advances in communications were being made across a very wide field and that Marconi's Wireless Telegraph Company was now in constant use by the shipping insurers in the city, and this in a day when the telephone linking his depots along the network was still regarded, by all but people like George and his disciple Edward, as a novelty.

Even nature herself seemed restless in that period, a mere twelve months or so marking the middle of the first decade of the new century. In Chile an earthquake accounted for thousands of lives, and within a year San Francisco was in ruins from the same agency. He thought, turning the pages and scanning headlines, 'I often told myself, in the old days, that I had caught the flood tide of an era but I hadn't. Just the ripples of a tidal wave that will change the face of the world before I've been in the churchyard a dozen years.' But then he congratulated himself on being young in the old century, for the options of an individual had been wide open then and not, as now, narrowed by consortiums and industrial groupings of one kind or another.

2

The social changes that preoccupied Henrietta were not discriminatory, as they had been a generation ago. Then a change of tempo was the business of men and the womenfolk, if they were aware of them at all, awaited the guidance of their masters in these matters, providing they deigned to give it. But even the rampart of male dominance was beginning to crumble and Swann women, dotted here and there about the islands, were among the first to appreciate the fact. Among them Helen Clarke, formerly Helen Coles, who had set Dublin tongues wagging by capturing a handsome groom several years her junior.

Most widows, she supposed, conscious of passing years and the looming menace of fading looks, would have married Rory Clarke with their eyes closed and so, probably, would Helen ten years before he led her to the altar, in the spring of 1905. But Helen, alone among the Swann girls, and almost unique among her contemporaries, had undergone ordeal by fire and the experience had taught her, among other things, to prospect ground over which she had decided to advance.

She did this during the waiting period between the beginning of Rory's storming courtship and the day when, clad in a gala dress of Irish green (as a widow whose previous husband had been decapitated by brigands she could not, she reasoned, wear white without sacrificing dignity) she threw her wedding bouquet from the carriage and set out for the new home Rory's father had given them as a wedding present, a handsome, Georgian building, standing in several acres of land near Crumlin, south-west of the city.

She was now, she assumed, beyond the Pale in two senses, having sacrificed Dublin Castle society by embracing the Roman Catholic faith during courtship, but she almost certainly reasoned that Rory Clarke was worth a mass, deep religious conviction never having been a feature of her upbringing at 'Tryst'. There were aspects of Rory Clarke, and even more of Irish political life, that baffled her during the first summer as the wife of a man who seemed to prize her above his pursuit of political laurels and popular acclaim, but one of the many lessons she had learned during her years in primitive surroundings was to look through rather than at local imperfections, counting only such blessings as were within immediate grasp.

They were, as it happened, many and various during those halcyon days of 1906 and 1907 and chief among them was the discovery that Rory's veneration of her was not, as she had half-suspected, a mere facet of his impulsive, many-sided character. It was rooted in a need to anchor himself to someone sufficiently mature to adjust to his moods and bolster a dignity that he continually placed at risk in his career as professional clown and sustainer of myths; to which could be added, she supposed, incidental roles as conspirator, ballad-maker and several other walk-on parts in the repertoire of the dedicated Home Ruler.

She had braced herself against a cooling of ardour on his part as soon as Parliament reassembled, and he returned to London to do his clamorous stint in the Irish members' attempt to focus attention on themselves and The Cause, but nothing like this happened. Instead he insisted that she accompanied him back across the sea to his head-quarters in Bayswater where, under his active encouragement, she came to preside over a kind of salon, frequented by some of the weirdest people she had ever met, not excluding head-hunting Papuans who were reported to practise cannibalism.

Members of Rory's set whom she entertained at Crumlin and Bayswater did not go as far as the Papuans in that respect but there were similarities for they fed, male and female, upon one another's vanities and extravagances, each competing for the title of Eccentric of the Season. She met and moved among wild-eyed Fenians who had served long sentences in British gaols, professors of Gaelic mythology, poets, dramatists, songsters, orators with and without official platforms, Barcelona anarchists, Welsh activists, explosives experts, courtesans who had seen the Celtic dawn and been purified by it, men allegedly wanted by the police of several countries and a handful of comparatively sober politicians with some pretensions to statesmanship.

They had two characteristics in common. Each of them talked incessantly to anyone who would listen, or even pretend to listen, and all of them seemed eager to achieve Celtic martyrdom and, via martyrdom, a few lines in a Celtic ballad. The shortest road to the second seemed to be a resounding act of violence involving assassination or demolition.

It was no wonder, Helen reflected, that Rory sought tranquillity in the few hours he could spare from such a babel and in these intervals she was strangely touched by his boyish gentleness, and a sensitivity much at odds with the violently extrovert personality he revealed in public.

He was, she discovered, a shy but rewarding lover, so unlike poor Rowley in his response to a little cosseting, so grateful for any active encouragement she gave him when the fearful cacophony had subsided and all the callers had left or had been carted off to bed by the flock of Irish servants they maintained at both houses, every one of them schooled in the handling of stupefied anarchists, poets and mythmakers. And being five years his senior, and a survivor of a real rather than an imaginary revolution, she had no hesitation in taking the initiative on these occasions, especially after she had discovered that his aggressive masculinity (like so many mantles he donned during his working day and convivial evenings) was light in texture. Unlike most of his guests, he had no head for liquor and sometimes, after she had sent the yawning servants to bed and opened a window or two, she would rouse him from a doze on the chaise longue and guide him upstairs. Once here, like her sister Joanna before her, she would help the master of the house undress and let him sleep it off for an hour or so, after which he would awaken, surprisingly sober and restrained, demanding to know where everybody had gone, what time it was, and whether

she should be up here ministering to him instead of presiding as hostess downstairs.

She made the most of these few intimate hours, taking
her cue, unconsciously perhaps, from her sister Joanna
and after, at her gentle prompting, they had made love,
she would talk to him about her adventures beyond the
seas, native customs, her happy-go-lucky girlhood under
the tolerant Adam at 'Tryst', all manner of things that
were unlikely, she would have thought, to interest a
man whose outward life was dedicated to a fiery crusade.
It was impossible, however, after rubbing shoulders with
so many fervent converts, to avoid mild infection of the
fever and Helen perforce absorbed some of the legends of
Ireland's frenzied obsession with the English quarrel. As
to forming some conclusions as to how that quarrel should
be resolved she soon abandoned that pursuit, for everyone
in Rory's circle had an individual solution and she lost
herself in the maze of theory and practice they debated
one with the other. Alone among their visitors the more
mature of the Irish M.P.s seemed bent on maintaining
their political alliance with the British Liberal Party and
thus obtaining for Ireland a measure of Home Rule. For
the rest, methods of ending Ireland's servitude depended
on a wide range of offensive measures, all the way from
the setting up of an unofficial parliament and refusing to
pay taxes, to plots to kidnap ministers of the Crown and
hold them to ransom.

In the quiet hours, when he was lying in her arms, she
would sometimes coax him to discuss his own theories
but he did not seem to have any, beyond a vaguely defined
dream of becoming the first president of an Irish Republic,
that he saw as a kind of latter-day Eden from which poverty
and injustice had been banished, everybody talked Gaelic
and national business was confined to celebrations and the
exchange of mutual congratulations.

She would think, in moments such as these, of the
tremendous gulf existing between men like her father,
her brother George and even her brother-in-law, Clint,

whose energies centred on money-making, and this charming boy, besotted by his own extravagant dreams and so steeped in the legends of Irish greatness (past and potential but never, she noticed, affiliated to the present) that noble orations replaced ideas and poetry, laced with pathos and humour, the writ of government.

Listening to him the age gap between them widened from five years to fifty, so that he seemed no more than a child, endowed with a rich and colourful imagination fed by tales of giants, dwarfs, magicians, knights and the distressed damsel that was Ireland awaiting deliverance from the fire-breathing dragon across the sea. And yet, coming to know the Irish, she understood very well why they responded to his speeches and pamphlets and why they identified him as a champion in Westminster.

His voice, musical and infinitely persuasive, had something to do with it, and his boyish good looks, too, with soft brown hair falling over a Byronic forehead and eyes that were always full of laughter, even when he was launched upon one of his tirades against centuries of English oppression. It made her wonder, sometimes, why he had singled her out from all the pretty girls of his constituency and she did not find a satisfactory answer until, one night, she put the question directly to him, expecting one of his prolix or jocular replies but getting, instead, an answer as close to the truth as she was ever likely to get. He said, "Because you're real. Because you've suffered and survived and that's rare, much rarer than you realise. For what happened to you wasn't something out of a book or a ballad. You experienced it, horror, bloodshed, the rattle of gunfire in your ears and the fear of death in your heart. I *live* these things but at a remove. How can I be sure I would show your kind of steadfastness if it happened? Knowing you, holding you, makes me believe I might."

"But does it *have* to happen, Rory? I mean, do your people expect to have to battle your way to independence, the way the whites fought to survive out there in China?"

"It's in the cards, Helen. We'll never get real independence without a fight. Oh, the real radicals, like your brother Giles, believe we should and will, but I know otherwise. How do I know? I feel it, here and here," and he tapped his heart and belly. And then he sat up and looked down at her in the early morning half-light and she noticed there was no laughter in the eyes and that he was wearing what she called his 'climax-of-oration expression' as he said, "*When* that happens, *if* it happens, will you be with me or against me?"

"I'm your wife, Rory. Why do you ask me a question like that?"

"Because you're English and your folks are English, and think like the English."

"How do the English think?"

"Arrogantly, overbearingly and inflexibly."

"Could any people be more inflexible than the Irish?"

"Concerning their right to govern themselves? No, they couldn't. But the English take it as their God-given right to govern everybody."

"Yet you married an Englishwoman, Rory."

"I fell in love with one and that's my good fortune right now. But if it ever became a choice I'd turn my back on you, Helen."

The laughter had come back into his eyes as he said this and he capped it by kissing her and running his fingers through her hair, so that she dismissed it as banter at the time. She was to remember it, however, when they returned to Crumlin for the summer recess and the tone of his house parties changed, so abruptly that it seemed to her someone had turned out the lights on all that gaiety, bubble-talk and vainglory at the London soirées.

The hangers-on dropped out of sight, along with the sportive ladies, the ballad-makers and the foreign elements, leaving only a hard core of ex-Fenians and poets, some of the former coarse, unsmiling men, heavy drinkers who never got drunk and some younger men who were teachers and journalists, with the ascetic bearing of young priests obsessed with the sins of the world. And these were quite unlike Rory in that they listened more than they talked. The social climate of Dublin was changing too, she noticed, and certain people, among them the older, more sober element among the Irish members at Westminster, were seldom seen at functions where, only the previous season, they and their wives had played leading roles.

She asked Rory about it when he was on the point of leaving to attend a meeting in the city one fine summer evening and he told her briefly that the party had undergone a severe shake-up and some of the moderates, who still trusted in the promises of the English radicals, had refused to enlist under the banner of Sinn Fein. It was the first time she had ever heard the phrase and she asked him what it meant. "The nearest translation is 'ourselves alone'," he said, and told her the story of the Irish servant who, sent to a fair to sell a horse, was absent several days and returned in a happy frame of mind, replying to every question about his absence and the money by repeating, over and over again, 'Sinn fein, sinn fein'.

"But what's the difference between a member of the Sinn Fein movement and a dedicated Irish Home Ruler?" she demanded. "You're all after the same thing, aren't you?"

"Not quite the same, my dear. And certainly not by the same road when it comes to the crunch. Some of us won't settle for Home Rule as they want it on the Statute Book, with limitations of one sort or another, and most of us are near done with talk. We've been talking, off and on, since 'ninety-eight – a hundred and seven years of talk! What Sinn Fein means to get is an independent republic, entirely separated from Britain."

"I take it you already belong?"

"My love," he said, "I'm a founder member."

She heard herself say, without consciously framing the words, "Is it an exclusively male society, Rory? Are any women enlisted?" and he cocked his head, giving her a humorously searching glance.

"I'd sooner have you with me than against me. Or neutral."

"But I couldn't be neutral, could I?"

"No, my love. Not if those people up north try and block Home Rule and it comes to a fight. No, you couldn't be neutral."

"Then I want you to know I wouldn't care to be, Rory. I was too long finding happiness to risk playing the fool with it."

The statement seemed to release some inner tension in him and he threw his arms round her, ignoring the presence of the coachman, who stood awaiting him on the steps just out of earshot. He kissed her twice on the mouth and stalked out, swinging his suede gloves in that characteristically jaunty manner of his and whistling a bar or two of one of Tom Moore's airs. She stood watching the gig bowl away down the incline of the drive, feeling at once disturbed and released, the way she sometimes felt after he had made love to her. Then, very thoughtfully, she turned back into the house and closed the door.

3

There were establishments less than a hundred miles to the east, on the other side of the Irish Sea, where lords and masters were not disposed to show as much confidence in wives and daughters. Social bastions of one sort or another had been under attack ever since Adam Swann sent his first waggons rolling, and in almost every sphere cracks were showing in the façade of mid-nineteenth-century felicity. One such bastion, however, resisted every attack, the determination of its male garrison hardening with the fury of each successive assault. Unrepentant reactionary or avowed radical, Philistine or enlightened, the inheritors of the tradition of male supremacy closed their ranks against any disposition on the part of their helpmeets to challenge the tribal doctrine in the chambers of the legislature, for here, it was sensed,

was the citadel of paternalism. In the home, still so
occasional as to be all but unnoticeable, random burrs
had stuck in the hedge of Victorian whiskers. A few privileged women, with private means, or impressive reserves
of stamina and resource, had secured for themselves a good
education and a handful of women doctors, still regarded
as oddities, had won the right to practise. Most other
professions remained closed to them and even in the fields
of commerce, where their services could be secured for
pennies, they were mostly confined to repetitive tasks,
requiring no particular skills or training. Yet even these
trifling advances were regarded, by men as a whole, as
straws in the wind promising a gale of frightful proportions
if the vents were opened another half-inch. The doctors
might waver. The educationalists might preen themselves
on a mild display of tolerance. The city gents, with one
eye on profit margins, might yield a little here and there.
But in the ranks of the lawgivers there was no sign of
weakening, if one discounted the lonely voice of the
Socialist Keir Hardie (he who had arrived at Westminster
a few years ago wearing a cloth cap as the badge of egality)
who had astounded the legislators by proposing that the
franchise should be extended to women.

It was as far as he got. The parties might hurl challenges
and insults at one another on the future of Ireland, on the
importation of Chinese indentured labour into South
Africa, on workmen's compensation acts, indeed upon any
other topic aired, at regular intervals, beside the indifferent
Thames. On this one thing there was solidarity. A
woman, no doubt, was capable of rising to impressive
heights as an individual. One could not entirely discount
Boadicea, Nell Gwyn, Grace Darling, Florence Nightingale and, of course, the dead Queen, now reunited with
Albert at Frogmore. But no man in or out of his cups could
advance the proposition that women, as a sex, possessed
the wits to make an unprejudiced decision at the polling
booth. They were not intended by nature to shoulder such
a responsibility, and that, praise God and John Knox,

was that! A few recalcitrants might deem themselves so endowed, might even venture to point out that a woman doctor with an Edinburgh degree was capable of exercising the same degree of judgment at the hustings as, say, an illiterate stonebreaker, with ten pints of ballot-box beer in his belly, but not even the progressive Mr. Asquith would endorse such a heresy, whereas King Teddy himself, an experienced judge of woman's capabilities, would have smiled on the proposition and switched the conversation to the season's prospects at Ascot.

All this being so it was predictable, when one such harpy founded a crackpot pressure group known as the Women's Social and Political Union in 1903, and opened her campaign of militancy aimed at securing women's suffrage, that a growl of anger rose from bearded lips in Highland croft and south-country mansion, followed by a smart redressing of male ranks in every city, town and hamlet of the nation. For this, they seemed to be saying to one another in suburban railway carriages, in horse and motor omnibus, at factory bench and behind a thousand counters – this was the first rumblings of a servile war and would be ignored at the peril of men in possession. This was an issue that cut clear across lines of party, church and rival schools of philosophy, and must be attended to with the despatch of a three-decker captain hearing murmurs of mutiny in the forecastle. The spark must be extinguished, preferably by persuasion but, if this failed, by the majesty of the law. If it were not, who could tell where it might end, and how long it would be before a man came home to find his dinner congealing on the kitchen stove and his slippers unwarmed, while his wife drew up a Bill of Rights in the front parlour? It was something too grotesque to be contemplated by anyone who used a razor. It had about it a horrid abnormality, like a black man commanding white troops in action, or the birth of a child with two heads capable of disputing one with the other and contempt for those who propagated such a proposition was not enough. In the face of further defiance on the part of Mrs. Emmeline Pankhurst and her handsome daughters, the law must act and the doors of Holloway open, offering the missionaries of misrule time to recant, to be forgiven and received back into an ordered society.

*　　　*　　　*

This view, crystallised in many a leading article, and expressed in terms of the ironic or the outraged on many a political platform during the period leading up to the radical landslide of 1906, had little effect upon the handful of militants grouped under their W.S.P.U. banner. Indeed, it was soon clear that the vanguard of the movement – 'suffragettes' as they were dubbed by some playful male journalist – had hit upon a means of self-advertisement that would have doubled the turnover of businessmen following a trail blazed by the vendors of Bryant and May Matches, Pears' Soap or Mazawattee Tea.

The bolder the foray on the part of the Pankhursts and their converts, the wider the acreage of print they won for themselves, and the more talking points they provided in first-, second- and third-class compartments of branch trains steaming citywards from the suburbs between seven and eight-thirty a.m. each morning. The progress of the Japanese War, and the toll of the San Francisco and Valparaiso earthquakes, ran poor seconds to the latest outrage of the suffragettes at a bye-election in the provinces or on the streets of the capital and some of the bulletins were all but unbelievable.

Frock-coated statesmen, rising to deliver addresses on matters of moment, like the disestablishment of the Welsh Church, or the growth of the German Navy, had not uttered a dozen words before they were assailed by Furies, old, young and middle-aged, rising from the body of the hall to pose that utterly irrelevant question, "Do you support votes for women, sir?" And as if this was not enough, redoubling their outcry when stewards dragged them from their seats. Nor did it stop at heckling, followed by ejection. Realising that their storming parties were physically unequal to the task of maintaining lodgments in public hall and Corn Exchange, the assailants resorted to a bizarre range of tactics, involving chains and padlocks (with keys secreted where no steward could search for them) bags of soot, bags of flour, the stinkbomb and even banners that unrolled before the statesmen's eyes like the writing on the wall of Belshazzar's palace and bearing much the same message. But in a tongue everyone present could understand.

Soon, as the usage of hall stewards became less chivalrous, and frustrations on their part swept aside the dictates of modesty, glimpses of petticoats and worse were vouchsafed public and press, so that the purists, currently campaigning for the closure of music halls in London, found new targets in the display of undergarments exposed to public view in many a parish and town hall, and sometimes on the pavements outside. But even outrage on this scale did not seem to lessen the determination of Mrs. Pankhurst's converts to make themselves heard, not even when persistent hecklers were down to their well-laced stays. Neither were these unseemly scrimmages confined to public meetings attended by Cabinet Ministers and other notabilities. By the time the year 1906 was drawing to a close the new banditti were roving the streets of the West End, scratching their slogans with diamonds on the windows of blameless tradesmen, marching en masse through the streets of the capital to one or other of their interminable rallies and generally hellraising on a scale that had not been witnessed in London since the week of the Gordon riots.

More and more arrests were made and more and more jubilant martyrs elected to go to gaol rather than pay fines, or give undertakings to return meekly to the seraglio. Most of them, indeed, seemed to glory in an arrest and a ride in the Black Maria, regarding a spell in gaol as a kind of promotion in the ranks of the politically enlightened. And while Fleet Street editors made no bones about where their sympathies rested in this David and Goliath contest, they lost no time in despatching their most experienced reporters and photographers to the scene of the nearest riot or vigil, even when the latter took place within a handcuff-span of Buckingham Palace railings. There came a time when a suffragette riot took precedence, in news value, over coverage of the latest match at Lord's Cricket Ground, and Mrs. Pankhurst and her daughters were thus accorded more space in one week than poor Florence Nightingale had won during her sojourn in the Crimea half-a-century before. National and international topics dwindled to a column, half-a-column and, occasionally, if Mrs. Pankhurst's storm troops had been unusually active or original, to a few inches. Clear across the land her name was heard in bar-parlour and corner shop, during pauses in the musical programmes of suburban soirées and on the terraces of country houses where guests, meeting one another for a few moments between meals and changes of costume, asked one another what the country was coming to when parties of six women proved capable, time and again, of prohibiting free speech and decorating the waistcoats of their opponents with all the ingredients that went into the baking of a Christmas cake. Or, elsewhere in the provinces, where eggs and flour were put to more conventional uses, seeking ammunition in the interior of a master-sweep's hearth-sack.

*   *   *

Adam Swann, watching the world go by and ruminating on these frolics from the vantage point of the Hermitage knoll at 'Tryst', knew his family well enough to make educated guesses at their likely response to Mrs. Pankhurst's campaign. Nowadays he was more domesticated and less informed on what was happening out on the network. Each of his children, passing into maturity, had engaged his mind on one level or another.

Hetty, he would judge, would recoil from Mrs. Pankhurst and her cohorts, seeing them as an admission of failure on the part of women everywhere to bring pressures to bear upon men by methods for which nature had endowed them. Apart from that she had never, in his experience, shown more than a passing interest in politics and would not have bothered to use the vote Mrs. Pankhurst sought to win for her. Politics, in her view, qualified as a male profession, like the Army, the Law and the Church. It was not a fitting occupation for a woman, even a woman luckless enough to journey through life as a spinster. An identical view, he imagined, would be held by his daughter Stella, over at Dewponds, for Stella Fawcett already enjoyed as much independence as Emmeline Pankhurst demanded. Everyone at Dewponds deferred to 'Mother', and he for one had never been fooled by the token deference she paid to that husband of hers, Denzil.

It would be similar, he imagined, in the case of his daughter Joanna, and his youngest daughter, Margaret. Both were essentially feminine, the one relying on her instincts to regulate the balance between herself and that rackety chap she had married, the other endowed with a disposition that would immunise her against the doctrines of women like Emmeline Pankhurst and her valiant daughters. For he thought of them as valiant, remembering the courage and confidence it required to challenge established British practices, particularly those as firmly-based as those at Westminster, so that he saw the campaign as rather pitiful, fearing it could never prevail against such fearful odds. Yet, deep in his heart, he applauded them for their spirit, and even more for their ingenuity. All his life he had hated humbug, especially humbug in high places, and where was humbug more deeply entrenched than among the legislature? Giles, no doubt, would discover this in due course. Until he did, poor wight, let him continue to regard the Mother of Parliaments as the womb of human progress and not a creaking stage, where practised posturing advanced men far more swiftly than originality or virtue. Life had taught Adam Swann many lessons, among them the hopelessness of setting off in search of the Holy Grail ill-equipped and under-capitalised.

His mind continued to probe of the possibilities of Pankhurst alignment within the family. His daughter-in-law, Gisela, would be found among the neutrals. She had never sought equality with men, least of all with George, whom she regarded as the new Galileo, but Lydia, Alex's wife, would regard the campaign with contempt, seeing it as the negation of all the disciplines she had seen practised inside the prisoners' base of a barrack square. He was not so sure about his daughter Helen. Years ago, no doubt, she would have taken Joanna's view, but her experiences in China had changed her in a way that might encourage her to admire the courage and tactics of the W.S.P.U. and their leader. A woman who had shot a man at close range, and in cold blood, would be unlikely to regard the soot-spattering of a Cabinet Minister's waistcoat as a cataclysmic event. Word had reached him that Helen was adjusting to the Irish set and the liveliest activist among the suffragettes would be eclipsed in extravagance by a man like Rory Clarke. As for support on the distaff side of the family, he thought he could count on two – Giles' wife, Romayne, and his adopted daughter, Deborah, now helping her husband, that pleasant chap Jeffs, to run a tinpot newspaper in the west. Both women, he felt, were likely recruits for such a crusade. Romayne because she had always been a rebel of sorts, Deborah because, alone among the Swann womenfolk, she was what he could accept as an educated woman, whose involvement with the underdog went back to the early eighties, when she and W. T. Stead and that tub-thumping evangelist Booth had challenged the white slave traffic here and on the Continent. But musing thus he thought gratefully, 'Thank God I'm old enough to be objective about issues of this sort,' and thankfully turned the page to the Stock Exchange listing.

4

He came far closer than he imagined. At the precise
moment he was sunning himself on the terrace of his
Hermitage two far-reaching decisions were being made in
the family, each involving, more or less directly, Mrs.
Pankhurst and her troupe of wildcats. Less than twenty
miles away, in a rented flat at the top of Northumberland
Avenue, within easy walking distance of Giles Swann's
new workshop, man and wife were soul-searching on the
subject of his maiden speech in the House. Meantime,
some two hundred miles to the west, in the sleepy seaside
town where Milton and Deborah Jeffs had lived since
quitting the London scene, mail from London was pointing
them towards changes that had been in their minds for
some time now, ever since they had received a tempting
offer for their weekly newspaper from the Harmsworth
group, who led the newspaper field in the peninsula and
were engaged in adding local weeklies to their empire.

They had been very happy down here, all but out of
range of national controversy and engrossed in purely
parochial affairs, where they felt their influence was often
sufficiently powerful to decide an issue. Both, in their
younger days, had worked in Fleet Street, Milton as a
feature writer on a range of radical journals, Deborah as
one of the first woman journalists in the Street, serving
under W. T. Stead. With the prospect of marriage, a
vague dissatisfaction had settled on them, reaction in some
degree to all the misery and strife they had chronicled,
and when Milton proposed to realise every Fleet Street
man's secret dream – that of owning and editing his own
broadsheet – Deborah had encouraged him to take the
plunge.

Since then they had vegetated, or so they thought of it,
moving molehills in preference to mountains, with no
thought of returning to the London scene until events
conspired to make them take a closer look at the probable
course of the years left to them. Former friends of

Deborah, drawn into the Pankhurst maelstrom, wrote regularly of the mounting fury of the suffragist campaign, and one of Lester Harmsworth's scouts offered them a handsome profit for the newspaper, enough to enable Jeffs to buy a footing in a much more important journal serving a wider area of population. The coincidence caused the hidden wishes of both of them to surface simultaneously. Milton had said, "It's at least double what I would have asked if I had ever put it on the market. Money is no object to the Harmsworths when they want a thing and a man ought to think twice about refusing a profit of this kind if it falls into his lap. We built this paper up from scratch, remember? It was no more than a local newsheet when we moved in, and if we could do it once we could do it again, before we're too old and too lazy to try." But then he had paused, regarding her thoughtfully, "Only one thing stops me wiring acceptance, Debbie."

"What's that, Milton?"

"You. You and young Deany. We've had a good life down here. And a useful one too, in a modest way. Maybe I oughtn't to quarrel with the kind of luck I've enjoyed ever since I ran into you."

They were well accustomed to talking things over and pooling points of view. There was no paternalism here, for Jeffs' respect for his wife's intelligence dated from the moment he read her articles in the *Pall Mall Gazette* on the sale of fourteen-year-old children to rich old roués. He added, "You've been thinking of a change yourself, haven't you? Ever since the W.S.P.U. began to steal the headlines?"

He was right. She was fifty now, a time for reappraisal, and while she, like him, had found fulfilment in publishing their own journal, she had a sense of the years slipping by at an alarming pace since her son had passed from cot and toddling stage to boyhood. They still called him 'Deany', a diminutive of Houdini, the nickname he had acquired as a particularly active baby who had to be watched throughout his waking hours, for he seemed to be born with a working knowledge of escapology. He was away at school now, her half-brothers' old school on Exmoor, and a change of venue would not affect him much. The flow of letters she had received from former colleagues, inside and outside the Women's Social and Political Union, had stirred her deeply, as had press accounts of the rough-handling the campaigners had received at political meetings. She said, "How long do you suppose Asquith and those other politicians will hold out against the franchise of women, Milton?"

"Indefinitely," he assured her. "Make no mistake about that." And then, shrewdly, "You'd like to play a part in it, wouldn't you? Well, come to that, so would I. They get practically no press support and I see what's happening to them lately as a national disgrace. It's the domestic equivalent to the hammering we gave those poor devils in South Africa. That's what's disturbing about this country. The average Briton, from Prime Minister down to the layabout in the street, honestly thinks of himself as a standard bearer of human rights. But national arrogance, a century of commercial success, suzerainty over a quarter of the world's surface and a navy capable of blowing any rival out of the water, seems to have blinded a majority to aspects of human dignity. Did you know even Hungary has universal franchise?"

"No, I didn't."

"Then say what you have in mind. Irrespective of this Harmsworth offer."

"It's my age partly. With luck I've got around twenty years left to play a part in affairs, to use what talent and experience I've got to alter things, to try and change them for the better. It can't be right to spend them writing about the Withy Brook overflow, and the decaying fabric of our infants' schools in this backwater. Sometimes . . . sometimes I feel an itch to head back to London, to find out things for myself and write about them . . . where are you off?"

He paused by the door, smiling at her over his shoulder. "To wire Harmsworth," he said. "And just for the record I've had the same itch for a year or more and lately I've been scratching it raw."

5

The problem, similar in so many ways, yet with undertones more far-reaching concerning each of them, was not so easily resolved by Giles, mulling over his notes in the first-floor flat they had leased from a departing Tory member for a Welsh constituency.

It was conveniently central and they had been lucky to get it, but already both of them were missing the soft, south-west wind over the Rhondda uplands, and the singsong lilt of their constituents. In London, Giles felt, a man could lose his identity if he wasn't careful and his initial reactions to the fulfilment of a dream that had preoccupied him since his early twenties, had been oddly deflating once L.G., and another Welsh Liberal, had introduced him to the House of Commons at that first jubilant assembly, following the February landslide.

He had always thought of it as a very solemn place governed, of course, by tradition but generating a kind of magisterial impulse that conditioned the mood of the entire country outside. Everything that happened to ordinary people began right here beside the Thames and one was almost tempted to speak in whispers once the portals had been crossed and one found oneself rubbing shoulders with men whose names had been familiar to him since boyhood. But the sense of majesty was soon dissipated, perhaps by L.G.'s gentle raillery, and he recalled now that David Lloyd George never had been the least impressed with the place. He had called it crabbed when they met here one afternoon as long ago as spring, 1879, Giles an awed thirteen-year-old, tagging on to a bunch of sightseers, Lloyd George, seventeen and clad in rough country clothes, making his first-ever visit to a building that would dominate his life and destiny.

"It's more of a club, Johnny Peep," he said, "and no club is worthy of stardust. Think of it as a workshop if you can, where policies are hammered out, as upon a bench. Fashioned, refashioned, recast and more often than not rejected after infinite palaver among the journeymen. We get things done, of course, but never in the way we hoped or imagined. We have to compromise one with the other in order to make progress and that's in the nature of things, there being more than six hundred of us, all trying to catch the spotlight."

"I've never known you compromise over anything you regarded as important, L.G.," but Lloyd George had replied, "Well, never in front of an audience, lad. But here? You'd be surprised, shocked even, until you come to understand how essential it is."

There was one issue, Giles had noticed, concerning which most of his closest associates were prepared to compromise upon, and that in the company of men whose policies they had attacked for years while in opposition. No one, excluding that saintly old Scotsman Keir Hardie, seemed disposed to make a party issue out of women's franchise, and it distressed him that this should be so, for he had long since been convinced that it was a vital plank in the efforts of the Liberals to broaden the stage of democracy.

Down in the valleys Romayne had already played a part in forming a local branch of the W.S.P.U. and he had encouraged her, even though the response among the miners' wives had been apathetic. It seemed quite monstrous to him that women as intelligent and socially aware as she or Debbie were denied a voice in the nation's destiny and his misgivings were not dispelled by L.G.'s bland assurances on the subject.

"It's all a question of priorities, Johnny Peep," he reasoned. "It will come, you can depend on that, but in its own good time, when we've dynamited our way through centuries of rubble half-burying the body politic. There are so many issues that I see as vastly more urgent. National insurance, pensions for the old and disabled, reform of the House of Lords, higher education and opportunities for the poor, public ownership of certain national products, a basic minimum wage, the relegation of the very idea of tariffs on to the bonfire, and don't deceive yourself that Free Trade won't be in danger from time to time. Home Rule for Ireland, to shed that packload of trouble, all manner of things, many of them linked to the future of your miners and their families. We simply haven't the Parliamentary time and that's a fact, and the tactics of Emmeline Pankhurst aren't doing much to persuade the electorate that women can be trusted with the vote."

"But what else can they do?" Giles had argued. "They've tried lobbying and talking for a generation without gaining an inch. At least they've brought the matter into the open."

"Kaiser Wilhelm is a star turn at doing that but it doesn't make him more credible in the Chancellories of Europe."

He had gone away less than half satisfied, to discuss it all again with Romayne and discovered, as he had expected, that L.G.'s arguments made no impression upon her. Sometimes it struck him that she did not trust the man and this pained him a little, for he still regarded L.G. as the greatest campaigner for reform in the land. She said, "It isn't important what L.G. thinks, Giles. You're a Member of Parliament now. What do *you* think? Honestly and deeply, down in your heart?"

"You know what I think. That all women over thirty ought to have the vote now. And that a Commission should be set up to consider extending it to women over twenty-one. You couldn't get the public to swallow a mouthful that big in one gulp but it could be done in two."

"Would you be prepared to say that in public?"

"Of course I would. I only played it down at the election because L.G. warned me it wasn't wise to raise it until Liberal policy had been decided on the issue."

"And now?"

"There's absolutely no hope that the W.S.P.U. will win enough support in the House to get a bill through the Commons. As for the Lords, why they'd throw it out in ten seconds."

"Then if you believe in it, sincerely and utterly, why not introduce it into your maiden speech?"

He did not answer at once. The possibility had occurred to him but he had shelved it, half agreeing with L.G. that there were so many more important priorities. He said, finally, "I've roughed out my speech. It's devoted almost entirely to the miners' minimum wage. After all, the miners put me here and I owe them the honour of the first salvo."

"Their wives helped and I'm not talking about work in committee rooms and so forth. I mean by keeping their homes and families together, year after year, often under impossible conditions. You owe them a salvo, Giles. Wouldn't it be possible to slip in some reference to a wife's right to have a say in the family's future?"

He looked down at his notes again. "I don't know. I should have to think about it very carefully."

She did not press him further, knowing he was already under some strain concerning the prospect of the speech. His platform confidence, she noticed, varied from shuffling nervousness to a buoyancy where he could dispense with notes altogether and hold an audience for an hour or more. It depended entirely on atmosphere. If he could sense sympathy in the upturned faces he could race away in galloping style, garnishing a theme with all kinds of anecdotes, some from the mountain of books he had scaled, others from personal experiences. But there were times, as now, when the prospect of hostility or indifference could make him sound humdrum or even dull. All the best of his speeches were made in the valleys, where the great majority of his listeners were men whose cause he had espoused as a youth during his first visit to Wales, so that sometimes she thought his father was right when he told her, "Old Giles ought to have settled for the Church. They need people like him, with his kind of innocence and integrity. Politicians can do without it, for politics is a dirty business most of the time. A politician who won't hit below the belt is at a disadvantage."

He came to her briefly the day he was to make his parliamentary debut and said, "Well, I took your advice. I slipped in an oblique reference to the W.S.P.U. campaign."

"Just how oblique, Giles?" she asked.

"I'll read it to you tonight, when it's all behind me. I'd prefer it that way if it's all the same to you. I'm going over there early. I want a word with L.G. before the debate. He's promised me ten minutes before lunch."

"Good luck, Giles," she said, kissing him, glad now that they had agreed she should not avail herself of an opportunity to hear him from the Ladies' Gallery and thinking, 'He'll be more relaxed when he gets back late tonight and I can convince him he wasn't half as bad as he imagined.'

But then, when she slipped out for a walk along the Embankment after their help, old Mrs. Robbins, had come with the shopping and could keep an eye on the children, she had an unlooked-for opportunity to read at least part of his speech, the important part, hours before his return. A *Star* news-vendor was standing opposite Cleopatra's Needle with a contents bill clipped to his board and the legend on the poster read, in handwritten script, '*STIR IN COMMONS – LIBERAL PLEDGES SUPPORT FOR SUFFRAGETTES*' and she fumbled in her purse for the halfpenny, taking the paper across the road to read under one of the globes glowing there beside the plinth.

It was not much of a stir. Whoever scrawled that contents bill must have been desperate for an eye-catching item but it made her start to see the heavy print of the lead-in that began 'Today, in the House of Commons, Mr. Giles Swann, newly-elected Member for Pontnewydd, caused a brief uproar during his maiden speech in support of the second reading of the Minimum Wage Bill . . .' And underneath, a side-heading arrested her eye as it swept down the column, '*Liberal Pledges Support for Labour Motion*'.

She folded the paper, aware of a quickening of her pulse and a painful thumping of her heart, and almost ran back across the Embankment and under Charing Cross arch to the flat. She had a near certainty that he would be there, long before he was expected, and in need of her, but when she let herself in and called, "Giles! Are you there, Giles?" only Mrs. Robbins poked her head over the banister and hissed, "*Shsh*, M'm! I on'y just got the baby orf . . . It's his teething, like I said." She waited a moment to regain command of herself, then mounted the stair slowly, holding the newspaper close to her breast.

*   *   *

He managed to buttonhole Lloyd George in one of the corridors after enquiring for him with mounting desperation.

"You did promise me a few minutes, L.G. Run your eye over it, no . . . not the first page, that's along the lines you advised . . . the piece I've written in," and when the Welshman glanced at it, casually at first but then with keen attention, "One of us has to say it, L.G. You think it, but won't make it public. I don't necessarily want your approval, certainly not your official approval. But if you think it's letting you down I'll wait for Keir Hardie's motion."

"You realise what it implies. For you, I mean, and that's all it concerns really, for you'll not win anyone over at this stage. Not even the odd waverer."

"What *would* it imply. To me?"

"Any chance of patronage. Now and for a long time to

come. No one cares to hear a change in policy so much as hinted at in a maiden speech. They'll forgive dullness, confusion even. But not originality. It doesn't become new boys!"

"You're urging me to take it out?"

"Not necessarily. You know where I stand on the issue, and I was reckoned a firebrand when I first came here. I disappointed them, however. My instinct was to lay low and watch points until I learned my way around."

"And that's your advice to me?"

"If you like, Johnny. Most of them do, you know. What I'm saying is you have to make a deliberate choice between principle and discretion, and that's a choice you must make yourself, without me pointing you one way or the other. What time will you be speaking?"

"Early on. About three-thirty, I was told."

"Well, then, skip the preamble. Take a breath of fresh air in the park and think it over."

He went out into the pale spring sunshine, cutting through Queen Anne's Gate, then across St. James's Gardens to the path circling the lake with its nesting island. The park was all but deserted at this time of day. At the nearer end of the wooden bridge a woman who looked about seventy, probably one of the many professional scrubbers from the Treasury or the Admiralty buildings judging by her cap and sacking apron, was feeding crusts to a small circle of ducks. He stopped to watch, taking in the woman's coarse, reddened hands, swollen finger joints and badly ·broken nails, and the abstracted look on the craggy features under the crooked peak of the cap. A square of greaseproofed paper that held her lunch or breakfast lay on the seat behind her, and close by a carpet bag, that was almost surely her scrubbing brushes and mopping cloths. His eyes travelled slowly down to the dipping hem of the skirt, noting the broken boots that concealed a fine array of bunions judging by the bulges near the toes. He thought, 'She's probably worked at scrubbing office floors for sixty-odd years and she'll stick it another five. After that it'll be the infirmary at best . . .' but then, his glance moving up again as she chirped "Chick-a-dee, chick-a-dee!" to the swarming ducks, he noticed a ring all but buried in the mottled flesh of her left hand and a burning curiosity to know something of her possessed him. He said, touching his hat, "Good-day. Are these your regulars?"

She turned and looked at him levelly, a hint of mockery in her eyes.

"You could call 'em that. They know me any road. I on'y got to call to 'em. There's a rare lot after it today. That'll be the dripping. They like dripping and I don't alwus 'ave it."

"Bread and dripping. Is that all you bring?"

She looked not so much surprised as mildly outraged. "Lumme, what *else* on their screw?" and she jerked her head towards the offices in the background. He felt in his pocket and took out a half-a-crown, offering it shyly. She looked hard at it and then up at him. "Nice of yer, gov', and I know yer mean right. But we never begged."

"We?"

"Not me, not Thompson. Nor none o' the kids when I was around to fetch 'em one. I'm working and I've got a room. There's plenty who could use that 'arf-crahn sleeping out on the Embankment."

The rebuke, for he accepted it as such, shamed him. He put the coin back in his pocket, saying, "I'm sorry. Is Thompson your husband?"

"Was. Watchman on Grimshaw's buildin' sites for forty-odd years 'til he caught his death, winter before last. Never missed a night until the bronchitis got 'im. Then lay there worrying about it all the time. I told 'em that when I went to collect the half-week's screw they owed 'im."

"How many family have you?"

"On'y two, now. 'Arry's in the army. Middlesex Reg'ment and he'll sign on for another twelve years if he takes my tip. Minnie's married to a streetlighter

and they got five kids. I told both of 'em to watch out
lars time I saw 'em. God knows how many working days
I lorst wi' kids comin' and goin'."

"Coming and going?"

"We buried five. 'Churchyard luck' Thompson called
it when they went straight orf, tho' he never said it about
'em when they got parst the first stage."

The incredible hardships of their lives, together with
their matchless fortitude, struck him like a blow in the
stomach. Her age, and still scrubbing. Thompson,
gasping his life away and worrying about his job, as a
night-watchman on around twenty-five shillings a week.
Seven children, five dead in infancy. He said, "Have
you finished work now?"

"Finished?" She scratched a mole on her chin, a
gesture of mild surprise. "Gawd no, Mister. I got me
offices in Oxford Street now. I knock orf around four an'
go 'ome for me tea an' kipper. Rose'll 'ave it all ready."

"Who is Rose?"

"Another White'all scrubber. We share the room
fifty-fifty. Whoever's first back puts the kettle on."

"What time did you start work this morning?"

"Five. I do second floor, Adm'lty. Bin doin' it twenty
years now."

"Do you mind telling me how much they pay you?"

"Why should I? Regular rate. Tanner an hour."

Big Ben boomed the hour and she wiped her hands on
her sacking apron. "I gotter go now, Mister. Nice 'avin'
a chat. Alwus someone to chat with in the park."

He handed her her carpet bag and touched his hat and
she mocked his gallantry with a jaunty twitch of her cap.
He watched her trudge away towards the Mall, her
bunions causing her to roll slightly as she put her weight
on her heels and the sides of her feet. He thought, 'She's
better than ten sermons and fifty blue books. What the
devil do the bishops and the economists know or care about
the Mrs. Thompsons? Yet they keep the whole lot of us
going, the way the miners do. But miners qualify for a

vote!' The memory of a recent visit to Henley Regatta returned to him, the river teeming with blazered young bucks displaying their prowess with the sculls, every man jack among them entitled to a say in who ran the country, although few of them would ever do a full day's work in their lives. Certainly not a day beginning before sunrise.

He sat down on the seat where Mrs. Thompson had eaten her dripping sandwiches and reread the paragraph he had shown Lloyd George, hinting at support for Hardie's bill to extend the suffrage to women. It sounded apologetic, an aside in the main purport of the speech that was concerned with the economics of the coalfields. He detached the sheet, took out his pencil, struck it through and wrote, in its place:

And now, at the risk of seeming to introduce an irrelevancy into the argument, I am putting on record, in my first speech to this House, my resolve to fight not merely for a basic minimum wage for the men who dig the nation's coal at the risk of their lives but the right of their wives to join them in having some small say in the nation's affairs, women now classed, like all women in this so-called free society, as second-class citizens, wise enough to raise the nation's children, strong enough to work upwards of fourteen hours a day, but disqualified, for ever it would seem, from a voice in the future of their children, or the regulation of the rewards of that toil. And I do this in my first speech advisedly, for I believe that every Member of this House, rising to his feet to address it for the first time, should avail himself of the privilege of making an unequivocal declaration of his intentions and the fundamental beliefs that were factors in bringing him here. My intention is to battle for universal social justice in this realm. And my fundamental belief is that all adults attaining maturity should participate in the counsels of the nation. The Honourable Member for Merthyr Tydfil is, I understand, preparing a bill to put that right into the statute book. He will have my unquestioning support, as has the bill before us at this moment.

*   *   *

They listened to the earlier part of his speech with a mixture of indifference and lazy tolerance. No more than about a hundred and fifty of them and of those, he would judge, about a third either dozing or preoccupied with thoughts of their own. Very few of the front bench were present but he could see L.G. sitting bolt upright, and paying him the compliment due to a protégé. But then, when he came to the sentence admitting irrelevancy, there was a mild flicker of interest, and it struck him that a few of them might be academically interested in the quality of the maiden speeches, much as sixth formers and cricket colours would bestir themselves to watch the performance of a very junior member of the team brought in as a substitute at the last moment.

The flicker widened. He saw one member nudge his neighbour, so that when he came to the passage dealing with his conception of the duty of a newly-elected member to make a declaration of intent, his real audience had increased to about three score. Lloyd George did not stir. He continued to sit bolt upright, intent on not missing a word.

At the mention of the Honourable Member for Merthyr Tydfil's forthcoming bill, a kind of growl rose from the thinly-packed opposition benches, then spread like a flame to the front bench of the Liberals, where he saw the man next to L.G. turn and gesture, without, however, deflecting the Welshman's attention. When he sat down the response, that began as a growl, increased to a sustained buzz and at least two members were on their feet trying to catch the Speaker's eye. From the area of the House where sat the small knot of Labour members came another sound, not a cheer exactly but a vocal stir that might have been a muted chorus of 'Hear, hear' and 'Bravo'.

The moment passed. Somnolence regained possession of the chamber and he sat down feeling a little foolish yet satisfied, deep within himself, that he had made the gesture . . . Mrs. Thompson's gesture, really, so that his mind returned to her for a moment, scrubbing her way down the worn stairs of some third- or fourth-storey office block in Oxford Street, knuckles gleaming as she tightened her grip on her brush, sacking apron spattered with suds, her dead husband's cap still at a jaunty angle. The thought made him smile.

An usher was plucking his sleeve and handing him a folded slip of paper. He opened it and recognised L.G.'s writing. The scribble ran:

Some might say you've burned your boats, Johnny, and perhaps you have. But I'll refer you to Stevenson – Alan Breck's defence of the roundhouse, remember? 'David, I love you like a brother. And O, man, am I no' a bonny fighter?'

4

Anniversaries and Occasions

THE MOMENT HE OPENED HIS EYES AND, RAISING
himself on his elbow, satisfied himself that Hetty was still
asleep, he hoisted himself carefully out of bed, buckled on
his leg and crossed the room to widen the chink of light
filtering through a gap in the curtains. He stood by the
window gently scratching his chest and noting the promise of another fine day, rare at this time of year. It
seemed to him a good omen for, despite close involvement
with his affections, he was not anticipating his programme
with much pleasure. Strong winter sunshine, of the kind
augured by a clear sky over the Weald and the jocund
glitter of frost points on the hedges, might help to dissi-
pate the glumness a man of his age had every right to feel
at the prospect of lunching two gaolbirds. Especially
when his guests happened to be an adopted daughter and
a daughter-in-law.

Paradoxically (he had always been known to possess
a somewhat eccentric sense of humour) the association of
the word 'gaolbird' with his kith and kin made him grin.
Swann history, so far as he was aware, had no earlier
record of gaolbirds, but he thought it probable, if one
could have searched diligently, that they had existed,
and if this was so it was probable that their offences had
been more serious than a refusal to pay a small fine for
demonstrating on the doorstep of the Prime Minister.
'Might have been looting,' he told himself, massaging his

lower thigh where, on mornings like this, the stump of his leg was tormented by the straps, and the word 'looting' alerted him in the way the word 'gaolbird' had, setting memory bells jingling in the attics of the brain so that he lowered himself on to Hetty's dressing-stool in order to answer them in comfort. He was exploring the nearest attic in a matter of seconds, recovering something that had lain dormant there for a long time. Loot that he himself had acquired fifty years ago this month on a battlefield in India. A ruby necklace of thirty magnificent stones that had, in fact, launched him as a haulier and could therefore be regarded as the original source of all he possessed.

Twenty-nine of the stones had gone their way, some to provide initial capital outlay, others to enrich the Spanish whore his partner Avery had prized until she was murdered by her partner. One remained, set in a ring Henrietta still possessed but only wore on great occasions, although he knew she was attached to it because he had seen her take it from its resting-place in the dressing-table drawer from time to time and contemplate it, remembering, no doubt, an evening over a bivouac fire under the Pennines when he had shown her his loot.

Curiosity stirred in him and after another glance to satisfy himself that she still slept he opened the drawer, foraged in it and drew out the ring, holding it between his finger and thumb in a way that made it take fire in the early morning sun. He thought; 'I wonder if she remembers how I came by it? Or what might have resulted from the discovery that it escaped the clutches of the East India Company by travelling home in the kit of a time-expired lieutenant?' His train of thought ran ahead, all the way down the years to the present moment, eight o'clock on a bright January morning in 1908, when he was debating how to tell her that he had persuaded Giles, and his son-in-law, Milton Jeffs, that it was in both their interests to keep away when the girls were turned out from Holloway.

She had taken it hard at the time. All that publicity,

all those pictures in the papers and the final shattering news that she had a daughter and daughter-in-law serving time in gaol, but he had found it possible to make allowances for her. She had come a very long way in fifty years. Further than him some would say, for she had always valued the respect of neighbours, an aspect of county life that had never bothered him. As to the girls and their offences, he made very little of that. If they cared to sacrifice their dignity shouting and brawling outside that priggish chap's house then good luck to them for it was time somebody pricked the bubble of party complacency. Some of those chaps who had ridden to glory on the Liberal landslide of two years ago already saw themselves as the Lord's Anointed, and all who differed from them as the agents of Baal. He was old enough to understand that politics, especially party politics, were not as clear-cut as that. Even starry-eyed old Giles was beginning to learn this, having been consigned to the wilderness for taking an independent line on women's suffrage.

There remained, however, the placating of Hetty and he wished with all his heart to spare her the embarrassment that would surely follow his announcement that he had told Giles and Milton he would meet Romayne and Deborah and give them the meal they would need after a month on skilly. For there was surely no sense at all in either husband showing up at the gaol gates. Giles would be recognised by the press, and his presence, and relationship to one of the prisoners made public. Milton Jeffs, as a freelance journalist, could not afford personal involvement when the editors he worked for regarded Mrs. Pankhurst and her acolytes as hell-raising harpies, deserving all they got in the way of official correction.

He saw Hetty stir and stretch and crossed over to her side of the bed, the ring concealed in his palm.

"I've got to make an early start," he told her, by way of a preamble, and when she asked where he was going he said, casually, "Over to Holloway. To meet the girls. I promised Giles and Milton I'd deputise for 'em as a welcome committee and I daresay you think I'm a damned old fool to involve myself, but better me than them. Matter of fact I told 'em so when they were here earlier in the week."

She did not protest, as he had expected, but she looked very troubled. "Isn't it their responsibility rather than yours?"

"Yes, I suppose it is. But it won't do Giles any good with his party to have his name linked with Romayne. She went in under her maiden name but the press would start digging if he was seen greeting her outside the gaol. There's bound to be a bit of a stir when they emerge. Wouldn't surprise me if they didn't have a band."

"I'm sure it's quite the silliest thing I've ever heard of," she said, "and I told Deborah so the last time I saw her. All this fuss over a vote! She's a married woman, with a ten-year-old child, and it's high time she knew better!"

He was tempted to remind her of the quarrels they had had over Debbie in the past, notably when the girl was caught up in that *Pall Mall Gazette* scandal about child prostitutes; but decided, instead, on a flank attack. He opened his hand, displaying the ring resting in the palm and at once her eyes widened.

"What are you doing with my dress ring?"

"Remembering," he said.

"Remembering what?"

"How I came by it. Fifty years ago."

"What do you mean by that?"

"It just crossed my mind that I could have served time in prison for taking it, along with those other stones. That or been cashiered at the very least, for I robbed the John Company of around thirteen thousand pounds. We started the business on the proceeds in case you've forgotten. It makes what the girls did small beer, wouldn't you say?"

She took the ring from him and sat up, contemplating it.

"You told me you found it on a battlefield. That isn't stealing, is it?"

"It would have been considered so if I had been caught with it."

"But you fought for it, Adam."

"The girls fought for that month they got. The difference is they believed in what they were fighting for and I never did."

"But you've said over and over again they won't get anywhere with all this uproar."

"That isn't the point, Hetty. It's the fight that's important, and the convictions behind it. That's important all right. It was important to people like Catesby, our Polygon manager, who went to gaol for his share in the industrial riots back in the 'fifties. And to those farm labourers down in Dorset, who were transported for trying to form an agricultural trades union. Everything has to be fought for by somebody. When there's no one around to fight that's the time to watch out, for the men on top will do what they damned well like with all of us. I happen to think Mrs. Pankhurst and her troops are on a wrong tack, strategically that is. There's nothing wrong with what they have in mind and they'll achieve it. In your lifetime, probably." He braced himself. "Listen here, Hetty, will you do something today? To please me rather than them. Will you come up to town with me and *be* there when I meet them? It would mean a lot to them but even more to me."

"Why, Adam?"

"For a variety of reasons but one will do. I'd like your company."

Her expression softened and he knew there was nothing wrong with *his* strategy. "Very well, since you wish it. How long have I got to get ready?"

"I want to be there at noon sharp," he said, "so we'll have to hustle."

*　　　*　　　*

He had promised her a stir, and possibly a band, but she had never expected anything on this scale. It was like mingling with a crowd awaiting the passage of a royal procession or a Lord Mayor's Show, and it was difficult not to be infected by the air of expectancy and excitement among the crowd. She looked about her with lively interest, leaning out of the cab window when he pointed out Mrs. Pankhurst and Mrs. Pethick-Lawrence, whom she instantly recognised from pictures in the newspapers. They did not look like women whose business was public uproar, who encouraged others to smash windows and commit physical assault on members of the Cabinet; more like the women who attended her croquet parties at 'Tryst'. They were neatly dressed in white and each wore a ribbon across the breast, printed with the slogan '*Votes for Women*'. They looked pleased with themselves too, she thought, watching them move among the crowd smiling and shaking hands and when she mentioned this to Adam, he said, "They are pleased. So would I be if the Government gave me a thousand pounds' worth of free publicity."

Then another woman emerged from the ranks of supporters, all of whom were dressed entirely in white as though, for pity's sake, they were on their way to a wedding. The newcomer, young and pretty, wore a kind of apron that draped her from neck to hemline but it wasn't really an apron. It was a placard, advertising a march and mass meeting, with the information, '*The greatest number of free tickets ever issued for a public meeting – You march from Victoria Embankment. Assemble 12.30.*' And above, in heavier type, the obligatory slogan, '*Votes For Women*'.

She had no idea until now that so many people were caught up in the business, having thought of it as the preoccupation of a few intellectuals, women like Debbie, and eccentrics like Romayne, yet it was obvious the movement embraced all classes and all ages. Four girls, carrying a large 'Welcome' banner, were obviously shop girls or housemaids and Henrietta, judging this by the quality of their clothes, wondered how they had found the opportunity to slip away from their work, and what penalties their truancy might involve. Policemen were everywhere, and strangely tolerant, she thought, contenting themselves with keeping the main thoroughfare open.

And then, just as he had warned, a uniformed band arrived to take its position at the head of a procession that was forming, a dozen or more men with trombones and bassoons, and a police sergeant positioned himself in front, as though he was band-master.

Then, across the width of the roadway, there was a stir, rippling outwards like a wave, so that it gusted stragglers back to the kerb. Adam said, briefly, "They're out! But I don't know how we're expected to contact them in this jamboree. Giles and Milton might as well have come after all, for they couldn't be identified in a crowd of this size." He struggled out of the cab, then turned to hand her out, saying to the cabbie, "I'll be going on to the Norfolk Hotel as soon as I pick up my passengers. Can you wait round that corner? I'll make it worth your while."

"I'll do me best, gov'nor," the man said, and began to edge his way along the road away from the gaol gates. And then the band struck up and the procession began to move, Cockney urchins prancing alongside the ranks and indifferent policemen flanking the column of whiteclad women. She said, as they scanned the moving ranks, "It's more like a celebration. Can you spot either of them?"

"No," he said, "and it begins to look as if we've travelled up for nothing," but then, wearing darker clothes that singled them out, the dozen or so martyrs began to pass, and she saw both Debbie and Romayne marching in step some fifty yards behind the band.

They looked wan and tired and their presence there, jostled in a street · procession instead of comfortably settled in a cab irritated her, so that she left Adam for a moment, struggling ahead of him and catching Deborah's sleeve and shouting, above the blare of brass, "Your father has a cab! We're taking you to the Norfolk for luncheon."

Debbie turned, looking very surprised but then smiled as she shouted back, "We can't fall out, Auntie! Tell him we'll catch a cab at Headquarters and meet you there In half-an-hour or so."

"But how *are* you, for heaven's sake?"

"We're fine But very hungry!" and Romayne, on the far flank, raised her hand in greeting.

Adam caught her up, very much out of breath.

"Did you get a word with them?"

"They're coming over to the Norfolk in about half-an-hour. Is that leg bothering you?"

"Like the very devil."

"You're too old for this nonsense and I shall tell them so!" and she piloted him back to the cab, helping him to hoist himself inside and giving the driver instructions to make his way to the Norfolk.

He was badly winded and done up, she noticed, but he managed to grin, saying, "You know, I believe you're enjoying this, Hetty!"

"Oh, no I'm not," she snapped, "but it's lucky you insisted I came along. I really don't know what things are coming to . . . all these people here to meet a batch of women just let out of prison. I do wish I could begin to understand."

"Ask Debbie," he said, "she'll enlighten you, no doubt," and he settled back to regain his breath and she saw his left hand at work massaging the flesh where the straps chafed his leg.

Suddenly, and for no reason that she could think of, she wanted to laugh. 'It really is too absurd,' she thought, 'for he's turned eighty and I'm sixty-eight and here we are driving away from Holloway prison to meet a pair of hot-heads who refuse to grow up. They were far less trouble when they were children, for then either Phoebe or myself were on hand to tell them to mind their manners, and smack their bottoms when they got too tiresome! And really he's no better, but there's more excuse for him, for men never grow up and no woman with her wits about her eve expects them to!'

But she told herself, none the less, that he was right about her enjoying herself, in an odd sort of way, and she *had* seen Mrs. Pankhurst and Mrs. Pethick-Lawrence in the flesh and that would be something to talk about at her next soirée or garden fête. And it was thinking this that enabled her, in some respects, to come to terms with what she had thought of, until then, as a family scandal. Whatever was going on in the world you could always be sure that somewhere, in some capacity, a Swann or two would be involved in it, and there was comfort, she supposed, to be derived from that. Most women her age had settled for the lace cap and serenity but with a family like hers you could put those things right out of mind. She was feeling almost gay when the cab dropped them at the Norfolk and they went in to freshen up and study the menu against the arrival of the gaolbirds.

It was much later, after the girls (as she still thought of them) had been fed, reclaimed and taken away by their husbands, when they were preparing for bed that looked very inviting when the lamp was lit and the fire made up, that she said, "That ruby necklace you talked about — it isn't the same really, Adam!"

"Tell me the difference?"

"The difference is," she said, "you made sure you weren't caught!" That made him laugh, as she knew it would, and he went on chuckling after the lamp was out and they were abed, watching the shadow play of the flames on the ceiling. It pleased her to score over him in that way once in a while. It proved she wasn't as rooted in the past as it sometimes pleased him to think.

2

She had another opportunity to recant when the spring came round and she was faced with the prospect of marrying the last of her daughters to a man she had not even met until Giles produced him like a rabbit from a conjuror's hat on a sunny morning in early April.

Giles was now accepted as the family ambassador, an

amiable broker for all kinds of delicate missions involving the in-laws and the grandchildren. Everybody took his goodwill and tact for granted, and even the Boer War breach between him and Alex seemed to be healing as evidenced by the fact that both Alex and his wife Lydia were careful not to refer to the embroilment of Debbie and Romayne in that fracas on the doorstep of No. 10 Downing Street.

He excelled himself on this occasion, appearing in the sewing-room during the Easter recess and saying, mysteriously, "I've got someone I'd very much like you to meet, Mamma. It took a lot of persuasion on my part to get him here, poor chap, but he's here now, out there talking to Father. We ran across Father down by the knoll."

She was not immediately aware that he was referring to his prospective brother-in-law, Huw Griffiths, but then his sly smile gave her the hint and she said excitedly, "That miner? Are they *both* here? Is Margaret with you?"

"No," he said, "I thought it might be easier on both of you if you give him a chance to speak for himself. So did Father. I warned him I was bringing Huw a week ago, but don't scold him. I made him promise he wouldn't say a word to you."

"It's . . . it's quite certain, then? The girl has really made up her mind?"

"They want to be married very soon. As soon as can be arranged." Then, "She was worried about your reactions, especially after that 'think again' letter you wrote her. But at least she didn't get married in Wales, and present you with a *fait accompli*. They've been engaged for over a year now, ever since he came out of the pits."

"You're saying he isn't a miner any longer?"

"Look, Mamma, there's nothing degrading about being a miner but it so happens Huw isn't. He's my agent, and we pay him five pounds a week and that's riches in the valley."

495

"It can't be riches to Margaret. Doesn't she know she's entitled to a share of her grandfather's money?"

"She knows, but she doesn't want a penny of it. Not now and not ever. She says it would destroy Huw's confidence in himself as a provider."

"That's a very silly point of view, isn't it?"

"Not to her. Not to Huw either. They've got a little house near ours at Pontnewydd, and they're perfectly content to leave things as they are. It's their decision."

It surprised her a little to find Huw Griffiths' determination to take this line. Indeed, it elevated him a little in her estimation for at least it proved the man was not the fortune-hunter she had assumed him to be. She said, briefly, "Show him in, Giles. We can't keep him on the doorstep."

"No. Wait a minute, Mamma," he said. "I've got something I'd like to show you first," and he unbuckled the strap of a briefcase he had thrown on the sewing-table, extracting what she recognised as one of Margaret's sketch-books. "Have a look at these. Particularly the one of Huw Griffiths. He's changed now but I want you to see both versions."

He opened the sketchbook and thumbed through a number of drawings, mining village scenes apparently, for the pen, brush and crayons (Margaret had used all three) portrayed serried rows of narrow little dwellings, looming machinery, dark landscapes studded with debris of one kind or another, and here and there the face of a child that reminded her of Spanish children in a picture by a painter called Murillo that Adam regarded as one of the best in his collection.

"She paints *this* kind of thing down there?"

"All the time. She says it's more exciting than painting woods, fields and flowers, subjects that occupied her before she came to the valley. This is Huw, about the time they first met."

She studied the picture carefully. It showed her a powerfully-built young man sitting on an upturned wash tub in an unkempt garden, and although she knew herself to be no judge at all of paintings or drawings she was not proof against the impact this one made upon her. It was one of humour, frankness and powerful masculinity, all caught, magically to her way of thinking, in the subject's expression, and the set of his shoulders as he turned towards the artist, as though she had called, "This way, Huw! No, not *at* me, over my shoulder! I'm here but you're only half-aware of it and are looking at something to my right."

"This is him? This is Huw?" and when Giles nodded, "Why, it's . . . it's quite splendid! I mean, I always liked her drawings, even when she was a little thing, but this . . . why, it might have been done by a real painter!" and at that he laughed and closed the book, returning it to his briefcase.

"I'm glad you think so for we all do. And now I'll get in the original but treat him gently. He's very shy with the ladies."

'And I don't believe that for a moment,' she thought as Giles went out, closing the door, and her fingers itched to get at the sketchbook again and take another look. She did not, however, remembering her dignity, and the solemnity of the moment, and when Giles returned with the prospective son-in-law in tow she realised that he was shy, despite those merry black eyes and wide smile, one of the widest and warmest, she thought, she had ever seen on a man, especially a man as big and impressive as Huw Griffiths.

It was his size rather than his shyness that impinged on her, however, for she had always thought of Adam as an exceptionally well-made man, and here was someone who could top him by an inch or more and with shoulders a yard wide. Giles said, acting the impresario with just the right amount of light relief, "Well, here he is, Mamma. Your latest son-in-law, and a wild Welshman down to his bootstraps. Don't let her scare you, Huw, boy. She never did me, for you can talk her round in no time if you set about it the right way!"

Henrietta said, blushing, "Hush, Giles, for heaven's sake! You'll have Mr. Griffiths thinking me a perfect dragon! Please sit, Mr. Griffiths, and get the sherry from the cupboard, Giles . . ."

But Adam, it seemed, had anticipated her and came over with decanter and glasses, saying, with a wink in Giles' direction, "I'm sure Huw could do with a drink today, even if everybody in his part of the world pretends to be a teetotaller."

It was surprising after that how effortlessly she adjusted to the situation, a situation that, contemplated in advance, would have promised embarrassment all round. Giles helped, of course, as he always did on these occasions, but Huw Griffiths had begun to shed his awkwardness before his sherry glass was empty and she found herself viewing him as she might have viewed a handsome, well-set-up man forty-five years ago, in other words, as her youngest daughter must have when she first met him, and who could blame her wanting to paint his portrait? Why, it made her feel young and spry again just to be in the same room with him, and she blushed again when she caught Adam's eye and realised, confound the man, that he knew precisely what she was thinking, even if Giles, for all his book learning, did not. She not only approved his figure and bold good looks, she liked his lilting accent and the way his glance softened whenever Margaret was mentioned. All her early prejudice against him crumbled under the assault of his masculinity and she found herself comparing him with the Adam Swann she remembered when she was a bride-in-waiting at Derwentwater all those years ago. The upshot of it all was that Huw was talked into spending the night at 'Tryst', in order that he could make preliminary arrangements for the wedding at Twyforde parish church in early June.

The prospect of another family wedding exhilarated her. She would have thought that she was past the age when this could be so, for it was years now since she had seen one of her sons or daughters married in the old flint church down the road. Stella, her eldest, had been married there as long ago as 1881, and after Stella, Alex. Then Helen and finally, when she was turned thirty, Deborah. George had married abroad, Giles in the city, and Hugo at that fashionable church in Belgravia. Joanna, silly girl, had not had a real wedding at all, just a churching after her runaway match with Jack-o'-Lantern, whereas Helen's second marriage (performed in what Henrietta thought of as a Papist church) took place in Dublin. Now there was only young Edward left and she supposed he would be married wherever his wife happened to live, so she was determined to make the very best of the occasion and spent many happy hours choosing Margaret's gown and her own ensemble.

She wept a little at the ceremony – just for convention's sake – but admitted afterwards that Margaret had proved the prettiest bride of them all, whereas when it came to sons-in-law, Huw Griffiths finished a long way ahead of Denzil Fawcett, poor, dead Rowland Coles and his brother, Jack-o'-Lantern.

The occasion roused romantic echoes that persisted long after the wedding breakfast and excitement of the departure. The renewal of youth, bestowed upon her by the advent of this big, smiling Welshman, remained like a benediction, so that when Adam (surely he must have been subtly aware of her feelings!) mooted the idea of a sentimental journey into the past she could have hugged him, for nothing could have suited her mood more exactly.

It was a brilliant June morning, a day or so after they had all dispersed, that he said, over the breakfast table, "How do you fancy retracing your steps for a week or two, Hetty? It's grand weather, and this place seems as empty as a mausoleum now that every last one of them has moved out. Suppose we do one of our network tours, the way we did those summers after I learned to walk again?"

"Oh, I'd *like* that, Adam!" she said eagerly. "I'd like that very much indeed! We need a change, both of us, and there's nothing to keep us here. But where would we go, exactly?"

"Wherever you like," he said, eyeing her merrily, "the west, for you always liked it down there, and then up north to the Lakes, looking in on Bryn Lovell's boys in the Mountain Square en route. Then up into Scotland if you've a mind to, for it's years since I was there and George tells me Higson and his sons are still scooping up the groats in the Lowlands. I'd like to see just how he goes about it for I always had faith in that young rascal ever since we rescued him from the brute of a sweep in this very room."

It was clear that his mind was working along similar lines and that Margaret's wedding had struck chords in his heart that conjured pleasant melodies out of the past. Like him, she thought of the people he mentioned, not as they were now but as they were in his heyday, when the network was battling for its life in all corners of the land, and he was always hurrying to beleaguered sectors to give aid to his hard-pressed lieutenants. Bryn Lovell's boys must be approaching their thirties now and she knew they were doing well in the Mountain Square, where George had installed them after his reorganisation of the territories. And Jake Higson – she remembered him well, as the one asset salvaged from that frightful shambles on the 'Tryst' hearthrug in the early 'sixties, when Jake's fellow apprentice had been dragged dead from her flue. And since they were travelling north she had other stopping-off places in mind but thought it wiser to say nothing of them now lest he should tease her as a sentimental old biddy, just as if he wasn't as bad in his own special way.

One of the agreeable characteristics of Adam was that, having made a decision, he never lost a single moment implementing it. His holiday proposal had been mooted on Monday. By Wednesday midday they were off, travelling by Southern Railway as far as Salisbury, where they spent a pleasant night with the Rookwoods in what was still called, on the company's maps, the Southern Square.

She had heard a great deal about 'Young' Rookwood, the very first of Adam's Thameside scavengers to make his mark, and looking at the solemn, portly man over his impressively-laid dining table she wondered why, in heaven's name, Swann viceroys still referred to him by that silly name, for she judged him at least twelve years older than Alex, her eldest son, and that would make him fifty-seven. He and Adam talked little but business, booming about here it seemed, with Rookwood's full quota of mechanically-driven vans on the road, but she took a fancy to his gay little wife, another Hetty, and when the men were lingering over their port made so bold as to ask her how she and 'Young' Rookwood had met and married.

"He was our boarder," Mrs. Rookwood told her, "when he first came to these parts as a . . . well, not much more than a boy. Do you know anything about his past, Mrs. Swann?"

"I know he was an orphan, brought into the business as a vanboy by Mr. Keate, our waggonmaster. Keate was always rescuing orphans in those days."

"Ah, the marshal's baton in the Swann knapsack. But there's rather more to it than that. The poor boy spent all his spare time trying to discover who he was, and his failure bothered him so much that he never would have proposed to me if my mother hadn't given him a series of pushes! After that I persuaded him to concentrate on his future rather than his past. I expect your husband will have told you how well he's done down here, and I can tell you he's been a wonderful husband and father."

The story, she thought, had all the hall-marks of a Mudie's Library book, so she asked, "Do *you* ever wonder who he is, Mrs. Rookwood?"

"No," she said, firmly, "I don't and never did! I wouldn't change anything about my life if I had to live it all over again but then . . ." and she looked at her shrewdly, "I don't suppose *you* would, would you, Mrs. Swann?"

"No," said Henrietta, fervently, reflecting what a pleasure it was to meet a woman who was not ashamed to sing her husband's praises in public and to regard him, as Mrs. Rookwood obviously did, as the equal of any man on earth. She had always spoken of Adam in that way but few of her intimates followed suit. Most of them carped at their men as soon as the door was shut on them and she sometimes got the impression they regarded her as very naïve, and fair game for any husband with a trick or two up his sleeve. All the same, she could not readily picture the solemn Rookwood as an ardent lover, although it was abundantly clear that he was an excellent provider, and had she known Mrs. Rookwood better she would have liked to have pursued the subject for curiosity about men in this respect had remained with her since marriage, and so few women would discuss it. Most of them, when they did, gave the impression that a man's demands on his wife, outside the purely domestic sphere, were tiresome and vulgar, and none seemed able to prolong the early excitements of marriage into later life. And yet, as she was ready to admit to herself any time since her wedding day in 1858, it had been of paramount importance to her, converting what might have been a humdrum marriage, of the kind that seemed the norm nowadays, into an adventure more exciting than any to be lived second-hand between the covers of a book. Even now, after all this time, she still felt a stirring under her heart when his arm went round her, or he inclined his weight against her. It would be very interesting to know if she (or he, for that matter) were singular in this respect. She made a mental note to raise the subject with Edith Wickstead again when she next saw her, for Edith's admission that she had once been in love with Adam had broken the barriers of reserve between the two women. They had few secrets from one another.

They moved off the next morning for Exeter and booked

into a hotel in the Cathedral Yard, within three minutes walking distance of the Swann depot in South Street, ruled over by that funny Westcountry character 'Bertie-boy' Bickford, nephew of an even funnier uncle, the late Hamlet Ratcliffe, he who had captured a circus lion, and died hauling a statue of Queen Victoria up the Exe Valley on the eve of the Golden Jubilee.

She had always enjoyed visiting the Westcountry. The lilting names of villages, and the buzz-saw brogue of the locals, fascinated her and she spent a pleasant day with Adam on one of Mr. Bickford's two motor excursion waggons – 'charrybangs' he called them, for some unexplained reason. The 'charrybang', puffing like a grampus at some of the inclines about here, took them all the way to Teignmouth and back in a day, and although she was half choked with dust, and felt as if all her bones had been put in a box and rattled like a set of dice, she enjoyed the experience, her very first aboard one of George's motor-waggons, vehicles she had come to regard as George's private invention, owing nothing to anyone else, alive or dead.

She remembered earlier, smoother rides in four-horse brakes, and when they retired to bed that night she ventured to ask Adam how it was that so many people preferred to be trundled about in this rough and ready manner, when they might so easily have relaxed on a horse brake.

"It's a lot faster for one thing," he said, chuckling, "and almost everybody wants to move faster and further afield these days. I shouldn't quarrel with that, I suppose. I built the business on speed and a point to remember is that those motors of George's are constantly improving in comfort and reliability. Ten years ago that thing we were on today would have broken down a dozen times and as for noise and vibration, well, it was a duckpond sail compared with a ride aboard that first juggernaut he brought home from Austria. In another ten years, I daresay, motors will be bowling along the roads so fast that you'll barely notice their passage. Some of the expensive private motors now can travel at fifty miles an hour, pretty well as fast as a train."

"Well, they won't get my custom," she said, emphatically. "If we do any more excursions on this holiday we'll hire a gig and you can drive, as you used to in the old days."

Bryn Lovell's boys, Enoch and Shad, met them at Newport and took them on to Cardiff, where the Mountain Square depot was now established. All the motor-vehicles about here, they told her, were concentrated in the coal, steel and tinplate areas of the south. They never used them in Central or North Wales, where road surfaces were poor, hauls were mostly agricultural and no one was in a hurry. She had never seen the mountain country of North Wales and persuaded Adam to break the journey north at Chester, hire a trap and make a leisurely circuit of the mountain country where, at a place called Bedd-gelert, he showed her the spot where Giles met Romayne, 'rescuing' her from a counterfeit drowning. It was the kind of prank one would expect of a minx like Romayne Rycroft-Mostyn and, judging by her recent performance outside No. 10, that had earned her a spell in gaol, she was still untamed, despite years of marriage to a gentle creature like Giles. She said, voicing her thoughts: "Have you ever come close to understanding that girl, Adam?" He said he had not, and neither, he suspected, had Giles, although it was fortunate for him he had been able to channel her nervous energy into politics.

"But doesn't that kind of publicity do him harm?"

He replied, after pondering the question a moment, "No, not in the long run. It would have ruined him a generation ago, but today almost any publicity is good publicity. It's the way the world's going, I'm afraid. Stridency is replacing commonsense. I imagine, in time, Romayne's involvement with the suffragettes will give Giles that extra boost which every public man needs, and Giles more than most, for he's a very modest chap and modesty is a handicap in a politician."

"But you advised both him and Milton to stay clear of that welcome party outside the gaol in January."

"Yes, I did, and you saw for yourself how wrong I was. You can still learn at my age, providing you keep an open mind."

It set her thinking, as did these stirring, age-old vistas about here, about the size of the tapestry they had woven about them in half-a-century of marriage. It was like a piece of embroidery that began life as a child's sampler and grew bigger and bigger until it was an epic scene, embracing every aspect of life. The name 'Swann' now seemed to her as permanent as Snowdon, whose bulk dominated every other mountain about here. They were now drawing near the scene of her first encounter with the real founder of the dynasty, and the place, some miles to the north of it, where she had suggested the device still used on all his vehicles, billheads and in all his newspaper advertisements. It hardened her resolve, when they entered the Polygon area of North Cheshire, to make a pilgrimage to the place where, on a hot July morning in 1858, she and her splendid destiny had merged on a desolate stretch of moorland.

He acceded readily enough. They travelled on to Manchester where her grandson Rudi, second son of George and his Austrian wife, Gisela, was winning his spurs, managing the depot sited at Salford. Here The Polygon's generous quota of petrol-driven waggons were fully extended over flattish terrain, serving both Lancashire's cotton interests and the vast volume of shipping that steamed in and out of Liverpool's docks.

Rudi, liveliest and most winning of George's flock, had always been a great favourite of hers, so that it did not surprise her much when, after handing Adam over to his manager to visit the new Ship Canal docks, he drew her aside and said, shyly for him, "I . . . er . . . I should like to ask your advice on something, Grandmam."

She at once jumped to the conclusion that the handsome young scamp had got into debt, and was seeking a loan, and was therefore dumbfounded when, the moment the office door closed on them, he said breathlessly, "Grandmam . . . I can tell *you*. Nobody down south has an inkling as yet. The fact is . . . I'm . . . well . . . married!"

"*Married!* And your father and mother don't know? *Nobody* knows?"

"Well," — and he gave something between a wink and a grimace — "Evie's parents know, for her father had to give her away. And her brothers and sister know, but nobody in the yard does, not even the foreman. I haven't even told Max, my brother, although I could trust him to keep mum until I'd sorted things out."

"But this is quite ridiculous, Rudi, and you must know it is," she said, severely. "I mean, why all this secrecy? And how did it come about? Your mother would be very upset indeed to think you have married without even telling her. And anyway, why are you telling me now?"

He said, avoiding her eye, "I've got to tell somebody and I knew I could rely on you. As for keeping it secret . . . well, it was all a bit of a rush, and my first responsibility, as I saw it, was to Evie." He looked up, a little desperately, "Can't you *guess* the rest, Grandmam?"

She could guess, and thought herself slow not to have guessed at once. "You mean you *had* to get married?"

"*No!*" He looked quite truculent, his expression reminding her vividly of George when he was thwarted as a child. "I didn't 'have' to get married as they say. We would have married anyway, as soon as I was thoroughly established here. I love Evie. I loved her from the first day I saw her sitting perched on that chair!"

"What chair?"

"That one over there, the high one by the ledger rest. She was a girl clerk, you see, taken on by Bagshawe, our chief clerk, when I was away on a trip. We take girl clerks now, like a lot of firms up here. They're cheaper for one thing, and the best of them are more conscientious than men. Evie's very sharp. She left school at thirteen to go in a mill but she had the sense to go to evening classes and learn book-keeping. You'll like her, Grandmam. She's not just pretty. She's so much, well . . . so much *fun!*"

She thought, only just succeeding in suppressing a smile, 'She sounds it, my lad!' but then the desperate sincerity of the boy touched her and she made a quick mental review of the probable consequences down south, once his secret was out. George, whose gallantries at Rudi's age were still remembered, would probably give the boy a dressing down and forget it, but Gisela, who had been at such pains to adopt English proprieties since she had left the Danube, would be very upset, seeing a marriage of this kind as a blot on the record. She said, "When did you marry, Rudi? And when is the child due?"

"We've been married six months now. The baby is expected any day. We've got a little house out at Timperley, a few miles from here and I'd love you to meet Evie, Grandmam, but maybe you would prefer to wait. I've got a picture of her here. It's a wedding photograph actually. She didn't wear white, of course. Naturally it was very quiet, just her mother, father and sister as witnesses. We managed to arrange it early in the morning."

He fumbled in his jacket pocket and took out a small, studio portrait of a girl with dark hair and merry eyes – George's kind of eyes – that looked out on life with confidence, and an expectation of jokes dredged from the small change of the day. She had, however, a very determined chin, a good figure slightly on the plump side, and her costume, an inexpensive one, was worn with panache.

"Weren't her parents very angry about it?"

He grinned, then wiped the grin from his face.

"Well, no, not really, or not once they understood how things were between us. I like them all. They're a very jolly family. He's a lock keeper on the Canal, and all her sisters and brothers are spinners in Rowton Mill. To be honest I suppose they think Evie's done well for herself but that's only to be expected, isn't it?"

"Yes, I suppose it is, but I hate to think of you hurting your mother's feelings. She thinks a rare lot of you boys. What exactly do you want me to do about it?"

"Break the news, as soon as you get back. Maybe the baby will have arrived by then and if it's a boy mother won't mind so much. She was always on at Max and me to get married and give her some grandchildren. I think she really worried about us staying bachelors so long."

It was true. She knew Gisela well enough to realise that the prospect of growing old without a tribe of grand-children would not appeal to her, or to George either for that matter. It really was a little odd that, with four children, they had neither sons-in-law nor daughters-in-law for two of Stella's boys were married now, and Alex's daughter, Rose, and Joanna's eldest daughter, Valerie, were engaged to be married this summer. Robert and Richard, respectively eldest and youngest sons of Stella, had so far produced three daughters between them, her first batch of great-grandchildren, but if, as she fervently hoped, Rudi's child was a boy, he would qualify as the first Swann great-grandson, so who cared whether he 'came across the fields' as her old nurse used to say? She said, "I'll do what I can but the very first chance you get bring that girl down to 'Tryst' for I'm sure I'd like to meet her and so would your grandfather. If it is a boy have you decided what to call him?"

"Sam. For Grandfather Rawlinson. After all, he'll be a Lancastrian, and Grandfather Sam did a lot to help my father when he was working to perfect his prototype up here."

She had forgotten that, Sam Rawlinson's part in sponsoring George at a time when he had quarrelled bitterly with his father, and it touched her a little that the boy should want to make this gesture. She had never been close to her father, always having regarded him as a bit of a ruffian, but there was no doubt about it, Sam's strong, mechanical strain was present in the family and his aggressiveness too, when you came to think about it.

"You won't say anything to Grandfather yet?"

"I won't say anything to anyone until I've seen your mother and that can't be for a fortnight or more. We're supposed to be going on to Scotland."

"How do I keep in touch then?"

"Well, tomorrow your grandfather has promised to take me to the place where I grew up, Sedley Mills. Then we shall return to Manchester and catch a train on to Ambleside and stay a day or so at The Glades Hotel before going on to Edinburgh."

She took out her purse and extracted a gold half-sovereign. "The day he's born put this in his hand and close his fingers over it. Then put it away somewhere. It's an old good-luck custom. Adam's father, the old Colonel, did it with all the children, right up to the time he died."

He kissed her, saying, "You're a good sport, Grandmam, and you never seem like a grandmother to me. More like a . . . well . . . like a sister."

It was worth more than half-a-sovereign to get a compliment of that kind.

3

It was surprising how little the vista beyond what she thought of as The Rampart had changed. The Rampart was a string of towns following the course of the great-grandfather of all railways, Stephenson's Manchester-to-Liverpool line over Chat Moss where, for weeks on end they said, Irish navvies had tipped thousands of fascines to form a base under the track. Here town and country met on the northern edge of the Cheshire plain, the vast jumble of mills, shops, warehouses, sidings and cobbled streets, straggling west in what now seemed one huge ugly city and beyond it, to the south, hedgerow land, ploughed furrow, neat black and white farmsteads, and the house where she had grown up, Sam Rawlinson's mock-Gothic lodge, known by millhands in those days, as 'Scab's Castle'.

She had no fond memories of Seddon Moss, the town where her father had made his first fortune, but the moor to the south of it was dear to her and she became very silent and absorbed as the trap rattled over the winding road towards the familiar clump of woodland on the horizon.

He respected her silence, having memories of his own, of a saddlesore young man riding north across the swell of gorse common fifty summers ago and coming upon a scene of riot and arson that turned him back, sick with disgust at the cruelty he had witnessed. Yet something sweet and wholesome had emerged from it, for it was only hours later that he came upon her in a dip beside a shepherd's hut and their life's odyssey, in convoy, had begun right there, weeks before the first Swann waggon, bearing its strange device moved out across Kent in search of customers.

"It was about here, wasn't it, Hetty?"

"No," she said, "a little further on. Just past the Nantwich fork coming this way."

He wouldn't have remembered, or not with that degree of accuracy, but was prepared to trust her judgment. The moment, he guessed, would have even more significance for her. He had taken a long time to evaluate her, some seven years if he was honest with himself. Until then he had been almost entirely absorbed in his work and the terrible demands it had made upon him.

"Here, Adam. Why, you can still see where the hut stood. There, over on the left, just at the foot of the dip."

It was true. An oblong of flattened gorse was marked out by what he could identify as the holes where the posts had been driven in, and he checked the horse and climbed down, helping her to alight and tethering the skewbald to a bush. They moved off the road and stood silently on the patch of open ground, holding hands lightly and seeing themselves, a little ironically in his case, as they had been the morning of the encounter. He said, finally, "Tell you something, Hetty. When I realised you were Sam Rawlinson's daughter I came damned close to leaving you to fend for yourself. The smoke from old Sam's burned-out mill was still on the skyline yonder, and I kept thinking of that boy he had ridden down in the town."

"What stopped you?"

"Oh, a variety of reasons. At least you'd had the sense to run out on him, and you didn't seem much more than a child at the time. Then you coaxed me into a more tolerant humour, thinking Birmingham was a seaport, and that story about deportment."

"I don't recall that."

"You don't? I'll never forget it. Something your governess taught you – 'Never accept a chair from a gentleman until you are satisfied it is no longer warm from his person!' And then again, I hadn't thought about a woman as a woman in more than a year."

"That isn't much of a compliment, is it?"

"A better one than it sounds. Emptying that well at Cawnpore, crammed full of butchered women and children, must have petrified my emotions. You started the thaw."

She wondered how much truth there was in this and how, exactly, she had appealed to him as a woman in that bedraggled green crinoline she was wearing, with her hair uncombed and mud on her face. Hardly at all, she would say, remembering his first embrace beside Derwentwater a few days later, that left her in a turmoil, but had not seemed to make much impression on him. She had worshipped him from the beginning, from the moment he hoisted her on to the rump of his mare and told her to put her arms around his waist, but responsive affection, of the kind that flowered early in their marriage, had not been evident until they were man and wife. Perhaps he was right. Perhaps the horrors of the Sepoy Mutiny had blunted his sensibilities and they had been sharpened, over the ensuing weeks, by physical access to her that had begun in a mood of tolerance and developed in a way that lasted them down the years. She said, "Hold me, Adam. Just for a moment," and he put his arms round her and kissed her gently on the mouth.

They climbed back into the trap and moved on over the crest towards the trees, catching a glimpse of the lodge turrets as they drew near and reining in at a spot where they could see the house through the trees. To her it looked much smaller than she remembered. To him it was one of the ugliest dwellings he had ever seen, a monstrous multiple marriage between domestic Cheshire, mock Tudor, mock Gothic and neo-classical, precisely the kind of monument a vulgarian like old Sam would erect to his brigandage and avarice.

"Great God!" he exclaimed, "no wonder you fled from it!"

"But I didn't, not in that sense, for it seemed a grand house to me. I fled from that awful man Goldthorpe Sam had decided I should marry in exchange for a loading bay area on Goldthorpe's father's land."

"Oh, yes. I'd forgotten the bartered bride angle." And then, with an approving glance, "Nobody would have married you against your will, Hetty. You've far too much spunk."

"I'm not so sure. It was touch and go until you spoke up for me. Come, I've seen all I want to about here. Let's get back to Warrington if we're to catch that train for I wouldn't care to spend a night hereabouts, not even in a shepherd's hut with you on hand. That's another thing I learned from you early on."

"What exactly?"

"To value comfort. I remember you telling me, when I remarked on the trouble you went to make a bivouac weatherproof and cosy, 'Any fool can be cold, wet and miserable.'"

*　　　*　　　*

The Glades Hotel, overlooking Windermere where they had spent their first night together, was still in business, but much larger and more pretentious than it had been half-a-century ago. They dined in the same room, where he had made her half-tipsy on claret and she had suffered agonies of embarrassment wondering how to tell him she was desperate to be excused. 'The miseries we inflict on ourselves at that age,' she thought, smiling as she recalled the relief attending the release of her corset tapes in the ladies' room.

It was still light when they took an after-dinner stroll along the lakeside, with the sun setting over Hawkshead and Coniston Water and the blue peaks of the fells on the far side of the lake. It was surprising, she thought, that they had never retraced their steps here in all this time, for her thoughts, all of them pleasant, had returned here time and again, remembering so much of that stupendous occasion when, or so it had seemed to her at the time, all the secrets of the universe had been revealed to her. And as she thought this she was aware of a rare spurt of rebellion against growing old, reflecting that their relationship had entered a new phase in the last few years, a burned-out phase she supposed, although his touch and nearness still awakened in her echoes of the fearful ecstasy of that splendid time.

The red-jacketed hall porter greeted them in the foyer, holding a buff telegram form, saying, "The telegraph boy arrived with it just after you and the lady went out, sir. There's no prepaid answer but the telegraph office is open until midnight if you want the boots to send a reply."

He took the envelope, drew out the message and read it with an expression of mystification, passing it to her and saying, "Can you make anything of this, Hetty? It's gibberish to me." She took the form and moved nearer the chandelier. The message read, 'SAM DESCENDED ON US TODAY STOP ALL EIGHT POUNDS OF HIM STOP LOVE RUDI' and she realised then that the telegram had been addressed to her and laughed outright, partly at the sauciness of the message, partly at Adam's baffled expression.

"What's the joke? What the devil is the boy driving at? It *is* George's Rudi, I imagine?"

"Oh, it's George's Rudi all right," and she began laughing again, so that he looked quite irritated for a moment and the porter, sensing domestic contention, moved away and pretended to be absorbed in the letter rack beside the receptionist's desk.

"There's no answer," she called across to him, and to Adam, "Come up to our room, Adam, and I'll explain."

His exasperation was really quite comic as she closed the door, laid down the telegram and said, removing her hat and veil, "It's really quite an occasion, Adam. Nothing whatever to scowl about. The arrival of our first great-grandson, no less. That's worth a telegram, isn't it?"

"Great-grandson? But, dammit, woman, the boy's a bachelor!"

"Oh, no, he isn't. He's been married six months or more."

"Six months you say?" He picked up the telegram and re-read it. "How do you know? And why is this addressed to you?"

"Well, it wouldn't have made much sense addressed to you, would it? He confided in me when you were out looking at the new docks. He married his book-keeper, a girl called Eve – I don't know what her maiden name was. I imagine they married a week or so after she discovered she was expecting his child."

"He told *you* that?"

"He had to tell someone, poor lad. They were hoping for a boy and decided on 'Sam', remembering how close Sam and George were in the old days."

He sat down on the bed. "Haven't George and Gisela been told yet?"

"No. They were going to be married anyway as soon as Rudi had settled in as manager of the depot but it seems – well, you know what young men are better than I do. It isn't that kind of marriage, however. They're very much in love and she looks such a pretty, forth-coming sort of girl."

"You've met her?"

"No. He showed me a picture of her."

Humour finally triumphed over his bewilderment and he smiled but then, giving her a steady look of appraisal, "I find that very interesting, Hetty. That a boy in that situation should confide in his grandmother, when he could have made his choice from a whole tribe of uncles, aunts, brothers, sisters and cousins. It establishes something important."

"Only that he needed someone to break the news gently to his mother."

"No, something beyond that. I could have done that for him. So could his father, or Max, his brother or even Giles, whom we all seem to use as a go-between. But he didn't, he went straight to you, and do you know why? Because he sees you as the real power behind the throne, the one person with the broadmindedness and authority to ease him and that girl he's married out of a ticklish corner. I've a notion any one of them would do the same if it came to the pinch, and that means you've kept overall command of 'em. Not as a grandmother but as a person, and it's a credit to you if you think about it. They'd confide in me soon enough if it was a business matter but a human problem, that's something different."

His eyes returned to the form again. "Sam, eh? Well, it's fitting, I suppose, for a first great-grandson. Your father would have been tickled. Especially by us getting the news here of all places. Come over here, you witch."

She came and stood before him and his big hands enclosed her tightly corsetted waist, inclining her towards him and then, in a way that was reminiscent of the man she recalled so vividly from the past, his hands slipped over the rim of the corset to pinch her bottom. "You're a very singular woman, Henrietta Rawlinson. I had a lot more sense than I realised when I scooped you off that moor, showed your father the door and brought you here to this hotel, as green a woman as a man ever coveted. By God, I'd give something to be that young again."

"Who wouldn't?"

"You'll always be young and this is proof of it," and he released her, folded the telegram carefully and put it in his pocket. And then, in the last blink of twilight reaching them from the darkening surface of the lake, she saw his eyes light up. "To blazes with trailing further north," he said. "Let's go south again, stop off at Manchester, meet that wife of his and wet the baby's head. After that I'll bow myself out and leave you to introduce Sam Swann to his grandmother."

5

Landmark

THE SWANN TRIBE, TOGETHER WITH THEIR LEAD-
ing henchmen dotted about the country, had many common characteristics, uniformity being the product of the
strain, as far as the family was concerned, added to Adam
Swann's skill in selecting deputies capable of measuring
up to his standards. Every one of them, to some degree,
were dogged and purposeful, not easily turned aside from
the pursuit of what they sought in the way of glory,
rewards and the satisfaction that stemmed from doing a
job well. In addition, almost all of them were capable of a
strenuous effort and an occasional sacrifice demanded by
loyalty to one another and to the firm, for they saw themselves as a unit constantly confronted by rivals and what
Adam referred to as 'the Johnny-Come-Latelys', whose
watchwords were quick profits, with no real regard for the
quality of service rendered. They had in common a
sense of living in the present, that promised endless
possibility, of being members of an élite among their
fellows, especially those (poor devils) who had the misfortune to be born the far side of the English Channel, so
that the pulse of nationalism, quickened by three generations of success, beat strongly in each of them, even in
Giles, who sometimes saw the strident nationalism of the
British as a threat to the harmony of nations. But that
was as far as it went in terms of collectivity, really no more
than a loose but effective alliance of some three thousand

men and a hundred or so women, who respected the past and embraced the present but gave little thought to the future and were therefore not equipped to anticipate the rhythms of destiny.

Adam, the patriarch, had the advantage of all of them, in this respect. He had lived far longer than most of them and the jeopardies of his youth had developed in him a deeper awareness of the wanton twists of fortune. A guarded optimist in most respects he had yet learned, over the years, to live like a boxer squaring up to an opponent of unknown reputation, poised on the balls of his feet and conserving his wind, even when he had an adversary sagging against the ropes. As a soldier and trader over more than six decades of high adventure, entailing so many brushes with sudden death and slow bankruptcy, he understood that it did not profit a man to underestimate the opposition, or over-extend himself, or squander reserves of patience. Someone or something was always lurking behind the hill to exploit any such lapse and he had tried, in his gruff, solitary way, to instil this precept into his children and employees. With very little success, however, for neither the Swanns nor their henchmen had had much personal experience with failure and even Henrietta could look back on the successive crises of the 'sixties with a sense of having met and surmounted them. As for the others, for the children and even the middle-aged among the pashas, not one of them could recall a time when Swann had not been a household word, when there had not been reserves of cash and credit in the bank and, above all, to a time when British citizenship did not carry, as it were, the golden star of precedence over every competitor in the world of commerce.

God knows, Adam sometimes thought, they had grounds for such confidence. Ever since the dawn of the new century, and particularly since the general advance of 1905–1908, family and firm had been riding high. George Swann was now acknowledged the most successful haulier in the country, with over two hundred petrol-driven vehicles on the road and still as many horse-drawn vehicles as his father had fielded in the days when the term 'horse-less carriage' was a carter's gibe. The Swann insignia was now seen in every corner of the country save only the Western Isles, where there was little or no profit in hauling, whereas the overall yield of the firm rose year by year, from fifteen per cent in 1901 to just over thirty per cent in the Swann Jubilee year of 1908. George had achieved his headstart and viceroy investors sometimes asked themselves where their wits had been holidaying in 1904, when he had been voted down by his fellow directors. Now his position was even more secure than his father's had been, for he was reckoned a general who had won not merely Waterloo but the peace that followed it. With his privately owned concern adding to the fleet of Swann-Maxie waggons at the rate of one a week there seemed little prospect of anyone coming abreast of him.

In other fields, seemingly remote from transport, the Swanns had made their mark. Alexander Swann, close confidant of the War Minister and acknowledged expert on small arms, was a force to be reckoned with among the polo-enthusiasts who still thought of Haldane's Territorials as a kind of last-ditch reserve.

Giles Swann, although a little-known back-bencher, cold-shouldered by the patricians of his party, was known to have personal access to two or three powerful men in the Cabinet, notably the Welsh Wizard and the pacifist, John Burns. He was also enlarging his grip on his con-stituents in the valleys where he was known as that rare breed of politician who could be approached anywhere, anytime, and the prospect of unseating him now was considered remote. Meantime Hugo Swann, war-hero, not only lived on in the after glory of earlier athletic prowess but had won fresh laurels at Netley Military Hospital. He was known as 'Flexer' Swann among staff and patients and there were some, among them the men he treated, who declared there was magic in his hands, a legend that his wife helped to foster among the splendid

ones who attended her fêtes and garden parties organised
on behalf of ex-servicemen.

Of the Swann girls, two had married men of substance,
and even Edward Swann, a solitary young man seldom
seen in the metropolis, had a high reputation as a mechanic
among manufacturers and exporters in the great Midland
swathe marked out on Swann's new maps as The Funnel.

And yet, into the heart and mind of the ageing Adam
Swann, head of the tribe, there stole, on this high tide of
fortune, a sense of unease as he stumped about his arbours,
flowering shrubs and exotic trees on that estate of his
sixteen miles south-east of London Stone, and if you had
taxed him with it he would have found it very difficult to
express in words. It was not that prospects, after so far a
run, were due for a change on that account alone, for to
accept this would have been admitting to superstition
and Adam was the least superstitious of men. Neither did
it stem from the stridency of firm and family but from the
mood of the tribe as a whole, that had now, seemingly,
made a complete recovery from the blight of self-doubt of
a few years ago, when sixty thousand farmers had beaten
them thrice in a single week. National preoccupation
with what he saw as the fairground aspects of the new era
might have contributed to his apprehension, for everywhere there was prattle about the garish stucco city they
had erected at Shepherd's Bush and were comparing, to
the former's advantage, with the Great Exhibition of
1851. And this, he thought, was nonsense, for alone
among them he could remember the Great Exhibition,
and its air of earnest exploration, whereas now, at this fun
parlour they called the White City, the most talked-of
exhibit was the giant flip-flap, a joyriding contraption of
extraordinary silliness. Then there was the ever-increasing
emphasis on outdoor sports, as if German and American
competition could be held at bay by an army of cricketers,
yachtsmen, prizefighters, jockeys, lady archers and lady
tennis champions. Tremendous coverage was given,
even in sober journals, to the antics of these tumblers

and less and less, or so it seemed to him, to the real business
of the nation, so that the British Empire might be going the
way of Rome when the approach of the barbarians failed
to deflect citizens from gladiatorial conventions in the
Coliseum.

The very titles of current successes in West End theatres
underlined the pervading frivolity of a nation hitherto
dedicated to the pursuit of profit – *The Merry Widow*,
A Waltz Dream, *The Flag Lieutenant* and *My Mimosa Maid*.
Slang was finding its way into the verbal currency of
debutantes and top-hatted city gents, as well as that of
street urchins. A serious campaign, aimed at extending the
franchise to educated women, was treated, by press and
public alike, as a lively sideshow running a close second
to the White City's flip-flap, so that sometimes he began
to equate London – in his day the most industrious city
on earth – as a new Vienna, awaiting, indeed sometimes
seeming to invite, total eclipse by Berlin and Chicago.

There had been a time, less than twenty years ago,
when he would not have wagered a sixpence on the prospects of a successful overseas challenge, but it did not
require a dedicated newspaper reader like himself to see
Germany and the United States as strong contenders for
the title of top dog today. Over on the Continent, he
sensed, people still had their noses to the grindstone,
whereas over here Bank Holidays, seaside trips, beanos,
regattas, day excursions by motor brakes, and all manner
of diversions were beginning to rank high on the programme of thirty-shilling-a-week clerks and even, he
suspected, collarless artisans, among whom were a
thousand or more Swann carters.

He was all for giving the underdog a fair crack of the
whip but underdogs ought never to forget that the only
road to advancement lay through the portals of application and self-development. Certainly not through the
turnstile of the White City or the nearest professional
football stadium.

He wondered sometimes how that tough old warrior,

John Catesby, he who had fought so hard and so courageously to establish the Trades Union Congress, would have regarded it. Contemptuously, he would say, remembering The Polygon manager's passionate avowal of the dignity of labour, but there it was – the sons of men whom Catesby had helped to liberate from stupefying labour in mill and factory were now more elevated by news that Britain had won four out of the first five prizes in the International Balloon Race than in improving machinery designed to strike a bargain between boss and hired hand. They did their work – shoddily if some of the new products he had handled lately were their judge – then rushed off to an athletic field somewhere, more often to watch than to play, for the gladiators who drew the largest crowds nowadays were professionals and even village cricket, they told him, was entering a decline.

Glum as they were, however, he kept these thoughts to himself apart from a hint or two to Giles, still struggling towards the Millennium, for it gave him no pleasure to puncture the self-confidence of George, Alex and Edward, and he saw little of the girls now they were all off his hands.

So it was, when George came to him with an invitation to occupy the seat of honour at the forthcoming Jubilee banquet he was planning for late September, he thanked him and accepted, saying, "You'll not want me to make a speech, I hope?" And at that George laughed and said he most surely would be required to speak, for he was down to reply to the toast 'Swann-on-Wheels, 1858–1908'.

"Who else could do it with your style?" he demanded. "Come to that, who else has survived to challenge the authenticity of all the I-remembers you'll weave into your text?"

"Oh, I daresay a few old crocks will shake the moths out of their festive rig on the promise of free liquor. Not poor old Keate, the original waggonmaster, for he's ninety and anyway he's a teetotaller. But I daresay a few old stagers like Bryn Lovell, Young Rookwood and

Jake Higson, will want to boast about their long-service records. Where are you holding it? At the George Inn?"

No, George told him, it was planned to take place in the largest of the new warehouses, specially decorated for the occasion, and every region was balloting for a deputation of twenty employees, for even the warehouse could not accommodate everyone who would want to come.

"There'll be over three hundred by my reckoning," he added, "and on the same night every region is holding its own celebration dinner. I've allocated a grant of fifty pounds to every depot."

"Wives?"

"A few of them. Would mother be interested, do you suppose?"

"I wouldn't care to be the one who told her she hadn't been invited," and noting George's smile added, "Why do you ask such a question, boy?"

"I don't know . . . maybe because I've always sensed she regarded the network as a rival."

"So she did. But your mother's far too sharp to turn her back on the Other Woman. I found that out when you were a toddler."

It crossed his mind then to wonder how much they knew of Henrietta's achievement when she had hauled the business out of the doldrums that time he lost his leg and was out of action for a year. Little enough, he imagined, for it was all so long ago, and so wildly improbable at the time, a transformation, overnight, of a feckless girl into a merchant princess and it gave him the bare bones of the speech George wanted him to make.

"Send her a card and all the trimmings," he said. "She'd appreciate that, boy."

2

Edith, he recalled, had once seen them as privateersmen, converging on the Thames to plan a string of piratical affrays, but when he reminded her of this, in the interval when they were milling around before taking their seats, she smiled and said, "But they've come *en masse* today, with their private retinues, so I see them a little differently. As trained bands, converging on the capital to squeeze the best terms out of the man who hires them. Or as a company of mercenaries, assembling under some old brigand like Sir Robert Knollys before cutting a swathe from Lower Normandy to Gascony."

He liked that and thought about it for a moment as he watched them exchanging banter round the seating plan George had fastened to a blackboard near the double doors. A White Company, well versed in the use of weapons, and masters of their own tactical skills, yet still needing the strategical direction of a veteran like George, a man they had come to trust and admire, forgetting the occasions when he had led them on unprofitable ventures and remembering only more recent triumphs in which every one of them had shared.

They had come here from every corner of the islands, bringing with them their local prejudices and babel of dialects but disposed, for once, to set aside old rivalries and frontier skirmishes for they would see themselves as meeting on neutral ground.

His eye roved among them, ironically but affectionately, revisiting their several beats and recalling, over half-a-century, the men who had planted the Swann banner in every shire of the four kingdoms. Higson and his band of Lowlanders and Highlanders, inviting ridicule by appearing in the kilt to which, no doubt, few of them were entitled. Their leader, Higson, was not among this minority. Adam recalled him as a rawboned lad of thirteen, with an accent that placed him no more than a mile from this spot, but none of the young bucks would have the temerity to remind him of his origins tonight. Higson's record was far too impressive. Within two years of crossing the border he had captured the Lowlands from the natives. In another year he had consolidated his gains. And in two years more he had won the Swann accolade, wresting it from that other gamin, Rookwood, who tonight moved among the upper echelons of celebrants like an exalted Palace flunkey, a cut above everyone save only George and himself, and only marginally below them in Swann seniority.

It was curious, he noted, how the ballot-chosen retainers took their several cues from the regional chieftains. Higson's lot looked like a score of moss troopers embarked on a border raid, whereas the men around Rookwood were a sober, respectable bunch, every man jack of them wearing gloves and evening dress, as though Rookwood had held an inspection on Salisbury Station before setting off for town.

Bertieboy Bickford's westerners were easily distinguished by their brogues and the volume of laughter, a heavy-jowled, redfaced, breezy troupe, who might have been recruited from Dartmoor and Exmoor smallholdings. The Lovell boys had travelled up with a covey of Welshmen, whereas Clint Coles' contingent were Irishmen to a man and gave the impression of having foregathered in advance at the George Inn, down the road, in order to fortify themselves for long speeches. Scottie Quirt was here from the North, with what seemed to Adam an entirely different breed, younger men mostly, many of them still in their twenties, and it struck him that mechanically-propelled vehicles would be unlikely to attract mature men, just as if the general post caused by Stephenson's railways nearly a century ago was being repeated all over again with the phasing out of the horse. Watching them, catching a word or two of their technical jargon, his mind returned for a moment to old coachman Blubb, who had been thrown on the scrapheap by 'that bliddy teakettle', that had reduced professional coachmen to the status of carters.

The elegant Godsall, of the Kentish Triangle, came up to pay his respects to Henrietta and as they exchanged courtesies Adam reflected that Godsall was probably the only bona fide gentleman he had ever enrolled as a manager. Now, they said, he drove about Kent in a big Daimler car, like the one King Edward owned, so that in a sense the ex-guardee was a link between the old cadres and the new.

He managed to have a word with his grandson, Rudi, down from The Polygon and accompanied, he was glad to see, by that saucy little baggage he had married in such a hurry. He said, addressing her, "Well, now, and who's minding my great-grandson tonight?"

"Our Lottie, Grandfather — my youngest sister that is," she replied, pertly enough. "But she wouldn't do it for less than half-a-crown and only then if we gave her permission to have her young man in until Mam comes at suppertime."

"Ah," he said, chuckling, "you Lancastrians are razor sharp when it comes to putting a price on yourselves. They always say Yorkshire folk have the edge on you but I never believed it."

"The difference is," she said, "on our side of the Pennines we don't mind parting with it once we've got it." And he thought approvingly, 'Young Rudi knew what he was about when he picked that lass and so, I'd wager, did she, when she jumped the starter's gun. But they're well matched, somehow, and that's half the battle at their age,' and he turned aside to have a word with Dockett, of Tom Tiddler's Land, one of the very few originals here tonight.

Then someone beat a gong and the company began to sort themselves out but the warehouse was so crowded that it took some time for guests to find their seats. In the hurly-burly he bumped into Young Edward, who looked very spruce in a London-cut evening suit, with a red carnation in his buttonhole and a blue silk colarette, embroidered with the swan insignia. "It's George's idea," Edward said, grinning. "I'm toastmaster, you see," and then, moving to one side, he displayed his partner, the most attractive girl Adam had seen in a very long time.

It was not that she was pretty, in the way most young

girls appeared to him nowadays, especially when they were dressed for an outing, or that her hair was a high, flaxen crown of exceptionally soft texture, or indeed that her eyes, a genuine violet, were veiled in long, curling lashes, so that she reminded him a little of Madame Récamier in David's portraits. She had intelligence as well as good looks in her smooth oval face, and a bloom on her cheeks that made him think of standing in his rose garden contemplating a handful of fallen petals and inhaling their sweetness. He thought, 'My word, she's a stunner! I wonder where he found her . . . ?' but then Edward said, "You've met Gilda, Gov'nor. She's Gilda Wickstead . . ."

"It was a long time ago, when I was in pigtails, Mr. Swann. You came up to the Crescents once or twice when Father was alive but I've been abroad since I left school."

He took her hand, enclosing it in both of his and thinking, 'Now why the devil didn't Edith tell me she brought this lovely creature along . . . ?' but then, his sharp old eye catching the way his son was looking at her, he knew the reason. The boy was obviously much smitten by her and Edith would prefer to leave introductions to him, providing he wanted to make them. He said, "My word, you're quite grown up. I didn't realise . . . we don't, you know, at my age . . . Abroad, you say? Where?" And she said Switzerland, where she had gone to learn French and German and later as a teacher of English at Tours University.

"But she's back for good now," said Edward, with a hint, he thought, of desperation. "We shall have to talk later, Gov'nor. George wants the top table seated. The caterers have been complaining to him that the soup will go cold," and they moved on, the girl inclining her head to him with an enigmatic little smile that encouraged him to whisper to Henrietta, as they took their seats in front of a side table bearing a gigantic cake surmounted by a silver swan, "Young Edward is hooked. Look over there, on the left, that girl in green next but one to Edith!"

He saw her look, frowning with concentration, for he was aware that she was concerned by her youngest son's extended bachelorhood. "It's Edith's girl . . . the one that came along after her boys were grown. She's . . ." but then George was on his feet, and Edward was calling for silence in order that grace could be said, and both of them were caught up in conversations with their neighbours, so that he judged the subject of ending Edward's bachelorhood would not arise until they were back at the hotel and preparing for bed. For that was usually Hetty's time for family inquests, confound it. She never seemed affected by the fatigues of the day.

*　　*　　*

A sustained clatter of china and cutlery, a nonstop hubbub of talk; the quality of the beef, the hundred and one quips sparked off by the rivers of champagne, ale, Madeira and port. This was a celebration dinner to be remembered and relished as Swann-on-Wheels entered its second half-century. He had never been much of a trencherman – the short commons of youthful campaigns had seen to that – but he had always appreciated good company and a collective sense of achievement and the latter touched him now like a shaft of sunlight, illuminating the long and adventurous road they had travelled together, since he stood on or about this spot (there were no warehouses, as such, in those days) and wished old Blubb, his Kentish manager, good luck on the first Swann Embassy to pass the gates.

So few were present who could share that memory. Keate, the aged waggonmaster could, of course, and Bryn Lovell, about his own age, called out of retirement by the stupendous occasion. Dockett, too, and Morris, formerly of Southern Pickings based on Worcester. And Edith, whose father had once managed Crescent North, plus two of the original yard staff, a smith and a night-watchman. A mere eight out of a company of over three hundred but it didn't matter all that much. There were memories enough to be bandied around and most of them got an airing tonight.

"Do you remember that damned awful winter of 'sixty-five, when we had floods in five southern regions and snow blocks on every road north of Birmingham?" – "Do 'ee mind old 'Amlet vetching that bliddy lion home and getting civic honours from the Mayor of Exeter? Nobody told 'is Worship the poor brute would've rin from a tomcat with a vull set o' teeth . . . !" – "Wass you born, bach, when Bryn Lovell hauled that Shannon pump up a mountain to pump the water out of Pontnewydd pit, then?" – ". . . Seven ton that turret weighed, or so I heard. But George always reckoned it as a shade over six" – ". . . I first smelled smoke when I was coming out of the weighbridge hut and next minute, *woof* – up she goes, and a Clydesdale goes tearing by . . ." Up and down the tables like the exchange of so many brightly coloured balls in a complicated party game that everyone could play, even young Kidbroke, fourteen-year-old van boy, who had drawn a lucky ballot paper in Southern Square, for only last week Kidbroke had been present when a Swann vehicle broke down on a narrow bridge over a Hampshire river and blocked main road traffic for nearly an hour.

And then the cake cutting and the speeches, amusing most of them, and well spiced with anecdotes, but one or two rambling and heard with impatience, so that when it came to his turn he thought, 'I must cut it short . . . They'd sooner flirt and guzzle than listen to me.' But there was complete silence when, in response to Edward's stentorian "Pray silence for Mr. Adam Swann, our Founder," he rose to his feet and put on his reading glasses in the unlikely event he would use his notes.

He thanked them all gravely for honouring himself and the firm and told them a little, just a very little, of what it had felt like to take the gamble he had taken as a rank outsider in the transport stakes of those days. But then, perhaps because he could sense their genuine interest, he warmed to his favourite theme, the marriage of capital and labour that had been his policy ever since he signed on his first two score hands, and that other Swann precept, selecting local men who knew their areas and potential customers for executive positions in most regions between here and the north. He told them something of the tight-rope days, of the first managerial conference a few months before the present managing director was born and how, on that occasion, "we came so close to bankruptcy that Mrs. Swann will tell you those weeks were responsible for the first patches of white on a head where anyone among you tonight would have difficulty in finding a single dark hair." But this reminded him of his original thoughts for a wind-up and he continued, interrupted by a few shouts of 'Hear, hear!', and a cry of 'No politics, please': "We hear a great deal these days, of Women's Rights, and a woman's eligibility to take a responsible part in running the country, so let me conclude by reminding some of you younger folk of a crisis this firm survived, as long ago as 1866, solely on account of the skill and courage of two women, both of them happily in our midst. I refer to my wife, and to Mrs. Tom Wickstead, who encouraged her to take over the personal direction of Swann-on-Wheels when I was abroad, learning to use this tin leg of mine.

"Very few here will remember that challenge, and how it was met, but some will – among them four of the originals, Keate, Dockett, Morris and Lovell, respectively waggon-master and managers of three regions at that time. For the truth is, ladies and gentlemen, I came home from Switzerland in June of that year expecting to have to start all over again but several surprises awaited me. The first was that there was more money in the bank than when I had left. The second was that Miss Wadsworth was no longer Miss Wadsworth but Mrs. Wickstead. And the third – spare Mrs. Swann's blushes – was that I had a three-months-old son I didn't even know about, who grew up to be the Member of Parliament for Pontnewydd in the Mountain Square! So be damned careful, all of you, how you approach the subject of Women's Rights in the future!"

It was probably the most successful joke that he had ever used to terminate one of his speeches and he took advantage of the laughter and applause to sit down and take a sidelong glance at Henrietta, who was indeed blushing, a rare occurrence for her these days. Everybody rose to their feet then and the cheer they gave him could have been heard, indeed *was* heard according to young Harry Hitchens, a vanboy who lived hard by, in Tower Bridge Road.

She whispered, laughing, "Really, Adam, you might have warned me."

"Not on your life. Haven't seen you blush in fifty years."

"Can you wonder, with you for a husband?" she replied. "But I must say they're all very kind, and I'm so glad I came. Do introduce me to that girl Edward's squiring. I'd like to look her over, for it's time he settled down like the rest of them."

But it wasn't that easy in the mêlée that followed, with so many of them passing in and out of the warehouse as they cleared the floor for the dancing that was to follow. He had a brief word with George, congratulating him on the smooth organisation of the dinner, and in tempting so many of them down to London. "Bright idea to have it right here, too," he added. "At a hotel or assembly rooms it wouldn't have been the same somehow. Hello, Milton, my boy, glad you could get here," and he greeted Deborah's husband, the journalist, who asked of George, "Have you told him yet?"

"No," George said, "I haven't had a minute. Tell him yourself and see what he thinks. He likes to pretend he's out of it but that's rigmarole. If we offered him a seat on the board he'd jump at it, wouldn't you, Gov'nor?"

"Don't deceive yourself as to that," Adam said, "I've done my stint. You're not thinking of enlisting Milton, are you?"

"In a way he is," Milton said, "but on a part-time basis," and as George moved away to welcome the five-piece orchestra they had hired, Jeffs said George had offered him a tempting screw to found and run a magazine for circulation within the network.

"Why, that's a perfectly splendid idea," Adam exclaimed. "Who thought of it?"

"Who else but Debbie? I earn a good living but the Street is a young man's life and a three-day week editorial job of that sort would be a wonderful standby. You approve of it, then?"

"Wholeheartedly," Adam said. "What will you call it?"

"We haven't decided. How about *The Swann Bulletin*?"

"Too dull," Adam said, "we've always had a reputation for quirkish titles. How about *The Swann Migrant*?"

Jeffs laughed, saying, "You really are on top of your form tonight, Gov'nor."

Henrietta, he noticed, was surrounded by wives and daughters, and he needed a breath of fresh air, so he slipped out into the yard and stood by the old horse-trough, reviewing a scene bathed in silver moonlight, with the outline of the new buildings stark and clear against the sky and, hard to his left, the slender tower of the belfry that was still the ark of the tabernacle as far as he was concerned.

Moved by an impulse he drifted across to it, aware of stirrings and giggles in the patches of shadow where, no doubt, some of the younger ones were making the most of their opportunities. He went in and tackled the winding stair, needing no light on ground as familiar as this and stumping his way up to the queer, octagonal room at the summit, where the door stood open and moonlight flooded the floor about the narrow casement. And then he stopped, sniffing Turkish tobacco and vaguely aware of a figure standing by the embrasure, looking out on the wide curve of the Thames. He said, jocularly, "Hello there? Who's been sleeping in my bed on this night of nights?"

The figure turned, moving into the moonlight and he saw to his surprise that it was Edith, her mantle thrown over her shoulders and a cigarette in her hand.

"You? Well, I don't know! What drew you up here, I wonder?"

"Memories, mostly. Whenever I thought of you in the old days, and it was every day before I married Tom, it was always here, Adam. Never at 'Tryst', and never out on the network," she said.

"I didn't know you were a smoker."

"Just occasionally, when I want to think. They're Turkish. Will you have one?"

"No, thanks, I'll stick to my cheroots," and he lit one, blowing the smoke up to the cobwebbed rafters as he said, gaily, "Edward introduced me to that girl of yours. She's a rare beauty, Edith. Tom would have been very proud of her."

"Yes, he was," Edith said, "although he didn't have long with her. He died before she put her hair up."

He might have been wrong but he thought he noted a drag in her voice, enough to prompt him to say, "You still miss him terribly, don't you?"

"Yes, I do. I thought it would get a little easier every day but it doesn't. Times like this, when all the survivors get together, are the worst. It wasn't so bad when the boys were at home but they had to move on. I was glad when George gave them a chance to prove their mettle in a busier sector."

"Well, you've got Gilda home now, I hear."

"Gilda isn't the same, Adam."

"How do you mean?"

She turned, drawing thoughtfully on her cigarette. Its aromatic whiff reminded him, momentarily, of the military base at Scutari, where he had spent a month recovering from a wound received in the Sebastopol trenches. "Your boy has proposed to her, Adam."

"He has? Well, I'm delighted to hear it, and Hetty will be too. She has a great deal of respect for you Edith, and I don't have to tell you how pleased I should be to acknowledge a daughter of yours as my own."

"I didn't say she'd accepted him."

"A girl as pretty as Gilda would be sure to keep a man on a string for a month or two."

"There's more than that in it. Gilda . . . well, she's different somehow. Very sure of herself. Too sure, I sometimes think. That's the penalty of over-educating a girl. It would take her a long time to settle down after all her travels abroad, and the kind of people she met and mixed with in France, Switzerland and Italy."

"Well, that's her prerogative. How old is she, exactly?"

"Twenty-two. She's already had half-a-dozen proposals. One was from a French count, I believe." Then, hesitantly, "I don't know Edward very well, Adam, but what I've seen of him I like. He seems a very practical lad, more like George than any of the others."

"He's practical all right. George tells me he's shaping up wonderfully."

"Sensitive? Easily hurt?"

"I couldn't say. No more or less than most lads his age. He's very dedicated to his work. That's all I could say. I didn't have much part in raising them, you recall. Right here was my family, up to the time I retired and by the time I did they had all grown up and most of them had gone."

"Well, I wouldn't like to see a boy of yours hurt or humiliated and I've even gone so far as to tell Gilda as much. If she means to marry him fair enough. If she doesn't I won't have her encouraging him too much."

It surprised him to hear her talking like this, indicating as it did the underlying reason for her presence up here alone, as if doubts concerning her daughter's romance had driven her here, clear away from the noise and high spirits below. He said, "Look here, Edith, don't you concern yourself. Edward's a grown man and must learn to look to himself in matters of this kind. Was that why you came up here? To mull it over in solitude?"

"Partly," she said, "but not altogether. I had a queer

sensation down there tonight, when they were all congratulating one another on the past, present and future
prospects of the firm. I can't describe it, exactly, but it
wasn't altogether removed from – well – a sense of foreboding. So silly on an occasion like this."

"Not so silly," he said. "I've had a niggle or two under
my own ribs just lately. Not about the firm, however,
about the country generally."

"Tell me."

"I can't, or not precisely. It's old age, I daresay, and
the rate of change I see about me. But the fact is, as I see
it, we're too damned confident, the whole boiling of us.
We've all had a wonderful run for our money, had it all
our own way for too long. As a trading nation, I mean. I
thought we would slow down and take stock when we got
that drubbing from the Boers a few years since but we
didn't. The minute we had 'em on the run we were the
same arrogant, overweening tribe of chest-beaters. It
never seems to occur to anyone that the Continental and
American competition is getting tougher every day.
There's a lot I don't like about the international scene
for that matter. These constant confrontations between
Russia, Austria, Germany and France, and our politicians'
tendency to stick our nose in, instead of minding their
own till and exploiting the tremendous potential in the
dominions and colonies. The Continent's business isn't our
business, and I never did trust the French any further than
you could throw the Arc de Triomphe!"

He had succeeded in cheering her up anyway for she
laughed, saying, "You don't change a bit, Adam. And
I'm glad, and so is everyone down there. Come, I've not
had more than a word with Henrietta, and if anyone finds
us up here in the dark the old rumours will start circulating
on the Swann grapevine."

"Not," he said, mournfully, "at my age. At yours,
maybe, for you don't look more than forty in moonlight,"
and he took her hand and led her across the threshold and
down the stairs into the brightly-lit yard, thinking as he

did of a time she came up here with some tomfool notion
of emigrating to Australia simply because she believed
herself hopelessly in love with him. 'But that was before
she met Tom,' he thought. 'After that I might not have
existed,' and it prompted him to ask her, as they crossed the
yard to the warehouse, whether she had ever told Gilda and
the boys about Tom Wickstead's past as a man who had
once walked abroad with a revolver strapped to his
wrist. "Never," she said. "What purpose would it have
served? Besides, he never was a bad 'un in that sense, not
even before I met him. He was only hitting back at a
society that had stamped on him and his. His father was
transported for twelve years for stealing a piece of cloth
to make clothes for his mother and sisters. His mother
died in the workhouse at thirty-five and his eldest sister
went on the streets, for it was a case of that or starve.
Incidentally, he named Gilda for her. It's ironic how the
wheel turns full circle, don't you think?"

He had no time to answer for, seeing them, half-a-
dozen people converged on them, but he thought about
it at intervals all the evening and later when Henrietta
said, as they undressed, "I had a talk with that girl of
Edith's. She seems terribly brainy – Deborah's sort of
braininess. I do hope Edward hasn't bitten off more than
he can chew."

He replied, a little grumpily, "If he has he can spit it
out. The same as we all have to from time to time. Turn
out the light, woman. I'm dog-tired and you ought to be."

And then, as she climbed into bed and settled herself,
he forgot Gilda and Edith too, his mind basking a little
in the splendour and fulfilment of the Jubilee, and all it
represented in terms of personal and collective endeavour.
As to the nation, he supposed it was like Edward, mature
enough to absorb any shocks and disappointments that
lay ahead and equipped to ride them out, the way he had
done since he came to this city to prise up a few of those
golden paving-stones they were always talking about in
the shires.

PART FIVE

Journey into Chaos

I

Win One, Lose One

IN THE LONG AFTERGLOW OF HER LIFE, WHEN warmth had stolen back into her bones, when she had adjusted, more comfortably than most women who had worn crinolines, to short skirts, sounding brass and the rootlessness of the post-war era, Henrietta Swann would challenge those who claimed that the old world died in August, 1914. Her memory calendar was at odds with those of her contemporaries, showing a discrepancy of some five years, and there was a logical reason for this. For Henrietta the onrush of the terminal sickness of the age began as early as the summer of 1909, when the first of a string of domestic catastrophes occurred, shattering her serenity and undermining her abiding faith in her destiny. And after that, in quick succession, came a long run of crises demanding more and ever more of her impressive stocks of resilience, and resource – and all this at a time of life when one could reasonably look for repose. For she had then entered upon her seventieth year and was ready, if only occasionally, to sit back and assume the role of an interested spectator.

It was not to be, however, and perhaps the scurviest trick fate played upon her at that time was to open the year with a discharge of Swann rockets designed to light up the achievements of the dynasty, enabling her to look back into the past and forward into the future with a grandiloquence that Adam had always found comic, particularly after she passed her sixtieth birthday and he came to see her as equating, on county level, with Victoria in that photograph showing her surrounded by a swarm of dutiful, popeyed relations, the least of them a duke.

The family firework display began on New Year's Day when the newspapers carried reports, some of them flatteringly detailed, of sovereign recognition of Hugo Swann, Layer on of Hands. The bombshell was not entirely unexpected. His wife, Lady Sybil, had been over at 'Tryst' in late autumn, dropping mysterious hints on the subject but neither Adam nor Henrietta, or indeed anyone else outside Lady Sybil's exclusive charity circle, had regarded them as pointers to the fact that Hugo, least promising of all the Swann boys, would be the first to attain the rank of knighthood, and even when she saw it in print Henrietta wondered, a little fearfully, if there had not been an embarrassing mix-up somewhere and Hugo's name had emerged from the hat in error.

For it seemed preposterous to think of dear, bumbling Hugo, one-time athlete, sometime war hero, latterly, she gathered, a kind of doctor's auxiliary at a hospital, as *Sir* Hugo Swann. She had never been one to minimise the achievements of any of her brood. Indeed, it had crossed her mind many times during the last thirty years that her husband's contribution to commerce should have earned him an official accolade of some kind. But Hugo, even in his heyday, when he sometimes brought home two trophies a week, had never figured in her dynastic daydreams. There was no reason why he should when he faced such formidable competition on the part of his brothers, three of them well advanced upon their careers and winning mention, from time to time, in the national press. Alex had earned his first headline as long ago as 1879, when he sent home an account of that battle with the Zulus at a place with an unpronounceable name. George had fought his way to the forefront on four wheels and carried, or so it seemed to her, the whole country with him, for she never saw a motor-bus or a motor-car nowadays without reminding herself that the very first of them, so far as she was aware, had arrived in England with George's baggage when he landed with his Austrian bride in 1885. As for Giles, his present place in the high counsels of the nation could have been predicted when he was a boy of thirteen, reading his way through his father's library at the rate of one tome a day. Even Edward, they said, nine years younger than Hugo, was considered a gifted engineer and currently a Swann viceroy in one of the network's most lucrative sectors. Was it to be wondered at that she had overlooked Hugo, a man who walked with a white stick and was followed about by an ex-rough-riding sergeant who barked like a collie every time his master had need of him?

Yet there it was – Sir Hugo Swann, honoured, it seemed, for his work among the human wreckage of that awful war in South Africa, the war that everybody had thought so splendid at the time but which was now dismissed as a faraway squabble that had been settled, in the way of all these colonial squabbles, by Earl Roberts' tact, Lord Kitchener's scowl and promises of good behaviour all round.

Even Adam, so rarely surprised these days, had been stunned by the news yet not so much as not to quarrel with the rumour that the honour was the result of canvassing behind the scenes on the part of Lady Sybil. He said when this story was relayed to him, "Once in a while, every hundred years or so, those honours brokers reward someone deserving by accident. Go down to Netley and watch him at work on patients. I did just that, admittedly out of curiosity, and I came away humbled. I'm not a religious man but I believe in some miracles. One has to when one hears a blind man preach a sermon through his fingertips."

He did not say this to her but his comments were repeated to Henrietta by Debbie's husband Milton. Neither did she take it up with him later, sensing that she would not comprehend any clarification he condescended to make and also (he was oddly touchy in some areas) that questioning on the subject would embarrass him. She was prepared, as always, to take his word on matters that baffled her and assumed, from then on, that Hugo's endowments, unlike those of his splendid brothers, had been hidden from her by an inscrutable Providence.

Adam's verdict was only part of the truth. Lady Sybil had, indeed, been tireless on Hugo's behalf, but his selection from a swarm of probables was really another kind of miracle, brought about by a flash of inspiration in the minds of what Adam called the honours brokers and what others called the Faceless Ones; an inspiration, lighting up the imagination of men rarely responsive to romantic impulses and national moods. Men who, for the most part, were guided by motives far too complex to be comprehended by the man in the market-place, who might regard Hugo Swann's services to the nation as more deserving than, say, the transfer of a small part of a large fortune to areas where its arrival would make the maximum noise.

But circumstances, on this unique occasion, combined to answer Lady Sybil's prayers. When the list of candidates for New Year's honours were being considered it was apparent, even to the Faceless Ones, that to elevate them en bloc would be to give substance to recent murmurs that knighthoods had ceased to be earned with anything but hard cash, discreetly distributed, later 'discovered' by the press. Thus it was that Hugo came to be seen as a kind of minority candidate, isolated among a swarm of contenders whose prospects, on the face of it, were infinitely brighter, almost as though the adjudicators had reasoned: 'As God is our witness, his claims upon us barely exist. He was once acclaimed by the great unwashed as a pot-hunter. He was careless enough to lose his sight in a conflict that is now regarded as a national blunder. He has since buried himself alive in an infirmary without so much as an M.D. to explain his presence there.

He has no influence anywhere, has never contributed a pennypiece to either great political party and his nod in anyone's direction would count for nothing in the way of preferment. But stay! We are overlooking the obvious! Sporting laurels, sacrifice on the field of battle and political anonymity are the very ingredients capable of producing a compound capable of exploding the myth that our rewards are bought and sold.'

So it was that Hugo's name went forth and Lady Sybil, bringing the news to him, was taxed to convince him that it was deserved.

"*Me? Knighted?* But it's quite absurd, Sybil! What have I ever done to get knighted?" he asked her, quite amazed.

"Hugo, dear," she said, taking his hand, "it's for what you've done right *here*."

"Here? In Netley? A bit of massaging?"

"Yes, dear, for . . . a bit of massaging. *They* see it as important."

She realised she could never hope to make him understand that and did not try. She had watched him expand day by day, coming to terms with his disability in a way that a man learns to adapt to the customs of a strange country and create, within himself, a sense of belonging. He had learned to dispense with eyes, not so much because his other senses had enlarged themselves but because, through his bones, sinews and nerve ends, he had regained his old ascendancy over competitors in the field.

"I couldn't accept, Sybil," he said. "The fellows here would see it as swank."

"That isn't so, Hugo dear. You *must* take it. There's a very good reason why you should."

"What reason?"

"Because it signifies official acceptance of the work you are doing here. I don't mean personally, but in the wider sense, of men like you helping and encouraging one another, of establishing the value of expert massage inside the medical profession, of proving that a man without sight can play a useful part in society. That's why I insist you accept, Hugo."

It was, of course, a shoal of red herrings. She did not give a button about the abstract aspects that tripped so glibly from her tongue but she understood the regenerated Hugo Swann well enough to realise that these were the likeliest means of overcoming his essential humility and she was right. He sat thinking a moment, hands resting on his enormous thighs, and presently he said, "Would it help to persuade them to set up that training centre I suggested? Would it convince some of those stick-in-the-mud army surgeons that a masseur and an osteopath isn't necessarily a quack?"

"I think it would."

"Very well, then. I'll accept."

"Thank you, Hugo. I knew you'd be sensible," and she was glad she could safely indulge herself in a smile of triumph and went her way rejoicing. For although she was glad for him she was even more relieved for herself, seeing the recognition she had won for him as the last and most impressive of the string of penances laid upon her for her share in encompassing his fate. She had no way of knowing that his enlargement since he had been caught up in rehabilitation work had been brought about by an almost parallel process, that his successes here had in themselves been acts of atonement for taking the life of a child on a ridge thousands of miles from Southampton Water. It was some time since he had been troubled by the dream that had returned to him time and again over the years, a dream of looking down on the face of an enemy in a slouch hat who lay flat on his back staring sightlessly at the sky and then, although manifestly a dead face, transformed its features into those of a child he had never seen, his own seven-year-old son.

2

The second rocket soared a month or so later when Edward, coming into the hall at a run, announced that Gilda Wickstead had at last capitulated and agreed to marry him at Easter.

The news, long expected but unaccountably delayed, delighted Henrietta, so much so that she found she could forgive the stupid girl for keeping everybody on tenter-hooks for the better part of six months. It was a relief to see the youngest of her sons released from the private pur-gatory to which that Wickstead girl had consigned him, and there had been times, over the last few months, when she could have shaken his beloved until her teeth rattled, notwithstanding her sincere regard for Edward's mother-in-law elect.

Time and again she had tried to coax from Edith the source of her own and her handsome daughter's reserva-tions on the match but no important information had been forthcoming. Edith hinted that the girl had been spoiled, first by her father, then by her brothers, that she wasn't ready for marriage, that she might not be content to vegetate in the English provinces after so much acclaim in foreign cities, and even that Gilda might have ambitions of her own that did not include marriage. It was this hint that alarmed Henrietta, for she had a suspicion that Edith, known to be sympathetic to the Pankhurst hell-raisers, was hinting that Gilda was a suffragette, as if two martyrs in one family wasn't enough to get on with. But Edith, challenged on this point, smiled and shook her head.

"A militant? Our Gilda? No, you can put that aside, Henrietta. If Gilda campaigns it will be for Gilda."

It was strange and rather chilling, Henrietta thought, that a mother could talk that way about her daughter, almost as though she neither liked nor trusted her. Gilda was exasperating, certainly, and probably more experi-enced mashers than Edward had succumbed to her undeniable charms, but she wasn't unlikeable, or even particularly vain. Reluctantly, for Henrietta was very fond of Edith, she put it down to maternal jealousy, of the kind she herself had sometimes felt (although never admitted to) for Helen and Joanna, when they were young, slim and pretty, and licensed by a tolerant father to play fast and loose with a troop of young gallants in a way that would never had been allowed a generation before.

But then, just when Henrietta was beginning to resign herself to having a bachelor son at the tail of the family, everything sorted itself out and she was plunged into preparations for what she thought of as the last of the first generation weddings, and grandchildren's weddings were not the same, for you hadn't the fun and the bother of helping to stage them. Henrietta always put as much effort into her sons' weddings as those of her daughters. It was a wonderful excuse to try out the very latest fashions seen in one or other of the dozens of costumiers' catalogues that found their way into 'Tryst' at all seasons of the year.

Her pleasure might have been muted had she known the background of Gilda Wickstead's hesitation, aired during a rare, serious discussion between mother and daughter a day or so before Edward came pounding into the house with news of his reprieve.

Edith had not enjoyed watching the son of her oldest and dearest friends waiting on her doorstep. Like Henrietta she would have preferred to take some positive action calculated to hasten a climax. Nothing would have given her greater satisfaction than seeing Gilda marry into the Swann family but all her life, as regional manager, as wife and as mother, Edith Wickstead had been excessively irritated by ditherers.

Just as Henrietta would have liked to have shaken a decision out of Gilda, Edith was sometimes tempted to apply a spur to Edward. Ordinarily, and she had got to know him very well during his managership of her old territory, he was a very practical young man but her daughter's presence seemed to reduce him to the status of a minor flunkey privileged to serve royalty. And this, she had long since decided, was quite the wrong approach to make to a girl of Gilda's temperament. She would have liked to have said to him, "Look, Edward, for everybody's sake, but mostly your own and hers, tell the girl to make up her mind on the spot. You've a great deal to offer, and all she is bringing to you are looks that won't last her a lifetime! If she turns you down then go out and find somebody who will make you a better wife, lad. If she accepts then in heaven's name assert yourself. A man who doesn't won't get far with our Gilda!"

In the event it was Gilda who herself raised the matter, admitting that 'she was fond of Edward but that was as far as it went'.

"Then it's not far enough," Edith said tartly. "Your commonsense should tell you that, girl!"

And Gilda replied, with one of her superior smiles that made Edith regret yet again Tom's insistence, before he died, that she should receive the best education they could afford, "On the contrary, Mamma, it's my commonsense that urges me to marry Edward as soon as maybe. Before he goes off the boil, that is, for I'm not likely to get a better offer here or abroad. I surely don't have to tell you the Swanns are better off than anyone else we know."

The cynicism implicit in the girl's reasoning was so much at odds with Edith's character that she came close to boxing her ears but restrained herself, saying, "That's no way at all for a girl your age to talk, Gilda! Either you care for the boy or you don't, and money, given enough to be housed, fed and clothed, should have little to do with it!" She saw her daughter's eyes widen.

She said, wonderingly, "You really *believe* that, don't you? But then, you're a romantic, and I'm not, so we aren't likely to agree about it, are we? Was Papa penniless when you married him?"

Not simply poor, Edith reflected, remembering how, in effect, she had had to do the proposing, but a man with a police record, who had served time in broad arrows and had been planning an act of theft when serving as one of her waggoners. Suddenly it occurred to her that here was an occasion when part of the truth about Tom Wickstead, so carefully hidden from the children over the years, might have a beneficial effect upon his daughter. She said, quietly, "He was not merely poor. He had seen the inside of a gaol and was busy hauling himself up by his bootstraps!"

She had expected that the information, regretted as soon as it was out, would have shocked the girl half out of her wits. All it produced was a shrug of Gilda's pretty shoulders. She said, "Oh, that isn't new to me, Mamma. Papa told me how you met and what he had been only a month or so before he died."

"He told *you*! *All three* of you?"

"No, just me. I was named for his sister Gilda, wasn't I? The one who went on the streets while he was in prison."

"He told you that . . . everything? About his father being transported, about his mother dying in the work-house?"

"Yes."

"But why? I mean, what possible motive did he have? And for not telling me that you knew? Did you pass it on to the boys?"

"I didn't pass it on to anyone. He made me swear I wouldn't but in any case it isn't the kind of thing one would boast about, is it? I thought about it, however. I thought about it for years, all the time I was away from home and you needn't worry, I'm not ashamed of it. It taught me more about life than I ever learned from books."

"What did it teach you? What specific thing, Gilda?"

The girl looked at her levelly. "It taught me that the very worst thing that can happen to anyone is to be poor. That's why I've finally decided to marry Edward Swann."

So there it was, and sitting, because suddenly she felt a little dizzy, Edith groped for the key that opened a door on so much about Gilda she had never understood. Her ability to detach herself from her surroundings. The tight control she had over her emotions. Her unusual reliance on her own judgments, so unlike the boys who had always, to some extent, leaned on her when they were growing up and going out into the world. In her presence now she felt deflated and oddly helpless, and yet, behind her confusion, there was a glimmer of hope that out of this they might find a bridge to a better understanding. She said, finally, "You do what you think best, Gilda. In a way I suppose I've misjudged you. I loved your father to distraction but I can't help thinking it wasn't very wise of him to confide in you without consulting me first. He probably had a good reason, or what he thought was a good reason. You were always more important to him than the boys. Maybe he saw you as that sister of his, born all over again with a better chance. If you'll take my advice you won't tell Edward. His mother and father know but they can be trusted. All there is left to say is if you do marry Edward do your very best to make him happy and to have the kind of marriage I had, and Edward's father and mother have had all these years. It's the only thing worth having in the end."

She got up and walked upstairs to her room. Unaccountably, and for the first time in thirty years, she wanted to weep. To weep for Tom and his sister Gilda. For all the wretchedness and deprivation they had suffered under a social system that valued goods and money high above human beings. Perhaps Gilda had it right after all. Perhaps the only ultimate sin was poverty.

2

The Swann firework display continued, at intervals, all through spring and summer to a time when the first shades of gold were beginning to show on the curling edges of the 'Tryst' chestnuts and the early south-westerlies – 'Sussex skies' Adam called them – came probing over the county border, reminding him that it was time to get his apples in and give his ornamental lake its annual dredging.

Edward's wedding, staged, to Henrietta's delight, in Twyforde Church rather than in faraway Northamptonshire, was behind them now and everybody had stopped teasing Hugo by prefixing his name with 'Sir', a family joke that bewildered Hugo's punctilious soldier-servant, whose chest expanded an extra inch every time he looked at his master nowadays, giving substance to Adam's remark that the sergeant was the most outrageous snob in the country.

One golden September morning Henrietta put on her shawl and carried the post down to the terrace of the lake, where Adam was superintending the drainage, a task that needed considerable care if the sluices were not to jam and his paddocks flood. He looked like a ruffled old heron standing there in his rubber thigh boots, issuing gruff directions to the gardeners, and when she called to him he waded out and joined her on his stone seat fronting the water, a seat that had once formed part of the original embellishment of 'Tryst' in the sixteenth century and had been rescued from a potting shed behind the stables.

"The mail looked important," she said. "Here is your quarterly report, one from Alex, who has gone over to Ireland, and one from Margaret, addressed to you for some reason."

He opened Margaret's letter first because he could see she was curious about it and drew out a cheque bearing his own signature, together with a letter and a photograph of the latest addition to the Griffiths family, a fat and very jolly-looking baby sitting on the obligatory bearskin rug.

He said, passing her the photograph and pocketing the cheque, "I won't get any peace until I explain. They can't be well off, so I sent her twenty pounds for her birthday. She's returned it, as she has returned other cheques I've sent her. I suppose it's time I took the hint and stopped playing fairy godfather. That husband of hers seems to have a surfeit of Celtic pride. She says they are several pounds a week better off now, for Giles made over his M.P.'s salary to Huw as his agent down there."

"I didn't know they paid Members of Parliament!"

"They've just started to, and I don't care to think what might come of it. They're a shifty enough lot as they are. Pay 'em for going there and we'll have some real blackguards scrambling for the cash. However, it doesn't surprise me. About Giles, I mean. He'll see it as a way of helping them and pretending it's a rise. I daresay that prickly young Welshman will swallow that."

His attitude to his in-laws often amused her. Ever since Joanna had run off with Clinton Coles in the middle of the night Adam had referred to him as Jack-o'-Lantern. Helen's first husband had been 'That pill-rolling Bible spouter'. Now the handsome Huw Griffiths was 'That prickly Welshman'. He was a little gentler with his daughters-in-law; George's wife, Gisela, was generally 'That nice gel', and Romayne 'The flighty one'. Alex's wife, Lydia, was still 'The Colonel's daughter', Hugo's wife, 'The Prima Donna'.

So far he had made but one jocular reference to Edward's wife, commenting on the astonishing self-possession she exhibited at the wedding in April. He named her 'The Ice Maiden'.

Alex had interesting news. He had been sent to Ireland, he told them, by Lord Haldane, Secretary for War, to make a survey of territorial recruiting prospects over there if and when the Irish Home Rule Bill was approved by Lords and Commons. When Henrietta, like so many others baffled by what successive generations of politicians referred to as 'the Irish Question', demanded to know whether Ireland would become an entirely separate country if the Irish at last had their way, he said: "Not for defence. Haldane is far too sharp for that. There will always be some of our chaps over there, if only to keep an eye on Paddy."

She left him then, to mull over the latest news from the

network and he unwrapped the latest copy of *The Migrant*, for Deborah's husband, Milton, had used the name he jokingly suggested when the quarterly journal had been launched.

It was, he decided, a thoroughly workmanlike broadsheet, well-edited, well-printed and full of interest to anyone like himself. He read, among other things, that George had just commissioned his four-hundredth motorvan and sent it out to earn its bread in The Polygon. There was also a quarterly report by the Managing Director and he went through it word by word, telling himself that affable old George sounded oddly pompous when he committed himself to paper. He mused, tucking *The Migrant* into his boot, 'He's got a right to feel smug, I suppose . . . He was a big jump ahead of all of 'em twenty years ago, when nobody, least of all me, believed in that snorting great engine he brought home from the Danube. But it won't do for him to go on thinking nobody can ever catch him up. There's always an outsider with a new trick up his sleeve, and there always will be. If there wasn't commerce would be desperately dull and he'd be the first to realise it with all that energy . . . Besides, it's clear enough now that everyone is latching on to the potential of commercial motoring and his presence out there in front is a challenge to 'em . . .'

He gave some final instructions to the head gardener and turned to make his way up to the house for lunch, looking round him with pride of a kind he had never experienced beside the Thames, for up there someone was always around to disturb his sense of order whereas here, now that his estate had matured with its imported trees and shrubs, he could keep strict control on the landscape and intended to do so, as long as he lived. What would happen to it then he could only guess. The only one of his sons who had inherited his taste was Giles, and he doubted whether Giles would ever be tempted to turn his back on his lame ducks and become a country gentleman.

He was wondering, idly, what kind of instruction he could insert into a codicil to his will concerning the future care of 'Tryst' and its treasures when he saw Henrietta emerge from the house and make her way, very swiftly for her these days, across the forecourt, turning her head this way and that as though she was looking for him. The moment she saw him she broke into a little trot and he called, "What's the hurry, woman? I'm coming . . ." but then his sharp eye caught the glint of tears in her eyes and he hastened his step, saying, "What is it, Hetty? What's upset you so suddenly?"

She said, breathlessly, "Wanted to catch you . . . tell you before you saw her . . . Edith's here . . . She's got news . . . dreadful news . . ." and she broke off with a sob, tears running parallel courses down her cheeks.

"One of her boys . . . ?"

"No, no . . . it's Gilda. Gilda and Edward. Edward came to her yesterday . . . Gilda's gone."

"Gone? Gone where?"

"He doesn't know. She just . . . well, left, in the middle of the night. They had a tiff, nothing at all so he said, and when she didn't appear at breakfast he went to her room and found that her bed hadn't been slept in."

His immediate reaction was one of profound irritation that something as trivial as this, a tiff between newlyweds, should provoke such an emotional response in her but then his impatience transferred itself to his son and daughter-in-law. Surely they were old enough to know that young marrieds who occupied separate beds in separate rooms could expect to quarrel and say things to one another that they would afterwards regret.

"I don't know what Edith can be thinking of to come posting down from Northamptonshire on this kind of excuse," he growled. "As for you, Hetty, there's no sense at all in you upsetting yourself over something of this nature. How long have they had to get used to one another? Three months? Four? They have a quarrel and she decides to teach him a lesson by going home to mother.

How many times would you have gone at her time of life if you had a mother to run to. Or if you hadn't been reasonably certain I'd tan your backside when I came for you."

"I don't think you understand," she said, "for it isn't like that at all. Gilda didn't go to Edith's and Edward traced her as far as Dover. She's gone abroad and from the note she left it's quite clear she intends to stay there! Let Edith explain . . . I . . . I just wanted to warn you that she seems to regard it as her fault, and that's nonsense . . ."

He thought, savagely, 'What the devil is the matter with everybody? Am I the only one about who isn't going senile? Hetty getting hysterical over a farce like this, and Edith, as sane as any woman I know, blaming herself for having a feather-brained daughter . . .' And suddenly that vague sense of unease that had been prowling about under his ribs for a long time now found an outlet, driving the sparkle from the morning. He said, gruffly, "I'll have a word with her, but this won't amount to anything, take it from me," and he stumped on ahead, mounting the portico steps two at a time.

3

A sense of deep, personal failure had attended Edward from the very beginning, from the first moment they were alone after the hurly-burly of the wedding reception, the plaudits and the send-off of trailing the usual assortment of threadbare slippers and old boots. And it was the more oppressive because he had no previous experience of personal failure and would have found it very difficult to put into words, even to old George, in whose shadow he had stood ever since he could remember. For until then he had been concerned with tangible things, with nuts, bolts, gradients, time schedules, metal stress, trade potential and profit margins, inanimates that responded to patience and logic, whereas Gilda, the prize that had fallen to him so unaccountably, and after so long a siege, did not respond to approaches that had solved his problems as an engineer, a regional manager and master of his trade.

In the first few weeks of their life together he tried variants of all the methods that had served him so well in the past. Flattery, bribery and a careful study of the opposition's defences; aggression, compromise, the storming salesman approach, favoured by George, and even craftiness, but all in vain. He had won her on paper and lost her in practice. Her very passivity was her strength and his weakness. His experience with women was no more and no less than that of most young husbands, but he had a conviction that an accomplished masher would have retired baffled from the single room she had insisted upon occupying as one of the articles of her surrender. Yet this is not to say she had denied him access to her on any occasion. She betrayed no sign of fear, shame or even embarrassment that he had expected when she was obliged to share his bed during their touring honeymoon into the west.

In the first weeks of married life in their new Birmingham home, surrounded by the highly-trained staff he had enrolled for her, she spent the time he was absent in reading, walking and writing letters acknowledging their array of wedding gifts. When they were together, on excursions about the city, dining or merely sitting by the fireside, she performed all her domestic functions faultlessly, acceding to his every wish save the one that began to obsess him. All he was to be granted, it seemed, was her presence. A beautiful slave, obedient to his every caprice but enjoying, by some feat of legerdemain, far more freedom and personal privacy than was available to her owner.

Turned back upon himself by her stillness and chilled by her impersonal acknowledgment of his affection, he began to change in a way that his intimates were not slow to observe. He had always been an amiable young man, unruffled by minor setbacks of the kind that came the way of every regional manager in the course of a working day. Now he became strangely intractable, given to gruff replies and short, explosive bursts of temper. And at the same time his methodical approach to problems involving consultation with senior subordinates and customers became casual and off-hand as he took to spending much of his time closeted in his office, leaving all but the major decisions to deputies.

That was before the weekly letters from Paris began to arrive for her, the first of which merely excited his curiosity, so that when he asked who had written it she passed it to him and he ran his eye down the page, discovering that it was written in French and turned at once to the final page to look at the signature.

"Who is this 'Clothilde'?"

"A friend."

The reply was typical of her replies to all his questions, polite but yielding nothing.

"What kind of friend?"

"We shared rooms."

"Where?"

"At Tours, when I was teaching English at the University. Her name is Clothilde Bernard."

"How old is she?"

"About my age."

"What does she write about?"

"Mutual acquaintances. Shall I translate?"

"No, no, it doesn't matter, I didn't mean to pry."

"You are not prying."

He forgot the incident almost at once but recalled it when, almost as regular as a Swann hardware haul to Coventry, identical-looking letters arrived, always from Paris, always on a Wednesday and always, presumably, from Clothilde Bernard, so that his curiosity concerning them became so intense that, taking advantage of her temporary absence one day, he opened her bureau and counted them.

There were twelve, all looking alike save the most

recent delivery, a bulkier package containing photographs. He took them out and found they were not the ordinary amateur photographs he had expected but professional pictures, depicting what looked like some kind of entertainment, a melodrama presumably, for they depicted dramatic confrontations between a young, spade-bearded man wearing evening dress, and a young woman in a ballet costume. The little ballerina, it would appear, was being victimised in some way, for the man in the pictured numbered 'one' was threatening her, arm upraised. In the picture numbered 'eight' she lay dead at his feet and he was being arrested by gendarmes, a revolver in his hand. He made nothing of these but a ninth picture interested him. It was a still of a young actor in the costume of the eighteenth-century and he looked very elegant and self-assured. It was signed 'Etienne' and below, in handwriting so full of flourishes that it defied analysis, was some kind of greeting.

He returned the photographs thoughtfully, wondering at her preoccupation with this kind of frivolity for over here she had given no indication of an interest in theatricals. But curiosity nagged at him so persistently that, when a thirteenth letter arrived, he asked outright what subject it was that Clothilde found so much to write about. She answered, quietly, "As I explained, what goes on at the universities. She is now at the Sorbonne, teaching drama. Upstairs I have some photographs of her work. Would you care to see them?"

"Yes, I would. Very much."

She got up from the table and glided away, moving as noiselessly as she invariably did, and a moment later she was back with the photographs he had already seen. He made a pretence of looking at them and asked, "Who is Etienne?"

"Clothilde's brother."

"Another university tutor?"

"No, a professional actor. There he is playing Monsieur Beaucaire."

"What has he written under the picture?"

"*Souvent femme varie – Bien fol est qui s'y fie.*"

"What does that mean?"

"Woman often changes; he is a big fool who trusts her."

"Was the picture meant for you?"

"Of course."

"You knew him that well?"

"We were friends."

"Is he implying you broke a promise to him?"

"Perhaps."

"No, not 'perhaps'. Surely this is a direct reference to you getting married."

"He made no proposal of marriage to me."

It did not tell him much but enough, once he had left for the Swann Bull Ring depot, to disturb him deeply so that he began to ask himself if she had been as frigidly unresponsive with Bernard as she had been with him since he led her to the altar. His wits were very woolly these days and he realised that, without further elucidation, he could make no real attempt to gauge the relationship that existed between her and this actor fellow.

As the days passed, however, the shadow of Etienne Bernard, and the childlike trust he had reposed in her, began to gnaw at him until uncertainty became unbearable. A week later he went to her room with the intention of reopening the subject and persuading her, if that was possible, to tell him more.

It had been customary, until then, for him to tell her when he would come to her after she had retired but on this occasion he said nothing and did not even knock when he entered her room, discovering her seated at the dressing-table in a silk shift, engaged in brushing her lovely, corn-coloured hair. The sight of her, so bewitching and vulnerable, disarmed him and he moved over to stand behind her, taking the brush and applying it in imitation of her own sweeping strokes. She made no protest and he remarked no change in her expression as he watched the reflection in the mirror but then, bending low, he kissed the nape of her neck, saying, "I've been a bear lately, Gilda. I don't mind admitting that I was jealous."

"Jealous of whom?"

"That actor chap, Bernard, the one who sent you those pictures. It's foolish, I know, for whatever he meant to you or you to him is of no consequence now. How could it be. It was before we met."

She said nothing, so he went on. "Do you mind if I stay?"

"If you wish it, Edward."

Her voice was so impersonal that it stirred in him a kind of fury. "If I wish it? Good God, of course I wish it! We're man and wife, aren't we? If I had my way we'd share a bed every night!"

"But that was agreed, Edward."

"I know it was agreed but I never imagined it would be like this, living together under the same roof but behaving as if we hardly knew one another. It's the craziest thing I ever heard of and no man I know would put up with it."

At least he had made some small impression on her. Her face flushed and for a moment it seemed as if she would match his anger, but then, with a shrug, she stood up and when she turned her features expressed the familiar and dreaded blankness of all the other occasions he had come here as a supplicant. She said, "I will go to bed. Come back if you wish. The door will be ajar," and lifting her nightdress from the eiderdown where her maid had laid it she shrugged herself out of the flimsy shift and raised her arms to replace it with the linen gown.

It was the smooth ripple of her breasts that stimulated him to a degree that nothing else could have done. He saw it, swift and infinitely sensuous, as the lifting of a curtain in everything about her that he had coveted, won and was now so infamously denied. He said, huskily, "Wait, Gilda!" and reached out, taking the nightgown from her and tossing it aside, then seizing her and crushing her against him with such impetuous force that she cried out involuntarily as her flesh came into contact with his clothes. Half distinguishable words, fierce but caressing, accompanied the kisses he rained on her face and shoulders and then, gathering her up, he hooked the open door with his foot and carried her across the landing to his own room. Once here, momentarily undecided how to dispose of his prize, he paused and set her down, turning his back on her for a moment to slam the door and turn the key in the lock.

The click of the tongue slipping home had a curious effect on him, proclaiming perhaps his unexpected victory over her reservations and his own apparent mastery of the situation. He said, gruffly, "Like it or not you'll stay here tonight," and began to pull off his clothes, tossing them in a heap on the floor.

She said, still very quietly, "No, Edward, not this way. I had your promise," but the sight of her standing there stark naked and proposing terms for a conditional surrender increased his sense of outrage. He found he was able to look at her in a way that had never been possible before, objectively and impersonally rather than the summit of all he had ever hoped for from women. His eyes took in every part of her, not sensually, as in her room a moment ago, but coolly and almost mockingly. He went on undressing but less hurriedly, retrieving his jacket and waistcoat from the floor, putting them over a chair and saying, as he sat to remove his boots, "Sometimes I can't imagine why you married me. Since you have, I've rights to exercise whenever I choose."

She remained perfectly calm, a fact that secretly astonished him in the circumstances.

"I've never denied you access."

"Aye, but always on your terms."

"On terms we agreed."

"I renounce them."

He had got as far as removing his trousers and she had him at a disadvantage. Her movement was like the spring of a cat. Before he could regain his balance she was at the door, had turned the lock and laid her hand on the door knob.

He caught her before she could pull it open, seizing her round the waist and dragging her back into the centre of the room where she writhed from his grasp and made as though to try again but he shot out a hand and caught her by the ankle so that she fell flat on her face, a flailing arm coming into sharp contact with the fender.

Her fall, and the metallic clang of displaced fire-irons, brought him up short so that he paused, suddenly aware of the farcical element in the quarrel, she sprawled naked on the carpet, he half entangled in his trousers.

"You aren't hurt, are you?"

She rose to her knees, her left hand holding her wrist where it had struck the metal. She looked so childish and pitiful that shame invaded him. The light of the bedside lamp fell on her back and her crouching attitude, with her hair touching the carpet, suggested the pose of a wounded animal.

"Gilda, it doesn't have to *be* like this! I'm sorry I treated you that way but in God's name try and understand how I feel. I love you and want you. Why can't we be like any other married couple? In God's name, why not?"

She rose slowly to her feet, still massaging her wrist.

"Let me see your arm."

She turned facing him and her eyes were blank.

"Do what you have to and let me go back to my room," and she began to walk slowly towards the bed.

Anger ebbed from him. Submission, on these terms, wasn't worth exacting. Sullenly he unlocked the door and threw it open.

"I'm damned if I'll beg, not even from you – wait, you can't go like that," and he stepped out, crossed the landing and entered her room, retrieving her nightgown and returning with it. She took it wordlessly and slipped it over her head. Then she went out, closing the door.

*   *   *

The moment he was certain she was not in the house he forced himself to think logically, rummaging in his mind for possible refuges at her disposal. He could think of none other than her mother's house in Northampton, so he went out breakfastless and summoned a cab to take him to the station, with every intention of boarding the first available train for Peterborough, and some half-formed plan of confronting her in Edith's presence. He did not know what her mother would make of it. He did not know what anybody would make of it. Their quarrel, seen in retrospect, was pointless and childish and while he had sacrificed his dignity she, in her mysterious way, had succeeded in rescuing hers. He was like a fugitive with the hounds on his heels, brought up short against a twenty-foot wall, and had no alternative now but to face the consequences of the ridiculous episode, already, no doubt, the subject of gossip among servants, who would know that she had fled during the night and that he had gone in pursuit without so much as a cup of coffee.

It was while he was standing in front of the departures board trying, with all his might, to focus his mind on the train schedules displayed there, that Garside accosted him, touching his cap and saying, "It's gone down, sir. I managed to get it on the workmen's train just after six," and Edward turned, wrinkling his brow and staring at the deputy stationmaster as if he had been a stranger and not a man with whom he had had scores of consultations concerning the despatch of freight since he came to the district as manager.

"What's that you say?"

"Madam's trunk, sir. The three-fifteen was on the point of leaving . . . matter of fact, I shouldn't have let her pass the barrier, but she was clearly in a great hurry to catch it. I got her on and put her trunk on the next train, as promised. It'll catch her up with that express label on it. Her cross-Channel doesn't leave until just after nine, sir."

His brain, completely fogged at Garside's initial approach, began to clear a little so that he was able to make some kind of sense out of the man's remarks. Gilda had come down here in the small hours with a trunk but had been unable to catch the three-fifteen save by jumping aboard when it was moving off on the whistle. To do this, she had been obliged to abandon the trunk and shout instructions for its forwarding to the obliging Garside, who had obviously recognised her and gone out of his way to help, probably because he regarded Swann-on-Wheels as one of the city's most important patrons of his railway. It was Garside's reference to the cross-Channel packet that baffled him. He said, carefully, "Is that three-fifteen a through train to the coast?"

"Yes, sir, though there's a longish wait at Victoria. Long enough for Mrs. Swann to get breakfast, I daresay."

"Thank you, Garside." He reached into his trouser pocket and drew out a half-crown.

"That isn't necessary, sir."

"Take it, man."

Garside took it with another salute. "Glad to help, Mr. Swann. The ladies will cut it fine, sir."

He went off and Edward, passing a hand over his unshaven chin, sat on a platform seat and made a tremendous effort to think clearly and purposefully. It was no use going after her. By the time he got to Dover (he remembered now that the early morning train from Manchester connected to Dover) she would be in France. It was no use trailing over to her mother's either or not yet, not until he had had time to think up some plausible story for Gilda's absence. As to the future, he had no wish whatever to explore that. The best course he could take now was to get himself shaved, make some kind of pretence to eat breakfast, and stop the news of her flight being broadcast to tradesmen who might well be numbered among Swann's regular customers. If that happened, the depot would get to hear about it within hours and the thought of moving among the clerks and waggoners as a newly-married husband, whose wife had fled from him in the middle of the night, was not to be contemplated.

He went out of the station, called a cab and drove home, telling the housekeeper that Mrs. Swann had been summoned away on urgent family business and that he had been to the station to send on her luggage. He had no means of knowing whether or not she believed him but she was a discreet woman and he could rely on her to relay the information, for what it was worth, to the other servants. She said, "The breakfast is cold, sir. Shall I get cook to send up some more?" and he said no, for he planned to follow Mrs. Swann after a visit to the depot, and would make do with coffee and eat on the train. He then dismissed her and went upstairs to shave, finding that he had to use extra care with his cut-throat for his hand was unsteady. He packed an overnight bag and came down again in ten minutes to drink a single cup of coffee. Then saying no more to anyone, he went out and walked the distance to the station. The depot could await a wire explaining his absence. In the meantime, the need to confide in someone was imperative and he could think of no one but his mother-in-law, Edith Wickstead.

2

Incident in Whitehall

HE WAS NOT ILL, OR NOT OF A SICKNESS THAT COULD be diagnosed and cured, yet those who remembered Edward Swann in the days of his apprenticeship, and his surge into the Westcountry with his brother George when the two of them had raised the eyebrows of every transporter in the country, began to think of him as a sick man for both his appearance and character had undergone dramatic changes in the last few weeks.

He had always been a ruddy-faced, well-set-up young man, quiet and deliberate in manner. Not too talkative, perhaps, but friendly enough, and a very good man to have beside you, behind you, or even over you in a crisis. He was more equable than George and more approachable than his father, someone who would always listen, who had time to spare for the lowliest employee in the sector, a gaffer, moreover, who was reckoned a first-class mediator in a local dispute and almost as good as his brother Giles at pacifying irate customers. Now there was hardly a trace of those characteristics that had played such a part in enabling this sector of the network to adjust to the 1905 realignment of frontiers and reshuffle of executives after the switch to powered transport. Moody and unpredictable, he slouched through his daily schedule like a sullen schoolboy harassed by an imposition, ranging off to the nearest public-house as soon as the yard shut down, not to royster, it was rumoured, but to sit in a corner drinking and snarling at anyone who offered to share his company.

The direct cause of the vast change in him soon got about, despite his mumbled stories of his young wife being on an extended trip abroad. "Completing her studies," as one senior clerk said to another when the subject was raised in The Funnel's counting-house, and his companion had winked solemnly as he said, "Studies in what, I wonder?"

It could not have been housewifery, for the Swann house at Edgbaston was closed and coming up for auction, its staff dismissed and its new furniture in store at the Bull Ring warehouse. When this proved to be more than a loading-yard rumour, and the young gaffer had taken to biting heads off in every direction, clerks, drivers, mechanics, waggoners and even customers shared the view that someone should take Edward in hand before the sector slipped to the bottom rung of the Swann ladder, to rub along with regions where the horse and cart predominated. Opinion was divided as to who that someone should be. One Barnes, a summarily dismissed loader at the yard, was heard to exclaim that it should be that flighty young wife of his, after she had been dragged home by the hair, given a hiding and put to work at milking the bile out of the gaffer. The senior clerk was more restrained. He let it be known that brother George should be informed of how things stood and summoned to give the region an old-fashioned going over. Older men said the Old Gaffer would have sorted it out in a trice, for he had always been partial to sacking from the top whenever things went awry in a particular region. None of these speculators were aware that George had already been called in and been told to mind his own damned business, that no one this side of the Channel knew where the flighty young wife could be located, that old Adam himself had made little or no headway with the boy and that Edith Wickstead (still 'Gaffer Wadsworth' to the oldest hands about the place) had twice waylaid her son-in-law and urged him to put her daughter out of heart and mind before his life went sour on him.

Edith came as near as anyone to making a breach in Edward Swann's glowering defences when she said, with her Yorkshire forthrightness: "The girl's not worth a glass of cold gin, lad, and I would have told you that before you married if there had been the slightest prospect of you heeding me. She was hopelessly spoiled from babyhood and had her own way in everything until her father died. By then it was far too late to get it into her head that she wasn't somebody very special, destined to become a great actress or a king's trollop."

It was the word 'actress' that made Edward look up and he at once demanded to know if Gilda had always had an ambition to go on the stage.

"It was one of her grander fancies and the most persistent of them. She appeared in school plays, and had a good deal of amateur experience abroad, I believe. But everyone knows that kind of life needs real talent and far more stamina than she possesses, drat her. I thought she had put aside all thoughts of it when she married. For security," Edith added, "she even had the gall to tell me that!"

Edward said, in a low voice, "She never pretended she was in love with me. She was honest in that respect. But I got the impression she preferred me to any other man she had met. I didn't know about that chap Bernard until later."

Edith had been on the point of interrupting and telling him, with some notion of shock therapy in mind, that what Gilda had preferred was not Edward Swann but Edward Swann's prospects, including his share in his grandfather's fortune but his mention of Bernard checked her.

"I never heard of anyone of that name. Who is he? And how do you come to know about him?"

He told her the story of the flow of letters from Bernard's sister, and the little he had learned from Gilda of the man who sent the inscribed photograph. "It was brooding about him that sparked off that silly row," he said. "I got it into my head that he had been her lover in France but I don't think so now. Since you mention her being obsessed with the stage other things seem to fit."

"What kind of things?"

"The kind of books she read, for one thing. Plays they were, mostly, by Shakespeare and so forth. And French writers too . . . especially a chap called Molly something."

"Molière?"

"Yes, that was it. She used to read him aloud when I wasn't around, or so the housekeeper told me. She was always dressing up, too. She'd spend hours up in her room, messing about with costumes of one sort or another. Not real clothes, you understand, but well – fancy dresses. As a matter of fact, I thought it odd that she left most of her own clothes behind and took all those costumes away with her in that trunk. Could it be that she was still set on being an actress?"

"I would have thought so once but not lately. There's no security on the stage and she's sharp enough to know that."

"But if she thought she was good enough – I mean, to become someone like Ellen Terry, wouldn't she have decided that money would come with success?"

"It's possible, but listen here, lad, I didn't hunt you down for the purpose of discussing my daughter's castles in the air but to persuade you to get a hold of yourself. You tell me you've had no success with your enquiries in France and I certainly haven't a notion where she is or what she's about. Neither do I care as things are, but your father and mother are my oldest friends and I feel badly enough about this to go to work on you. Sooner or later, if she doesn't turn up, you'll be well advised to get shot of her on grounds of desertion. It might take a long time but you're young enough to live through it. And for another thing, why don't you buckle to, and drown your misery in work instead of drink? That road is no way out, not your way at all events. I'd offer you a home with me but it's too far from your depot. Suppose you rent a house locally and I come over and run it for you?"

He shook his head. "It's kind of you, Edith, but I need time . . . time to ride it out, and either find her or forget her. It's not just . . . well . . . losing Gilda. God knows that's bad enough, and there isn't an hour when I don't think of her and want her. It's looking such a damned fool, knowing everyone at the yard and out on the network and in the business men's clubs about here sees me as someone who married a girl as pretty as Gilda, showed her off everywhere I went, then woke up one morning to find she'd ditched me like an old pair of boots."

He paused frowning. She said nothing so he went on, "I don't have to tell you the name of Swann stands for something up here. The Gov'nor and George saw to that. How will people think of us now, I wonder? Or me particularly? A man who couldn't even stop his own wife walking out on him after five months of marriage?"

"Most people won't think of it at all, lad. Most people have forgotten it already. Or would do if you'd let them."

"But how am *I* supposed to think and feel in these kind of circumstances? I mean, what does everyone expect me to do? Dance a jig in the Bull Ring?"

"I imagine people who count expect you to write her off like a bad debt. One that costs far more to collect than it's worth, and it's her mother who is telling you this. Those letters you mentioned. Did you try the address on them?"

"I'm not that much steeped in liquor," he said, with a touch of his newly acquired asperity. "I wired and wrote five times, and when the letters came back I hired a man to go over there and check on the place. The woman who wrote to her had gone, leaving no forwarding address."

"And the universities? At Tours and in Paris?"

"He went there too. They couldn't help, or maybe they didn't choose to."

"Well, at least promise me one thing. Keep in touch, and come over for the weekend whenever you feel like it. Maybe you won't but it's better than going home to 'Tryst', and a lot better than drooping about by yourself with your head in a tankard."

*   *   *

A few days after his conversation with Edith he turned a corner and came headlong into collision with the realities his mother-in-law had urged him to face.

It came about in a curious way, when he found himself in the New Street area one Saturday afternoon, with more than two hours to wait before George's train arrived. He had been surprised when George had wired saying that he was coming up for the weekend. He knew that his brother was heavily engaged with what promised to be an important development in powered transport, although it was one that, so far as Edward could determine, was unlikely to profit private enterprise. George, it was whispered, had at last talked his brother Alex into arranging a test-haul, made under the auspices of the Automobile Association, of a battalion of Guards from Aldershot to Hastings in a variety of motors, and Edward could only suppose that George saw advantages in the publicity. He did not know that Edith had written to his brother the day she had left Birmingham, urging the Managing Director to look to his crumbling defences in The Funnel.

Time, now that Edward had lost all interest in work, hung tediously on his hands. He spent most of Saturday morning in a public-house, had lunched there on bread and cheese and finally drifted down to the station where, checking George's wire, he noted that he could not arrive until around four in the afternoon. It was now two o'clock, and his fuddled head, and the sour taste on his tongue, disinclined him to return to the bar. It was then, only a few steps from the station entrance, that he saw the bill-boards outside the Biograph Theatre.

He had heard, in a general way, about these biograph entertainments, moving pictures depicting news and fictional tales flashed on a screen in a darkened auditorium, but he had never had the time or inclination to visit one. Grudgingly he examined the advertisements outside the narrow little hall, wedged between a warehouse and a shop, a display of garish posters proclaiming the new wonder of the age and hung in a frame, under the canopy, photographs of the kind of entertainment promised within. It was some sort of desert epic, featuring Arab sheiks and camels, and away in the back of his mind he connected them with those pictures Gilda had been sent from France. The similarity caused him to take a closer look and he isolated a picture about six inches square, showing a fierce-looking Bedouin photographed in the act of thrashing a prostrate woman with his whip.

Like the pictures in Gilda's letters it had about it the trappings of improbable melodrama. The gestures of the victim, hands raised, eyes wide with appeal, dress disordered, revived memories of the entertainment he and his brothers had once derived from a magic lantern, and he was on the point of moving on when something in the woman's face checked him so that he looked again, peering very closely at the blurred image, then wrinkling his forehead with disbelief.

The woman on the ground reminded him vividly of Gilda. She had Gilda's wealth of hair and Gilda's smooth, oval face. She had Gilda's petite figure, too, and he thought, 'It's almost surely a fancy . . . I'm beginning to have hallucinations . . .' But he paid his money and went in none the less, groping his way to a seat facing a blank screen centred by a small, circular light. Then the hall went even darker and somewhere towards the front a piano began to tinkle as a series of flickering images trooped on to the screen. Isolated here in the dark he forgot his miseries, his lifelong interest in technology absorbing him as he witnessed a moving photographic record of a steeplechase in which the horses seemed to

cross the screen powered by clockwork mechanism and all
the stewards and sightseers had the same jerky gait and
gestures, even when they raised and lowered their straw
hats. A mild sense of wonder invaded him, that it was
possible to make pictures move in this way, and he began
to enjoy the intimacy of the place as he watched first some
French Army manoeuvres, then a seaside scene and
finally a swift tour of the Earl's Court and Anglo-French
Exhibition.

The round-up of news pictures was followed by a display of conjuring and then some mimed comedy in which
an actor fell into a pond, and, having emerged, pranced
about on the bank shaking his fist and mouthing oaths at
mocking witnesses. Then the screen went blank for a
moment and after an appreciable pause projected a
frame announcing the main attraction, subtitled in
English, *The Terror of the Desert*.

It was, Edward soon decided, a very silly story, concerning what seemed to be an expedition into the Sahara,
attended by a caravan of camels and horsemen, and led
by a wildly gesticulating young man who spent most of
his time spurring up and down the line of march mouthing directions at his underlings. Once, when the face of
the leader was grossly enlarged, it had about it the same
hint of familiarity but again he dismissed this as fancy or
coincidence. It was only when, after the travellers had
encamped at an oasis, and the horseman entered his tent,
that he sat up with a jolt that almost projected him from
his seat. The woman rising from a silken couch was either
Gilda or Gilda's double. He identified her not only by
face and figure but even more surely by her mannerisms
and that gliding walk of hers.

It was an extraordinary sensation sitting there watching a shadow play involving the woman he had loved to
distraction, since the moment he met her at Edith Wickstead's home nearly two years ago. It was as though he
was dreaming an exceptionally vivid dream, in which
were incorporated elements of amazement, a deep yearn-

ing and the wildest kind of farce, far more improbable than the scene in his room the night she left home. But then, before he could determine whether or not he was in the grip of some self-induced deception of the senses, the action of the epic changed and the oasis was attacked by a horde of Arab horsemen, who succeeded in scattering the expedition and abducting Gilda, who was carried away on the saddlebow of a bearded chieftain, whose eyes rolled like those of a man in the grip of an epileptic fit.

There followed a short series of scenes, more or less connected, showing the chieftain's impetuous siege of his prize and her ultimate consignment to the harem where, in the presence of half-a-dozen fat, inscrutable-looking women, she alternately raised her hands to heaven and collapsed sobbing on a couch. This orgy of despair lasted, perhaps, five minutes, before the Arab chieftain arrived with the obvious intention of thrashing his captive into submission but hardly had he begun the work when the gesticulating horseman turned up again, firing endless volleys of shots from his revolver and accounting, so far as Edward could judge, for rather more than half the population of the town. The chieftain went down as he tried to escape with the struggling Gilda, after which the cameras played on a fond reunion scene, with Gilda fluttering her eyelids as if they had been automatically-operated blinds, and the gallant pistoleer kneeling on one knee and running a scale of kisses up and down her arm.

Before he could emerge from his daze of incredulity the screen went blank and the lights came on and everybody around him got up and went out into the daylight. He had no power in his legs to follow them but sat there with his lips parted, gazing up at the blank screen, until a man in a rusty-looking frockcoat touched him on the shoulder and said, civilly, "Nex' show five o'clock, sir. Rich, weren't it?"

Edward hauled himself to his feet and said, "That . . . that actor and actress, do you know them?"

The man looked almost as astonished as he felt and

replied, "Lor' no, sir, I don't *know* 'em. I mean, 'ow would I? It's a French reel, rented for publick exhibition . . ." but then, "Wait a minnit tho', I got the contrac', 'aven't I? I'll 'ave a squint if you can 'old on a jiffy. Alwus 'as the names o' the leading actors on the contrac'." He pottered off into his little office under the balcony where the projectionist was housed, emerging again with a document that resembled a conveyance. "Now let's see. *Terror o' the Desert*. Made in Paris, like I said, tho' I dunno how they managed for sand and whatnot. They get up to all kinds o' tricks over there, same as the Yanks. Made by a cove called Jules Lamont, wi' – here you are, sir, – Monsewer Bernard Villon an' Mamerselle Fantine Grenadier. I remember we've rented several wi' the same team and the customers like 'em, judging by the takings."

"That picture you have in the foyer . . . the one of the two of them, could I buy it?"

"*Buy* it?" The man scratched his head. "Well, I dunno. I don' see why not, seeing this is Sat'dy, and we got to send this lot on to Mr. Hamilton's Picksherdrome at Wolver'ampton tomorrer. But they woulden miss one display picsher. What do you say to 'alf-a-dollar, sir?"

Edward gave him half-a-crown and they went into the foyer together where the manager removed the picture from its frame and handed it over. Edward walked blinking into the daylight and down to the station hall, noting that it wanted but twenty minutes for George's train to arrive.

He sat on the seat he had occupied the morning of her flight and studied the picture anew. It was like Gilda and yet it was not. The delicate moulding of her features were disguised under what might have been a thick coating of actor's greasepaint and distorted, to some extent, by her simulated expression of terror or loathing. She looked a little like a doll conceived by some malevolent scarer of children and yet one knew, at a glance, that she was play-acting and that the agonised look was a pretence and a poor one at that. He thought, dully, 'It's her right enough and she exchanged me for this . . . this mummery . . . She threw over the name Swann, and even the name given her by her parents, for one that goes along with this kind of nonsense . . .' Suddenly he was persuaded that it was not love for Bernard or anyone else that had urged her to decamp with that trunkful of theatrical clothes but the allure of seeing herself in this kind of role, a shadow on a screen, to be gaped at by strangers in places like that seedy little hall he had just quitted. It seemed incredible to him someone sane could make such a choice but in a way, at some distance below incredulity, it fitted her personality, for it was really no more than a gross extension of the self-deception she had been practising ever since he had known her and almost certainly, if Edith was to be believed, since her childhood. The yearning to be 'someone special' had milked her of all her natural feelings and responses, of the capacity to love and be loved, of obligations to anyone other than herself and this, in a roundabout way, accounted for her woodenness towards a man she had married.

Painfully and vaguely repugnant memories of their brief association returned to him like clumsy fingers probing a wound. Gilda accepting a gift. Gilda at meals. Gilda, with her lovely hair spread on a pillow and her body beneath his, but always with that blankness behind her eyes, as if, at the very moment of coition, she was transforming him into the person of that prancing horseman or eye-rolling sheik. Or perhaps not even that. Perhaps she was visualising herself drooping about a stage tent dressed as an Arab houri, wooed and whipped by other shadows. But always as a person uninvolved in life as it was lived by everybody but 'special people', always pretending to situations in which she was never required to be involved emotionally and as he thought this a kind of shudder passed through him.

The sensation was like the quenching of an unbearable thirst, rich, satisfying and uplifting, so that his memory revived for him a story old Phoebe Fraser, nanny to all the Swanns, had once read him and his sister Margaret, a story called *Pilgrim's Progress* that had promised to be dull because it was holy but had proved surprisingly absorbing and adventurous as the hero, Christian, journeyed to the Celestial City. He remembered with surprising clarity how Christian had ascended the Hill of Difficulty with his burden and struggled upward to the cross where the burden fell away, tumbling down, down and out of sight and leaving the pilgrim untrammelled for the road ahead. Sitting here, with the hissing din of the station in his ears, he could identify with Christian at that very moment, a man miraculously freed of a weight so intolerable that it clouded his mind to the business of the day.

Deliberately, and with a kind of dedicated joy, he tore the picture into small pieces and let them fall on to the platform. Then he glanced up to see George's train sliding in and George's face scanning the platform, and he grinned. It wasn't often anyone saw old George looking bothered.

*   *   *

The brothers had always been close. Closer than any of the others save, possibly, Joanna and Helen, so that it did not surprise him much when George understood the intricacies of the story so readily. He said, as they sat over a pint in Edward's favourite snuggery, "I don't know . . . marriage is always a bran-tub to a man who is interested in his job. I was damned lucky, considering, remembering the gambles I took before I fetched up with Gisela. I've played the fool since, come to that, and might have again if I'd ever found time. Work, that's the best tonic in the long run." And then, giving his brother a shrewd look, "You're pretty much behindhand from all I hear. Maybe I can suggest a short cut or two. Or would you prefer some other distraction? A music-hall, maybe?"

"I'd like to go down to the yard, providing you'd come

along. God alone knows what's got buried in those in-trays," and for the third or fourth time since he had met George at the station he raised his left arm and scratched himself vigorously. "As if I hadn't got enough on my plate," he said, ruefully, "I caught a flea in that sleazy little theatre!" George, predictably, threw back his head and laughed and Edward joined him. It was his first laugh in a very long time.

It was coming up to midnight when they returned to the hotel after six hours spent unravelling the muddle that had accumulated since the day Gilda had left. He was very tired but pleasantly so, a different kind of tiredness from that induced by liquor and by his long self-pitying walks through city and suburban streets. He felt very sleepy and far closer to George than he had ever felt, judging himself extraordinarily lucky that his brother's visit had coincided with the moment of revelation. He said, thoughtfully, "Do you see any future in that moving-picture business, George? I mean, will it ever amount to more than a showman's stunt?"

George replied, "Oh yes, there's money in it now, and there'll be a lot more as time goes on. Those biograph theatres are mushrooming in the London suburbs but I wouldn't invest in it, although I've been urged to by several claiming to be in the know."

"Why not then?"

"I suppose because I never did derive pleasure from play-acting of any kind. Our sort can't, and I can tell you why. We're too curious to go behind the scenes and find out what goes on. And then there's the folk associated with theatricals. They're crazy, nearly all of 'em. I mean, who the devil can begin to understand what makes a fine-looking woman like your missus spend her life prancing around pretending to be somebody else?"

He stretched his legs, enlarging on his theme. "I re-member once when the Gov'nor took us all to our first pantomime at the Lyceum. It was before you were born, I imagine. Old Alex, Stella, me and young Giles. Must have been somewhere around Christmas 'seventy-four or five. 'Jack and the Beanstalk' it was, and all the others were nearly sick with excitement. I wasn't. The show itself left me cold but I remember puzzling all the way home how the hell I could make a beanstalk grow in front of an audience and still keep 'em guessing. I worked out that it must be by a system of ropes and pulleys, high up behind the proscenium arch. It's odd how different people can be inside one family. You're the only one I've ever really understood. I suppose that's why I caught on about how you felt in that picturedrome, weighing that woman's worth against the network." He sat thinking a moment. "Shall I tell you something else? When he was your age the Gov'nor had trouble with mother but he was luckier than you. Or more ruthless, maybe. He nursed her round to his way of thinking. Maybe, given time, you could do the same."

"I'll tell *you* something," Edward said. "I wouldn't bother to try. I'm over it, George, and through with it. She can go to the devil for all I care," and he broke off, stifling a yawn.

"Go and sleep it off, lad. I'll have a nightcap and follow on. We'll have another crack at that backlog tomorrow. Our way of going to church!"

Edward left him in the lounge and George was still there, puffing on his cigar, when he heard himself being paged by a boy in a pillbox hat. He called, "Hi, my name's Swann. Who's asking for me at this time of night?"

The boy said, "I don't know, sir. The night porter has the message if you'll ask at the desk."

He lounged over to the desk, thinking, "The Gov'nor once told me the network was a seven-day-a-week, twenty-four-hour-a-day job, and he was right." Having identified himself at the reception desk he was shunted on to the hall porter who said, "It's a telephone message, sir. It came in about ten o'clock. The lady asked if you would ring this number, no matter how late it was."

He took the slip with some disquiet, assuming it must be Gisela in some kind of fix, for she was chary of pursuing him on his frequent lunges up and down the country. But then he saw that it wasn't his own number but one of the inner London exchanges, and tipped the porter to call while he went over and retrieved the second half of his whisky and soda.

He recognised the voice as that of Milton Jeffs, his brother-in-law, and was at once alerted by the strained undertones in Milton's voice as he said, "*George?* Thank God! Debbie wants to speak to you. Something urgent . . . bad news, I'm afraid. She found out where you were from Gisela and badly wants advice. Wait, she's here now." Deborah came on the line saying, "Something bad has happened, George. It's Romayne. She's been seriously hurt in a suffragette demonstration outside Parliament this afternoon."

"Is that all you know?"

"She was knocked down and ridden over by a van."

"Is she with you?"

"No, no, she's in Westminster Hospital. George . . . she isn't expected to live."

He could tell by the catch in her voice that she was fighting very hard to control herself. He said, bracing himself, "Take it easy, Debbie. Take your time. Tell me how I can help."

"I don't know . . . I've been at my wits' end trying to trace Giles. He's away in his constituency on account of that trouble they're having in the mines and nobody seems to have heard of the telephone down there. I've wired his home, of course, and Huw Griffiths, but there would have been an answer by now if they had been anywhere in the Pontnewydd area. I felt so helpless and I have to get back to the hospital right away. I dare not tell the old folk so I rang Gisela and she told me where you were. We've got to find Giles and bring him home as soon as possible."

"The Welsh police could help . . ." but she cut in,

sharply, "No, not the police! Not even in these circumstances," and he guessed that the police had been involved in what had occurred outside the Houses of Parliament that day. He said, quickly, "I'll find him. I'll hire a car and drive down. That's by far the quickest, for it's Sunday now and God knows how long we might be getting there by train. I'll find him and bring him back. By tomorrow afternoon at the latest."

"Thank you, George. I'd be very grateful. There's at least a chance that way."

"She's that badly hurt?"

"A fractured skull, so the surgeon said. She's not regained consciousness."

"Leave it to me. Go straight back to the hospital. And Debbie . . . !"

"Yes?"

"Don't even try to notify the old people. They can't do anything to help, or not yet, and remember the Gov'nor is over eighty."

"Very well, George. I'll be here if I'm not at the hospital. They might not let me stay . . . there may be no point in staying anyway. You'd handle Giles better than any of us."

"Not better than you, Debbie. But I'd waste time coming to pick you up."

He replaced the receiver and stood thinking, holding the full import of her message at bay while he grappled with the practical aspects of a night journey by road to Wales. They could get a powerful motor somewhere. Edward would know where, and it would take them the better part of the night to reach the valleys. If they were lucky, and found Giles, they could refuel at the Cardiff depot and make a dash for London. But even if they encountered fair weather, unlikely at this time of year, they would be lucky to reach London before dusk. For a moment he toyed with the idea of going over Debbie's head and trying his luck with the Cardiff police but thought better of it. Giles was probably a marked man in that part of Wales, torn by strikes and political dissension. His wife, with gaol sentences behind her, and the current one hanging over her head under the 'Cat and Mouse' Act, whereby suffragettes on hunger strikes were released and re-arrested, was not likely to engage much official sympathy. It was better, in the circumstances, to rely on Edward's local contacts and his own ingenuity.

He knocked on Edward's door and, getting no answer, went in, finding his brother heavily asleep. He would have preferred to leave him sleeping and shift for himself but that wasn't possible. He needed Edward's local knowledge if he was to get hold of motor transport at this time of night.

He shook his brother awake. "Sorry, old son, but I'm off my own patch and badly need your help. Who do you know around here who would be likely to lend or hire us a Daimler, or some motor with that kind of performance?"

Edward said, rubbing his eyes, "Grayson, the big brewer, has a Panhard. He's an old customer. So is Sir Alec Gratwick, the draper. He runs one of those new Silver Ghosts. It's a corker. But what's happened? What do you want with a car?"

"I'll tell you later. How friendly are you with Grayson?"

"Not very. I know Sir Alec rather better."

"He's in politics, isn't he?"

"Yes. He'll be the next mayor."

"Liberal or Tory?"

"Liberal. Rabid. He stood for a local Parliamentary seat last election."

"Then he's our man. Would your association with him stand for rousting him out and asking a favour of this kind?"

"If it was important. He's a good sort and has been on our books since the Gov'nor's day."

"Then take me to him and leave me to do the explaining. I'll tell you as we go along."

2

The demonstration had the makings of a fiasco from the outset. The opposition in Trafalgar Square had been exceptionally noisy and abusive, and even Christabel Pankhurst, Mrs. Pankhurst's daughter, had been unable to get a hearing. It came on to drizzle as they formed up at the top of Whitehall, flanked, as always, by police, mounted and afoot, but the police seemed to be in a neutral mood today, trudging along with bored expressions and fulfilling their invidious role as a shield against the rowdiest elements of the crowd, who followed the line of march closely, eddying from pavements to carriageway and sometimes getting close enough to jostle.

Before they had passed the Horse Guards Romayne realised how mistaken she had been in parading and volunteering to carry a banner. She badly needed rest. Three days out of Holloway, following eight on a hunger strike, wasn't a long enough interval to recuperate, much less to march, and the banner, heavy with rain, was a terrible burden. At the House, when Christabel was due to speak again, she would have to surrender it to someone but in the meantime she thought she could manage, providing there were no mêlées. In the course of their shuffling progress to a point level with Downing Street she had a chance to look about her, peering closely at the cavorting bully-boys and asking herself yet again what it was that made them care enough to turn out on a rainy Saturday afternoon in order to abuse a few hundred women waging a lopsided war on a Government that called itself 'Liberal' and had proved, against all predictions, more implacable than its predecessors up to the landslide in 1906. It could not be fear, that she supposed accounted for most of the world's cruelty. Or envy, that accounted for the rest. It was probably no more than a mild revolt against the boredom and pinchpenny economy of their own lives, for most of the men in the crowd looked like mechanics or labourers, cloth-capped in the main and half-tipsy probably, seeing that it was payday for the majority.

The street sign 'Downing Street' reminded her of earlier, happier days of the crusade, when she and Debbie had earned their first arrest and spent their first fortnight in Holloway. That was getting on for five years ago now and she had been inside three times since then and twice subjected to forcible feeding before someone thought up that diabolical 'Cat and Mouse' scheme, a method of prolonging the agony capable of converting a dedicated campaigner into a morose fanatic. She had not reached that point yet but she was nearing it, her entire being rebelling against the demands made upon her physical resources over the last few months; and again she thought of her stupid rejection of the offer to go down to Lynmouth, where the W.S.P.U. ran a rest home for released hunger-strikers. In her present condition she wasn't much use to the cause, dragged down by this terrible yearning for sleep and stillness, for the predictability of a humdrum day in her own home, with the children and Giles if he could spare time to comfort and counsel her.

He would have counselled her now, no doubt, and extricated her from this untidy scrimmage, hailing a cab probably, and cheering her with news of progress on other fronts, but he had been away in Wales when she emerged, unexpectedly, on the eighth day of her twenty-eight day sentence, and she realised that he had troubles enough of his own, with the valleys in revolt, a lockout at the mines, and money to be raised for families who were pawning bedclothes in mid-winter to fortify their bellies against another week without wages.

She envied him his inner serenity, his ability, acquired little by little over the embattled years, to absorb the trials and tribulations of so many, allotting each its proper place in a scale of priorities. She envied him his resilience too, and the dynamo of nervous energy that enabled him to move through a working day that would have prostrated more robust men. He had the knack, that so few of the militants seemed to acquire, of isolating injustices like microbes under glass and studying each objectively before deciding how to deal with it. But when the moment came there was never a time when his coolness deserted him and he was tempted to abandon one plan in favour of another promising more spectacular results, a very common failing among crusaders.

Someone in the crowd threw an egg that struck the banner pole just above her head and spattered the shoulders of the woman in the rank ahead. The procession halted for a moment, closing up from behind and while she waited, resting the butt of the pole on the road, the remaining traces of the egg slipped down the pole and over her fingers, sliming them and making the pole difficult to grasp. The yearning for sleep made her senses reel and the shouts of the crowd, apparently blocking the march ahead and being broken up by mounted police, merged into a long, incessant roar so that she thought, distractedly; 'I'm going to faint and I mustn't faint here in full view of these louts. I must find Debbie and tell her to take my place for a spell, but how can I do that without abandoning this greasy pole . . . ?' And then, as though boosted from the direction of Trafalgar Square by a strong wind, the ranks behind her began pushing forward and the woman ahead remained stationary so that the section in which she was marshalled split and spilled sideways on to the pavement, the column losing cohesion as the banner was torn from her grasp. A bellowing policeman cantered past and she dodged to one side, brushing a lamp-standard with her shoulder. Behind it, leering at her like a centaur, was a fat middle-aged man with beery breath and heavy blue jowls singing snatches of the music-hall song, 'Ta-ra-ra-boom-de-ay', and beating out the time with his furled umbrella.

Then a fresh thrust from behind flung her forward into his outstretched arms and the whiff of his breath was so pungent and putrid that she retched and all the time he kept chanting, 'Ta-ra-ra-*BOOM*-de-ay!', even when he lost balance and they rolled together in the gutter.

When she rose to her knees he had disappeared in a swirl of legs and she crouched there close against the lamp-standard, shaking her head to and fro and her unpinned hair fell across her eyes and the sour smell of her own vomit reminded her of the cell in Holloway, where the little Scots doctor, with desperate patience trying to insert the feeding tube between her clenched teeth, kept repeating, "Awa', lassie! Dinnae mak' me do it . . . Dinna *mak'* me . . ." she lost all sense of time and place and became isolated from the chaos all about her.

The two-horse van appeared out of nowhere, running wild and free it seemed, so that she half rose to her feet and tried to ward off the goring butt of its shaft with both hands. It bore down on her inexorably, however, and she had an impression of being lifted as upon a wave and tossed the full width of the pavement. And after that the sustained roar of breakers on a rockbound coast dinned in her ears and Giles' sunburned face peered down at her from the bridge arching the river Gladwyn near their old home in Caernarvonshire.

He looked so much younger than of late. No more than a youth and he had a pack on his back that he jettisoned to climb down to where she stood waist deep in the shallow water. She was aware of the terrible importance of touching his hand and this she succeeded in doing, but only just, so that she had to scrabble with her toes to reach the level of the road. But when she got there it wasn't a road, only that long, bare dormitory of the emporium in the north where she had once lived the life of a shopgirl drudge. And then the scene changed again and they were in the bedroom of their little stone house on the side of the hill at Pontnewydd, where their life began all over again in a spirit of tender camaraderie that was startlingly new in their marriage. And suddenly she felt glad and free and at peace with the world, smiling and enfolding him, pressing him close and assuring him over and over that this would be different for both of them and that here, in this drab little room with its faded wallpaper, she would conceive his child. The sound of the breakers assailed her again then, louder and terribly insistent, so that she held him with all her strength and presently a wave broke over them both completely submerging them. But when it receded she still had him close against her breast.

3

They got him there just as dusk was creeping up river and the lights of the Embankment were winking like a vast necklace lit by a moving candle against a background of murk. They were all three chilled to the bone, despite heavy coats and mufflers and both George and Edward tried hard to persuade him to get a hot drink inside him before he went in but he shook his head.

"No, George. Go on home and take Edward with you. You've done enough for me, and I'll never forget it," so they left him and drove the borrowed Silver Ghost over the bridge and down Whitehall to the Strand. George said, glumly, "By God, I need a stiff one. Let's stop at the Savoy and give her a chance to cool off."

*   *   *

Giles went in to the lobby and here Deborah claimed him, breaking away from a nurse and saying, fervently, "Thank God you're here! She's been conscious but only for a moment . . . long enough to ask . . ." She piloted him into a waiting-room being vacated by the last of the Sunday visitors and heavy with the scent of chrysanthemums.

"Is there any chance at all, Debbie?"

She lowered her glance so he went on, with surprising calmness, "You were on the march? You must have seen what happened?"

"Not really, I was away up at the front. The mob surged on to the road and cut the column in half. Romayne was further back, carrying a banner. Sit down a minute. You'll be able to see her but you have to know, you have to understand first."

He sat on a long wooden bench, drawing off his gloves, and slowly chafing his numbed hands. "I was at Tonypandy. They're in a bad way down there."

"We're all in a bad way," she said, bitterly. "What makes us think we're unique as a nation, when things like this keep on happening? Romayne was a fighter, Giles. She could have taken the rest-cure in Devon, with all the others who were turned loose, but when she heard Christabel needed backing for the rally she insisted on coming along. Don't blame yourself for not being here. This is a war on so many fronts."

She told him how the march had attracted the usual horde of layabouts, all looking for a wet Saturday afternoon's diversion. "It's the papers I blame. They keep whipping them on like a lot of foxhounds. The police were fair – they did what they could but there wasn't nearly enough of them. They broke up the procession opposite Downing Street and the van that knocked her down was a Black Maria, moving in to pick up the rowdies."

"How bad are her injuries, Debbie?"

"Spinal, and a suspected fractured skull. But they're not absolutely sure yet."

A young doctor approached and conducted them wordlessly through a maze of corridors to a ward containing about forty beds. There were screens around most of them, so that he assumed the patients here were all on the danger list. Nurses swished to and fro, absorbed in their own business. Lights burned low and from all around rose a low, persistent murmur of distracted protest. He thought, 'It can't be right for people to die without privacy. These places need looking to, like every other institution in the damned country . . . if she holds on I'll get her out of here somehow . . .' And then a sister, distinguished by her dark blue overall and small coif, came up and said, "She's conscious intermittently, Mr. Swann, but don't stay more than a moment. Don't talk either and only one of you, please."

Her head was swathed in bandages and she lay very still, her long, shapely hands spread on the coverlet in what he saw as a gesture of resignation. He lifted one of them and stood holding it and presently there was a slight break in the rhythm of her heavy breathing and she stirred, her eyes opening, closing, then opening again. He forced himself to smile and something in the refraction of her pupils, and a slight pucker about the lips, indicated that she was half aware of him. His heart thumped painfully against his ribs as he saw, or thought he saw, her trying to frame words.

"Don't talk. I'm here now, it's Giles, dearest."

The eyelids fluttered again and the tip of her tongue emerged to moisten her lips. He took a damp flannel from the bedside locker and drew it gently across the mouth and cheekbones. She looked surprisingly young, he thought, about half his own age, and her skin, emphasised by prison pallor, was smooth as wax. He remembered he had always been aware of the texture of her skin, ever since that first impulsive kiss she had given him when, as eighteen-year-olds, they had met under the looming bulk of the mountain at Beddgelert. He reckoned up the interval, a span of something over twenty-five years, but it did not seem so long. More like twenty-five months, a summer's morning a year or two ago and yet, in that space of time, her personality had undergone a dramatic change. In those early days she wouldn't have given a damn about women's suffrage, miners' pay or anything else save how to get her own way in everything. He wondered what agency had transformed her to that extent, from a spoiled millionaire's brat into a dedicated freedom fighter, willing to sacrifice all she had won from life for deeply-held ideals involved with justice and equity among people of both sexes and all classes. It could not have been his own influence on a personality that had once been as self-centred as that of her father and as feckless as a child, and his mind went back to that curious withdrawal of hers before they were married, when she had fled her father's home and found work in a draper's shop for a few shillings a week, eating the kind of food they fed paupers at workhouses. He wondered if, for all his love of her, and for all his book browsing, he had ever come near to understanding the impulses and aspirations of the brain behind that smooth, white brow. In a way, she was like a woman who had taken the vow and never gone back on it, and he wondered if the sense of dedication that had swept both of them down the years into this murmuring ward would re-occur in either of her boys. He doubted it. More likely it was unique, welling from some Celtic blend of fervour and mysticism in the genes of Cambrian ancestors.

Her eyes were open now and the tapering fingers tightened their grip on the ball of his thumb. He whispered, "Romayne? Romayne, darling?" The slow, painful smile confirmed his belief that she was conscious. She made a distinct sound then and he bent very low over the pillow, without releasing her hand. She tried again and this time he could just identify the word, a single syllable that, in the present context, seemed strange and very moving. It was only part of a word really, '*Pont* . . .', the Welsh word for 'bridge', but it had a message for him. She had been trying to say 'Pontnewydd', the name of his constituency, and it seemed to him that in the confused labyrinth of her lacerated brain, she had all but found her way back to the point in their lives where they had discovered fulfilment, both personal and public. For that was the word that had signposted them here to this parting.

Her head lolled sideways, just as the sister reappeared in the aperture of the screens. She lifted the wrist, stood poised for a moment, then looked across at him, shaking her head. She said, very quietly, "I'm so sorry, Mr. Swann." And then, "I knew her, knew you both. Will you come down again now? I'd like to have a word with you if I may. Mrs. Jeffs has left. She's been here almost continuously, ever since they brought Mrs. Swann in, but I persuaded her to go home. She needs food and rest."

He followed her down to the cheerless waiting-room, wondering vaguely what she could have to say to him, and when they had passed inside she closed the door and stood with her back to it, looking vaguely embarrassed.

"The porter is bringing some tea. He won't be a moment. You've had a terrible shock and a long hard drive from Wales."

"Mrs. Jeffs told you?"

"She didn't have to. We've all three met, you see. Just the once."

He forced his mind away from the memory of the angled, bandaged head upstairs, trying to identify the woman who stood watching him, her back to the door. She was Welsh. He could assure himself of that much by her accent, and she looked Welsh too, one of the blonde, less full-faced Celts one met occasionally in the valleys but more often in the north, about L.G.'s stamping-ground.

"You're from my constituency?"

"Near it. From Swansea. But you couldn't possibly remember me. It was so long ago. I was the cause of a . . . a disagreement between you and your wife in a London shop. You weren't married then, I believe."

"I'm sorry?"

"Don't be. It's of no consequence, or not to you, Mr. Swann. It's just that . . . well, it crossed my mind that it might cheer you a little to know. I was a millinery counter assistant in a shop in Oxford Street, and you and Mrs. Swann came in late at night to buy a hat in the window. I was tired and refused to serve her. Afterwards I fainted and you hustled her out. I never forgot about it because it was the turning point in my life. I suppose that was why I followed your career so closely, and Mrs. Swann's too, after she became so involved in the W.S.P.U. It's terrible for you that this has happened but it might help people to realise . . ."

She stopped, giving him time to absorb the astonishing completeness of the pattern involving three lives, perhaps many more. He remembered her now, a tall girl with blonde hair, who had been goaded to mutiny by Romayne's petulant insistence on getting a hat out of the window at past eleven o'clock at night after the girl had been on her feet for fifteen hours; the intervention of an outraged floorwalker and the girl, probably appalled by her outburst, fainting behind the counter. It was the night he broke off their engagement, seeing no kind of future in their association, but he had been wrong. The incident must have made an even greater impression on Romayne, for it was that which prompted her flight and enrolment in the ranks of the hard-driven. Indeed, her involvement in causes of all kinds had dated from that very moment. It seemed very strange and wonderful that this woman should be present to witness her sacrificing her life for yet another cause. He said at last, "How do you mean – a turning point?"

"I was sacked, without a character. It meant leaving the drapery trade. I took up nursing. I needed that push and Mrs. Swann did me a good turn because that wasn't any sort of life and this . . . ? Well, you'll understand – one feels useful, needed, more able to help. The way you help people."

"I wish she could have known."

"It was hopeless from the start, Mr. Swann. We did everything we could."

"I'm sure you did. What is your name, Sister?"

"Powell. I'm a senior ward sister, studying for my finals. I hope to get a matron's post somewhere in a year or so. In Wales, perhaps. There's plenty of need for trained nurses in that part of the country." She paused, turning to open the door in response to a knock. A porter came in with a tray of tea and she took it and dismissed him.

"It is very kind of you, Miss Powell."

"Nonsense. You can't leave yet. There'll be papers to sign in the office."

She poured his tea and handed it to him. It was scalding and strong and he sipped it gratefully. She said, hesitantly, "I wonder . . . would it seem impertinent . . . would you mind telling me why your wife became a militant? Was it because of your work as an M.P.?"

"No. She was involved in a variety of other lost causes long before I won the Pontnewydd seat. One of them was the pay and conditions of shop assistants. It began on account of you, on account of that silly business about the hat," and he told her of the sequel to the incident and how, a year after they had parted, he had traced her to a draper's sweat shop in the north.

"Doesn't it strike you as a kind of . . . well, a design of some sort? As though it was a plan, involving all of us?"

"Yes," he said, "very much so. That's why I wish my wife could have known."

"I'll get those papers. Please help yourself to some more tea."

"Thank you."

She went out, her starched skirts rustling like dry leaves underfoot and he sat hunched, his fingertips seeking warmth from the cup. There was, as she said, 'some kind of design', but what kind, and leading where, was more than he could say. He would have to think about it. Sometime when he felt less tired and drained and hopeless.

*　　　*　　　*

The day after the funeral he accepted his father's shy offer to take advantage of the frosty sunshine and walk through the woods to the plateau overlooking Denzil Fawcett's rough pasture at Dewponds. It was a walk they had often taken and one he seldom failed to appreciate for up here, in his father's genial company, they had discussed, over the years, every topic from hymns to haulage and poetry to poverty.

Adam said, as they emerged from the beech grove, "I'm glad you rejected that showy funeral they were planning to give her. Wouldn't have suited her nor you. Not your way of going about things."

Christabel Pankhurst had come to him with plans for a big W.S.P.U. turnout, but he had politely declined the offer, accepting only the magnificent wreath the movement sent her for the grave at Twyforde Churchyard. The cause was very dear to him. But not dear enough to encourage him to use Romayne's broken body as an advertisement.

They buried her a few plots away from his Grandfather Swann's grave. It was where he would wish to lie himself, a swallow's swoop from this corner of the Weald where he and all the other Swanns had been born and reared. It was the first Swann funeral in thirty years.

He said, bitterly, "I'm with them, body and soul, and have been, from the very beginning. I see it as the most important social issue of our time."

"It's important, I grant you."

"But not vitally so? Well, it shouldn't be difficult for you to see why it is to me. Enough to consider crossing the floor and joining up with the Labour Party. They're fully committed to Women's Suffrage. Our people are digging their heels in deeper every day."

Adam looked at him shrewdly. "You're saying you could quit the Liberal Party and still hold on to Pontnewydd?"

"Not at first, maybe. Eventually, I'd win it back."

"In the meantime you'd be prepared to split the vote and let a Tory in?"

"What does it matter, Tory or Liberal? A majority in both parties still regard women as serfs and demand passive acceptance of bed and bondage. How can you work alongside men of that kind? What do their clamours for reform amount to when they're made exclusively on behalf of the male half of the population?"

"Don't do it, old son."

"They've got some good men in that minority party. They go a lot further than we're prepared to go. Not just about this, about other issues."

"Ah, yes, I daresay and maybe that's why I'm doubtful. Not concerning their intentions but their hustle. I've read all their speeches and some of their pamphlets and they mean well enough. But there's something awry somewhere."

"Can you explain, Father?"

The climb through the last part of the woods had winded Adam. He found a convenient five-barred gate to lean upon and looked eastward towards the heart of the Weald and the sea.

"No, just an instinct. A prejudice, even."

"A prejudice against what?"

"Not against anything. A prejudice in favour of something. Of going about reform in the way the English radical always has, a nibble at a time."

"Does that mean that, deep down, you're with Asquith, that you don't feel the women should have the vote yet?"

"No, no . . . I'd give it 'em, but it's only a part of what wants doing and what will be done if we're not led astray by the grab-alls, the blowhards, and the peacocks."

"But this is a personal business for me now."

"So it is, but you're holding a long line, boy. Plan for a general advance. Don't spend yourself storming a single redoubt. The strongpoint will be over-run anyway in a general offensive."

Giles said, gloomily, "Power changes parties as well as individuals. I've seen it happening, ever since 1906. We aren't the same men as we were in opposition all that time."

"*You* are."

He turned aside from the gate and seated himself on a convenient log. "Tell you something else, my boy. I've been watching you ever since you were in short trousers. I've lived a long time, and kept my eyes open most of the time. There's Alex's lot, George's lot, and your lot. The Army, Trade and Politics. All three of you have had to contend with stupidity, greed, excessive caution, complacency and so on, and you've all worked out your own ways of tackling 'em. I like your way best. The quiet way. And so, in the main, does the country. Our people aren't fools. They soon learn to sort out the men they can trust and the men they can't. Takes 'em time but they learn and the difference between you and your friend Lloyd George is a case in point. You decide issues from conviction. His starting point will always be personal preferment. Folk find that out in the end. Go back to your miners and get on with your job. That's my advice for what it's worth. Well, I've had my breather. Let's get on before it clouds over."

They walked together across the winding heath path, in companionable silence for the most part, but when they reached the briar-sown track down to the curve of the river, where it rejoined the 'Tryst' boundary, Giles said: "What did you mean, precisely. 'Unless we're sidetracked by grab-alls, peacocks and blowhards'?"

"I was looking well ahead. You can do that objectively at my age. I can't say I am reassured by what I see, for civilisation as a whole or for us in particular. Forty . . . thirty years ago the twentieth century seemed a golden age but it's like most things we mistake for gold at a distance. When you touch it it's pinchbeck. Things seemed to be getting better all the time. Machines were going to give everybody more leisure. Poverty was going to go the way of feudalism. Universal education was going to work wonders. You must have heard it all in your line of business?"

"Things have got better, haven't they?"

"In some respects. We still resort to eighteenth-century diplomacy in our chancellories. And then think of the scramble for Africa, and this naval arms race between us and Germany. I sometimes wonder where it will lead us all. Down the Gadarene slope if we don't look sharp. Mind, we've always had to contend with the gluttons. I once knew a merchant in The Polygon who boasted of running his business on boys and old men. He sacked the boys the day they finished their apprenticeship and paid the old-stagers half the current rate, since it was that or the workhouse. You can legislate against that kind of thing nowadays but you can't frame laws against secret treaties made by the idiots who find reassurance in music-hall ditties written on red, white and blue scores. Those are the jokers who worry me the most and the sickness is spreading fast. It started here, back about the time you were born, and it's taken hold in Potsdam, Paris and even Washington. All over the West people who should know better think money and prestige are the touchstones. They aren't and you've only got to read the history books to prove it."

"What are the touchstones, Father?"

The old man knitted his brows. "Ah, now you're asking. Respect for human dignity, maybe, and for Donne's dictum – 'Each man's death diminishes me.' Mercifully there's still evidence of that here." He paused as they drew level with the river, low for this season of the year and fringed with frosted brushwood sparkling like a long row of Christmas trees. "As for your loss, try and regard her as the French view the loss of Alsace-Lorraine – 'Speak of it never, think of it always.'"

Giles reached out and touched his father's arm. "A walk with you is the best tonic I know, Father."

"Glad somebody thinks so. If you can serve any purpose at my age one shouldn't complain."

"You're good for a long time yet, Father."

"A year or so, given mild winters," and in his bones he believed it, for at eighty-two he had less aches and pains to bother him than many men twenty years his junior.

He would not have believed, however, that he would live to see yet another royal funeral.

3

The Last Rally

IT WAS THE FINAL RALLY. SURELY THE LAST HE
would live to see and perhaps, who knew? the last
occasion when a constellation of kings, princes and grand
dukes, garnished, gilded, splendidly mounted and serenely
untroubled in their Godgiven right to occupy the centre
of the world's stage, would use the passing of one of their
number as an occasion to catch up on family gossip and
practise a little harmless skulduggery on one another
once the royal corpse was decently below ground at
Frogmore.

There was no logical reason why he should view it in
this cryptic manner, or none save that slight stir of uneasiness somewhere near the bottom of his rib cage, the
pulse he had sometimes referred to as 'the little feller in
here' when expressing undefined doubts about a project.
This was no cause, however, for foregoing the occasion
to celebrate (for that was how Henrietta regarded it) his
own longevity and go posting up to town to bribe or
bully one or other of his old cronies to find him a
place on a balcony or a window overlooking the funeral
march.

He saw it as a rally of the privileged, most of them
stemming, in one way or another, from the loins of that
gloomy German chap Albert. 'The stud house of Europe',
Napoleon had called the House of Coburg. For here they
were, a whole shoal of them, in their frogged tunics,

glittering orders and absurd headgear, assembled to pay homage to a corpulent man whom some thought of as a peacemaker and others a mere womaniser, but whose death that summer had caught everyone off balance. For these days a monarch was not reckoned old at sixty-nine. After all, the fellow's mother had reigned almost as long and even his great-grandfather, Farmer George, had made eighty-plus.

Yet there it was. He was gone, and his bright new halo with him, and Adam could find cause to regret him, for, just as he had grown to dislike his tetchy old mother, he had come to respect her roystering son for the dignity and despatch he brought to his job when he was summoned after such a long and frustrating wait in the wings.

He did not know whether most people had had time to adjust to his style, so different from Victoria's, with its opening of social doors, and the application of shrewd personal judgment in foreign affairs, sound but not showy. At least, the foreigners respected him in a way they had never respected his mother. Somehow he had taken the measure of them, especially of his nephew Wilhelm, with his fierce upturned moustaches and loud-mouthed braggadocio. He had brought to his job the dignity that had been lacking for nearly three centuries, since the time Elizabeth rallied the nation at Tilbury.

Mainly, of course, they were here to show off their plumes but he suspected there was another reason for their assembly. Deep down the more responsible of them were genuinely worried by his abrupt departure from their midst. He was, in essence, a kind of stabiliser in the chancellories, a factor that had to be reckoned with in small matters and great, and it was no time for the vacuum to be filled by that unassuming Prince George, whose experience, outside the navy or a pheasant shoot, was very limited.

It might well be, of course, that he too would surprise the cleverdicks. He was known to be an amiable man, anxious to play out his life on a low key. Most of them, no doubt, would hope that he would continue in this way, enabling time for their personal plans to mature, but with a Coburg one could rarely take such things for granted. Nobody had rated Albert very high when he married Victoria two generations ago yet he had succeeded in surprising most people, just as Edward, his scrapegrace son, had only a few years back.

Meantime they composed their expressions and marched a dutiful slow-step, eyeing one another with a certain caution.

*   *   *

They did these things superbly well, did the English, he thought, his mind returning to Victoria's funeral in 1901, and her glittering Jubilees of '87 and '97. Weather as good as this, of course, was sure to increase the demand on vantage points, so he went up to town the day before and was in position before the procession set out from the palace at nine sharp. Yet even he, used to such spectacles, had not anticipated a show on this scale, with eight kings and a royal duke, riding three by three, followed by five .heirs-apparent, forty imperial or royal highnesses, seven queens, and ambassadors from every country on the map.

They had talked about Queen's weather at the Jubilee but here was King's weather, with the sun riding high in a cloudless sky, temperatures soaring into the seventies, and not even the lightest breeze to ruffle the white plumes of Kaiser Wilhelm's field-marshal's hat as he reined back slightly to give Cousin George the precedence demanded by protocol. He was worth a look, this plunging grandson of the old queen, who was reported to have said of Britain, "I am proud to call this place home . . ." But it didn't seem to stop him reviling it when he was in one of his 'encirclement' moods. They said he had a withered arm but if it was true it didn't show. His right hand held the marshal's baton, his left the reins of the docile grey he was riding and, as at his grandmother's funeral, he seemed to be on his very best behaviour, although even a mild-mannered man might have been forgiven irritability under all that sweaty clobber he was wearing.

The leading trio passed, the new King, Wilhelm and the dead monarch's only surviving brother, the Duke of Connaught, and in their wake the kings of Denmark and the Hellenes, brothers of the widow, flanked by her nephew, Haakon of Norway, and after them Alphonso of Spain, Manuel of Portugal and a mourner wearing a silk turban whom he had some difficulty in recognising as Ferdinand of Bulgaria.

He thought, cynically, 'Well, they carry themselves well enough, I suppose, but they're always getting bombed or shot at. And that chap Ferdinand has to bolster himself by calling himself "Czar" and buying Byzantine jewellery from a theatrical costumier . . .'

His sharp eye roved beyond to the next trio, Franz Ferdinand, heir to old Franz Joseph's ramshackle empire, God help him; Yussuf, heir to the Sultan's Turkey; and a tall, less showy man who seemed to Adam to sit his horse as an expert. He recognised him as Albert, King of the Belgians, and thought: 'He's the only one among 'em embarrassed by all this and wishing to God he was anywhere else . . .' His scrutiny returned to the corpulent Franz Ferdinand, who had replaced Prince Rudolf, after the poor bemused devil shot himself and his mistress in a hunting lodge, and placed such a fearful strain upon Habsburg flunkeys to explain how it happened. And an equal strain on the credibility of the journalists, obliged to select one of a dozen contradictory theories.

The great thing about an occasion like this was that it gave a man an opportunity to ponder the infinite variations in the pattern of the Continental carpet as it unrolled, little by little, year by year. Not by everybody, of course, but by the privileged like himself, who kept pace with events, who had lived a long, long time, and who was endowed with a selective memory. There wasn't one of these gilded popinjays concerning whom he could not have told a story or two they would have preferred forgotten and it gave him a feeling of thankfulness that he had been able to pick his own way through life, unfettered by protocol and tradition, responsible to himself, his family and his work force certainly, but to no one else alive. And as he thought this there came to him a conviction that he was watching a cavalcade out of a dead century, mounted in an era long before that of universal male suffrage, and the rise of the new commercial aristocracy, the twin nineteenth-century forces that had made these people as obsolete as dodos.

Japan was represented by the brother of the Emperor; Russia by the Grand Duke Michael; Italy by the Duke of Aosta (what fancy handles they attached to these royal jugs!); then came Carl of Sweden, Henry of Holland, any number of Balkan nabobs and in their wake a flock of grand dukes, petty princelings and top-hatted civilians from the world's republics. His old friend, Lord Roberts, was there, as always upon these occasions, together with as colourful a display of military detachments as he had ever seen assembled in line of march – Coldstreamers, Gordon Highlanders, Household Cavalry, lancers, dragoons and hussars of every crack Continental regiment, and even a handful of gold-epauletted admirals. And between these and the swarm of British office-holders, all in their traditional best bibs and tuckers, a typically British touch – the dead man's charger, that had never once been called upon to charge, followed by his wire-haired terrier, 'Caesar' led by an academic-looking chap in a college gown.

It was all very splendid, a little too splendid for anyone like himself, who had walked by night among the London destitute, reflecting sometimes upon the strange idiosyncrasies of a race that valued its dogs and horses above most of its children, and spent far more on the dead than the living. For this was really no more than a dazzling reflection of an East End coster's funeral, paid for by the indigent widow out of her twopenny-a-week insurance policy. People were the slaves of their tribal rituals.

*   *   *

The heat was beginning to distress him so he made his way through the crowds to the Strand and thence to his hotel where he took a tepid bath and, after that, a light luncheon and a refreshing afternoon nap. By twilight he was back at 'Tryst' and Henrietta, perhaps remembering earlier homecomings, came down the yard steps when the coachman (he had never let George talk him into selling his carriage bays and replacing them by a motor) was giving the horses a rub down. She led the way across the hall and into the dining-room where it was dark and cool and he regaled her over supper with a detailed account of the procession, noting that even here, in deference to the servants he supposed, she had tied a black crepe bow on the sleeve of her blouse.

"King George, what kind of man is he, Adam?" she asked. "I don't recall much about him. It was always his brother, the one who died, who was going to be king."

"George? He's all for a quiet life and I hope he gets it. But I doubt it very much after a close look at the poor chap's relations," he replied.

"You mean they'll make trouble for him? But how could they? I mean, after all, he's King of England now."

"King of Britain, my dear. I'm always afraid you'll say that in front of old Phoebe Fraser, who went to such frightful pains to get it straight with the children."

"Well, Britain then. Are you referring to that silly man, the Kaiser?"

"Him among others," Adam said.

"Oh, he's just a braggart," she said. "The King will

soon put him in his place. And as for all those others you were telling me about, well, they wouldn't care to pick a quarrel with us, any one of them."

"No," he said, stifling a yawn, "I don't suppose they would, Hetty. I'm quite worn out. It was so devilishly hot in town. Shall we make an early night of it?", and he rose, foregoing his final cheroot of the day and the stroll in the forecourt he enjoyed at this season of the year.

But sleep, perversely, evaded him and he woke up soon after midnight and slipping on his dressing-gown went downstairs and let himself out of the tall windows opening on to the balustraded terrace he had built along the front of the house during his renovations twenty years ago.

The front of the house was bathed in moonlight and between the lilac clumps, at the head of the drive, he could see as far as The Hermitage beyond his artificial lake. It was very quiet out here, and reassuring too in an odd sort of way, for the presence of the old house behind him, and the broad, down-sloping vista studded with imported trees now growing to an impressive height and looking as if they belonged here, gave him a sense of permanence and stability. 'I shall hate leaving it,' he thought, 'not the network and the family so much, for the one is in safe hands with George and Edward, and the other will manage. But this . . . these coppices and fields and flowering shrubs that smell of England all the year round . . .' As his mind returned to that gun-carriage and the empty saddle of the royal horse . . . 'How much longer can *I* expect? I've already overstayed my welcome by several years but, by gum, I've had a wonderful innings and ought not to resent making way for others. If only they'll learn to value it – this corner of an old landscape, and the way of life that goes with it – peace, order and progression . . .'

He looked up at the sky, searching for familiar stars and it occurred to him for a moment to contemplate the infinite, something he rarely did. *Was* there anything to follow? Did it matter one way or the other? He had never had any deep convictions about it and felt no special need of them now that his time was running out.

He extinguished his cheroot in a flower urn trailing geraniums and went in, closing the windows. A few minutes later he was back in bed and drifting off to sleep, his arm resting across the generous hip of his wife, who stirred slightly and murmured something unintelligible.

4

Snowslide

THE SHOCK OF THE BAD 1911 MIDSUMMER FIGURES
had them reeling. Not even the older and least venturesome men in the network had experienced a slide of this
length and steepness. They were all aware that they
were passing through a bad patch after the relaunch of
six years ago, but the consolidated bi-annual returns,
privately circulated among them, converted speculation
into furious self-questioning.

No region was altogether exempt from the dip although
some, mostly rural territories, seemed to be holding their
own better than others. The overall drop in turnover was
slight but that only made the January to June profit
margin look more preposterous than ever. For the hard
facts were profits had fallen to a miserly five and a quarter
per cent, compared with eight and a half in the preceding
six months, and sixteen per cent in the corresponding
period last year.

George did what everybody expected him to do,
calling for regional reports and convening an extraordinary general meeting for the second week in July.

The favourite excuse, of course, went under the
heading of 'a general business recession'. It had a comforting vagueness and could be laid to the door of German
competition, plus the unsettled atmosphere overseas.
After that, a close second, came the old whipping boy,
the weather, for the winter had been long and wet,

particularly in the north and west, and as recently as February some of the busiest regions had had a third of their vehicles in the repair shops. Higson, in the far north, for instance, thought he could be forgiven a falling-off in his rural areas, where the snow falls had been heavy and his quota of motor-vehicles seldom penetrated, but it seemed odd that Bertieboy Bickford, whom all of them thought of as a yokel, came close to finishing top of the regional poll, an almost inconceivable circumstance in these days, for the Western Wedge was jocularly referred to as 'the turnip patch' and Bickford, operating in the Western peninsula, must have had his fill of sloughed roads and flooded valleys.

The cancer seemed to be located mainly in the flattish, densely-populated areas, where lorries had all but super-seded the horse, and industry was still expanding; regions like The Polygon, The Funnel and the Scottish Lowlands. It was on the figures from these regions that George concentrated during his two-day exile in Adam's tower, whither he retired as soon as he had ridden out the initial shock.

At first, with regionalised bleats spread the whole length of the trestle tables he had rigged up, he could discern no real pattern in the slump, nothing to show why the blight should have struck so savagely and so quickly. At last he began to see that it was high time he made some sweeping reassessments, not only of national transport trends and Swann-on-Wheels as an enterprise operating within those trends, but also of himself, a man of forty-seven, hitherto of cool judgment and with nearly thirty years' experience under his belt.

*   *   *

George had always seen himself as a pioneer, in advance of other pioneers, a man ready to look ahead, so that he had succeeded in pulling something out of the hat well in advance of his viceroys, even the few gamblers out along the network. His tenacity and unswerving belief in himself had gained for them all that impressive start over every competitor in the field. But he supposed now that that start had been altogether too impressive, encouraging him to sit back and live off his fat, and it soon became obvious to him that he had lost his place in the vanguard.

The evidence of these unpleasant conclusions were everywhere, but particularly telling in his newspaper cutting file where he found evidence of advances that would have put a cutting edge on his curiosity a few years back. There were those London 'H' type 'buses, now operated by the London and General Omnibus Company as far as Hampstead. There was news that the last L.G.O.C. horse 'bus was due for retirement in early autumn this year, and the same company's spectacular success in the private hire field, where even councils composed of men who had never ridden in a motor were commissioning 'bus excursions for schoolchildren. There was Morris's amazing advances down at Oxford, and Austin's breakthrough with his baby car, that had somehow caught the imagination of a public unimpressed by the impossibly expensive, carriage-built vehicles of ten years ago. But beyond all this there was the flood of new, high-performance foreign cars on the roads, the Renaults and Unics, the Napiers, the Charrons and the Panhards, pouring from continental workshops where, he suspected, commercial vehicles, capable of outpacing and outhauling the best of Scottie Quirt's Swann-Maxies, were already over their teething troubles and promising formidable haulage competition in the near future. Indeed, it seemed that the very name 'Swann-Maxie' had an old-fashioned ring about it, like last year's slang, so that he gave a thought to that other and infinitely more adventurous form of transport, the staggering advances made in the conquest of the air over the last two or three years.

There was no commercial future in air transport, or

none that he could discern. A machine that was still unsafe for a man was unlikely, in the foreseeable future, to enter the haulage field. Yet George Swann, his mind conditioned to evolving patterns of transport over three decades, could sense the impact aeroplanes were beginning to make on a public that had for so long regarded the motor as a rich man's toy. The public mood was changing, year by year, and month by month, ever since Blériot made his cross-Channel flight in the summer of 1909, and that human dynamo Northcliffe (quick as a fairground barker to spot a crowd-collector) had initiated his air races. Even ballooning was now no longer regarded as a happy-go-lucky way of breaking one's neck. The Germans were reported to be making impressive progress with airships, led by that dedicated aeronaut, Count Ferdinand Zeppelin. And here perhaps air haulage was at least a possibility.

Swann-on-Wheels, once accepted by every transport man in the country as first in the field, was no longer 'in the frame' as the bookmakers said. Was even in danger of slipping to fourth or fifth place in the national table.

What was to be done about it? How could the plunging downward trend in Swann's graph be halted, levelled off, and encouraged to rise? Or what common factor could be isolated as the arch villain and placed squarely in the dock? He had often been baffled, but never this baffled. He turned back to his viceroys' reports, beginning with the Eastern Region facing the North Sea, and ending with the turnip patch, where Bertieboy Bickford, with his assortment of outmoded men-o'-war, frigates and pinnaces was still holding his own.

It was pondering this – Bertieboy's curious immunity from the slump – that suggested an answer. Not the whole answer, certainly, but a hint that there must be a common factor in the falling off in orders and the sharp drop in profits. Bertieboy, largely concerned with bread and butter hauls over rural routes, and fobbed off with teams and vehicles that were already obsolete in the north and midlands, none the less enjoyed a built-in advantage over all his rivals with the single exception of Clint Coles, operating on the far side of the Irish Sea. He had, so far as George could discover, no serious competition. Some seventy per cent of his customers (a cross-check with accounts established this) were either farmers or merchants marketing agricultural goods of one sort or another, and there was something else that seemed, against all probability, to be operating in Bickford's favour, something that was not difficult to assess if you knew his beat as well as George knew it. Bickford's territory was served by a very poor road system, that had changed surprisingly little from the coaching days. The gradients thereabouts were fearsome. Indeed, it was for this very reason that few Swann-Maxies were seen in the peninsula, and these two factors had to have an important bearing on the exemption of the Western Wedge from the general depression.

He turned back to the detailed reports from The Polygon, The Funnel and the Scottish Lowlands and suddenly the general pattern of the dilemma emerged. *In areas where the ground was favourable to the motor, where distances between cities were short, where potential customers were thick on the ground, the amateur was emerging as a successful challenger to the professional.*

Not individually, of course. Nobody running a fleet of transport vehicles, powered or horse-drawn, had cause to lose an hour's sleep over the odd Johnny-Come-Lately who built or bought a single motor-vehicle and advertised himself as a haulier of goods. These people had always existed, even in his father's day, and they had never succeeded in making a dent in the Swann economy. But that, possibly, was because there were so few of them and most of them were locally based, operating no more than a few miles from the waggon sheds where they kept their decrepit carts and stabled their ageing beasts. A glance at his brother Edward's report convinced him that this was no longer the case. In the Birmingham–Wolverhampton area alone Edward had listed thirty-seven one-man operators, and according to his son Rudi, up in The Polygon, an almost identical swarm of parasites was skimming the cream from the house-removal trade.

Spurred on by a sensation of discovery he did a rapid cast of the number of one- or two-vehicle operators in these three regions alone and the total frightened him. Country, seaside and beauty-spot excursion promoters – in several regions summer excursions had yielded a rich harvest for Swann-on-Wheels since they were introduced a generation ago – together with prominent local trades-men involved in every kind of traffic from haberdashery to undertaking, there were no fewer than six hundred and eight competitors in three of Swann's busiest regions!

*   *   *

His sense of humour returned to him as he thought, with a grin:

> 'Each bug has a lesser bug upon his back to bite him
> And that flea has a lesser flea, and so ad infinitum . . .'

and the tag prompted him to do yet another sum, this time concerned with the number of firms and factories in the Metropolitan area known to field their own motor transport. The result was equally daunting. In the Home Counties, according to the latest check, seventy-four former customers had, within the last two years, an-nounced that from here on they were equipped to do their own haulage.

Here it was then, the elusive common factor that he sought. Lesser bugs proliferating across the country plus a new breed of merchant who had seen the light that George had seen beside the Danube twenty-five years ago and were using it to find a way towards cutting trans-port costs.

He went over to the window, propping his elbows on the stone sill and looking out on the view that had always offered his father a challenge, the broad brown curve of the Thames below London Bridge, with its steady flow of river traffic down to the forest of shipping at the docks. He had his conundrum and he had to solve it, before he got bogged down in the slough of generalities that would emerge from the meeting in two days' time. He thought, 'I can't solve it here. I've studied those reports until my eyes ache and those chaps out there are each concerned with their own patch. It isn't fair to expect them to see the picture as a whole. That's *my* job and, by God, it's time I tackled it.' The line of thought suggested another. He reflected, 'At the Gov'nor's age a man is entitled to live on his memories but I'm not much more than half his age. Somewhere in the 'seventies, when he was the right side of fifty, he must have faced a dozen challenges equivalent to this one. I'll take a walk and get the smell of this damned slum out of my nostrils,' and he flung himself out and down the narrow staircase to the yard, then towards the bridge, thick with horse and motor traffic.

His steps led him via Cannon Street to the top of Ludgate Hill, then down past the Old Bailey and Snow Hill in the direction of Smithfield Market. It was a long time since he had passed this way on foot but in the days of his heir-apparency, more than twenty years before, he was often on the prowl hereabout, drumming up new contracts among the wholesalers, hoteliers and restaurateurs who frequented the great meat market from first light.

He had never been much of a walker, doing most of his thinking in cabs or suburban trains once he was clear of the yard, but it was soon apparent to him why his instinct had chosen this particular route through the city's most congested area on a hot July morning with the promise, by noon, of another scorching day. He was checking, half-consciously, the city's traffic patterns, comparing the flow up and down these streets with the groundswell in the same location in his youth, and soon found confirmation about the general drift towards the use of powered vehicles. In the old days these streets were choked with hansoms, four-wheeler growlers, flat drays and high-slung waggons, some of them bearing the Swann insignia, all moving at a snail's pace through a complex of thoroughfares laid out in London's reconstruction after the Great Fire of 1666, when the city's population was no more than a seventh of today's. Now, although there were still a few cabs to be seen, and more than half the moving commercial vehicles were horse-drawn, the motor was very much in evidence and he recognised at least a dozen different makes in his progress between St. Paul's and the Holborn Viaduct. Squat, hooting taxi-cabs nosed their way through all but stationary lines of two-horse drays and vans, and even the horses seemed to have adjusted to their blare and rattle. He remembered a shoal of urchin crossing-sweepers here, darting between traffic blocks in peril of their lives, but now a single old scarecrow represented the ancient calling. The noise had a different note too, a more strident, less musical orchestra, punctuated by intermittent toots of the bulb horn and the squeal of brakes, whereas the acrid smell of crushed manure, although still evident, was moderated by the fumes of exhaust and the smell of dust spiralling from the rubber-tyred wheels of the newcomers.

A small tribe of street arabs, mounted on what seemed, at first glance, a string of soapboxes, debouched from Snow Hill at a rattling good pace and sent him skipping into the gutter, clutching his straw hat and bringing him into contact with an iron lamp-standard. He turned to curse at them as they slowed to a stop but then, screwing up his eyes against the fierce sunlight, he checked himself, for it seemed to him there was something very novel about the six-wheeled conveyance that had come close to upsetting him.

It was more than an urchin's soapbox, of the kind one saw in every city and suburban street where youngsters were at play. To begin with, it was non-rigid, its steering apparatus housed on what looked like a small, elevated raft on which the steersman sat on a biscuit box nailed to the main structure. Behind him, carrying a total of four passengers, three girls and a boy, was the carriage itself, two linked fish-crates, with the glitter of scales still on their boards and he noticed also the astonishing lock the design of trolley gave the steersman. Using his right foot as a means of propulsion, he brought the whole thing round in a tight circle as he shouted in high, nasal Cockney, "Everybody aht! 'Arry, Floss, 'Arriet – look sharp, an' stand by ter tow her up for the nex' trip!"

Three of the tiny passengers scrambled out. The fourth, a little girl about five, sat hugging her knees and crooning with glee as the older boy added, "Orl right, leave Ada be. She don't weigh nothing," and he seized the looped cord fastened to his steering box preparatory to hauling his trolley up the incline.

George sauntered over, saying, "Hold on there – just a minute, boy. You've got a nippy little runabout there. How'd you come by it?"

The older boy, who wore a cloth cap with the peak at the back, said, with that mixture of amiability and insolence only met with on the streets of the capital, "Well, I didn't nick it, gov. Ast the kids if you like. Knocked 'er up I did, lars night." And then, with a craftsman's pride in his work, "She ain't bad, is she? Turns in 'arf 'er length and seats the 'ole bleedin' fambly. Get aht of it, kid, and let the gent 'ave a proper squint at 'er."

The sole remaining passenger climbed out and joined her brothers and sisters as George, bending low over the steering platform, peered between biscuit box and foremost fish crate to observe that the front axle was part of a perambulator, with its original wheels bolted to the chassis. He moved along its length and inspected the coupling, a length of steel wire running through a pair of sizeable staples and then turned to the engineer, saying, "She's first rate. Best I've even seen and I'm in the trade. Where did you get the idea for that steering-gear?" He had been on the point of saying 'articulation' but realised that the word would mean nothing to the boy who had clearly arrived at a means of improving the lock by the application of commonsense.

"Well, I 'ad the pram chassy and I thought I'd try it on for a change. There's five of us, see, and Mum won't let me aht if I don't take the bleedin' tribe. My ole 'bus woulden take no more'n three an' you coulden turn 'er on the pavement." He gave George a long, speculative look and added, half-mockingly, "You wanner try 'er, gov? You c'n take over for a tanner."

George Swann was probably the only middle-aged man in London who would have accepted such an offer. He said, chuckling, "Why not? Can you leave the girls with your brother for a minute?"

"I c'n lose the four of 'em fer a tanner," the boy said, and with a brief, authoritative nod at his brother and sisters he began lugging his trolley up the slope to a point where the pavement levelled out.

It was a very narrow side street, free of traffic for the moment and almost clear of pedestrians. The few that were there were obviously Londoners to a man and acclimatised to eccentrics, for they gave George no more than a glance when he seated himself behind the driver and went shooting down the hill at the pace of a fast-trotting horse.

They had almost reached the waiting children and were slowing down appreciably when George shouted, "Bring her round – full circle!" and the boy did, leaning heavily to his right as the linked soapboxes swung the full width of the pavement and stopped. He said, warmly, "My word, she's a corker!" and then, extricating himself, "What's your name, boy?"

" 'Ere, what's the catch? No names no pack drill my Dad alwus says."

"All right, no names. What'll you take for her as she stands?"

"You got kids? You wanter buy it?"

"I've got kids and I'll buy if you'll deliver. How about five bob, and an extra shilling for delivery?"

The boy now looked more suspicious than ever but then, having tried and failed to guess his patron's motives, he grinned and said, "You're 'avin' me on, ain't yer?"

But George rummaged in his trouser pockets and brought out two half-crowns and a shilling. "I'm not having anybody on. Here's the money . . ." Then it occurred to him that so original a boy deserved an explanation and added, "Do you know Swann-on-Wheels, the hauliers?"

" 'Course I do. Everybody does, don't they?"

"Do you know Swann's depot, in Tooley Street?"

"You bet."

"Well, my name is Swann and I deal in everything on wheels. Here's your money and you've given me an idea worth more than six shillings. I'll go to ten if you'll have that soapbox in my yard inside the hour. Now will you tell me your name?"

" 'Ardcastle," the boy said, pocketing the silver, "but I still don' know what you're at, gov."

"I'll tell you, Mr. Hardcastle." But then, to George's mild distress, the smallest of the boy's sisters began to blubber, and was at once joined by the girl he had addressed as Ada who wailed, "But it ain't yours to sell, Arty, it b'longs to all of us, don't it, 'Arriet?" And the eldest girl said, in an aggrieved tone, "We helped yer make her, didden we? We did, didden we?"

"Yerse, yer did," said Arty, with unexpected mildness, "but I c'n start knocking up another the minnit we get 'ome. The back 'arf o' that pram's still in the yard, ain't it? Besides, you c'n 'ave a tanner all rahnd if you'll give me an 'and over the bridge. Then yer can buy enough gob-stoppers to make yerselves bleedin' well sick, so 'old yer row, will yer?" He turned back to George, "Ten bob it is, then? You coming wiv us?"

"Er . . . no," said George, wrenched from a speculation of a network served by a fleet of Arty Hardcastles, "I'm going ahead by cab to make sure you aren't turned away at the yard gate, but before I go, and in case we miss one another, would you mind telling me when you leave school?"

"In a fortnight, thank Gawd."

"Got a job lined up?"

"Sort've. My Dad's a porter at Smiffield. Reckons he c'n get me taken on as an errand boy with 'Enson's, 'is firm."

"How much will that pay?"

"'Arf a crahn a week. Couple o' bob more in tips maybe. Depends on me rahnd. West End's all right, 'otels especially, but the 'olesalers is stingy. I know, see, I done a bit o' delivering before school summer-time."

"Well," George said, "I can pay you twice that and you can start on a suburban round where some of my vanboys make ten shillings a week in tips alone if they look lively. Here's my card. Show it to the Tooley Street weighbridge clerk but don't part with it. Give it to your father and get him to bring you along first week of the holidays."

The boy took the card and examined it carefully. Then putting his fingers in his mouth he produced the most earsplitting whistle George had ever heard. A taxi-cab, bowling along the Old Bailey, braked hard and George said, "Thank you, Arty," and walked towards the cab.

*　　*　　*

Unlike his father, George was not, and had never been, a man of quick decisions. In this respect at least they were complete opposites for, whereas Adam would, almost invariably, act upon instinct, George would contemplate each factor in any problem and then form a pattern in his brain. Once formed it was seldom subjected to adjustment.

It was so in this case. The pattern had been all but complete when he was nearly overset by Arty Hardcastle and his articulated soapbox in Snow Hill, but he had been unaware of it. The final piece in the jigsaw was missing and without it the pattern was not applicable. Now it was, however. Arty, turning that tight circle on the pavement with his full load of passengers still safety seated, had struck the spark that had fired George's train of ideas, for it occurred to him on the instant that here was the real answer to all that niggling local competition and that formidable drift of trade away from wholesalers and manufacturers converted to the notion of owning their own transport and saving costs.

The answer had two parts. One was concerned with manoeuvrability, afforded by the housing of vehicular power forward in a compact unit with independent steering; the other was a matter of stowage involving linked vehicles in the form of trailers. Together, he decided, they could revolutionise one's entire concept of road haulage, for so far the mulish rigidity of a vehicle, driven in streets designed solely for horse traffic, had applied severe limits on the size of the following container, it being impossible to employ a motor over a certain length in the sharp turns and angles met with in the old towns and congested cities of every region in the network. An articulated vehicle, based on Arty Hardcastle's precept, promised far greater mobility and more mobility meant more overall length allowing twice as much stowage. And this, in turn, meant cheaper hauls over long and short distances.

It did not take him long to evolve a detailed plan — a few hours at the sketchboard, a ten-hour session with Scottie Quirt (summoned by telephone from his Manchester workshop) and finally a long discussion with Withers, the chief accountancy clerk, roughing out an approximate estimate of the initial outlay partial conversion required. His sole remaining concern was to convince the viceroys, summoned to discuss the crisis, each of them, he suspected, in a suitably chastened mood.

Swann-on-Wheels had never concerned itself much with records, that is to say, with data that might prove invaluable to a historian of the firm in the distant future.

It had never once occurred to Adam, or indeed to George, that developments over the years, and changes in policy generally, would be likely to concern anyone but themselves and their current work forces. For both, in their time, had been men of the present and the future, apart from what it was likely to yield in increased turnover, could be left to itself. Thus George Swann had worked, year by year, developing the commercial motor. In the accumulation of day books and minute books and old ledgers stored in the depository adjoining the new counting-house, one could have found any amount of data concerned with the day-to-day running of the firm but very little relating to the inspirations, doubts and arguments of individual members of the firm. There were, in that small depository, maps by the score marking regional frontiers old and new, ledgers in which diligent searchers could have discovered the ratio of profit and turnover in every part of Britain, details of the rewards of men who administered and operated them and careful records of expenditure on plant and rolling stock, from the day Adam Swann sent his first three-horse waggon into rural Kent with old coachman Blubb on the box. But the real heart and bones of the enterprise were not to be found in these day-by-day recordings, not even in the master minute book, started by the head clerk Tybalt, in December, 1863, when Adam first summoned his managers to help him surmount his first major crisis. Decisions were there but not the manner in which decisions were arrived at or the pressures that lay behind those decisions.

And yet, once in a while, a researcher of the future might have come across a nugget of gold among all this dross. Such a find lay in the laconic entry towards the end of the twenty-odd pages recording the business of the extraordinary general meeting of July 12th, 1911. It ran:

Resolved, by sixteen votes to three, no abstentions. That the sum of £50,000 should be set aside for the conversion of twenty motor vehicles to articulated lorries based on the accompanying sketches, a maximum of half this sum to be earmarked for the assembly of three new vehicles and subsequent research thereon. This total to be reviewed at the January conference, 1912."

There was no mention of Arty Hardcastle's soapbox and why should there be? The production of a child's soapbox, assembled from a discarded perambulator, a biscuit box and two fish crates taken by stealth from Billingsgate Market, had no place in the deliberations of some score of serious-minded transport men, each and every one of them worried by a sharp falling off of profits. And, in any case, when George laughingly displayed the soapbox to some of his colleagues as they trooped out into the yard at the conclusion of their discussions, the clerk whose job it had been to take shorthand notes of their deliberations was already on his way home to his young wife and baby in Clapham. He did not hear George say, to a puzzled group of executives, that included his own son Rudi and two of his nephews raised on a Kentish farm: "Take a good look at her, gentlemen. She cost me ten shillings. She's just cost you fifty thousand!"

2

Most of the third generation Swanns (they now numbered around a score) had a favourite uncle and had a poll been taken among them it is probable that Lieutenant-Colonel Alexander Swann, veteran of Isandlwana, Rorke's Drift, Tel-el-Kebir and various other engagements featuring thin red lines and slaughtered savages, would have emerged the winner. After Alex, no doubt, would have come Uncle Hugo (also performer of a deed that won the Empire, once winner of an entire roomful of athletic trophies and now *Sir* Hugo) but Giles, a mere politician, would have come third; a poor third, notwithstanding the fact that he was a playful, soft-spoken man.

Edward, who was not much older than some of the elder grandchildren, qualified as a courtesy uncle.

Uncle George, despite his jocularity and generosity at Christmas-time, was not a contender for the title. Perhaps, on account of his high spirits, the younger Swanns saw him as one of themselves, but there was one at least who did not, who entertained for him a respect approaching reverence. This was Martin, second son of Denzil and Stella Fawcett of Dewponds Farm and his regard for his Uncle George had nothing to do with Christmas stockings or birthday tips. It was based on his easy familiarity with a real live giant and dated from a summer afternoon around about 1890, when Martin, then aged about eight, had been invited into the old stable block at 'Tryst' to watch the Giant Maximilien, who lived there.

Martin had never forgotten that enchanting afternoon and in a way it had dictated the course of his life. For, alone among the Swann grandchildren, he came to share George's affection for the great shining monster, with its brassy lungs and blue breath, seeing it not as an ogre (and a very noisy, smelly and dangerous one at that!) but as the bondsman of his Uncle George, who told Martin that he had found him far across the sea, had since taken care of him, fed him with oil and given him a home in the tile-hung outhouses on the eastern side of the stable-yard.

Martin, soon a very regular visitor, thus grew to love both Maximilien and his master, seeing them as inter-dependent on one another. For he discovered, as time went by, that Uncle George came out here to commune with his servant at all hours of the day and night, giving as his explanation that Maximilien was a restless, thirsty fellow, who needed a great deal of exercise to prevent his joints getting rusty and that Uncle George, having found him scared and lonely in a strange country, was now obliged to keep him in good fettle against the day (not long now, Uncle George prophesied) when Maximilien would travel at a speed faster than any horse in the world could gallop.

For three years, until he was turned eleven, Martin did not believe this part of the story. He had never seen Maximilien actually move, that is to say, to step down from his wooden blocks, pass the stable door and cross the outside yard. He always looked as if he was about to do this but he never did, contenting himself with a kind of stationary dance that involved rapid movements of all his vitals and a steady spinning of his two immense rear wheels that sometimes turned at such a speed that the giant began to gasp and puff his blue breath into every corner of the stable. He was far too big, anyway, to pass the door, and while George assured him that he could take Maximilien to pieces and put him together again, Martin did not believe this either, having long since decided that the stable must have been built around him the day he arrived.

In the meantime, however, it was fascinating to stand here and watch Uncle George tend the brute, touching a knob here, pulling a lever there, applying his oil can to various joints in the giant's armour and sometimes polishing him with rags and leathers. Martin said, one day, "You're *jolly* kind to him, Uncle George, I mean, considering he doesn't *do* anything," and George had said, "Ah, but he will, as soon as he's ready and I give him the nod. You see, Martin, he's promised to make my fortune one day. Mine and your Auntie Gisela's, so naturally I have to keep him fit and good-tempered."

Martin accepted this as a reasonable explanation of his uncle's cheerful servitude but he could never have said at what point in his boyhood the brassy-throated Maximilien transformed himself from fairy-tale figure to fact of life. It must have been somewhere around the day he came over here, when he was thirteen, to find the stable doors swinging free and both Uncle George and the monster gone, the latter never to be seen around these parts again.

His grandmother told him what had happened.

Uncle George, she said, had taken the Maximilien away to Manchester, to show him to *her* father, and Martin's great-grandfather, Sam Rawlinson. It was more than a year later when Martin saw George again and asked him if this was true and he said it was, and that Maximilien had kept all his promises in the north and had even persuaded Grandfather Swann of his merits.

From then on a warm relationship developed between uncle and nephew, beginning with the admission that Maximilien was not a stray monster but a mechanically-propelled vehicle, and Martin's confession that he had known this for some time but had never liked to admit it in case he was forbidden the stable. He also added, with a grin, that he had earned several thrashings from his mother for coming here, for his mother, in common with all the womenfolk about the estate, regarded George's engine as a potential child killer.

It was some years after that that Martin was dramatically rescued from the never-ending chores of his father's farm and sent up to Manchester himself, there to work in Uncle George's engine shed, where any number of stream-lined Maximiliens were assembled and sent out to work on the roads.

The translation, from Kentish countryside to a clamorous northcountry workshop proved to be the most exhilarating experience of his life and while Uncle George's manager, the taciturn Mr. Quirt, was a heavy task-master, given to sudden outbursts of temper, he came to enjoy every moment he spent on the benches in the company of his brother John and about a dozen other apprentices.

John Fawcett, unfortunately, did not last the course and emerge as a journeyman mechanic. In his second year up north he developed asthma and was ordered south again, there to find open-air work in Swann's Maidstone depot, for Dewponds was not sufficiently prosperous to support three families, Stella's eldest son, Robert, having married and moved into the farm's tied cottage.

In the meantime, Martin, learning something new about the internal combustion engine and heavy coach-building each day, qualified as Scottie Quirt's favourite assistant, a fact that seemed to please George for every time he came up here – it was generally at least once a month – he called for Martin's progress reports and, having studied them, demanded of Scottie whether or not (family favouritism on one side) Martin could be given further responsibilities as head of the draughtsmen's section.

It was not often that Scottie paid anyone a compliment. His northern dourness compelled him to qualify any praise he doled out, or at least to preface it with a warning such as, "Ye'll no' get bigheaded aboot it!" Or, "When you've been at the trade as long as me ye'll have reason to ask yourself . . ." On this occasion, however, he was more forthright.

"The laddie's the best ye've sent me, there's nae doot aboot that! He doesna give a hoot how long I keep him at it when we're pushed and, by God, George Swann, ye've been pushing us hard lately, hae ye not? Aye, gi'e that lad a year at the drawing board and see what he comes up with."

"And after that?"

"Och, maybe he'll tak' on where I leave off, for the fact is I canna teach that boy any more."

It was the first time in their long and strenuous association that George had ever heard Scottie concede technical equality with anyone.

So Martin Fawcett went into the drawing office, emerging, from time to time, with some very practical blueprints aimed at various modifications, and it was to him, more than to anyone else, that Quirt turned when George presented them with a seemingly impossible challenge – the almost overnight conversion of a small fleet of Mark IV Swann-Maxies to articulated steering, with an engine thrust capable of providing the power to haul two loads in one. This, plus an edict to design and build three articulated trailer vehicles from scratch and do it all by the turn of the year, now less than six months ahead.

Scottie had argued vehemently that it could not be done, not even if they signed on a dozen extra mechanics and worked double shift. "Ye'll hae to choose between one or the other," he declared, "for ye canna hae both, man, in that span of time. Do you no' ken the size o' the task in these quarters, when there's no room to swing a cat?"

George conceded him the point regarding space. For a long time now the present quarters in Macclesfield had been badly overcrowded and the assortment of tin-roofed sheds in the yard outside had not kept pace with regional demands for more vehicles and faster repairs. He said, briefly, "Then we'll separate the projects. You stay here, and get ahead with the conversions, and Martin can build the prototypes in premises I'll rent for him in Leeds. You'd join me in backing him for the job, wouldn't you, Scottie?"

"Aye," said Scottie, judiciously, "I'd back any lad I'd trained. But yon more than most."

3

It was wonderful watching it grow. It was marvellous to watch it move, stage by stage, from a sheaf of sketches, blotched by oily thumb-prints to blue-print, and thence to the foundry, factory bench and carpenter's shed. But best of all was to contemplate it in the white glow of the unshaded lights after all the others had shed their overalls and gone home, to sense its assumption of a corporate personality from mere hunks of tortured metal and baulks of timber, so that it was no longer an artefact but a thing of sensibility and temperament, that needed to be tamed and schooled by someone who had created it from a thousand and one components.

Time ceased to exist for him. In some ways, indeed,

time telescoped, so that he was sometimes a child again standing beside the flailing, hissing Maximilien in the 'Tryst' stables, sometimes a journeyman mechanic working on his first real assignment, and sometimes the kinsman of men like Gottlieb Daimler and the Wright brothers, or Blériot and Captain Cody, whose pioneer flying feats over English shires had captured every headline in Fleet Street.

This thing had moods. Occasionally winsome and more often fractious moods. There were days when it was sluggish and inert, and others when it was wooden-limbed, like a sulky child being dressed for Sunday for an unwanted outing. There were times when it seemed to resist a stage in its assembly, so that it seemed like a huge, fractured pipe men were trying to reduce to its original pattern. When this happened Martin's landlady saw nothing of him for days together, for he would stay on the job all night, snatching a few hours' sleep on a bagged-out mattress in the drawing office and living on fish and chips and cocoa brewed on a burner.

But gradually it took on shape and form and a kind of looming grace, reaching almost from one end of the shop to the other, preening itself under its three coats of green and gold paint with the Swann emblem etched in black on the sides of the trailer. Then he would prowl around it, contemplating its immensity and the ponderous thrust that lay dormant under its downsloping bonnet, and he would picture himself driving it over the most punishing roads of England dragging a load that no Swann vehicle had ever hauled across a regional frontier in the fifty-three-year history of the enterprise.

Uncle George came north once a fortnight now, praising his tirelessness and ingenuity, and sometimes bringing messages from his Kentish homestead. In October, when they were well forward he commissioned Martin's chief lieutenant to begin work on the second giant and in early November, having been assured that Mark I would be ready to run by mid-December, he told his nephew that four regional viceroys were quarrelling furiously over the honour of putting the first articulated trailer van on the roads and he had been obliged to draw lots between his son Rudi in The Polygon, his brother Edward in The Funnel, Higson in the Scottish Lowlands and Rookwood in the Southern Square.

Word came, a day or so later, that Rudi had emerged winner so that the vehicle's trial run, exclusive of routine road testing, would constitute its delivery, entailing a short but stiffish haul over the Pennine ridge to the Salford Depot, a mile or so west of the cotton capital.

Work was all but complete by then and Martin left the finishing touches to the three apprentices and the painter, retiring to his littered office, that reeked of a hundred fish and chip suppers, to plan his route, George having told him that he had succeeded in persuading Scottie Quirt to delegate the honour of the first journey to the man who most deserved it. He paid Martin another compliment, the biggest compliment anyone had ever paid or was ever likely to, when he said, with a grin, "Have you thought up a name for her? We've christened every other vehicle in service, from pinnaces to frigates to Goliaths, so she'll have to have a name of some sort."

Martin said he hadn't thought about naming her although the team who had worked on her over the five months period of assembly had called her by a variety of names, all of them unprintable. George said, seriously, "Well, I'll always think of her as a 'Fawcett', so you'd better do the same from now on. And to make it official get a couple of nameplates stamped out and screwed to the radiator and trailer tailboard." He hurried off then to catch the London train for he could see Martin blushing through his rash of freckles and after the shed had closed down for the night Martin stayed on until nearly midnight, stamping out the name, first in letters four inches high but afterwards, afraid of seeming to put on side, reducing them to three.

*   *   *

The run was scheduled for December 13th and Quirt advised travelling empty. "If she jibs at some of those inclines at least we can get her off the road and send someone by motor-cycle to gie you a hand," he said. "Loaded she'll need towage and a brace o' waggons to offload." Martin thought the precaution unnecessary. She wouldn't jib at any incline and as for descents, there was no metalled slope on the west side of the Pennines that he feared, with his rim block brakes, revolutionary contracting transmission footbrake and equally novel handbrake controlling internal-expanding units on the rearward wheels of the forward section. There was a further feature Scottie seemed to have overlooked, the speeded up interchangeability of the enlarged driving sprockets, enabling the gear ratio to be altered to match laden or unladen running and varying road conditions. Up or down dale Martin Fawcett had no doubts at all about his four-ton Fawcett holding the road. He would have wagered all he possessed on this even before the road tests buttressed his faith in the giant.

On the day before he set out a bulky package arrived for him and was delivered to his lodgings. It turned out to be a handsome present from Uncle George, a heavy leather coat with stylish crossover fastenings, a vizored cap to match, leather gauntlets and a pair of aviator's goggles. There was a note attached in George's handwriting, reading, " 'Rich not gaudy, for the apparel oft proclaims the man!' Good luck. Uncle George and all at H.Q."

He was glad then the spanking new kit had not been sent to the sheds for he could never have waited to see himself in it and the result, reflected in the mirror of his landlady's wardrobe door, did not disappoint him. Cody and Blériot would have envied him the rigout; he looked more like an aviator than an engineer.

He rolled her out into the yard and backed her round facing the double gates ready for a flying start in the morning. She handled even more easily than he had hoped, as light on the steering as a Swann-Maxie with less than a third of her cubic capacity but there was no mistaking the chant of her three-cylinder engines. They sang of power and conquest, of even coasting along high plateaux and swift, controlled descents into the valleys. They spoke to him of capacity hauls of over two hundred miles a day, spilling goods into the four corners of the land with a speed and profusion that a fleet of his grandfather's waggons could not have achieved. They made the latest model from the Macclesfield sheds seem as obsolete as a Roman chariot and a seat on these leather driving-box cushions was a throne, elevating him to the status of king among road travellers. He climbed down and went round to the bonnet, glancing covertly at the shining letters of the newly-affixed nameplate, a just reward for all the hours of toil that had preceded this moment of triumph. He said to an acolyte, unable to restrain his exuberance, "My stars, but she's a beauty! She's the most beautiful thing I've ever imagined! And this time tomorrow, from here to Salford, she'll pull in the crowds wherever she rides!"

The man to whom he spoke, one Dyson, a carpenter who had bent and fitted her hood poles, was to remember this remark. Especially when his daughter brought him his illustrated paper towards the end of his lie-in the following Sunday morning.

His route was a double compromise.

By the shortest distance, and probing for low gradients and good, metalled roads, he could have knocked miles off his journey and as much as three hours off his time schedule, but he had to reckon on the near certainty of traffic congestion in the complex manufacturing centres stretching eastwards and southwards from Bradford through Halifax to Huddersfield and Oldham. He knew this ground well. Only by night, or on a Sunday, was it free of heavy haulage, up here mostly horsedrawn, and there was no certainty of an easy passage of any of the West Riding towns in mid-week. On the other hand, a more northerly and circuitous route up the valley of the Aire, bearing west by Haworth, then south via Hebden Bridge and Rochdale, presented serious hazards at the time of year. Most of the road ran over high, windswept upland, with the virtual certainty of ice on some gradients. There was, however, a third alternative, the compromise within a compromise, a more tortuous approach over the lower landmass enclosing the Aire gap, heading north-west for Keighley and beyond it to Cross Hill, where the road branched north to Skipton and south-west for Colne and the eastern frontier of the cotton belt. Thus, of the three alternatives, two offered virtual freedom from traffic and of these two the Keighley–Colne route promised the easier climb, although adding more than thirty miles to the journey.

It was this approach he finally chose, stowing two extra drums of fuel in the trailer, for he had no experience on which to base his probable petrol consumption. His own guess was that it would be nearly double that of the heaviest Swann-Maxie on the roads, particularly over the spine of England, but he was in no particular hurry and a series of long climbs and the twenty-mile drop into Lancashire might provide him with the answers to some of the many questions both George and Scottie Quirt would be sure to put at the inquest. And a searching inquest, with two other prototypes in the making, was vital, with a prospect of saving weeks of trial and error when fed back to the Leeds mechanics. It might also be generally useful to Scottie's men in the Macclesfield yard, for every six months or so modifications were adapted to the standard vehicle and not all of them came (by fair means or foul) from the brochures and workshops of competitors. Perhaps half were derived from personal experience within the network, sedulously circulated to the regions in the columns of *The Migrant*.

The morning was bright, clear and cold, with the thermometer hovering a couple of degrees over freezing point in the city, so that his hoped-for early start was delayed. There had been a sharp frost in the night and he decided to wait for the morning sun to get to work on the ice patches. The wind, coming from the west, was very fresh, altogether an exhilarating morning to begin an odyssey, and he set out about ten-thirty, heading west-south-west through Shipley and Bingley, well north of the Bradford suburbs and finding the road surprisingly open.

He was right about the Fawcett attracting attention. Errand boys whistled with surprise as he rumbled past and he saw one jot down the name of the vehicle in a notebook. He thought, smiling, 'That'll fox him for sure. Nobody but Uncle George and me, and the Leeds mechanics, have ever heard of the name applied to a motor.'

He made very good time, averaging around twenty miles an hour, and before starting the climb to Cross Hill and the Skipton junction he pulled in at a tavern and ordered a ham sandwich and a cup of coffee, occupying himself while the coffee was brewing by stamping about the yard and swinging his arms to restore circulation to his fingertips. The leather coat and gauntlets were a boon but it was still cold up on that high box. Only his feet were warmed by the engine and the coffee was so good that, after a reassuring glance at his watch, he ordered a second cup.

The sky had clouded over as he gained height and the wind freshened, veering to the north-east. There were still patches of ice here and there but he travelled most of this section in second gear, driving with excessive caution. The trailer was inclined to snake a little when he built up speed and his mind was occupied, as he went along, with ways of how this problem could be tackled satisfactorily. Probably by adjustments to the coupling, he thought, as the crossroads came into view a mile beyond the village of Steeton.

From here on it was almost all downslope, a stretch of about eight miles into Colne and the prospect of flatter ground from then on, together with the near certainty of heavy traffic, slow-moving in these narrow,

Lancashire streets, after he reached Nelson and Burnley and turned south for Rochdale.

He pulled in to the side of the road at the summit and fed ten gallons of fuel into the tank, using his tin funnel with a filter but impeded somewhat by the ever freshening wind that whipped the hood of cabin and trailer causing them to exclaim like sails and spraying a fine rain of fuel over his gauntlets and the engine cowling. He rolled the cask back and up the plank slide to the trailer tailboard, thinking that it might have been wiser to bring along an apprentice to do the chores, but not seriously, for this was an experience he did not care to share with anyone, not even with Uncle George or Scottie Quirt, whose brains had contributed far more than his to the creation of the monster. There were parts of it, however, that were indubitably his, so that the name was not really undeserved. He looked westward down the long, straight stretch of road he was to travel and thought: 'Longest route notwithstanding, I've made rattling good time. At this rate I'll be in Salford by late afternoon, and Cousin Rudi and I can celebrate with a pint and a dish of Lancashire hotpot!'

Then he was off again, tackling the decline at about twenty-two miles an hour but changing down when he saw the long squiggle of ice crossing the road diagonally from south to north where a streamlet had frozen during the night. He had not expected ice this side of the Pennines. Almost always the eastern side was the colder but it must be the wind blowing in from the North Atlantic.

He felt the skid and heard the distant toot of the horn at the same instant. A hunting horn it was from somewhere on the fell away to the left and a second later, as he was steering into the skid on the shoulder of the hill, he saw the hunt streaming diagonally across his front, a straggle of about twenty riders less than a hundred yards behind the pack and clearly in full cry, for they were pounding over the frosted turf at a cracking rate, the huntsman out ahead, horn to his lips.

The spectacle did not distract him. He was too good an engineer for that but he wasted a split second gauging their probable line and trying to judge where, precisely, they would cross the road bounded by low stone walls, no obstacle to experienced horsemen and certainly none to the scrambling pack that went at it in a bunch and were all over the road in a matter of seconds.

He had to brake harder then and out of the corner of his eye he saw the leading horsemen pulling on their reins and one or two of them cavorting parallel with him as the horses, baulking more at the Fawcett than the wall, swung left on a downslope. It was then that he went into the real skid, a long, skittering slide left, right and left again, and he had a moment to be afraid; not for himself but for the Fawcett, for it flashed across his mind that this would be a ridiculous way to conclude his odyssey, broadside on against a loose stone wall on the eastern slopes of the Pennines.

The landscape lost coherence for him then, at the moment of the first impact. He was hunched over the steering column, wrestling with the heavy vehicle as with a Mastodon and it was not answering to any of the directions transmitted through his hands and feet. It was like an elephant that had run wild, lashing out with its immense hindquarters and grinding everything in its path. The hunt foamed up on the far side of the wall and about a dozen laggards among the pack were still spewed over the highway, running it seemed in all directions, as though to escape the thundering passage of the vehicle, now almost broadside on with its trailer ricocheting from the base of the wall but always, impelled by its own weight and anchored apex, returning for more punishment.

Then, as though the whole world was turning topsy-turvey, he lost all sense of direction as the cabin heeled over, was checked by the pull of the trailer, half-recovered its upright position and finally somersaulted twice, ending up on its nearside wedged between the two walls and piled in the form of a barricade across the full width of the road.

He had a sense of being picked up by the heels and shaken, a vanquished rat in the jaws of a terrier, and experienced a single spasm of fear as he saw, all about him, a soft orange glow and smelled the reek of blazing fuel. His last conscious thought was of that unstowed reserve drum in the trailer, surely the main contributory factor to this holocaust, and his lips framed the word, "Fool . . . *fool!*" as he remembered that he was the man who had placed it there, without so much as a brace or a piece of rope to hold it in position against a contingency like this.

5

Stella

GEORGE HEARD THE FULL TRUTH BY TELEPHONE
from Rudi, who had received it from the police at Colne
who, in turn, had got it from the infirmary surgeon
examining the charred bundle they brought in for him to
certify as dead.

By then Rudi was in Colne himself having rushed there
by motor-cycle, arriving, chilled to the bone, about dusk,
when a team of corporation men were still trying, without
much success, to clear the road six miles to the east. Rudi
telephoned before notifying Scottie Quirt and the Macclesfield depot. Shocked half out of his mind he still realised
it was his responsibility as Polygon viceroy, and com-
missioner of the new trailer, to pass the information to
Headquarters and ask for instructions.

He could sense his father's numbed horror over the
two-hundred-mile gap between them, and when George
remained silent for something approaching half a minute,
he said, urgently: "You did get it, sir? You . . . you heard
everything?"

George replied, in a voice that seemed to come from the
other side of the world, "Yes, Rudi, I heard. It's awful
. . . frightful . . ." but then, rallying a little, "You're at
Colne? Then go out to the scene of the accident. Talk to
the police, to anyone who was early on the scene. To the
master of that damned hunt if you can find him. Get all
the information you can. Every scrap, you understand?"

"Yes, sir. I'll stay on overnight."

"Arrange to stay indefinitely and I'll join you for the inquest. I'll get someone to stand in for you at the depot. Meantime I've got to tell his mother and father."

"Can't someone else do it? The police? Grandfather, perhaps?"

"No, son, it'll have to be me, for I was the one who took him from that farm. Stay on the job, there's a good lad. And thank you for letting me know so quickly. Don't bother with Scottie, I'll see he's notified from H.Q."

"Right, Father. Goodbye."

"Goodbye, son. Leave word where you're staying with the Colne police."

He rehooked the receiver and sat motionless, forcing himself to assemble the factors fed him by Rudi into some kind of sequence. A head-on collision with a hunt in full cry on a Pennine slope. A pile-up, with that immense weight bearing down on the buckled cabin and the man inside it. The first puff of flames, a soft explosion, then an inferno, far too fierce to permit hope of rescue, even if the nearest horsemen could have got to him in time. He remembered the last time he had seen Martin, only a few days ago, and told himself how splendidly the boy was coming along, and what an asset he would be to the network in the years ahead. Now he was not a person at all, just a blackened corpse lying in a corporation mortuary two hundred miles to the north, awaiting a string of coroners, solicitors, witnesses and jurymen to pronounce upon the circumstances of his death. And after that, he supposed, a coffin would trail south, containing all that remained of Martin Fawcett, one-time farmhand, lately someone of infinite promise and charm.

He drew a jotting pad towards him and wrote a few instructions for the head clerk, calling a vanboy and telling him to deliver the note to the counting house at once. The network viceroys at least would have to know in advance; they would never forgive him if they learned it from the newspapers. And thinking of newspapers he rang for

Jeffs, his editor, who came close to breaking down when he heard the news and said, in answer to George's query: "Fleet Street will get on to something of that kind very quickly. Local correspondents will wire in stories by tonight but there won't be any, most likely, in a place the size of Colne. Probably staff men will go over from Manchester, certainly one on behalf of the Northcliffe press. He'll feature this as his front page tomorrow."

"As soon as that?"

"Almost surely, George." He looked at him steadily. "It means Stella and Denzil will have to know tonight, doesn't it? Would you like Debbie and me to drive over with you?"

"No, this is something I've got to cope with alone. Thank you all the same, Milt. Go on home and arrange for Debbie to go down to 'Tryst' and tell the old folks in the morning. There's no need for them to know yet. The London papers don't get there until around eleven o'clock. Tell Debbie I'll be there by then."

He dragged himself up and across the yard from his ground-floor office block near the weighbridge to the spot where his Daimler was parked. The mechanic in charge was polishing the windshield. George said, gruffly, "Leave that, Rigby. Is there enough petrol in the tank to take me down to 'Tryst'?"

"It's half full, sir. I checked a minute since."

He got in and waited for the man to swing the starting handle. Then, tuning the engine, he drove slowly through the main gates and headed south into the thick of the Old Kent Road traffic. The Daimler's oil lamps battled with a low swirl of river mist as he nosed his way carefully into the southbound stream.

He had one meagre slice of luck. Bumping down the length of unsurfaced track from river to farmyard he saw the wink of a lantern in the byre on his right and pulled up, opening and closing the door softly and treading over frozen ruts to the byre. Denzil was inside, anxiously watching one of his Guernseys. The shed reeked of warm, country smells, touched with a whiff of disinfectant. His brother-in-law looked up as he entered, his broad, red face expressing surprise as he said, "George? You here, this time o' night? Stella never said . . ."

"Where is she, Denzil?"

"In the kitchen. I've only come out to look before locking up." He nodded at the cow beyond the rail. "She's through it but we had a worrysome hour or two. Vet was here twice since she started, around noon. Twin heifers. Alwus look for trouble with a pair. Still, she'll do now, I think. Take a look at 'em," and George peered beyond the lantern ray to see the mild-eyed Guernsey munching at her rack, one calf at her udders, another curled at her feet in the straw. He said, with a rush, "Listen, Denzil, I'd sooner break it to you here . . . alone. Martin was . . . was killed today, up in the Pennines . . ."

"Killed? Marty!" His head came up so sharply that George heard the cricking sound of his neck. "How?"

"He was driving one of the new vans from Leeds and skidded on an icy road trying to avoid a hunt. He was dead before they got him out. Rudi telephoned from a place called Colne."

He watched the farmer ride out the shock. His weather-beaten face first drained itself of colour and then a heavy flush returned to his pendulous cheeks as he raised a hand and rasped the palm across a day's stubble.

"My boy? Dead, you say?"

George nodded and stood waiting. The only sounds that broke the stillness of the byre was the lisping suck of the calf and the champ of its mother at the rack. Presently Denzil said, "When did it happen, George?" George said he wasn't sure but it was probably early afternoon. The van Martin was driving was brand new, one that he assembled himself and partially designed on his own drawing-board. He added, "He was keen, Denzil. The keenest lad we ever had in the machine shops. It's a frightful thing to have happened, the first man we ever lost on a motor run. I don't know much about the circumstances except that there was a fire . . ."

"A fire? On the road you mean?"

"The vehicle caught fire but Martin was almost certainly dead when the flames reached him, or so Rudi says."

Denzil was staring at him aghast and he knew why. Within yards of where they were standing Denzil's own father had died in a fire, trying to save his cattle when the farm was gutted. That was before he married Stella, something like thirty years ago. Stella had told him how, on that occasion, Denzil had carried his father's body to an outhouse down the approach lane and afterwards she had watched over him all night while he slept on sacks in a shed behind the piggeries.

"We'd best go in now and tell his mother, Denzil."

"Nay, I coulden do that."

"You don't have to, I will . . ."

"*No!*" The farmer shot out his huge hand and caught George by the wrist. "Let me think on it a minute . . . Burned up, you say? . . . I can't tell her that. She's alwus been afraid o' fire, ever since we lost Dewponds that time. Every time she smells smoke she makes me go out an' do the rounds. No, I dassn't tell her that, not yet any road."

George could hear his breath wheezing but soon, rather sooner than he expected, his brother-in-law recovered some sort of grip upon himself. He said, finally, "You wait on. Wait in the yard. I'll go in and break it, best I can. It'll be better comin' from me, seein' she was always dead against them boys goin' up there in the first place. Wait on 'till I come."

He plodded slowly out of the byre, closing the door and moving across the beam thrown by the Daimler's lights towards the kitchen. He went in and George saw his shadow move against the muslin curtains of the big, low-beamed room.

It was a room, he recalled, that his sister had helped Denzil to rebuild when she was a girl of about twenty, slowly emerging from the shock of that disastrous first

marriage to a vicious wastrel over the Sussex border. He
understood then why she had opposed the exodus of her
boys from this farm and this plodding way of life. Everything that was real and important to her was right here, in
this flowering corner of Kent and everything beyond it,
even 'Tryst', where she had been born, was alien and
charged with menace. She had renounced home and
family the night of that fire, identifying herself body and
soul with that lumping great chap, Fawcett. Why and
how nobody had ever discovered. Not even his mother
who had done all she could to encourage the unlikely
match.

About five minutes passed. The sweat on his forehead
and under his arms struck cold and he shivered, making
the effort of his life to resist the temptation to leap into
the motor, reverse madly up the lane to the river road, and
drive off into the night. Presently Denzil came out and
called, not to him but to someone working in a milking
shed on the far side of the yard. Robert, Denzil's eldest
son, emerged, shouting irritably, "What's to do now?
I'm milking. Charley's gone and I said I'd finish!"
But his father called again, sharply this time, and Robert
stumped across the cobbles to join him and they stood
talking for a moment in the doorway before Robert went
in and Denzil came across to the byre. He said, "Woulden
it be better if you left it? If you just drove off, and come
back in the morning?"

"No, it wouldn't, Denzil. The papers might be full
of it in the morning and even if you keep them from her
busybodies from the village are sure to come posting up
here falling over themselves to tell her the gory details.
No, no, I don't want that, and neither do you if you think
about it."

"Ah, come on in, then, but don't say more'n you have
to for she's taken it bad. She's taken it real bad, George."

She was in her customary place at the head of the long
oak table, as though about to preside over supper. She
sat bolt upright and her plump round face was perfectly

blank, almost as though she was asleep with her eyes open. She gave no sign when he moved around and took a seat close to her, furthest from the fire. He took her hand, coarsened by years of farm work, and held it tightly. It had always been difficult to equate her with the elegant sister he remembered in the days when they were all growing up together at 'Tryst' and she was reckoned the belle of the county and the best horsewoman for miles around. The Stella of those days had died before she was twenty and this heavy, practical, unsmiling woman had taken her place. He said, brokenly, "I'm sorry, Stella . . . sorry," but could say no more, lowering his head so that he was only half aware of her sudden, incredibly swift movement up and away from the table. He only realised that the hand he had been clasping had been whipped away, as from the fangs of a snake. He heard Denzil and Robert cry out together and a combined rush of boots on the slate floor. There was a sudden flash and a shattering report, blinding and deafening him and then, as his chin came up, he saw Stella struggling with her husband and son, the latter with one hand on the gun forcing the barrel towards the floor. Then, very suddenly, she went limp, her knees buckling as she pitched forward and would have fallen had not both men grabbed her, Robert throwing the twelve-bore to the floor. The kitchen was half full of smoke and the reek of gunpowder made him cough and splutter. Robert said, breathlessly, "Leave her, Dad. I'll see to her. I'll carry her up. Fetch Dolly fer Chrissake! For Chrissake run an' fetch Dolly!"

George subsided on the bench, the noise of the shot still singing in his ears and through a haze of smoke he saw Robert lift his mother as though she was a slip of a girl and move ponderously towards the stairs. He was unable to help him. There was no power in his legs. The big kitchen clock ticked on and a Welsh collie, that had scampered for cover when the shot was fired, emerged cautiously from beneath the table and arranged himself carefully beside him, slowly wagging his bush of a tail.

Dolly, Robert's brawny wife, hurried in and went straight upstairs. Then Denzil returned, wordlessly picking up the gun and breaking it open. "T'other barrel weren't loaded," he said. "That must be young Dick. On'y Dick's vool enough to leave a loaded gun about the place."

"Did she mean to kill me? Or was it to scare me out of the house?"

"God knows. She had the gun on you any road, and if Bob hadn't been mighty quick . . ." He ran his hand over his stubble again, making a sound like a hand-saw. "It's all on account of what the boys did, I reckon, leaving here to work on those motors of yours. She's never been the same. She never got used to it and alwus blamed you for it. She told me just now you killed him, same as you shot him but she didn't mean it, not really."

"How do you feel about it, Denzil?"

"Not the way she does. It was what they wanted, or young Marty wanted any road. We had letters from him saying so and his brother woulden come back to a farm, not now."

"That's how it was, Denzil. I'd like you to believe that. I'd like you to try and make Stella understand that. Martin was a born engineer and was first-class at his job, right from the start. He wouldn't have been happy doing anything else. Do you think you could convince her of that?"

"No, I don't, but I'll try, once she gets over the shock."

"There'll be an inquest. I'm going up for it. Would you or Robert like to come?"

Denzil shook his head. "No, neither of us. We're busy here, dawn to dusk. You can't leave livestock same as you can motors. Besides, what purpose would it serve, seein' the boy's dead?"

He sat down heavily as Robert came clumping down. "Dolly'll stay with her while I take the mare and ride for Doctor Fowler. Maybe he'll come, or maybe he'll give us something to quieten her. Meantime you'd best take a gill, Dad. You, too, Uncle George." He went over to a cupboard in the big dresser and took out a bottle and two cups, pouring into the cups and adding water from the iron kettle beside the hearth. "I'll be back in less than an hour, providing he don't keep me waitin'."

His father raised his head. "Watch out for ice on that footbridge. Don't try and ride over, get off and lead. We've had trouble enough for one night."

"I'll mind the ice. You drink up. You, too, Uncle George."

He went out, a big, strong, very capable man, ideal to have around in a crisis. Something about his gait reminded George vividly of the Adam he remembered from childhood. He thought wretchedly, 'They've all got more Swann than Fawcett about 'em. That must be because Stella's the dominant partner . . .' Slowly he reached out for the liquor and lifted it to his lips. It was sloe gin judging by the taste, and well matured. The cloying stuff warmed his belly and soothed his throat, still irritated by the whiff of gunpowder. The big clock, inevitable as doom, ticked on. The collie's tail maintained its steady, friendly whisk. He said, finally, "We'd best keep this to ourselves – the gunshot I mean. It could lead to her being put away somewhere. The old folks must never hear about it. I can't face them right now. Debbie is going to cope with telling them in the morning . . ." He heaved himself up, "I'll keep you informed, Denzil. And be sure the newspapers are kept from her. Come to that I wouldn't read them myself if I were you. They'll play it up, if I know 'em."

He felt drained and useless. All his striving since he had recoiled from that June balance sheet had amounted to this, a favourite nephew burned to a cinder. His own sister trying to blow his head off with a twelve-bore. He went out, reversed the Daimler down the lane and straightened her out on the river road. He let in the clutch and drove off into the frosty night.

2

Down the years, good and bad, the Swanns had demonstrated that they could ride out the buffets. Hugo's blindness. Stella's disastrous first marriage. The death of Giles' wife in a street riot. These sombre events had been absorbed into the mainstream of life. Not forgotten, of course, but shelved, like bills that were inconvenient to pay on demand, and never featuring in the conversational traffic of a family as large and gregarious as the Swanns of 'Tryst'.

So it might have been with the death of Martin Fawcett, and that despite the furore in the press, had the boy's mother been seen to mourn the boy with dignity, to divorce the tragic incident from her long-standing grudge against George concerning the nature of his work and his involvement with George's concerns rather than his father's. But the shattering report of that gunshot seemed to have released tensions within her that no one suspected were there, least of all her easygoing husband, and her big, capable son, known about Dewponds as Young Master. Her physical prostration lasted no more than forty-eight hours, and in the days that followed, at least to the farmhands and villagers, she seemed to potter about her chores much as usual, but those close to her could not fail to note an abrupt change in her manner and a marked increase in her taciturnity that had passed for matter-of-factness since she had renounced the role of county belle for that of farm wife on a three-hundred-acre holding.

She was not seen at the funeral in Twyforde Churchyard a few days after the tragedy but then no women were present inside the family. There was no occasion for display when, at the very moment of interment, the leader writer of *The Times*, and his opposite number in Northcliffe's *Mail*, were at war with one another on the vexed question of heavy road traffic, the one declaring that the appearance on the nation's highways of motorised giants represented a menace that almost justified re-introduction of the Red Flag Act; the other holding that an occasional mishap of this kind was a small price to pay for the dramatic spurt Britain's motor engineers had achieved since that idiotic piece of legislation had been repealed, enabling the country to regain its lost lead over Continental competitors.

George watched the controversy from the touchlines, resisting, on the advice of the editor of the Swann broadsheet, the temptation to contribute a letter pointing out that the accident could never have occurred had the master and hunt servants involved shown a little common-sense, or made an allowance for Martin's difficulties in braking a heavy vehicle on an icy gradient.

He growled, when he ran his eye over the spate of letters from the hunting shires. "Here's proof, if we wanted it, that the English value the life of an animal at twice that of a man earning his living. If Martin had run clear through that damned pack, and killed a dozen or more, you would have heard baying from Channel to Border. As it is, seeing the kid sacrificed his life for them, they vent their spleen on the vehicle! In the name of God, what do they imagine keeps the nation fed? Trade, or the entrails of foxes?"

But Milton Jeffs said, quietly, "Let it ride, George. No one can stop the motor now. There was the same uproar when the railways carved up the fox-hunting country. Ask Adam if you want confirmation of that."

He was sometimes tempted, indeed, to consult his father on the current turn of affairs, and more particularly on his own inclinations as regards further development of the Fawcett trailer but he held back. The old people had taken a series of hard knocks lately, what with Romayne's death, and the moonlight flit of young Edward's giddy wife, and at their age they would lack the resilience for which both had been noted in the past. So he kept clear of 'Tryst', waiting for the press controversy to die down and be replaced by another, the public hazard of low-flying aeroplanes over cities. But the unease at Dewponds persisted, as he learned from Debbie who was often over there, trying to coax Stella out of the doldrums. She said, early in the new year, "Poor Denzil's worried half out of his wits. He says she's so tetchy he hardly dares open his mouth and they both seem to be sleeping badly. Did you know Stella was abnormally scared of fire?"

"Not until the night I was there. Denzil told me then. He said she has him up going the rounds every time she smells a bonfire. It's understandable, I suppose, seeing that Dewponds once was burned to the ground, and old Fawcett lost his life in the outbreak."

"Well, it's gone beyond that according to him. He tells me she has him out of bed as often as three times a night and when he's hard to rouse she goes on the prowl herself. I got the doctor in again and he prescribed for her but Denzil says no one can lead Stella to medicine. Most of it goes down the sink according to him." She paused, regarding him sympathetically. "There's another thing, too. She knows the full circumstances of Martin's death. One of the farmhands blurted it out and was sacked for his pains. How do you feel about calling in and asking Giles to talk to her?"

It was an old Swann nostrum. When the medical profession had had its fling they usually sent for Giles, the family wiseacre. He had a knack of coaxing secrets from closed minds and finding unsuspected paths out of an impasse, but he had no luck as regards Stella. After an unresponsive hour with her he told Denzil: "I can't reach her. Not yet, anyway, for I daresay that doctor's right. The shock came at a bad time for her, when most women of her age are finding it difficult to cope. However, I'll prescribe for you if you'll heed me."

He looked shrewdly at his brother-in-law, not liking his haggard features and the sag in his belted belly. He had lost, at a guess, upwards of twenty pounds in the last few months, and it was obvious that interrupted sleep was taking its toll. "Get her into a nursing home for a month or so and I'm not talking about an asylum. It's more of a retreat, a place I know at Broadstairs. They just sit about and are cosseted during convalescence. It's expensive but she can afford it. She's never touched that money of Grandfather Sam's, has she?"

He admitted this was true. There had been times, Denzil said, when they could have used her private capital, but he had never asked her for it, not even during the severe agricultural depression of the 'nineties.

"Why not, Denzil?"

"I had my reasons. She come to me when she was in bad trouble. I never dreamed she would but she did, forsaking your lot for this, and a hard and toilsome life mostly. I wanted her. By God, I wanted her, ever since I was a boy, but I never wanted her father's money, or her grandfather's, come to that. We've made do and rubbed along happily enough until now and we'll come through this I daresay, without packing her off anywhere."

He looked around the yard. "She rebuilt this place with her own hands. You woulden know about that, being no more'n a boy at the time but she did, or the pair of us did. Laid every beam, every brick and every tile. You take her from here and she'll get worse instead of better."

"I'm not thinking so much of her. You put in a fourteen-hour day and you need your sleep, man."

"Aye, I do," Denzil said, "but there are times when a man must go short of it and this is one of them. She's been a wonderful wife to me and a fine mother to the boys. What sort of man would I be to pack her off to some kind of hospital at the first sign of trouble? She never had a day's illness in her life until now."

"But this is a different illness, Denzil, a mental illness. Temporary almost surely, but something you can't expect to handle alone. Why don't you think about it?"

"I'll think on it," Denzil said, but Giles knew he would not. Brood, possibly, but not think, for he was not equipped for that kind of thinking, any more than was the village practitioner who brought her bottles of medicine from time to time. Giles said nothing of what was uppermost in his mind, that brief murderous attack that he had dragged from George the last time they discussed Stella's plight. Among them all, however, he came nearer to understanding his sister's dependence on this three hundred acres tucked in a fold of the Weald. It had saved her reason once, a long time ago, and perhaps it could do so again. Spring was on the doorstep, the busiest season of the year for people living off the land. It was possible, indeed likely to his way of thinking, that the demands of a lifetime, grafted on to the very bones of their existence, would reassert themselves as soon as the longer days came round. Hard routine work, as he knew by bitter experience, was the only real anodyne. Providing one had faith in what one was about.

*   *   *

They had entered into a conspiracy to keep it from the old people, soft-pedalling whenever the subject arose and one or other of them paid a call at 'Tryst'. When Henrietta asked a direct question they would reply with half-truths. Stella was slow to shake off her depression and reassert herself as mistress about the place. Denzil had taken it more philosophically, helped no doubt, by the confidence he reposed in his first-born, Robert, and that cheerful village girl Robert had married a year ago. Dolly, they added, was expecting her first child in early spring and the presence of a grandson or granddaughter about the farm would prove a compensatory factor – it often did, in these cases, Debbie argued, wondering how much a man as shrewd as Adam was taken in by this kind of prattle.

Debbie had less misgivings as regards Henrietta. Martin, gone from these parts several years now, had never been as close to her as most of the grandchildren, boys like his brother Robert, the first of them, or Gisela's tribe, who had grown up down at the old millhouse at the foot of the drive. Or perhaps she reserved her deepest sympathy for George, whose habitual grin was rarely seen these days.

But Deborah was in error as regards the impact Martin's tragic death had made upon the woman she had long ago accepted as a mother. Henrietta had never learned to ride the buffets fate had in store for everyone. For so long a stretch, all through her young and middle years, she had walked in sunlight and had come to expect it as the right of the circumspect. True, Hugo's blindness, and a son-in-law's violent death in distant China, might have counselled wariness in these matters but these sombre occurrences, sad as they were to contemplate, had taken place far across the sea and Henrietta's world was local and enclosed.

The death of young Martin was something else. She saw it not only as a shocking waste of a young life but as a kind of culmination to the swarm of tribulations that had beset the family of late, an unlooked-for plague at her time of life. They had begun with that shameful abdication of Edward's wife, a blow not only to his pride but to hers, for it seemed monstrous that any girl should seek to exchange a lifetime as a Swann vicereine, in Henrietta's eyes the most envied future available to a woman, for a career as an actress. Then followed the death of a daughter-in-law in a vulgar street riot and while Henrietta could not help but feel this was a likely outcome of trespassing on male preserves, she was not insensitive to the misery it inflicted upon the most sensitive of the brood, even though she had long abandoned any attempt to understand what went on in the overstocked head of a genius. For that is how she had thought of Giles since he was a child.

Hard on the heels of all this came news that the firm was going through a very bad patch and in a way this information disturbed Henrietta more profoundly than the wounds inflicted on Edward or Giles, for these were of a personal nature. Adam's admission that Swann-on-

Wheels was in rough water was like a hint that the British Empire itself was in jeopardy, or that the Bank of England was expected to close its doors in a week or so. In a way it cast doubts upon Adam Swann's infallibility and this struck at the very roots of her faith in the stability of life. It was symptomatic too of all she witnessed, and more that she sensed, about the times, so different, so very different from those of her middle years, after Adam had been miraculously restored to her and his affairs had been seen to prosper to a degree that put him alongside enterprises like Pears' soap, Lipton's and all the other businesses she saw advertised on hoardings and public transport.

The signposts of change were there for all to see. Nicely-brought-up girls had taken to marching about the streets with banners. Divorces in high places no longer proscribed the departure of parties concerned to Boulogne. And half the families she knew had exchanged carriage and pair for a variant of George's nine-day-wonder that had once been confined to the stable block but had now, it appeared, spawned a thousand and one children, encouraging folk to swarm here, there and everywhere like itinerant salesmen. There was no sense, so far as she could see, in any of it.

And then, as if to confirm her worst fears on this particular issue, they came to her with news that Stella's boy, Martin, had been crushed to death by one of these monsters. Both crushed and burned she understood, although she was at pains not to enquire into the details and it was clear then that the family was undergoing a series of plagues, like the affliction visited upon the Egyptians in Exodus, and that this was a hint that even a dynasty as firmly-based as hers was mortal and that the troubles besetting them were designed, perhaps, to chasten her pride.

She even took to attending church more regularly, and tried hard to persuade Adam to do the same. In this she failed, but having, as it were, renewed her nodding acquaintance with God, she set herself to relearn the habit of prayer as a possible means of warding off further disasters.

It was not easy after all this time, a lifetime of worshipping Adam rather than the nightshirted Jehovah of her girlhood. He seemed so remote and, just lately, so implacable, and phrases to address Him were hard to find if one was looking for anything more than the public approach set out in the Book of Common Prayer. She would have liked to have consulted Adam on her route (after all, he was recognised as Britain's most famous router) but she knew, instinctively, that he could not help her much as regards the best way to propitiate the Almighty. He had never been a churchgoer and she suspected that he had no real belief in survival after death or, for that matter, in the existence of a divine plan and even this, contemplated in the abstract, was strange, for he was certainly what she thought of as a *good* man, and a good Christian, too. Always, ever since the day she had met him up on that moor, he had concerned himself with the troubles and deprivations of the poor, as recommended so insistently in the gospels, but that did not seem to help. What she needed now was a guide along once familiar roads where, unfortunately, the Swann-on-Wheels insignia counted for little.

She could not bring herself to consult the rector, who occasionally came to dinner at 'Tryst'. She had always thought of him and his predecessors as semi-dependants and social inferiors, men who would look to her and hers for help in their routine labours about the parish. What she required, she felt, was an ecclesiastical equivalent of Adam, say an archbishop or, at least, a bishop, and the bishop of her diocese had never been to dinner. Now that she came to think about it he had not even attended one of her At Homes, croquet parties or garden fêtes.

There seemed no reason, however, why this should not be remedied and she broached the subject to Adam when she was drawing up an invitation list for a dinner party she was planning for her birthday. His response was irreverent. All he said was, "Why the bishop? What's he done to deserve it? I can't ever recall having set eyes on the chap, though from all I hear he'll probably take you up on the invitation. He's a rare gad-about, I'm told, and a good judge of wine." And then, with a twinkle, "If he accepts let me know well in advance. I'll look out something special for him, for I wouldn't like him to spread it around that our cellar wasn't one of the best in the diocese."

But then, before she could think of a way of coaxing a qualified spiritual comforter into the house, disturbing hints reached her that Stella was making very heavy weather of things and behaving very oddly on that farm of hers a mile up the river. She took it for granted that Stella's eccentricities could be attributed to the meno-pause and not, as Debbie was inclined to think, delayed shock regarding poor Martin's death in the north and there were grounds for this supposition. From all she knew of her daughter, particularly since she had shaken loose of that scoundrel she had married in such a hurry, Stella was not a person to let a misfortune like this disturb the rhythm of her life for long. What temperament she had possessed as a girl she had shed, like her social background, the minute she married that lumping farmer's son, Denzil Fawcett. Since then, somewhat to Henrietta's dismay, she had identified herself with the yeoman class and was now, Henrietta would have said, the least imaginative of all the Swanns and as practical as, say, George or Edward. On Henrietta's occasional visits to Dewponds she had seen her as the undisputed mistress of the place, with a sharp tongue for everyone, male or female, who did not measure up to her standards of efficiency. But nobody there, least of all Denzil, would regard this as unnatural. Denzil had never recovered from the shock of having acquired her as a wife, where the Swann bossiness had clearly asserted itself as soon as Stella had learned the rudiments of husbandry. For more than a quarter of a century now Stella's word had been Holy Writ on Fawcett acres, and

it was therefore disquieting to hear that her recent behaviour was the subject of gossip among local chaw-
bacons and Twyforde villagers. For it was through these
freely available sources that Henrietta learned more of
what was happening at Dewponds than anyone suspected.
Stella had, it seemed, abdicated authority over the staff
and spoke very little, even to Denzil or Robert, her eldest
son. In the daytime, Henrietta learned, she kept to her
room or chimney corner, leaving the preparation of meals
to a slut of a girl she employed, but by night, or so it was
rumoured, she more than made up for her withdrawal.
Sometimes as many as five times between lock-up and
dawn she made her rounds of the homestead and farm
buildings, obsessed by the fear of a second disastrous fire at
Dewponds, and here again Henrietta would have liked
very much to have consulted Adam on what was best for
the girl. She was restrained, however, by Adam's own
preoccupation of late, and this was yet another source of
disquiet, causing her to wonder if his age was not beginning to tell on him at last, despite his apparent fitness for
a man about to enter his eighty-fifth year.

He gave no outward sign of senility and his step, notwithstanding an artificial leg, was as brisk as a boy's.
His eyes were clear too, clear enough to read small print
without spectacles, and his last spell of illness was so long
ago that she had forgotten its nature. And yet, when she
thought hard about it, there *was* something different
about him, a hint or two, no more than that, of his
daughter's opting-out of affairs other than those relayed
to him second-hand in his newspapers and journals. He
enjoyed his solitary walks about the estate and his contemplation of the pictures, furniture and valuable china
he had assembled over the years. He liked his books too,
and whenever the weather was bad could always be found
in the library, absorbed in one or other of the hundreds of
leather-bound tomes they had inherited from the previous
tenants of the house. Meantime she had no complaint at
all regarding his temper. He was invariably kind and soft-

spoken in his dealings with her yet she could not but feel, since about the time their recent spate of troubles had begun, that she had lost touch with him, that they had moved appreciably further apart than the era when he had been disposed to demonstrate his approval of her in a very practical way.

It occurred to her more than once when she was lying beside him in the great Conyer bed (her recent anxieties had revived her old trouble of insomnia) that here, possibly, was a reason for his new-found stillness. Perhaps a man's need of a mate and a good deal of his appreciation of life, disappeared when his senses were no longer capable of being stirred by a woman and this was more likely to be true in the case of a man with a mind as well-stocked as his for it might well enable him to find all the stimulus he needed in the contemplation of abstracts that had never interested her very much. But she could do no more than guess at something as complex as this and even the bishop, if she finally lured him to 'Tryst', could hardly be consulted on a subject so personal and delicate.

Thoughts such as these, deeply nostalgic and tinged with sadness, were drifting across her mind like cloud wisps in the small hours of the first day of spring, when the wind, gusting in from the south-east and circling the wooded spur behind the house, had banished all prospect of sleep and given her a couple of hours to pass before she could slip from the room and brew herself an early dish of tea in the kitchen. He had been reading until very late and had not come to bed until long after she had retired but he was sleeping soundly now and in the first glimmer of dawn she turned and looked at him, wondering how a man with so much behind him, and so brief a span ahead, could relax so completely.

He did not look more than about seventy, with his clear skin and firm, slightly aquiline features. His hair, although snow white now, had never receded and his teeth, surprisingly, were as preserved as those of a man in his thirties. She thought, pettishly, 'It's not fair . . . the way some men stop themselves ageing, just as if they were empowered to slam the door on time . . . No woman can do that, or not once she has lost her shape child-bearing and is running to fat, and her hair has thinned and turned grey . . .' But then, chiding herself for taking advantage of his repose to find fault with him, she forced herself to remember the good times she had had with him right here, in this vast bed, the bed that he always declared had been used as a mating couch for that old pirate Conyer and his haughty-looking wife, for whom he had named this house more than three centuries ago. And they had been good, too, those gay, rollicking hours when she was in her early twenties and he was in his mid-thirties, and but recently embarked upon his glorious adventure.

She had always thought of this room and particularly of this bed as a refuge from the family and the external pressures of his life and hers, and in those days he had taken such a delight in her and all she had to offer, which was really no more than he had taught when he had married an eighteen-year-old goose as green as grass, totally ignorant of what men wanted most from a wife. And remembering this she took heart a little, reminding herself of the astonishing durability of his satisfaction in her, for he had never once wandered off in search of fresh pasture. There had always been the network to hold him and after the network her own supple body, and the two had sufficed to keep him to her and hers over a span of more than fifty years.

She supposed she could give herself some credit for that and, indeed, for surviving this long as his partner. Almost all the women she had known in her youth and middle-age were dead or widowed, and here they were, in comparatively good health, getting on for fifty-four years after their first encounter on a heath a few miles north of her father's house . . .

She was wide awake now and could see through the chink in the curtains that it was all but light outside. There was no prospect of dropping off again so she eased herself cautiously from bed and slipped into her favourite bedgown, a silk one emblazoned with gold and silver dragons that he had bought for her from a tea importer years ago.

She would try her luck at tip-toeing downstairs and making that much-needed dish of tea without disturbing him and, testing each old floorboard before putting weight on it, she got as far as the door before he stirred, heaving himself over and shouldering her share of the bedclothes but not waking, or not so far as she could determine, for his breathing at once became regular again and she was able to lift the latch and slip into the corridor, leaving the door ajar rather than risk another rattle.

It was much lighter in the kitchen, with its uncurtained east-facing window and it took her no more than a minute to bring the water in the iron kettle to the boil and lay herself a tray. The big, solemnly-ticking clock told her it was coming up to six and in the brief interval she allowed for the tea to brew she stirred up the fire, for the kitchen, opening directly on to the stableyard, was full of draughts. It was then, in the act of stabbing at the smouldering log with a poker, that she heard the step outside and at once, without a split second's pause for rationalisation, she was gripped by panic.

It was not unreasoning panic either. Her memory, travelling backwards at the speed of light, reminded her of an almost identical situation, a little tableau set out in this same high-ceilinged room at approximately the same hour of day, in which there were two principals; herself and Denzil Fawcett from Dewponds.

He was 'Young' Denzil then, a lad of around twenty, who had walked here through wind and rain with news that he had come upon her daughter Stella drenched through and hysterical after her mad flight from the Moncton-Prices over the county border and now she knew, with horrid certainty, that the scrape on the gravel outside was a variant of those same circumstances, betokening yet another period of wretchedness.

She was so sure of this that certainty robbed her of any surprise she might have experienced when she crossed the room, drew the bolt and threw open the door. It was not Denzil who was climbing the short flight of steps from the yard, however, but Denzil's son, Robert, the eldest of her many grandchildren.

She said, without preamble, "Something's wrong, isn't it? Badly wrong! Come in and speak quietly. The maids will be up and about in less than an hour."

He came in, leaving a trail of mud on the slated floor, saying, "I wouldn't have said anything to anyone but you or Grandpa . . . I would have made some excuse. But seeing you're up and about . . ." And then, looking wildly distracted, he broke off.

"What is it, Robert? What's happened?"

"It's mother. She's wandered off again. God knows where this time, for father's no idea how long she's been gone. We've searched the buildings and the fields on both sides of the river but there's no sign, or wasn't when I left."

"When was that?"

"Under half-an-hour ago . . . Dad's scared, Gran . . . She wasn't wearing her dressing gown and she usually does, or so he says, when she's on the prowl. She'll be chilled through time we find her, and God knows who might run across her meantime. I thought I'd make sure she wasn't here before I got everyone out looking and talking about it."

He sat down and gave her a despairing look, the kind of look his father had given her all those years ago when he came scratching on the door on an even gustier morning with news that Stella had run away from her husband and was being dried, fed and cared for over at Dewponds.

"Was it that silly notion of fire again, Robert?" and he nodded, adding, more to himself than to her, "It can't go on . . . Father's fair done up after weeks of it, and damn it, I'm not much better, as you can see, what with everything to see to. But he won't hear of . . . of sending her away anywhere. The doctor says it'll pass, given time, but I keep remembering that place Uncle Giles thinks she should go."

"What place is that?"

"A kind of special hospital. At Broadstairs, I think. A swanky place, that charges a lot. But like Uncle Giles says, what does the money matter? We can't watch her twenty-four hours a day. Not Father, not me, nor Dolly either with her expecting any minute."

She wanted very much to comfort him. She wanted most desperately to give him aid and advice, to command the situation in the way she had when his father made an almost identical appeal to her years before he was born. But she had lost the knack of command somehow and neither words nor plan suggested themselves. She could only sit there chafing her hands, reflecting that, on Robert's testimony alone, it would soon be post-office gossip in the village and every farm kitchen for miles around, that Stella Fawcett had lost her wits and taken to wandering the country-side in her nightdress, and that there was talk of 'putting her away somewhere'.

She said, finally, "How long, Robert . . . ? I mean . . . when did it begin? Seriously, I mean?"

He replied, glumly, "Ever since she heard. Ever since they told her about Marty and she took that shot at Uncle George."

A wide variety of rumours had reached her via local gossip but the most alarming of them had not included this.

"*Shot* at him? Stella shot at *George*?"

He looked badly bothered for a moment but then he shrugged. "We all decided not to tell you but I can't see as it matters now. You would have found out sooner or later."

"Tell me. Tell me exactly what happened."

He told her and when he had done she bowed her head. She felt so weak and sick that she could hardly answer him when he said, rising, "Look, I'd best get back. Maybe you could send the groom and gardeners over to help look."

She managed to say, in a whisper, "No, don't go! Not until your grandfather hears . . . he'll decide who is to know and who isn't . . . I can't, I can't even think straight just now," and she dragged herself out of the kitchen and up the stairs, wondering if she had the resolution to rouse Adam and tell him that his daughter had lost her wits and was a danger to herself and everyone about her.

Standing there, her hand on the door latch, she thought, 'The last time this happened he was away. I had to cope with it quite alone and I did, very successfully. Where on earth has all my courage gone?' and she went in to find him in the act of strapping on his leg.

"Get dressed," he said, shortly. "Get something on and leave this to me."

"You heard?"

"Enough."

"Robert wants some of the servants to go over and help search."

"Robert can want. I'll deal with it."

"But Adam, it's terrible . . . terrible . . ."

"It could be worse."

"Shall I get Phoebe to tell Chivers to harness the trap?"

"No trap. I'll ride over."

She thought, 'I envied him repose an hour ago . . . now it's his coolness and courage . . . At eighty-four he's still got more than any man alive!' She dragged herself across to the dressing-table and sat staring at the forlorn reflection in the mirror.

As he was struggling with his riding boots she said, "What can you do anyway, at your age?"

"Whatever has to be done, Hetty."

*   *   *

There was still no trace of her when he rode into the farmyard. Denzil was there, looking like a man dragged

from a deep sleep. He stood rubbing his eyes as Adam
said, stormily, "Why in God's name didn't you or George
tell me about that shooting incident? Hadn't I the right
to know?"

"George wanted to keep it from you. It didn't seem all
that terrible at the time, just a flare up of . . . well . . .
temper and a spite against George. She never wanted the
boys to leave the farm and work on those motors and she
was right, I reckon. But I sided with George. It seemed
the best thing for them at the time."

"Never mind that, tell me exactly what happened last
night."

"Nothing particular. She was restless, same as usual,
and I must have dropped off, I was that worn out. I
woke up about five and found her gone. I went down and
looked around but when she wasn't in the house . . .
when I realised she was in her nightdress and nothing
else, I roused Robert and Dolly. Robert got the two hands
to search the farm buildings but there was no sign of her,
apart from that one footmark."

"What footmark?"

"The one in the cow pat down by the bridge. It don't
mean she crossed the bridge, does it? I mean, she might
ha' turned aside and gone along the tow path. Charlie
and William are looking there now."

He said, dismounting, "See to the horse. I'll take a look
myself."

He went behind the barns and across the short stretch
of pasture to the footbridge. The wind had dropped and
the sky was overcast, promising a spatter of rain. At the
approach of the bridge only a few yards on the farm side
of the first plank, he found the tell-tale cow pat. It carried
the clear imprint of a naked foot but he could find no
subsequent footprints in the hard-packed slope leading
down to the river. The water was fairly high, running
three feet or so below the level of the bridge. During several
wet springs in the past he had known the bridge covered
and old Fawcett, Denzil's father, had often had trouble

with flooding about here. He went back up the bank to the bridge and began to cross it, testing the handrail on either side as he went. The middle section was looser than the approach sections, a single two-by-four batten, nailed to stout posts sunk into the river bed. He leaned hard against it, and felt it give a little, then harder still, steadying himself by the upright until the rusty nails yielded and the rail nearest the farm sprang loose, one end of the section holding it in place but leaving a gap over the deepest section of the river. He went on over to a downsloping field where there was a couple of hen-houses, abandoned now for Robert had moved the nest boxes nearer the farm. There was a lot of litter about here, broken planks, a sheet or two of corrugated iron, and a pile of mouldering straw raked together as though for a bonfire. He stood there looking down at it for several minutes, his heavy brows drawn together in thought. Then, with a glance over his shoulder, he took out some matches, stooped and set the straw alight. It blazed up for a moment before subsiding into a spiral of yellow, pungent smoke. He went back across the bridge and met Charlie and William, the two farmhands, returning from their unavailing search of the tow path.

"A section of that handrail is loose. Take a look at it. I'll tell Mr. Fawcett myself."

The men looked startled but Charlie moved swiftly to the bridge and he saw him jigging the loose section. William said, "There's smoke over there, zir . . . there by the old hen-houses," and Adam said, "I know, but I've looked there. Who made a bonfire there yesterday?"

"Nobody so far as I know, sir. Master Robert was pulling down the shed but didn't get to finishing the job. You can ask him yourself, sir."

"I will. Take Charlie and try the southern reach as far as the stone bridge where the road passes over."

"Yes, Mr. Swann."

He went back to the yard where Robert was standing talking to his father. "I've sent the two hands downstream as far as the road bridge. I'm going back now and I'll get my own men to search downstream towards the islet beyond 'Tryst'." Then, looking hard at them, "If she's found, leave Dolly with her and come straight over. Come in any case if she isn't found before noon."

He led his horse over to the mounting block and heaved himself into the saddle. They watched him ride away at a slow trot and Denzil said, in a low voice, "I know what he's thinking. He's sure she's in the river but I'm not letting myself think that. Not yet, any road."

*   *   *

They found her close to the spot he had anticipated, where the river made an ox-bow opposite the little islet that Henrietta always referred to as Shalott. The stream here was shallow, running over what had been a ford and still was in summer. Roots and branches, washing downstream, had piled up to form a dam and she was lying near the far bank in about two feet of water, half-concealed by a curtain of trailing briars.

Boxall, the groom, brought her ashore and laid her under the screen of willows that lined the bank. Her passage down the river had not disfigured her in any way. In her sodden nightgown, and with her tawny hair streaming loose, she looked like one of those women in a pre-Raphaelite painting. Expressionless and make-believe, as though she had never been anything more than a painter's model. Looking down at her, after they had freed her hair of twigs and bracken fronds, there came to him, with the poignant sadness of a blackbird's song in mid-winter, the memory of a little girl toddling beside him to the summit of the wooded spur behind the house forty-odd years ago and the sound of her voice trying to say the word 'foxglove' when he pointed to a clump and told her they were his favourite wildflowers. He said, "Go back, the pair of you, and fetch the dogcart. I'll stay here and watch. And you can tell Phoebe Fraser to break the news to Mrs. Swann. Don't be longer than you can help, although you'll have to go the long way round. That dog cart is too wide for the bridge." And then, as they shuffled off, "One other thing, apart from telling Phoebe. Keep it to yourselves, you understand? If anyone asks I'm still looking."

They went off at a fast walk and he sat down on a drift log, his mind conjuring with the kind of questions a coroner would be likely to ask. He thought, savagely, 'They'll need priming, every one of 'em, and there's not much time before the tongues start to wag. George will be here by dusk and George will see it my way. As for the others, they'll damned well do as they're told and say what I tell 'em to say!' It was very quiet and still here at this hour of the day. A few birds rustled in the thicket about the dam and the stream sang as it rippled round the breast of the islet. He thought of his father, who often came here to paint in watercolours, and wondered if the riverside scene would ever hold anything but dismal memories for any of them in the future.

6

The Strategist

When all three of them were present, quietly awaiting his pleasure, he had second thoughts about Hetty and said, addressing George, "I'll fetch your mother. I don't care whether she's equal to it or not. She'll have to know what we're about," and he clumped out into the hall before George, Denzil or Robert could protest. Henrietta was in the sewing-room, hunched over the fire, an untasted cup of tea on the table beside her. He said, "You'd better join us, Hetty. There's something you have to know, along with the others. It won't take long. Then we'll talk things over among ourselves. Just you, me and George, for Denzil and Robert will want to get back and make their arrangements."

She rose and followed him back into the drawing-room, taking a seat George offered her by the hearth and pulling her shawl close about her shoulders. George stood with his back to the fire. Denzil and Robert sat close together near the window as though poised to flee his silent wrath.

He said, clearing his throat, "There are things you have to know and I don't want a word of this mentioned outside this room. I'll have my say and after that it's up to you to pick holes in it. However, as I see it and with ordinary luck there shouldn't be any trouble, for the fact is, fair means or foul, I mean to squeeze a clear verdict of accidental death out of that coroner and I can only do it with your backing. You don't have to worry about that doctor. He'll know precisely what's in my mind and I think I can rely on him. First of all let me deal with that broken handrail on the bridge."

Robert spoke up, a hint of truculence in his voice. "That rail wasn't broken yesterday. I was over there several times during the day and I'd have noticed."

"Noticed it was loose?"

"I didn't look at it that closely."

"Well, your man will bear me out. One end was swinging free." He glared at them. "I made damn sure it was before I sent him to look at it."

"You pushed it? Pushed it hard?"

"Hard enough to make a gap. And while we're at it you might as well know it was me who relit that straw beside the hen-house."

He heard Denzil hiss. Robert was staring hard at the floor. There was silence in the room until George shuffled and Adam, swinging round on him, said, addressing him as though he was a child, "Don't fidget! Get glasses and pour Denzil and Robert a stiff tot of whisky. I'll take brandy, so will your mother. Help yourself if you care to join us."

George did as he was ordered. The heavy silence continued, broken only by the chink of decanter on glasses. Robert took the drink gratefully but he had to push the glass into his father's hand. He said, at length, "I was working on that hen-house most of yesterday. I piled the rotten straw but I don't recall setting a match to it. I was going to but I thought of mother and I left it."

"I'm not asking you to say you lit it. You'd had fires there before by the look of the ground. Nobody is likely to press the point if you say there was a bonfire stacked from straw out of the roosts. I'll say it was smouldering. On oath, if necessary."

George said, hoarsely, "You'll have to be more explicit, Gov'nor. Robert and I are getting your meaning but I don't think Denzil is, are you, Denzil?"

Denzil looked up as if seeing them for the first time. He took a gulp of his whisky and said, "She walked into the river. That footprint proved as much, didn't it?"

"Not one of us is in a position to prove anything one way or the other. All I'm aiming to do is to stack the evidence in favour of an accident. If there's reasonable assumption of that, seeing who we are, the coroner and jury will go our way. She's your wife, Denzil, and your mother, Robert, but before that she was my daughter and I'm damned if I'll have her branded as a suicide." He paused momentarily, glaring round the circle. "I'll say more. I'll never forgive any one of you who mentions that shooting incident. If that comes out there's no other verdict they could return, so bear it in mind, all three of you."

"They aren't likely to call George as a witness," Robert said. "Why should they?"

"They might. On account of the big fire at Swann's yard."

"Great God, Mr. Swann," Denzil burst out, "that was years ago! What's your fire got to do with my Stella drowning herself in the river?"

"Who knows whether it had to do with it? Who knows whether she didn't get started on this line long before that, the time of the Dewponds fire? Three fires, two of them fatal. Her father-in-law dead in one, her son in another. And in between half her father's property goes up in flames. Wouldn't that give a sick woman in shock a morbid fear of fire? Wouldn't it give coroner and jury good grounds for thinking so? That's all I need and I mean to get it. You'd best be clear on that, all of you, for if necessary I'll fight for it in open court."

The force of his personality held them in thrall. They were silenced by his vehemence and again there was a long silence in the room as he glared at each of them in turn.

"Well? I'm asking for holes in the theory. If you see any now is your chance to point them out before somebody else does."

The whisky seemed to have steadied Robert. He said, setting down his glass, "Neither Charlie nor William noticed that loose handrail. It's true they hadn't crossed over today but Charlie particularly was surprised and said as much. He was across there yesterday, carrying new planks and taking back the old ones I prised loose for him."

"Would a man with his arms full of planks notice a thing like that?"

"No, but neither Charlie nor William will be called, will they?"

"Not if I can help it. I've already given a list of witnesses who could help to the constable and their names weren't on it. I'll give evidence myself of finding her, and of seeing that rail and that smouldering bonfire. Denzil will have to tell them how he missed her and searched the farm buildings. No more than that so far as I can judge, save to bear out the doctor's testimony."

George said, "What will that testimony be?"

"That depends on him."

"Not really. If you've dropped this number of hints you will have gone further, just that much further. You saw him when he certified death. What did you say to him?"

"What would you expect in the circumstances? I primed him, much as I'm priming you."

"But it isn't the same, Gov'nor. He's not in the family."

"In a way he is. In a way the coroner is, and the locals on the jury will be. Prejudiced in our favour that is, so where's a conflict of evidence to come from? Only the collie that followed her down to the river knows what really happened."

There was another pause. Then Denzil said, pleadingly, "Tell it your way, Mr. Swann. Tell it the way you want it told and talked about afterwards."

"Is that necessary?"

"I have to hear it. Hearing it maybe I can believe it. Now, and for the rest of my days."

"Very well, Denzil." The querulous note had gone from his voice. He sipped his brandy and set aside his glass, moving over until he was close enough to lay his hand on his son-in-law's shoulder.

"Listen, my boy, and listen carefully. None of us know and none of us will ever know but this is how it *could* have been. There's no secret about how Stella felt as regards fire. I daresay it was how your mother felt until the day she died after watching your father die trying to save his cattle all those years ago. Or how *I* felt, watching my lifework go out in smoke beside the Thames. Or how George feels, come to that, when he thinks on young Martin in that wretched trailer up in the Pennines. There's nothing strange about that. It's how any of us feel deep down about something that threatens anything near and dear to us. Besides, she was in the change of life. The doctor will testify to that. Under that kind of stress, multiplied a hundred times maybe by Martin's death, fear of fire dominated her thoughts, night and day. That's real enough, for it kept you and Robert and Dolly on the jump ever since the night George broke the news to you. But this time there was a fire of sorts, a glow from a dying bonfire across the river, and the river was running high. She went over to take a look and put too much weight on that rail. There's a strong current midstream when the river is high. Strong enough to carry her two miles downstream. Why do we have to assume it was anything but an accident? If it didn't happen that way it happened some other way, brought about by factors we'll never know. Not us nor anybody else. Finish your drink, Denzil, and go on home. Take two of those pills the doctor left for Stella. They didn't help her but I daresay they'll ensure you a night's rest."

He went back to the fireplace and picked up his glass. When nobody moved he went on, "There's only one thing more I'd like to say and doubtless Hetty will join me in saying it. It has nothing to do with today's wretched business, or the misery you've had to face in the last few weeks. It counts for much more than that, son, and as I say, it comes from all of us here, but especially from me and her mother. You've been a good husband to her from the beginning. All this time, ever since you helped her through that other piece of foolishness, Stella has had a good life and a full one. Try and bear that in mind. It doesn't come everybody's way and the fact that it came hers, after such a bad start, was your doing. No one else's, just yours, do you hear?"

They went out then and George walked with them into the yard where their trap was waiting, lamps glowing in the light swirl of mist closing down from the spur above. He watched Robert help his father into the passenger seat and climb up himself, gathering the reins. Then, after the little rig had clattered through the arch and passed round the rhododendron clump at the head of the drive, he walked slowly back, hands deep in his pockets. The Gov'nor had given them their rations, plenty enough to get on with for the time being. But he had a queer certainty that his own were still awaiting him inside the house.

*　　　*　　　*

They were much as he had left them, his mother seated by the fire draped in her shawl, her face puffed under the eyes, her cheeks flushed by the brandy he had forced on her. But he noticed that the old man held himself poker-straight and thought, meeting his steady glance, 'By God, but he's a hard man to follow! How can any of us *feel* a gaffer so long as he's around?' Adam said, with the merest trace of anxiety in his voice, "They won't let us down, will they?" and he said no, they wouldn't. Robert had got the message and would rehearse his father carefully in what to say and what not to say in the witness box. Adam said, "Right, then, now I can move on to you and your mother. Not about what's said in public, or gossiped around concerning your sister, but about things in general. It's time somebody spoke up and as long as I'm around I'll not shirk the job, not even tonight. Help yourself to another drink if you want one."

"I don't need another drink, Gov'nor."

"Well then, sit, for this will take time," and George sat. "It's about drift. Drift and muddle and woolly-mindedness generally. I've held my tongue until now, hoping one or other of you would take the initiative, but you haven't. Not you, nor Edward, nor Alex, who must have noticed what was happening to us since we ran into this string of setbacks. I don't count Giles. He has enough on his plate without worrying overmuch about us. You were ready to push on with that articulated trailer and I've not heard a word about it since young Martin was killed on the prototype. Have you shelved it?"

"Not shelved, exactly. We halted production on the other two."

"Was that a Board decision or yours?"

"It was mine."

"Then it underlines everything I've been thinking. Tell me something else. That new vehicle was going to put the old firm back on its feet, wasn't it?"

"It would have done that."

"How? In a few words, that your mother can understand."

"Well, articulated vehicles can operate where we're meeting our stiffest competition – in congested towns designed for horse traffic, for it's there that one-man operators are hauling our goods in driblets. Apart from that, a trailer would more than double the weight of haul per vehicle. Only that way could we check the drift of big firms to organise their own haulage fleets. We could deliver faster and far cheaper."

"It's much as I thought. But after Martin was killed you didn't push on?"

"No."

"I've never heard such damned nonsense! That isn't what I'd look for in a son of mine." His disgust created in him a need for further stimulation. He went over to the decanter and poured himself another brandy. "See here, it all adds up to what I feared. You're all losing your nerve and looking over your shoulders and it won't do, d'ye hear? Why should we expect nothing but fair winds? The best of us run into squalls from time to time but that's no damned reason for putting back into port, like a lot of frightened amateurs. We're *not* amateurs! We're the toughest and most experienced professionals in the game, and I thought I'd lived long enough to establish that beyond doubt. Do you think *I* never had self-doubts? I did, time and again, but I never let 'em make a nincompoop out of me. What's scared us so badly? Lay it out for yourself, clause by clause. Edward's flighty wife makes a fool of him so he takes to the bottle and let's his region go to the devil. Oh, I know he's over it now, but my information is he still spends too much time in pubs instead of casting round for a wench to give him something better to think of in his off-duty hours. Clause two: your sister-in-law gets herself killed in a street fracas, but that's her business not yours and certainly not Swann's, as a firm earning its bread and salt in the open market. Clause three: we have a big drop in profits and you hit on a way to turn the tide, but the first sign of danger and difficulty you run for cover and keep your head down, hoping the trouble will go away of its own accord. That boy Martin was a casualty but you can't expect to come through everything, every hazard, unscathed, the way you did when you stole a march over everyone by mechanisation, and it ought not to have led us here, sitting round like a lot of undertaker's mutes feeling so damned sorry for ourselves that instead of fighting back we cry into our beer. With commonsense, and a bold front, it could have been avoided. On your part and Denzil's. On Giles' and Deborah's too, if either of 'em had had the damned sense to come to me and give me the facts."

Henrietta spoke up, the first word she had uttered since Adam steered her into the room. "They were trying to save us worry, Adam. You're eighty-four . . ."

He made a savage gesture with his free hand. "What the devil's my age got to do with it? I can still think clearer than any of you! I'm proving it now and I'll prove it at the inquest tomorrow. Stella was sick and sickness needs treatment. I can't say whether she could have recovered or not but that isn't the point. My complaint is that every one of you, saving Giles maybe, let your personal problems make fools of you and that talk of sparing me grief is no more than a face-saver."

Avoiding his eye, Henrietta said, in a whisper, "They meant well . . . What else could they have done?"

His jaw shot out. "I'll tell you since you ask, Hetty. George here, and Denzil and Edward and Deborah, and Alex, too, as head of the family. They could have put their heads together and evolved something practical instead of hushing it up and going at it piecemeal. That's what a firm and family is, or should be. But I blame you most of all, George, for you were the most like me in a rough and tumble. At least, I always thought so. I'm not so sure now. Well," he drained his glass, "it's not too late. At your age your mother and I had our share of setbacks but we turned things in our favour and you can if you put your mind to it." He stopped for a moment, looking baffled, as though he had mislaid the thread of his argument and was too disturbed to hunt for it but the check was temporary and George, sensing this, said nothing. The fire rustled. Outside the wind got up again and went to probing the tops of the avenue limes, seeking its familiar passage through to the chimneys that had re-sisted its siege for three and a half centuries. Hearing it at work George thought, 'He's like this house . . . rooted and braced, for all his eighty-four years. Who would suppose he had just dragged his own daughter from the water and was waiting to hear her death pronounced upon by outsiders? The worst affront you could offer him would be pity.'

He said, at length, "That's not all, is it, Gov'nor?"

"No, though I'm speaking out because somebody has to and there's only one excuse for your muddle-headedness to my way of thinking. It's the times, the way the whole damned lot of you are going about things lately. Not just here but clear across the world. You're all sleep-walking and if you don't prick yourselves awake you're in for a God Almighty tumble. For here we are, with everything to make a new world and a new society, but all people with money in their pockets are concerned with is a month at the seaside, the next country house-party, Fanny's coming-out dress, a search for gentility and soft living generally Even the international apparatus we rely on to keep the garden-party going is as antiquated as feudalism and not nearly so efficient, and this attitude has a nasty habit of spreading down, to the city clerk, whose main ambition nowadays is to hoist himself another niche up the social scale. Not that there's anything wrong with that – as a spur, for it's what makes the world go round. What's wrong is the way he goes about it. Not by hard work, clear thinking, self-education and self-reliance, but by putting on airs, currying favour with the fellow above him, and learning how to talk with a plum in his mouth. It's all a sham and I hate shams wherever I find 'em. I hate backsliders too, so if you'll take a tip from me, George, you'll go out of here and do some hard thinking and hard planning, the way you used to before you had things too easy. And you can pass that on for what it's worth once we've got tomorrow's business behind us." He turned his back, spreading his hands to the fire as though signifying by this gesture that he had finished.

George turned to his mother. "Could I telephone Gisela and say I'll be staying overnight and going home after the inquest?"

"Of course. We'd be glad. Find Phoebe and tell her to air the bed in the big guest-room."

"I'd sooner have my old room. Is that possible? Without too much trouble?"

"Of course it's possible. Tell her to get a girl to make up

the bed and put a bottle in." She glanced at the clock. "They won't have all gone to bed yet."

"I'll see to it then, don't you stir."

He went out without another word and they heard him climbing the back stairs that led to Phoebe's quarters in the east wing.

She said, "You hit him too hard, Adam."

"I had to. I got through to him. That's what matters."

"Haven't you anything saved up for me?"

He seemed to her to relax a little.

"Certainly no broadside, Hetty."

"Ah, but something?"

"Advice. It can wait until this wretched business is behind us."

"That isn't necessary." She chose her words carefully. "I was wondering . . . would it be possible for me to . . to come with you tomorrow?"

"To the inquest? You could face that?"

"I'd prefer it to waiting here alone and hearing a second-hand account. George isn't the only one who has been waiting for things to go away of their own accord."

He looked at her tenderly, feeling a pity for her that he had been unable to feel for Denzil, or even for Stella lying under the poplars with her hair enmeshed in the flotsam of the river.

"It's different for you, Hetty. Nothing I said applied to you. When you were young and spry you faced up to things better than any woman I know."

"You're not young, Adam, and you still don't shrink from them. Not even from something as bad as this."

"I'm a very obstinate old cuss."

"I don't think it is a question of age. I was thinking back, when Robert came to us to say she was missing — back to that time of Stella's other trouble with the Moncton-Prices. You were hundreds of miles away then but I managed."

She could have reminded him of other occasions, many of them, when she had faced trouble squarely and alone, and made decisions most women of her acquaintance would have shirked making. The fire had died in her now and deep down she could isolate the agent that had extinguished it. It was not age but pride, and a very counterfeit pride indeed compared with his. Flabby, overweening pride, that most people would call conceit.

She said, "Part of what you said to George applied to me. For years now I've thought of myself not only as privileged but deservedly so. Bad things just didn't come my way. Not because I was lucky but because I was sharp. Well, it isn't so, and I see that well enough now. If the others must have a share in what happened to Stella I'm not blameless. I should have visited her more and found out for myself how things stood. The reason I didn't would be hard for you to understand."

"Tell me if you want to."

"The truth is I lost patience with her long ago, ever since she sold out to the Fawcetts to the degree she did and let herself go. As a woman, I mean. I was never able to see it for what it was, a rejection of all she had thought of, up to that time, as the strictures and conventions of her own class, or that it was a natural result of what happened to her as a young bride."

"That isn't true, Hetty. Damn it, you steadied her up by young Fawcett. Do you imagine I didn't know you handed her to him on a platter?"

"Not for her sake, for my own. I would have married her off to a tinker if necessary. Later on, when I realised she didn't give a button for her waistline, or the clothes she wore, or even the way she came to speak, I think I began to despise her. It never once occurred to me that she really grew to love that farm and what it stood for, or that in her own way she loved Denzil as much as he loved her and coming to his level was the best way of showing it. Well, it's too late to alter that now, except to be kind to the boy, and do what I can to nurse him through the next year or so. God knows, I mean to do that." She got up, discarding her shawl. "I'll see Phoebe about George's room. Will you be long?"

"No, not long."

He caught her hand as she passed him and pressed it to his lips. There was no point in trying to eradicate her sense of guilt now but he would set about the job shortly, just as soon as the page was turned on tomorrow. And after that somehow, by some means, direct or devious, they would fight their way through to a peaceful close.

2

She thought of him then as performing the office of the Dutch boy in that old story about the hole in the dyke. A man more resolute and steadfast than any man in the world, self-dedicated to the task of averting a catastrophe, and although she was emotionally involved in every word they were saying, and aware of the covert glances they stole at her from time to time, she had eyes only for him and no more than a cognisance of the others who followed one another into the witness-box, or those who sat mute, listening to the dismal tale.

She had never previously attended an inquest and the formality of the phraseology startled her. It had an archaic touch, like something out of Magna Carta – " . . . Touching the death of Stella Fawcett . . ." "draw near and give your attendance . . ." as though they had been staging a pageant instead of establishing, if it could ever be established, how the first child she had borne came to disappear in the middle of the night and reappear as a corpse two miles down the river.

She followed the drift of each witness. The long-faced doctor, who told of his examination of the body, then of his visits to Dewponds for the purpose of treating a woman in shock. The pills and potions he had prescribed. His professional opinion of the deceased's state of mind between

675

the date of his first call in December and the twenty-first day of March. He had treated her for insomnia. He did not consider the 'deceased' as ill or not in the accepted sense of the word. Under stress, certainly, but not ill.

She could not get used to hearing Stella described as 'the deceased', as though everyone was under an obligation not to speak her name aloud, and she wondered if this oddly impersonal term bothered Denzil too, or whether he was too bewildered and shocked to relate it to the woman he had worshipped since he was a boy. They got little enough out of him anyway, so that she wondered if George was right about Robert rehearsing him in what he had to say. He told them that his wife had been 'upset' by news of her son's death and that all their married life she had had a very real fear of fire. Pressed gently by the coroner he admitted that this fear was based on the fact that Dewponds had been burned to the ground and that the fear increased when she learned that fire had played a major part in the fatal accident last December. He identified the body taken from the river as that of his wife. He had last seen her when he went up to bed on the night of the twentieth.

The coroner, whom she recognised as a local solicitor whose wife, a rather twittery creature, had attended her garden parties, was very considerate and seemed genuinely touched by Denzil's distraught manner. He said, gently, "You searched for her personally when you discovered her missing, Mr. Fawcett?"

Denzil replied, in a scarcely audible voice, "Aye, I looked around. I didn't think much to it. She'd often get up and poke around after lock-up."

"You never heard her threaten to take her life?"

"Take her life?" He seemed outraged. "Lord no, sir, she never once said anything o' that sort." And then, "She never said much about anything save the work on the farm. Not lately, that is."

She glanced across at Adam, awaiting his turn to enter

the box, and now wedged between Robert and George, legs crossed, arms tidily folded. He gave no sign that Denzil was on dangerous ground and unlike herself, was clearly indifferent to the glances of jurymen and those standing at the back of the hall although he must have known almost everyone of them by name. In a curious way, even when sitting there, he dominated the proceedings, much as he had dominated her life for more than fifty years. He had a presence everyone else lacked and she wondered if he had always had it, even as a boy, or whether it was something that had settled upon him about the time he made history in the Crimea and India shortly before he met her, and later developed to a degree that empowered him to set all those wheels in motion across the country.

Surprisingly, to her at least, George was called, and she compared father and son, seeing them alike and yet curiously unlike, for George, although in full command of himself, lacked his father's air of authority, his ease of manner and natural amiability showing through even here. The evidence he gave was brief. He told of bringing news of her son's death to his sister in December and the manner in which she had received it but no one could have guessed, from his reasoned tone and calm expression, that he had come within an ace of violent death himself on that occasion and the reflection turned Henrietta's thoughts to the hatred Stella must have felt for him at that moment. *Was* she mad? Were they all hard at work trying to conceal the fact and, if so, was such deception wrong under the circumstances? Perhaps so. The solemnity of the proceedings, here in this stuffy parish hall, had made its impact on her and the flutter of uncertainty about the propriety of their concerted suppression of the facts inclined her to glance back at Adam as though for reassurance. His expression was as unchanged as his posture. He might have been listening to an Act of Parliament being read aloud, or a prose recital at one of her winter soirées, so that she thought, chillingly: 'Would he look like that if they were discussing my death?' and she bowed her head for, at that moment, he seemed as remote as the God she had tried to approach in her prayers just lately.

She caught the last few words of George's evidence, something about the big fire at the yard at that time, and saw him leave the stand, to be replaced by his nephew Robert. Robert, poor lad, was clearly under strain and she knew why. He was a truthful, literal soul and it was upon him that the burden of sworn fiction would lie most heavily. Even the voicing of a half-truth, if that curious story about the fence and the bonfire qualified as such, would not come easily to him.

They asked him the same question as they had asked his father, had his mother ever threatened to take her own life and he answered in the negative emphatically and with a certain defiance. He then told of his search of the buildings and assumption, planted by a footprint, that his mother had gone down to the bridge, some little distance from the farm. Could he give any reason why a woman haunted by a fear of fire should have gone in that direction? She saw Adam's head come up sharply as he turned his dour gaze on his grandson; Robert said, carefully, "Yes, sir, there was a reason, to my mind at least. We had been burning straw on the far bank near an old hen-house. Maybe the wind had whipped up the bonfire."

It made a disproportionate impact, producing a low sustained buzz from the body of the court and she saw, out of the corner of her eye, Adam's features relax to resume their former impassivity. She saw the coroner's next question as the crux of the whole enquiry. The constable, in earlier evidence, had mentioned a loose rail in the bridge. Was the witness aware of such a rail and if so when? She could sense the expectancy of everyone present to his answer and at length it came, as if dragged from him. "One of my men pointed it out to me that same morning. I hadn't noticed it before. The rail was four to five years old and the bridge often gets flooded. Maybe the nails holding it to the upright were rusted."

"Thank you, Mr. Fawcett. Call Adam Swann."

It seemed so silly, so ritualistic to say that, with Adam no more than five yards away, and a surge of impatience passed through her. Let Stella be buried, quickly and decently, like everybody else who died. What business was it of strangers or acquaintances to pursue enquiries into her state of mind, her obsession, her very movements up to the moment of her death? But the moment passed as Adam straightened himself and clumped up to the stand, his artificial leg echoing on the bare boards and, now elevated some two feet above floor level, his dominance was even more profound so that she saw him as a kind of Moses passing judgment on Aaron's calf-worshippers. It comforted her enormously just to contemplate him, a man older in years than anyone in the court but secure, utterly so, in his authority, and replying to polite questions in a way that implied they were not merely irrelevant but vaguely impudent.

"You are the father of the deceased?"

"I am."

"You were leading the party that recovered her body from the river?"

"I was."

"You visited the farm early on the day of her death?"

"I did."

His steadiness affected even the coroner. "Er . . . could you tell the court anything you noticed on that occasion relative to this enquiry?"

"I noticed a loose rail on the parapet of the footbridge. One end was secure, the furthermost end. The near end was loose. Slight pressure on it produced a gap measuring about a foot. It was at a point over the deepest section of the stream."

There was no hint of irresolution here. He was stating plain, incontrovertible fact and she knew they would believe him in every particular. It was impossible not to believe him. It was as though he was telling an assembly of attentive children that the world was round, that the sun rose in the east and set in the west, that two and two made four and it was profitless to imply that it could ever be otherwise.

"You drew the attention of others to that rail?"

"I did. But before that I crossed over and went down to the half-dismantled hen-house mentioned by the previous witnesses. There was a smouldering bonfire of damp straw. No flame, just smoke."

"Thank you, Mr. Swann. As regards finding the deceased — I am sorry to have to distress you — but it is necessary I establish precisely where and how the body of the deceased was recovered."

"You cannot help distressing me. In company with my groom and gardener I recovered my daughter's body from a pool formed by flotsam just above the ox-bow, about a mile below 'Tryst'. It was on my land. We brought her to the bank and I waited while my employees went back to the house for a vehicle. It was about three p.m. on the same day."

"Thank you, Mr. Swann. I don't think it necessary to ask you any further questions. Neither, I think, will it be necessary to call further witnesses."

He stepped down, still impassive, still holding himself erect, and resumed his seat between son and grandson. There was a moment's silence, broken only by the soft riffle of the coroner's papers and an apologetic clearing of throats. He said, at length, "The facts in this tragic case would seem to be clear. This unfortunate woman, not in the best of health, and dogged, it seems, by a fear of fire, left her bed in the small hours of March the twenty-first and seemingly began to cross the footbridge between Dewponds Farm and her husband's land on the west bank. What happened precisely cannot be known but the existence of a loose handrail, and a smouldering bonfire beyond, would seem consistent with the fact that she was on her way to investigate and slipped or fell into the river. If the jury wishes to retire to consider the facts as given by witnesses they may do so now."

7

Interception

IT WAS BETTER, FAR BETTER THAN HENRIETTA HAD hoped when she made her resolve at the termination of the inquest.

After the funeral he seemed to her, although not to others less close to him, to sag. It was then that she found herself able, in some small degree, to feed back to him a little of the fortitude they had borrowed from him after they came to her with news of a drowned daughter.

There was no possibility of restricting the funeral to a private ceremony, of the kind that had been achieved when Romayne was buried here three years ago, for here was a local tragedy and Stella, child, girl and farmwife, had been very well known in the rural community. Her funeral would have attracted a large assembly of unofficial mourners had she died a natural death so that no one was surprised to find the little church full to overflowing.

They followed, these unofficial ones, at a discreet distance, when the cortège procession wound its way past the yews to the extreme south-east corner of the churchyard which the Swann clan had appropriated to itself. Henrietta, glancing aside from the committal, sensed their silent sympathy and realised a good deal of it was for the Fawcetts, who had farmed here for centuries. The Swanns had been here a mere fifty-two years, reckoned almost nothing in the mind of a rooted rural community. She

thought, 'I wonder if any of them remember the circumstances of her birth, the first evening her father and I set
eyes on "Tryst"? For had it not been for that I doubt if
we would have ever bought a place so far from that slum
of his beside the Thames . . .' But then her mind, seeking
a less melancholy pivot, returned to a warm evening in
April, 1860, when a carriage horse called Dancer ran
away with their carriage and upset them against the
stone pillars of the drive, thereby bringing on her labour.

She was able to draw some small comfort from the
solidarity of the Swann clan. All save Alex and his wife
were present, Lydia having wired to say he was on active
duty in the far west of Ireland and found it impossible to
get leave of absence and travel over in time. But Joanna
had come, bless her, although such a poor sailor, apolo-
gising for Clinton's absence. One of the younger children
had been down with scarlet fever, she said, and Clint was
due, that same day, to fetch her home from the isolation
hospital. She caught Joanna looking intently at her
father as the sexton's team withdrew the bands from the
grave and thought, 'She's probably thinking this will
knock years off his life but she doesn't really know him.
None of them do, save me. Not even George.' It was later
that week, when Adam, seeking consolation in the spring
glory of his flowering shrubs, was away from the house,
that she had occasion to put a rather different interpretation on Joanna's searching scrutiny of him at the graveside.

Joanna had been prevailed upon to stay over for a few
days after news came that her daughter Mary was con-
valescing satisfactorily. It was seldom now that 'Tryst'
saw much of her or her younger sister, Helen. Both, it
seemed, were fully occupied with their social life in and
around the Irish capital and the journey, by sea and land,
was long and tedious. She looked well enough, Henrietta
thought, but preoccupied for Joanna, least complicated
of the brood, so that she was not much surprised when Jo,
having established that Adam was clear of the house, said,

"Could we have a chat, Mother? About something . . . well, bothersome. I'd appreciate your advice. Before I approach Papa, that is."

Henrietta said, guardedly, "How bothersome?"

"Bothersome enough. I badly need advice."

"About Clinton?"

"No, nothing to do with Clint this time." A fleeting smile lit up her plump, pretty face for an instant so that Henrietta guessed her daughter was remembering another time, twenty-three years behind them now, when she had sought, willy-nilly, counsel from her mother concerning her pregnancy before the stage-managed elopement that had earned Clinton his family nickname. "It's about Helen."

"She's well . . . happy?"

"She's well. I never saw her looking better in my life. Happy? I couldn't say really, although she must be to go to the lengths she did to look after that rascal she married."

"Just what do you mean by that, Jo? I thought you and Rory got along very well."

"We did. I always thought him a bit extravagant but most of the Irish are. And he certainly transformed Helen after her terrible time in China. But now – well, I daresay you know how things are in Ireland since they passed the Home Rule Bill."

She didn't know, not really. Politics had never interested her and just lately, with blows raining down on them from all directions, she had not been disposed to give a rap for Irish squabbles. They were not new to anyone of her generation. All her life Ireland had been in a turmoil over one thing or another. She said, "What leisure have I had just lately to worry about Ireland's troubles? Haven't I enough of my own to go on with?"

Joanna looked uncomfortable and said, "Oh, well, I'll not worry you. I'll have a word with Papa before I go back."

"You'll do no such thing, or not if it's something likely

to upset him. Good heavens, child, he's had his fill of worry recently."

"Yes," Joanna said, knitting her brows, "I see that well enough. But this . . . well, I'm not sure it should wait. He might even want to know."

"Let me be the judge of that."

Joanna seemed to weigh this in her mind before she said, reluctantly, "Very well, I will, providing you'll give me your solemn word to tell nobody but him, no matter what. Will you give me that promise?" She smiled again, adding gently, "You aren't all that good at keeping secrets, Mother."

"I can keep certain secrets," Henrietta said, grimly, and led the way into her sewing-room, carefully shutting the door.

* * *

It was Mary's restlessness that accounted for Joanna's inability to drop off to sleep that particular night. The doctor had not been summoned then and the girl's flushed face and temperature had been put down to a feverish cold, so that Joanna, finding at one o'clock in the morning that sleep was likely to evade her, slipped out of bed and stole along the corridor past Alex's room to take another look at her daughter before going downstairs and brewing herself some tea.

There was no other reason for her to be abroad for she was usually an excellent sleeper and the evening, apart from some slight anxiety regarding her youngest child, had been a pleasantly convivial one. Both Alex and Helen were guests in the house and it was some time now since she had had such an opportunity for a family gossip. She saw Helen frequently, whenever her sister drove into the city, sometimes with Rory, now that he had lost his parliamentary seat, but more often with her maid in order to do some shopping. Alex, however, was a much rarer visitor and the day she heard he was in Belfast she telephoned the mess, suggesting he spent the weekend with them. He agreed readily, promising to be there on Friday evening and stay until Sunday. It happened their conversation coincided with one of Helen's half-day visits to Dublin and Joanna, meeting her for an hour, and telling her that Alex was due down for the weekend, suggested that she and Rory might like to come over again on the Saturday for lunch. She was surprised when Helen looked doubtful and said, "I'd like to, for I haven't seen Alex in a long time. But I should have to consult Rory first."

"About having lunch here? With your own brother?"

"Yes. Rory's funny that way. Maybe he has guests and he hates to entertain in my absence. Suppose I telephone tonight and let you know?" and that was how it was left.

Helen rang through late that same evening, just as they were going up to bed, saying that she would not only like to come to lunch but asking to stay over for the night if that was convenient. Rory, it seemed, was due to speak at a political meeting in Tipperary and would be away from home. She added, after a long pause, "Will Lydia be with Alex?"

Joanna told her not. Lydia accompanied Alex on all his longer tours abroad but had not come to Ireland for Alex, she gathered, was not here on a regular tour of duty but on some special assignment to do with his territorials. "He'll only be in Ireland about three weeks," she added. "Then he goes back to London to prepare for another tour in Malta or Cyprus, I forget which . . . But I'm sure he'll be pleased to see you. It's a pity Rory can't join us."

It was not, she reflected, all that regrettable. On the few occasions they had met, she noticed that Rory Clarke, who came as close to embodying the traditional elements of the stage Irishman as anyone she knew, and Colonel Swann, the dedicated, humourless professional soldier, had very little in common, either as relatives or acquaintances. For herself she was sorry Lydia would not be present, for Lydia had a mellowing effect upon stuffy old

Alex but it would be pleasant, she thought, for the three of them and Clinton to have a cosy little dinner party at home, with the odd man out in Tipperary. She put Alex in the best guest-room and Helen in the old nursery on the other side of the house, a comfortable enough billet for the one night, and Helen duly arrived by train about midday on Saturday and was met by the family Belsize and driven back to the house for luncheon.

The two sisters and brother had little in common beyond memories of 'Tryst', in the days before either of the girls were married. Alex was six years Joanna's senior and nine years older than Helen, and they had seen very little of him in their girlhood, when he was away campaigning in various parts of Africa and India. Sometimes he had been absent for years at a stretch.

Alex seemed to get along very well with Clinton, however, and the two men talked animatedly over the political aspects of impending Home Rule, with particular regard as to how it was likely to be received in Ulster. Joanna would have thought this political talk would have bored Helen but this was far from being so, indeed, Helen seemed better informed on the subject than either of them. She remarked also a subtle change in her sister of late, wondering why it had escaped her during recent meetings. She was tense and animated and talked incessantly of Ireland's prospects of settling down once Home Rule, now in the process of becoming law, was a fact, so that Joanna thought, ruefully, 'Time was when she was only interested in clothes, bicycling, tennis and beaux, but some of Rowley's terrible earnestness must have rubbed off on her after all. She's beginning to sound like a regular bluestocking . . .' And then, watching her sister closely, 'One thing is for sure – she doesn't know that husband of hers, despite all the billing and cooing they do whenever I see them together. She obviously takes his political claptrap seriously. It sounds as if they talk Irish politics in bed . . ' But then, being Joanna, she chided herself for uncharitable thoughts, for the truth was that Rory

Clarke had undoubtedly been the saving of Helen a few years back.

All the same, in view of the way Irish politics dominated the occasion, and the time Alex took answering the complicated questions Helen put to him, it proved a dull weekend for her as hostess, particularly as Mary, her youngest, had come home from school complaining of a headache, and had been hustled to bed with a temperature before dinner.

They all went upstairs at about half-past eleven and Clint, who had drunk more than his nightly quota of port, Madeira and brandy, was snoring in a matter of minutes. Joanna heard the clock at the far end of the crescent strike midnight, then all the quarters through to one-fifteen before she got up without disturbing him, slipped into a gown, and went along the corridor to look in on Mary.

Her eleven-year-old was asleep but very flushed, she thought, telling herself she must call Doctor Connolly in first thing in the morning and leave Clint to drive Helen and Alex to the station to catch their trains.

She had moved over to the window with the object of raising the sash an inch or two, when her attention was caught by a motionless vehicle parked almost opposite, close against the gardens. There was no cab rank there and at first she thought it must be a private conveyance awaiting a passenger higher up the crescent. But then, as she turned away, a vague familiarity with this particular cab made her take a closer look.

It was drawn by two horses, the hindquarters of which were revealed in the circle of light thrown by the street lamp but the cab itself was in shadow. She thought, wonderingly, 'But it can't be! For what on earth would Rory's fancy equipage be doing out there at one-thirty in the morning? If Rory had driven it there he would have knocked, and if he hadn't why had Helen come to Dublin by train, when the coachman could have driven her here as usual?'

Without precisely knowing why the very presence of the motionless vehicle disturbed her, the more so as there did not appear to be a driver in attendance and the fact that the curtains of the interior were closely drawn. It almost surely *was* Rory's cab, for she had always thought of it as one of her brother-in-law's stage properties, a low-slung, extremely elegant little carriage, shaped like a shell, with gilt mountings now reflecting gleams of lamplight. It was usually drawn by a pair of matched bays, fast-movers but superbly trained by Rory himself. The horses, unfortunately, were in so much shadow that she could not be absolutely sure, but if Rory's cab had been copied by one of the fashionable Dubliners it was curious that the owner should station it almost opposite the house in the middle of the night.

She stood there a moment longer, coming to no conclusion, but then her ear detected the scrape of a foot on the back stairs, hard left of her daughter's room, and she moved over to the door, watching through a chink the section of corridor opposite the all-night gas jet that illuminated this side of the first storey. If it was not one of the servants she could only suppose the person climbing the stairs, and very cautiously by the sound of it, could only be Rory, although how he had gained entry into the house without knocking she could not imagine.

It was not Rory's shadowy figure that came into view, however, but Helen's, moving a step at a time and without benefit of candle, and Joanna was so surprised that she came close to hailing her but checked herself. She followed her out, however, as soon as Helen had passed beyond the gas jet and watched her progress as far as the next circle of light thrown by the outside lamp through the landing window opposite the guest-room occupied by Alex. And here, to Joanna's increased bewilderment, Helen stopped, hand on the door-knob, head on one side as though listening intently

It flashed through Joanna's mind that her sister was sleep-walking and the memory returned to her of a woman teetering on the edge of nervous collapse, whom she had encouraged to climb into bed with Clint when they were at 'Tryst' shortly after Helen's return from Peking. And yet, there was no real indication of sleep-walking here. Indeed, her sister's carriage and movements were those of a person thoroughly alerted to her surroundings. And then, while Joanna still watched, Helen turned the knob and slipped inside, leaving Alex's door ajar.

She was not out of sight for more than twenty seconds, hardly time enough for Joanna to come to terms with the fact that she was not dreaming herself, and when she emerged, recrossing the shaft of light adjoining the main landing, Joanna saw that she was holding something flat and bulky close against her breast.

The strangeness of what she had witnessed, a sister prowling about the house like a burglar, seemingly for the purpose of purloining her brother's luggage, did not register on Joanna at first. She told herself, standing there with one hand gripping the edge of the door, that there had to be some innocent explanation of what she had seen and again the thought that Helen was acting under some mysterious pressure returned so that she thought, desperately, 'I can't challenge her here, right outside Alex's door, and within earshot of Mary . . . she might scream or struggle and that would rouse the servants as well as Alex and the child . . . And yet, I can't leave it there, without finding what she's taken from Alex's room and why . . .' But then Helen herself decided her next move by passing round the wide curve of the stairhead to descend by the main staircase and this served to increase the mystery, for her own quarters, in the old nursery, lay in the east wing of the house approached by the corridor matching this one. Whatever purpose Helen had in mind it was clearly not to take her spoil back to her own room and realising this her sister's eccentric behaviour made a connection with the presence of that motionless cabriolet outside.

She knew then, with a small spurt of relief arising from decision, precisely what she must do. If Helen had some notion of leaving the house, and passing whatever she had stolen to the driver of that cab in the crescent, she must be headed off and this was still possible, providing she moved quickly and quietly. The back stairs led directly to the kitchen quarters at the rear of the house and these were partly on ground-floor level occupying a semi-basement area, with one door opening on the tradesmen's alleyway and another into the enclosed yard bounded by high brick walls. Access to this part of the house – already, or so it would appear – visited by Helen that night, was direct by the back stairs but indirect by the front hall to which Helen was now descending. Moving quickly Joanna passed into the corridor and hurried down the stairs as far as the green baize doors, double doors here to prevent cooking smells rising to the bedrooms. She passed one and put her hand on the other, holding it open an inch or so, to give her a clear view of the kitchen.

She was just in time. Steps, less cautious now, approached from the servery and the door opposite opened, revealing Helen holding what looked like a small leather portmanteau fastened with a brass lock in addition to straps. There was a light in the kitchen and she could see her clearly. In the old days Joanna had always been known as 'the pretty one' for Helen's complexion was sallow, and her eyes were deepset, emphasising high cheekbones, but seeing her now, with her dark hair streaming, and a flush of excitement on her cheeks, she looked, Joanna thought, beautiful. She stood framed in the aperture for a moment before gliding into the room, putting the case on the scrubbed table and emitting a kind of sigh that enlarged itself into a startled gasp as Joanna flung open the second door and stepped through it.

For a moment they stood regarding one another and then Helen's expression crumpled so that she suddenly looked like a child, caught in an act of mischief. "You've been following me?"

"Why not? This is my house and I've a right to know what you're about taking things from Alex's room," and she laid a hand on the case, anticipating Helen's swift movement towards it. There was a silence. She could see her sister's breast heaving under her ruffled nightgown and loosely-tied robe. Helen said, slumping down in a chair, "What's the use? How could you possibly understand?"

"I understood last time."

"That was different."

"And this, whatever it is, concerns Rory Clarke, and all those fancy ruffians he consorts with? Well, I realised you were committed to him, but not to this extent, not to the extent of raiding your brother's room in the middle of the night. It *is* Rory's cabriolet outside? And he's waiting, waiting for you to hand him this, whatever it is."

"He doesn't intend stealing it. We aren't pickpockets."

"Great God!" Joanna burst out, "how can you do this? Creeping about the house and taking things from the luggage of a guest in someone else's home? What on earth has Rory done to you to make you so much as think of behaving in this way? Keep it, copy it or look at it, what does it matter in Heaven's name?"

"As I say, you know nothing about these things. Nobody English does, not even people like Clint, who have lived and worked here all this time."

"You're English, aren't you?"

"Not any longer."

Joanna sat down facing her. She kept both her hands on the case and noticed that they were trembling. "Then tell me. Tell me if you can. What's in this case that makes a thief out of you?"

Helen looked across at her, very levelly. "A list of the military depots he's visiting, with inventories of the arms and ammunition held in each of them. I said I'd get it for Rory to look at, no more than that I swear. Then I was to return it and Alex wouldn't have known a thing about it. No one could have held him responsible for the information in there getting to us for no one would have known how we came by it."

"'Us'! 'We'! You talk as if you were fighting some kind of war and Alex was the enemy."

"We are fighting a war, or will be the moment the British implement the Home Rule Bill. Doesn't it mean anything at all to you that those people up north are buying guns from Germany and drilling openly in the streets? With encouragement from Parliament and the army? Haven't the Irish the right to know what's going on, when more than half the senior officers at the Curragh sympathise with the Protestants in Ulster and won't even try and stop them when they start a civil war?"

"No, it doesn't matter to me. All I know is I can't ever ask you into my house again. That matters terribly, to me if not to you!" She took a deep breath. The kitchen was large but it felt unbearably close tonight. "I saw you on the back stairs before you went to Alex's room. That means you were down here earlier so you'd best tell me why, before I rouse Alex and Clint. And I'll do that I swear, unless you tell me exactly what you had in mind. Well?"

"Don't do that, Jo."

"You're saying Rory and his friends are prepared to do violence to get at these papers?"

"I'm not saying anything of the kind. All I want you to understand is *why* I took it, what it could mean in terms of other people's blood. I did come downstairs earlier, to unbolt the back door for Rory won't stir from the cab until I give the signal."

"What signal?"

"What does it matter what signal? I can't give it now. You've spoiled everything by interfering."

"*Interfering?* Wouldn't anyone in my position interfere in these circumstances?"

She was some time answering. Finally she said, in a low voice, "Yes, I suppose they would, Jo. In your circumstances, that is." She turned away, her expression infinitely troubled. "You've always been good to me. I hate hurting you, and I realise how it must look to you but . . . this . . . it means everything to me, just everything, you understand?"

"No, I don't, Helen. You tell me if you can."

"It proves I'm *with* them, don't you see? It would make all the difference to my life. And nobody need ever know. Alex is asleep and I could give you my word of honour that case will be back in his room in less than an hour."

Joanna jumped up, tucking the case firmly under her arm. "It'll be back in five minutes. And no one, least of all Rory, is coming into this house to pry. I'll make sure of that," and she went into the scullery and reshot the top and bottom bolts on the door leading to the alley. "Now you can make whatever signals you please, for I shan't leave you until you're dressed, packed and out of the house."

"You won't do this one thing for me?"

"Of course I won't! Not for your sake, for Rory's or for the king of the Cannibal Islands!" She glanced up at the kitchen clock, noting it wanted a couple of minutes to two. "I'll give you fifteen minutes to leave. After that, if you haven't gone, I'll wake Alex and tell him what you've done and why. I'm not leaving you down here either, to open that door again and use my kitchen as . . . as a plotters' den. Get up and get dressed. I mean to see you upstairs and out of the house."

They went through the hall and up the main staircase, turning down the corridor to the old nursery. She stood wordlessly by the door and watched Helen dress and it was as if a terrible weight was pressing on her breast. In ten minutes they were back in the hall and she pulled the lobby curtains aside and looked out. The cab was still there. She said, "Draw the bolt and turn the key. You can let yourself out," and at that Helen turned and she was surprised, and a little startled, to see tears streaming down her face.

"We've been close a long time, Jo."

695

"All our lives. You think this is easy for me?"

"No, no, it can't be, but you still don't understand. Rory's committee, especially since he lost his seat and joined the staff . . . well . . . they didn't trust him before. They don't trust any of Redmond's men. But they trust him now. Him but not me. Because I'm English."

"Dear God, it can't be all that important, Helen! It just can't!"

"To stand well with Sinn Fein? No, that isn't important. Not on its own it isn't. But can't you understand, Jo, it's all I've got to offer Rory. I'm years older than him, and I've never had your looks. And I can't give him children. It's too late for that."

She had a glimpse then of the hidden pressures at work in the relationship of this ill-matched pair; one a man consumed by his own conceit, his mind lost in the fog of Celtic legend and the real and fancied injustices practised upon these people, the other a woman whose entire being was centred on a younger man's flattery and probably unable to think straight once he laid hands upon her.

She said, "I understand in a way but it doesn't make any difference, Helen. You must see that, besotted as you are with that man. From here on we've no choice, have we? You go your way, I'll go mine," and she moved past her to withdraw the bolts of the front door. And then, as the night air struck chill on her, she remembered something else that might be important.

"I'm returning that case. You'll have to tell me where it was in Alex's room. It wouldn't do for him to find it had been moved in the night."

"You won't tell him then?"

"I don't know. It's something I'll have to think about."

"It was on his chair. He isn't very careful for a man with his responsibilities."

Was it the vaguest of threats? Or a last-minute warning? Did it mean that, from here on, Alex was a marked man as long as he moved unescorted about Ireland? Joanna didn't know. Suddenly she was too tired and too depressed to think about it. Instead she watched her sister descend the steps and stand hesitating under the street lamp. Opposite the cab door opened and somebody got out but she did not wait to identify him.

2

Back at 'Tryst', Henrietta's first reaction was of intense relief that she had prevailed upon Joanna to tell her, without piling this additional load on Adam's shoulders. It was enough, as she had found to her cost of late, to put a bold face on one's own troubles without meddling in the affairs of factions, sects and nations. Her spirits lifted for she recognised, in her interception of Joanna's tale of woe, an opportunity of service, a way leading back to the summit she had occupied in her youth when, by common consent, Adam had confined himself to his business and she to hers, that of steering the family through the crosscurrents of the years.

She said, unequivocally, "Don't mention a word of this to your father. You'll not so much as hint at it, is that clear?"

Joanna, looking pained and puzzled, said, "But surely I have to, don't I? I mean, suppose Helen or Rory come here on a visit? And suppose that visit coincides with one from Alex and Lydia?"

"I'll deal with that if it arises but I'll not have your father worried, you understand? It was right of you to tell me, and right of you to act as you did. But this is as far as it goes, do you hear?"

"And Alex?"

"There's no point in saying anything to him either. You know that in your heart, Jo."

She paused, recalling an earlier family quarrel that had never really healed, one between Alex and Giles in connection with that awful war, and the misery that had emerged from it for Hugo. What would be served by widening the family breach to include Alex and his sister,

697

who were unlikely to meet again for years? Ireland, confound it, could look to itself. For her part, having lost a grandson, a daughter-in-law and a daughter in swift succession, she was concerned with what remained. Nothing else mattered. She said, "Listen Jo, Alex and Lydia are sailing for India in a week or two. I was sorry when I heard but I'm right glad now. Let it pass. Leave it where it is." And then, dejectedly, "You and Helen – I suppose you'll keep yourselves to yourselves from now on?"

"How else could it be?"

"No other way. But it's sad just the same. And very stupid, too, if you think about it. Meddling in men's affairs is always dangerous. What did it bring Romayne but a messy death? What purpose does it serve any of us in the end?" She mused a moment, aware that Joanna was watching her intently. "A woman should have more than enough to absorb her, especially if she has children to rear."

"Helen has no children."

"No, and more's the pity, for if she had she wouldn't have made such a fool of herself. Think yourself fortunate, Jo. Go back to yours and forget this happened. That's my advice, and that's what I want for all of us."

"Is that all you have to say, Mama?"

"Almost all." She got up and went over to the fireplace, lifting a photograph framed in silver from its pride of place above the hearth. Adam wasn't overfond of a display of family photographs – 'sentimental clutter' he called them, much preferring to decorate his walls with oils and water-colours acquired in his forays up and down the country, some of them worth a penny or two, or so he claimed. She took his word for it, but this group photograph meant a lot to her. It was a silver wedding photograph, taken on the lawn in September, 1883, and they were all there, every last one of them, together with the three senior in-laws, Denzil, Lydia and Gisela, and the first brace of grandchildren, Robert and Martin Fawcett. Sixteen all told, less than half the Swann muster today.

She studied the group, forgetting Joanna was still there. Jo and Helen were sitting crosslegged in the foreground, sixteen and thirteen respectively and very conscious, judging by the exceptional solemnity of their expression, of the great occasion. She said, passing the picture to her daughter, "It doesn't seem long ago, does it? But three of that group are dead, and now Helen is dead to you. That makes four. Providing you wish it so, that is."

"Are you really saying I should pretend to myself it never happened?"

"I don't know. It's for you to decide. You and Helen, as you get older, and fewer of you are left who remember how it was at 'Tryst' when this picture was taken. I can't tell either of you what to do or what not to do at your age, with homes and husbands of your own. Apart from sparing your father more worry, that is, and I'm in no doubt about that. But I can tell you something I've learned here in all these years. The family is the only thing worth a row of beans in the end and that's about the only thing in life I learned in advance of your father. I'll tell you something else. When I was a girl, I thought the only sons worth having were soldiers. I don't think so any more. No woman does once she's gone to the trouble of bearing children, and, what's a great deal more tiresome, raising them until they can stand on their own feet. You think hard about that. Helen and you were as good as twins once. Well, I'd value that high above a piece of foolishness hatched up by men, for men never grow up anyway, or not in the way women do." She took the photograph back and rehung it, glancing as she did at the mantelshelf clock. "Go and find your father. Tell him luncheon will be ready in about twenty minutes. He has to be coaxed to eat just now."

*   *   *

As soon as Joanna had left she went over to her bureau beside the window, taking out her address book and leafing through it until she came to the 'C's. She could rarely remember these outlandish Irish addresses and even when she did she couldn't spell them without a copy. When she came on Helen's address she put a marker in the book and sat thinking, grateful for a brief interval of solitude. But presently, having watched Joanna pass beyond the lilac clump and cross the area of lawn where it sloped down to the lake, she took up her pen and began to write, continuing to do so until she had filled one sheet and half another.

The words came easily, for somehow the act of writing restored to her some measure of the authority she had once wielded but had lost since the brood had grown up and gone about their own affairs.

My dear Helen,

Thank you for your letter about Stella and for the lovely wreath that arrived in time. We did not expect you to travel over at such short notice and by now you will have received the newspaper I sent, explaining everything, or everything that matters.

You might like to know your father was wonderful throughout it all. Without him I can't imagine how Denzil and I would have managed, but he feels it as much as either of us, and so does George, who regards himself as responsible for what happened. But this letter isn't about Stella. What happened to her, all the sadness and waste of it, is behind us now and can't be altered, one way or the other. That doesn't apply to you and Jo, however, and I've told her so a moment since, together with advice – that I mean to see she takes – to never breathe a word of it to her father or Alex. That way, given time, you can both pretend it didn't happen. You can do that with most things if you've a mind to, for I have and still do where there's no other way out. And there isn't for you and Jo, or not as I see it. But even supposing either or both of you can't or won't, this is to say that *I* mean to, because that way, if you ever want to come back here, with or without Rory, there's nothing to stop you, and why should there be? This is still home for all of you and as long as your father and I are alive I mean it to stay so.

She signed and sealed it and put it in her tray among a dozen others, each acknowledging wreaths and messages of sympathy. It was the only letter there, she reflected, that really said anything.

To Adam and Joanna, slowly climbing the drive in sunshine that was exceptionally strong for the time of the year, the luncheon summons seemed very sonorous, almost like a judgment.

8

As From a Pinnacle

IN THE TWO YEARS LEFT OF THE OLD WORLD, AND
what some (half-forgetting that Teddy had been replaced
by the blameless George) would call 'The Edwardian
Afternoon', Adam watched as from a pinnacle, armoured
against the byblows of fate and able, to some extent, to
disassociate himself from all but the process of growing
old and that detached curiosity about men and their
affairs that had made him the oracle others thought
him.

He was like a veteran general, with countless battles
behind him, who was yet peripherally caught up in the
current war and in receipt, from time to time, of scribbled
despatches brought him from afar. And having, as it
were, studied their content he would listen gravely, or
sympathetically, or half-humorously, to what the messen-
gers had to say and then prophesy, so that they went away
stimulated, or sobered, or mildly fortified by his wisdom.

In the late spring, summer and early autumn months
he could usually be found out of doors, pottering about
his Hermitage museum, or seated on a log in one of the
patches of wild wood that varied the pattern of his planted
areas, or on one of the stone seats or balustrades that em-
bellished his demesne. But when the rains came and the
winds went whooping over the Weald, he retired to his
study fireside, browsing among his books.

He was here, one day, when Deborah called for consolation as regards her old and trusted mentor, W. T. Stead, lost on the *Titanic* and last seen, so survivors said, absorbed in a book as the great liner, symbol of all the new technologies, poised for her final plunge, making nonsense of the claims that she was unsinkable.

"Her sinking seems to me symbolic of all I've observed over the last few years," he said, shaking his head. "Of my generation, too, I suppose, tho' to a lesser extent. For my lot were improvisers, whereas those who came after us – like George – relied on sums worked out in the office instead of in the market-place. Sad that Stead had to be sacrificed to their pride, however. The old warrior deserved better. Reading a book, you say? Well, that was in character, I suppose. He had a high opinion of you once. What did he think about you and the suffragettes?"

Deborah replied that he didn't really approve, for Stead's violence was always confined to words and edited words at that. "But he was a bonnie fighter," she added, "and I'll always remember him as that."

"Me too." And there returned to him, over an interval of thirty years, the memory of a distraught man awaiting him in his turret at the time of the *Pall Mall Gazette*'s strident campaign on behalf of child prostitutes, served up to satyrs for five pounds a hymen, a man he had been ultimately to champion.

"Well," he said, by way of valediction, "Stead won most of his battles, so maybe the pen does have the edge on the sword."

She knew then that he was debating with himself the old imponderable. Did the end ever justify the means? Or did the end get grotesquely distorted by the means, in their case assaults on the person of the Prime Minister, on the Lossiemouth golf links, the slashing of the Rokeby Venus in the National Gallery, a bomb in the house of the Chancellor of the Exchequer, another against the walls of Holloway Prison and the militants' Calvary. She had pondered this herself many times, waiting, pinched with hunger, to be released under the Cat and Mouse Act but had never arrived at any irrevocable decision. Yet she knew that he had and tried to coax it from him.

"You're wavering, Uncle Adam. You've probably decided we're our own worst enemies."

"No, no, not that, for no one can say you didn't give the pen a fair trial," he replied, smiling. "Why, I was reading your pamphlets forty years ago. Aye, and averting my eyes from the first knickerbocker suit too! It's just that sometimes I wonder if Britain is the best place for you. In France you would have been home and dry long ago, riot being the staple diet over there."

"But that isn't why they hate us, is it?"

"No, it isn't," and his eyes twinkled for a moment.

"Why then?"

"Because you deny what's meat and drink to the politician. Patronage. He can't get along without that. But tell your friends not to despair, my dear. The moment the Government of the day finds it convenient to pat your heads instead of kicking your backsides, you'll get your vote."

He had one of his rare visions then, of a time when every pair of hands, white and gloved, red and calloused, would be needed at the pumps, and out of it, no doubt (providing the ship of state did not follow the *Titanic*), might come universal suffrage, so effortlessly perhaps that even Mrs. Pankhurst would be caught on the hop. But he said nothing of this to her, for he knew that she, and that clever husband of hers, and George, and all the rest of them, did not believe in his Armageddon.

*　　　*　　　*

One of his most regular visitors these days was George. A George, he was glad to note, who had recovered most of his natural ebullience once he was satisfied he had stolen yet another march over his competitors by shunting his Swann-Maxie fleet into regions where they could do the kind of work Swann's one-horse pinnaces had once done, leaving the heavy hauls to his latest nine-day won-

der, the articulated trailer, an improvement on the prototype that had cost Martin his life on a Pennine slope.

There were far less Clydesdales and Cleveland Bays on
the Swann roster nowadays, and horse-drawn transport
was now confined to local runs, or over routes where, even
yet, motor-vehicles jibbed at the terrain.

A visit from George was usually an ego-booster to the
prophet on the pinnacle. For a long time now he had been
aware that his advice was no longer sought out of deference but as insurance, in premiums George had been more
than willing to pay since the night he rehearsed them in
the parts they were to play at Stella's inquest. You could
say that for George, he thought, and it was one reason why
he backed him to stay out in front.

Just as Debbie kept him up to the minute on what was
happening in the suffragette sector, and Giles briefed him
on the national issues, so George kept him abreast on the
latest trends in transport.

Their relationship had deepened and broadened appreciably since Stella's death. The partnership had steadied
of late, not only because George had evaluated his shrewdness and steadfastness but because Adam had at last adjusted to the stupendous changes in the transport scene
since the arrival of the self-propelled vehicle. George saw
himself as a master of tactics but when it came to strategy
he was always ready to defer to a man who carried in his
head a large-scale map of Britain, and indices of all the
products that kept the country in the forefront of the
world's trading nations.

*   *   *

It was different again with the younger children, whom
he saw less frequently, or with one or other of his many
grandchildren, who saw him as a kind of eccentric sage,
excessively tolerant in most areas but obstinate and
adamant in others and sometimes giving advice of a kind
they did not comprehend at the time.

It was this way with his daughter Helen, devilishly wary, he thought, when he quizzed her on Southern Ireland's response to Carson's bloodcurdling threats from Ulster. When she told him the Catholic South was recruiting to raise a force capable of confronting the Orangemen, he said, "Will you carry a message from me back to that husband of yours, my dear? Tell him to leave the sealing of this business to the British. I speak as a Home Ruler from Gladstone's day and that bill is law. Only one thing can stop you going your own way now and I'll tell you what it would be – if you people jump the gun *ahead* of Ulster and put yourselves in the dock!"

She was still digesting this when he added, with a smile, "You can remind Rory Clarke of something else. Tell him that your mother's mother was as Irish as the shamrock, and landed penniless in Liverpool ahead of the potato famine. So you've really no call to feel an exile over there."

In truth she had forgotten and it made her thoughtful during the remainder of her stay. It went some way to explain, perhaps, her identification with the Irish and her tendency, since her second marriage, to look at history through Irish eyes, and she said to him, on the last day of her visit, "You're as English as anyone I know. What made you back Home Rule all those years ago? You never set eyes on your mother-in-law, or so Mamma tells me."

"No, I never did, but I served in Ireland in the 'fifties, a year or so after the 'Great Hunger' as they call it, and I understood their grievances. It didn't take me all that long to realise the English had been asking for this how-de-do for seven centuries. Bad as things were they weren't peculiar to Ireland and the Irish. You're looking at a man old enough to recall seeing men transported for poaching and petty theft. Not all were from County Cork and County Mayo. Some were from Hampshire, Dorset and right here where we're sitting."

* * *

Giles called less often, spending an occasional weekend at 'Tryst' between his parliamentary chores in Westminster and Wales. Adam felt great sympathy for a man who, at the age of forty, had been robbed not only of the woman he loved but also his faith in British democratic traditions. There was no more talk of Giles joining the Labour Party, however (although the presence of Keir Hardie as his constituency neighbour at Merthyr Tydfil was a permanent temptation) but he was disenchanted with the conformity of the Liberals. He said, when they were discussing Women's Suffrage one day, "Do you remember what Abe Lincoln said on the practice of slave-owning before the Civil War out there – about it being impossible for a nation to remain half-free and half-slave? Well, that's how I've come to feel about us. For as long as we deny women the vote how can we prattle on about the home of the free, Father?" When Adam said he should use the analogy in a speech in the House, he replied, with a smile, "Oh, I plan to. The next time we get a debate on the issue. And don't think I begrudge the chances of preferment I've given up by identifying myself with the suffragettes. I owe that much and more to Romayne, wouldn't you say?"

Adam said, gently, "You still miss her, don't you?"

Giles nodded. "The only relief I get from the permanent ache is in the valleys, doing what little I can for the people who sent me to London."

"Well, you can warm your hands there, boy," Adam told him. "Personal local representation is the only justification for your profession and from what I hear and read most of 'em up there forget as soon as they've counted the votes." And then, taking a chance, "Have you ever thought of marrying again, my boy?"

"Oh, I've thought of it," Giles said, and then, perking up somewhat, "I might even surprise you and mother one of these days."

And before very long he did, confounding them utterly, by turning up, uninvited, with a very pleasantly disposed but rather sad-looking woman of what Henrietta described as 'a sensible age'. Giles introduced her as Sister Gwyneth Powell, presently on the staff of Westminster Hospital, whose home was close to his headquarters at Pontnewydd.

Long before he told them how they had met on the night of Romayne's death (he withheld the story of Miss Powell's part, years ago, in that flare-up over a hat in an Oxford Street store) they had wholeheartedly approved of her, although neither Giles nor Gwyneth hinted at anything more than friendship and mutual political sympathies. Even so, when the carriage taking them back to Bromley Station was out of sight, Henrietta said, "Well, Adam?" And there was no mistaking the matchmaking gleam in her eye.

"I'd put it at odds on. In less than a twelve-month, m'dear." And then, "When will I learn to mind my own business? I advised him to remarry the last time he was over. If it goes off at half-cock I'll feel responsible."

"She seems very steady and sensible," Henrietta said, disregarding him, "for my part he could go further and fare worse."

2

He had his silent visitors too, what he called his Grace and Favour tenants whom he encountered pottering about his terraces and coppices, or taking a breather up on the wooded spur, or when he was immersed in his newspapers on the knoll behind the Hermitage museum.

There was the pair of nuthatches, rare in these parts, who nested in the bole of an elm and were, he would have said, the least demanding of his charges, for their neighbours, an army of tits, were forever swooping on the bird tables he had set up hereabouts, squabbling among themselves for the fat he hung there and the split maize he spread upon the ground. Every kind of tit – great tits, with their neat black skullcaps, blue tits by the dozen and an occasional crested tit or marsh tit, though only once did he catch a glimpse of the long-tailed variety. There were finches, too, a swarm of them, but one particular chaffinch, who seemed to him not only extraordinarily long-lived but unusually perceptive, for he ignored the largesse on the tables and always made a personal approach for crumbs of cheese Adam balanced on his boot. He told Giles – the only one among his children who shared his tolerance for this army of blackmailers – that Joe, the chaffinch, not only knew the whole range of cheeses but could distinguish between his sound and his artificial leg, distrusting the latter's stability, for if, by chance, he put cheese on his left boot, Joe would execute a furious little dance about his feet, waiting for it to fall. But if he placed it on his sound leg he would hop right up and eat it on the spot, waiting until Adam spread his hand with more cheese, when he would perch on his thumb.

Giles, smiling at this recital, said, "It's queer, I always thought of you as a city man. You seemed to belong in that slum beside the Thames in my younger days and I can remember you jeering at city merchants who turned themselves into squires the moment they made their pile. At what point in your life did Wordsworthia set in?"

"Around the time of that yard fire, I imagine. I was seventy then, late in the day but not too late. I saw everything I'd slaved for for over forty years go up in smoke in two hours and it struck me then, for the first time, I think, that everything but land, and what thrives on it free and wild, is a short-term credit, likely to be called in any time. I begrudged every day I spent there after that."

Just beyond the plank verandah of The Hermitage was a buddleia and on hot days he would move out there to watch the butterflies skirmishing round every blossom. Red Admirals, Peacocks, Tortoiseshells, Commas, and his firm favourites, the local Chalkhill Blues, all making a Donnybrook Fair of the bush. He sometimes watched them for thirty minutes at a stretch. But the birds and the butterflies, with the single exception of Joe, the cheese connoisseur, took him very much for granted, whereas his

warier tenants did not, regulating their comings and goings by the degree of solitude he enjoyed.

There was the old grey badger, whose set was inherited
from a line of ancestors stretching back to a time when
this part of the Weald formed the western margin of the
Rhine estuary. He was a suspicious old codger and it
took Adam months to win his confidence, but once this
was achieved Old Blubb (his grizzled, flattish head and
wary looks reminded Adam vividly of Blubb, the ex-
coachee who managed the Kentish Triangle in the 'sixties)
took him very much on trust when he poked around looking for fresh bracken for his set. On the spur behind the
house there were other familiars, an old dog fox that had
learned the hunt never drew this near the house and rarely
ventured off limits. Adam would watch him upwind,
'loping along like a Pathan scout', Adam observed, and
wearing a self-satisfied grin on his return from a successful
hunting foray and he thought, as he watched, 'I'll wager
he's led every local pack about here a dance or two in his
day, but they'll never catch him now. He's like me, a
born survivor.'

Down on the banks of the stream that he had diverted
from the river to keep his lily-ponds filled, he often saw
otters, voles, herons and the comical long-tailed field mice
who seemed to live mainly on insects they found on the
wild irises, although Adam knew their winter stores of
food were treasure houses of berries, nuts, peas and grain.

It was watching these tenants of his, over a period of
months and years, that went some way towards adjusting
his views about the world outside, for he reasoned – 'They
manage their affairs much better than we do. Stick to
their own patch and never kill, save for food. Whereas,
look at us. We've been roaming and pillaging ever since
we came out of the trees and it'll bring us down in the
end.'

And then, when the evenings grew shorter, he would
take to going into the house, and paid visits to his in-
animate friends. Here, too, he had his favourites, some of

them under glass and never handled save by himself or a fellow connoisseur. There were many examples of the English and Irish glass blowers' art, opaque glasses with twist stems, baluster stem glasses with a royal monogram, a pair of magnificent Jacobite goblets, engraved with the image of the two Pretenders and a flagon showing the Stuart rose with six petals.

He was less zealous of his silver-ware, extending to Henrietta and Phoebe Fraser the privilege of keeping the pieces bright, but the maids were forbidden to handle his china after one dropped a Derby comport and made the mistake of trying to excuse herself by saying, "I was in that of a rare hurry, sir." He was usually very tolerant with the servants, but Rachel, the culprit on this occasion, got a tongue-lashing. "If the man who had made the comport had been in that of a hurry," he roared, "you wouldn't have had the privilege of laying your hands on a piece of craftsmanship made by people who took their work seriously! From now on *I'll* do the china dusting in this house, and that's an order!"

It was one of his very rare flashes of temper for usually the mere contemplation of his treasures brought him serenity. He loved to ponder the moulded decoration in the form of mermaids and festoons on his George I salt cellars, the fan and chrysanthemum motifs on his early Worcester glazes, his choice pieces of Nantgarw, Pinxton, Coalport and Rockingham, but above all some of his late eighteenth-century English furniture, pier tables, pole-screens, rosewood veneered tables inlaid with brass, japanned corner cabinets, the Torricellian barometer in the hall and his magnificent breakfront bookcase, veneered with curled mahogany, measuring nine feet, two and a half inches by twelve feet five inches and holding nothing but calf-bound books, the earliest an atlas, dating from the sixteenth-century, the latest a first edition of *Gulliver's Travels*.

He could tell how and when he had acquired each piece; by cajolery, by hard bargaining and sometimes (for he was a shrewd and a not altogether scrupulous collector) by pretending to do a customer a favour by relieving him of something he regarded as inherited junk. There was very little in the house that was made outside Britain. "We're the finest craftsmen in the world," he would claim, adding with a characteristic touch of cynicism, "At least, we were, before chaps like George got it into their heads that everything had to be done at the double!" And when George reminded him that he, too, in his heyday, had advertised the speed of his deliveries in the press, he said, "So I did, but I had more sense than to treat a consignment of Worcester china as if I was hauling a load of turnips. Look at our insurance files if you want proof of it. No, no, I reckoned one claim a month was excessive and proof of bad bedding-down or sloppy off-loading."

If there was one part of his collection that afforded him more contemplative satisfaction than another it was his picture gallery, where, he would claim, "There isn't a canvas that won't treble in value before you boys trundle me up to that churchyard yonder, some that haven't done so already for that matter."

If he was prejudiced in favour of English silversmiths, English and Irish glass-blowers and English cabinet makers, he was more catholic in his taste for paintings. Up here, along the wainscotted walls of the east and west galleries, or concentrated in the big drawing-room where there was a north light, he had several Dutch masters, including a Van Huysum, two Fragonards, a Claude and a Cranach, besides a selection of English landscape artists, among them a Constable that he had bought at an auction – "Held on a day when a timely blizzard kept everyone with a longer purse away from the auction mart!" He took great pleasure in his English landscapes for they reminded him of his forays up and down the shires since his first prospecting trip on horseback, in 1858. In addition to Constable, artists like Crome, Cotman, Richard Wilson and Bonnington were well represented, reproducing the four seasons and most areas of the country, and when some of his more pernickety visitors expressed regret that he had never been able to get his hands on the work of one or more of the greats, a Leonardo, a Rembrandt or a Velasquez, he would protest, "But, damn it, I didn't haul goods across Italy or Holland or Spain! I made my living right *there*, in *that* narrow country lane, dragging a ton of goods over *that* very hill, or fording *that* particular river and often in *that* kind of weather!"

It was a strange kind of conceit but they left him to it. After all, he was a very old man and could be forgiven his eccentricities.

9

Upon St. Vitus's Day

ON THE TWENTY-FIFTH OF JUNE, 1914, A THICK-
set, middle-aged man wearing the uniform of a general of
the Austro-Hungarian Army, set out on the first engagement of a three-day assignment in the province of Bosnia,
in south-east Europe.

Plumed, girdled, fiercely moustached and over-
bemedalled, he accompanied his wife, Sophie, in a drive
from the small spa of Ilidze into the capital, Serajevo.
His approach was greeted with respectful acclaim on the
part of the mixed population of Serbs, Croats and Turks,
and the Serbo-Croat shout of '*Zivio!*' betokened his
welcome. But that was no more than his due as heir
apparent to the Austro-Hungarian throne.

In the local bazaar, where he and Sophie did a little
shopping, the crowds were so thick that his entourage had
to clear a path for the visitors, but one man, a narrow-
face, slightly-built nineteen-year-old did not shout '*Zivio!*'
He was too absorbed taking stock of the couple he was to
shoot dead three days hence, on Saint Vitus's Day, June
28th, a Serbian national holiday.

The movements of these three people, the Archduke
Ferdinand, his morganatic wife, Sophie and their slayer,
Gavrilo Princip, over the next seventy-two hours were to
have a direct impact upon the lives of every man, woman
and child in Europe; to some extent, every man, woman
and child then living on the planet, and succeeding genera-

tions; to a time long after the hauling firm of Swann-on-Wheels had been forgotten. Because of them, because of their momentary impulses and trivial decisions within this short span of time, ten million Europeans were to die violent deaths within the next four years. Double that number were to live out their lives as chronic or partial invalids. Empires would dissolve, national frontiers would undergo drastic changes and crowned monarchs would become hunted fugitives. Yet neither of these two men, momentarily within touching distance of one another, were aware of more than a tiny fraction of those whose lives were cut short by their encounter. Their encounter that day, or their ultimate confrontation three days later.

*   *   *

The ensuing two days were spent by the Archduke witnessing the manoeuvres of twenty-two thousand troops in the mountain country near the capital; by Princip, the assassin, in brooding, conferring with fellow assassins and visiting, for the purpose of renewing an oath, the grave of a dead revolutionary called Zerajic, buried in that portion of the Serajevo churchyard reserved for criminals and suicides.

At the conclusion of the army manoeuvres the Archduke, well-pleased, wrote, "I had been convinced that I would find nothing but the best and my expectations were fully confirmed by the outstanding performances of all officers and men." On the same day, Princip, together with two fellow conspirators, wrote a postcard to a common friend living in Switzerland but what they wrote is not recorded.

*   *   *

Far away to the south-east, in Punjab mountain scenery more dramatic than the Bosnian crags, Alexander Swann's occupations during these corresponding days of June had something in common with these men.

715

Seven thousand feet up in the foothills of the Himalayas, breathing an atmosphere rarefied not only by the mountain air but by the social graces and taboos of the British Raj, Lieutenant-Colonel Alexander Swann had occasion both to brood and to write, as he studied the reports of a batch of young officers undergoing a course of instruction in a climate that their fellow subalterns, sweating it out on the plains, would have envied. For Simla, the summer residence of the Viceroy, was, by European standards, the most civilised and salubrious town in the sub-continent of India at that time. A visiting artist had written of it, "Everything here is so English . . . one would fancy oneself in Margate."

Unfortunately, however, Alex was too dedicated a man to enjoy the mountain air, or anything Simla had to offer in the way of social amusements. Never much of a mixer, he was currently engaged on work that distressed him, both as a highly-specialised professional soldier and as a rationalist. For he too, in a sense, had been engaged in reviewing and his conclusions were less euphoric than those of Franz Ferdinand in faraway Bosnia. The field work of the candidates, he decided, had been sloppy in the extreme, but if possible that sloppiness was exceeded by their written work. Putting them together he was hard put to it to find a single student eligible for a recommendation to a staff college.

This was bad enough, out of a course of twenty-four. What was worse was the underlying reason for the overall poor quality. The young men selected were either favourites, with some kind of backstairs influence, or regimental failures, the kind of men a busy colonel would not miss for a month or so, and one reason or the other accounted for their presence here. Otherwise it was very unlikely that they would have been detached for the course in the first place. In addition nearly all the candidates were cavalrymen.

Take Willoughby-Nairn, for instance, typical of the kind of subaltern Alex had encountered all over the Empire during the last thirty years. Twenty-three, the younger son of a guardee and an Admiral's daughter; educated Eton; gazetted to a smart regiment on passing Sandhurst at his third attempt. Cherubic-looking, easy-mannered, a great favourite with the ladies, the winner of innumerable polo cups and pig-sticking trophies but running slightly to fat, despite so much outdoor exercise. A proven toper in the mess. Much given to skylarking. Supremely satisfied with his own modest attainments and his future. As a soldier in the field recklessly brave, no doubt; as a leader of men worthless; as a trainer of soldiers worse than useless.

His pen hovered over Lieutenant Willoughby-Nairn's character summary at the foot of page three of his report and he would have given a month's pay to write a truthful assessment of this arrogant young puppy, who embodied all that he most detested in the service. But by now he knew his limitations, both as a small-arms fanatic and as the son of a tradesman. He wrote, "In my view this officer is not temperamentally suited for staff work," and left it at that.

He said rather more in his daily letter to Lydia, for his wife was his emotional safety valve on all these occasions. Of the class in general he wrote: "God help those led by these men in any scrape with a modernised army. Their sole hope of survival would be the elimination of their platoon commander in the first brush and his replacement by a time-serving N.C.O. I use the word 'platoon' rather than 'squadron' advisedly. What nobody here seems to realise is that, in a war with any disciplined force, every man jack among them would serve as an infantryman. I warned my class of that one day last week. Those who were awake looked at me as if I had uttered a blasphemy, as indeed I had in their view . . ."

An overbold monkey, one of the many he had heard thrumming on the iron roof over his head all the afternoon, made a quick grab through the open window at a bowl of fruit on the ledge and suffered for Lieutenant

Willoughby-Nairn's shortcomings. Seizing the first opportunity to release his inner tensions Alexander Swann, square peg in a round hole, smashed his fist down on the intruder, clipping the end of his tail. The monkey fled, screaming with rage. Alex picked up his pen and resumed writing.

The incident afforded him no more than temporary relief. Soon, shuffling his reports, he rose and made his way through a labyrinth of corridors to the Mall outside, threading his way down the winding road towards the barracks. Past block after block of some of the ugliest administrative buildings in the world, monstrosities raised on girders held together with stanchions and roofed with corrugated iron. Architectural eyesores that had been described as 'pyramids of disused tramcars'. Past the premises of military tailors, past estate agents, a bank, two provision merchants, a very English-looking church, Peliti's Restaurant (where you could learn who was cuckolding whom), and as he went rubbing shoulders with Pathans, Sikhs and Tibetans, with strolling Europeans, civil and military, and a string of panting rickshaw drivers. He had eyes for nothing and nobody. The accumulated weight of his misgivings bore on him like a heavy burden. A few high-ranking officers had been impressed by his reiterated pleas for increased fire-power. Had it been otherwise, he would not have been here, marking the test papers of the Willoughby-Nairns, but he knew, and they knew, that his sponsors, men of Haldane's and Roberts' calibre, would not be confronting the enemy if and when the challenge came. That would fall to the Willoughby-Nairns, mostly to men half his age, who thought of him, most of them, as a prig and a bore.

It was the price, he supposed, of having seen so many men needlessly sacrificed in a dozen campaigns; that, plus the misfortune of being born of a practical mother and an imaginative father and of having inherited their commonsense, but not their humour.

He went on past the trim houses of the Little Tin Gods,

with their Sikh guards and their regimented rows of
lupins, on down the Mall in the general direction of the
vice-regal palace. His steps led him instinctively towards
the range, silent at this hour of the day when parades were
over and Europeans took their ease.

The armoury was housed in a long shed, a hundred
yards beyond the guardhouse. He acknowledged the
salute of the sentries and passed inside, pausing to glance
through the barred window of the building and seeing
there something that mildly surprised him, at least enough
to penetrate the gloom that had tormented him since he
sat down to mark those test-papers. A shirt-sleeved lance-
corporal was at the bench, coiling belts of heavy machine-
gun ammunition and something reverential in the
youngster's movements arrested him. The gun, dismantled, lay on the bench but the lance-corporal was
wholly absorbed, coiling the belts like a bride-to-be
winding ribbons. Alex went inside and the young soldier
– Alex judged him to be no more than twenty at the most –
sprang to attention, his arms held stiffly by his sides,
thumbs in line with the seams of his breeches.

"Are you the armoury guard detail?"

"No, *sir!*"

"What are you doing here? Are you on duty in the
guardhouse?"

"No, *sir!*"

"Did you strip that Vickers?"

"Yessir."

"You were given authority?"

"Sergeant of the guard. *Sir.*"

The young man seemed petrified in the presence of
a lieutenant-colonel. He held himself poker straight and
when he spoke his lips moved like those of a ventrilo-
quist's dummy.

"All right, lance-corporal. Stand at ease."

The man relaxed, muscle by muscle. It was like
watching someone thaw.

"You're interested in the heavy-machine-gun?"

"Yessir."

"But not a qualified machine-gunner?"

"No, sir."

"Then who taught you to strip a gun?"

"No one, sir . . . I . . . I watched . . . watched it being done during the course, sir."

"Then you must recognise me as the instructor?"

"Yessir."

"What are your duties on the range?"

"Setting up targets, sir."

"But you have never actually handled a gun until now?"

"No, sir."

"Could you reassemble it?"

"I believe so, sir."

"Do it then."

He took a seat on the end of the bench, watching the lance-corporal's expression. His body was at ease, or nearly so, but his features were still frozen into a blankness bordering on that of an imbecile. Yet gradually, as his hands closed over the dismantled pieces of shining metal, the expression changed, the hard, staring look softening to one of dreamy absorption. The oil-stained fingers, long and supple, moving very rapidly but with infinite precision. The only sound in the hut was the soft click of metal as the gun took shape. Alex glanced down at his watch, then at the man's hands, then at his watch again. The operation occupied one minute, fifteen seconds. He said, "What's your name, lance-corporal?"

"Hunter, sir."

"How long have you been out, Hunter?"

"Two months, sir."

"Where do you live in England?"

"Kent, sir."

"What part of Kent?"

"A place called Hildenborough, sir."

"Then you probably know my father's home, 'Tryst', near Twyforde?"

"Yessir." There was a pause. "I used to deliver telegrams there, sir. Before I enlisted."

It was an odd coincidence. He must sometimes have seen the boy, pushing his red bicycle up the steep drive from the old mill-house, for telegrams from the Tonbridge office were constantly arriving at 'Tryst', especially in the years before his father had installed a telephone.

He sat pondering a moment, Lance-Corporal Hunter having stepped back a pace and resumed his at-ease posture, head up, legs astride, hands clasped behind his back.

"Automatic weapons fascinate you, Hunter?"

"Yessir."

"Since when? You never saw one during your recruits' training."

"Since I was a kid . . . a child, sir. I once watched a demonstration at a tattoo."

"Where was that?"

"At Hythe, sir."

"You have applied for transfer to a machine-gun section?"

"Yessir. But there's a long waiting-list, sir."

"Are you sure of that, Hunter?"

"So I was told, sir. Sergeant Topham, sir."

"Strip that gun down again."

The young soldier leaped forward, his hands seeming to tear the segments apart but he laid each of them down on the bench with infinite care. The operation was completed in under the minute.

"I'll recommend you personally, Hunter."

The lance-corporal's jaw dropped an inch, but then, his reflexes reminding him that this was disrespectful, it snapped shut again.

"Thank you, *sir*."

"Where is your sergeant now?"

"In the guardhouse, sir."

"Thank you, Hunter. Expect to begin training to-morrow after first parade. I shall be here. I'll arrange your course of instruction myself. Now reassemble the gun."

"Sir!"

He did not wait to see it done but went out without a backward glance, his step appreciably lighter. The weight had lifted from his brow and he thought, making his way over the scrupulously-swept asphalt towards the guardhouse, 'What the devil does it matter if the Willough-by-Nairns of this world go to their graves without learning the difference between a lance and a Vickers machine-gun? Providing, in places like there, here and on home stations, there are waiting-lists of Lance-Corporal Hunters?'

*   *   *

On Saturday, June 27th, the heir to the Austro-Hungarian throne and his wife, Sophie, presided over a formal banquet served in the dining-room of the hotel at Ilidze.

The night was warm. Windows were thrown open. Outside on the lawn the band of the Serajevo garrison played Schumann's 'Traumerei', a phantasy on 'La Bohème', a Léhar medley and the obligatory 'Blue Danube'. The guests ate soufflé, lamb, fillet of beef, roast goose and fruit. They drank French wines, the local Mostar and Hungarian Tokay. Towards midnight, Franz Ferdinand remarked he was glad his Bosnian visit was almost over, and someone suggested that the brief visit to the capital scheduled for the following day should be cancelled and the archducal couple should make an immediate return home. Then, being persuaded that Serajevo dignitaries would be hurt and disappointed by the cancellation, a decision was reached to adhere to the original schedule. The hands of the dining-room clock moved up to midnight. The day of St. Vitus had begun.

2

That same night, at round about the same hour as the Archduke's dinner guests were doing justice to their roast goose, Edward Swann was eating a less exotic but appetising home-cooked meal in the dining-room of his mother-in-law, Edith Wickstead, near Peterborough, Northamptonshire. He had company but it was not Edith's and although unaware of it at the time Edward too had a surprise immediately ahead of him. For he, too, in a very small way, was the target of a conspiracy.

Although outwardly himself again, encouraging his brother George's colourful comment that "He's blown his nose, dusted himself off and emerged the same good old go-steady-think-twice Edward again," he had been changed inwardly by his wife's desertion and in a way that even George, his mentor over many years, was unqualified to judge. The real trouble with Edward was that he had absorbed, one could say, a quadruple dose of ancestral practicality. From his French grandmother, Monique d'Auberon, daughter of a Gascon pastrycook, he had inherited the same strain of hard commonsense that ran so richly in the veins of his father and mother and had been present, in full measure, in the blood of his maternal grandparents, one a Lancastrian millhand who had made two fortunes, the other an Irish peasant, whose commonsense told her she should seek her pot of gold in Liverpool rather than County Kerry.

The same strain, to a degree, ran in all the Swanns but with nothing like the same urgency, and whereas it stood him in very good stead as an engineer, and a man of business, it made it almost impossible for the same man to rationalise his wife's dream of becoming a celluloid goddess.

For a brief spell, after watching, openmouthed, Gilda's eye-rolling and cavorting on the flickering screen of that little picture-house in Birmingham, he had been comforted by the acknowledgment that he had made the

---

biggest mistake of his life by falling in love with her. He was not in love with her any longer.

This was how things stood with him when Betsy Battersby was unleashed upon him for Betsy, it could be said, was the price Edith Wickstead paid to get her conscience out of pawn, a brawny, cheerful, uncomplicated Yorkshire lass, her favourite among a tribe of nieces and great-nieces left behind in the North Riding when she moved south to take over the old Crescent territory in the 'sixties. Edith, missing her own family when the boys grew up and Gilda went abroad, grew to like Betsy's undemanding company, particularly when Tom was out about his business, and after Tom's death she became a frequent visitor, giving her great-aunt a hand with the house chores so that Edward, also a frequent visitor, came to think of her as a family hanger-on, midway between a domestic help and a house guest. While under the spell of Gilda, however, he never saw her for what she was, a well set-up girl in her mid-twenties, that is to say, some ten years his junior. She had flaming red hair, light blue eyes that always looked pleasurably surprised, regular if slightly heavy features, a generous mouth, much given to laughter, and an excellent figure that Edith always thought of in Adam's terms as 'promising', recalling that neither he nor Tom had cared for wraiths, much in vogue during their courting years. Tom, she remembered, had always admitted that 'he liked plenty to catch hold of' and Betsy Battersby certainly came into this category of women.

The idea of deploying her against Edward, however, as a kind of consolation prize for the manner in which a real slut, her own daughter, had served the poor boy, did not occur to Edith until she had had an opportunity to make a full assessment of the harm Gilda had inflicted on him and this she was only able to assess by instinct, after Edward's response to the first letter from America.

It arrived out of the blue, about two years after Gilda's flight to France, telling a tale that the truant might have borrowed from the Arabian Nights. Her films, it seems, had been seen in America and an agent had negotiated a contract enabling her to travel all the way to California to make a costume film about the French Revolution. This, so Gilda reported, had led to other films and a better contract, so that she was now in receipt of the equivalent of a hundred English pounds a month, with the promise of much more to come. She had changed her name again and was now known as 'Gilda de la Rey'.

Reflecting that there was surely substance in the adage that the wicked prospered like the green bay tree, and remembering also that she had always been inclined to doubt the validity of that contradictory saw about virtue being its own reward, Edith read the final page. It scouted a proposition that, as they were unlikely to meet again, Edward should supply grounds for a divorce and was set down, Edith thought, as though this was the bestowal of a royal and gracious favour upon an unworthy subject.

She took the only course open to her, telegraphing Edward to visit her and discuss the matter and was not surprised when he growled, after scanning the relevant page, "Let her whistle for her divorce. I'm over it now and I'm damned if I'll make it public. Just don't answer the letter, Edith."

She said, gently, "That's precisely how I felt about it at first, but then it occurred to me you might be cutting off your nose to spite your face. Divorces, nowadays, aren't the end of the world, as they were in my day, and this would be undefended and wouldn't create much stir. Anyway, look at it from another standpoint. You might want to get married again some time."

"When that happens you can certify me," he said. "Don't answer it, Edith. Hasn't she caused both of us enough grief?"

She said, carefully, "I know you're over it, Edward. I know also that you must ask yourself sometimes why and how you came to fall in love with a girl as heartless and self-centred as that. I'm glad Tom didn't live to see the way she turned out. However, be honest with yourself. You've got red blood in your veins and you're only in your mid-thirties. What do you propose to do about women for the rest of your life?"

He said, without meeting her glance, "I don't need women in that sense. If I did I could buy one."

"But that's not you, is it?"

"How do you mean 'not me'? Look here, Edith, you were gaffer of a region here and must have seen most things. You know that men who want a frolic can get one, providing they've got money in their pockets."

"I know that, yes. But it wouldn't be your way and you've probably found that out for yourself."

He was silent, so she said, with a sigh, "Very well. I won't answer it. But if she writes again I'll re-address the letter to you and you can decide for yourself whether or not you read it."

He left her in an ill-humour and she suspected he was going to drown his sorrows. In spite of what the family were saying about him it was clear to her that he still had some to drown. But then, within minutes of his departure, her spirits lifted, for Betsy arrived with luggage and asked if she could stay a week or so.

"It makes a rare change," she announced, "for down here it's free and easy, and back home I'm faced with a choice of playing nursemaid to other folks' babies or filling my time with chapel activities. That's the two alternatives open to old maids in my part of the world."

"I'll never think of you as an old maid, Betsy," said Edith and Betsy replied, cheerfully, "No more will I until I'm the wrong side of forty. It was hot and dusty in the train. Can I pop up and have a bath before supper?"

She was calling from the top of the stairs in five minutes. "Auntie Edith! There's no more than a sliver of soap in the dish. Can you throw me a cake?" and Edith, getting a new tablet, took it to the stairhead where Betsy was standing naked on the landing.

It was her nakedness that fired Edith's imagination.

Somehow it had never previously occurred to her how
comely Betsy might look without clothes that were
usually home-sewn and out of fashion. With her flaming
red hair reaching as far as her broad buttocks, her high
bust set off by a waist that looked two inches narrower
than it did when she was dressed, she looked like a Viking's
bride and she thought, with a mild rush of excitement,
'By God, if young Edward could see Betsy now it would
do more to put that stupid wench of mine out of mind
than any amount of soothing talk on my part. Or tumbling with whores, for that matter . . .' But all she said
was, "Here's your soap, Betsy. And over supper remind
me that I've a proposition to put to you."

"What kind of proposition?"

"We'll see, shall we?"

*   *   *

On Saturday, the 27th of June, about the time the
archducal guests assembled in the Ilidze Hotel, Edward
Swann appeared at his mother-in-law's door in response
to an invitation for a weekend stay.

He was met by Betsy, who said that Auntie Edith was
visiting a sick friend a mile or two nearer Peterborough,
and wouldn't be back until after dinner

"She asked me to cook for you and it's almost ready.
Give me your grip and I'll take it up while you treat
yourself to some sherry." And without waiting for his
response she grabbed his bag and tripped upstairs where
he heard her humming a snatch from the music-hall song,
'Won't You Come Home, Bill Bailey?'

In the dining-room a meal was laid for three. There
was, he noticed, a bottle of champagne in the ice-bucket
and he thought, 'What's Edith celebrating, I wonder?
She doesn't generally run to champagne. Maybe it's
her birthday.' He said to Betsy as she reappeared, "Is
it Edith's birthday, Betsy?" and Betsy said it was not but
it happened to be hers.

"I'm twenty-eight," she said gaily. "Isn't it awful? But I'd sooner have a birthday here than home, for our house is strict T.T. If my father thought I was guzzling champagne he'd come down here and fetch me home with a flea in my ear."

"He could hardly do that to a daughter of twenty-eight, could he?"

"Oh, yes he could. I don't know whether you know the north well but they keep a rare tight rein on the women up there, much tighter than down here. It's still a patriarchal society, and pi-faced with it."

There was something about Betsy that amused him. It was difficult to believe that she was twenty-eight.

"How do you mean, pi-faced?"

"Well, everything revolves round the chapel. No one goes to the theatre, no one is supposed to drink and cards are the Devil's prayerbook. That's why I spend as much time as possible with Auntie Edith. She's fun, but my people don't really know her. They think she's a semi-invalid, and she plays along with it just to get me here. That's jolly sporting of her, don't you think?"

He hardly knew what to think. For the first time despite her ingenuousness, she was registering upon him as a woman, not all that much younger than himself, a woman with an air of a lively, mischievous child about fourteen radiating a boisterous cheerfulness that was difficult to resist. He said, "Well, make the most of it, Betsy. Join me in some sherry before you serve and we'll follow up with the champagne. How long is Edith likely to be?"

"Oh, not more than an hour or so, but she insisted we weren't to wait dinner. I've roasted a duck and it will be spoiled. I'll have the sherry, tho', and then dish up. Shall I put on the gramophone?"

"If you like." He looked across at the big horned phonograph on a side table, noting that it was an American model, an improvement on George's latest and George was an Edison Bell enthusiast. "That's new, isn't it?"

"Auntie Edith gave it to me for my birthday but I'll

have to leave it here. A phonograph is only one up from a pack of cards in our house."

"You could get round that. Why not buy a sacred recording and try breaking 'em in with the 'Hallelujah Chorus'?"

It was the closest he had come to making a joke in a long time and she made it seem a better one than it was, exclaiming, "Why, that's a wonderful idea! They might even progress, eventually, to Gilbert and Sullivan. But I've only got the one cylinder and that's ragtime."

"*What* time?"

The word meant nothing to him and she looked surprised. "Ragtime. Bouncy stuff played fast. It's called 'Alexander's Ragtime Band'," and she hummed the first line or two of a jerky little tune that he immediately recognised as a recent vanboys' favourite at the yard. "I'll put it on. If it winds down while I'm dishing up turn the handle quickly for they sound frightful when they run down, like a rhinoceros with the belly-ache."

She switched on, downed her sherry at a gulp and bounced off into the kitchen, where he heard her singing an accompaniment to the whining, oddly fascinating rhythm of the scratchy recording. He thought, pouring himself another sherry, 'She's a rum sort of girl. Her cheerfulness rubs off on a chap somehow yet it doesn't sound as if she has much of a life, poor beggar . . . no idea Edith's folk up north were straitlaced . . .' and as he thought this he felt relaxed and grateful to her for the lift she had given him. For nowadays there seemed to be nothing much in life but work and sleep.

Her home cooking, to a man who lived mostly in chophouses, was a discovery; brown soup, duck, trifle and Stilton cheese, eaten with some crisp brown biscuits she had made. Over their second glass of champagne he said, "Don't you have a young man, Betsy? Someone like you should, surely? More than one, maybe."

"Most women are married at my age," she said, "and I've come within shouting distance of hooking someone three or four times in a row, but it always fizzles out. Not on my part, on theirs."

Her honesty made an immediate appeal to him, especially as she illustrated the admission with a wry face but then, as if to demonstrate the fact that she had survived her disappointments, a chuckle.

"I can't understand that. Let's face it, you're pretty, you're good company, you're a first-rate cook."

"Ah, I daresay, kind sir, but I'm also considered flighty," and he had to laugh as she went on, "I am too, but we aren't here for long, are we, and I honestly can't see why most people have to make such heavy going of it." Then with a flicker of embarrassment, "Was Gilda flighty? Surely she must have been to run off like that, all the way to America."

"You know about me and Gilda?"

"Not *you* and Gilda, or only the very little Auntie Edith's told me. But everyone knows Gilda by now, don't they? I mean, she's famous. I saw her in that French Revolution picture at the Bijou, in Peterborough. Auntie Edith took me."

He was jolted by this. It had never occurred to him that other people took Gilda's posturing seriously and as to Gilda de la Rey or whatever she called herself being considered famous it seemed to him quite preposterous. He said, thoughtfully, "What did you think of her?"

"I thought she was awful. I mean, that kind of thing isn't real acting, is it? No more than a lot of put-on eye-rolling and bosom heaving. I'm sure I could do better than that myself, although maybe it isn't her fault."

It struck him then that she must have known Gilda before he did, visiting here as a child and probably being patronised, as by a governessy sort of cousin. It would be difficult, he thought, to think of two more dissimilar women than his wife and Betsy Battersby. He was pondering this when he heard her say, "You don't like talking about her, do you?"

"Not much, but it doesn't matter with someone like

you, that is, someone who knew what she was like before she was married. What *was* she like? When you met her after she came home from the Continent?"

"Lah-di-dah," Betsy said, promptly. "Very pretty, of course, and clever, but I never liked her. She wasn't interested in anyone but herself. Anyone could see that in a twinkling. I thought then, 'Any man who marries Gilda Wickstead will be asking for trouble.' I'm sorry if that offends you but you did ask for the truth."

"It doesn't offend me." He got up. "I'll help you clear and wash up before Edith gets back."

They cleared the table together and while relieving her of a heavy tray he noticed the pleasing swell of her breasts. It made him think fleetingly of Dulcie, the over-ripe barmaid at The Mitre, where he drank in the evenings sometimes, and he thought again, 'I'm damned if I know why some lively spark hasn't snapped her up long ago. She'd have a lot to offer to the right man.' Far more than most, he decided, standing beside her at the sink and watching her closely as she washed dishes, for every time she straightened up after lifting plates from the water her fine breasts rippled and the evening sun, filtering through a side window, made her hair glow like red-hot cinders. 'By God,' he told himself, looking away hastily, 'I need a woman and no mistake!'

But when they had gone back into the dining-room she asked him if he knew the Bunny-hug and the Turkey Trot. "A girl I know taught me. She goes to all the hops at the drill hall but there'd be hell's delight in our house if I went there, with or without an escort. Did you ever learn to dance?"

"Formal dances," he said, "when we were kids. We had a teacher call for the girls and she used to rope me in as a partner. I never took to it."

"I could teach you. You can dance to ragtime; in fact it's better. Here, roll that rug up and I'll put it on again," and mildly surprised at the pleasurable anticipation of learning the Bunny-hug with Betsy as a tutor he did as she asked and soon they were prancing around the room to the whine of the phonograph and he realised that she was quite an expert, although the new dances did not seem to consist of more than skipping and jogging, steps that he found no difficulty in improvising.

"I say, you're jolly good!" she said, pausing to rewind the handle. "You've got a natural rhythm and you lead well. We'll show Auntie Edith when she gets back. Come on, let's try again." He put his arms round her and noticed that her cheeks were flushed with the champagne and that she seemed eager that he should hold her close, and soon he began to perspire gently, not so much by reason of cavorting in a confined space but on account of the fact that Betsy's sturdy thighs collided with his at every turn and hover, so that he found it difficult to sustain belief in her innocence. 'She may have been reared in the Baptist tradition,' he told himself, 'but she's picked up the basic technique somewhere.' Then the phonograph ran down again and when she made no move to wind it, but remained in his loose embrace, he thought, 'I'd be a fool not to make the most of this – a man must have a bit of fun sometimes,' and he kissed her mouth, enlarging his grip in a way that supported most of her weight.

She did not seem to mind in the least. On the contrary, when he adjusted his position so that he could run his hand across her breasts, she gave a definite wriggle of approval and it crossed his mind that his next move should be a suggestion that they write a note for Edith and go for a spin in his car as far as the nearest woods.

He had no opportunity to put the question, however, for as soon as his hold relaxed slightly she renewed it and began kissing him back in a way Gilda had never kissed him and then he was sure, somehow, that he had been excessively naïve about her, and that she had almost certainly had a wide experience in this particular pastime. He managed to get as far as "Why don't we . . ." but at that moment the front doorbell rang loudly and she exclaimed petulantly, "Now who on earth can that be . . . ?"

and detached herself and went into the hall, where he heard her talking to someone on the doorstep.

She came back holding a folded note in her hand. "It's from Auntie Edith," she said, triumphantly. "She sent it over by Timothy, Mrs. Burrell's little boy. It's to say Mrs. Burrell can't manage with that leg, and all the children to see to, and wants Auntie to stay over for the night until Mrs. Burrell's sister arrives from Devizes."

"What did you tell the boy?"

"Well, what could I? There's four children to feed and get off to school in the morning."

"You mean you don't mind staying here alone?"

"I'm not alone, am I? Auntie said you intended staying until tomorrow night."

"So I did but – well, in the circumstances . . ."

"Oh, fiddlesticks to the circumstances," she said emphatically. "If Auntie doesn't mind, I'm sure I don't for I'm enjoying my birthday. How about you, Edward?"

He said, with a laugh, "You're a rare tonic, Betsy, especially to someone down in the dumps. You're sure you don't mind me staying over?"

"I'd like you to. I'll cook you a slap up breakfast in the morning and maybe you'd take me a ride in your car, for I've never ridden in one in my life."

"You mean you want to go now?"

"Oh no, not now. The morning will do. If I've waited twenty-eight years to ride in a motor, I can wait overnight."

There was simply no resisting her and it astonished him that he had hardly noticed her on his previous visits here. He said, "We've had enough dancing on the sort of meal you provide. Let's treat ourselves to a glass of Edith's port and take it in the parlour." He picked up the decanter and two glasses and followed her into Edith's cosily-furnished snuggery where he settled himself on the sofa. It was growing dusk outside now and a feeling of well-being stole over him as she drew the chintz curtains and paused on her way back to him to inhale the perfume from a bowl of roses Edith had set on an occasional table. He had few doubts now as to what was expected of him and when she passed in front of him he reached out and grabbed her, running his hands over her plump bottom and saying, gaily, "Edith's got a nice sense of timing. Sit on my knee, Betsy."

"I'm no light-weight."

"And all the better for it."

She said, teasingly, "I thought you preferred skinny girls. Gilda was skinny."

"Oh, to the devil with Gilda. Let's forget Gilda for a bit."

"All right."

"Any man in his senses would want you, Betsy, and that isn't the champagne talking," he said pulling her down, gathering her up with a kind of desperation so that she laughed.

"Here, hold on lad! We've got all night, haven't we?"

She began to settle herself close to him but he said, running his hand over her hair, "I'd like to see you with those pins out of your hair, Betsy. You've got wonderful hair. Let it loose now. It must look even more wonderful freed of that comb and all those pins," and she looked at him seriously for a moment, her head on one side and then, getting up again, "I'll have to do it upstairs. It's quite a business. Wait here, I won't be five minutes."

He could feel his heart thumping and was aware of the constriction of his starched collar that seemed to be choking him so that he was strongly tempted to take it off, together with his jacket, but he thought; "Here, that's taking too much for granted." But then he heard her step on the stairs and she came in as he was in the act of getting up, her hair cascading over her shoulders and wearing a voluminous pink bathrobe, sashed about her waist and reaching down to her bare feet but sufficiently open at the top to display her breasts.

"I was hot after all that food and drink and dancing," she said, equably, "and you must be too. Why don't you take your jacket and collar off while I pour us some port?"

It was as though she had found some secret spring in his character, releasing a man charged with an abundance of tenderness and affection. He had always been reckoned the most dour and inarticulate of the family, "Closer to old Sam, in his mellow period, than any one of them," Adam would say of him, and then his late-flowering high spirits had been checked and turned back by the monstrous assault on his pride.

What began as a kind of mutual dare, with undertones of body hunger on his part and high spirits on hers, transformed itself, in a matter of seconds, into a genuine giving and receiving.

He said, touching her neck with the tips of his fingers, "You're beautiful, Betsy! You're the most beautiful woman in the world."

"You don't have to say that. In fact, you don't have to say anything. I needed you and you needed me. I've thought about you a lot. You're not feeling guilty about me, are you?"

"I'm not in the least guilty, Betsy. Just grateful. Would you like me to go and come over again when Edith's back?"

"You want to?"

"No, I don't want to. I want this to happen again as often as you want it to. But I can't expect that in the circumstances."

"You mean Gilda?"

"I mean Gilda. She'll divorce me in time but when I can't say. And I wouldn't want you to be mixed up in a divorce."

She considered this a moment, looking thoughtful, but the strain of concentration was too much for her and presently she smiled. "It's late," she said, "too late to go into all that. Would you like some tea?"

He laughed. Always, he thought, she would demonstrate this priceless gift of being able to sidestep the imponderables and find fulfilment in the moment, and the small change that emerged from the moment. "No," he said, "I don't want tea, Betsy. The only thing I want is you."

3

It was doubtful, Rory Clarke had once told his English wife, whether Ireland would ever be free without more blood-letting and that meant getting arms for the South. Watching, clause by clause, the tempestuous progress of the Home Rule Bill, she had argued, "But if it goes through, if you get what you've been fighting for all this time, would you ever vote for bloodshed, Rory?" and he replied, gravely, "No. I'd do all I could to stop it. We're not assassins."

They were not so squeamish in the Balkans.

At dusk on June 27th, about the time Lieutenant-Colonel Swann was watching Lance-Corporal Hunter strip and reassemble a Vickers machine-gun, and while his brother Edward, abed in England, was discovering the hitherto unimagined charms of Edith Wickstead's hoydenish niece Betsy, five students, the eldest of them no more than twenty, met their schoolteacher mentor, twenty-three-year-old Danilo Ilić in the park at Serajevo, after a final consultation at a neighbouring coffee house.

Ilić handed four of them a bomb, a revolver and a dose of cyanide. To the fifth, Cabrinović, he gave a bomb and a phial of poison. The poison, as it turned out, was all but harmless but the bombs and guns were lethal, even in the hands of amateurs. Their use on the Appel Quay a few hours later were to herald a million fusillades clear across the world. Not least in Ireland, where bombs would burst and guns blaze long after the rest of Europe had sickened of killing.

Helen's humiliating failure to serve Sinn Fein interests in the matter of the stolen brief case had effectively blocked her admission into the inner councils, but it had one bonus. It had strengthened her relationship with Rory for he was all too aware that she had at least tried, that she had been prepared to jettison family loyalties for his sake. And this was all that mattered so far as he was concerned.

From then on she enjoyed his complete confidence, even if she was disbarred from accompanying him on his endless journeyings about the country, and had perforce to remain the far side of a locked door when officers of the movement assembled in her home for conferences. Yet she did not resent this exclusion. Rory trusted her and she resolved to build upon his confidence by what could be described as pursuing an intensive course in Irish grievances, readily available to her in his well-stocked library.

She never read novels or a fashion journal nowadays. Her reading matter was entirely confined to pamphlets, newspaper clippings that Rory had pasted into albums that he referred to as 'The Score', to local histories and government surveys devoted to the economics of Ireland over the last century or so, and she was appalled by what she read.

There were accounts here of evictions, abortive risings, rent strikes, Fenian forays and the savage penalties all forms of protest had provoked. There was the horrifying story of the successive potato famines of the 'forties, and the steady drain of Irish immigrants overseas, mostly via coffin ships sailing out of Cork for the New World where, she imagined, whole areas must now be populated by fugitives from Mayo and Kerry. For those who survived, that is, for it seemed to her, reading grisly accounts of epidemics and ill-found voyages, that only half the emigrants lived to begin life again elsewhere.

It was desperately gloomy reading but it strengthened the bond between man and wife, for he came to see her now as a convert in her own right, brought to the light by her own convictions rather than by wifely obligations. The time would come, he told her, when he would persuade his colleagues to see her in this way, and not as a potential informer in their midst, as they tended to regard every Englishwoman domiciled in Ireland. But it would need time, for the long story of revolt in Ireland was blotched with betrayals from within.

This was how matters stood when Rory returned from his survey of Ulster in the early summer of 1914, shortly after the mutiny at the Curragh, where Ulster-born officers succeeded in obtaining from the British Government a guarantee that they would not be called upon to fight fellow Protestants in the north.

He had gone there half-doubting the stories of extreme militancy among the Orange Lodges, and the martial preparations said to be on foot by the Carsonites, aided and abetted by the British Unionists and aimed at recruiting an army capable of resisting Home Rule by force of arms. He returned a despondent man, his worst fears confirmed, he told her on the night he came home to find her waiting for him. Ulster was virtually mobilised and it was high time – almost too late, maybe – to take this undeniable fact into the strategical considerations of Sinn Fein.

"I went there supposing they had a few hundred sporting guns and surplus Continental discards," he said, "but our sources in Belfast soon changed that view. In April, over at Larne, they ran in thirty thousand rifles and bayonets and three million rounds of ammunition. Right under the noses of the police and coastguards, and Carson, they say, now has a hundred thousand volunteers pledged to fight. How will the National Volunteers stand up to that?"

"By running in an equivalent armament you've always said," she reminded him, but he replied, with an impatient gesture, "Aye, that's what I said, Princess, but I spoke out of turn. Our Continental agents tell us they can lay hands on enough rifles to equip the Dublin brigades now drilling with broomsticks but in our case, without big money interests behind us, it'll always be cash in advance. Where would we lay our hands on that kind of money? For my part I'm bled white, and so are the few of us who started out with capital. It costs a great deal to raise and equip an army of starvelings."

"I have money, Rory."

He looked at her with a half-smile. "Your private nest-egg, hatching in an English bank? No, Princess, we're not that straitened ..." But then, his grey eyes regarding her with a curious intentness, "I've never asked about your means. It wasn't my business, for I had more than enough before all these demands were made on me. I know of your father's marriage settlement but as to capital – how much have you got under your own name?"

"Fourteen thousand," and judging by his expression it was a far larger sum than he had anticipated. "Mostly it's my share of Grandfather Sam's legacy and I've never touched it. It's grown over the years."

She rose and rummaged in the top drawer of her bureau, returning with her bankbook and a typewritten list of investments that George's lawyers sent her each quarter. The bank statement showed a credit balance of over eight thousand. The last quarter's estimate of investment yielded another six thousand, four hundred and eighty pounds. He returned the documents. "I couldn't accept this. It represents all you've got, doesn't it?"

"No, Rory, not nearly all. I've got you."

"But, God in heaven, woman, this isn't your quarrel."

"If it's yours, it's mine. What would that money have done for me if you hadn't rescued me from myself a dozen years ago? Arrange for that shipment in cash. By the time it arrives I'll guarantee you fourteen thousand. I don't know what a shipload of German arms would cost, and I don't suppose you do at this stage. But it's a sizeable contribution by any standards, isn't it?"

He said, taking her hand and studying it, much as a fortune-teller might, "You're a strange creature, Princess. I've always thought so, ever since you told me about that part you played in the Peking shindig. But I love you and need you, as few men ever loved or needed a woman," and he raised her hand to his lips and kissed it. "I'll make no promises one way or the other until I've put your offer before them, but I'll tell you this. Spurn it or accept it as manna from heaven, I'll never forget you offered it." And then, with the ardour and despatch of a groom carrying his bride over the threshold he scooped her into his arms and marched out of the room and up the broad staircase. It was ample reward for the money, she reflected. Particularly for a woman who had recently overlooked her forty-fourth birthday.

* * *

The Appel Quay ran above the river Miljacka, dividing the ancient city of Serajevo and on the morning of June 28th, St. Vitus's Day, both sides of the thoroughfare were lined with spectators, assembled there to see the Archduke's motorcade pass on its way to the City Hall.

Spectators were more numerous on the north side, for there was shade here. On the river side the crowd stood in blazing sunshine, heads turned west towards the station as the first of the six cars came in view. It was here, close together, that three conspirators were positioned, Mehmedbasić, the one Mohammedan in the plot, young Cabrinović and Cubrinović, both nineteen-year-old Serbs. Across the road stood Popović, the fourth assassin. Further along, again on the river side, Gavrilo Princip was posted. Ilić, the mentor, moved among the five, keeping up their courage, urging them to be firm and sure-handed.

The procession passed Mehmedbasić unscathed. The Mohammedan boy fumbled, or lost his nerve, thinking himself watched by a policeman. But when the second car, containing the Archduke and his wife Sophie drew level with Cabrinović, next of the group, a small black object sailed in an arc to pitch on the folded hood of the car, roll off and explode with shattering force. The procession halted abruptly and the Archduke stepped out unharmed, hurrying back to inspect the damage done to the following car, where one of his entourage was bleeding profusely from bomb splinters.

Further along, beside the Lateiner Bridge, Princip continued to wait but he, too, had no luck. The procession restarted and passed him at speed. The other assassins, with the exception of Cabrinović, who was hauled, vomiting, from the river into which he had jumped, dispersed. Bombs and revolvers were discarded as Serajevo's one hundred and eleven policemen moved in, broadcasting news of the heir-apparent's miraculous escape. But Princip retained his weapons. He had the nerve of a dedicated revolutionary but what was more important, at this juncture, he had more patience than his fellow-conspirators.

*   *   *

Far away to the north-west, where the Kentish Weald was dreaming under sunshine as hot as that flooding the Appel Quay, Adam Swann, a few days beyond his eighty-seventh birthday, took it into his head to take his daily constitutional on horseback.

Only when the temperatures were high, and he found walking excessively tiring, did he venture afield mounted nowadays. In the spring and autumn he could walk, indeed, he preferred walking, and in the winter he stayed indoors. But sometimes in the summer the fancy would take him to feel a horse between his knees again and Henrietta, watching him from the terrace, shook her head at this exhibition of an old man's obstinacy as she saw him ride his mare down the drive as far as the old mill house, then over the low bank, into the coppice that marked the northern boundary of the estate.

He rode well and confidently, she thought, for so old a man but then he had never liked to be driven, not in carriage or dogcart, and certainly not in one of George's motors.

"When a man has to depend on others to get him around

he's done for," he told her, the last time she suggested it was time he put his mare out to grass. She did not argue with him. She was well aware, as indeed were all who knew him well, that he had always accepted the loss of a leg, at the age of thirty-eight, as a personal challenge to his mobility.

He rode north-east along bridle paths and through a stretch of woodland in the general direction of Dewponds, looking about him with satisfaction and noting not merely the quality of his son-in-law's crops but the profusion of what farmers would call weeds but what he thought of, these days, as the summer finery of the Weald. Charlock glowed among the barley and here and there a cornflower added its splash of blue to a patchwork of green and gold. And on higher ground, where a straggle of oaks and beeches crowned the hogsback that separated farm and estate, the woods were en fête with a hundred thousand wild flowers, from foxgloves taller than himself, to tiny outcroppings of bugloss and toadflax under the hooves of the mare.

He thought, with satisfaction, 'I notice these things now. Years ago, when I used to ride this way to East Croydon Station I took little heed of them. The scent, maybe, but not the sparkle and glory of it all.' But that, he recalled, had been a time when he despised the city gent who made his pile, kissed his farewell to the counting-house, and set about turning himself into a country squire. He was far more tolerant now, far more appreciative of the fact that Kent, the oldest settled shire in the islands, was still largely rural, with its panoramas of field, coppice and wood, its red-tiled oast-houses and hopfields, its old, crouching farmhouses that had been supporting life hereabouts since the days of the Plantagenets. Men who worked the land, men like his son-in-law Denzil, and his grandson, Robert, were not qualified to judge their heritage, save in terms of what it would yield. But to a townee like himself it was a rare privilege to be here, with strength enough to sit a horse and savour the richness of the countryside.

He had a mind, as he descended the slope beyond the woods and glimpsed the roof of Dewponds among its screen of elms, to pay a friendly call on Denzil, and drink some of his cider, but he thought better of it on meeting Robert, driving a wain up to higher pastures east of 'Tryst'.

He called, "Hello there! You've got a fine crop, Robert. The weather's been good to you this year."

Robert, reining in, replied, "Arr, it's fair to middling. If we don't pay for it in July, as we generally do."

Adam smiled, reflecting that he had yet to meet an optimistic farmer. He said, changing the subject, "How's your father, my boy?" Robert said he was well enough but not as active as he had been in happier days at Dewponds, and as he said this he looked speculatively at his grandfather, probably reflecting that his eighty-seven years sat upon him more gracefully than his father's fifty-four. He said, however, noticing Adam's jaded mare, "Isn't it time you put that old nag out to grass, Granfer?"

"We'll be put out together," Adam told him, genially, as he swung about and rode alongside the creaking wain. "In a year or so maybe, depending upon how much we get of this kind of weather."

Robert glanced at the clear blue sky. "It'll hold for a time yet," he said, phlegmatically, and lifted his hand as their ways parted and Adam moved back into the shade of the woods, letting his mare crop wherever she felt inclined and easing his legs from the stirrups. 'That's the trouble with being Robert's age,' he reflected. 'You think it's there for good and you don't appreciate it, any more than I did at his time of life. But now, with no more than a summer or two ahead, you hoard it, ticking off each week as a score against time.'

Away in the direction of the village the sound of church bells reached him, intruding, though not discordantly, on the murmur of the woods. He thought, 'I've been lucky, I suppose. Luckier than most, despite this damned leg and that frightful packload of work I carried all those years. I've survived and that's about all a man can expect at my time of life.' And then, glancing at his watch, he saw that it was coming up to eleven and his newspapers would be coming up from the village. It was time, perhaps, to see what was afoot elsewhere, for keeping pace with events was always important to him. He gathered up his reins and set off up the winding bridle path to the summit where, a mile below, he could see 'Tryst' dreaming its way through another June.

*   *   *

The Serajevo dignitaries, putting as bold a face as possible upon the outrage on the Appel Quay, had their fulsome say, trying to look as if they did not comprehend their distinguished guest's comment, beginning, "I come here to pay you a visit and I'm greeted by bombs . . . !"

There would be no more bombs, Governor Potiorek assured him. The Bosnian capital was not swarming with assassins, and the young madman who had thrown the bomb was now under lock and key. The route for the visit to the museum had been changed. There would be no tour of the narrow streets and, after lunch and a brief visit to the hospital to see how the wounded officer was faring, the Archducal couple would entrain for home. To interpose between any potential assassin and the heir-apparent, however, Count Harrach surrendered his seat and took his stand on the running-board. He would have done better to inform the Archduke's chauffeur of the change of route.

For a second time that morning the fate of the world rested at point of balance. Then the chauffeur made a right turn into Franz Joseph Street and Governor Potiorek, realising the driver was in error, shouted that this was the wrong way and the driver stepped on the brake, preparatory to reversing.

It was, to the hovering Princip, a heaven-sent opportunity. He was standing within yards of the stationary car and he acted with the promptitude of a trained soldier, stepping forward and firing two shots before he was seized and overwhelmed. The car reversed, straightened up and sped away down the Appel Quay. The Archducal couple remained sitting bolt upright so that it seemed yet another assassination attempt had been foiled. But then Sophie, shot through the stomach, collapsed and a thin stream of blood spurted from the mouth of the Archduke. Seeing it, Count Harrach enquired anxiously if His Imperial Highness was suffering badly. Franz Ferdinand sagged murmuring *"Es ist nichts . . . es ist nichts . . ."* repeating the three words over and over again. They were the last he uttered. The door had slammed on an era. At eleven a.m., fifteen minutes after his wife had died, His Imperial Highness, heir to the Austro-Hungarian Empire was dead.

* * *

At the precise moment the physicians were probing the fatal wound in an attempt to extract the bullet, Adam Swann, founder of an empire more in tune with the times, opened the first of his Sunday newspapers. There was plenty there to interest him but little he did not expect to find. Jo Chamberlain, unforgiven arch-enemy of the radicals, and scapegoat of the whole sorry mess that had emerged from his policy in South Africa, was ill and not expected to live. Repercussions of the master-builders' lock-out in January were still reverberating round the industrial world. Madame Caillaux, wife of the ex-premier of France, and last in. the long line of French *femmes fatales*, was to stand trial for the murder of the editor of *Le Figaro*. The wildest speculations were being made as regards Ulster's threat to fight rather than accept the Home Rule Bill, that had passed its third reading in the Commons a month ago.

He had followed the recurrent Irish crises of the last few months with keen attention, salted with the pinch of cynicism he reserved for Irish affairs. There was not much, he decided, that he didn't know and couldn't predict about that particular witches' brew. In response to the shipment of arms at Larne, or so the Dublin correspondent claimed, Irish Nationalists were now drilling openly in the capital's parks and public squares. Everybody over there was huffing and puffing and what seemed to him a disproportionate amount of space was devoted to the prospect of civil war. There would be no war in Ireland. Neither, in his view, would the northern Protestants be bludgeoned into accepting the Bill for a united and independent dominion, with freedom to go her own way in all matters but defence and a small British military presence would be maintained at strategic points. The Ulstermen had too much money and influence behind them and some kind of compromise would be struck in the end. He thought, remembering the music-hall Ireland of his garrison days in the early 'fifties, 'The whole damned lot of 'em are bored stiff without something to encourage them to strike attitudes and write their maudlin ballads. Wouldn't surprise me if local blacksmiths in the south weren't being sounded on the prospect of manufacturing pikes and much good they'd be, facing the Mausers that idiot Carson has shipped into the north.' Impatiently he turned the page devoted to the impassioned pleas of correspondents on both sides of the Ulster border and passed on to scrutinise the latest Stock Exchange quotations.

In many ways he was a sage and prescient judge of other people's quarrels but he could be forgiven for having no inkling that one of his children, who had sunned herself on the very spot through lazy summers more than three decades behind her, had squandered her entire inheritance in an attempt to equalise the spurs of the two fighting-cocks beyond the Irish Sea.

I O

Heatwave

Robert Fawcett was a good weather pro-phet. "It'll hold for a spell yet," he had told Adam, look-ing at his barley crop ripening under a June sun and so it did, right on through the succeeding month and into that new phenomenon on the calendar, the seaside holiday season, commencing with Bank Holiday.

Day after day the sun blazed across the Weald, tem-peratures soaring into the eighties on the Fawcett pas-tures, where cattle browsed in the shade of the field cop-pice, tails swishing, heads down to parry the swarm of fat flies. Day after day the heat haze hung over the teeming capitals of the Swann regions – Edinburgh, Cardiff, Dublin, Birmingham and Manchester – the sun baking the slippery pavements and the water-carts, abroad at first light, doing little or nothing to lay the dust swirls raised by Swann tyres and Swann hooves, so that work in the high population areas became a penance and the viceroys (being of the minority who could anticipate the seasonal rush) slipped away telling one another and their families that it was wise to take a break while the splendid weather held.

George and Gisela, the youngest of their family long since off their hands, went abroad to visit Gisela's sisters and brothers-in-law south of Vienna, before moving on into the Tyrol for a breath of mountain air. They were just in time to see the Archducal catafalque leave for

Artstettin, surrounded by far less pomp than usually attended the obsequies of a Habsburg. Gisela's brother-in-law, who stood with them to watch it pass, explained the modesty of the display.

"They've never forgiven him for marrying a commoner," he told George, mildly interested in yet another Balkan furore. "They're saying here that those anarchists will get a medal from Prince Montenuova, the Lord Chamberlain and a rare stickler for protocol." And when George, a fluent German speaker, reminded him of the newspaper headlines, he declared, "Oh, there's talk of bringing Serbia to book for her share in the conspiracy but it won't amount to anything. The court party is relieved to see the back of Ferdinand and that woman he would marry, despite all the fuss there was here at the time."

George, watching the coffins trundle by on their way to the Westbankhof, attended only by such nobility of the realm who chose to defy the Chamberlain's posthumous snub, thought, 'I remember old Maximilien Körner telling me that Flunkeydom would choke the Empire in the end and it seems he was right. These fellows look more like a troupe from a musical comedy than soldiers,' and he turned away to retrace his steps to the hotel, where Gisela was packing for the Tyrolean expedition.

*　　*　　*

Mid-July also saw Giles playing truant, despite the backlog of parliamentary business that had accumulated as the summer recess loomed. He had urgent business in the valley, where yet another strike threatened, and when he had done what he could to head it off until tempers cooled, he stole an extra day and used it to drive his new wife, Gwyneth, into Pembroke, that little England beyond Wales, where they walked over the stretch of coastline that had seen the last invasion of England at a time when his grandfather, the old Colonel, was still a boy.

Hand in hand, they explored the Pencaer peninsula

HEATWAVE

jutting from the North Coast and he told her something
of the forlorn descent of a few hundred French starvelings
in February, 1897. He seemed more relaxed these days
and the expedition emboldened her to ask a question
that had been dormant in her mind ever since their
marriage, just a year ago. Reminding him that he still
held the lease on his first wife's house in the mountains at
Beddgelert, and that he had not revisited North Wales
since Romayne's death, she said: "Would it distress you,
Giles, to take a holiday there with me? I'm as Welsh as
a leek but the truth is I've never been to the mountains."

He replied, with a smile, "I've no melancholy memories
of Romayne, as she was then, when I met her up there
thirty years ago. Nor as the woman she became, when we
started from scratch down here in the south. Yes, I'll
take you there during the next recess if you've a fancy to
see Snowdonia. I'll show you the very spot where we met
at the bridge over the River Glasn when I was eighteen.
For the fact is, I don't really see you as two women in
that sense."

"How then?"

"More as the complement of one another, I suppose.
You began where Romayne left off and I sometimes half-
believe that it was meant to happen that way. How else
did it come about that our paths recrossed an hour or so
before she died?"

She thought about that all the way back to London and
it did not strike her as fanciful. She had but two memories
of Romayne Swann. One of a spoiled and pettish young
madam, standing at her counter just before closing time
on a Saturday night and demanding the window display
should be half-dismantled in order that she could buy a
hat; the other of a wan, waxen little figure in soiled
clothes, rushed into her casualty ward after a street riot
in Whitehall. A willing sacrifice, she would always think
of her, to male intolerance, and the way things were
shared in a man's world and in a way the impressions
fused, especially here in Wales, the ancestral home of both

749

his wives. She supposed something of this kind lay behind his remark. As a champion both of Wales and women, he could not be unaware of the fusion and she thought, gratefully, 'He's almost over it now, and I've helped in an odd sort of way. It really does look as if it was planned.'

George was home in time to stand in for his son Rudi, viceroy of The Polygon, who decided, in the last week of July, to take his wife and young family on a trip to the Isle of Man. He did this each year and had come to regard it as an extension of his own holiday, for up here, among the shippers and the textile men, he could feel the peripheral pulse of the network better than anywhere outside the capital, The Polygon having been his youthful stamping ground and one of the oldest of the Swann manors.

Young Rudi, a dynamo hereabouts, left his father a string of last-minute instructions, just as if George had been an apprentice to the trade to whom had been granted a little brief authority, but he did not complain. The boy was shaping up well after that furtive marriage of his and he wasn't surprised when Rudi was back a day before he was due with a new idea and a rumour that a Continental war was brewing.

Rudi, it seems, had run into old Albert Tasker in a Douglas hotel and had learned from him that there was every likelihood of a boom in textiles by the time harvest was in.

"Tasker is one of the biggest shippers about here," Rudi told him, "and he's given me good information on foreign markets in the past. 'If you hold any Continental stocks unload 'em, Young Swann,' he told me. 'If you don't the bottom will fall out of 'em inside a month.' "

But George, recalling his Austrian brother-in-law's comments on the occasion of the Archduke's funeral, replied, "My advice to you, Rudi, is stick to hauling and don't dabble in stocks. If you've money to invest plough it back in the business, as I do. And you can tell old Moneybags Tasker next time you run across him that your father had his ear to the ground on the Continent less than a month ago. There'll be plenty of huffing and puffing but no more than a skirmish or two, this year or next year. It's all bluff on Austria's part and I daresay the Serbs will call it. What was the other revelation granted to you in the Isle of Man?"

"Oh, that," said Rudi, grinning, "that's more in your line. Why have we never opened an Isle of Man depot? The name 'Swann' doesn't mean a row of beans over there and the local hauliers have it all their own way."

It was true. In the original and successive partitions of Britain the Isle of Man had been overlooked by both his father and himself, and he saw at once what Rudi was angling for, a Polygon concession, based on Douglas, with H.Q.'s authority to expand.

"What have you in mind? Two or three teams to break the ground?"

"Teams my eye and Betty Martin," retorted Rudi, using one of the Lancastrian expressions picked up from his wife, "over there they have a road trial course and no one so much as looks up when a motor passes. Let's start off with a brace of Swann-Maxies for house removals. I've got an option on a depot in Douglas at a hundred a year. A brewery that's being wound up."

"Then cost it and send it down by tomorrow's post. I'll talk it over with the head clerk."

"I costed it on the boat," Rudi said, handing his father three handwritten sheets clipped together. "It's legible. The crossing was flat calm."

He took the papers, forbearing to say what came to mind, that Rudi, at twenty-seven, was barking at his heels even more impatiently than he, in his own day as heir-apparent, had barked at Adam's. The boy was cocky enough and needed no further encouragement from him, but it was a story to make the Old Gaffer chuckle the next time he looked in at 'Tryst'.

* * *

Edward Swann was another who succumbed to the lure
of the heatwave. On his mother-in-law's advice he took
Betsy Battersby down to Cornwall for a week – "In order
to get to know the girl," she added, "for you seem very
much taken with her and I'll not have you blaming me
for a second fiasco."

Edward, sharp enough in matters of business, entertained no suspicion at all that she and Betsy had been
plotting since the night she absented herself from home
leaving Betsy to make the running. Betsy had worked a
miracle on him and he had already asked Edith to write to
Gilda in California, telling her she could have her divorce
as soon as possible.

They drove down to the Westcountry in his new Lan-
chester, travelling as Mr. and Mrs. Swann and exchanging a wink every time they signed the hotel registers.
He wondered sometimes what his circumspect mother,
and Betsy's chapel-going family, would make of it if
news of the liaison reached them but the prospect did not
bother him much. Somehow, come hell or high water, he
intended to marry Betsy Battersby and neither he nor she
was prepared to wait on the law's delays. As he reminded
himself more than once during that hilarious trip, at
twenty-eight she was old enough to know her own mind.
As for him, life owed him a ration of fun.

*   *   *

There was one Swann who did not respond to the
brilliant weather but sat it out in his private Mount
Olympus, scanning bundles of newspapers and occupied,
for the most part, with his own sombre reflections.

Adam Swann had never been one for holidays and it
would not have occurred to him to uproot himself and
travel in a stuffy railway carriage to the coast. Or cross
the Channel in search of a change of scene. Up here on
his knoll, with every tree in full leaf, and the scent of
honeysuckle coming out of the woods, he had all the pas-

toral pleasures on tap, plus his own bed to sleep in at nights. He had, too, all his treasures to hand, and his wife by his side. Indeed, the only thing he did not have to cushion his old age was peace of mind, for, despite everyone's dismissal of the European crisis as just one more display of Balkan fireworks, he sensed, deep in his heart, that things were drifting in a way that promised trouble. The newspaper editors, it seemed, did not share his sense of unease but his famous 'little man', who still lived an inch or so above his navel, was agitated. He supposed that Sir Edward Grey was as familiar with the antics of foreign diplomats as he was himself, but there seemed to him a very ominous note in Russia's championship of the Serbs and Germany's encouragement of Austria to use the assassination as an excuse to overawe Belgrade. The devil of it was, France was closely involved too, and seemed likely to exploit the crisis in order to reopen her eternal inquest on the provinces torn from her in 1870, and while he agreed with the wiseacres that no responsible statesman would be such a fool as to use a Balkan assassination to promote a European war, an upset on this scale could play havoc with trade.

And then there was Ireland, where almost everybody was acting the goat, and that solemn ass Balfour, leader of the Opposition, seeing political advantages in backing Ulster, was encouraging army officers to defy a law approved by a majority of nearly a hundred in the House. If they didn't watch out over there those crazy Fenian outrages would begin again, followed by repression and an end to all hope of peace.

It was not the slightest use confiding his misgivings to Henrietta (she probably did not know where Serbia was) and everyone else seemed to be off on holiday somewhere. Towards the end of the month he had to take himself to task, reasoning – 'Why the devil should I lose any sleep over their concerns at my time of life? I've so short a time left!' And so, in the end, he left his newspapers unread and concentrated on his own borders, now a riot of colour

753

and scent and a beanfeast for the bumble bees, whose drone was continuous every time he pottered to and fro about the more regimented sectors of his estate.

He was here, on a morning in late July, admiring some particularly fine clumps of lupins west of the forecourt, when Giles drove up and, without bothering to go into the house, left his motor at the head of the drive and hurried over to him looking, thought Adam, more pre-occupied than usual. Adam spared the boy a sympathetic thought, reflecting, 'He's the only one among 'em inclined to shoulder everyone's troubles but his own. But I'm glad he had the sense to marry that woman and start again.' As he thought this he did his usual little sum about the age of such sons and daughters who visited him, surprised to realise that the grave-looking, soberly attired 'boy' now approaching him was well into his forty-eighth year.

Giles said, "I looked in at The Hermitage on the way up. You're usually there at this time of day reading your papers, aren't you?"

"Indeed I am," Adam said, "but I've given myself a holiday from them. To tell the truth I can't make head or tail of what's happening any more, can you?"

"Russia's mobilising," Giles said, grimly. "That's official, although it missed the morning papers. I'm very concerned, Father. Things are getting out of hand, and I . . . well, the truth is I find it helps talking to you. That's why I drove over. I only got back from the valleys yesterday. Shall we take a turn in the rose-garden before lunch?"

"By all means. There's a rare show this year. Every-thing is responding to this sunshine. So that fool of a Czar has given way, has he? Well, that'll set the cat among the pigeons and no mistake, for as like as not the Kaiser will follow suit, and after him, France." He checked his stride, contemplating for a moment the result of full-scale mobilisation across Europe. "You think there'll be war?"

"Grey seems to think there might be. Some of our people are beginning to hedge."

"You mean the Cabinet is divided?"

"Right down the middle, I gather from the people I talked to last night."

"But good God, boy! If she's fool enough to square up to Germany without provocation, why should it concern us?"

"We're under an obligation to protect France's Channel coast. Not an alliance, a military arrangement. No more and no less, so far as I can discover, for they've kept very quiet about it. Nobody seems to know the true nature of the understanding, not even Asquith, and Lloyd George himself is confused. He told me last week all would depend on what happened to Belgium if the Germans attack France."

It struck him then, as it had many times over the last few weeks, that politics lacked the precision of business, that hardly anyone practising politics had the ability, or even the wish, to think things through, as he and George and the regional managers were required to do when confronted with a choice of alternatives on a haul or contract. They invariably followed a policy of drift, leaving all the final decisions to civil servants and soldiers.

"What you're saying," he said, slowly, "is this. If Germany tries to get at France through Belgium, we're in, like it or not?"

"That's the general opinion at Westminster," Giles said. "What would you make of it in those circumstances?"

He was a long time answering. He had seen many battlefields, had experienced the dragging pain of wounds, had witnessed, in the Crimea and India, scenes that would turn the stomach of the most enthusiastic flag-flapper in the country. Yet he realised that here was a question of principle that could not be dismissed in the way both he and Giles had opposed the South African War. The German Junker was a bully and a brute. Three limited wars, against Denmark, Austria and France, had established that beyond doubt, and an easy victory following an invasion of Belgium would prove fatal to smaller nations and the security of the world in the years ahead. Beyond that, what would it feel like to sit here in Kent, with a triumphant Germany dictating peace terms in Paris and her jackboots stomping in Channel ports only a few miles away?

He said, at length, "I hate wars. Always have and always will. Small and local, or as big as this promises to be. But there are times when a man has to fight, as we found in India in '57. You can't stand aside and let might take over from right. If it was anything more than a straightforward confrontation between jingoes in Potsdam and Paris, I'd fight and so will Grey if I know the man. You say the Liberals are split. Where do you find yourself, Giles?"

Giles replied, unhappily, "With you, Father, in those circumstances, and I told L.G. as much."

The sound of the lunch gong reached them from the house, telling him that Henrietta must have seen Giles' car and hustled. Adam rose stiffly from the arbour seat and paused to inhale the scent of a full-blown rose cresting the trellis work of the pergola. "That's a smell of youth," he said. "Youth and renewal."

They sat on after lunch, mulling over one thing and another. The navy's preparedness. The part, if any, a small professional army like Britain's could play in a war involving the clash of millions. How the Empire was likely to respond. What a professional like Alex would make of it and how long it was likely to last, and Adam snorted when Giles said a matter of weeks was the general estimate.

"Why do they say that?"

"The cost. The City men say nobody could face expenditure on that scale for long."

"That's damned nonsense," Adam said. "Once war hysteria is aroused they'll find the money to keep it going, and anyone who supposes modern Germany isn't a tough nut to crack is a fool. We were bogged down for months before Sebastopol and half a century later it took us three years to round up sixty thousand Boer farmers. No, my boy, once it gets going it'll be a fight to the finish, with half the world involved and casualties running into millions. The pity of it is that most of those damned fools poised on the brink have never heard a shot fired outside their game preserves. You saw what a local war cost Hugo."

Giles said nothing and Adam changed the subject.

"How are you and that nice woman getting along, eh? They say second marriages stand a good chance if one of the partners has been happy in the past. You were always very much in love with Romayne. Does that make it easier?"

"I've been lucky," Giles said, and then, with a smile, "Luckier than you in one respect. For I've run across two women who were prepared to take me on trust." He got up. "It's time I got back."

"There'll be a debate in a day or so, I imagine?"

"On Monday, depending on circumstances. I think Grey will make a statement to the House."

He said, on impulse, "Could you use your influence to get me a seat in the Members' Galleries if I come up to town? The public gallery will be packed."

"I'd do my best, providing you don't think . . ."

"That it would put too much strain on me? You let me worry about that. If that chap Grey speaks I'd like to hear him." His eyes filmed over and Giles, watching him closely, wondered what he was thinking. He went on, after a moment, "I've seen pretty well everything that's happened in the last seventy years or so. Three monarchs buried, two Jubilees, the Charge of the Light Brigade, the fall of Sebastopol, the well at Cawnpore. This will reduce 'em all to a sideshow. I'll see you to the door, boy."

They passed out into the blazing sunshine and he watched Giles manoeuvre the car in a tight circle to descend the drive. Soon the only evidence of his visit was a small dustcloud hanging over the old mill house. Henrietta came out and stood beside him.

"He looked very worried," she said. "It isn't his marriage, is it?", and suddenly, mercifully, he was able to make a grab at his vanishing sense of humour as he said, with a chuckle, "You have a way, my dear, of reminding one of essentials. No, no, it isn't his marriage. That's booming along, just as I predicted as soon as I set eyes on that woman. It's other people's worries, Hetty, and that's Giles – too old to mend his ways."

2

Despite Giles, who had sat here ten years now, Adam did not often honour the House with his presence. It had never, at any time in his life, had majesty for him and latterly he had come to regard it as a kind of clearing-house for specialised interests. But today was different. Old and cynical as he was, he was caught and held by the terrible tensions of the Chamber, sensing all about him a strain that had nothing to do with the high temperature outside, or the presence, in Whitehall and all the converging thoroughfares, of the crowds drawn there by the mounting expectancy of some cataclysmic change in their lives.

He glanced about him, his keen eye ranging the Government benches immediately below where he could spot a few of the men who had contributed to his daily ration of news this century, isolating the bland, slightly clownish face of Asquith. Beside Asquith, fidgeting a great deal, was the familiar figure of Lloyd George, a man he had never trusted, despite his patronage of Giles, and beside L.G., Sir Edward Grey, on whom most of the attention would be focused today.

Grey looked his part. A patrician, whose handsome profile had survived on into middle-age, and who was clearly under very considerable strain for every now and again, glancing at his notes, he tightened his mouth, as though what he was about to say was distasteful to someone who took his pleasures quietly beside English trout-streams and who was said (it was hard to believe) to be able to imitate over a hundred English bird calls.

Winston Churchill was down there, looking cheerful and slightly roguish. Haldane was there, champion of his son Alex, still far away in India, a rather Prussian-looking fellow, who had once made the statement that Germany was his spiritual home and was almost certainly regretting it today. And across the floor, crowded today with extra chairs, the lions of the Opposition, Balfour and Bonar Law, who had made fools of themselves over Ireland, and among the small Labour cohort, two men who stood out, Ramsay MacDonald and Keir Hardie, one looking like an arrogant young clansman, the other, whose integrity had always earned Adam's respect, like the prophet Elijah ascending to heaven in a chariot.

Those fellows will oppose war, he supposed, Belgium or no Belgium, but they already had the look of men who had enlisted in a lost cause. MacDonald looked fierce and defiant but there was tragedy in the eyes of Hardie.

The place was packed to the doors, every gallery full to overflowing, there had never been so many assembled under this roof since Gladstone's day. Well, that was war and the rumour of war.

Grey was on his feet now and there was stillness, shattered momentarily by the sudden and distracting clatter of the Chaplain's stumble against the extra chairs as he backed away from the Speaker. In a clear, level voice, and with no more than an occasional glance at his notes, he began by asking the House to approach the crisis from the standpoint of British interests, British obligations, British honour, proceeding from there, in the same measured tone, to describe the nature of the military 'conversations' with France. No secret engagement existed. No agreement had been entered into to bind or restrict Britain's course of action if France found herself at war with Germany on account of her treaty obligations to Russia. "We are not partners to the Franco-Russian alliance . . . we do not even know the terms of

759

their alliance. What does exist is our naval agreement with France in consequence of which the French fleet is concentrated in the Mediterranean, leaving her northern and western coasts absolutely undefended . . ."

*   *   *

George Swann, at that precise moment, had made his initial dispositions, had descended from his tower and was sunning himself in the yard, all but empty seeing this was a Bank Holiday.

There was nothing more he could do.

For who among his competitors, he reflected, had been granted a kerbside view of the Archduke's funeral in Vienna over a month ago? Or how many had received a direct tip from a source as reliable as old Albert Tasker up in The Polygon, to unload stocks before they plummeted? Yet he had ignored both warnings and it had fallen to his aged father to remind him that, in the event of war, a firm owning a fleet of heavy transport vehicles, and relying on three hundred trained mechanics to drive and service them, was a likely candidate for either bankruptcy or millionaires' row, depending upon how he disposed himself.

Within ten minutes of hanging up his receiver George was on his way to the yard. Within an hour of arriving there he had drafted a comprehensive telegram, running to three hundred words, to every viceroy in the network, giving them basic instructions about stockpiling motor spirit, conserving of machines and manpower, and half a dozen other matters that would alert them to the situation. Most of them (excluding young Rudi) would be as bemused as he had been by the long spell of blazing sunshine.

His imagination, once alerted, worked like a shower of sparks on a scatter of combustibles. In a memorandum, designed to follow his telegram by express post, he covered every conceivable contingency, from the commandeering

of his vehicles by government agents, to the mass enlistment of his mechanics in one or other of the specialised
army units that had proliferated since the General Staff
had conceded the self-propelled vehicle a place among
their priorities. He thought, sitting on a makeshift seat
used by waggoners for their lunch break, 'That's about it,
until I can see Scottie Quirt and get an estimate of future
production out of him. They can't close us now, providing
those chaps out in the shires follow my guidelines. Given
luck, we might even squeeze some contracts from the
military and make a killing out of it . . .'

*   *   *

There was no doubt now which side of the fence would
see Grey's elegantly trousered leg first. The cheers,
breaking from the ranks of the Tories opposite, confirmed
as much when he asked what attitude the country might
take to the presence of the German fleet bombarding
French ports a few miles away and then, borrowing lavishly
from Gladstone's oratory, he underlined his point by
declaring unequivocally: "Could England fail to take her
stand against the unmeasured aggrandisement of any
power whatsoever?"

Adam, his eyes focused unwinkingly on the elegant
figure at the despatch box, thought: 'It's all over now . . .
we're in it sure enough . . .' And then, as Grey reiterated
our pledge in favour of Belgian neutrality, 'And why not?
Had the fellow any real alternative? Has any one of them
down there, including that leathery old fox Earl Roberts,
perched up there in the Strangers' Gallery?' And suddenly he felt old and tired. He extricated himself from his
cramped seat and made his way into the lobby and thence
into the yard where the sun beat upon the necks of ten
thousand Londoners almost blocking the movement of
vehicles.

Giles must have seen him go and caught up with
him as he stood with head bowed beside the plinth of

Cromwell's statue. "Are you all right, Father? Can you get back to your hotel alone . . . ? I can't leave now but I warned Arscott, George's chauffeur . . ." But Adam, straightening himself, muttered savagely, "It's the heat. No air in there . . . I'll be all right, my boy. Get about your business." But Giles would not and hurried off to the place where Arscott had promised to wait. Within minutes Arscott was back and helping Adam into the seat beside the driver's, with Giles standing by anxiously. He said to the chauffeur, "To the Norfolk, if you can get there, and then home," and to himself, 'I'm too old for crowds,' as the car nosed its way south-west through thinning crowds, circling Victoria to approach the Strand from Piccadilly and Haymarket, for it was useless to attempt a more direct route.

He thought, watching the surge up and down the pavements, 'They're with Grey, every last one of 'em. You've only got to look at their faces to see that and it's curious, really, when the very lives of some of 'em are at stake.' But then it occurred to him that it was not so curious after all, for the country, apart from that South African business and a string of tinpot colonial wars fought by professionals, had been at peace for ninety-nine years. Too long, maybe, for anyone but old stagers like himself to understand what there was to war beyond cheering and bugle calls and an escape from office drudgery.

3

The news reached them all in driblets. Via the shrill cries of newsboys, via the clatter of the telegraph, via the measured predictability of the post, or the timeless wag of tongues.

Alexander Swann, far away on the Indian plains, heard it with relief, for he had been sure the Liberals would rat at the last minute.

Edward Swann learned it from the banner headlines of his evening newspaper, carelessly scanned while he was awaiting his turn in the bathroom at a Bristol hotel, where he and Betsy had stopped off for the night on the final evening of their Westcountry jaunt. He called through the open door where, a moment ago, he had heard her splashing and singing, "Change your tune, Betsy! There's going to be a war after all," and her tousled red head appeared round the door-frame.

"Will you be going for a soldier, Edward?"

"Not so long as you're available," he said, and she came in, pink and naked, and went to drying her hair as he read her Sir Edward Grey's speech, adding a few random comments of his own.

She did not seem interested and neither, for that matter, was he. With a woman of Betsy's proportions standing there without a stitch to cover her it was difficult to get excited about the tread of armed hosts. She said, "It could make a difference to us, couldn't it? I mean, nobody will bother much with divorces if there's a war to write about. Not that I care, mind. They could say what they liked about me, so long as I was sure about you in here," and she lowered the towel and touched her breast.

He thought about that a moment and then decided that she was laughing at him, so that instead of assurances he gave her a smart slap on the behind and spun her round, saying, "Get dressed, woman, while I have my scrub. I reserved a table for seven and the head waiter said he couldn't promise to hold it. It seems everybody's celebrating as well as us."

*   *   *

"England's peril is Ireland's opportunity," Rory had told Helen more than once but she had thought of it as a sentiment that belonged to Napoleonic times and the abortive rising of '98. Until the Bachelor's Wall affair that is, for that, more than any tribulation out of the past, impinged upon patriots in a way that penetrated the haze of ballad and legend. Rory and his friends were now facing a straight choice; submission, and a compromise with Ulster, or militancy of the kind British troops had showed when they tried to capture the arms landed at Howth in the last week of July. Three civilians killed and thirty-eight wounded, half of them seriously. Surely an outrage deserving of a dozen ballads, justifying an equal ruthlessness on the part of the Volunteers.

They got most of the guns away in the mêlée. Over a hundred of them lay snug in her own cellar at this moment but then, it seemed, an appeal to arms suddenly became the currency of politicians all over Europe and the Bachelor's Walk massacre was forgotten by the British. She said, when confirmation came that England considered herself at war with Germany and Austria, "Will the Irish fight too, Rory? Will your people put away their private quarrel until there's an end to it in France, or wherever they fight?"

"Here's one who won't, by God! I hope the Kaiser gives them a drubbing and then, maybe, we can make terms with the Germans."

She said nothing to this. Away in the back of her mind issues that had once been stark and clear were getting blurred. It was not easy for anyone growing up in Victoria's England to visualise the English at the mercy of a conqueror, any more than it was credible to contemplate a man like Rory taking a pot shot with one of those contraband rifles at, say, Alex, over here to keep the peace. And apart from that, having lived among the Irish for so long, she could not bring herself to believe that a fight of that magnitude would not encourage them to think of Ulster and Ulster's Volunteers as small beer. All the same, the news increased her sense of isolation over here and sometimes she yearned, more than anything in the world, to slip into town and make her peace with Joanna, to sit down in her drawing-room and have a good old family gossip.

*   *   *

For the rest, in the enduring blaze of sunshine, the news touched them but lightly. Joanna, in Dublin, Margaret, in the valleys, Deborah in London and Lady Sybil in her elegant house overlooking Southampton Water, may have reflected, with a certain amount of relief, that their husbands were too old, and their sons too young, to be eligible for service in the field, and in any case it seemed unlikely to last more than a month or two. Or so all the experts were saying. They were not the kind of women to take war-fever seriously. Joanna was too placid and Margaret, with Huw for a husband and Giles for a brother, too indoc-trinated with anti-militarist theories to wave Union Jacks, or buy wool for soldiers' socks. Deborah, who for years now had suffered physical affront at the hands of men, was inclined to regard the entire male sex as too pig-headed to deserve sympathy and even said so on a postcard to Henrietta from Folkestone, where she heard the news during their annual holiday. "Let them discover what it's like to be hounded," she wrote. "Maybe it will teach them something." And as for Lady Sybil, busy, as usual, organising garden parties and theatricals for Hugo's patients, she had reservations on the subject of patriotic displays, remembering, possibly, a tented hospital in South Africa and a young man on a bed with bandages over his eyes.

*   *   *

It was otherwise with Adam. For a day or so after that spell of dizziness in the House towards the end of Sir Edward Grey's speech, he rested, saying very little and responding hardly at all to Hetty's flow of speculations about the likely involvement of her tribe of descendants, now totalling some thirty-odd. Alex would be home earlier than expected, no doubt, and some of the grand-children might be silly enough to offer Lord Kitchener their services but it would be over by Christmas, wouldn't it? He said, briefly, that he hoped so and bestirred

himself, going out on to the terrace and taking the winding
path up to the summit of the spur where the old Colonel's
summerhouse, constructed of half an up-ended whaler,
still stood. The path was steep and taxed him severely
but he managed it somehow and sat gratefully on the plank
seat, wheezing slightly and resting his mottled hands on
his knees as he surveyed the north-western segment of
the Weald basking in its sixth week of unbroken sunshine.

It was cooler up here. A faint and welcome breeze
rustled the leaves of the beeches and oaks behind him and
jostled the pink and white bells of the tall foxglove spires.
Blackbirds sang and finches quarrelled in the thickets left
and right of the shelter, and away across the full expanse
of his estate, beyond the larch coppice where his third
son had been sired, beyond the white blur of the old mill
house, where, years ago, his second son had lived with his
Austrian wife, he could just glimpse, through the shimmer
of heat, the grey-brown blob that was the capital of the
world, now feverishly involved with the concerns of
lesser capitals across the water.

For a while his imagination conjured with those far-off
places, so that he saw, in his mind's eye, endless columns
of encumbered men marching, marching, marching
towards points of collision with one another. As a man of
war he could identify with them at all levels. With the
braided generals, with sweating privates, wondering when
the next ten-minute halt would be called and they could
ease the dragging weight of the equipment from their
shoulders; with cannoneers riding their limbers and light
horsemen freeing their feet from stirrups and flexing their
thigh muscles; with toiling teamsters half-asleep on the
box-seats of their waggons and even with the clamorous
children lining the dusty roads to witness the passage of
the cavalcades.

It was so old a pageant and so poor a cause. Poorer
than ever in this day and age, when men should have
learned the art of governing themselves without resorting
to chaos. And yet . . . there was the kernel of that chap

Grey's speech: "If France is beaten to her knees, if Belgium fell under the same dominating influence, then Holland and Denmark, I do not believe we should be able to undo what had happened to prevent the whole of the west of Europe falling under the domination of a single power . . . we should, I believe, sacrifice our respect and good name and reputation before the world and should not escape the most serious and grave economic consequences . . ."

He was right, of course, particularly his reference to economics, for that was what it amounted to in the end. Economics. In other words, to pounds, shillings and pence, to marks, roubles, dollars, francs and kroner, by which men lived and died and without which, with a world population running into hundreds of millions, everything would come to a halt.

Well, they would have to make what they could of it without his help, for it was doubtful indeed if he would live to hear a cease-fire and that, when you thought about it, was a comfort at eighty-seven. In the meantime he would seek his comfort elsewhere. In the movement of those mottled foxglove bells ringing a noiseless peal across the Weald. In the society of Hetty who, like himself, belonged to an older world. And in the contemplation, perhaps, of having done his stint as best he could, without treading the next man underfoot.

He inhaled the rich scent of summer and reminded himself that this, at all events, qualified as something eternal.

He closed his eyes.

ALSO BY R. F. DELDERFIELD AND AVAILABLE FROM CORONET BOOKS